HOPE

Unexpected FATE

Bleeding LOVE

When I'm With YOU

HARPER SLOAN

Hope Town Books 1-3

Cover by: Sommer Stein with Perfect Pear Creative Covers
Photo: B2 Photography
Formatting: Champagne Formats

ISBN-13:978-1539660088
ISBN-10:1539660087

Unexpected Fate

Cover Design by Sommer Stein with Perfect Pear Creative Covers
Cover Photography by Scott Hoover
Editing by Ellie with Lovenbooks.com
Formatting by Champagne Formats

Bleeding Love

Cover Design by Sommer Stein with Perfect Pear Creative Covers
Cover Photography by Perrywinkle Photography
Editing by Ellie with Lovenbooks.com and Emma Mack
Cover Models : BT Urruela and Laura Chwat
Formatting by Champagne Formats

When I'm With You

Cover Design : Sommer Stein with Perfect Pear Creative Covers
Cover Photography : Perrywinkle Photography
Editing : Jenny Sims with www.editing4indies.com &
Ellie with Lovenbooks.com
Formatting by Champagne Formats

CORPS SECURITY

FAMILY TREE

REID

AXEL & IZZY
NATHANIEL "NATE"
DANIELLE "DANI"

BECKETT

JOHN "BECK" & DEE
LIAM

CAGE

GREG & MELISSA
COHEN
LYNDSIE "LYN"
LILLIAN "LILA"
CAMDEN "CAM"
COLTON "COLT"

COOPER

ASHER & CHELCIE
ZACHARIAH "ZAC"
JAZON "JAX"

LOCKE

MADDOX & EMMY
MADDISYN "MADDI"
EMBERLYN "EMBER"

HARRISON

DILBERT & DAVEY
STELLA

NEW YORK TIMES & *USA TODAY* BESTSELLING AUTHOR

HARPER SLOAN

Playlist

Kiss by Kiss by Brett Young

Got It by Marian Hill

All The Way by Timeflies

I Will Wait by Mumford & Sons

At Last by Etta James

Breathe You In by Dierks Bentley

They Don't Know About Us by One Direction

Trumpets by Jason Derulo

Jealous by Nick Jonas

Thinking Out Loud by Ed Sheeran

Say You Love Me by Jessie Ware

I Want You by Nick Jonas

Waiting Game by Banks

To PornHub and PornMD.
Seriously.
And all the 'stars' that grace their pages.
For helping making all those kinky moments pop just *a little* more.
I tip my hat to you.
Especially you, bendy girl, **you** are amazing.

Prologue

"AXEL REID, DON'T YOU DARE!" my mom exclaims. Then she yelps when my daddy charges through the front door.

"Don't I dare what, Princess? No way *that* boy is going near my girl. Look at him! He looks like he can't wait to creep on my daughter!"

"Well, there is no need to scare him to death!" she mocks.

My cheeks heat instantly when I see Dane start backing away from the porch. My hopes of being able to actually *go* to my senior prom are starting to go up in flames.

Poof.

Just like that.

Not that I should be surprised about it. Mom did her best to calm Daddy down, but we should have known better. He took one look at me and stormed over, only to return ten minutes later looking like he does now.

So embarrassing.

"You need to stop this nonsense right now, you big lug, or you'll be sleeping on the couch," Mom fumes.

"Like hell I will, woman!" Daddy roars at my mom.

I watch her face get sharp. He stops long enough to sling one of—that's right, ONE of—the rifles he's carrying over his shoulder, where it lands next to the other one he already has over his other shoulder.

Only my mom would be brave enough to deal with him when he's in "Protect Dani from everything with a penis" mode. He looks absolutely ridiculous. He has two hunting rifles now hanging by their leather straps over each shoulder. He has two handguns strapped to each thick thigh, two on each side of his belt, and various knives along the way. His shirt, which he thinks is hilarious to wear when I attempt to go out on a date, says *I kill things . . . and eat them.* I know it's a hunting shirt—for animals, not teenage boys—but Dane doesn't.

Mom moves in front of him, standing in the front doorway and blocking his path, where Dane is still slowly retreating. She's been dealing with this way before they even had me. He's . . . protective. I guess that's the nicest way to put it. Well, she calls him protective. However, I call it possessive, overbearing, controlling, demanding, and jerky.

"This is her senior prom, Ax. You wouldn't let her go last year." She pauses when he grunts. "And I'm sorry, but you won't be stopping her this year. She has a right to experience this. And Dane is a nice boy. Right, Dane?" she yells over her shoulder.

"Uhh . . ." he stammers, causing my daddy to grunt some more.

"The boy doesn't even know how to talk, Izzy. I bet he will be nothing but handsy and think with his little pecker. Nope. No way. Not near my baby girl."

Oh. My. God. I wish I could just fall into a hole right now. I try to see over my parents to find out if Dane heard that, but with Daddy basically being a giant, that's not happening.

"You did not just say that!" I yell at his back.

Daddy turns around, his movements awkward with how many weapons he has strapped to his body. His green eyes, so like my own, slant and harden. He looks down at my dress for the thousandth time since I came downstairs and doesn't even bother hiding his displeasure that it's showing too much of my body. Even if it is about as tasteful as it gets.

My strapless, red dress has a sweetheart neckline, and everything he calls my "girly bits" is covered. There isn't really any cleavage. Well, okay, there is some, but surely with my lack of being busty, you couldn't even call what *is* showing "cleavage." His first problem was with how much of my legs was showing. Then I made the mistake of turning around without my wrap on. That's when he saw that the dress was completely backless to my bra line. Well, what it would be if I had been wearing one. Which is clearly when he lost his mind.

"You look just like your mother did that night twenty years ago when we finally came back to each other. Right down to those strappy shoe things. And I guarantee you, Danielle Reid, any teenage boy who doesn't bat for the other team will be thinking thoughts I'll cut his dick off for. No. You aren't going with that boy, and that's final."

I harden my eyes, and his narrow even further.

I put my hands on my hips, and he squares his shoulders, his rifles clinking together.

I raise one brow, and he mirrors the action.

"Daddy."

"Dani."

"I'll cry."

"No, you won't. You have more balls than that."

"Want to bet?" I attempt to muster up some tears, knowing that he won't be able to handle them, but before I can force the first one out, my brother jumps into my line of sight and blocks our standoff.

"Yo, Dane! You just run along now. Dani is unfortunately feeling a little under the weather. Ebola. Or the flu. I don't know. It's really ugly and you probably don't want to be around this. The boils—they could pop at any moment."

"You did not just do that," I heatedly whisper, fuming at his nerve.

Nate turns and smirks at me. "Oh I just did."

"I can't believe you two!" I spin to look at the one person who can help me. "Mom, seriously?"

Her expression softens, and she just shakes her head. "I'm sorry, Dani. I tried."

"You two," I start, pointing between my older brother and father. "You just can't leave it alone? I'll be eighteen in a few months. What are you jerks going to do then?"

"You're not dating, Danielle. Not ever."

"Oh yeah, Daddy? And how realistic is that crap?"

"Watch your mouth, little princess."

"Mom?"

"I'm so sorry, Dani." She walks over and wraps me in her small arms.

I could probably really cry now a lot easier than when I was trying to fake it, but I've never been one of those girls who weep constantly. It would be easier to just go upstairs, take off the dress mom and I spent hours looking for, scrub off the light makeup she helped me apply, and pretend this night didn't happen.

An hour later, I'm sitting in my bedroom, still wearing my perfect dress. My makeup is still done and my hair is still flowing in long waves. And I'm no less mad at the men in my life than I was earlier. I've considered climbing out my window. I've considered asking my best friends, Lyn and Lila, to come help me escape. But what would be the point? Rambo-Dad already scared away my date, the only boy left in school who had been willing to ask me even though his friends had warned him about my father.

I lie down on my bed and stare up at the ceiling. Maybe I should go away for college. I planned on living at home while I attended Georgia Tech, but there is no way I can deal with this stuff any longer. If my father had things his way, I would be shipped off to become a nun. Or he would buy an island and make it an all-girls cult.

"Uhggggg!" I yell to the empty room.

"Seriously, Dani-girl, things can't be that bad."

I jump up when I hear the deep, gravelly, insanely sexy voice coming from my bedroom door. That voice. My lord. The things it alone does to me should be classified as illegal.

My hair slaps me in the face, a good handful landing in my open mouth, and I hastily pull it out before I turn to where *he* is standing.

My lord, he's beautiful. He's always been. My heart speeds up when I take in his smirking face and the mischief dancing in his brown eyes.

"Cat got your tongue?"

I shake my head.

"Speechless?"

I shake it again.

"Do you really have some flesh-eating, boil-slash-Ebola-like sickness?" he laughs.

I narrow my eyes at him, and his rich laughter booms through the room.

"I'm just kidding, Dani-girl. Come on. Get yourself ready and let's go rock this prom."

My jaw drops again. "What?"

For the first time, I notice that he's dressed in a perfectly tailored tux. My eyes travel down his tall form to his shining, black dress shoes. On the way back up, my eyes hit the corsage spinning around his finger before I look back up into those gorgeous eyes.

"Let's go, beautiful."

"Does Daddy know you're here?" I ask, not moving from my spot.

He sighs, steps into my room, and walks over. His cologne, Gucci Black, wraps around me. He's worn the same scent for years. I perversely sniff it every time I hit the mall with Lyn and Lila. That scent—it's my undoing.

He grabs one of my hands and gives my knuckles a kiss before placing the corsage around my wrist. He gives my hand a squeeze before letting go. Placing his strong hands on my shoulders, he presses down until I'm seated on my bed. Kneeling before me, he takes my feet one by one and fastens the straps of my black heels before standing and grabbing my hands, again, to pull me to my feet.

The whole time, I act like a freak and just gape at him.

What in the hell is going on?

"Ready?" he asks.

"Uhhh . . ."

"Right. You're ready," he laughs, grabs my hand, and pulls me through the house, down the stairs, and into the entryway of the house, where my parents are waiting.

Mom has her camera ready, forcing us to take some pictures, for all of which I'm sure I'm just standing there in a daze. I think I smiled in them, but I was too busy trying to figure out what the hell is going on. Daddy smiles big and triumphantly the whole time, like he's won some battle here.

"Oh, good. You got here," Nate mumbles through a sandwich he's stuffing down his throat.

I shake out of my stunned stupor and look over at him. "You did this?" I ask with disbelief.

"Well, duh. Can't have my little sister miss her prom because of some boils. Plus, I knew this guy," he says, pointing at our father, "wouldn't mind *him.*" He takes another bite before he looks over my shoulder. "And I know *he* isn't going to try to pet the cat."

"Nathaniel Gregory!" Mom gasps.

"What? Why do you think Dad acts like he does? Just because I'm willing to say the words doesn't mean you have to freak out."

I look over at my mom, who has turned bright red.

Daddy laughs at her embarrassment and pulls her into his arms. "Are you sure we didn't drop that one a few times as a baby?"

She slaps his hard stomach and shakes her head. "You look beautiful, honey. Have fun, okay?"

I smile at her and move my eyes to Daddy to judge his mood.

He just smiles at me. "I trust *him.* He won't let any of those pimple-faced, prepubescent boys touch a beautiful hair on your head. Have fun, sweetheart."

I walk over and give them both a hug, standing up on my toes as far as a can to whisper my gratitude in his ear. He's annoying, overprotective, and possessive of his girls, but I love him and I know he comes from a good place.

"Uh, excuse me? Do I not get any little-sister love here? I'm the one running this show, you know?"

"You're such a dork, Nate," I laugh and give him a hug before turning back to my date.

He's standing by the door, talking in low tones to my daddy. I can't hear him, but he's still smiling, so I'm guessing there isn't any talk about dismemberment going on. He looks over, his smile deepening and the lines around his eyes crinkling. Something moves behind his eyes that darkens them slightly, but he looks back over at Daddy, finishing up their conversation.

"Ready, Dani-girl?" he asks a few minutes later, making my heart speed up again.

Holy. Crap.

"Yeah. I'm ready." Or at least as ready as I'll ever be.

That night, while dancing to Brett Young's "Kiss by Kiss," I knew I would never be the same. I could feel the jealous waves coming off every female in the room as *he* held me in his arms. Of course, I had a man and not a boy as my date. Five years older than I am and very obviously not a teenager.

Being held in his arms was a dream come true. His scent invaded my lungs with every inhale. His eyes twinkled as his smile held me hostage. I knew I would never love a man as much as I love him.

Yeah. That was the night I confirmed what I had always known. What I had always felt.

Cohen Cage owned my heart and I never wanted it back.

Chapter 1

Dani

Four years later

UGH.

I swear to God, if he wakes me up like this one more time, I'll kill him.

Like, really kill him.

Throwing back the covers, I jump out of bed, shivering when my bare feet hit the cold hardwood floor and the cool air hits my fevered skin. Then I march—because really, when you're in a snit, you shouldn't just walk. Full-on toddler-like stomping needs to ensue. The door, yanked open and flung back, bounces off the wall with a loud *thwack.* Then I stomp some more down the hallway until I hit his door. Then, because this is completely normal behavior for a twenty-one-year-old chick, both hands come up and I bang the hell out of his door with both fists.

"You no-good, dirty pervert! I swear to God, Nate., I hope you get a flesh-eating STD and your dick rots off!"

I can hear him laughing at me through the door. The freaking sicko.

"Turn that crap down, Nate!" I yell before a big cough takes over and I have to pause while hacking up a lung . . . or two.

Does he turn it down? Nope, not that low-down, dirty dog. He turns it up and the sounds of female moans, manly grunts, and skin slapping echoes through his doorway and into the hall.

"You're disgusting!" I scream, doubling my efforts to break down his door so I can kill his sick porn-watching ass by kicking my feet between beats of my fist. "When I get in there, I'm going to beat your head in with your porn collection. Go to town on your thick skull with one of those DVDs until it all just explodes! Nasty dirtbag!"

"Little princess, what in the hell are you doing?"

I spin around and march over to where my father is standing. His hair is standing on all ends, his eyes looking tired, and his expression is a mixture of confusion and exhaustion.

"*That* in *there* is exactly why I need my own place. Do you know how disgusting it is waking up to the sounds of your own brother beating his junk? I swear, Daddy, I'm going to kill him!" I end my rant and instantly deflate, coughing a few times. "I just want some sleep. I feel like crap and I literally just fell asleep, and now, the king of pocket play is at it again. Can we just buy him a hooker? Please, Daddy! Let's get him a hooker."

His lips twitch, and his arms unfold from his chest, opening wide for me to fall into them. Which, of course, I do. I'm not ashamed that I'm still very much a daddy's girl.

"We aren't getting your brother a hooker. They're too classy for his ass."

I laugh and hug him tighter when his gruff chuckles vibrate through his chest.

"What's wrong with my girl?" he asks, pulling me back and looking into my eyes.

"Nothing. Just a little cold. I'll be fine . . . *with some sleep!*" I yell towards Nate's bedroom. And, of course, dissolve into a coughing fit that has my overprotective father narrowing his eyes.

"Go on back to bed, little princess. Let me deal with your brother. I'll have Mom come up and check on you." He gives me a strong hug and spins me toward my room. Then, almost like my words just hit him, he says, "And no more talk about moving out. Not happening."

Ugh.

Seriously. He's told me since I was a little girl that I would never leave his house because I was his little princess and, if he couldn't watch out for me, then all the dirty, thieving, no-good men of the world would get their hands on me.

To say that growing up with Axel Reid as a father was a little . . . tough, would be an understatement. Don't get me wrong. I love my daddy. But he is protective with a capitol P. Possessive of "his girls," which is what he calls Mom and me—to the point where he would probably kill a man who looked at us cross.

I love him . . . but sometimes, I want to strangle him.

That being said, I know that, if I ever needed someone in my corner, no questions asked, that person would be my daddy.

I shuffle back down the hall. Now that I know that Nate will be handled and the rush of trying to kill him has started to fade, I realize just how bad I feel. I came home early yesterday from what was supposed to be a girls' weekend at Lyn and Lila's apartment with them and Maddi Locke. We had the best weekend planned of makeovers—and by that, I mean me dying and cutting their hair—junk food, and a Gossip Girl marathon. It wasn't an hour into the night when I felt like I had been hit by a truck.

Maddi made sure I got home okay, and I crashed instantly.

I drop down into bed, pull the covers over my head, and try to ignore how bad my body hurts.

"What's wrong, Dani?" Mom whispers a little while later after walking into my room and closing the door softly behind her.

I can still hear Daddy yelling at Nate from down the hall, but at least the damn porn sounds have finally stopped.

She sits down, and her cold hand presses against my forehead. "Sweetheart, you're burning up. Tell me what's bothering you."

"I'm okay, Mom. I just need to sleep," I mumble and burrow deeper into the pillows.

"What you need is a doctor, little princess," Daddy grumbles from the now open doorway.

"Go away," I groan and try to ignore them so I can go to sleep.

"Go away my ass," he snaps.

I hear him bend down and kiss Mom before whispering to her low enough that I can't understand him. Another kiss—gross—and the sounds of him walking away.

I finally start to drift off with my mom's soothing touch rubbing my back and she begins to hum softly. Of course, that is short-lived, because not even two minutes later, I'm being wrapped up like a burrito cocooned in my blanket and lifted off the bed. I don't have to open my eyes to know that Daddy is getting his way. The scent of leather and cinnamon hits my nose, and I hear his rough complaining.

"Go away, you said? I didn't know you could read my mind, little princess. I'm going to take you away . . . right to the urgent care clinic."

What did I tell you? Protective to the nth degree.

"Whatever," I grouse with a small smile and allow myself to fall back asleep, knowing that he will take care of me.

A few hours later, I'm back in bed with a scowling father standing over me and holding my medication. Scowling because he knows that, if he hadn't pushed the issue, I would have laid my ass in bed all weekend and gotten worse.

The plus side, though, was the promise from the doctor that the cough medicine would have some pain relievers in it and I would be feeling better shortly.

I swallow the pills and then reach out to take my cough syrup from him. His frown deepens when I start coughing instantly. Come on though. You try to take that crap like a champ. It's disgusting.

"Sleep," he shoots out roughly. He sets the empty medicine cup down on my nightstand and proceeds to tuck me in like I'm five again. Every inch of my body up to my neck is covered, and the blanket is pulled tight as he tucks it around me.

"Is this really necessary? I swear I have to move out. Pretty soon, you're going to try to feed me from a spoon again."

His bright-green eyes shoot up from where he's tucking the blanket in around my feet. "Do not tempt me, little girl," he says with all seriousness.

I have to get out of here. Lyn and Lila said that their lease is almost up. We've been toying with the idea of getting a big, old house together. *Their* dad, Greg Cage, is almost as bad as mine, but he still lets them leave the house. They think it's sweet that mine is so protective, but when the role is reversed and it's their dad pulling something crazy, or their brothers—all three of them—they don't find any humor.

"Not moving out, Danielle."

"You can't stop me, you know," I remind him around my yawn, hunkering down into my warm bed.

"Sleep," he demands before he slips out of the room.

So. Annoying.

But do I even give moving out a second thought? Nope. I smile, cough, smile again, and then fall into one hell of a deep sleep.

Chapter 2

Dani

"HEY, DANI-GIRL."

I smile.

"There's that beautiful smile," the voice says, and my smile deepens.

"Jesus Christ. What the hell did they give her? Izzy!" another voice booms. "The fuck did that bottle say? She's out like she's in a goddamn coma!"

I frown when my father's voice enters my heavenly dream.

Good lord, what is he doing in my dream? Daddy shouldn't be here. Not when I finally have Cohen Cage in my bed. Well, besides the fact that that would be sick, he would kill Cohen if he caught him putting a hand on me. Literally. Cohen would be dead.

"I'm sure it's fine, Axel," Cohen says softly. "Mom sent me over with some soup and some show that the girls have been going nuts over. I don't mind sitting with her."

Ha! Yeah right. Sitting with her would mean that Daddy would trust something with a dick near his daughter. Regardless of who it is, that would never happen. Yup—definitely dreaming.

"Yeah, sure, son," he stutters.

I can just picture him rubbing the back of his neck with a helpless look.

"Let me go call that stupid kid doctor and see what the hell he did to my little princess. I knew he didn't look old enough to be out of med school."

"You got it," I hear *him* mumble, and the bed dips.

I listen as my father's footsteps stomp out of the room and the door shuts softly behind him. Ah. Finally. My dreams of *him* never last long enough, and there is no way I want to share good dream time with my father in the picture.

I have a feeling that, even in my dreams, he would be like a giant shield against any man who even breathed in my direction.

"Dani-girl," he whispers in my ear. "I have your favorite soup from my mom here. Why don't you open those beautiful green eyes and take a bite? If you do, I promise I'll even sit here and watch a few episodes of Game of Thrones with you."

"You furrr real?" I slur and open my eyes slightly before quickly closing them when the bright light from the sun hits my tired eyes. "You can't be real. You're in my dream bed, Cohen!" I reach out and pat his stubbled cheek a few times, trying to get my eyes open and focused on his face. "You can't be here. What if Daddy catches you? Wait. Why are you dressed? You're not usually dressed when you're in my dream bed." My hand drops from where I was rubbing all over his face and starts to roam over his cotton-covered chest. "You can take it off. I won't bite." I giggle and start to trail my hand lower to get this stupid shirt off him.

God, he feels like heaven.

A surprised noise somewhere between a choking gasp and a shocked stutter comes from his mouth, which is followed by a groan that rumbles against the palm I have resting against his chest.

I bite my lip, thinking that I can at least try to do something seductive. They're always doing it in the books I love to read. Even if I never understood what's hot about lip nibbling, I might as well give it a go.

"You're so hard," I whisper in awe as my hand continues to palm his pecs, his abs, and everything between. "And warm," I add, nuzzling in close. My head moves to his shoulder, my hand still rubbing his hard stomach, and I pull one leg up to wrap around his hips.

"Jesus Christ," he moans when my leg hits his crotch.

"Are you hard . . . everywhere? My dream is going to stop soon.

It always does. You should just tell me now. Then, when I wake up, I won't be disappointed because I once again missed all the good stuff." I sigh deeply. "I bet you're huge," I giggle.

"Fuck. Me," he whispers on a prayer.

"That would be nice too."

"Dani-girl, what in the hell has gotten in to you?" He lifts his body and moves out from under me, lightly swatting my hands when I start to grab after him. "I'm just . . . uh . . . I'm just going to go to the bathroom." He stands from the bed.

I drop back with a pout. "But we were going to fuggle," I complain.

He turns sharply to ask, "The hell is a fuggle?"

"Duh. It's a cuddle fuck," I giggle and reach for him again only to stop when he walks away and starts to pace.

"Jesus fucking Christ."

I was having the most beautiful dream. Well, every dream that involves Cohen Cage is beautiful—overwhelmingly beautiful. And trust me. There have been *a lot* of dreams over the years with him as the sole star. Each and every one of them ends in disappointment, though, when they stop before he can get to the good stuff.

This one, even though it lacked the erotic content that usually partners with a Cohen sex dream, was different—it felt so real. God, what I would give to have him in my arms *that way* for real.

"You coming back to the land of the living now, Dani-girl?"

I still instantly.

Holy shit.

"Uh . . ." I stammer.

"Yeah. There's my girl," he laughs. "Let me go call your dad and let him know you're awake. I thought he was going to lock himself in your room earlier when your mom said they had to go. She tried to tell him you would be fine, but you know how your dad is."

Why can't I clear the cobwebs in my head?

"Anyway," he continues, "they had that charity function for local Wounded Warriors that Maddox runs to go to. If it would have been anything else, I don't think she would have been able to get him out the door. You should have seen it, Dani. I've never seen your dad deflate so quickly." He laughs to himself, and I feel him shift before the bed lets up when his weight is removed.

Oh. My. Gosh!

Cohen's in my bed. Like, really in my bed. I don't think my panic level could get any higher than it is right now. I frantically search the murky depths of my memories to see if I can piece the last few hours together.

All I remember is Nate and his disgusting wake-up call, Daddy dragging me to the doctor, and my Cohen dream. Holy crap. That was a dream, right?

Opening my eyes, I look over to where he's standing with his phone against his ear. He looks up and gives me that panty-melting smile, and I feel myself flush instantly. Blush like an innocent schoolgirl. How. Embarrassing.

He shakes his head a few times and moves his attention to my dresser full of pictures while waiting for the call to connect. I use this time to study his handsome face.

He's always been an attractive person. When he was a kid, he had that youthful perfection. His skin always looked flawless and he carried a good tan all year long. His brown hair, until he enlisted in the Marines, carried that sexy shaggy look any female worth her salt would get an itchy palm that just begged her to run her fingers through. Now, he keeps it slightly longer than regulation with a buzz on the sides. It brings out the sharp angles of his jaw and cheekbones. Not to sound like a freak—hey, maybe I am—but I've been studying this man for so long that I could probably draw him to exactness from memory alone.

What all his good looks really do is make him look like one deliciously sexy man who puts me in a state of constant arousal when he's around. His dark-brown eyes look over at me again, and he raises a brow when he sees that I'm still looking at him, but he quickly glances away when I'm assuming my dad picks up.

"Axel," he starts only to pause and roll his eyes. "She's fine. Awake, tired, and I'm sure getting more annoyed by the second that I'm reporting to her father . . . Yes, sir . . . I'm positive I'll get an earful as well . . . No, sir . . . I'll get her to eat something as soon as I get off the phone . . . No, she hasn't taken her meds yet. She just woke up, uh . . . She just woke up." He looks over at me almost uncomfortably before looking away.

Weird.

I start to cough, and he rolls his eyes.

"It was just a cough, Axel. She's already back to scowling at me. Yeah, I'll get the soup and her meds and demand she doesn't move a muscle indefinitely. No, sir, I'm not making fun of you."

When I laugh, Cohen shoots me another look. This time, he's warning me to hush before my daddy goes nuts.

"Yes, sir. She's fine. I'm sure she going to listen because she knows that's best too. Okay. Yes, sir. Bye." He shoves his phone back in his pocket and shakes his head. "Your dad. I swear that man still thinks you're six and riding a bike for the first time. Remember when he wouldn't even let you attempt to ride it without training wheels before he had a fully stocked first aid kit attached to his back?"

We both laugh at the memory of just one of his over-the-top parenting moments.

"What are you doing here?" I ask, waving my hand around the general area of my bedroom.

"Nate. Well, Nate indirectly. He called me earlier." He raises one shoulder in a shrug like that should be enough.

"Yeah? And that explains what, exactly?"

"Oh shut up, brat," he teases. "He mentioned, in between his bouts of hilarity over the morning craziness at the Reid house, that you were sick, and I figured I would come bring you Mom's soup and keep you company. You know, like old times."

"Old times?" I question, confused.

"You know. I used to always sit with you when you were sick."

"Cohen, the last time I was sick, I was, like, ten and you had no choice since we were the only two with the flu and our parents didn't want us spreading it to our siblings."

What in the hell is going on here? For a couple of years, he's treated me with a friendly indifference. Not rude, but never . . . this.

"Still, it helped," he smirks.

"Yeah, it did."

Of course, he probably thinks it helps for an entirely different reason than it actually did. I was beside myself the whole week we were basically quarantined together. Not because I was sicker than shit and miserable. I *was* sick as hell, but I was in heaven. Absolute euphoria because I was alone with Cohen—just him and me—for a whole week.

There is seriously something wrong with me. Besides the obvious. In case you haven't guessed it, I've been madly in love with Cohen Cage since I was a little girl—I think I was six when I realized just how much I loved him and he was ten. That childhood crush has grown over the years into something that is so big—so soul consuming—that even I feel like it will crush me at times.

And the worst part is that he's completely blind to it.

Chapter 3

Cohen

I'M DEFINITELY IN WAY OVER my head here.

I look over at Dani, who is now peacefully—thank God—sleeping again, and drop my head back on the pillows stacked up behind my back. What the hell was I thinking rushing over here? As soon as Nate called, laughing his ass off over how he woke his sister up, and let me know just how sick she was, I couldn't seem to stop myself from getting here as quickly as possible. Mom didn't even bat an eye when I asked her how to make her soup—the same soup she's made for each of my siblings and me every time we were sick. She did ask why I needed it and left it alone when all I said was, "Dani." I didn't miss the look in her eye though.

Curious but hopeful.

It really should have been a concern. How could she possibly be okay with me rushing over to Dani? Someone who is almost five years younger and has never made it a secret, even though she thinks she has, about how she feels about me.

Sure, there was that one time. I think the twins, Lyn and Lila, had just turned sixteen—Dani was around fifteen—when she whispered her feelings towards me with a intensity that no teenager just coming into herself should ever understand.

I'll never forget it. Never. Of course that was a defining moment for our relationship—not that she knows that.

"I'm going to miss you, Cohen. I know you don't look at me like I

look at you, but one day, you're going to come back and I'll still be waiting for you. Waiting for you to see me like I see you. Mark my words, Cohen Cage. One of these days, you're going to be mine. And until you're ready . . . I'll be here. I'll be waiting."

Her husky whisper replays in my mind like it just happened moments ago. I haven't forgotten a single word. Not a single one. Over the years, they would come back to me at the worst-possible times. When I would be out on a date—boom, there they were. Instantly, that chick would morph into a vision of Dani so clear that I struggled not to reach out and run my fingertips down her cheek. When I was in the middle of one of the biggest games in my football career, there they were—a hushed whisper that carried over the roaring crowds. And it would never fail—I would look up from a huddle and there she would be standing with my family, screaming louder than any other person in the stadium.

And most recently, when I was in the middle of a warzone, gunfire flying all around us, bombs exploding, and the dust burning our eyes and lungs. Right in the middle of that Hell-on-earth chaos, I would hear her words trail through my thoughts right when I needed an extra push of strength or, God forbid, hope.

I think that was the moment that I realized the enormity of it and that confession whispered all those years ago. Right or wrong, whatever it is between us would always be bigger than I understand. It's something that was so unexpected—that feeling, craving, desire, to make her mine. It's something I've almost felt guilty about over the years. Not only because of how close our families are, but because, until the last few years, it's something that was very inappropriate to feel towards someone that young.

When she woke up earlier—or at least I think she was awake—and started rubbing her body against mine, I thought I was going to come in my pants. That hasn't happened to me since I was a teenager just learning how to control my random pop-up erections.

I have no doubt that it was the pain meds in her cough syrup making her act like that. She's always gotten weird on narcotic pain meds. But when her warm body crushed against my side, I had a hard time telling myself that she wasn't in her right mind. Trying to convince myself not to react was impossibly hard. Then her small but firm tits pressed against my side and it was almost game over.

Her tits had been straining the confines of her small, white tank top since I'd walked in the door. Her nipples were pebbled to firm tips just begging for me to wrap my lips around them. Did she have small nipples that matched her size or would they be large? Are they light pink in color or more tan? Would she taste as good as the promise of her has hinted at when I finally pull them deep into my mouth and tease her with my tongue and teeth?

Yeah. Ever since *that* moment, I've been as hard as steel and ready to pound into her small body.

Yup. I'm in way over my head here—so far over that I'm shocked I haven't drowned yet.

"Fuck me," I groan, pressing my palm against my cock, willing it to calm the fuck down.

If her brother—or, worse, her father—were to come in here right now, I have no doubt that I would be put in the hospital with the force of their beatdown.

She shifts, and I look away from Game of Thrones, where the little dude—or "imp," as she and the girls call him—she is always raving about, is playing with his whore.

Jesus, is everyone getting some action?

After making sure she got her meds, I heated up Mom's soup and called her brother to see if he would be home soon. Of course he said that he was too busy on his date with the Carver twins to come home and take care of his sick sister. One thing about Nate—he loved his sister, but he loved pussy more.

Axel and Izzy had left for their night for the charity event, the same one my parents and all the other parents from our group would be at. Axel had already planned on being out all night with Izzy, something about a bed and breakfast, so I told him that I would stay here with Dani and make sure she was okay. There is no telling Axel Reid that his adult daughter can take care of herself.

If he had any idea about the thoughts I've had about his daughter, there is no fucking way he would have left me alone with her. No. Way.

"Coh," she moans and moves in her sleep. Her legs shift, and she moans again.

Fuck! How the hell am I supposed to not get messed up over this? I jump off the bed and pace around her room. Looking around, I try to find something to focus on that will help me move past the fact that she is clearly having some heated dream.

Cuddle fuck. What did she call it? A fuggle? I shake my head and wince when my cock swells even further. Fuggle. What in the hell is that supposed to mean, anyway?

Focus, Cohen. Focus on something other than your desire to bury yourself balls-deep in sweet Dani pussy.

I look around her room for anything to form some sort of distraction. Her dresser is full of pictures. There are some of her and my sisters. Some pictures of Maddi and Dani alone. Some of Maddi, the twins, and Dani together. More pictures of her and Liam Beckett—her best friend other than my sisters. My eyes go past the pictures to the canvas paintings she has hanging up around the pale-blue room, and I know without checking that they're some of Ember's, Maddi's little sister. She has a huge chaise lounge-type sofa thing in the corner by her floor-to-ceiling windows that overlook their backyard and lake. It has a worn throw tossed carelessly over the back, and a book has been thrown on the ottoman.

That chair would be the perfect chair to take her on, I muse. *I would put her on her knees, facing the back, her elbows bracing her body against it, and take her hard. Goddamn, I could sink myself so deep into her tiny body.*

Okay . . . Quickly moving my eyes past the chair, I look back at her sleeping form. Her tan skin looks flushed, her full lips are parted slightly, and her chest is rising slowly. Just like an angel, my Dani-girl.

An angel sent from Heaven who is without a doubt always going to be my greatest temptation.

Chapter 4

Dani

COHEN WOKE ME UP TWICE while I slept to have me take more medicine. I don't remember much from that night, just that he never was far from my side when I woke on my own and he played with my hair until I was able to fall back to sleep after a good coughing spell. Well, that's a lie. I remember dreams so vivid that I'm still getting hot and bothered over them.

He was gone when I woke up the morning after, and for once, I didn't have to wake up to Nate beating his junk with porn on surround sound. It's been four days of sleeping off and on. Every time I close my eyes, though, it's all about Cohen.

Sluggishly, I pull myself from bed and make quick work of showering and getting ready for the day. I've missed way too much work, and even though I have the coolest boss in the world, I can't afford to miss much more. Especially now that, after all of this, I'm even more convinced that I have to get the hell out of my parents' house.

Grabbing my phone, I press the screen and wait for Lyn to pick up. One half of my best-friend duo since birth, Lyndsie Cage has been my go-to for everything—and I mean *everything*. She loves the fact that I have a ridiculous crush on her unattainable brother. She encourages my love for him. God, I love the little head-in-the-clouds dreamer.

"Yo, bitch!" she laughs, and I smile.

"What's up, hooker?" I throw back.

"Nothing much. Lila just left to head off to school. I swear she is never going to graduate," she jokes.

"Yeah, well, that's what happens when you're going after your doctorate, Lyn. I think she has to sign her soul away for the next twenty years or something," I snicker.

I couldn't be prouder of Lila though. She has always told us that she is going to be a doctor; I guess we all just assumed she meant the medical kind. It wasn't until the summer of our junior year in high school, when we were all working at a local day care, that she decided she had found her calling. She didn't just want to work with kids. Nope. Not our Lila. She wanted to own, operate, and specialize in a day care for handicapped and special-needs children. Ever since then, she's had one goal in mind. Her dual degree in special education and business management have had her eating, sleeping, and breathing school since graduation.

"You aren't far off, I'm sure. Anyway, what's up?"

I hear her fiddling with stuff in the background and visualize her puttering around her bathroom, getting ready for work as well. She probably has her thick, black hair up rolled in a bun on the top of her head while she makes sure her makeup is two hundred percent perfect.

"Nothing much. Just getting ready for work. I feel like I've been off forever. Has the place gone up in flames since last week?" I ask, only half joking.

"Not really," she giggles.

Oh shit.

"Lyn," I warn. "What did he do now?" I probe, dreading her answer. The last time I took a week-long vacation, I came back to work to a nut house.

"Well, where do you want me to start? You should know by now that, just because he has calmed down some over the years, when he gets some wild hair, there is no stopping him."

"Start from the beginning," I spit out through my teeth.

Using my shoulder to hold the phone, I pull my black pants over my hips, step into my favorite four-inch, black-suede heels with the gold-studded bowtie adorning the top. They're freaking fabulous, and with the “must wear at least one item that is gold” requirement at work, they work perfectly. Of course, my feet will be screaming before the day is over, but at least they’re going to be screaming while looking badass.

I’ve worked for Dilbert Harrison for the last two years. Dilbert Harrison also lovingly known as Uncle Sway. He’s the most over-the-top, not-a-care-in-the-world, fun-loving, and flamboyant man I know. I’ve heard stories about how, when we were younger, before he and his partner adopted their daughter Stella, he would prance around with a long, blond wig and heels taller than any of our mothers would brave wearing. Even Aunt Dee, who always has the coolest heels, wouldn’t even touch them.

But his fun-loving, not-a-care-in-the-world personality can also be a little larger than life at times. I mean, hello. Because of him, the whole sidewalk outside the salon and a few other local businesses, including Corps Security, is painted gold with flecks of glitter.

“Well, first he decided that we needed to touch up the flooring. Since we had to close down because the paint fumes were a little much for the clientele trying to relax the last time he touched it up, he was doing it in sections with a huge box fan bungee-corded to the rolling front desk chair. Then Samantha almost broke her neck when she tripped over the extension cord, so I talked him into waiting until we closed and stayed until four in the morning helping him touch up the damn floor. I told him he needed to consider having a laminate company custom make him some gold glittered flooring and maybe it wouldn’t need touching up. I believe he might be considering it.” She stops, and I hear her moving around her house.

“Is that it?” I ask, knowing that there is no way that’s all.

“Nope,” she states but doesn’t elaborate.

“Okay?”

“Then he decided we needed to have theme Fridays. Dani, theme fucking Fridays. You are going to shit yourself. This week, he wants a burlesque-type theme. He actually wants all of us girls, plus Jonathan—the new guy that started while you were out—to dress up in complete burlesque gear. If he could get away with it, I think he would even incorporate some sort of dance number into the end of every hour."

"You're joking?" Son of a bitch. I knew better than to leave Sway unattended for too long. I've always been able to keep a leash on his wilder-than-normal ideas.

"Not at all. He even mentioned something about a pole-dancing class to teach us how to move before we had a stripper-slash-Vegas-showgirl day. Dani, he mentioned headdresses. Head. Dresses!" she yells in my ear.

"I'll talk to him when I get in. Maybe I can talk him out of this."

"I wouldn't put any money on it. He's already taken an ad out in the local paper. He's gone off the deep end ever since they wrapped filming of the reality show for *last season* and started their pre-filming for the next season. Sway All the Way is definitely making him battier than normal, and you know, once the show airs it's only going to get worse."

"God, Lyn. Can you freaking believe that is actually happening? I'm going to die when the first show airs." I slap my palm against my forehead when I remember what happened during the first episode's filming.

"Well, that's your own fault for not rescheduling my brother's haircut for a non-filming day," she laughs.

"Jesus, he's going to see it, isn't he? Do you think we can break all the televisions he could possibly be around before it airs? Luckily, Daddy already said he wasn't watching that 'chick shit,' so he will remain blissfully unaware."

"You can only hope, Dani. I don't know what the big deal is though. It isn't that bad."

"Uh. I basically have 'I'm daydreaming about running my hands through your hair while you fuck me' written all over my face and then I stupidly admitted my feelings to the producers during our camera interview!" I shriek.

"Ew. Don't be so dramatic, loser. You didn't look that obvious, and I'm sure they won't even show that part of the interview. It was the first show. They have to . . . I don't know . . . introduce the place and all that is Sway first. They wouldn't start off with your crazy ass lusting after my brother."

"You don't know that," I challenge.

"Yeah, and you don't know they will do anything different. Calm your tits. Look, I have to go and finish up my makeup. I've got a wedding party of five coming in today, and if I want to grab up all those hopeful bridesmaids' business, I have to look like hot shit so they know I'm capable when the time comes for them to not be the poorly dressed extras in the wedding. Marketing is such a bitch sometimes."

She doesn't even give me a chance to say bye. She just clicks off the phone. I can imagine she is going all out on her makeup—not that she needs it. Lyn is stunning. But she always gets a little eccentric when it comes to wedding makeup. She's convinced that the bridesmaids are living in some jealous fog and, when they get makeup done by her, meet their Prince Charming, and then in turn have their wedding in the plans, they're going to somehow remember the girl who made them stunning and created that snowball effect.

Yeah, Lyn is also the most confident person I've ever met, and she's convinced she can do anything. Since she's booked for more weddings of repeat bridesmaids, I have to kind of agree with her logic here.

Burlesque- and showgirl-themed days? Good lord, it's going to be a long day.

Chapter 5

Dani

AS PREDICTED, IT IS INSANE the second I step foot inside of Sway's. The madness starts with Sway and ends with Sway. Madness and insane being the keywords.

"Sweet heavens you, my little belle! Sway was imagining you on your deathbed! When that hunky father of yours—stop looking at me like that, you would have to be blind not to see how hunky he is! Anyway, when he told me that my Danielle-Bell was sick, I was so worried. Darling, you look like you've lost weight. Weight, I will remind you, that you did not have to lose. Such a tiny little tinker." He spins me with two hands on my shoulders, and I have to work hard not to bust my ass when my heels struggle to keep up with the rapid movement. "It's a good thing you have your mother's lush bottom or you would look like a stick. As it is, you look like a stick with a great ass."

He spins me back around and looks down at my chest. Oh here we go. Reaching up to my black blouse, he unsnaps the two buttons that kept me decent and nods to himself when my red bra is peeking through the opening.

"Perfect. Now give the girls a little tuggero and we're done. I'll make sure to put some more weight on you, Belle."

"You do realize that this would be considered sexual harassment in most work environments," I remind him. Again.

"It would. But lucky for you, I haven't swung for the kitty cats once in my life. I think, for the harassment to be sexual, I would have to actual want to get in those pants, darling. The only pants I ever want to get into happen to be carrying far different equipment than you, sweet girl." He laughs and smacks my rear when I turn to walk to my station.

"Good God, Pops! Do not talk like that!" I hear Stella yell as she walks in from the back room, where we do all of our color mixing. "That's just . . . No, that's just too much, even for you. I don't ever want to think about my dad's junk or my pops lusting after it." She rolls her eyes and walks over to give me a hug. "Hey, you. I missed you around this circus."

"I heard that, Stella!" Sway laughs and struts to the front of the studio in his glittery, gold heels—heels that, as predicted, are taller than mine.

"I wasn't trying to hide it, Pops!" she yells at his back.

Ah. Never a dull moment at Sway's.

I was busy doing Karen Oglethorpe's hair for about twenty minutes before the cameras walked in. Of course. Film day. I must be completely off my game if I had already forgotten the filming rotation.

I loathe film day.

Not only are the cameras always in my way when I'm trying to do hair, mix color, and move between the washing station or the blower station, but the producer and his people are freaking annoying. Devon Westerfield. He's been a constant presence around the salon since this time last year, and I think I might actually hate him more now than I did then. Not because he's a bad person. He really isn't. He's doing his job just the same as I am. But it's because of him that I might publicly, in front of millions, make a fool of myself when the reality series goes live.

"Ah! Danielle Reid. Aren't you a sight for sore eyes," he says and leans in to give me a light hug. "You know Don and Mark?"

"Hey, Dev. Nope, I don't think I've had the pleasure," I respond with fake enthusiasm.

"Hmm. Oh that's right. You weren't here the other day when I brought them by to meet everyone. They're my assistants this go-around. Here to help with the crew and also with anything small to large that I might just be too stretched thin for." He starts looking around, and I can tell he has already forgotten about me.

"Okie dokie, Devy boy."

Returning my attention back to Karen is effective enough in getting him off my back, but the two shadows-to-be stick around. I pause in my brushing of her color and look up.

"Is there something you two need?" I ask in annoyance.

"Well, Devon said you were the go-to person here. Manager and head stylist of Sway's. We just thought—" the short one—Don, I think—starts, but I interrupt him before he can get started on his crusade to get me to tell him how to do his job. They're all the same. Devon has been through more assistants than I can count in the year and a half I've known him.

"One thing to know and remember, boys: I don't have time for you to act like you don't know your head from your ass. Nice to meet you and all that, but please don't act like the last few idiots who all but licked the ground Dev over there, walked on. It won't earn you points with him. In case you haven't noticed, he's a little tunnel-vision prone, and I assure you that it won't do you any good to try and fuse yourself to me." Dismissing their shocked faces, I look in the mirror and give Karen a wink, earning a giggle from her in return. She loves it when the girls around here are sassy.

They mumble something under their breaths, and I turn to give them a sharp glare, which of course they miss because they've tucked their tails again to run after an order-barking Devon.

Two hours later, I finally have a chance to go grab a quick bite to eat. Well, I would have if Sway hadn't yelled from the front that I had a call-in that would be here in fifteen.

I hate call-ins. Since I'm one of the best stylists in the local area, my appointments are booked weeks out. But there are a handful of people I always allow to call in, and Sway wouldn't have said yes to them had it not been one of those select few.

Mentally, while shoving as much of the sandwich Stella grabbed me when she did a lunch run down my throat, I try to figure out who could be coming in. I know it's not Nate or Liam; I cut their hair last week. Daddy doesn't need a cut since I did his the other day. I've seen the others it might be recently enough. I pause with my last bite to my mouth when I realize who it will be—the only person who I haven't cut in a while.

Cohen. Freaking. Cage.

Son of a bitch. I know I told Sway no more scheduling or allowing him to come in on a film day.

"Breathe, fancy pants," Lyn whispers in my ear on her way towards the back breakroom. "He hasn't been a biter since he was a kid." She continues walking with her laughter trailing behind her.

I'm going to kill Sway, I think to myself before going to wash up so I can prep my station.

I have just put down my trimmers when I feel it.

That magnetic charge that floats over my skin, heating every inch and leaving a trail of awareness in its wake. That pull that has always been connected to one man. I shiver and give myself a pep talk about how to treat him with friendly indifference while there are cameras around. Of course they have been filming a few things that the cameras mounted all over the room can't capture perfectly. I have already tripped over one of the assistant asshats twice today.

"Dani-girl." His voice, that rich rumble of masculine excellence, washes over me and I shiver again before cursing under my breath. The rumble of his low laughter tells me that he definitely didn't miss that little move.

Kill me now.

"Hey, Coh," I say with a smile. "What brings you in? Last minute, I might add." I pat the chair before walking around and holding the back while he sits down.

When his scent hits my nose, I almost come on the spot. Lord, he smells good. I wonder what he would smell like while his body covered mine, all sweaty from hours of good lovemaking. I run my fingers through the longer lengths on the top and feel my cheeks heat slightly, thinking about doing the same when his face is buried between my legs.

". . . needed a trim."

Shit. I missed what he said because, naturally, I was thinking about him naked. Naked and thrusting into my body. Naked and feasting between my spread thighs.

"You feeling okay? I thought Nate said you were better?"

"Uh, I'm fine. Just—is it hot in here?" I fan my face and avoid his eyes.

He's silent, so I take that as a sign that it's safe to bring my attention back to him.

Big mistake there. His knowing eyes are boring right into mine. The chocolate depths sparkling in a way that makes it clear he has a good idea about where my mind was going.

"Did you hear what I said, Dani-girl?"

"Of course I did, Cohen. What, did you think I was standing here daydreaming?" I joke.

"Well, yeah, that's exactly what I think." His eyes darken and he smirks a devilish grin. "Did you know you talk in your sleep, Dani?" he asks, and I drop my comb.

Oh, God. Shut up, shut up, shut up. This is not happening. No way.

"No, I don't," I childishly snap.

"Dani, you do. So, yeah, I do think you were standing there daydreaming. Want to know why?" He uses his booted foot to move his chair so that he's facing me, and then he leans in so that his face is dangerously close to mine. Even when he's seated, his head is almost level with my own. Curse my horizontally challenged self. "While you were zoning off into space with your fingers running through my hair, you had this smile on your lips. The same smile you had the other day when you were dreaming. About me, Dani. And don't deny it, because you don't moan my name if you're dreaming about another man. Yes, Dani, you very much do talk in your sleep." He smiles again before leaning back and looking down to his phone. "Clean up my neck please, cut the length off the top, and give me a buzz on the sides. Other than that, you're clear to continue with your thoughts."

I must have been standing there like an idiot because he looks up from his phone, laughs to himself, and, with one tan hand, reaches out and pushes my mouth closed.

"You're going to catch flies that way, Dani-girl. One day, maybe you can clue me in on what those dreams are about."

Drives me insane, the control he has over me. There isn't a single person in the world, other than Cohen, who can turn me into a ridiculously stupid, sputtering fool. My normal confidence disappears. And clearly, he isn't as oblivious to my feelings as I originally thought.

How in the hell am I supposed to handle this?

Wait a minute. Cohen or not, I'm not going to let him pull my strings when I know he is just doing this to make me feel uncomfortable.

So, time to call his bluff.

"Why? You planning on doing something about it?"

He looks up sharply, clearly not having expected me to actually say something in return since he was going for shock value.

"Try me," he demands, his voice thick and even deeper than normal.

I throw my head back and reach out to run my fingers thought his hair again, just barely suppressing the shivers. Curling my fingers slightly so that I can grab a good hold, I lean in and pull his head back at the same time. With my nose just a hair away from his and our breaths mingling together, I say, "Cohen, you couldn't handle the truth of my thoughts when it comes to you and we both know it. So how about *you* let *me* know when you're ready for me to *clue you in.*" I give his hair a light tug and smile when he swallows loudly and shifts in his seat. "Ready for that trim?" I ask with a wink, and I'm rewarded with his groan.

I have no idea how I do it, but I manage to get through his cut without coming unglued. I can see Lyn trying to get my attention from across the room. Stella had to leave after she overheard my words to Cohen because her giggles were getting the best of her. Cohen has remained silent the whole time. His eyes though . . . They're speaking louder than his words ever could.

They haven't left my reflection in the mirror since I started. I can feel them every time I shift. When I stopped to go grab another comb after I dropped my fourth one, I felt his gaze follow me across the room to Stella's station. The few times I stopped cutting to meet his eyes, the heated promise written all over his face almost did me in. I almost just said 'fuck it' and climbed on his lap to have a go regardless of the people watching our every move.

I finish the last buzz of my clippers around his right ear and move to brush all the stray hair off. "All done," I say softly and unclip his cape.

He stands, shoving his phone in the back pocket of his jeans, and walks over to stand in front of me. I continue to pretend I'm busy with the cape I just removed, brushing stray hairs off here and there, when his hand comes up, his finger and thumb hitting my chin, and my face is lifted until I have no choice but to look in his eyes.

"Do not tease me, Dani. It's not a game you want to play if you don't intend to follow through."

"I-I wasn't . . . I wouldn't," I stammer.

"You did, and I have no doubt you'll have the brilliant idea to do it again. The next time you allude to those dirty thoughts I know you have about me, don't think for a second that I won't drag you to the closest bed to show you just how fucking dirty they'll get." He leans close, his scent hitting my nostrils, and I involuntarily inhale deeply, earning me a rumbled chuckle. "What you don't know, Dani—because contrary to what you think, you don't know me well enough to assume what having me would really be like. But I promise you this: every little thought that you have had that causes you to moan my name while scissoring those perfect legs back and forth, praying for completion—it would be so much hotter than you could ever imagine." He gives me a soft, sweet kiss against my temple that has fire racing from that spot all over my body until it ends in the awareness that I'm pretty sure I just came in my pants.

Chapter 6

Dani

"YOU WOULDN'T EVEN BELIEVE IT if you had seen it with your own eyes." Lyn laughs and points across her living room at me. "I'm not joking at all, Lila. It was ridiculous. It was even making me hot and he's my damn brother. Of course it wasn't *him,* but the whole sexual chemistry taking over every ounce of space in the whole room. It could have turned on a monk." She laughs again and takes a big pull of her wine.

"I knew you two would be explosive," Lila jokes.

"You have no idea, sister. It was out-of-this-world insane. The whole time she was cutting his hair—and ignoring him, I should add—he just kept glaring at her like he wanted to throw her over his shoulder and drag her out of the salon."

"Cohen did that?" Maddi asks in shock.

"Yup. Swear it. But don't worry. If you don't believe me, just wait until *that* episode airs. I shit you not, Devon was about to have a heart attack. He hit television gold with that right there." Lyn takes another swallow and giggles to herself.

"Ohmigod. Ohmigod! Shit. Lyn! How could you let me act like that when they were filming? How could I forget that? Oh no, oh no. This isn't good at all." I jump off the couch, knocking Maddi's legs off from where she had them resting on the coffee table, and start to pace the room. "Lyn! He's going to have to see that again. People we know are going to see me saying that to him."

"So?" she says with confusion.

"What's the big deal, Dani? So what? You finally opened your mouth and gave him a little something to think about. You shouldn't be ashamed about that," Lila, ever the voice of reason, argues.

"I shouldn't be ashamed?! This is Cohen. Your brother, my brother's best friend, the same Cohen that I've been hopelessly in a state of lust over for *my whole life!*" I scream.

"Someone is a little dramatic today," Maddi says with a sigh.

"I'm not being dramatic! I'm being realistic. What if things get weird?" Things are so going to get weird. The next time I see him, I'm just going to run the other way. It will be safer than trying to act like I'm not completely humiliated. Or that I have completely humiliated him.

"Realistic would be you shutting the hell up and realizing that maybe, just maybe, my big brother finally has his eyes wide open when it comes to you," Lila adds.

I look over at her, catching Lyn nodding emphatically out of the corner of my eye. Maddi sighs again and voices her agreement.

"You all think this way?" I ask the room and get three yeses. "Okay. Say I believe you. Now what?"

"Easy!" Lyn yells, almost falling out of her seat with her excitement. "Now we make *him* the one that is craving *you.*" She nods to herself like this is the best advice in the world.

"And how am I supposed to do that?" I ask the know-it-all currently sloshed off Asti.

"Just leave that to me, Dani. Just leave it all to me."

If I were in my right mind, maybe I would be alarmed here, but because we are on our third bottle of Asti, I have to agree with her and let myself believe this is a brilliant plan.

Ready or not, Cohen. Ready. Or. Not.

"This is a stupid idea," I complain under my breath and look over at Lyn.

"This isn't a stupid idea. This is an awesome idea. As sexy as you are, you've always been clueless to your own sexuality. You dress the part, look the part, but the second *the part* is shoved in your face, you start doubting yourself. I get it. Years of trying to get someone's attention makes you feel like you're lacking something, but I assure you that isn't the case. So . . . this will help to bring out some of that confidence. Would I lead you the wrong way here, Dani?" She ends her speech and puts both of her hands on her hips with a huff.

"Pole dancing, Lyn?"

"What? It's technically a gym activity. I did tell you we were coming to the gym. I just didn't tell you what for. Doesn't matter. Sway brought it up, and after doing a little research, I found out you get the workout of your life during these classes, so just think about it as a positive-type thing. Even if you can't open that brilliant mind of yours up and see that I'm right."

"Let's get this over with."

She gives me a bright smile and pushes herself out of the car. I give myself another pep talk and try to convince myself that this isn't going to be a mistake. She's right about one thing: I could always use some more gym time. Tiny or not, I won't stay firm with all the sweets I eat.

"Is this even something I'll be able to do, Lyn? I mean, we all can't be tall warrior princesses like you and your amazon sister." I laugh, but I'm dead serious. I'm five foot two on a good day. The twins tower over me. Always have. They have upper-body strength that could rival a grown man, and mine is more like that of a small child. "I'll never be able to get off the ground," I mutter to myself as we walk through the door to the studio.

The first thing I notice is that it's really cool in the room. Like, instant nip boner. I bring my arms up to cross around my body and pray that no one sees my headlights beaming. Lyn confidently marches ahead of me and waves to Lila, Maddi, and Stella. I give them a wave of my own and quickly cover myself up. How am I the only one freezing my ass off here?

"You girls ready to learn some moves?" Lyn asks the group with a huge smile.

"I'm just here for the workout. Mom says this is an amazing way to keep your body toned in a fun way," Maddi says with a smile. "Of course she would think that since she used to strip herself." She laughs when all three of us look at her in shock.

"Emmy? Aunt Emmy? Sweet little Emmy who has a husband so protective and possessive of her that he makes my dad look like a choirboy? That Emmy?" I ask, causing her to laugh even harder.

"Yup. Hard to believe, right? She doesn't talk much about it, but they have never kept secrets from us. They told us a few years ago when we were getting a lecture about what life choices can do to people. Or better yet, how some choices can lead to bad shit and even worse shit. Whatever. I forget the whole point of it, and when you think about it, it's what brought Mom and Dad back together, so it's kind of romantic." She waves her hands and turns to walk into the room I'm assuming class will be in.

"Did you just call stripping . . . romantic?" Lila giggles after Maddi.

"Oh shut it, Doc. It really is. I'll tell you the whole story later, but basically, some stuff went down and Mom got all weird and ran away. Dad found her at a strip club of all places, and when she went to, you know, strip, he jumped on the stage and carried her out of the place over his shoulder. See? It's romantic."

"Uh, Maddi . . . if you think that's romantic, I would hate to see what happens when you have someone send you roses." Lyn snickers.

"Roses are boring. And overrated," Maddi snaps back.

God, I love my weird friends.

Twenty minutes later, I hate my weird friends.

We, of course, were the first to arrive. The room—a long, white rectangle—has ten poles going down a line and all facing the huge, daunting, floor-to-ceiling mirror. After the five of us filed in and were introduced to the instructors, Sarah and Felicia, they asked us to sit tight for a second while they waited for the other ladies who had signed up for the class. Who, of course, were late.

And now, here we are. After stretching every possible muscle in our bodies, the music still low, Sarah and Felicia got to work on some basic instructions. Instructions my short-as-hell ass was just struggling with.

“You want me to do what?” I ask Sarah again.

“Sweetheart, get it out of your head that you can’t do this. It isn’t about upper-body strength so much as it is about core strength. You’re using your arms to pull, but you are pushing off with your feet, all the while using your core to hold. Don’t focus so much on the mechanical stuff. Let your body do the work, and shortly, your mind will follow.”

“How is my body supposed to climb this thing again?” I ask, watching Lyn, Lila, and Stella slowly worm their way halfway up their poles. Maddi—the little slut—is already practically hanging from the ceiling. Of course she would be a natural.

“Watch,” Sarah says and grabs the pole with one hand. Then she reaches up and grabs the pole right above her other hand. She continues to alternate hands until she’s standing on her toes. Then she mimics the movements with her feet. And just like that, the monkey-slash-instructor is in the air. She elegantly lands back on her feet and, with a wave, says, “Now you try.”

It takes me a few times, but the next thing I know, I’m halfway up. “Woohoo!” I yell and stupidly remove my hands from the pole. My eyes widen about two seconds before I’m ass to the ground and once again cursing the pole.

“Next time, don’t get so ballsy,” Maddi laughs from the other side of the room, still twirling and swirling like she was made to be attached to a metal pole.

Okay, once I am out of my head, it really isn’t so bad. It only takes me a few more times before I feel confident to try something new.

“Well done, ladies! Now it’s time for the good stuff.”

Oh, hell.

Another ten minutes and I’m having more fun than I ever thought was possible. I’m covered in sweat, but the moves we’ve learned against the pole—and some off the pole—have my body humming with confidence. Okay, Lyn was right. Not that I’ll admit that to her.

I laugh when I see Lyn twist her body and almost fall off the heels on her feet. After about thirty minutes, we are told to shed the gym shoes for the heels we were asked to bring. Looking straight ahead to the mirror, I have to say that I look hot as hell.

My body looks tall with my five-inch heels, my legs long, tan, and toned. My gym shorts are looking more like sexy boy shorts at this point since they've all but ridden into my vagina. I'm normally not proud of my less-than-spectacular tits, but my small boobs are pushed up with my sports bra, and with the way I'm breathing, those barely-a-B cuppers are heaving like a busty pro. (Okay, so a B cup might be pushing it.) My cheeks are bright with all the exertion I've been putting out, my light-green eyes bright and shining with excitement, and my hair, which was in a long, perfectly stylized ponytail, is now looking more like a messy but sexy up do.

"All right, ladies. Class is almost over, so now it's time for the fun part. Each of you, grab a chair off the far wall. I want you to use that chair and pretend that it's whoever you need it to be. Work it like you mean it. Roll your hips, pop that ass, and make it mean something. Pole dancing isn't just a dance of seduction. It's an art form in how to get a man to crave you like you're the air he needs to breathe. Like, if he can't have his hands on you right that second, he is going to die. Make that chair crave you, ladies."

When she turns and changes the music, I look over and read the name off the iPad screen—Marian Hill's "Got It." The music starts off with the perfect beat to warm my body with. Her sultry and seductive voice feeds my newfound confidence. It isn't long before I'm lost in the sounds pulsing through the room. I move with ease and ignore the burn in my muscles when I bend over and grab my ankles with my hands, shaking my ass in the air . . . right where the object of my desire's face would be if he were sitting there.

With that image fresh in my brain, I end the dance giving it all I have. My hips are rolling and undulating in a feverish nature, so when I catch my refection in the mirror, even I have to admit that it's hot. Standing up, I run my hands from my neck, over the sides of my tits, and down to my inner thighs.

The music owns me.

It isn't until the song ends and the girls around me start to clap that I remember where I am and stand up quickly.

"Well done, Dani! I knew you had a little slut in you yet!" Maddi whoops from the corner where she is standing with Stella and Lila, who are giggling.

"Very good, Dani. If I didn't know better, I would have thought you weren't even seeing that chair, right?" Lyn knowingly jokes and throws her arm over my sweaty shoulder.

I don't say anything. Not even when Maddi keeps cracking jokes. Stella laughs a few times, but her focus is quickly lost when we walk out of the room and she sees that the gym filled up with hot guys since we went into the class almost two hours ago.

"Oh my God," Lila laughs.

"Uh oh," Maddi giggles.

"This is going to be so freaking good," Lyn chuckles just seconds before my elbow is grabbed and I'm spun around before looking at a very angry Cohen Cage.

"Shit," I mutter.

Chapter 7

Cohen

IT SHOULD HAVE BEEN AN easy workout. Chance, my roommate and ex-Marine brother, said that I needed to get my shit in gear and get off the couch since I would be shipping off in two weeks.

The plus side of being in a unit that was as dark as it gets is that we aren't reporting to a base every day and dealing with shit day in and day out. We report, but it isn't to a base in the middle of the public eye. No, our shit is buried deep. We have once-a-month training missions that can last up to two weeks. Those keep our skills sharp and our bodies ready.

We were lucky this time. Normally when we're needed overseas, things have gotten worse than they can control. Then we come in and clean house.

This time, we're being sent in with notice, which always means we're going to be gone for a long period of time with no set end date. We could be over there for a few months or over a year. Mom is her normal freaking-out-but-staying-strong-and-supportive self. Dad, I know, is worried, but he won't speak a word of it. He's been there. The Special Forces unit I'm in is almost a carbon copy of the one he served on almost thirty years ago. He is more aware of the reality that I might not come home than anyone else is. But he also knows that this is very much a part of me and wouldn't dream of being anything less than supportive.

Chance served with me during our last deployment, but when we were ambushed and, in turn, he was injured, he was discharged honorably and has been heading up the personal security end of Corps Security ever since. We've been roommates on the home front ever since boot camp, and I wouldn't have it differently. He's just as much of a brother to me as Cam and Colt. He's been so busy in the two years since moving to town, often out of town for long periods, that he has rarely gone out with all of the crew.

"Yo, Cohen. Isn't that Maddox's daughter?" Pause. "Uh . . . and your sisters? And Axel's kid?"

My head was already turning when he mentioned one of Maddox's girls, then a little quicker when he mentioned the twins, but the second he mentioned Dani, my head snapped so rapidly that it's a shock I didn't break my own neck.

"What in the hell?" I ask, not expecting an answer.

"Damn, you didn't tell me the girls were looking like that these days," he grumbles and lets out a deep, "Umphh," when I elbow him in the gut.

"Shut the fuck up," I snap. "Is that the fucking pole dance room they just went in?"

"One in the same, brother," he laughs on a sharp exhale. "Did you have to give me all your strength, fucker?"

"Don't be such a baby. I hardly touched you."

"Hardly touched me. Well, Superman, you don't know your own strength."

I spend the next hour and then some fuming, imagining what is going on behind those doors. The more I think about it, the more I fume. I take it out on every piece of equipment I hit. I push my body to the edge just to get some of the anger out before the girls get out.

To make matters worse, what I thought would be a good idea to get my curiosity out of the way backfired in a big way. Ten minutes ago, I thought it was brilliant to just peek. Just a little peek to make sure there wasn't anything crazy going on. But that peek will forever be branded in my memory as one of the hottest things I've ever witnessed.

Dani coming unhinged and all but fucking the air between her and one black, metal chair.

I've been fighting a raging boner ever since one of the facility's staff members came and shut the door, giving me a warning about dis-enrollment if I am caught again.

Ever since then, her body and the way it looked, moved . . . Fuck me. I've been picturing every way I would take her when I finally hear Chance's voice break through my fantasy.

"Don't look now, Iron Man, but the girls have emerged, and now, they're all hot, flushed, and sweaty," he whispers down at me from where he's spotting my lifting.

I slam the bar home and leap off the bench, pausing to punch him in the gut again before I stomp through the gym.

"Oh my God," my sister, Lila, laughs.

"Uh oh," I hear Maddi giggle.

I don't even look at them.

"This is going to be so freaking good," Lyn chuckles right as my hand snags Dani around her tiny elbow and forces her to turn until her startled eyes are looking up into my own.

"Shit," she mumbles.

"What. The fuck. Was that?" I seethe.

"What was what?" she hedges.

"Do not fucking play games with me. You went into there to do what? Knit a sweater?"

She narrows her eyes but doesn't speak. I can hear my sisters laughing and look over to give them a hard stab of my eyes. I would never talk down to my girls, but right now, they're pushing the limits of my patience.

"I know what goes on in there, Dani-girl," I say and point behind her in the direction of the pole dancing room. Every man in this building knows what goes on in that room. We've been watching fine-as-hell chicks go in and out of there for years. The instructors alone are enough to keep some of these douchebags going for years in jack-off fantasies. "What I want to know is what in the *fuck* you think you're going to do with what you learned in there, Dani? Hm? Who in the hell is he?"

I can't stop the shit coming out of my mouth now. Ever since that night in her bed when I watched her sick with a fever dream all night with my name escaping her lips, all I've been able to think about is Dani. The only thing I've wanted is to throw her over my shoulder and take what my body keeps screaming is mine.

But it isn't mine.

Not yet. If I weren't about to ship off for a future unknown, I would throw her down and take her right fucking now. The only problem is, as much as I want her, I won't take something when I can't give her anything in return. And unfortunately, right now, I can't give her anything but the next two weeks. For a woman like Dani, that would never be enough. However, that doesn't mean I'm going to sit on my thumbs and let her show that sweet body off, work herself in preparation for someone else.

I do *not* think so.

"That isn't any of your business," she huffs and pulls her arm out of my hold.

"You don't think?" I ask, narrowing my eyes to slits.

"I don't think. I know."

"That's where you're wrong, baby." I step into her space and wait for her to make the next move.

"I'm not wrong, Cohen. Realistic. I'm not the one who's afraid. I haven't been afraid to admit how I feel for a long time. You, on the other hand, well . . . I'm sick of waiting for you to come to terms with it. Time to move on." She crosses her arms, and I want to groan when it brings attention to her tits. I've always been a breast man, but even though she isn't huge, there is more than enough to fit perfectly in my palms and I've been thinking about it for way too long.

"I'm not afraid of you," I scoff.

"You're terrified," she challenges.

"You're delusional."

"Ha! As if. Have a good workout, Cohen." She reaches up and pats my cheek, still trying to play off this indifference. If her palm didn't linger a little too long on my stubble, then I would possibly believe her.

What happened to my sweet Dani-girl?

I watch with a slack jaw as she turns, her long ponytail slapping me in the face, and struts out of the gym. My sisters, Maddi, and Stella all trail behind her, laughing.

Chapter 8

Dani

MY BODY IS SHAKING SO badly that, once we clear the gym's front doors and get out of sight of the windows, I almost collapse.

"I am so proud of you," Lyn says, reaching out to take my black heels out of my hand so I don't drop them. You do not drop Louboutins on the ground. Ever.

"Holy crap, that felt . . . amazing! I mean, I kind of feel like I'm going to puke, but holy crap!"

"Told you. Confidence. It means everything when dealing with men."

"When did you get so smart?" I ask her, trying to calm my heart down after that showdown with Cohen.

"When you started letting your hormones take over your common sense."

"Bitch," I laugh.

"Slut," she smiles.

That night, I'm pretty sure I am still feeling the adrenaline of my Cohen showdown. He sent me a text shortly after that simply read, "We need to talk," to which I responded with a very mature, "No we do not." He didn't reply, but then again, that isn't Cohen's style. When he wants something, he just takes it. I have a feeling that, the next time I run into him, there will be a whole lot of taking.

Daddy was up when I came home, but I'd left the heels in the car and pulled on some sweatpants and a hoodie over my normal workout gear. He narrowed his eyes, but didn't say anything. I swear that man knows everything.

It is most definitely time to move the hell out.

"Dani?" I hear Mom yell from the kitchen.

"Hey, Mom. What's up?"

"Nothing much, sweetheart. I just wanted to let you know your father and I are going up to the mountains next weekend." She looks up from her dinner prep and gives me a smile.

My mom, even at her age, with some gray hair mixed into her dark-red locks, is beautiful. You would never guess that she has two children. She's just a little taller than I am, but where I got all slim and small, she has the curves. I'm pretty much an exact replica of my mom—which is why Daddy has called me his little princess since the day I was born. Mom is his princess, so it makes sense.

"And you're letting me know this because you're worried Nate will starve?"

She gives me another smile. "No, my smartass daughter. I'm letting you know this and telling you that there are some boxes in the attic that you can use and giving you a heads-up that I'll have your very loving but overprotective father hours away and unknowing for four days. Plenty of time for you and the girls to get you packed up and moved into their new townhouse. Melissa and I checked it out this afternoon, and it's in a gated community, so when your father does become aware that you moved out on a sneak attack, he will only be upset for a little while."

I look up at my mom and have to fight back the emotion. Not because she is basically kicking me out—lovingly, of course—but because she is giving me the one thing I have been basically begging for.

"You're helping me escape?" I whisper.

"I'm not helping you escape, sweetheart. That would imply that we've been holding you hostage," she laughs. "I would keep you home for as long as I could, but I know you need to fly. And if I don't help make sure it's at least done in a way that your father can't argue about when he does find out, then you're never going to convince him that you aren't his little toddler just learning how to walk. He was made to protect you, baby. He loves you and it comes from a good place, but even I can admit it's time."

"What about Nate?" I ask.

"What about him? That big old baby wouldn't know what to do without me to wash his clothes and feed him."

I laugh because she is not wrong.

She turns and walks over to the sink to wash her hands. After drying them off, she walks over to me and gives me a big hug. I soak up the strength of her love and pull back to look into her eyes.

"You're okay with this? He's going to be so mad," I laugh.

"I'm okay with it. And your father mad isn't a bad thing if you know how to calm him down," she jokes with a wink.

"God, Mom! That is so gross."

We both laugh, and I thank my lucky stars that I lucked out with such amazing parents.

"Why don't you go change out of your gym clothes and those sweats you think fool anyone with. Then you can come down here and tell me what's going on with you and Cohen."

I gasp and look at her in shock. "What? How?"

"Oh you silly girl," she says and tucks a piece of hair that fell from my ponytail behind my ear. "Not only have I been watching this unfold for years, but I watched him all but fly out of here the morning after he stayed with you. Not only that, but the twins are chatty with their mom, and their mom is chatty with me."

"Oh, God. This is so embarrassing."

"I don't see why. Just because I haven't been screaming it doesn't mean that I haven't been your biggest cheerleader when it comes to you ending up with Cohen. Go get changed and come fill your mom in. I think we have about an hour before the men come looking for food."

I make my way up to my room and think about everything she just said. Obviously, the girls didn't know or they would have said something today. I can't believe she and Melissa went through all of this trouble. Especially knowing that Daddy is going to hit the fucking roof when he comes home to find I've moved out.

This should be fun. Maybe I can talk the camera crew from work into following me home. You know, for video evidence if he snaps and starts to go all Hulk-raging mad.

"Start from the beginning, Dani. I'm having a hard time following here. Lyn said what now?" Mom asks and hands me the spoon to stir the sauce.

"Okay, so we might have had too much wine, but she had some brilliant idea that all I need to do is work on my confidence when it comes to my . . . sexual side, and then the rest of it will fall into place with Cohen."

"And she said this because why? Because you've been a little shy with him lately?"

"Mom! Yes. It's been terrible. Ever since he was here with me when I was sick, things have just been weird. It's like my body is hyperaware of him when he comes around. Then boom, I turn into a mute freak."

She laughs, stirs the noodles and moves over to work on the salad. "Sweetheart, that—everything you're feeling—is completely normal. You and Cohen have been traveling two different roads on the way to this point for so long that it only makes sense that there will be a head-on crash when you finally connect. You should listen to her. She's right."

"I am listening to her. That's why we went to the pole dancing class," I mumble.

"You did what?" she asks, shocked.

"We went to a pole dancing and sensual empowerment class at the gym. It was a lot of fun, but it really worked. And . . . uh, Cohen was there when we left."

"Oh wow. And how did that go?"

"I think my heart is still about to beat out of my chest."

She laughs and reaches over to pull me toward her body. "That, my sweet girl, is the calm before the storm. If you think that is powerful, just wait until you're hit with it full force."

I shiver and she laughs.

"What are my girls in here gossiping about?" Daddy says, coming into the room and around the island to give me a kiss on the forehead and one to Mom that has me looking away.

"You two really need to remember that some things can't be unseen," I gripe.

"Little princess, just how do you think you got into this world?" he asks and then booms out a laugh when I cringe.

I look over at Mom, who gives me a wink, and shake my head when Daddy continues to laugh.

I watch them both for a little while and pray, not for the first time, that one day I'll have what they have.

Hopefully one day soon.

Chapter 9

Dani

"DAD IS GOING TO KICK your ass," Nate grumbles under the weight of my favorite reading chair that he and Liam are carrying up to my new bedroom.

The townhouse that Mom and Melissa picked out for the twins, Maddi, and me is a lot more than just that. It's a freaking townhouse on crack. It's a five-bedroom, three-story, huge-ass house located in one of the best gated communities around. She clearly downplayed it. I expected them to have put the house in their name, which I would have had a huge problem with, but Thursday morning, I had a call from the realtor asking me to meet him in his office on my lunch break. Seems my mom and Melissa had gone above and beyond. They had put first and last months' rent as a down payment and wouldn't even entertain the arguing. Emmy had been there with them. Three against four should have given us good odds—but then they brought out the big guns and started to talk about 'the dads' finding out and what would they say if we weren't in the best of the best.

Whatever.

We signed the lease, all four of us, and in less than thirty minutes, we were handed the keys.

It was amazing!

It's been two days since Mom took Dad up to the mountains, and I've enlisted Nate and Liam to help me get the heavy stuff out of my room. Mom told me to take all the furniture, but I felt too bad about it knowing that, if Daddy came home to an empty room, he very well might have heart failure. My new bedroom suite is being delivered tomorrow. Maddi and I went in on the living room stuff and entertainment systems. Lyn and Lila picked up the kitchen and patio furniture.

"If he kicks my ass, what's going to happen to you? You're the one who helped me move out!" I laugh when his face pales.

"Don't be such a baby, Nate," Liam says, continuing to lift the chair up the stairs.

I give him a smile. Liam Beckett, Aunt Dee and Uncle Beck's son, has been my best friend for so long that I couldn't imagine moving out and not having him here to witness this moment. I've been begging for him to come help hold my dad back so I could make my escape for years. I've always been close with Liam. Our mothers have been friends forever, and since we're close in age, we just kind of became buds. We were born close together, so we were lucky to grow up together and hit each grade in the same class. There was one year—third, I think—that we weren't in the same class. Mom and Aunt Dee say all the time that I cried for weeks until they realized I wouldn't stop until the school moved Liam into my class.

I don't believe it for a second. Even if there is home video footage of it somewhere.

"Lee, where did you put the keys to my car?" I call up the stairs, where he and Nate climbed with my reading chair.

"I don't know, Dani. Look by the front door table thingie!" he yells down.

"It's an accent table, doofus!" I yell back.

"What the hell ever that is," I hear him grumble.

I spend the next few minutes looking all over for my car keys. I need to get the last of my clothes and shoes out so I can start organizing my closet. My purses and the first, second, and third waves of my clothes and shoes came over early this morning. The girls left to get dinner a little while ago, so I knew they wouldn't be any help.

"Where the hell are they?" I grumble, looking in the coat closet before moving into the living room, which is just off the entryway, and bending over to look under the couch.

"Looking for these?"

I jump when I hear Cohen speak in a gruff tone just behind me. Coming off the floor with a squeal, I land right in his arms, my back pressed firmly against his chest and his arms clasping my arms to keep my steady.

"You jerk! Are you trying to give me a heart attack!?" I yell as I push back against him and try to move away. I realize my mistake instantly when I feel him go statue still and his harsh intake of breath against my ear. Then I feel him, really feel him, hard and hot against my back, and it's my turn to groan.

"I wasn't trying to sneak up on you." His hips move almost as if they have a mind of their own. "You just didn't hear me call your name."

"Can you let me go?" I ask.

"Why, Dani-girl? Scared?" He hums when I push back lightly and roll my hips.

"Hardly. Just depends on if you want Nate and Lee to see you manhandling me when they come down here." I'm only half joking. I wouldn't call what I'm feeling scared. Well, not scared of him. Scared of the enormity of these feelings? Absolutely.

"I'll hear them coming," he responds.

His hands shift, and then he spins me so that we're facing. I look up until our eyes meet, and my breath comes out in a whoosh.

"You're so beautiful," he mumbles.

"Thanks," I reply lamely. Thanks?

He laughs and drops his head some, his brown eyes becoming so dark that they're almost black.

And that's when I hear dumb and dumber with the worst-possible timing in the world arguing about real tits versus fake tits, stomping down the stairs. Cohen drops his forehead against mine, gives my arms a squeeze, and then steps back. I watch, baffled, as he reaches out and holds my car keys up. Mutely, I take them from his hooked finger and watch as he walks away, over to my brother and Lee and starts to weigh in on their conversation.

Humiliatingly enough, he sides with the fake tit side.

Cohen

I could be agreeing that the sky is green and the grass is blue. I have no fucking clue what these two are talking about. I enter in and pretend I have a care about the topic, grunting when I feel would be appropriate, and steal glances over at Dani as she drops her shoulders, her head dropping and her eyes focused on the floor in front of her. She looks so deflated. I just want to pull her back in my arms and take that kiss that was just seconds away from finally happening. Take her in my arms and promise her the world.

But then I remember why I've been holding back and realize I made the right move. She gives me a sad glance before squaring her shoulders and walking out the front door.

I finally tune in to the conversation around me and shake my head when I realize what they're talking about.

"If you prefer fake tits, then something is wrong with you, Nate," I say and sigh. "There is something to be said about feeling a woman, all woman, in your palms and you just can't get the same feelings when you can feel a bag of fluid rolling around under your fingertips."

They both look at me like I'm a fool, and I look between the two of them while playing my words back in my head, trying to figure out what the hell their issue is.

"Dude, two seconds ago, you agreed with me when I said big, huge, fake tits is the way to go." Nate reaches out and puts his hand against my forehead before continuing. "Are you feeling okay there, big guy?"

Belatedly, it hits me that Dani might have heard me, and I groan.

Shit.

"I'm fine, asshole. I just have a lot on my mind." Which isn't a lie. I have a shitload of things I need to do before I leave, and on top of all that, this thing, whatever it is, between Dani and me has me running in circles around myself.

"Sure you do, Coh. Do you need anything?" Nate asks, no trace of humor left in his tone.

"Nah. Just need to work on things myself. I've got some loose ends I need to tie up before I leave. Mom and the girls are having a hard time with it. Cam and Colt haven't said as much, but I know they're worried, and Dad is being Dad." All true. I leave out that I also need to figure out what the hell I'm going to do with Dani too before I leave. If I leave things how they are, knowing I'll be gone for a while, I'll constantly be thinking about it. If anything, I need to sit her down and at least explain why I'm holding back when it's clear we both want this.

Well, it's clear to me that I want her and she wants me. I'm guessing she has no clue the depth of my desire for her.

"Makes sense. Don't worry though. We'll watch out for the girls," Lee, ever the peacekeeper and do-gooder, says.

If Dani were best friends with any other guy, I would probably shit a green brick of jealousy, but not with Liam. He's helped me chase off more guys than I can remember, and I have no doubt he will continue when I leave.

"Thanks, Lee." I slap him on the shoulder and give him a nod before I head to the door in search of Dani. I almost run into her when she comes back in with a stack of shoeboxes taller than she is. "Whoa, Dani!" Reaching up, I snag a few boxes and smile when her flushed face comes into view. "Show me to your room?"

She nods, walks around me, and moves up the stairs. I watch her firm ass with rapture with each step I climb behind her.

Yeah . . . we definitely need to have a talk.

Chapter 10

Dani

I CAN'T DO THIS ANYMORE. I just can't. This hot-and-cold shit with him. Me suddenly forgetting how to act like a normal adult around him. All of it. I'm just so tired of it all.

I've always known he would be stupid to love. I've known it since before I made that last tumble ass over elbows and landed in a mass of limbs. I knew before the fall that it would be a painful tumble, but I still jumped and fell in love with him regardless.

"Dani, look at me," he implores when we step in to my room and place the boxes on the floor of my walk-in closet. "Please," he adds.

With a deep breath, I turn and look him in the eye. Gone is the boiling lust, and what's taken its place is acceptance that we won't ever be.

"Talk to me," he pleads.

"What do you want me to say? You know how I feel, Cohen. I've told you before. I know you heard me in my sleep when I was sick. Plus, there is this . . . thing between us. Bottom line—you know how I feel and it isn't your fault that you don't return those feelings." I sigh and sit down on my chaise lounge, which Nate and Lee just placed in the middle of my room. "I'm tired of feeling like I need to run or act a certain way around you. It used to be easier to hide the way I feel."

"I don't want you to hide. Not from me."

I feel my brows pull in at his words, confused by the mixed signal.

"I don't want you to be anything but yourself around me," he continues. "I just don't know what to do about this, Dani. I know what's right here. I know what I should and shouldn't do when it comes to you. It's just getting harder to keep those lines from blurring."

"What are you saying, Cohen? Spit it out in plain terms so I don't get your words mixed up and seek hope when there isn't any to be found."

His face hardens, and he takes a step towards me, leaning down, placing his hands on either side of my hips, and not stopping his body until his face is level with mine. His harsh breaths hit my lips, and I lean back, only to stop when his body follows the movement.

"When you were fifteen and you sat in my parents' basement, you told me that, one day, I would see you the way you see me. You told me that you would be waiting, Dani. Waiting for me to become yours and you mine. I wasn't ready, but that doesn't mean that I didn't see you and haven't seen you every day since and thought about what it would be to have you. You told me you would be waiting. You sat there with all the courage in the world and laid it out there, Dani. Are you telling me now that you take it back?"

"You remember that?" I gasp.

When he starts talking next, I swear that my heart stops. Shock. But complete wonderment. His voice, a pitch higher, whispers the words I said to him almost eight years ago verbatim. I should know—I practiced them for weeks in the mirror before I worked up the courage to actually say them to him. They were words I would never forget. Especially since he treated me with the indifference of a good friend after—until recently.

"I'm going to miss you, Cohen. I know you don't look at me like I look at you, but one day, you're going to come back and I'll still be waiting for you. Waiting for you to see me like I see you. Mark my words, Cohen Cage. One of these days, you're going to be mine. And until you're ready . . . I'll be here. I'll be waiting."

Holy shit.

"Holy shit," I repeat out loud when he stops talking. "I can't believe you remember that."

"I will never forget it," he vows.

"What does that even mean?" I throw back. Once again, here he goes with his hot-and-cold shit.

"That means exactly that. I won't ever forget it. Just because I haven't acted on this chemistry between us doesn't mean I don't want to. Back then, I couldn't. You know that it wouldn't have been appropriate with our ages. And now . . . Now, I don't even know what it is because my head is in a million different places right now. But one thing I know is that I'm getting ready to leave. I'm getting ready to leave and, Dani, I just can't put you in the position of being in limbo for months, years, who knows, just so that I can feel what *you* feel like." He drops his head against mine and sighs. "I've never wanted someone as fiercely as I want you, Dani-girl."

The tone of his voice is so heartbreaking that my chest clenches.

"I wish it were a different world. One where I wasn't leaving and our future wasn't unknown. If it were, you would have been mine already." He gives me a sad, small kiss against my forehead—not pulling back for a few beats. He looks me in the eyes again before pulling himself up and walking out the door.

Well, if that doesn't suck, I don't know what does.

I might be grasping at straws here . . . but what he didn't say was that we didn't have a future at all. Just that he wasn't sure what it was.

It's not much hope—but it's something. And that was more than I had an hour ago.

Chapter 11

Dani

Two weeks later

"DANI!" NATE YELLS UP THE stairs, his impatience clear as day. He just got here two minutes ago to pick me up and he's already reached his patience level.

"What?"

"You need to stop putting all that shit on your face so we can get going."

"I'm not 'putting that shit' on my face, Nate!" I yell back as I recap my mascara and go over my lips again with bright-red lipstick, giving myself one more look to make sure everything is perfect. I have to look perfect today.

Summer has come to stay in Georgia. If my daddy saw me now, I'm sure he would have a fit over my outfit. I'll have to deal with him later, but he won't be able to do anything but complain about it by then. My jean shorts are just shy of what I would consider normal. They cover everything but show a lot—and I mean a lot—of leg. My red tank top is tight and gives me just enough of cleavage.

I look hot.

Really hot.

My legs look amazing. Like, off-the-charts ahhhmazing. The shorts matched with my heels make them look longer than they are. Weeks of working daily at the gym and a few more pole dancing classes have them toned to perfection, and thanks to the sun, my tan is the perfect shade of dark. My long, chestnut locks are hanging down my back in soft waves, giving them that "I woke up like this" look even though it took me almost an hour to get each curl perfect. But my makeup might take the cake. Maddi did it before she left the house, going heavy on my eyes so that my green peepers would pop like crazy. I'm not vain, but I can safely admit that I look hot as hell.

It really is a shame that I look this good and I know it might not do any good. I'm frustrated. Ever since that day in my room, Cohen has been like a ghost. Any chance I thought I might have had to try to further our conversation was just kicked like a bug. He just disappeared.

Okay, he didn't disappear, but he didn't exactly make it so that we could ever be alone to have a private chat. Nope. If I tried, he just wasn't having it. He was hell-bent on keeping his distance, and that shit is ending tonight.

Nate pulls up to the event hall—a rustic, old log cabin—and grunts a few times when he looks over at me, clearly trying to tell me by his caveman speech that he isn't happy about my outfit.

"What is your problem?" I ask, crossing my arms across my chest.

His eyes narrow, and he grunts again.

I give him a few grunts of my own. What the hell? Maybe he'll understand what I'm trying to express verbally if I try to dumb it down to alpha speak.

"What are you doing?" he asks with his head tilting like a confused dog when I grunt a few more times.

"Well, dear brother, I'm trying to see if I attempt to vocalize as you and our father do that maybe you'll answer me back. Clearly, I have no idea what has your panties in a twist today. You've been all snappy snapperson since we left my house."

"You."

"Uh . . . can we add a few words to that, maybe a dramatic pause for flair and express a coherent thought that is well thought out and planned to make sense so that it can be understood and processed?"

"God, you can be such a bitch."

I smile. "Oh? You say that like it's a bad thing."

He sighs and looks out the front window.

"Seriously, Nate, what's going on?"

"It's nothing, Dani. I'm taking my bad mood out on you. Doesn't help that you're dressed like a tramp just to gain Cohen's attention."

I look down at my outfit again. I don't think it's trampy. Sure, it's showing my legs off and my top is tight, but I'm hardly indecent.

"Okay, tramp might be too much, but couldn't you have worn something that, I don't know, covers all of that under your neck?" He gestures wildly to my body.

"You're being ridiculous. And I'm not wearing anything *for* Cohen. It's summer, in Georgia, and, like, over a hundred degrees. I'm pretty sure this is considered overdressed by most."

Okay, so I'm lying. He knows it. It could be considered slightly manic in my desperateness to get some sort of reaction from him.

"You're only going to get hurt, Dani," he whispers so low that I almost miss it, and hearing him confirming my biggest fear brings tears to my eyes.

"You don't know that," I argue weakly.

He does know that though. Cohen's his best friend. Regardless of the fact that he probably doesn't like that I've always crushed on him, he's never tried to stop me. Until now.

"What do you know, Nate?"

He doesn't say anything for the longest time. He just continues to look out the window, taking in all of our extended family as they mill about the parking lot and outside the venue. I follow his gaze when I see it soften slightly and see Ember Locke waving at our direction. Her face falls when Nate doesn't acknowledge her and she looks over at me. I give her a weak smile but bring my attention back to my brother.

"He's bringing a date, Dani."

And cue heart stop.

It just drops right into my stomach.

In all the years I've loved Cohen Cage from afar, he's never, not once, brought one of his dates around the family. I'm not stupid. I know he dates. He practically has girls falling over themselves to get his attention. But throughout the years, he's never brought them around. And with everything that's been going on between us for over a month now, I really didn't think he would stoop this low just to get me to leave him alone. Maybe he didn't mean to leave a trail of hope in his little goodbye speech the other day.

"What?" I gasp.

"You heard me, Dani. Don't make me say it again."

"Is it . . . is it serious?"

"He's bringing her, isn't he?" He looks over, and I can tell he hates that he is hurting me right now. "I've only met her a few times. She's nice enough. I honestly don't know her or their relationship well enough to tell you any more. He's bringing Chance, too."

"Oh," I say, looking back out the window.

"Yeah, oh," he parrots, reaching over and grabbing my hand to give me a strong, reassuring squeeze. "Come on, little princess. Let's get this over with."

When we make it inside, things are predictably insane. Whenever we all get together, things tend to go that way. I love my family, but sometimes—like right now—they're just too much.

The room is huge, set up that way to ensure plenty of space for the number of guests they plan on attending. Numerous tables are scattered throughout the middle of the room, with some space for the food tables, DJ, a bar, and a huge stage set up across the room. It's typically used for small, local concerts and some wedding receptions. I guess you could consider it country chic, with the log cabin look from outside continuing inside. They've added crystal chandeliers to the vaulted ceilings and carried the décor to the table settings. Mason jars full of wildflowers are at each table, American flags sticking out the center of each, with a red-white-and-blue theme for each table. My attention goes back to the large stage, which takes up the whole back end of the room. It's covered in a thick, red curtain—and I officially decide that it will be my escape later.

Obviously, Mom, Dee, and Melissa went all out. I see Mom at the far side of the large room talking to Dee and Emmy. She's waving her arms around like a windmill, so she's clearly worked up about something. Daddy is standing by the bar with Beck and Asher. He looks up when we walk in. As always, he knows when one of his girls is near, and I have no doubt, judging by the way his eyes go hard, that he knows I'm upset. Or he's noticed my outfit. I give him a bright smile, which he doesn't buy for one second, and I move around Nate to go find Maddi.

She left the house almost an hour before me to come and help set up. The girls had spent the night back at their parents' house so that they could spend more time with their brother, so I knew they wouldn't be here yet.

Liam stops me before I even get two feet into my quest for Maddi to say hey and gives me a big hug.

"Are you okay?" he asks, not even breaking to say hello.

Another infuriating side effect of being surrounded by overprotective alpha males is their inability to leave well enough alone. They sense that one of the females in our group is upset and they just can't *not* try to fix it.

"Stop, Lee. Don't turn on your protector crap right now. I get it enough from Nate and Daddy. I'm fine. Just fine," I snap.

"Uh, right. I'm just . . . I'll just go find Zac and Jaxon now." He holds his hands up in a mock surrender and walks slowly backwards. Away from me and my special brand of crazy.

I watch him walk away until he stops where Asher and Chelcie's boys are standing with Cam and Colt.

"Aren't you a happy camper. You were fine an hour ago. How could your day change so swiftly?" Maddi laughs, coming up to my side and wrapping her arm over my shoulders.

I allow myself two seconds of soaking up her support before I duck under her arm, grab her hand, and drag her through the tables and out the back door.

"What in the hell," she mumbles, struggling to keep up with me. Which is laughable, really, with her long legs against my short ones.

I let the back door slam behind us and pull her farther behind the building and the dumpsters. No way I'm chancing anyone overhearing us.

"What has gotten in to you, Dani?" Maddi inquires when I finally drop her hand.

"Did you know that Cohen was bringing a date?"

"Do what? You're kidding, right?"

"Dead serious," I all but yell. "Nate just told me in the car that he was bringing someone. That's all I know. But, Maddi . . . surely it's serious if he's bringing her here! Oh my God, oh my God. I need to leave. That's what I need to do."

"Actually, you should probably just try and calm your shit down and stop acting like the world is over. It's Cohen. I'm sure that she is just a friend or something. I don't know, maybe she's homeless and he is bringing her so she can get a meal. Maybe she is part alien and using him to get to know our culture. Whatever the case may be, you freaking yourself out over it isn't going to do a bit of good."

"Why do you have to make so much sense?" I ask sarcastically after she stops talking.

She, in turn, gives me a glare that would make her father proud.

"Aliens? Really?" I laugh.

"Oh, shut up. And you know I make sense because I'm the smart one. Plus, with the twins not here yet, someone has to keep your ass from overacting. Oh! I know. Let's call Lyn. She'll know what's up."

She pulls her cell out of her back pocket, and after a few seconds of fiddling with it, she presses it to her ear.

"Hey," she says into the phone. "Are you alone?"

This is ridiculous. I should just leave now and save myself the gut-crushing pain of seeing another woman in his arms.

"Is Cohen bringing a date?" she whispers and looks around the side of the dumpster.

"No one is coming, Maddi," I whisper back.

"Then why are you whispering too, smarty pants?" she snaps and turns her attention back to her phone call. "I know that, Lyn, but Nate told Dani that he was and now she's freaking the hell out . . . I don't know where he heard it . . . No . . . Well, then who is she?"

Oh shit. It's true. I should definitely leave. Maybe if I cut through the woods to the industrial park, some nice trucker will take me to Mexico.

"Oh really? Oh . . . yeah . . . No . . . Shit. Okay. Bye." She looks down at her phone before looking up at me. Her eyes hold nothing but sympathy.

"It's true?"

"Looks like it," she whispers before pulling me into her arms. "Okay, plan B. Let's turn this frown upside down. So he's got a friend with him. We don't know anything else, so let's just pretend they're friends and just friends. Lyn didn't know much. Just that her mom told her that he's brought her by the house a few times this last week. That's all she knows. Let's try not to stress about it, okay? You, my friend, look hot, so let us just enjoy the day. You continue to be hot, and aside from being polite, ignore him and his special friend. There will be plenty of other guys here tonight, so it's time to get your flirt on. Do you need me to go sneak you some booze?"

"Maddi, I'm old enough to drink. I don't need you to sneak me anything anymore." I laugh.

"Right. Well, it's time to act like you could care less and have some fun. Don't let this hang over you—not tonight. Tonight is about making sure Cohen knows his family loves him before he leaves. No sad faces or jealous eyes. This thing between you two will work itself out, I promise."

"Yes, sir, Maddi, sir." I salute her, and after a few giggles, we take off on a mission to practice my acting.

I've always been good at acting.

Even if I feel like my heart is breaking inside.

It isn't his fault I feel this way and he doesn't. Or I should say that I feel this way and he isn't willing to let himself.

One thing's for certain though. If Cohen Cage wanted me like I want him, he never would have let it go this long without taking it. Taking me and never letting go. Instead, he's just playing more games in his quest to keep me at arm's length. Because *he* is making decisions about the future without even considering that maybe I believe he's worth waiting for.

Time to put on my big-girl panties and pretend that the other half of my heart isn't going to be in the arms of another woman.

Chapter 12

Dani

"LITTLE PRINCESS, WHAT THE HELL are you wearing?" Daddy rumbles, taking my beer out of my hands. "No," he snaps, playfully slapping my hand and takes a sip.

"I don't think so," I laugh and grab it back.

He raises one dark brow but doesn't make a move to take my drink again. He had the hardest time when I turned twenty-one and could legally drink. He kept switching out my beers for apple juice the whole night.

"Want to tell me what has you down so I can go fix it?"

"Nothing is wrong, Daddy," I mumble into my cup.

"Right. You get that I wasn't born yesterday, yeah?"

"Oh yeah, I know that. You were born, like, fifty years ago."

I snicker to myself when he starts bristling. He hates to be reminded that he's over that fifty hump. I've seen pictures of him when he was my age, and honestly, if it weren't for the light peppering of gray, you would never know he was fifty-one. He's still one of the largest men I've ever met. He towers over Mom and me at six foot six, with muscles that have only gotten bigger and bulkier over the years. It's clear to not just me, but every friend I have had over the years that my daddy wasn't just hot when he was younger—he still has it.

"Don't think I didn't notice you going solid when the twins got here. Did you girls get into a fight? Does this mean you need to come home now?"

I roll my eyes and laugh. He's been trying to find reasons to get me to move home ever since he got back from his trip and realized I was gone. For a whole day, he wouldn't leave my living room. I think he would still be there if Mom hadn't shown up. All it took was her to whisper in his ear, and just like that, they were gone.

Of course the first conclusion he comes to is that the girls and I are fighting. He probably wishes we were. Which is really silly because one thing about Lyn's, Lila's, and my friendship—we don't fight. We never have and I don't see it happening any time soon.

Okay, well, time to divert his attention.

"Nope. We're fine. It was . . . uh, cramps, Daddy. You know, period stuff."

He looks horrified. Which was the goal. Daddy doesn't talk female issues. I asked him once to grab me some tampons from the store one day. He threatened to take Nate's car away if he didn't go instead. Nate came back thirty minutes later and threw the box at my head, cutting me right above the eyebrow and losing his car anyway for hurting me. To this day, I like to leave tampon boxes in Nate's car.

"Uh . . . yeah. I'm going to go over here with the guys and talk about football and boxing. You know, guy stuff."

I smile to myself when he walks away. God, he's too easy.

"Cramps, my ass," Liam laughs, throwing his arm around my shoulders and pulling me close. His strong hold makes it clear that I'm not getting away without talking to him.

I take a deep swallow of my beer and look up into his chocolate eyes.

"I don't think they're dating, if it makes a difference. He's hardly said one word to her, and she is sticking close to Chance's side. Chance, who I'm guessing isn't dating her either, looks like he would rather be anywhere else than glued to her side."

I look across the room where Cohen is talking to his brothers, Camden and Colton. As if he senses my gaze on him, his eyes meet mine, and he frowns when he sees Lee's arm around me. His eyes move back to mine, and even from the distance, I can see them heat. That fire that burns across my skin.

Okay, so he still wants me.

What the hell ever.

"Yeah, that right there. A man doesn't get jealous of someone he knows is just a friend if there isn't something else there, Dani. I've told you this a million times over: he's scared. Think about it and you know I'm right. His parents, your parents, all of the relationships mixed in that would go insane if you two got together. Sure, it could have a happy ending, but he isn't going to upset the fold. Not when it could just as easily go bad."

"It wouldn't go bad, Lee." And it wouldn't. I know it with everything I am that it would be a flawless love.

"You can't know that. Not for sure, anyway. Regardless of what your stubborn little heart tells you, you can't predict these things."

"Are you telling me I should give it up? Give him up?"

"Never, Dani. I would never tell you to give him or your feelings for him up. You know my parents' story. Dad never once gave up on Mom, even when it seemed fruitless. What I'm trying to get at, but clearly doing a terrible job of, is that if you believe with one hundred percent of your soul that he's your other half, don't you dare stop until you've had a taste of it."

Oh shit. My throat is burning. I swallow thickly and nod my head, not trusting my words.

"Do you think he knows how bad it is?"

"That you're in love with him and that you don't just want him to fuck you?" Liam guesses correctly.

"Yeah, that."

"He isn't stupid, Dani. He knows. Or at least he has an idea. Look, before, it wouldn't have been good for him to even entertain the thought. You were too young. I'm not saying that isn't an issue for him now, but you're almost twenty-two, so I don't think that's it. You know him. You know how important his family . . . this family . . . is to him. All I can tell you is to talk to him. He leaves tomorrow. Just talk to him. I know you guys talked before, but obviously, you didn't talk enough. Make him hear your points, and don't leave anything out. You say that he's saying no because he's leaving . . . well, don't let that stop you. If it's really that simple, then go for it."

"What about that girl?" I question, my mouth having a hard time getting the question out.

God, he's right. I'm eaten up with jealousy over her. She's pretty. Blond, busty, and tall. Everything I'm not. She is my complete opposite in every way.

"Who? The date? Yeah . . . something tells me you really don't have to worry about her. Seriously, Dani. She hasn't gotten up from that table he parked her at when he got here. If a girl were here with a man like him, you better believe she wouldn't be leaving his side. In case you haven't noticed, there are a few overly horny men in this room."

"You're so sick." I laugh and look up at Liam's smiling, handsome face. "What would I do without you, Lee?"

"Probably get lost in life, Dani. It would be tragic. Just confused and walking in circles around reality all of the time."

I throw my head back and laugh. How absurd the thought is. He knows I'm as independent as it gets. But he's halfway right. Just like without the twins, I would be lost without Lee in my life. My skin tingles, and I stop laughing to look around the room. Cohen's stopped talking to his brothers and is scowling over at Lee and me. His hand grasping his beer is turning white around his fingertips.

"Uh oh. Could the bear just come out of hibernation? Looking at his prey for the first time since a long, cold, lonely winter?" Liam snickers.

"Shut up," I hush, punching him hard in the stomach, only to pull my hand back when his rock-hard abs cause millions of little tingles to shoot up my arm. "Did your body just break my hand!?" I screech when the pain won't stop.

"The hell?" I hear growled, and before I can react, Daddy wraps me in his arms and looks at my hand. I let the familiar scent of leather and cinnamon calm me down, and I fight back the stinging tears and burn in my throat. "Liam Beckett, did you break my daughter?!"

"Oh come on. She hit me! I didn't break her. Well, my perfectly chiseled body might have hurt her slightly. But it wouldn't be an issue if she would learn how to keep her hands off of me."

"You little shit," I laugh over my father's shoulders.

Liam laughs loudly, "I'll go get some ice for the big baby."

"Don't call my little princess a baby!" Daddy yells after Liam.

"I'm fine, just hit him weird," I say to soothe his worry.

"How many times do I have to tell you not to hit like that? I could see your form was off all the way across the room. Should have gone for the crotch. Always go for the crotch, Dani."

Oh lord, here we go. He's been teaching me how to kick a man's ass since I was five and Zac stole my doll. Of course, his first lesson was for me to always go for the crotch.

"Daddy, I wasn't trying to hurt him. We were just joking around."

"Joking around? You aren't supposed to *joke around* with boys. I need to look into that island. Ship your ass off," he grumbles under his breath.

It's going to be a long night.

Four long-as-hell hours later, the parents have all left. Which was a relief. Not that it isn't fun to have everyone around, but I know we're all ready to let loose and enjoy the night. They wanted to keep the beginning of the evening just the close families. More intimate so that way we could all spend some time with Cohen. Through the hours, more of our friends came—some of Cohen's from school and some from Basic Training. Everyone is ready to make sure he enjoys his last night home for the next year. This is his second deployment, and I don't think it will ever get easy.

Cohen joined the Marines after he finished his football career at University of Georgia. He probably could have gone pro, but he's always wanted to follow his father's footsteps and join the Marines. Then again, for a boy who wore a cape for the majority of his childhood, it makes sense that the hero inside him would win.

The first time he went overseas, I was depressed for months. Worried, sad, and heartbroken. It was hard to watch his parents struggle with their worry and his siblings deal with the fear, and everyone in general just had a hard time knowing he was fighting in the middle of a war zone.

Like his father, mine, and the rest of the father figures in our close-knit family, Cohen was special ops, and when he was deployed, it was lights out for communication. It was months until we finally heard an update from him. In the thirteen months that he was gone, he was able to call home twice.

This time, he already warned his family that this would most likely be a longer tour. A longer tour and even less of a chance that he would be able to get in contact with us often.

I would be lying if I said that I wasn't terrified for him. Not because I have doubts in his abilities, but because of the very real fear that, no matter how trained he is, something terrible could happen to him over there.

"What's got that frown on your face, Dani-girl?"

God, that voice.

I suck in a deep breath when I feel Cohen sit down next to me. His smell instantly surrounds the dark haven I've escaped to. I thought I was doing a good job hiding back here. The party had gotten pretty rowdy when the parents left. Usually, I would be right there with them, but with Liam's words still floating around in my head, I just needed a moment to myself. To collect my thoughts and figure out a way to get him alone so I could force another talk.

When no one was looking, I walked behind the stage curtains, plopped my ass down in the middle of the floor, lay back, and let the vibrations of the DJ's music lull me and the darkness wrap around me like a comforting hug.

"Nothing, Cohen. Just thinking."

"Thinking about what?" he pushes.

"Are you scared?" I ask, sitting up on my elbows to look at him.

He turns his head but doesn't speak.

Given this opportunity to take him in, I don't waste a second. His dark eyes are looking directly into mine. Searching for what, I'm not sure, but one thing I'm certain of is that he isn't looking at me like a man who has a girlfriend should. Or whatever she is. His hair is freshly buzzed along the sides and slightly longer on the top, which makes me wonder who cut it for him since I know I didn't. He usually keeps it a little longer, perfect for all the times I've imagined running my fingers through it when I'm not in the middle of cutting it. The light beard he was sporting all year is gone, which allows his strong jaw to show. I love it when he shaves, but I also love the look of his beard. Every time he swallows, his jaw flexes in this sexy way I've never been able to control lusting over. Jaw porn. With Cohen, it's a very real thing.

I am staring at his lush, full lips when I realize I have been basically lusting over his face since he sat down. Shit.

When my eyes meet his, I expect to see humor at busting me, but all I see is the mirrored hunger I know is dancing behind my green eyes. His are heated, a deep fire blazing behind them. He isn't even attempting to hide his desire for me.

I hold my breath, waiting while the world stops spinning around me, and I go for it. Clearly, he's taken off guard when I all but leap off the stage flooring and into his lap. My legs fall on either side of his hips, my hands dive into that freshly cut hair—enjoying the prickle of the buzz against my palms—and my lips are on him before he has a second to figure out what my intentions are. He's solid and unmoving. If it weren't for his strong hands holding my hips in place, I probably would have gotten up and run away.

Pulling my lips off his motionless ones, I look into his shocked eyes and feel a heated blush of embarrassment wash over me.

"Oh my God. I'm . . . I . . . I shouldn't have done that."

He doesn't say anything, but he also doesn't let go of my hips when I try to move off him. It takes me a second for the reality to hit me—I'm sitting in the shadows, straddling a very shocked Cohen Cage.

Holy crap. Okay, so maybe I really was reading too much into the last couple of weeks.

"I . . . I don't even know what to say. I'm sor—"

My apology never leaves my lips, because in a split second, his hands tighten, pulling me harder against his body, and his thick lips crash down on mine. The feel of him, the reality of a kiss I've dreamt of since I was old enough to crave it, is so overwhelmingly perfect that I feel it all the way to my soul.

"We shouldn't be doing this here," I gasp against his lips, knowing that I don't mean a word of it. If he stops, I just might die.

"Can't stop, Dani-girl. Now that I finally know what you taste like . . . I can't stop," he moans when I shift my weight against his lap.

I can feel the truth in his words against my core, and I can't stop myself from rotating my hips against his hardened length.

"Jesus. I knew you would make me come undone."

His lips are back on mine. Caressing, lightly nipping between his teeth, before his tongue slides along the seam and demands access to my mouth. Our tongues dance together, almost as if they were made for each other. My breaths dance with his in a heated tango.

It.

Is.

Glorious.

"Your girlfriend," I pant, trying to pull back but knowing it will be impossible to let this go.

"Not my girlfriend."

I pull back and look into his hooded eyes, "She came with you, Cohen."

"*She* isn't with me. She came because she is the widow of one of the men from my unit, Dani-girl. She is here because she has no one else and she's had a hard time recently. But *she* isn't who I want in my arms. Good lord, woman. Shut up and kiss me."

Well, alrighty, then.

When I still don't move, his hands slide up my sides. His thumbs brush over the sides of my breasts, causing my nipples to harden painfully, before his hands cup my face. His fingers go into my hair, his thumbs lightly caressing my cheeks, while he studies my face. I have no idea what he sees there, but it must be enough, because seconds later, he pulls my face to his and devours my lips.

There is no other word for it. He takes my lips in a kiss so brutally perfect. His tongue duels with mine with effortless control.

It takes my sluggish mind only seconds to get with the program. Seconds, minutes, hours—I have no idea. It isn't long before I'm working his shirt over his head and his hand is working its way into my shorts.

"Dani, we need to stop," he groans as his fingers roll against my core, lightly pressing against my swollen clit before he pushes two thick digits deep within my wet core.

"Can't," I gasp against his mouth and dig my fingers into his shoulders. "Don't want to."

"Not here. Anyone could find us." He's right. I hate it, but he's right.

"Cohen Cage . . . I swear to God that I'm going to go insane if you're going to leave me like this."

He doesn't say anything. His eyes are back to searching my own.

"I've waited forever for this," I whisper.

His eyes close, and he drops his forehead against mine.

"Forever," I repeat.

"Shit," he groans. Then he pulls his fingers from my shorts, helps me right my clothing, and helps me stand with his hands against my hips.

I watch in confusion as he grabs his shirt and pulls it back over his head before he starts to pace around in the darkness.

Good job, Dani. Way to scare him off with your freakish admission that you've always waited for him to shove his hands down your pants. I bet he's trying to figure out the best way to run as fast as he can without hurting my feelings.

Well, too late for that.

"Listen, I'm just going to go . . ."

His head snaps over to mine, and within seconds, I'm back in his arms. He just holds me tight against his body. When his body starts to sway with the music coming through the stage's thick curtain, I struggle to keep up with his mood changes.

Until I hear the song the DJ is playing.

Brett Young's "Kiss by Kiss."

The same song I had my first dance to with him four years ago. The same song that has always reminded me of him day after day and year after year.

His lips go to my temple and he places a lingering kiss there before sliding his jaw down to rest it there. His breath against my ear is coming in deep pants as I hear him singing the song lyrics. Lyrics that will forever have a new meaning to me.

"And every time you look at me I just want to hold you. *All my life*

I've been waiting for you. Little by little falling for you."

Oh. My.

I pull back and look up into his handsome face. His lips curl slightly in a smile that seems to say, *Well, I guess the cat's out of the bag now.* His eyes hold mine as he waits to see what I'll do with his admission, and he pulls me deeper in toward his body. As if he's afraid I'm going to run.

As freaking if!

"I fell for you a long time ago, Cohen Cage. I've loved you my whole life."

His face relaxes, and he lets out his breath. When his forehead drops against mine, I brace myself for his rejection.

"Dani-girl," he groans like a prayer for strength.

Which is when it happens. When he realizes just who he has in his arms. And he starts to pull back. This is going to change everything between us. This final rejection. If the families find out—my brother, his siblings . . . Oh, God, Liam was right. This is going to be terrible.

"I have to go check on Megan. Make sure Chance can take her home."

And just like that, he's walking away from me, pulling the curtain to the side, and jumping down off the stage.

I didn't think it would hurt this bad. But having something I've wanted, desired, *craved,* in my arms for just moments only to have it ripped away is more painful than never having him.

Because no matter the obstacles we would have had to face, having him there, realizing that we really are just as perfect as I'd always imagined and knowing I'll never have it again feels like someone just died.

To top it all off, I was so close to what promised to be the most powerful orgasm I've ever experienced.

"Shit."

After dropping my ass back down to the floor, I curl my legs up and wrap my arms around them before laying my head against my knees.

Well, doesn't this just take the cake for shit outcomes?

Chapter 13

Cohen

ONE COULD SAY THAT I had a moment of insanity. An out-of-body experience that I was helpless to stop and just had to let happen. Maybe I could say it was the beer? No. No matter how I try to excuse what just happened between Dani and me, it would be a lie.

She was exactly where I wanted her.

She looked so beautiful when I walked in this afternoon. Her body showcased in those short-as-hell shorts. Those perky tits I love so much standing out in her tight tank. And those heels. God, what I wouldn't give to know what it felt like to have them digging into my back as I pounded into her.

It took everything I had not to rush her right then and there. But I stuck to my guns and kept my determination to stand back. If things were still there when I got home, then we would explore this.

"What am I doing?" I mumble to myself, jumping off the stage and into the party that had been going on around us, careful to hide the fact that my cock is about to claw its way off my body to run back to Dani.

Cam spots me and shakes his head. Colt, who's standing next to him, gives me a thumbs-up, which I return with my middle finger. He and Cam laugh so loud that I can hear them across the room and over the music.

It takes me a second to get through everyone and to the table I left Megan at. She looks just about as miserable as she was this morning when I stopped by to make sure she was okay. Jack should have been shipping off with us, and I know that's a fact that hasn't escaped her notice. It's been hard since we lost him, but no one has suffered harder than Megan. Well, maybe their four-year-old daughter, who keeps asking for her daddy.

A little over a week ago, she called me because she needed help with something around the house. When I got there and saw just how bad things had gotten, I stepped in and continued to stop by—just basically made sure she knew she wasn't alone.

"Hey, Megs," I say with a smile.

I drop down in the chair next to her and look over at Chance, who has been keeping her company—or as he likes to call it, "watch duty." Chance, like I did, served with Megan's husband.

I think I've always known that I would eventually join Corps Security. When my aunt Melissa got custody of me after my mom died—then, shortly after, met Greg—it didn't take long before I was adopted by both and calling them Mom and Dad. They have been a huge part of my life, and I honestly look at them both as my real parents. I was around three when they started dating. He has helped shape me into the man I am today. Since then, I've come a long way from the little boy who wore a cape everywhere and wouldn't shut up about dick piercings.

"Hey, Coh."

She looks at me briefly before turning her attention back to the people around us. I lean back and take in the room. Since all the parents ran out before things could get a little crazy, the makeshift dance floor is crowded with the pulsing bodies of my closest family and friends. The room is full of people enjoying life. That is all she would see. Happiness she doesn't have anymore.

"Are you ready to get out of here? I think Chance has been ready for a few hours now." I laugh when he nods an emphatic yes.

"I am, but I don't want to take you away from your family right now. You should enjoy your time home before you leave."

"And I will, Megs. I can come back, or Chance can take you home."

It takes me a little longer than I would like to get Megan to agree to go home with Chance. He'll make sure she gets home, takes a sleeping pill, and is okay before he heads back to our apartment.

I stop over with my sisters to let them know I'm leaving with the truck and to catch a ride with Cam and Colt. They don't pay any attention to me, but they nod their heads. After checking with my brothers one last time to make sure they know to take the girls to their house before they head home, I head to my last stop and that red curtain hiding my prize is just within my reach.

I might be crazy for this. Hell, if Axel found out that I was about to drag his little princess off to my apartment for a night of debauchery, he would cut my dick off. Or maybe chain me to the back of his big-ass truck by my Prince Albert. Not exactly a pleasant thought. I reach down and rub my poor junk at the thought.

"You sure about this?" I hear right before I'm about to walk up the side stairs that will take me back to the cloaked darkness behind the curtain.

I look over to see Liam leaning against the wall, his arms crossed over his chest, but no doubt he would push off and attempt to kick my ass if he felt I was about to hurt Dani.

"Liam, mind your business."

"Yeah, that's not going to happen. That girl back there, the one you left ten minutes ago, doesn't think you're coming back. I would have known that even if I hadn't peeked behind the curtain to see if she was okay. I'll give you this time because I can tell you had every intention of coming back to her, but you hurt her again and, friend or not, family or not, I'll fucking kill you." He ends his rant by stepping right into my personal space, and it's taking every ounce of control I have not to punch him right in the face. "She's my best friend, Cohen," he whispers. "You aren't stupid. You know how deep she feels for you, and if you would take two seconds to not be terrified about it going bad, you would be able to admit you feel the same way. Either do something about it or leave her alone so she can get over you."

"It's not that easy, Liam. I'm leaving tomorrow. Leaving. I know you know just as well as I do that I might not come back this time. Right or wrong, consequences be damned, there isn't much of anything that could make me stop now. Did I expect this? No. But that doesn't mean it isn't welcome. I tried to keep my distance. I denied us both, but I can't anymore. I won't hurt her. I could never hurt her."

"All right. I might take back my earlier assessment. You might be stupid after all. Make sure she is clear with whatever is about to happen and what it means to you, Cohen. Because if you don't, you're going to get her hopes up, and when you leave without making something, anything, clear, it will crush her more than just you being deployed will." He turns and walks off, grabbing Maddi on his way by her waist and playfully throwing her over his shoulder before marching onto the crowded dance floor.

It should be said for the record that I am far from stupid. I thought I was doing the right thing by denying us this. I thought that it would be easier for both of us if we didn't take this attraction any further.

One thing and one thing only is clear now.

I want Danielle Reid.

And right or wrong, I will have her.

I just need to make sure she knows I can't make her any promises about our future. Not with too much unknown standing in our way. When I get home, we can sit down and figure this stuff out, but for now, I need to find out if the fantasy of her lives up to the reality. I have a feeling that it will be even greater than I ever could imagine.

I don't know what I expected when I came back to where I left Dani, but seeing her sitting in some kind of protective ball definitely wasn't it. My Dani is strong. She wouldn't ever feel the need to turn in toward herself. Hell, if she weren't happy with me, she would have marched out there and kicked my ass herself.

"Dani-girl?" I implore, walking up to her still form and crouching down next to her. "Talk to me, baby."

She's quiet for a second, and just as I lean down to pull her into my arms, she catches me off guard with an elbow to the gut.

"You jerk. I told you not to leave me like that. I'm two seconds away from shoving my own hand down my pants to finish what YOU started."

Her eyes flash, giving me just enough time to prepare for her launching herself from her position. My arms go around her seconds before I fall back. Then I roll until I have her trapped under me with no way to get away.

Leaning down, I make sure she is focused completely on me before speaking. “I don’t know what’s gotten you worked up, Dani-girl, but I told you I was coming back.”

“No you didn’t, jerk-off. You said you had to go check on Megan. You said you needed to make sure Chance was taking her home. Now tell me how was I supposed to know in Cohen’s world that mean you would be right back? You know what? Just forget it . . . Get off me so I can find my brother and have him take me back home.”

She’s lost her damn mind.

“That isn’t happening.” I push my hips against hers so there is no doubt in what I’m about to say. “For years—years, Dani—you’ve been parading around this flawless body and teasing me with something I couldn’t have. For weeks, we’ve been dancing around this attraction. I’ve had a taste, and now, I need my meal. So what we’re going to do is get off this damn floor, walk out the back door, and I’m going to get your sweet little ass to my bed quickly. I mean it, Dani. Years I’ve thought about what your pussy would feel like with my cock deep inside you, and I’m not giving that up now.”

Her eyes widen hilariously. Those stunning, light-green orbs look at me with so much shock that, if I weren’t so frustrated, I would laugh. Okay, so maybe I should have handled that a little better

Yeah, smooth I am not.

“What?” she breathes. “What happened to you saying this wouldn’t happen?”

“I’m man enough to admit I was wrong and I’m open to discussing this again. Now get ready, baby. It’s going to be a long night.”

Chapter 14

Cohen

THE WHOLE TWENTY-MINUTE DRIVE TO my apartment is done with silence and sexual tension so thick that it's choking. My cock is testing the strength of its confinement. With every inhale, I can smell her arousal, her desire for me, and it's driving me insane with lust.

"Do you think we should talk about this, Cohen?" she asks weakly, like she would rather talk about anything else but knows it's smart that we at least lay some communication out.

"What do you want me to say here, Dani-girl?"

"The truth would be nice. Is this just some game to you? Or is this more? I'm not asking for the world, Coh . . . but I don't think that I can just give myself to you if it doesn't mean something to you. I'm so confused with your no-and-then-yes games."

I don't answer right away. I need to make sure she understands me, and there is no way I can get my point across if she is staring out the window and freaking out instead of looking at me. I need to see her eyes, to know that she is here with me and not running into her head to hide.

After parking the truck, I pull my seat belt off before reaching over and undoing hers. She looks over at me sharply before I grab her and pull her into my lap. My hands instantly go towards her face so I can hold her attention. My fingertips dance against her silky hair, her cheeks feel warm against my palms, and those stunning eyes stare out at me—she looks terrified out of her mind.

"You silly girl," I laugh. "What are you so scared of? I'm not the big, bad wolf. Although, I wouldn't be opposed to eating you up."

"Oh, God, that was corny," she chuckles.

"You would like that though, wouldn't you? Do you want me to eat you first, or do you want to be my Little Red Riding Hood and go for a long, hard ride?"

"Oh. God. Stop, Cohen. Those lines . . . They're terrible."

I snicker before leaning in and giving her a hard, bruising kiss. I don't take my time, but I do make sure that, with that one kiss, I dominate her mind.

"You wanted to talk, baby, so let's talk." Now that I've loosened the mood up a little, it's time to lay this out there so she doesn't have any confusion that I want her.

"I don't think I can. Not with you . . . with your . . . Jesus Christ." She starts to rub against my erection and drops her head back to rest in my hands, which are still framing her face.

"How about this?" I groan when she starts to grind down harder against my throbbing cock. "How about we get upstairs before I fuck you in my truck? I'm ready to play, Dani-girl, and there won't be anything quick about it. You either start talking now or get the hell up and in my bed."

"Bed," she pants, giving me another hard rotation of her hips against my lap.

I crush my lips against hers and help her ride out a few more rolls of her hips, pushing up against her to give her just enough friction to drive her insane, before pulling the door open and grabbing her hand.

"Last chance. Once I get you through that door, I guarantee I won't be able to stop."

"If you stop right now, Cohen Cage, I'm going to die."

I laugh and bend at the waist, and with a shoulder to her belly, she's up and over as I take off up the four flights of stairs as fast as I can with her giggles trailing behind us.

Chapter 15

Cohen

IT SHOULD BE SAID THAT I have fantasized about this moment for years. Right or wrong, it's the cold, hard truth. I've wanted this woman in every way possible, and tonight, I will finally get to stop craving and *take*.

Dani Reid has been the spotlight of every jack-off session I've ever had. Recently, those sessions have gotten a lot more play. She's consumed my mind. I keep picturing what color her nipples will be. How her pussy would glisten with her juices when I spread her legs wide. How it would taste to sink my tongue between those swollen lips. What kind of pussy would she have? Would it be bare? Maybe she would have a hint of that burnt-brunette hair I can't wait to wrap around my fist when I'm pounding into her from behind.

Every single image I've made up in my mind pales in comparison to the real thing. Seeing her body spread out against my black sheets, every inch of her tan skin covered in a slight blush, which I know isn't from embarrassment from being nude before me, but from her arousal. And Christ, the smell of her. When she stood before me and removed her clothing like she didn't have a shred of inhibition, I almost swallowed my tongue. Then she laid herself down on my bed, spread her legs, and let me take my fill. That was when her scent—that mouthwatering smell of her arousal—hit my senses. I take another deep breath and groan when my mouth waters.

"I was going to take my time and enjoy every second of this, but if I don't taste you right now, I'm going to go out of my mind. I need your pussy against my tongue and your come in my mouth. Tell me I can have you, Dani." I lick my lips and wait for her to respond.

Her eyes darken, that beautiful light green turning an emerald shade, and she nods her head. "I think you're a little overdressed though," she says confidently.

I feel my cock grow painfully hard when I watch her hands grab her small tits and pinch her nipples. If it weren't for the slight tremble in her hands, I would believe this fearless act.

"Baby, stop doing that or it's going to be over before it starts." I groan when she withers against the mattress. "God, that's hot."

Her eyes blaze. My words give her the push she needs. "Stop doing what?" she laughs. Then she trails one hand down her slim stomach and wastes no time dipping her middle finger into her core.

"Fucking hell," I grunt, reaching for my belt.

Her eyes burn with need with each move my fingers make as I deftly remove my belt, pull my shirt over my head, and start unbuttoning each button on my jeans.

Slowly.

So achingly slowly.

So slowly that I can feel each second as if it were a drum beating through the room.

She continues to dip one finger in and out of her soaked pussy. Daring me with each thrust to take her, finish what she's started. The hunger inside me is starting to take over, cloud my vision with one goal in mind.

Take.

Take and take until there isn't anything left for her to give me.

Her eyes widen when I pull my cock out of my pants and let them fall down my legs before I kick them aside. Those beautiful eyes of hers move from my cock and up to meet my eyes. Once, twice, and one final time before her movements still and she throws her head back and laughs.

Laughing at my cock.

Never has that happened to me before.

I look down to make sure that nothing's happened to him since

I so carefully tucked him in this afternoon, but I don't see anything standing out. Same thick, tan skin. Same groomed manscaping.

And then it hits me. I drop my head, and with a heat of embarrassment flushing over my already fevered skin, I know what is going through her head, and it's just as funny as she thinks it is.

"You . . . Oh my God. You did it. Oh, wow," she hoots, choking on her words from laughing so hard.

"Can't say I've ever had a chick laugh at my cock before, Dani-girl."

"Well, I'm not just any chick! It's not my fault that . . . that . . . Jesus, Cohen, our parents tell stories about you always talking about that . . . well, THAT!" She finishes by pointing to my dick, which I'm still stroking even though she is basically laughing at the poor thing. "How many do you have, Cohen?"

"Enough." I smirk, sobering her instantly when she sees the intent in my eyes. "Enough that there is no fucking way you're going to be complaining when they're inside of you. You're going to love it, Dani. Each time I push in deep, you'll feel all four of them against your tight walls. You'll be begging me to take you harder so that the bar right here," I say, pointing to the one at the base of my dick, "rubs your swollen clit and the hoop knocks on your core. Each time I push in, you're going to feel them rubbing your tight walls. I'll have you begging for more, but for right now, it's just *enough*."

I bend down, grab her ankles while I pull her body to the edge of the bed, and spread her legs wide in the air. I hum my approval when I see just how wet her pussy is. She's practically weeping with her need for my cock.

"Dani-girl. Do you want my tongue or my cock?" I ask while trailing both of my hands down the legs I'm still holding wide. My fingertips lightly tease the skin behind her knees, traveling closer to where I want to bury my face—and then my cock.

She rolls her eyes back and moans but doesn't answer me. That's fine. I'll just give her both. Pulling her by her hips, I kneel on the floor. Then I smile up at her when she lifts up on her elbows to watch me.

"I'm going to eat you until you come in my mouth. Then I'm going to eat some more. And only then will I climb up this perfect fucking body and give you my cock. One thing you need to remember though, Dani-girl."

She holds my gaze, her skin flushed but her eyes alert.

"When I slam my cock inside your body, when my balls slap against your ass, when I finally take you, it means you're mine. Do you understand that?"

"God, yes," she pants. "Yes, anything . . . yes."

"That's good, baby," I hum and then lower my face to her pussy.

The first swipe of my tongue has her flavor bursting against my taste buds, and I groan before latching on and pulling her clit deep in my mouth. After playing with her until she's screaming and seconds from her release, I pull back, loving the feeling of her trying to push my head back down with her hands.

"You taste so fucking good," I moan, nipping her lips and the inside of her thighs with my teeth, causing her to scream out. "I can't wait to have my cock deep inside this cunt." And with that, I return my mouth to her body and I don't stop until she is screaming my name and coming against my tongue.

Only I lied and I make her go three times before I climb off the floor, grab her boneless body by the shoulders, and pull her with me deep into the bed. I don't give her a second to pull back before I drop my mouth to hers and spread her juices against her chin and lips. She kisses me with a hunger that matches my own, and I'm not sure if it's because she is just as worked up as I am or if the taste of herself on my mouth has her just that much hotter for me.

"Do you want my cock?" I ask.

"No," she pants. "I *need* your cock," she says breathlessly.

"Fuck yeah, you do."

Completely lost in the ecstasy of Dani, I absentmindedly stretch a condom over my cock, careful of the jewelry that was being laughed at earlier, and then I reach down, line up our bodies, and push myself balls-deep with one measured thrust. It isn't until she cries out, in pain and not pleasure, that I realize what I just did. Or better yet, what I didn't do, because if I had known I was her first, I damn sure would have had a little more finesse.

"Shit, Dani-girl. Fuck. Why didn't you tell me?" I take her head between my hands and will her to open eyes that she had slammed shut when I entered her body, and look at me so I know she's okay. My cock, still hard and deep within her tight pussy, is begging me to start thrusting. Demanding that I start to take her in the way my body has craved. But right now, I need to make sure she's okay, and there is no way that my body humping her like an animal will be anything close to okay. "Baby, look at me."

"I'm okay," she whispers, rolling her hips experimentally. "I just needed to get past that pain, but really . . . I'm okay."

"Why didn't you tell me?" I search her face, knowing she's brushing the pain under the rug. "If I had known . . ." I shake my head, because in reality, I was just so drunk on her that I'm not sure I could have stopped. "Baby, you have to talk to me."

She huffs out a breath, her cheeks getting red with embarrassment. "What would you have liked me to say? 'Hey, Cohen . . . before you *finally* fuck me, just thought you should know I'm a pathetic twenty-one-year-old virgin.' You know, stereotypical romance novel bullshit where the chick gets the guy only for him to freak when he realizes she is 'an innocent.' *Then* he runs as fast as he can because he wouldn't dream of ruffling a few feathers. News flash, bucko! I wanted my feathers ruffled. And I wanted them ruffled by you!" Her chest heaves when she stops talking, and her eyes go wide. "Did I just say all of that?"

"Yeah, Dani-girl. You sure did." I laugh and adjust my hips. My cock, still buried deep inside her body, twitches with the movement. "Just so we're clear here, I wouldn't have run the other way. I would have been more careful when I took you."

"Right. Well, can you shut up and fuck me now?" she whines when I shift again, and I feel the ring through my cock head brush against her womb.

I laugh, and her eyes narrow.

"Does it still hurt?" I ask with all seriousness.

"It wouldn't if you would move!" Her eyes are hooded and her breath is coming in quick pants by the time she finishes her sentence.

Her pussy clenches down when I shift again, and I drop my head to her neck to give her a little bite. She rewards me by hiking her legs around my back, hooking her ankles, and digging her nails into my shoulders on a moan. I pull back and rest my forehead against hers so that I can look into her eyes as I take her. Take what is mine and mine alone.

God, it feels better than I thought it would to know that no other man has ever been here.

I pull out just an inch before pushing back in and she doesn't flinch. She is looking at me with complete love. I pull back a little more each time, and it isn't long before my body is thrusting into hers in quick successions. I wish I could make this better for her, but her pussy is so tight that it was milking my cock before I even started to move, and now that I have, I know I won't last long.

I reach down between us and start to put pressure on her clit. The second my fingers start to move in sync with my thrusts, her screams get louder, and it's only seconds before she throws her head back and my name is leaving her swollen lips as she comes long and hard around my cock.

Four thrusts later, with my balls against her ass and my cock as deep as I can go, I come, and with her eyes locked to mine, I realize that I was a fool to think I could have ever lived without this.

Chapter 16

Cohen

"WHAT HAPPENS NOW, COHEN?" SHE whispers into the darkness surrounding us.

She has one leg hooked over my hips with her thigh resting against my spent cock, the other lying against the bed. Her chest is pressed against my own, and her forehead resting against my neck. The hand she was using to draw circles on my chest for the last twenty minutes stills with her question, and I use the arm I was holding her close with to tighten my grip.

I knew she was working things out in her head, so I let her take her time and waited for the questions I knew would come. I have a few of my own that hit me like a burst of clarity while I stared into her eyes and felt her body take every inch of me. Things I thought I would be able to wait for when it came to her. Things I have no fucking clue how I'll be able to turn my back on and leave in the morning.

I have an inner battle warring inside me now. One side knows with no doubt that she is meant to be right here—naked in my arms with her heart beating against my skin. Then there is the other side. The logical side. The one that's afraid to take it past tonight, knowing how many other lives it will affect. It's not just the Cohen and Dani show. It's our families, siblings and everyone else in the tight circle.

Battle or not, the side that will win all depends on the woman in my arms.

"Let me see your eyes, Dani-girl." I dip my chin and wait for her to move her eyes to mine.

Her face is void of emotion, but her eyes aren't hiding a thing from me.

"Tell me, honestly, what you want to happen now."

"Honestly?" she questions.

"One hundred percent. One thing you need to understand about this from here on out is that, if you plan on telling me what I think—and hope—you are, then honesty is the most important thing. I can't go into this without knowing what's going on in that beautiful head of yours."

She's silent for a beat; all the while, her eyes never stop their hopeful begging.

"I never want to let you go," she sighs, and I offer her a sad smile because we both know, come morning, she's going to have to. "I don't want you to leave, but I'll support you any and every way I can. I want to be able to be yours even when you aren't here but know that, when you come back, you're coming back to me. I want you to be able to go with the confidence that I'll be waiting for you if . . . if that's what you want, of course."

God, she couldn't be more perfect.

"Anything else?" I probe, moving one hand up to run my fingers down her cheek.

"I don't think we have enough time to get into everything that I want from you, Cohen. Let's just put it this way. I want you. I want you and everything that comes with it."

"Dani," I sigh. "I leave tomorrow, baby. I leave tomorrow and I can't even give you an estimate on when I'll be home. It wouldn't be fair for me to make you mine and demand that kind of commitment when I can't even be here for you. I won't even be able to contact you, Dani . . . How is that going to work? How is that fair to you? I don't want you to have to sacrifice for me—for us."

"When it comes to love, it's always worth the sacrifice. Always. One thing my parents taught me was that when you find the reason for your heart to beat, you don't ever let it go, and if, for some reason beyond your control, you have to, you fight with every breath in your body to have it back. You are worth that to me. You aren't asking me to give anything up, Cohen. I've loved you my whole damn life . . . What's a few more months of waiting if I know you're coming back to me?"

Each time she tells me that she loves me, it's on the tip of my tongue to return the words to her. I feel them, but I damn sure don't want her to think that I'm just saying them to parrot them back to her. Knowing Dani and the reservations she already has about my feelings towards her and with *us,* she would probably think that way too.

"What about our families?" I muse out loud. It needs to be addressed. I don't want it to become a big elephant in the room. Or, God forbid, her to want to hide this thing between us. First of all, with as often as everyone is together, it would be next to impossible. And I want to be able to show her off as my girl. Show her off and let the world know she is mine. I can't do that if she is worried about what will happen when we go public.

"What about them? Your sisters have been rooting for us to get together for years. Nate knows—or at least he knows about how I feel for you—and he's never said anything other than for me to be careful. I'm not sure that Cam and Colt care, to be honest. As for our parents . . . well, I don't know about them. What do you think?"

I give her a smile, and I'm instantly rewarded when her full lips tip up and she gives me one of her own. "Baby, I think that, when I get home, your father is going to kick my ass, because there is no way I can give this up. Here is my honesty. You ready?"

She nods her head.

"I want you to think about this from every angle, because that's what I've been trying to do. I would be damn proud to have you on my arm, in my bed, and to share my life with. I understand it's going to be a fight when it comes to your dad, but that's a fight I'll take if you're by my side. Our moms, yeah . . . that's not something you need to worry about. Trust me, baby. They'll start planning a wedding the second you and I let them know where we stand. My dad just wants me to be happy. And I guarantee you he will have my back when it comes to your dad. As for Nate, we don't need to worry about him either. I'll handle him. Sounds like my sisters aren't going to be a problem, and my brothers will be right there with Lyn and Lila."

I pause and shift our bodies so that she is lying under my body, her legs spread wide and her hips welcoming the pressure of my own. "The only issue I have here is knowing that I'm leaving tomorrow, and in doing so, I'm leaving you and what is most definitely starting between us. I'm not the type of man who likes knowing that his woman is alone, and if you needed me, I wouldn't be here. I don't like knowing that, if you're sad, I can't make it better. If you're sick, I won't be there to make you better. If you're scared, I can't chase away your nightmares. Bottom line, I won't be there for you, and that isn't something a man like me can stomach easily." I drop my head, give her a small kiss, and pull away, looking into her bright and hopeful eyes. "But, Dani-girl, I'm also a selfish man, because even knowing all of that, it doesn't make a difference. It's you and me, baby. You and me against the world."

I wipe the tear that leaks out of her eye before it can trail down her cheek to the radiant and very happy smile that has spread across her lips. Even when I drop mine to hers, the smile remains. And later—much later—when she is moaning my name, it still never slips.

My girl, my Dani-girl, is happy.

"You're mine?" she asks.

"Yeah, baby. And you're mine."

With a full but heavy heart, I hold her all night long. My eyes never once leave her sleeping—and still-smiling—face. I memorize every inch of her, from the way she feels in my arms to how she smells like wildflowers in the rain. When she moans in her sleep and huskily whispers my name, I know that, when I leave tomorrow, I'll be fighting every instinct I have to run back to her. It's going to be an uphill battle, but this will be one worth every second of yearning, because in the end, when I come home and she's right back in my arms, I'll be the luckiest bastard alive.

Chapter 17

Dani

IT'S HARD TO SEE THROUGH the tears clouding my vision. To see through the sadness my heart feels as I watch him get dressed. Watching him pack his things. Pull on his boots or grab his jacket. All the things I won't be watching again for months. Little, mundane tasks I'm trying to sear into my mind so I'll never forget. How his fingers look when he's hooking his belt through his jeans. How his brow furrows when he's trying to figure out how to get a little more space out of his carry-on. Even though I know he will come back to me, knowing that we're starting something so beautiful off with a big, ugly fog surrounding us has me in pieces.

He looks over when he finishes zipping the last zipper and gives me a sad smile. I'm sure my eyes are looking at him exactly as his are gazing into mine. Like this is it and if we don't see each other again, then we should make this second last a lifetime.

I bring a hand up and angrily swipe away a tear. I hate crying. It's a sign of weakness, but I'm helpless to stop them. My heart, while full to bursting with the knowledge that he is mine, is breaking.

"Dani-girl," he says on a sigh. "You're killing me with these tears."

He sits on the bed and pulls me into his arms. When his strong arms wrap around me and the comfort that always comes when he's near sinks into my skin, I only cry more.

"This isn't goodbye," he vows.

"Never goodb-b-bye," I stutter.

"It's 'see you soon,'" he whispers.

"Every time I close my eyes," I promise.

We don't need words after that. What more needs to be said? I have to believe that, even brand new, we have the kind of connection that can beat anything.

He holds me in his arms for another ten minutes. Ten whole minutes that I feel complete. When his phone beeps, letting him know that his parents are on the way, he gives me a deep kiss before pulling back and standing from the bed.

"Stay as long as you want, Dani-girl. I like knowing you're in my bed even if I'm not here." He stops when I let out a big sob-like hiccup. Leaning down over where he placed me in the middle of the mattress, he gives me another long and deep kiss. "See you soon, my heart." With one more kiss, he stands, grabs his stuff and walks out the door.

I'm not sure how long I stay in the middle of his bed, surrounded by his scent and the memories of the night before. It isn't until Liam shows up and wraps me in his arms, causing my sobs to double in force, that I realize the sun has long since set and Cohen is likely gone by now.

"Wh-what are you doing here?" I ask when I'm finally able to calm down.

"Cohen sent me a text a little after nine this morning. Told me that, if I didn't see you by lunch, I was to go find Chance and get the key to the apartment. Lunch came and no Dani, so here I am. Come on, little princess. Let's get you home."

Lee turns his back when I move the covers off my naked body, throwing my shorts and one of Cohen's shirts over his shoulder. When I pull the cotton tee over my head, I know instantly that it must be the one he wore the night before. The scent of him, so fresh and powerful, almost brings me to my knees. I have to bite my lip to keep it from wobbling and victoriously keep the tears at bay.

"Here," Lee says with a smile. "I grabbed a few more and the body wash and the bottle of that shit he wears off the counter in his bathroom."

When I look at him like he's lost his mind, he laughs, throwing the body wash, cologne, and three shirts he was holding in my arms.

"What? You were standing there sniffing that one like you wanted to rub it all over yourself. Might as well make it so you can have some to last." He shrugs his shoulder, collects my purse from the floor next to the nightstand, and takes my hand before leading me out of the apartment.

Chance is fixing some food in the kitchen when we walk out. He gives Lee one of those manly head-jerk things and me a small smile.

"See you around, Dani."

I nod, but I know I won't see him around much. Not now that Cohen is gone.

God, he really is gone.

"Do you think she's dead?" the voice asks, and I feel something sharp poke my hip.

"No, but I think she smells like she is," another voice replies.

"It does smell . . . funky in here. I wonder, if we move her, what's going to be growing on those sheets."

"Ugh, Maddi—you're so gross!" Lila snaps.

"Shut up, you two," Lyn mumbles.

I feel the bed dip, but I pull the sheets over my head. "Go away."

"Fat chance in that happening. Time for some tough love, bitch," Lyn snaps before pulling my comforter off my body. "Seriously, Dani. It's time to take the shirt off."

"No."

"Oh yeah, it's happening. Either you can take it off on your own accord or I'll be forced to cut it off. Do you want me to cut the shirt? Huh, Dani? Do you want me to cut it into tiny pieces?" Lyn barks, standing from the bed and placing her hands on her hips.

"You wouldn't dare!"

"Try me. It's been three days since Cohen left. Do you see Lila and me moping around the house? No, you do not. You're acting pathetic, and it's time to snap the hell out of it."

What the hell? Who does she think she is?

"What the hell, Lyn! Who do you think you are to tell me that I shouldn't be upset?"

"I'll tell you who I think I am! I'm your best friend, but I'm also *his* sister. I get to live this right along with you, but I have the added benefit of watching you fall apart all the while I'm holding my worry about him in because I don't want to make you snap any more than you already have."

Oh.

"I love you, Dani. I'm so happy that you and Cohen had that before he left, but right now, you have to stop acting like he isn't ever going to come home because he will. He will, Dani. I swear." Her eyes start to water, and I want to kick myself for making her feel worse when I should have swallowed my upset and been there for them.

"I'm sorry," I offer weakly. And I am. It hurts still, having the memory of his body holding mine so fresh, but she's right. I'm grieving him as if he won't ever come back.

"Go get a shower and you can get your ass to work today so I don't have to deal with Sway going nuts over you missing another filming day."

I nod my head and climb out of the bed. When I go to pull off Cohen's shirt, I look over my shoulder to where she is standing. Maddi and Lila must have dipped out the door while we were talking. She raises one of her black, perfectly sculpted brows and looks down at my hand on the hem. I narrow my eyes and instantly decide that this shirt—and the others I'm sure she doesn't know about yet—will be hidden well.

And I'm not even ashamed of the smile I have when I drop some of Cohen's body wash on my loofa and start to get lost in the memories.

Memories that will keep me going long after he comes home.

Yeah . . . totally normal.

Ten hours of hell later, I'm ready to kill someone. I'm missing Cohen terribly, but that feeling was exasperated tenfold by Devon, his two idiots, and—God love him—Sway.

Devon wanted to know when "the romantic drama hunk"

was coming in next, which was brought up when it was clear there wouldn't be anything show-worthy happening in the salon today. Lyn went nuts and threw one of her eye shadow pallets at him.

Devon's "assistants"—and I use that word loosely because I haven't seen them actually assist with anything—wouldn't stop being icky. The short one actually picked his nose, twice, and the second time almost had me throwing up my lunch when I saw him eat it. Then the other one . . . I can't put my finger on exactly what about him I don't like—but it's there. And his openly staring at every female in the room doesn't exactly give him any checks in the pro side.

And then Sway.

I might actually kill him.

Really.

I was in the back mixing some color for Jenna Nixon's pink touch-up when he came up behind me and tried to measure my bust. Like, full-on threw one of those measuring tape things around my body and told me to stop wiggling so he knew what size he needed to order for burlesque day at the salon.

I do not fucking think so.

And okay, I might have been a little overdramatic when I elbowed him in the stomach, but he crossed a line with the measuring tape.

Needless to say by the time the workday was over, I was more than ready to call it a night. If I'm this bad after just three days, I hate to think what I'll feel like as more pass.

And it's with that thought that I find it.

I find the reason I need to solidify that strength I need. A reason to smile again.

I'm not sure how I missed it earlier, but I wasn't exactly in the right frame of mind the morning he left—or each day after for that matter—so it makes sense that I didn't see it before. Tucked in one of the side pockets of my purse is a white envelope, sealed, with my name scrawled in masculine writing on the outside.

Not just my name.

The name only one person calls me.

Dani-girl

My chin wobbles when I hold the letter that Cohen must have tucked in there at some point the night before he left. Part of me wants to rip into it and devour each word. But the sensible part of me wants to savor each word knowing that these are going to be the words I need to keep me going.

Dani-girl—my sweet Dani-girl.

You have no idea how long I've been watching you sleep. I feel like, if I stare at you for the rest of the night, it might be enough to last me until I came home, but even as I write this down, I know it wasn't enough.

It's funny how I've lasted almost twenty-six years without knowing what it felt like to have you in my arms. I've had your naked body against mine for one night and I know it was a feeling that I will struggle to be without. I don't know a better way to explain it other than it just felt like you were always meant to be there.

My dad used to tell me that your father used to get so pissed when we were kids because wherever I went, you weren't far behind, and whenever we were in the same room, I was always watching you. He told me once that, even back then, it was like we had some invisible cord pulling us together. I don't think I understood it until last night. I've always used excuse after excuse to push the feelings I had for you aside.

Anyway, my point is, while I was sitting here in the dark, watching you sleep, it hit me how much it's going to rip me in two when I have to walk away from you in the morning. Seeing you in my bed, sated and flushed from just taking you again, will be something I think about for nights to come.

It was unexpected, baby, but it was fate. It's our unexpected fate, and I have no doubt in my mind that this happened at the perfect time, for us, even if it sucks knowing I won't hold you in my arms for a while, I'll carry the memories of last night with me every second of every day that I'm gone. And when I come home, I'm not sure I'll ever let go of you.

Danielle Reid, you've burrowed your beautiful soul right into my heart.

Stay strong, my beautiful Dani-girl, and know that, wherever I am and wherever you are, I'll be thinking about you. Know that, when I get home, there won't be a second that passes that I don't show you just how much you mean to me. I was a fool to push this connection we have away for so long, and for that, I'm sorry, but now, it's you and me against the world and there isn't anything that could take that feeling away from us now.

Remember, I'll see you soon—every time I close my eyes.

Love,

Cohen

When I finish reading the letter, my eyes are wet with tears, but this time, they're tears of acceptance that I can and will make it through Cohen's deployment, and when he gets home, it's going to be him and me against the world.

And I can't freaking wait.

Chapter 18

Dani

Two months later

"DANI!" I HEAR LILA YELL up the stairs.

I smile to myself because I know what's coming. The same thing that's been happening every single Saturday at nine o'clock in the morning for the last two months.

I look at the red roses sitting on the corner of my desk and smile. I do the same when I pass the dozen on my nightstand, and then again when I reach the end of the hallway and see the other dozen that will be replaced today on the accent table right before the stairs.

For the last two months, like clockwork, I've gotten a delivery of a dozen red roses. There's never a card, but I don't need one. There is only one person who would send me such an extravagant gift every week. When the first delivery showed up, it was the morning after I had read Cohen's letter, and it was the fortification I'd needed. The girls didn't say much—not at first. Then, when it was clear I wasn't going to jump off the deep end, they took me off suicide watch and started in with the questions.

I told them what I could without giving them the intimate details of Cohen's and my relationship. We were together and would remain together until he got home. I explained to them that I wasn't going to mention it to anyone else past them and Lee. I didn't want to rock the boat. They don't understand or agree, but for now, they've left that alone. I think part of me is still worried that this is a dream. That

Cohen will return and either change his mind or realize that it wasn't what he thought he felt. But also, I am selfishly waiting until I have his strength by my side before I tell everyone else.

And by everyone else, I mean my father.

"I went ahead and signed for you. That delivery dude is creepy as hell." Lila hands me the flowers with a roll of her eyes. "I swear my brother has gone soft," she mumbles under her breath as she walks away.

"Where are you headed today?" I ask while taking a big whiff of the flowers.

"I picked up a Saturday class for some extra credits."

"Damn, Lila! Aren't you worried that you're going to burn yourself out one of these days?" Flowers forgotten—well, almost forgotten—I look over at her with concern. She's been going hard for so many years that I really never stopped to think that maybe she might be pushing herself a little too much. "What's the rush, babe?"

"It's just something I need to do, Dani. I don't know how to explain it any other way. I just keep picturing all the kids that need my help and I don't want to give them anything less than one hundred percent."

I give her a smile before placing the flowers on the table just inside the entryway. Walking over to where she's picking at her nail polish, I wrap my arms around her and give her a big squeeze.

"You're going to be awesome, Lila. You would be awesome even without all these extra years of school, but with them, you're going to be unstoppable."

She smiles but doesn't acknowledge my words. "Do you want to catch some breakfast before you head off to meet Lee?"

"I'd like that. I feel like all I've been doing lately is working. Ever since Devon had to rush back to Los Angeles and he left Don and Mark in charge, things have been a little intense."

We walk down the hall and into the kitchen. Lila plops down on the barstool as I go straight to the fridge and start pulling out the ingredients I need to make French toast. Lila doesn't cook—ever. Not unless we want to be vomiting for weeks. The last time she tried to cook dinner for the house—when we had the brilliant idea that we should do a rotation so one single person didn't have to do all the cooking—she started a small grease fire, burned noodles, and made cheese toast without removing the plastic film over the slices.

Needless to say, with all her smarts, cooking just isn't something she can do.

"How are you doing with things?" she asks, breaking the silence.

"I'm okay, Lila. I really am. I know I got a little over the top when he first left and I'm sorry for that. It wasn't right for me to do that and not be there for you and Lyn. It's just—I can't even describe it. We've known each other forever. Been solidly on that 'just friends' line that I never imagined how different it would be to finally have him. Even if it was just for a few hours. Those hours . . ." I pause, remembering every second of my night in Cohen's arms. "When I was with him, it was like everything was right in the world."

"You sound like a cheesy Hallmark card," she giggles.

I laugh. "You're right. God, I'm pathetic."

"No, you aren't. I understand what you're saying, even if it is gross to think about it being with my brother."

"Do you think its crazy? This instant connection between us?" *I* don't think it's crazy, but I know how others might see the swiftness of our relationship. I've been lusting after him for so long that I'm sure I look pathetic to most. I know I never dreamt that he would return my feelings.

Lila studies my face for a beat, her expression giving nothing away, before she speaks. I don't know why, but between her and Lyn, I have always thought that Lila didn't exactly want Cohen and me to get together.

"I don't think it's crazy, Dani. But I'm worried about you. He's my brother, but you have always been like a sister to Lyn and me. I'm worried that things might get . . . sticky."

"Meaning?" I push hesitantly.

"What's going to happen when he comes home?" she asks, not answering my question.

"The same thing that would have happened if he were still here. We're going to tell everyone together and then, hopefully with their blessing, continue to see where our relationship goes."

"Okay. Well, what's keeping you from telling everyone now? I'll be honest, I don't agree with your wanting to keep a lid on it."

I'm trying to keep my temper in check. I know she's just trying to think logically, but that doesn't mean I'm not allowed to get frustrated with her lack of faith.

"You're afraid he's going to change his mind, aren't you?" she asks when I don't say anything,

"Never," I spit venomously. "Look, I don't want to fight with you, Lila, but I have faith in your brother that he never would have even opened this can of worms if he didn't mean it. But I will admit that I can see where you're coming from. It might be easier for me to say something now and deal with calming my dad down while Cohen is home. I know one thing for sure: when he comes home, I want to be able to focus on us becoming us without having to worry about hiding and being scared of what others might think. So I guess I'm not going to keep this to myself." I sigh and try to suck down the small panic I have from knowing what kind of chat that will be with my dad. "I'll tell my parents about it next weekend at dinner." I nod a few times before stopping. God, I must look like a bobblehead.

Her eyes widen. "You're going to tell your father—the same father that locked you in the house when Toby Gilbert tried to take you to the movies when you were seventeen and chased the kid out of the house with a chainsaw—that you and Cohen are together?"

"Hey—the chainsaw wasn't on," I laugh, remembering how embarrassed I was.

"Dani . . . he still chased a man down with a freaking chainsaw and all Toby wanted was to take you to a movie. We're talking about telling your father that you and Cohen are together *together,* and I'm pretty sure no one is going to believe that you two have something that doesn't involve touching."

"I know, I know," I sigh. "But I figure it would be better to tell him now and give him a while to get used to it before Cohen comes home."

"Oh, God. He's going to kill him. You know that, right?"

"He wouldn't kill him knowing it would hurt me. Hey! What's with the back-and-forth crap here? Five minutes ago, you were questioning my logic on not saying anything. Now, you don't think I should."

"I think that's before I realized what telling Axel you're dating his best friend's son would do to said best friend's son."

"It'll be okay. It will."

She gives me a weak smile, which tells me that even she doesn't believe my lie to myself.

God, this is going to be a nightmare.

Lee came over later that night with my brother. We were supposed to go out to a local sports bar for dinner, but by the time they got there, I was so tired that all I wanted to do was crash. I feel like I've been running on empty for the last few weeks, grasping at any kind of sleep I can find.

We're all camped out in the living room. Lee and I are sitting on the couch, my head in his lap while his fingers brush my hair, pulling me halfway to dreamland, when my phone rings for the second time in five minutes.

"It says 'private,' Dani," Nate says from the recliner next to us. "Want me to answer it?"

"Yeah, whatever," I mumble with a wave of my hand, not really caring. Anyone who needs me that bad could just call the house.

"'Ello?" Nate booms into my phone. "The fuck?"

Something in his tone draws my attention, and I look over at him. His eyes are locked on mine, but other than the sharp look he's throwing my way, he appears to be relaxed.

"Yeah. Sure thing, *bro.* I think you might want this, Dani." Nate extends his arm with my phone and waits for me to take it, looking at me like he can't figure out what's going on.

"Hello?" I question, trying to shake the lingering fatigue away.

"Dani-girl," I hear, and my eyes shoot to Nate before closing tightly and letting his voice wash over me.

Oh my God!

"How . . . how are you calling me? Did you call your parents? Your sisters or brothers? Oh my God! Are you okay? You're calling because something happened, aren't you?"

"Slow down, baby," he laughs. "I missed you. That's all."

Well, so much for holding my shit together. Those three words almost cause me to come undone. I give Nate another look, begging him not to freak out until I can talk to him. He gives me a hard one back but doesn't say anything.

"I miss you, too," I breathe while getting off the couch and walking out of the room.

Right when I'm about to shut the door into the front bathroom to get some privacy, I hear Nate boom at Lee, "Did you fucking know about that shit?"

"I'm guessing I have some explaining I need to do to your brother when I get home," he laughs, completely unconcerned about Nate's freak-out.

"That's an understatement at the moment," I laugh when I hear something thump on the other side of the door followed by Lee's whine of pain. "Don't worry. I'll talk to Nate."

"You shouldn't have to deal with that alone, Dani. I hate that I've left you in that position." He pauses, and I can hear his breathing pick up. "Fuck, I hate this. If you want to wait to say something, I won't hold that against you. I meant it when I said it was you and me against the world."

"I can handle it." And I can. Plus I wasn't joking when I told Lila earlier that it would be best for me to soften the blow a little when it comes to my father.

"To answer your earlier question, no. I haven't and won't be able to call anyone else. I'm going dark, baby, and I know this might be the last chance I get to call home—I needed that call to be to you. I couldn't go without making sure I told you some things. Things I should have said before I left. God, I sound like a fucking sap. I can't explain it better than me needing to get my head straight before our next mission and the only way I could accomplish that was to talk to you."

Ho-Lee-Shit.

"Oh . . ."

"Is that a good 'oh'?" he laughs, the connection getting a little fuzzy.

"If your sisters find out, they're going to kill me."

"No, they won't. If they do, you just tell them that their brother loves his girls, but he loves his woman more."

Wait a minute.

"Do what?"

He laughs again, the sound like a balm for my soul. "Dani, what do you think we're doing here?"

"Uh, talking?"

"Yeah, baby. Talking. You going to tell me how much you love me?"

"You already know how much I love you," I jest.

"I do. And now you know I love you."

"Even if I didn't, the weekly flowers are sure doing a good job at showing me."

He's silent.

Silent for so long that I pull my phone away from my ear to make sure we didn't have the connection drop.

"Dani. I haven't sent any flowers."

"Don't be silly, Cohen. Of course you have. They've been coming every Saturday since you left. Who else would send them?" I feel what can only be a described as a flash of fear wash over my body. Oh my God. If Cohen isn't sending them, then who is?

"Flowers . . . yeah, those aren't my thing, Dani. They look beautiful for a little while and then they start to stink before they die. When I show you how much I love you, it damn sure won't be with something that's going to die in a week."

Oh. My.

"Put your brother on the phone. Now," he barks.

I jump at his tone, the fear I started to feel only seconds before rushing into my system, and I almost drop the phone because my hands are shaking so badly.

I rush out of the bathroom door and almost tumble over my brother, who is standing there, looking guilty, with a cup in his hand. A cup I'm sure was just pressed against the door like the ghetto little spy he is. I mutely hand Nate the phone and step back until I bump into Lee. He looks down at me with concern, and I just shake my head, not trusting my words.

I listen through the roaring in my ears as Nate responds to what Cohen is saying in clipped tones. His eyes shoot to mine a few times, the anger that was there at first now turning to concern.

"I'll take care of it," he snaps and hands me the phone again.

"H-hello?"

"Don't worry, baby. Your brother knows what to do, and he'll take care of everything. Is Lee there too?"

I nod my head but then remember he can't see me. "Lee's here."

"Good. Ask him if he can stay with you for a while."

"I'll do that."

"I love you, Dani-girl. No one is going to mess with that. No one. Don't worry, okay?"

"I'm not worried." And I'm really not worried. I'm not. I am terrified.

"Liar," he whispers. "God, I hate that I can't be there to protect you. This is killing me, Dani. It goes against everything I feel to not rush to you."

My heart breaks, the fear I felt instantly dimming. "I'll be okay. I promise. I'll make sure I'm not alone and the guys will watch out for me. I'm . . . I'm going to tell Daddy about us and, well, this. He won't let anything happen to me, Coh."

"That's a good idea. Might mean he kicks my ass a little harder when I get back with all that time he will have to stew on it, but it will be worth it to know that you're safe." He doesn't even hesitate. Not one second, which would have made me think he doesn't want this.

"Tell me you love me, baby. I have to go."

"I love you, baby." I smile.

"Yeah," he sighs. "And I you."

"See you soon," I whisper.

"Every time I close my eyes."

I don't move the phone away from my ear. Not when I hear the click or when Nate starts to ask his questions. I just smile to myself and let it sink in.

Chapter 19

Dani

PREDICTABLY, THINGS GOT A LITTLE insane after that call. Nate demanded to know what was going on between Cohen and me. I was honest with him, and in the end, he didn't have a problem with it more or less, just that I had kept from him.

Okay, that might be a stretch. He knew how I felt, of course, but he was shocked that Cohen had taken it that far without at least talking to him first. Then I had to explain to my irrational older brother that he isn't my keeper.

Don't ever tell a man who was raised by alpha males that he isn't the keeper of his baby sister. It isn't pretty and there is usually something that gets broken in the process. This time, it was my coffee table when I pushed the big ape over for telling me that I should be locked away on an island of Barbies and Big Wheels.

Yeah. I'm always going to be the baby sister.

That being said, justifiably, what he did have a problem with was the unexpected and unknown sender of the weekly flowers. I told him everything I knew about the delivery guy and how many had come, showing him the ones that were still around the house. Each of the vases held a big, black bow tied to the center of the glass vase. Black wouldn't have been my first choice, but when I'd thought they were from Cohen, it hadn't bothered me. Now, it makes me skin crawl.

And that was before Nate had found the first microscopic-looking wireless camera in the arrangement.

"You're moving home," he booms through the room. "That's fucking it. No. You're not staying here one more second, Danielle!" He starts pacing around my bedroom, his hands clenching in tight fists at his sides. Bringing out the full name is his way of showing me that he's serious.

I don't think so. No. I finally got out from under my father, and there is no damn way I'm going back. Especially now, it would only be a million times worse.

"I'm not leaving my home, Nate."

"Don't be irrational, Dani!" he screams in my face.

Lee, who was quiet until now, steps between us. "Be pissed, I get that, but don't you dare talk to her like that."

I give him a squeeze before things get too intense between him and Nate. Won't be the first time, and it damn sure won't be the last.

"Look," I start and step around Lee so that I can make sure Nate knows I mean every word I'm about to say. "I'm not going to leave. First of all, if whoever is sending the flowers is watching me, they'll see that and follow. I'm comfortable here. We're safe here. Lee can stay for a while, right, Lee?" I turn and wait for him to nod. "And I'll tell Daddy what's going on. I won't be put out of my own house because of some stupid flowers."

"Flowers with goddamn cameras in them, Dani!" he yells.

"Tone, Nate," Lee reminds him.

"Shut the fuck up, Lee."

"Would you both shut the hell up?!" I scream.

"What the hell is going on here?"

Oh great. I look over at my mom and smile sweetly. She narrows her eyes, and I know she doesn't buy it for a second.

"Do you want to tell me now or wait until your father gets in from unloading the car? He's always freaked me out with that sixth sense he has when it comes to his children. Imagine my shock when I'm trying to enjoy a glass of wine and a nice game of Candy Crush when your dad comes rushing in the room and demands we leave *right this second* because he knew you needed something. Of course, he couldn't tell me what it was you needed, so we had to stop off for just about everything he could buy at Walmart, the only damn store that's open at eleven on a Saturday. So . . . before he gets in here and I have to hear him gloat about being right, why don't you tell me what has your brother doing his best Axel Reid impression? Hey, Liam," she finishes with a smile. "Don't you look handsome tonight."

Jesus Christ, it's going to be a long night, and all I want to do is go to bed.

"Don't worry. His bark will be a lot worse than his bite," Lee whispers in my ear on a laugh. He's quick to move away before my dad walks in the room though.

"Hey, Daddy," I smile when he pushes into the room. "Shouldn't you be in bed by now? You know, past your bedtime and all?"

"Don't be a smartass with me. What's going on?"

"What makes you think something is going on? Nate and Lee were just watching a movie with me. Normal boring night."

"What makes me think something's going on? Besides the fact that a father always knows when his little princess needs something? How about your brother over there?" he states and points to Nate.

Nate, who is standing farther away in the middle of the living room, pacing back and forth and muttering to himself. His fists are clenched and his face is flushed with anger.

"Oh . . . poor guy. I told him that 'N Sync wasn't getting back together. He took it really, *really* hard."

Lee lets out a boom of laughter. My mom snickers to herself and rubs her hand down my dad's back.

"Dani," Nate warns. "You tell them or I will."

"I don't think—" I start only to be interrupted by Nate when he drops a bomb in the middle of the room.

"Why don't you fucking start with you and Cohen and then get to the flowers and cameras, *Danielle.*"

"The hell is he talking about?" Daddy rumbles.

"Uh, about that."

"There better not be any of *that* to be *about,*" he fumes.

"What does that even mean?" I ask.

"Don't you be smart with me. Start talking."

I sigh and look at my mom for some help, only to get a small nod and smile. Lee isn't much help either. He walks over to the couch, sits next to Nate, and waits—the popcorn we forgot about in their hands.

"Shit," I mutter.

"Mouth!" Dad explodes.

I narrow my eyes and have to resist the urge to stomp my feet.

"Start. Talking."

"Ugh! This is ridiculous. Well, this is definitely not how I saw this going. Thank you, Nathanial. You might as well sit down, Daddy."

"I don't want to sit down," he argues.

"Now who is acting like they're a child," I tease.

His face softens for a second before he remembers why he's upset.

"Okay. So it's probably best if I just rip it off like a Band-Aid, right?" No one speaks. "So . . . Cohen and I talked before he left and we decided that, when he comes home, we're going to see where we stand."

Daddy looks at me, his eyes blinking a few times as my words float around in his mind. I can see him trying to figure out what I just said, and then I watch when it finally sinks in. His tan face turns beet red and his nostrils start to flare. His eyes go even harder before he explodes.

"THE FUCK YOU SAY?"

Oh boy.

"Axel, baby, calm down."

"I won't calm down."

"She's an adult. You *know* Cohen, and I know that he would never do anything to hurt her. Ever. So your normal excuses of them being up to no good aren't going to work. Not with him. You've known that boy since he was three years old. If there is anyone you shouldn't have to worry about, it would be Cohen Cage."

"I also remember all that boy would talk about was his dick, too!"

"I think you're twisting those memories slightly. Plus, it was his father's dick." Mom burst out laughing when Lee and Nate start choking on their popcorn.

Serves those little shits right for trying to enjoy this clusterfuck.

"Izzy," my fathers warns.

"Good lord, Ax. You were never this over the top when we were their age." She laughs and then walks over to where I'm standing. Her arms come around me and her mouth goes to my ear. "He'll get over it, but don't back down."

I get a big squeeze before she walks over to Nate and slaps him over the head.

"Don't laugh at your sister."

"Where are the girls?" Daddy asks when no one makes a move to further the conversation.

"Maddi is spending time with her sister. She said she's been missing her lately. The twins are out. And before you even think about it, yes, they know and they're completely okay with it."

"I don't like this," he grumbles.

"And you don't have to. But it won't change anything, Daddy. I think it's time to let me live my own life and stop acting like I'm a little girl."

"That's not going to happen. I'll work on it, but I won't make any promises that I won't be having words with him when he gets his ass home. Long words, Dani. Words that may or may not involve me showing him my gun collection. Now sit down and tell me the rest."

"Actually . . . I think YOU might want to sit down for this part."

Chapter 20

Dani

TWO NIGHTS AGO, I HAD to vaguely tell my father that I would be dating when Cohen came home. I think that, if had it been any other person, he wouldn't have accepted it as well as he did. Well, I say, "accepted it," but I heard him when he stepped in the kitchen to "get a beer" and boom into his phone at who I can only imagine was Cohen's dad that his son was "going to violate my daughter and that shit better not happen."

That conversation went a lot better than the flowers and cameras one went. To say that my father lost his shit would be a vast understatement. It took my mom offering him God knows what for him to finally leave. I try to tune them out when she starts whispering in his ear to get her way.

Not something I want to think about.

Nope.

Never.

So here I am, two days later, and I feel like I'm about to climb out of my skin.

Daddy has decided to appoint himself as my personal bodyguard. And if that isn't enough, the lingering exhaustion I've been feeling for weeks has hit an all-time high. Or I guess it would be low. I've been falling asleep at work. In the shower. You name it. I was eating dinner, which was cooked by Maddi and delicious, the other night with the girls and fell asleep in my bowl! In. My. Bowl! Who does that?

I'm over it.

At least he agreed to let Chance accompany the girls and me to the Loaded Replay concert tonight in Atlanta. God, I would have killed him if he had shown up. He pulled whatever strings he has and our shit tickets have been swapped out with V.I.P., front-row tickets. Of course, his stipulation was that our group of five—me, Lyn, Lila, Maddi, and Stella—turn into a party of six. Chance was going or we weren't.

For tonight, Chance will be an honorary chick because I am not missing this show.

Loaded Replay hit the scene huge a few years ago. They're a mix of old-school classic rock and new-school flare. There isn't a single band out there currently that has what they have. Of course, it doesn't hurt that their lead singer is a chick who is smoking hot and she's backed up by three damn fine men.

Maddi has been *in love* with their drummer, Jameson Clark, since the first day she saw a picture of him. Tall, built, blond Adonis. He really does look like a rock god. Lead guitarist Weston Davenport, brother of lead singer Wrenlee Davenport, is the fan favorite though. He looks like a rock-n-roll version of Liam Hemsworth, right down to that killer smile. I've always thought that their bassist, Luke Madden, was fun to watch. He has that boy-next-door look to him, but his eyes just scream trouble and mischief. Bottom line—you can tell there is something about Loaded Replay that just screams badass.

To say we're excited would be the understatement of the year.

"Thanks for agreeing to this," I tell Chance when we load into his Expedition to head over to the arena.

The girls are in the back, going on and on about how they're going to get the attention of one of the band members. I tune them out and focus on picking at the frayed holes in my jeans.

Where Lyn, Lila, Maddi, and Stella decided to go with their Slut Barbie looks, I kept it simple with skinny jeans, a flowing chiffon shirt, and my favorite knee-high, leather boots. I looked good, but I also looked like I wanted to be comfortable and not pick up potential bed-warming friends.

"Yup," he rumbles.

"You don't talk much, do you?"

He looks over briefly before returning his attention back to the road. "I don't think you've been around me enough to make that assumption."

"True. But so far tonight, I've said hello and gotten one of those man chin-lift greeting thingies. I asked you how you were and you grunted. I asked if you liked Loaded Replay and I got another grunt, and when you were ready to leave, all you said was, 'Truck,' and walked away. So you're right—I don't know you that well, but I think I actually can safely make that assumption correctly."

He looks over again. This time, his stoic face is grinning. "I can see what the attraction is now."

What an odd thing to say. "Excuse me?"

"I never could understand why Cohen would go on and on about you—no offense—but I get it now. You've got some fire under all of that innocence."

Oh. "Wait. Cohen would go on and on about me?"

"Clueless," he laughs. "You're right about one thing: I don't talk much. But that doesn't mean I don't watch. That guy has been watching you for as long as I've been around. And I don't just mean looking at you a few times when you walk in a room—the second that you walk in, his eyes never leave you. Always thought he was crazy, but I get it."

"Uh, I'm glad?" What am I supposed to say here? *Thanks for understanding why he is attracted to me?*

He shakes his head and continues to drive with his smirk in place. Such a weird man.

Since we were a little late to leave, when we finally get to the arena, they have already started letting people in. Every inch, from the ticket-holders at the entry to the ushers standing at the seating doorways, is crawling with fans. No, crawling would be a bad word for it. There literally isn't an extra inch to move. Everyone is yelling, beers are spilling, and the air around us is full of excitement to see one of, if not the, hottest bands in the country. Most of the chicks are in various stages of slut. Because Wrenlee Davenport, with her undeniable beauty, which is matched with one hell of a set of pipes, there seems to be an even mix of both men and woman milling around. A group of teenage shits almost cause me to drop to the ground when they go running through the crowd. If it weren't for Chance catching me at the last second of my stumble, I would have been on the ground.

No one even bothers to talk. It wouldn't do any good. Chance grabs my hand, I turn and grab Lyn, and I watch until we're all connected. This should be fun. Lyn gives me a look that tells me that she won't be letting go even if we go down. She wouldn't, either. If she goes down, the heifer will take everyone down with her.

Ten minutes later, we finally make it to our seats—best freaking seats in the house—and that's only because Chance finally had enough and started shouldering his way through the crowd. He isn't a bulky guy like my brother, but he is tall, and what he lacks in bulk, he makes up for with his general attitude. I probably would have gotten out of the way, too.

"I'm so fucking pumped!" Maddi screams, waving her fist in the air.

"Me too! Oh my God. Do you think we can get the guys attention? I'll probably piss myself if Weston looks my way. Like, legit piss myself." Lyn starts to fan herself with her hand, and her eyes roam around the stage just feet in front of us.

"That's disgusting," I laugh.

"Nope. I wouldn't piss myself. I would probably come in my pants though!" she exclaims.

"Jesus Christ," Chance grumbles.

I laugh and continue to look around the packed venue. Everyone around us is vibrating with the same crazy energy I've felt since we pulled into the parking garage. It's hard to contain the excitement you feel when you know you're about to see a group so huge perform. I tune out the girls, ignore an uncomfortable Chance, and just soak it all in. My earlier exhaustion is long forgotten.

The lights dim thirty minutes later, and the opening act, an all-female rock band called Carnage, is now working the stage. I'm not a huge fan, but the girls are, so while they jump and scream, I join in the fun. Honestly, I just can't wait to see Loaded Replay.

"Holy shit! Here they come!" screams Maddi and Lyn.

As if they heard them scream, all the lights go off, and after a small pause, there is a heavy drum beat that fills the air. Just *thump, thump, thump* fills the space and takes the excitement in the crowd to explosive levels. It doesn't last long as a solo beat until I hear and feel the bass line that makes my skin breakout in goose bumps. And seconds later, the electric guitar rift that lights the air around us has the girls next to me acting like they're hormonally challenged. The second the lights stream onto the stage, lighting up the four members of LR, Lyn and Maddi have tears streaming down their faces—the freaks. Stella is bobbing her head in tune with the beats, her long, brown hair swishing around her angelic face. Lila is laughing at her sister's and Maddi's antics, but she keeps peeking at the stage.

Elbowing Chance, I try to get his attention to let him know I need to use the restroom, but his eyes are transfixed on the stage. Well, not the stage. He's looking dead on at the stunning lead singer. The same lead singer who is holding his gaze with a wicked gleam in her bright eyes.

I must be the only one in the whole damn place who isn't acting like a bitch in heat.

Whatever. I don't want to miss more of the show than I have to, but if I don't pee now, I'll be pulling a Maddi and really embarrass myself. Chance doesn't even notice that I'm leaving until I'm already through the row of screaming fans and turning to walk up the ramp. I look back and catch his pissed eyes before I give him a sassy wave and walk off. Hey, when a girl has to go, she doesn't wait around.

Okay, so leaving the man who is supposed to be watching me for the evening wasn't my brightest move. I'm sure I'll have to deal with him being pissed when I get back—or worse, I'll have to deal with my father if he tells him. I've always been an independent person, so having to rely on someone else to babysit me isn't my favorite pastime.

I make it back to the seat, having only missed one song, but predictably, Chance is fuming.

"Don't pull that shit again, Dani. I like my balls right the fuck where they are. Your father wants me here for a reason, so don't act like a child and ignore that."

He's right. I know he is.

Wisely, I nod my head before turning my attention back to the show.

But I also don't mention the weird feeling I got when I was walking alone through the arena.

Chapter 21

Cohen

FUCK ME, I HATE BEING here.

I hate every day I'm away from home and stuck in this fucking sandbox.

Every day I'm here, I feel like I lose a part of my soul.

My worry for things at home have hit an all-time high, and if it weren't for my training, I would have been dead days ago when we hit an ambush of gunfire and bombs.

The only thing that is keeping me going is the knowledge that it might be over soon. We got word a few hours ago that, if things start to turn around, we could be home as early as two months from now. Two months is a whole hell of a lot better than the seven months this mission was projected at.

God, I can't wait to get home.

I've felt this pit in my gut since Dani told me about the flowers that have been showing up at her place. This feeling I'm helpless to correct. A feeling that has been screaming at me to get my ass home as quickly as I can because something is wrong.

My girl needs me and I'm completely fucking helpless.

Chapter 22

Dani

THE LAST THING I WANT to deal with on a Monday morning is camera crews and a manic Sway. No. That's not right. I don't want to deal with them any day, but today, I'm in bitch mode and I just can't seem to shake myself out of it. Every look someone gives me, even if it's just a smile, has me wanting to punch something. I can't decide if I just need more sleep or if I should kill Maddi for keeping me up all night with the noises that were coming out of her room.

I had considered going over to Cohen and Chance's place. I've escaped to Cohen's bed more times than I care to admit since he's been gone. More so since the Loaded Replay concert two weeks ago. I'm sure my family and my roommates are starting to notice my lack of attendance here lately. Chance isn't exactly the best company either, but we've become good enough friends that, between the grunts and hard looks, he's kind of fun to be around. Okay, fun isn't exactly the right word for what he is. He fills the void of loneliness the girls just can't. He talks to me about my concerns when it comes to Cohen and his "going dark," and since he's lived that life, it's reassuring to hear from him that it just means Cohen is on mission and needs to stay focused.

So here I am. After a night of no sleep, contemplating if I would be able to get away with murder.

We're on filming day two million seventy-five—okay, I kid—and

I'm about to shove these cameras up Sway's ass. Of course, it doesn't help that Lyn decided to call out because she was partying all night long, causing me to have to spend almost an hour rescheduling all of her clients. The new chick, Samantha, was a no-show, and Sway has been doing fucking cartwheels around the salon because of some heels that went on sale at Saks.

Yeah. I'm officially just having a crappy Monday.

And Devon is still gone, so Don and Mark have been up my ass all day. Okay, I take that back. Don has. He doesn't bother me as much as he did when we first met two months ago, but that doesn't mean he doesn't annoy the ever-loving shit out of me.

Mark, on the other hand, is silent and broody, and he generally makes it his life mission to let me know that I'm not working the camera like I should be and how the show all depends on us following the scripted points Devon wants us to hit. That is usually followed up by me reminding the idiot that it's a reality show, not a scripted sitcom.

But together, they both give me the creepiest vibes ever. I can't decide if Mark and his silent "I hate the world" vibes are worse than Don and his creepy little winks and smiles.

Today freaking sucks. I look over at a scowling Mark and think, again, how many ways I could make his death look like an accident. His newest scowl is because I wouldn't ask my last male client out on a date and make it look like I had been pining after him for months.

As freaking if.

"What has gotten into you, sweet girl?" Sway asks when he is finally able to stop dancing around.

"Just feeling a little low today," I mumble and continue to stock my station.

"Do you need me to kick the cameras out today?"

I look over at him, shocked, because Sway would never kick the cameras out. He loves every second of this reality show crap. His handsome, caramel skin is etched in concern. Dark, perfectly sculpted brows are pulled in, and his eyes show love and compassion. He runs one of his—manicured, of course—hands over his buzzed hair and waits for me to answer.

"I'm okay. Promise. Just keep that one away from me," I tell him and point over at Don.

"You got it, darlin.' Just promise Uncle Sway that, if you start looking any more blue, you'll take that skinny ass home." He wraps his arms around me, his silk blouse cool against my cheek.

"Promise," I sigh, soaking in the comfort I didn't realize I wanted or needed.

In all honesty, for the last two weeks, I've just started feeling . . . weird. I think a lot of it has to do with the fact that I miss Cohen and hold some resentment towards life because he was taken away from me right when we had finally gotten somewhere. Everyone seems to be doing just fine and I'm little miss broody. I hate feeling this way, but it's almost like I'm helpless to stop those thoughts.

I just want him home.

"Well, hello, my sweet child."

I smile to myself when my mother's soft voice enters my brooding.

"Hey," I sigh and let all my stress drain from my body when she wraps her arms around me and gives me a tight hug. "What are you doing here? Did I miss an appointment?"

"Since when do I need an appointment to come and take my only daughter out to lunch?" she smarts.

"Oh, my bad," I laugh. "Sway called, huh?" I correctly guess. That man can't help it. He hates seeing any of his girls upset.

"He sure did. He also told me he would handle your next two clients and that I wasn't supposed to bring you back until I've checked out the new sales at Lenox Mall. He also told me that, if you argue about missing work or upsetting clients or whatever of your 'outrageously cockamamie' excuses are, I'm supposed to tell you he has your father on speed dial and won't hesitate to call him." Her smile is huge, her jade-colored eyes flashing with humor.

I peer over her shoulder and look at a smiling Sway. He gives me a wink before spinning on his heels and returning to his conversation with Don. God, he's such a meddler.

"Well, I guess, since the boss man has spoken, I have a free day to spend with you."

She laughs softly. "Go ahead and do what you need to get ready, baby. I'm going to go bother Sway for a little while."

"Stay away from the cameras, Mom. You know Daddy would shit himself if you ended up some weird, fake twist in the story line. Knowing how these idiots work, you would end up being Sway's new lover and the reason that he is leaving his husband and daughter. Scandalous stuff. Just downright indecent!" I throw my hand over my chest and mock outrage.

I make quick work of cleaning up my station and making sure I have everything together for tomorrow's clients. Mom is still busy laughing and chatting with Sway when I walk up to the front desk. Don is nowhere to be seen, but Mark is standing next to one of their camera crew members with his arms crossed and a scowl firmly in place. I'm sure he's pissed that I'm leaving in the middle of a film day. Well, what the hell ever. I know it's childish, but I can't stop myself before I stick my tongue out.

I win this round.

"God, I'm stuffed," I laugh, pushing my plate of wings away from me before I can grab another one. This happens every single time Mom talks me into coming to Heavy's, her favorite barbeque place in town. From the way Dad talks, she's been hooked on this stuff like crack since before Nate was born.

"Well, give it here. No sense in letting those wings go to waste."

I laugh when she pulls the plate I just discarded in front of her and finishes it off in record time.

"I have no idea how you stay so tiny. You should really be at least five hundred pounds."

She looks up, her eyes shining. "That's because I work out every night."

"Yeah, right! I've never seen you step one foot in the gym . . . Oh. My. God. Don't say anything else. Some things can't be unheard, Mom!" Ugh! I do not want to think about how she works off all this damn food. Nope. Not thinking about it.

"What?" she says in shock, but she still has that devilish smirk. "Your father bought me one of those stair thingies."

"An elliptical?"

"Yes?"

"You don't even know what it's called! I bet it's not even out of the box," I laugh.

She wipes her fingers off on the wet napkin and laughs at me. "Moving on, sweetheart. Why don't you tell me what is going on with you? I called the house the other day and Lyn said you were out. I thought . . . Well, I thought that you and Cohen . . . I guess I'm just wondering what's going on."

"Why does everyone keep asking me what's going on? I'm fine. I was a little upset—okay, a lot upset—when Cohen left, but I'm fine. Really."

"Dani, you aren't fine."

I look at her—really look at her—and notice how concerned she looks. All the humor she held on her beautiful face is long gone and she's looking at me like she can see right through me.

I sigh. "I miss him, Mom. It really just is that simple."

"I see."

"I know we haven't talked about it since Daddy freaked out, but are you really okay with this? Cohen and me?"

She reaches out and takes the hand I was resting against the table. "Honey, I couldn't be more thrilled. I only ask because you haven't seemed like you're handling this separation well, and trust me—I understand."

I give her a sad smile because I know all about how well she did not handle the separation from my dad all those years ago.

"It's just . . . The girls mentioned that you haven't been sleeping at the house, and even though I know it isn't my business, I guess I'm just concerned and being nosy."

One thing I love about my mom is that she is super easy to talk to. I know that, when I tell her that I've been sleeping over at Cohen's apartment, she might not like the idea, knowing that Cohen doesn't live alone, but if anyone will understand where my head is in all of this, it's going to be her.

"You promise not to tell Daddy? *You* will understand, but him? No, he most definitely will not."

Her brow furrows, but she nods her head. I know she doesn't like keeping things from him, but I hope she can keep this to herself.

"I've been sleeping at Cohen's place."

She doesn't say a word.

"In his bed. It's just . . . Okay, I know this is going to sound insane, but there's just something inside me that makes me *have* to be near him. I never imagined I would miss him this much, and being in his space, his bed, surrounded by his things . . . It just makes this emptiness I constantly feel a little easier to bear."

"Oh, sweetheart." Her eyes start to water, and I know it's only seconds before she turns on the waterworks.

"Please don't get upset. I really am okay. It's just been a little of an adjustment. I haven't been sleeping well, and it just all caught up on me this last month, but when I'm in his bed, I sleep like the dead. I swear it makes no sense. We had just come together and decided to take a try at a relationship. Our time was so limited before he left that it might as well have just been seconds. How is it possible to miss him so much?"

She doesn't waste a second. My chin starts to wobble a little, so she is instantly on my side of the booth and pulling me close to her.

"You know about when your father left for his tour? I was a mess, Dani. Not just because of everything that happened after—losing my parents, our first child—even though those were enough to send me over the edge into the deep end. I was a mess because I didn't have the one person who gives my heart a reason to beat. Don't for one second downplay that feeling or its significance. Let me ask you this. If you think that you're having a hard time without him, how do you think he's handling everything? Do you think it would do him any favors to know that you're suffering when he isn't here?"

"No, Mom, I don't think it would." And honestly, it wouldn't. If he knew how upset I was about his being gone—knowing that was one of the major reasons he didn't want to start this between us—then it would do nothing but cause a distraction. "Of course he doesn't *know* that, though, and doesn't have a way of knowing how I'm doing."

"My silly little girl. I'm sure you don't realize this because this is really the first time you've loved someone with so much power behind it. When your other half is in pain, you always know."

"How am I supposed to just not miss him?" I ask.

"You aren't supposed to stop missing him, Dani. But you can't let that desire to have him near take over your life. You're pushing away your friends, you aren't coming to family dinners, and hell, you haven't even talked to your father in a few days. Something that I promise you he hasn't missed. You have to keep living your life, but living it in a way that you have that knowledge that he's coming home to you and this separation isn't forever. I lived twelve years thinking that I wouldn't ever see your father's face, Danielle. I know pain, and I know what it feels like when you feel like you have no hope left. These feelings you have aren't even close. You and Cohen, darling girl . . . You two have been fated from the beginning, and there isn't a damn thing that could take that away from you."

"What does that mean? We've been fated from the beginning?"

She takes a deep, shuddering breath and lets it out on a whoosh. "Let me tell you a little story. One that I hoped I never had to tell you, but one I think will help you understand why I am certain this thing between you and Cohen is much bigger than you even understand."

She takes the next thirty minutes to tell me all about her first marriage, one I knew she had but never ever knew the terrible details. Daddy doesn't like to talk about him, her first husband, and now that I know the hell my mother lived through during those years, I completely understand.

"You see, when I finally left my ex, I really didn't think I had hope left, Dani. I had Dee in my life, and she probably would have been my savior for the rest of my days, but I still felt empty. Then, when we moved here, to Hope Town, that was when Greg came into our lives. He had known Dee for a while, and as you know, he served with your daddy. I always used to ask myself why God was so cruel to make me spend all of those years without your father, to take our first child away, and bring all of that pain. It wasn't until years and years later, when I was sitting on the back porch during one of our family parties, that I realized what the big picture was. And let me tell you, I would have lived through all of that again if it would end in the same outcome."

"I don't understand," I tell her.

"Let me finish, sweetheart." She shifts in her seat and pulls something from her jacket pocket. "I took this that day. The sun was so beautiful that I just had to get a good shot of it. It was bouncing off the lake and outlining the dock and the trees around it, God, it was stunning. Here," she says and holds something out to me.

I look down, not sure what to expect, and gasp. I don't remember the moment. I was too young, but I recognize us instantly. She's right. The picture outlines the dock and the trees surrounding their property line to perfection. It also highlights the two figures sitting at the very end of the dock. I must have been around six or seven in this picture. It was the year I convinced my mom it would be a brilliant idea to cut my long, thick hair to my chin. Cohen, even at eleven, was so much larger than my tiny frame. We're sitting close, our heads touching temple to temple, and his scrawny arm is wrapped around my shoulders. I have no idea what we were doing or talking about, but it's clear in that picture that there was something so loving about the two of us.

"Even at a young age," she continues, "he was always drawn to you. If you were hurt, he was there. When Nate was being . . . well, Nate, he was always around to make sure whatever upset you was fixed. And the same went for him. Even as a baby, if you knew he was around, your sweet, chubby face would light up. You and Cohen have been a long time coming, and I know that everything that has ever happened in the past was to make sure this moment, every moment since then until now, was going to happen. It's fate, baby. I used to think it hated me, but I just realized that it works with the bigger picture. I never would have met Greg if it wouldn't have been for everything I went through, but I also wouldn't be able to be the mom you need—the one with the experience of what you're going through—if I hadn't lived it myself."

"Oh, Mom," I gasp and choke back the sob that so desperately wants to escape.

"I guess my point is, you might not feel whole right now, and, sweetheart, I understand why, but you will soon. Fate won't keep you two apart when it's been so clear that together is where you're meant to be. Hold strong and don't let this pain of missing him make you push everyone else who loves you away."

Clutching that picture to my chest, I let her words sink in and vow to do better at this whole "missing someone" business.

Chapter 23

Dani

AFTER ALL OF THE EMOTIONAL heaviness at lunch, we decided to spend the rest of the afternoon shopping. Even though it's a pastime I know my mother loathes to an extreme, she knows that it's something I love. I didn't realize how much I needed some mother/daughter time, and now that she's opened up my eyes to how well she knows what I'm going through, it's easier knowing that I have her to talk to about everything I'm feeling with Cohen being gone.

The sun is starting to fall behind the trees by the time we make it back to the complex where Sway's is located. Even with the late hour, the parking lot is far from empty.

Mom pulls her car next to mine and gives me a big hug. "I want you to come to me if you start feeling down again, Dani. Don't let it fester until you're being dragged down with exhaustion. Miss your man, but don't mourn someone who's coming back to you."

"Promise. I love you," I respond, feeling lighter for the first time in weeks.

I don't think I realized how much I needed this. I just don't feel like I can talk to the girls about this knowing that they're missing their brother just as much as I am. Lee doesn't understand even though I know he would try. And Chance is just . . . Chance.

"I'm going to go and see your father before I head home. Do you want to come with me? I know he would love to see you."

"I'll be over in a little while. Let me drop all of these bags in my trunk and head in to tell Sway I'm going to take tomorrow off. I think I just need a mental day. One that's away from those damn cameras."

"All right, baby."

She walks away, waving at Sway through the floor-to-ceiling windows on the salon and heading through the door to Corps Security, my dad's company he co-owns with the rest of his buddies. It's not lost on me that he probably loved it when I started working right next door so that he could keep his eyes on me.

Absentmindedly, I walk behind my car and toss in the bags that hold the clothes I did not need to buy. My mind is still on the afternoon and everything my mom and I talked about. It isn't until I step between the cars that I notice the piece of paper sticking out from the driver's side door, flapping against the window with the light breeze.

Reaching out, I snag the slim paper and look around. Shrugging off the feeling of being watched that crawls up my spine, I unfold the paper and almost lose my lunch.

YOU ARE SUPPOSED TO BE MINE, BITCH. YOU TAKE MY FLOWERS WITH A SMILE ON YOUR FACE, BUT SPEND YOUR TIME CRYING OVER SOME MOTHERFUCKER THAT ISN'T EVEN THERE. I HEARD YOU TODAY! YOU ARE MINE, DANIELLE! IF YOU THINK SOME OTHER MOTHERFUCK WILL HAVE YOU WHEN YOU BELONG TO ME—YOU ARE DEAD FUCKING WRONG.

I must be screaming. That's the only thing that makes sense, because not even seconds after my shocked and terrified hands dropped the note, I see my daddy, who is followed by Greg and Maddox, barreling through the door of his office and charging across the parking lot. Right as my head slams against the ground, I feel my body being lifted and cradled in his strong arms as he rushes away from that piece of paper, which is now being clutched between Greg's fist as he and Maddox look between each other with trepidation written all over their faces.

"She's going to the fucking hospital and that's the end of the discussion, Izzy. You didn't fucking see her, Izzy! Her head slammed against the ground, goddamn it!"

Damn, my head hurts. I push myself up from the couch in my dad's office and look around at the worried faces. My dad is crouched down on his knees in front of the couch, and my mom sitting on the armrest above where my head was just resting, her hand lying on his shoulder. I'm sure she is trying to calm him down. Maddox is leaning against the desk, and Greg is pacing the room.

"I'm okay," I say, but it comes out like a moan when my head starts to feel like it's spinning. "I think."

"See! She doesn't even fucking know if she's okay. Let's go, little princess. Time to go see the doctor." He jumps to his feet and goes to grab me before my mom reaches out one slim hand to stop him.

"Calm down, Ax. Let her speak for herself before you go crazy." She turns to me with concern etched on her face. "Sweetheart, is your head bothering you?"

"A little." I stop and look up to Greg, the last person who saw the message. "Do you have it?" I ask him.

"Yeah, baby girl. Don't worry about a thing, okay?"

A look I don't even attempt to process passes between him and my dad.

"I think it might actually be a good idea to go get checked," I moan. Then I lean over and lose my lunch all over my dad's feet.

Dad freaks out. He's convinced that I'm broken and someone needs to fix me. My head is hurting more from his continual barking at the staff at the urgent care clinic. My mom just sits back and lets him do his thing. She told me a long time ago that she learned her lesson when it came to him. He's going to over-parent and be protective to a point of annoyance and there just isn't a damn thing that will change him.

"Hello, Ms. Reid. I hear you took a nasty spill this afternoon," the young doctor says when she stops in the room. She smiles sweetly at me before looking over and seeing my parents. Her face instantly goes hard. "Mr. Reid, I presume?" At his nod, she continues. "I hear you've been giving my staff a hard time today."

I giggle, and Mom snorts a laugh out.

"Hello, Dr. Webb," I say after reading her jacket and effectively cutting my father off before he can start in on his rants. "It wasn't that bad. Just a little bump when I hit the ground. Lingering headache."

"Don't forget you threw up, Dani. Remember."

"Yeah, Daddy, I know. I was there." I roll my eyes and look up at the doctor.

"That's what they said. Your scans look fine, and aside from the contusion and obvious concussion, I would say you're fine. I'm going to write you a prescription for some low-dose pain meds that will be safe to take in your condition."

"Jeeze, Doc. You make it sound like I'm dying." I laugh and then wince when my head throbs.

"Oh, I'm sorry. Bad habit I guess. I know pregnant woman don't usually like us to refer to them as having a condition." She laughs, looking down at her chart, and doesn't even notice that the room has gone electric.

"I'm sorry?" I whisper. "What did you say?"

She looks up, noticing my expression before looking over at my parents. I don't know what she saw there since I'm absolutely terrified to look at my father.

"Oh, I am so sorry. I didn't realize. With your lab work and the date listed as your last menstrual cycle . . . I'm sorry. I just assumed."

"What are you saying, Doctor?" my father spits out. I can literally hear the force he had to use to get the words through his lips.

"I'll need to talk to you daughter in private, and then, when she's ready, she can choose to share the information we discuss as she sees fit. I do apologize, Mr. and Mrs. Reid."

I don't move my eyes from my lap. I keep my head down even through the struggle of my mom physically pulling my dad out of the room. I don't move when I hear him yelling out in the hallway or when I hear something crash. Not even when the door clicks loudly when the doctor shuts herself in the room with me.

The whole time, my mind is spinning.

Pregnant?

Surely, she's wrong. She must have someone else's chart. I remember the question about my last period. I just opened the app on my phone and put what it said. My periods have always been erratic, so I never even gave it a second thought.

"Danielle? Is it okay that I call you Danielle?"

"Dani," I mumble.

"I'm sorry?"

"It's Dani. I've always hated Danielle. Sounds like a mouthful, so I go by Dani. It works. I don't get any annoying nicknames. I'm just Dani. Dani Reid. That's me. Holy shit, am I freaking pregnant?!" I end my verbal vomit on a scream that makes me wince.

"I take it this is a surprise?"

"Very much so," I tell her, starting to freak out a little.

"How about I go get our portable ultrasound machine and we get a little look. Might ease your mind and make it seem a little more real. Well, once the shock wears off."

I nod my head, but I don't speak.

Pregnant.

Holy shit. Cohen is going to freak.

And my daddy is going to go apeshit.

Chapter 24

Cohen

THE NIGHTS ARE SO LONG here.

I'm left with nothing but longing to be home with my family and with Dani in my arms.

It gives me nothing but time to sit and think.

Think about the time I lost with Dani because I was too busy pushing her away.

Time I'm losing now because I'm over in this fucking hell, hunting terrorists.

And the worst feeling of all is that growing ache in my stomach that tells me I have to get home soon. I can't explain it any other way. It's a daily struggle to push the feeling aside so I can concentrate on my job and make sure I don't get blown the fuck up in the process.

One thing is for certain in all of this. This time away from Dani has proven one thing to me. That one night I had with her in my arms will never be enough.

I roll over on the hard ground and close my eyes, and just like the night before and every one since I've been here, I see her smiling face.

Chapter 25

Dani

THE DOCTOR COMES BACK IN the room, dragging some weird-ass computer behind her. She flips the light off before she has me lie back on the exam table, and she puts my shirt over my stomach before I can get over my shock. My leggings are wiggled down until they are resting just above my crotch. And then I let out a yelp when she squirts some goo on me.

"Sorry, Dani. I don't usually run the ultrasounds, so I must have grabbed the gel that wasn't in the warmer," she mumbles more to herself than to me.

I look down to where her hand is moving some wand-looking thing around in the disgusting goo. This is so nasty. All of this work for her to tell me that she read something wrong.

I have almost convinced myself that there was no way she could be right. Hell, Cohen used a condom every time, so surely there is no possible way for me to be pregnant. I haven't been throwing up. Everything has been normal. Just because I don't have a regular period doesn't mean I'm knocked up.

I am about to open my mouth and tell her just that when the oddest sound echoes through the small room. "What the hell?" I question at the noise. It sounds like thundering hoof beats.

"Well, that, Dani, is your baby."

She sounds so pleased that I can't help how my eyes narrow before the shock hits again. Jesus, it's just the night for shocks.

I hesitantly look over at the monitor she's pointing to before my heart stops for a beat before picking up. I have no idea what the heck I'm looking at. I just know it's the most beautiful thing I've ever seen in my whole life.

My baby?

Cohen's and my little miracle.

The doctor starts pointing to everything and explaining what I'm looking at. Every word she speaks, I soak up like a dying woman. Already head over heels in love with the child I was convinced only seconds before couldn't even be possible.

Holy crap. I'm going to be a mommy?

Even through I'm scared out of my mind for what this means for my future—my future with Cohen—I let the love for this child wash over me and smile the brightest smile I've probably ever had.

"So . . . surprised but happy?" she asks.

"Very." And I am. I really am.

"The baby's father? I can print these images for you."

"He's overseas. But I would love to have a few copies so that I can show him when he gets home."

"Of course. Do you know when he is expected to return? If you would like, just come on by when I'm on shift and I'll make sure you guys are able to sneak a peek at this little one. You're measuring right at twelve weeks, so unfortunately, it's too early for a gender screen. But come back in a few weeks and we can see if that little one wants to give you an early show."

"Thank you," I breathe roughly when she hands me the printouts of my baby and moves to turn the lights on. "Hey, Doc?"

"Yes?" She looks over after she washes her hands.

"Do you know if there is a back entrance you can sneak me out?"

She throws her head back with a laugh and shakes her head. "I'm sorry."

"It's okay. He's just a little . . . overprotective."

"I noticed." She laughs. "I'll step out and give you a minute. Congratulations, Dani. I want you to be careful. You shouldn't be alone tonight because of the concussion. You also need to follow up with your gynecologist later this week. Is it okay to have your parents come back in now?"

"Uh, yeah. Can you mention to my dad about my headache or something? It should keep his temper in check if he knows he can't freak out. Gives me a day or so to let this sink in."

She laughs but agrees.

When the door opens five minutes later and my mom walks in, she immediately wraps her arms around me. I can tell she's crying, but I wasn't expecting to see a huge smile on her face when she pulls back. She leans in and gives me a kiss on my forehead.

"I love you," she mouths.

I look over her shoulder and see my daddy. All six feet six inches of him, his tattooed arms crossed over his chest, and every vein bulging in his neck. His face is beet red, and his breathing is erratic.

Daddy is pissed.

"I love you, Daddy."

"And I love you, my little princess," he says, deflating some. Then, almost as if he remembered why he was so worked up, he stands tall again and his veins pop back out. "But I'm going to kill that motherfucker who touched you."

Mom gives me a squeeze, and I stay silent. Because really, what am I supposed to say to that?

Predictably, Daddy wouldn't take me home. He didn't say a word, even through all my complaining. Mom just giggled in the front seat. My head was killing me, so I wasn't willing to put up the fight. But I wasn't staying. My plan to call Lee the second we got over there was foiled when he answered and said that he was on a date.

My father thoroughly enjoyed watching me stew in my anger over being held hostage by him.

"Fine. I'll call one of the girls."

"The fuck you will, Dani! You might not remember how this night started, but I sure as hell do. Until we figure out what is going on with these flowers and now that note—you aren't leaving my sight."

"I'm not staying, Daddy. I'm perfectly safe at home. And if it's a problem, then Lee can stay with me."

"Liam doesn't own as many guns as I do," he snaps, crossing his arms over his chest, again, in his international Axel sign for "don't mess with me."

"Lee is also a black belt and could kick even your ass."

"Liam wouldn't be able to do shit against a knife or gun, Dani. You're safe here. I can keep you safe."

"I'm safe at home!" I scream.

"I know you're not going to argue with me, your father, who happens to own a fucking company that specializes in fucking security, that you're going to be better off without me watching over you. News flash, little princess: there isn't a single person that I trust to keep my little girl and future grandbaby safe."

His eyes soften slightly when he mentions the baby, and I just know that, despite his anger, which I'm sure will make another appearance, he's going to love this baby just as much as he loves Nate and me.

"Don't you look at me like that, Dani. I'm still going to kill that asshole who knocked up my little girl."

I'm not sure what it was in his tone that made me look back over at him. "What? I can tell you have more to say."

"I didn't want to get into this while everything that happened today is still so fresh, but I have to say . . . I'm disappointed in you, Dani. I never thought that you would do something like this to Cohen. I just hope that, whoever that bastard is, he's worth the trouble he caused. I might not have told you, but I couldn't have picked a better man for you to end up with than Cohen, and when he finds out you're pregnant with another man's child, I don't see how that can end well."

He turns and walks out of the room. His words hit me right in the gut before they slam directly into my heart.

Another man's child? What in the hell!

I don't even take a second to process my anger. I grab my cell out of my purse and search for the number I need. It doesn't take long for the call to connect.

"'Lo?"

"Chance? Can you please come get me?" I hiccup through a sob.

Chapter 26

Dani

CHANCE DIDN'T ASK ANY QUESTIONS. He pulled into my parents' driveway thirty minutes later and honked the horn. I didn't even pause. I got my purse, grabbed the bag with my meds, and walked out the front door. I could hear my dad yelling when I jumped in the passenger seat and slammed the door before locking it.

Chance looks at me with questions in his eyes before he looks past me to where I'm sure my father is fuming.

"If I drive out of here right now, is it going to get me killed?" he asks.

"Possibly."

"Right. Well, seeing as I like being alive and I plan to keep on breathing for a while longer, I'm going to step out of the truck and have a chat with your dad."

Before I can stop him, he opens the door and steps out.

Shit!

I can hear them talking, but not what is being said because the window is up and the hum of his engine is drowning them out. Hesitantly, I reach over and press the down button until the window is cracked slightly.

" . . . just came because she called me and sounded upset. I owe it to Cohen to make sure she's okay, sir. No offense, but if she isn't okay here, then I'll step in."

"Is it yours?" my dad barks.

"Is what mine?"

"The baby."

Chance looks over his shoulder at me. His face is stoic, but his eyes flash in warning. Warning of what, I'm not sure.

"I was unaware that Dani was expecting, sir."

"Cut the bullshit, Chance. Are you sleeping with my daughter? With your roommate's girl? Do you think I don't know about the nights she's been sneaking over to your place?"

Holy shit. This is bad.

"Axel!"

I look between the two men standing toe-to-toe in my parents' driveway to see my mom running down their porch steps.

"You need to step away right now. This, all of this, is none of your business, and as much as it kills you that it isn't, it's time to shut the hell up before you cause your daughter more pain. We will have words later about what you're accusing her of."

God, I love my mom.

Chance doesn't give him a second to reply. He steps away, turns, and walks back to the driver seat.

Mom calls his name and gets his attention before he can shut the door. "She needs to be watched tonight after her fall. Wake her up every few hours. I trust you to take care of her?"

"Yes, ma'am." He shuts the door and backs out of their driveway.

I can tell he has plenty to say, but he's keeping quiet.

"I'm sorry, Chance," I whisper.

He doesn't speak, but he reaches out and grabs my hand, holding it tight in his and giving me just what I need at the moment.

Someone else to be my strength.

The second we got back to the apartment, I took off to Cohen's room. By the time my head hits his pillow, I was ready to crash. Chance gave me the time I needed—and wanted—to be alone. The only time I saw him was the two times that he woke me in the middle of the night.

I can't believe that my own father would think so low of me. Even through my hurt that he would even say such a thing, I can see where the thought sprouted. Cohen's been gone, and by his own account, he knows I've been coming over here. It makes sense, even if his lack of faith in me is heartbreaking.

I don't realize I'm crying until I feel the bed depress.

"You want to talk about it? I'm not good with the chick shit, but I can try to help."

"I think you've guessed that I'm pregnant?"

"Figured as much when your dad was about to rip my head off and assumed I had slept with you. I thought he knew you and Cohen were together?"

I sigh. "You should know him well enough to know that, when he's mad, he gets . . . irrational. I guess he didn't consider that it was something that happened before Cohen left. And everything that happened today, with the note and then the baby bomb, I guess he just lets his emotions get the best of his."

"I won't insult you by questioning if this is Cohen's or not, but you do realize that it's going to be on the top of everyone's assumptions that this baby isn't his?"

"I've waited for him my whole life, Chance. Everyone who knows me knows that. I just can't believe my own father . . ." I trail off and leave it hanging. No sense in beating a dead horse.

"Why don't you tell me about the note? Then give either your girls or Liam a call. You need your friends around you, and honestly, Dani, I like you enough, but I don't know how to be the shoulder you are bound to cry on at some point."

I laugh and take a deep breath, willing my hurt feelings not to fester into tears. "Yeah, okay." I tell him all about the note and what I remember it saying, which isn't much, but he promises to check with the guys at work to get more details. In the end, I feel a little better just having someone to talk to, but I decide that he's right and I need my people.

Not knowing what to say to the twins yet, I pick up and dial Lee, knowing that he can help me sort my head before I call them. Having just dropped his date off, he agrees to head on over to the apartment.

I can tell he wants to ask questions, but he hangs up with the promise to be over shortly.

“Well, you really managed to go all out in the drama tonight, Dani,” Lee says, leaning back against the headboard and opening his arms so that I can rest against his chest.

“Can you believe I’m pregnant, Lee?”

“Honestly? I can’t say I’m shocked. I mean, it’s Cohen.”

“What the hell does that mean?” I laugh.

“The man wore a cape for, what . . . like, twenty years. He’s some super-secret black ops marine. I’m pretty sure he could kill me a million different ways—the man is just born to have super everything.”

“We used a condom, Lee.”

He gags. “I love you, Dani, but I don’t want to talk about that shit. Let’s just leave it at shit happens and his super sperm battered down the shield.”

I slap his stomach. “God, you’re disgusting.” I settle back down for a second before I push up and spin to look at him. “Do you think Cohen will think the same thing my dad did?”

Lee doesn’t say anything, which doesn’t help the trepidation I already feel. “I’m not going to lie to you, Dani. From the outside, without all the facts, it looks shady. But you said it yourself. Your dad didn’t even know how far along you are.”

“I would never betray Cohen like that.”

He smiles. “Yeah, I know that. It’s a shitty situation, Dani. Wait until Cohen gets back before you start to worry about it. I will say, I wouldn’t keep this from the girls.”

“I didn’t plan on it. I just need to process things. I’ll call them tonight.”

“Sure thing, babe. Come on. Let’s get some rest. I came straight here after a night out with Stacy. I’m fucking beat.”

Lee and I managed to get a good few hours in before the knocking started. Chance left a note that said that he was over at Megan’s and would be back later. He's been spending a lot of time with her lately. I teased him about finally dating, something I've never seen him do, but he told me that it isn't anything other than helping her out with her daughter. I push back my normal embarrassment and guilt when I think about my first impression of her. Now, having met her, I know she is just a grieving woman who needs her friends.

I step out of Cohen's room and walk to the door. When I look through the peephole, I smile and shake my head at the noise four fists can produce against one door.

Well, that didn't take long.

I open the door right when Lyn is about to bang on it again and just barely dodge her fist.

"Damn, Lyn!"

"About time, bitch," she snaps.

"Hey, Dani." Lila gives me a hug and follows her sister into the apartment.

"Where's Lee?" Lyn asks, looking around.

"Right here. God, could you be any louder. I was out with the screecher before I came over here, and God, my head hurts."

All three of us look over at Lee and gawk.

"I can't believe you went out with her crazy ass again," Lila snaps. "The last time you went out with her, didn't she go on and on about how many babies she wanted to have with you AND detailed out their names and what they would look like?"

"Christ, you must love crazy," Lyn mumbles.

"Oh, shut up. It wasn't that bad. Plus, I was horny."

"You're disgusting," Lila sighs.

"All right. Enough of this shit. What's going on with you?" Lyn says.

"What makes you think something's going on?" I hedge.

"Don't play me for a fool. First of all, you don't come home at all last night. You don't answer your phone. Your car is still at the salon! And if that isn't enough, when we went home to Mom and Dad's for dinner, Cam was going on and on about how he and Colt overheard Dad telling Mom about how you got some fucked-up letter after work today. *Then* he said that you had to go to the emergency room. If that's not enough to know something is most definitely up with you, then you're insane." She takes a deep breath, and for the first time, I see through her anger and the worry she must have had all night for me, instantly making me feel guilty.

Taking a strengthening breath, I point to the couch. "You two might want to sit down."

Chapter 27

Dani

"SO LET ME GET THIS straight. You got some fucked-up letter at work and proceeded to pass out. You went to the doctor, found out my brother knocked you up, and then your dad flipped his shit and accused you of basically being a slut?" Lyn finishes her rehashing of my last twenty-four hours with a dramatic sigh. "Wow. When you decide to go for the shock factor, you really put your all in it."

"I'm going to be an aunt?" Lila says breathily.

"Holy shit, we're going to be aunts!" Lyn screams, and I wince when her loud tones hit my ears.

"Did you just register that little nugget? What part of 'my brother knocked you up' didn't register that fact?" Lila smarts.

"Oh, shut it, Lila! I'm in shock here."

"So . . . I take it you two don't share my father's immediate reaction?"

They both stare at me with a mix of outrage and sadness. Like I've lost my damn mind, which is a feeling I share with them both at the moment.

"You've been in love with my brother for years, Dani. Even if that weren't the case, you aren't the type of person who strays when you're in a relationship. Regardless of where the other person is, you're loyal to your very core."

I smile at Lila's words. I didn't realize how badly I needed to hear that they believed me.

"I'm sure he regrets it, Dani. You know your dad. He's hotheaded, and as protective of you as he is, I'm sure the 'whole letter on the car, falling and getting hurt, and *then* finding out he's about to be a grandfather' took a toll on him. Yeah, I think it's safe to say he was probably tipping over the boiling point." Lyn reaches over and rubs my hand. "That doesn't excuse it. You have every right to be upset. I just can't figure out why you wouldn't call us." She gives me a sad smile, but there's no judgment in her gaze.

"I needed to be around Cohen. I'm not even sure I realized it at the moment, but the second I got here—surrounded by his things—I don't know how to explain it. I just felt like I was . . . home."

Lila has a big dopey smile on her face, and Lyn is looking at me in complete understanding.

"You still could have called us, Dani. We would have been here in a second. Did you think we would be upset or something?" Lyn pushes.

"It has nothing to do with that. I promise. I was still wrapping my head around it all myself. I wanted to be here, alone, and spend time with Cohen the best I can without him being here. My God, I sound like a complete nut job," I groan and drop my head into my hands. "He left here thinking he had one type of girl and he's going to come home to me being a complete basket case. Who comes over to their boyfriend's place so they can sniff his shit and hug his pillow?"

They both throw their heads back and laugh. The tension is broken just like that.

My girls get me. They always have, and that will never change.

"How about we spend the rest of the night doing girly shit and binge-watch some old One Tree Hill shows?" Lila asks as she stands to give me a big hug.

"At the risk of sounding even crazier . . . can we do that here?" I ask.

"Sure thing. I mean, I don't think smelling my grungy brother will be quite as comforting for me as it is for you, but I'm down." Lyn laughs. "We need to get some junk food too. Fatten you up already! I can't wait for you to have a cute little belly. Oh my God! I still can't believe my niece or nephew is cooking away in there."

I stop, causing them both to bump into me in the middle of the hallway. My jaw goes slack and my eyes wide.

"Holy shit. I'm gonna get fat!" I spin, grab the nearest body, and shake her shoulders. I can hear Lyn laughing her ass off behind an equally shocked Lila. "I'm going to be a big freaking whale by the time he gets home. He left me all skinny, toned, and hot, and he's going to come home and I'll be like, 'Oh hey, big boy, guess what? I ate a whale and you knocked me up!'"

Why are they laughing so hard? Can't they tell how much I'm freaking out here? There is no damn way he's going to want me all fatty mcfat fat.

"This is going to be terrible," I groan and turn my back on two of my best friends, who are losing their sanity with how much they're laughing. When I hit Cohen's room, I crawl back in the center of his bed and wrap my arms around one of his pillows.

"You're a mess, Dani. Cohen isn't going to just stop loving you because you have a belly. Plus, I hear some guys actually find it even more attractive. Stop freaking out over something you have no control over. Warning though, he will be shocked. I know my brother, and he might just pass out when he finds out."

I gasp and shoot up to my elbows to glare at Lila. "Do what?"

"Do you really think he's going to not even be a little shocked when you tell him that he gave you a little going-away present? No man would be able to take that kind of news without a little shock, Dani. Don't worry about it. It's all going to be fine. One thing about Cohen, and you know this, is that boy was made to be a father. He's always looked forward to when he will settle down and start a family. I think it comes with the whole idolizing our dad thing."

"What the hell are you talking about?" I question her.

"Just ask Lyn. When we were busy planning our weddings and what big, bright futures we would have as kids, Cohen would always tell us about how he couldn't wait to get older. He would be a hero just like Dad and have a house full of kids and a woman he loved to warm his bed. Of course, I never understood the last part." Lila finishes and sits down next to me, pulling the pillow from my body and shoving it behind her head. "He's going to be so happy it's you, Dani."

I look at her for a beat, letting her words sink in, before I feel a big, crazy smile take over my lips.

Well, that all sounds like a dream come true.

Hours later, we are still sitting in Cohen's bed. Junk food is spread all over the comforter and season two of One Tree Hill is starting on Cohen's television. Thank you, Netflix, for making girls' emotional television binging so much easier.

Lyn and Lila did what they do best. They took my thoughts out of my head and made me stop freaking out. Every time I got quiet, they would knock every doubt I had out of my head.

We spent time looking at the ultrasound pictures and talking about baby names and what he or she would look like.

I am hoping for a boy who will have his father's strong features and gorgeous, brown eyes. The girls are hoping for a girl so that we can dress her up in all of these adorably cute outfits they already started looking for.

"Look at this one, Lila," Lyn squeals and turns her phone to show Lila whatever new outfit she found online.

"Hey, Dani," I hear from the front of the apartment, and I almost jump out of my skin.

"Holy shit, he scared the crap out of me," Lyn says with her palm pressed to her chest.

"You and me both." I climb over Lila and make my way down the hallway to where I think I heard Chance's voice. Right when I come out of the hallway and into their large, sunken living room, I halt in my tracks and feel my body lock up with tension.

Chance walks my way and gives me a reassuring squeeze on my shoulder before he continues down the hall. I turn and see him step into Cohen's room and shut the door behind him.

Well, I guess that means the girls won't be coming to my rescue.

With a deep sigh full of dread, I turn, square my shoulders, and face my father.

"You look like you're ready for battle, little princess," he says solemnly.

"That's because I feel like I'm gearing up for one."

"Dani—" he starts, going to take a step towards me . . . until I hold up my hand to pause his movement.

"I think it would be best to stay over there, Daddy. This can't be fixed with a hug."

His eyes close, and I can tell how much it's costing him to hold himself back. I have no doubt that he regrets what he said, but the fact remains that, however fleeting, the thought went through his head.

"You all but called me a whore, Daddy. Your own daughter. The one you raised to believe in the power of love, and despite your over-the-top protectiveness, I found that love. That once-in-a-lifetime soul mate connection you and Mom have. I never, not in a million years, expected that from you."

His face softens, "Baby," he sighs. "I'm so sorry."

"Do you really believe that, after loving Cohen for as long as I have, with the first hurdle our relationship is faced with, I would run to another man?"

He shakes his head, his eyes never leaving mine.

"I can understand that you're having a hard time with the fact that I'm not a baby anymore. I haven't been one for a long time, but I always knew you would struggle with letting me go until you literally couldn't hold on anymore. But what I can't understand is why you reacted the way you did."

"Please, my sweet little princess, let me hold you."

I'm not sure if it's the slight tremor in his deep voice that causes the first tear or if it's the one of his own sliding down his face, but the second that tear falls, there isn't a thing I can do to keep him from crossing the room.

"I needed my daddy," I sob into his chest. "I needed you and all I got were accusations I never in my life thought you would throw at me. I needed you to hold me and tell me that everything would be okay and that you loved me. But you pushed me away and it broke my heart."

"God, Dani. Please stop." His arms tighten around me, and I feel my feet lift off the ground. His head drops to my shoulder, and I feel him take a deep breath.

"I can't breathe," I gasp and squirm against him.

He gives me another squeeze before he lightly drops my feet back down. When he pulls back and I get my first look at his red-rimmed eyes, my heart breaks a little.

"I don't know how to forget what you said to me, Daddy," I sigh. "I expected your shock. I expected your anger at Cohen. But most of all, I expected your love."

He clears his throat. "Sit down, little princess. I think, maybe, I can help with that."

I follow behind him and sit down on the worn, leather recliner. Daddy sits next to me in the matching one, and I wait for him to talk. I have no idea what he thinks can give me—maybe some insight on how he reacted to my pregnancy—but I wait.

"I don't think I can explain just how it feels to grow up with shit parents, Dani, but the ones I had—they were as shitty as it gets. I never wanted you or your brother to know how bad it was for me when I was growing up. Never wanted that for you, but I think you need to hear some of it . . . to understand why I am the way I am."

I lean back and wait for him to continue. It's his show now.

"My parents . . . They were never sober. They were never not high off some drug. They never talked to me with anything other than hate. That was my life until Social Services took me and I ended up in the system. That wasn't much better, but I wasn't beaten and I ate enough that I didn't starve. But it was lonely, Dani. It was terribly lonely. Until I met your mom. Trust me when I tell you that I know exactly what you mean when you talk about a once-in-a-lifetime soul mate. That was and is your mom for me.

"You know about me being deployed and what happened to me and your mom during those years and the ones that followed. But I don't think I've ever told anyone, outside your mother, what it felt like when, years later I found out that our baby didn't make it. God, Dani . . . To hear how your mother suffered killed me, but to know that part of us had died gutted me. I know the rational side of it. I went to a few therapy sessions with your mom to have those quacks throw it out there in terms I could understand. For a child who grew up the way I did, to live that lonely life void of love, a child with the woman I loved more than life, was my second chance. I remember the day your mom told me, all those years after, and sitting on the dock behind the house, vowing to God that, if I was blessed with more children, I would never stop protecting them. I would give them the love, safety, and life I never had."

He stops and wipes a tear that escaped my eyes. I don't speak. We sit in silence while I wait for him to compose his thoughts.

"I know I take it to a level that is just too much when it comes to you, Dani. I look at you, seeing so much of your mother, and I'm reminded of that sweet, stars-in-her-eyes woman I left all those years ago. That I left to a life of hell for years. I see the pain I couldn't protect her from, and it makes me hold you just a little tighter. I think I rationalized with myself that, if I just held on as long as I could, you would never know that kind of pain."

"I still don't understand how you could even think that I could do something like this to Cohen, Daddy. How I could cheat on him?"

"I don't think that, baby. I didn't think it then, and I don't think it now. There is no excuse for what I said. I'm not disappointed in you. I'm disappointed in me. I was scared, Dani, and that's the simple truth. I was terrified when I heard them say you were pregnant. All of those old wounds just sliced right open, and what I felt all of those years ago came back tenfold. Only this time, it was my girl, my little princess, and I was terrified to my core."

Never in a million years did I expect that from him. My father? The big, bad Axel Reid was scared? Nope. Never.

"The second you left and I realized what I'd said, I wanted to chase you down, but your mom said that I should give you time. Well, actually, she screamed at me for being a jackass. I'm always going to look at you as my little girl, Dani, and there isn't anything that could change that. I'm damn proud of the woman you've grown to be, and I love you more than life itself. I can't tell you enough how sorry I am for letting my emotions and temper get the best of me."

"You hurt me," I tell him.

"I know, and it kills me."

After hearing where he was coming from, my heart settles a little and I understand where he was coming from. Even if it still hurts, I know it's more because the words are still fresh in my mind. He's always been hot to the touch when he feels things deeply. That's just how he's wired. And honestly, if I had been thinking clearly, I probably would have anticipated a reaction like his. Doesn't make it okay, but I can't hold a grudge because he was blinded by the pain of his past.

"I love you, Daddy."

"I love you too, little princess."

"You have to let me fly now," I whisper.

"I know I do. I know. I don't want to let go, Dani, but at least if I have to I know you'll be in good hands."

"You're really okay? With Cohen and me . . . and the baby?"

"Yeah, sweetheart. I really am. I'm scared, I won't lie about that, but I'll work on not projecting that on you. Just don't expect me to change overnight. My little girl having a baby of her own? Jesus, Dani." He pauses, stands, and pulls me up so he can give me a kiss on my forehead before wrapping me up in his strong arms for another hug. "I'm still going to kick his ass. You know that, right?" he says, his voice rumbling against my ear that's pressed against his chest.

"No, you won't."

"Oh really? And why is that?" he asks and pulls back to look at me, his green eyes shining.

"Because you won't hurt me like that."

"I'm still going to yell at him. Maybe even throw shit," he counters.

"Yeah, now that I can see."

He doesn't stay long after that. I know the girls are probably about to bust down the door to make sure I'm okay. I walk him to the door, my heart feeling so much more whole since he came by. With the promise to come over for dinner the following night, he leaves me with a hug.

With a smile on my face, I walk back down the hallway, feeling much lighter than I did earlier. Things aren't just going to be magically easier from now on. There's the small fact that Cohen doesn't even know he's about to be a father, but I have no doubt in my mind that he will be able to see this miracle for what it is.

At least, that's the hope I will wrap myself in until he returns.

Chapter 28

Cohen

EVERY FUCKING DAY, I START to resent the life I always thought I wanted. Fighting a war I don't see ever ending is starting to pay its price on my sanity, and my heart is starting to feel heavy with every passing second I am away from home.

I miss my family. My parents, sisters, and brothers. I hate knowing that they are at home worrying about me and my safety. I know every time I'm away in training or deployed that my mom doesn't sleep well and my dad has nightmares. My sisters do better, their belief that I'm invincible helping that. And my brothers hide their worry in beer and sex.

But worst of all, I miss Dani.

It's hard to believe that something I never knew I was missing would take root and make it impossible to imagine leaving her again. I know without a shadow of doubt that this will be my last deployment. When it comes time to reenlist, I won't regret my decision to stay home and start my life with her.

It sounds fucking nuts, but after all of this time away, I know where my future is, and it damn sure isn't in a big fucking sandbox, getting shot at daily.

The second I get home, I'm going to pull her father aside and beg for her hand in marriage. Then make my girl mine forever.

I smile when I think about the future we're going to have. That right there has been the only thing that's kept me sane. Years, so many damn years, I pushed these feelings away, and there's no way I'm going to waste a second more before I make sure she knows how I feel.

"Yo! Cage, boss man told me to make sure you got this. Came over urgent a second ago."

I look over when Ferguson hands me a folded piece of paper. I unfold it and realize it's an envelope with just my name on it.

"The hell is it?" I snap, wanting nothing more than to get some sleep.

"No clue. He took a call, took some notes, then stuffed it in here and told me to find you ASAP. So I found you and did what I was told. Now, take the shit so I can get some grub."

I snatch the envelope from him and walk away. I've never cared for Ferguson, but he's a damn good soldier.

We were lucky tonight. Things were winding down here, and we finally made it to base camp after having been gone for three weeks on another mission from hell. I will be able to have a shower and actually eat food that doesn't taste like hard shit.

Walking away from the mess hall, I quickly look for the building we were using as mission control for our unit. After shutting the door and enjoying a second of silence, I open the letter.

I had hoped you would be home by now, but I'm assuming this was a multiple-mission assigning and you're looking at closer to a year. Fucking sucks, brother. Wrap up what you can and get home. Your girl needs you. I don't want to fuck with your head over there, but I can't impress it harder. I wouldn't be bothering with this if I didn't think it was necessary. Do what you need to do. Wait it out and hurry it up, call or fucking write. But she needs you *and it should be something that's handled sooner than later. I'll keep her in my sights the best I can, Cohen. Stay safe.-Chance*

With trembling hands, I refold the note and try to calm myself down. I've known something was wrong. I've felt it since the day I left. That feeling has turned my gut into a constant pain. Feeling like I've been needed at home is nothing compared to knowing I'm needed and not being able to do a damn thing about it.

"Fuck!" I roar and slam the door open hard enough that the very foundation the room is build on is sure to feel its force.

I set off for my CO and pray that he can tell me how the hell to speed this bullshit up so I can get home to my girl.

I'm not sure what I look like when I approach my CO, but he is more than accepting that I need to get a call home. Typically, we don't get the opportunity to contact anyone back home. Our missions are like that. We need our focus to be spot-on. Anything else would result in one thing. Our death. We're out "hunting" for weeks and months at a time. Searching for our target, sleeping with our backs against each other, hiding whenever we can. Crawling through the desert in conditions that are as bad as it gets. We eat, sleep, and breathe with the single-minded focus of a warrior. A killing machine. When situations at home cause our focus to waver, they're willing to do whatever it takes to point our focus back into the tunnel-vision mindset of a robot. Which is essentially what we're trained to be.

And with my mind spinning with a vague-as-fuck message from home, things would end up dire if I were hunting. Chance fucking knows better than to send some fucked-up shit like that. He knows that the only thing it would do is take my mind from the mission and make me become consumed with worry. Something I can't afford to have happen.

CO Krajack has me stuffed into a room with a secure line home in minutes of my handing him Chance's letter. My first call—Dani.

With each ring that goes unanswered, my heart starts to pick up speed, and my palms are so wet from the dread I feel pouring out of me that I almost drop the phone.

"Mother FUCK!" I thunder through the silence surrounding me.

"Breathe, soldier. Pick someone else and fucking call them," Krajack grinds out from the doorway behind me. "Won't do a bit of good to sit there acting like a little girl. Try your father."

CO Krajack and my dad served together. They spearheaded our unit, and Krajack made it his life's goal to see it turned into the baddest of the bad. Having him know Dad didn't make life easier for me when it came time for training. If anything, he pushed me harder than anyone else. But he's also the only one who would know me well enough right now—and correctly guess that I am way too fucking close to tearing the shit out of anything that gets in the way of me finding out what's wrong with my girl.

I nod, grabbing the satellite phone and pressing the buttons I need to in order to connect me with Dad's cell, praying that he answers.

"Cage," he barks.

"Dad," I say in a way I know he will instantly know I need him.

"Son?" His tone instantly alert.

"Tell me why I got a letter from Chance telling me to get the fuck home because Dani needs me? You know I can't deal with this shit. If she needs me home, I'm going to be wrapped up in that and—god dammit! You know, Dad. You fucking know how my head is going to be if I don't know what's going on." I feel Krajack place his hand on my shoulder and give me a firm squeeze.

"C-man, I don't know. Mom and I just got back in town the other day. I know something happened when she left work the other day, but Axel hasn't briefed me yet."

"Fucking shit," I mutter.

"You got the call. Call Axel, son. As much as I miss my boy and would love the time to talk, you need to get your head on straight so you can get the hell home. I love you, son."

"Love you too, Dad."

He rattles off Axel's cell and, after the promise that I'll keep my focus, says goodbye.

I hang up, give Krajack a stressed look, and make another

call—hoping and praying for answers this time.

It takes one ring for Axel's cell to connect.

As if he's been waiting for my call.

The dread in my stomach intensifies instantly.

"Cohen."

Not a question. He's been waiting.

"Had Chance call an hour ago. I figured you would have called sooner than this."

"Don't play games with me, Axel. I know you have your issues with me right now, but do not play games with me. I don't owe you an explanation, but my first call went to Dani—where it should have gone. Then Dad, who couldn't give me shit, so here I am, calling you and hoping you shut the fuck up with the warnings about your daughter and give me what I need to know. Is my girl okay?"

He doesn't waste a second. "Respect the hell out of you right now, Cohen. It's not a secret that Dani means the world to me and, if I could keep her under my wing for the rest of my life, I fucking would. But," he sighs, "I was reminded that it's time to let go and let her fly. Pleased as fuck that she's flying to a man I admire and that I believe is man enough for my girl. Just fucking remember, she was my girl before she was yours. There are things going on here that are much bigger than you and me. Things that I have no right in passing on to you, but I can't stress it enough that you need to either get home or get ahold of Dani."

"Ax—"

"I know what it's like to be over there, Cohen. To make sure your focus doesn't waver and that you don't end up dead. I've lived that shit, so I fucking *know.* But I wouldn't have gotten word to you if I didn't feel it was needed. Dani's threats have picked up in a sense. Flowers stopped, but she got a letter the other day that makes me believe things are more than just an admirer. As much as it kills me, she doesn't need or want her father right now. I know how Krajack works. You'll be over there for years if he doesn't wrap shit up. He picks your missions wisely. Some to keep your training sharp and some that are more than needed to help stop this motherfucking war. What I can't stress enough is that what doesn't serve a purpose need to be dropped so you can get back stateside. Move your missions up in order of importance and get home to my girl. She's safe and I won't let that fact change. Not now and not ever."

"What the fuck! How is that not supposed to mess with my head, Axel?"

"That wasn't the purpose, but you need to know that shit's going down that doesn't look like it's going away any time soon. You need to know that your clock isn't going to just keep ticking and that it's time to get the fuck home."

"You're telling me that I shouldn't be worried some freak is after my girl and that I should be home?"

"What I'm telling you is that you need to turn into that little invincible shit you were as a kid. Do your job and do it quick. Then get the fuck home."

"You have to know this isn't going to do shit but make me worry about her."

"*I* won't let shit happen to her," he vows.

"You better not, Axel. I know you love her. That can't be argued, but I would die for that girl. I would die for her and kill any motherfucker who harms a hair on her head. I'll talk to Krajack and see what needs to be done to cut our time here down."

"You do that," he says, and the line goes dead.

I drop the phone on the table, more confused than I was before I called home. All of these vague hints and half tells. Not one thing I can grasp that makes me feel confident that she is okay until I get home.

"He's right, you know?" Krajack says from my side. "We pick and choose between training exercises that serve no purpose other than to sharpen your skills and those that eliminating the enemy. I was hoping to have four to seven more months left with you over here, but with this intel, I'll do my best to cut that in half. Best I can do. Keep your head where it needs to be, Cohen. I can't afford for you to lose your focus."

"I appreciate that, sir." I sigh with resignation that I'm stuck here and my girl needs me.

This is going to be the hardest next few months of my life.

Chapter 29

Dani

Three months later

THINGS HAVE BEEN A LITTLE easier these last three months. I still miss Cohen, but shortly after I found out about the baby, he was able to get a message through e-mail that he would be home soon. Of course, his soon was in the next few months, but that was better than the unknown timeframe we had been working with since he left.

With the push of strength that his short e-mail gave me, I felt like I could face the world. We still didn't know exactly when he would return, but we knew it would be soon.

Things at work have been easier, too. When I got back after my fall, Sway was predictably in his extreme mothering mode. He would only let me work half days, and those days that I did work were always light. No coloring or heavy treatments. I was restricted to cuts and the like. Actually, now that I think about it, he hasn't let me do a color in almost a month. Every single time, he intercepts my client.

Devon wasn't too happy about losing his star drama maker, but he worked it in as me being too depressed to work because of my lover having broken my heart.

Whatever.

Surprisingly, Don's been the annoying one this time. He seems to think my sole purpose in life is to make his job easier by making sure I do things for ratings alone. He wants certain shots, or for me to do one of the lines he has written to give the show more drama, or the one time he asked me to fake a fight with Stella and fake slap her.

I don't fucking think so.

Mark's actually been the voice of reason this time. He joined me for lunch in the breakroom a few times before they left to go back to California, and I like to think we had some sort of a friendship. I gave him some pointers on how to win over the girl he's been dating. I guess you could say I have a soft spot for the guy now.

Of course, they haven't been around for almost two months. There was apparently a big issue with Devon's production team back home. Some big-time embezzlement stuff with the higher-ups, and until they could recover some funding that was stolen, they had to pause filming. Last we heard from Sway was that today would be their first day back. I am looking forward to seeing them. I hope that Mark was able to use some of my tips to get closer to his girl.

Unfortunately, one thing that didn't stop in the last three months was the weekly flower deliveries. They picked up about two weeks after the letter that was found on my car. So far, they've been impossible to track, always paid for with a prepaid Visa, and the order placed online. Maddox, the IT guru at Corps Security, has been struggling to actually nail down a location since whoever is actually placing the orders is smart about covering his tracks. So far, the orders have been placed in different locations all over the globe. Well, according the IP addresses, that is.

Needless to say, things have been a little on edge with no answers.

Between Lee and my brother, there has always been someone sleeping at our house. Dad had what already was a top-of-the-line security system replaced with one I still needed a manual to figure out. He's gotten even worse since I started showing. It's like my belly's growing—the sign that the baby is in fact very real—kicked his protective tendencies into overdrive. That tangible sight was all it took. He went as far as to steal my car keys two weeks ago and demand that I let him pick me up for work from that day forward. That was short-lived and got him in the doghouse with Mom for almost a week.

Never a dull moment with him.

Another thing that has changed is my new friendship with

Megan. I really feel terrible about my first impression of her when I thought that she was dating Cohen. She's become a huge support and go-to person for advice. Chance told me that my friendship and the bond she can give me over my pregnancy has given her something to focus on, and he thinks it's helping her heal. She has her moments, but I think he's right.

"What are you going to wear today? Planning on showing off that adorable little bump for the cameras?" Megan asks from where she's lounging on my chaise lounge in the corner of my room.

I look over at her in the mirror I'm using to fix my makeup. She has Molly, her adorable four-year-old daughter, bouncing on her feet with a smile dancing across her beautiful face.

"I think so. Now that I'm over that weird 'I'm not fat—I'm pregnant' stage, I find myself wearing the tightest things I can find just so I can show it off."

"Dani?" I hear Molly say in her singsong voice. She sounds like a little angel. "Can I play with your jewsree?"

"Sure thing, tink." I ruffle her blond curls when she skips towards my dresser.

"You know she's going to destroy your jewelry box again," Megan laughs.

"Eh, let her have at it. I moved all my valuable pieces after the last time. I swear she broke my heart with those tears. I almost told her she could have my grandmother's hand-me-down pearls!" I tease.

"Tell me about it. I would probably give that girl anything she wants with just the smallest tear. God help me, she's spoiled rotten."

"Nah, she's just well loved." I give her a smile and pull on my tight, black blouse. It hugs my belly perfectly, and the pencil skirt makes my legs look great. I've been putting on a little weight in my thighs, but now that I look closely, I just look curvier. My breasts, on the other hand, have really benefited from my pregnancy. I actually have cleavage without having to use a damn good expensive bra to get. "How are you doing, Megs?" I ask, pulling on my black silk blouse.

Today is the second birthday of her late husband since he passed away. It's a testament to how far she's come since the sad girl who was at Cohen's going away party. She's smiling today when I fully expected her to be locked in her house, crying.

"I'm doing a lot better, Dani. Really, I am. It gets easier every day that passes. I still miss him like crazy, but I'm trying to follow your lead and see the beautiful things in life and focus less on the things that I can't change. I was a mess when he was deployed during my pregnancy with Molly. I still don't know how you're able to wake up every day with such a positive outlook."

I look over at her with a small smile. "I don't know if it's so much of a positive outlook or the knowledge that, regardless of what life throws at me, I've been blessed with what life I've lived. I can't spend my life worrying about what might be or what could have been. I lost a lot of time with Cohen. We had one brilliant, eye-opening night together, and it might sound ridiculous, but if that was the last night I ever have with him, I'll cherish it forever."

She gives me a nod, and I know she understands. We've talked about her holding on to her happier memories and letting go of the hard ones. She understands where I'm coming from.

I know it sounds stupid. One night of us being an "us" was all it took for me. I could have had an hour and the outcome would have been the same. He's the other half to my heart. It's been like that for as long as I've known him, and no time frame could change that.

I look over my bed at the photo I had blown up and framed in a huge display of just how much I miss the man.

The image my mother gave me months ago—the one of Cohen and me sitting on my parents' dock almost twenty years ago. The one that proves that we've been building this connection for longer than we both could even imagine.

I spend a little more time with Megan and Molly before I have to head into work. After hating the cameras in my face for so long, it's going to be weird embracing them today. Megan was right. Now that my bump is one hundred percent recognizable, I want the world to know about my little baby.

"Hey, Sway," I say when I walk into the salon.

He spins on his solid-gold—with glittered embellishments on the heels—stilettos and gives me a big smile.

"Oh, darling girl, come and let Sway rub that belly! My lord, I love babies. Stella!" he screams, and I watch her wince.

I swat his hands away when he tries to open the top buttons of my blouse.

"Yes, Pops?" she responds with an eye roll. "God, leave her tits alone! Sometimes, I wonder if you're not really straight."

"Don't you give me that 'tude! I'll go get your dad next door and have him remind you that you're supposed to be sweet to me. I'm just trying to make sure little mama gets her tips. She's got four male heads to work on today." He gives me a wink.

"I'm always sweet to you, you weirdo."

I laugh at them and move around Sway and into the madness of the salon. Looks like a full house today, too. All eight stations are busy—minus Sway's and mine, of course.

"Where are the cameras at, Sway?" I call over my shoulder as I head to the breakroom to throw my purse in my locker.

"On the way, little mama."

I manage to get myself in order and a good head start on Mrs. Cartwright's highlights—without Sway seeing me doing color—before I hear Devon bang his way through the door.

"Ah! If it isn't my favorite home away from home! Are my little bees ready to buzz today?"

I roll my eyes in the mirror, causing Mrs. Cartwright to giggle.

"Hey, Dani," Don says from right over my shoulder. "We're going to need you to look over these story lines."

I spin on my amazingly kickass black heels and look down at Don. Yeah, down at him. My heels make me *maybe* right at five foot five and he's still shorter.

"I've already told you, Don. I don't do fake. If you want someone to beef up your show, then hire an actor."

"Holy shit, did you swallow a beach ball?"

Oh no he did not.

I might be rounder and my belly might be a very noticeably pregnant, but I am not *that* big!

He's looking at me with the strangest look on his face. As if he's mad about me being pregnant.

"What did you—" I stop talking when I hear a crash in the front and turn my head to see what happened. Mark is bent over to help the cameraman who looks to have tripped and dropped his equipment up.

"Son of a bitch, Troy! Do you have any idea how expensive those cameras are?" Don yells and walks away from me.

"God, what's up his ass today?" Maddi says, sidling up to my side. She drops a makeup brush and bends over to get it before giving me her attention. Her hand, as usual—it's always her first reaction when she's near me—goes to my belly for a small rub. "Maybe he's worried about the camera adding ten pounds and you looking like a whale," she smarts, and I give her a shove.

"Shut up. Stop using my paranoia to mess with me."

"Incoming," she says oddly and moves back to her station.

I give Mrs. Cartwright a look before glancing up in my mirror and seeing Mark walking over.

"Hey, Mark," I say with a smile.

"Dani. Uh, you're pregnant?" He's looking at my stomach like it's about to jump off my body and smother him.

"It would appear so, Mark," I laugh. "I didn't get a chance to share the news with you before you left."

He clears his throat, looking pained.

So weird. "Everything okay?"

"What?" He shakes his head. "Oh, sorry. Just a lot on my mind. Things back home were crazy. That girl I was telling you about? Yeah, not sure if it's going to work out. She wanted . . . well . . ." He points to my stomach, and it hits me. She wanted kids and he must not have.

"Oh, I'm sorry, Mark. Don't worry. There's tons of fish in the sea. Hey, how about we grab lunch today? Catch up and all that?"

The whole time I am talking, his eyes keep wandering back to my stomach. Damn, the guy must really have an issue with kids.

"Probably not today. Lots of stuff we need to catch up since we were gone for a while. Hey, did Don talk to you about the story lines we want to try and hit with this round of filming? They would probably jack up the drama, good for ratings and all that."

What the hell? He knows how I feel about that crap.

When I don't answer, he looks down at my stomach again before sharing a look with Don and walking away without another word.

So. Freaking. Weird.

I look over at Maddi, and she looks just as confused as I am. She shrugs one shoulder and then turns back to the young girl she's giving makeup tips to.

I return my attention to my job. It isn't long before I realize the day is wasting away and I still haven't eaten a thing.

"Hey, Maddi? I'm going to order some Chinese. You want in?"

I walk around and get orders from a few more people before placing the call. If I don't eat soon, I'll most likely take off my arm between clients. I would rather just go out and get it myself, but Dad was clear that I'm not to leave the salon alone—for anything.

I am in the middle of cleaning out my brushes and wiping down the area in front of my mirror when I hear the door ding and I look up to see the blessed food delivery.

"I could give you a kiss. I'm so hungry," I tell the young Chinese man.

He doesn't say anything, just roughly shoves the heavy bag in my hand and thrusts the receipt in my hands. I sign it, add the tip, and shove it back. Maybe a little harder than I intended, but damn. What's it take to get a little friendliness?

"Have a nice day," I mumble.

Of course I'm ignored and he's right out the door a second later.

I look around, thinking that maybe I have some sort of "don't talk to me" vibe since there isn't anyone near me except for our receptionist, Kat.

"I'll be in the breakroom if anyone needs me. I think I have about forty-five minutes before my next client gets here."

"Sure thing, Dani."

I drop the bag down in the middle of the breakroom and make quick work of pulling off the staples and opening the large, brown bag. Expecting to find our lunch order, I'm momentarily shocked by what I see inside. Then, when what I'm looking at sinks in, I jerk my hands back towards my body.

I feel like I'm drowning. The sound of my blood pumping ferociously through my body is making my ears cloud. My eyes tear up and my vision gets foggy. I must be screaming something fierce, because the next thing I know, the door is slamming open and Sway, along with half of the other stylists, come barreling in.

Sway grabs my shoulders and tries to get me to talk through my hysteria. "Child! Good heavens. What has gotten into you?"

I go slack, and I feel him adjusting his grip to keep my body from falling to the floor.

"Stella? Talk to me, ella-bella!"

I focus on Stella over Sway's shoulder, and the look of terror on her face does nothing to help my panic. I start to gasp and struggle against Sway. I have to get out of here.

"Someone go next door to CS and get some help."

I don't hear anything else after that. My body decides that it's had enough and just shuts down. My cries silence, my tears dry up, and I just go slack.

My focus stays straight ahead, but I don't see anything. My mind is too busy focusing on what I saw inside that bag.

The baby doll snapped apart with red letters against the torso.

Their words forever branded in my head.

An image I will never, as long as I live, forget.

YOU WILL PAY WITH THAT BASTARD BABY'S LIFE.

Chapter 30

Cohen

GOD, IT FEELS GOOD TO be home. I've been back stateside for the last week, having to debrief up north before I was able to get my ass back to Georgia. It was an impossibly hard week because I knew I was within a few hundred miles of holding my girl. I didn't have time to call and check in with Dani. I knew that, the second I heard her voice, it would be game over, so I stayed the course and checked in with my dad and Axel as much as I could. So far, nothing's changed.

My first stop home should have been Dani's, but I figure she is at work, and that gives me some time to get a shower, change out of the clothes I've been traveling all day in, and get to her for what I hope will be a welcome surprise.

I pull my truck up to the apartment and lean back with a deep sigh. Fuck if my body doesn't relax within seconds of parking my truck. Especially now that I know there will be no more of this leaving shit. I officially have been let go from the program. No more gone for months, going dark with no chance of talking to the ones I love back home. And most important—no more leaving Dani.

We can finally focus on growing our relationship. Making her mine. And I'm never going to fucking let her go. In the back of my mind, I've worried that she's had enough waiting, given up on us before we could even get off the ground running, but I've pushed it aside and kept hope.

There is no way that, after all of this time, when we finally have our shot and it will be over before we even get started.

Reaching over the back seat, I grab my bag and climb down from my truck. Then I pause to stretch before I bound up the stairs two at a time. I drop my bag, dig for my keys, and open the door.

The smile on my face dies instantly when I walk into the living room. Every single fear I've had since I left comes back but with a soul-crushing force.

My girl.

My fucking Dani-girl is wrapped up tight in the arms of the man I've considered one of my closest friends for years. Her back is to me, her head is tucked into his chest, and his arms are wrapped around her tight. He looks up when the door opens, and I can't even look him in the eyes because of the red haze clouding my vision.

I didn't think it could get worse. Nope. Never in my wildest nightmares did I think it could be worse than seeing her in the arms of another man. But when she turns at the noise and I get a good look at her, my world stops spinning. Right here, it just stops with an intensity that rocks my foundation.

"The fuck?" I bellow, the sound booming through the room, bouncing off the walls, and making Dani flinch.

"Huh?"

I look from her stomach—her slightly rounded and very obviously pregnant tiny bump of a stomach—and I feel my lip curl in disgust.

"And here I figured you would be waiting with your arms wide open." I throw my bag down and turn my back on them both.

I hear her gasp just as the door slams behind me. I don't even pause. The lump in my throat is burning and my eyes are watering. I blink, willing the show of emotion to stop, and thunder my way back down the steps and into my truck with a swiftness that shouldn't be possible given the way I'm feeling right now.

I just left my heart on the floor up there while my future fell around me.

After hours of driving around, the sun setting in my rearview mirror, I find myself pulling up to the one place I know will give me some peace.

My parents' house.

Cam's and Colt's trucks are gone, so at least I know I won't have to deal with them. As much as I would love to see my brothers, right now, with my mind as volatile as it is, it would be a reunion they don't deserve.

Dad's truck is parked right next to Mom's minivan. The lights are shining brightly out the windows and onto the front lawn. I sit in my truck for the longest time, still trying to calm my mind.

My throat still locked down with a lump the size of Texas.

I don't even know how to process what I saw when I walked into my apartment. Dani looked so lost—until she turned to see me—and I still can't place the emotions that crossed her face, but she almost looked guilty. A feeling I never thought I would see from her. I've struggled with the way I've felt for her for so long, but never once did I feel guilt.

Then, when I saw her belly . . .

Even with the flash of betrayal, I couldn't help but notice how beautiful she looked with that sign of life growing on her tiny frame.

All the dreams I used to get me through almost seven months of deployment of the future we would live—together—gave me the focus I needed to push through the pain of missing her. All of it, just like our start, is over before it began.

I jump when I hear a knock on my window and look up to meet my dad's concerned, blue eyes. I'm not sure how my mind knew that he was what I needed, but the second I see him, I let the emotions that were threatening to burst through tear through me.

"Dad," I lament. My shoulders start to shake, and I don't even care that the tears are starting to fall from my tired eyes.

His eyes narrow and he pulls the door open. I climb out, slap my arms around his back, and, for the first time since I left home, let him be my strength.

"Jesus, C-man. What in the hell is going on?" He pulls back, runs his hand over his thick, graying hair, and then grabs my chin, forcing my eyes to his.

"I just left the apartment," I sigh, getting a hold on my emotions. "I'm sorry. I was doing a good job at keeping my shit together."

He just looks at me, confused, before a flash of understanding flickers through his eyes. "I see. I know it must be quite shock. I'll admit your mother and I were just as surprised." His tone gives nothing away, clearly letting me run this show.

"I don't understand. I can't even seem to wrap my mind around what I saw, let alone everything that I'm feeling right now."

He gives a soft laugh. "Yeah, it was a shock for me, too, when it happened to your mom and me."

I'm explaining what seeing Dani like that did to me when his words register. "What?"

"When I first found out she was pregnant, shock was my first feeling, hands down, but then, when I realized what our love had created . . . Fuck me, that was one of the most incredible feelings in the world. I'll admit it even made me cry, son. No shame in how you're feeling."

"What?" I repeat, shocked.

"Christ, Cohen. Did finding out you're about to be a dad knock you stupid?"

"What?" I offer lamely, that feeling I had finally rid of in my gut returning.

"Uh, so I take it you didn't just see Dani?"

"Yeah, I fucking saw her—wrapped up in Chance's arms," I snap.

His brows crinkle and he looks at me, waiting for me to continue.

"Wrapped in his arms, Dad. What more do I need to give you. They looked cozy enough that I didn't stick the hell around."

His eyes harden, and he shakes his head. I wasn't expecting the hard hand against my head.

"The fuck!" I shout at him.

"The fuck about sums it up. I never thought I would say this to you, but damn, you sure did fuck things up big time with that idiot move."

"What the hell are you talking about?" I ask, rubbing my head. "That hurt, old man."

"You really thought she's with Chance? Had been with Chance? Son, she's six months pregnant. Do the fucking math."

"Yeah? I left almost seven months ago."

"Did you even pay attention in school?"

My mind starts spinning, trying to remember what little I know about the female reproductive system. When the truth hits me—hard—I have to stabilize myself with one arm on the truck.

"Yeah, son. Some stupid shit about the adding two weeks here, taking the time of conception and then adding some weeks—I don't really know how the hell it works, but I assure you that she is very much pregnant with your baby. Trust me. It was a shock to us as well, but not once did we lose the faith you did in your girl."

"I fucked up," I exhale deeply.

"You sure did. Come on. I'm shocked your mother hasn't broken down the door to see you, and we need to give Dani some time to cool off before you rush over there. I guarantee you, if she's anything like her mother, the lack of trust you held for her will piss her off, maybe more than it will hurt her. Either way, you have some serious making up to do."

He walks away, muttering something about raising me better than acting like a douchebag.

Chapter 31

Cohen

"MY HANDSOME BOY!" MY MOTHER screams when I walk in the door. She slams herself into me and gives me a hug tight enough to knock the wind out of me. Then she follows it up with a slap on the side of my head that rivals my father's in pain.

"Dammit, Ma!" I exclaim and move away from her vicious hands before she can get another slap in.

"I heard every word, you silly boy. How could you even think that?" She jabs her fist on her slim hips and gives me a hard look. "I can't even imagine what she's feeling right now. Not after the day she had."

"What does that mean?" I ask.

"Oh no, you don't. She's fine where she is. For now, you're going to tell me how in the world you could even think that she had been unfaithful."

Jesus. Where do I even start?

I follow my parents into the kitchen, where Mom starts a pot of coffee. Thirty minutes later I have it all laid out.

My rush to get home, the exhaustion that months of stress and worry had placed on my shoulders, and the feelings that seeing her with another man had rushed to the surface.

"I snapped. There isn't an excuse, but fuck. I let my jealousy get the best of me."

"Not an excuse, but it's forgivable, Cohen. It couldn't have been easy being away when you knew that you're needed at home. I get what you're saying, but that still doesn't explain how you rushed to the thought that she was with another man," Mom says with a sigh. "It wasn't right, but given everything you've been through, I understand."

"You need to talk to her, son. Don't let this fester," Dad adds when she finishes talking.

"I know. I know."

It's been four hours since I walked in and assumed the worst. The fact that *I'm* about to be a father hasn't even settled in now that the relief that I was horribly wrong is still fresh in my system.

"Do you want to talk about it, son? How you're feeling? I know it's a lot to take in."

I look over at my dad and sigh. Not for the first time, I realize just how lucky I am that he found my mom and, in turn, found me. He's been my rock since I was three—my hero—and the man I've always hoped I could just be half as good as.

"I'm going to be a father," I gasp, holding on to the countertop with a white-knuckled grip. "Holy shit," I breathe.

Dad laughs, and Mom smiles. It isn't lost on me that they're excited about this news.

"Do you know if it's a boy or girl?" I question.

Dad opens his mouth to respond, but Mom beats him to it. "I talked to Izzy about it last week and she said that Dani had refused to find out. She said that she didn't want to know unless you were right there with her to find out at the same time. She held strong on that she didn't want to know until you were home—or obviously if she went into labor. Izzy said that Dani believed that you were going to be missing so much that she didn't want to take that away from you." Mom smiles and leans against my dad's side.

"Shit," I puff, once again feeling the extremes of my rushed judgment.

Even through everything she's been going through alone, she still put me and my feelings ahead of her own. I'm sure she wants to know what we're having, and that she wanted me there badly enough to wait for something that huge is humbling. And it makes me feel like an even bigger jackass for even thinking that she had been with another man. The girl saved herself for me for almost twenty-two years.

"I think I need to go to my girl," I state. "Shit. What if she's so pissed she isn't even willing to hear me out?"

"Son, the one thing I know from experience is there is no problem too big for true love to conquer. Just take a look around you. Everyone you know has been faced with a challenge in their relationships. Challenges that, even at the time, felt unbeatable, but if what you had—for however brief before you left—gave you even a sliver of promise that I think it did, then you don't stop until you fix what's broken."

When I don't speak, Mom picks up where he left off. "You've been pushing her away for years, my sweet boy. I know you struggled with how you felt for her, so it was no shock for me when I found out that you two had finally come together. I hurt for you—so badly—when you had to leave before you two even got started, but I knew, I just knew, that you two had that 'staying power' kind of love that I felt when I met your dad. Nothing—and I mean nothing—can change that. You're going to screw up—that's a promise—but all that matters is that you work your hardest to fix it." She walks over and wraps her arms around me. Standing on her toes, she kisses me on my stubbled cheek. "You, my darling boy, need to stop thinking that you aren't allowed to feel the way you do for the woman you love. It was only a shock to her hardheaded father, but according to Izzy, he's admitted how to-the-moon happy he is that his baby girl has found a man he truly thinks is worthy of her love."

That feeling I had in my throat earlier comes back, but this time, I'm able to clear my throat and push it down. Hope is blossoming in my chest at her words.

"I know you're eager to go find her, but I think we need to address a few things before you leave, son . . . alone." He gives Mom a look, and she returns it with a small, worried nod.

"I'll leave you two. I love you, Cohen. I'm so happy that you're home safe."

I give her a hug, bend to kiss her cheek, and follow my dad into his office.

He shuts the door behind him and walks to lean against his desk. "You aren't going to like this, Cohen."

"I figured as much when you mentioned this needed to be done without Mom. I'm guessing she doesn't know?"

"She knows enough that she's aware of the issues that have been going on. However, she doesn't have a single clue at how dire they've become as of today. I've got to say, you have incredible timing, son."

He takes a deep breath, and without thought, I steel myself for whatever news he has to share with me. I'm guessing that it has everything to do with that ominous message from Chance and the chat with Axel. The one that was instrumental in having Krajack rush my assignments and my ass back home in record time.

"You know about the flowers. The first note she got was shocking enough that it's had everyone on high alert. She hasn't been alone, not even for a second." He walks around the desk, hits a few keys, and turns the computer so I can see the scanned document.

YOU ARE SUPPOSED TO BE MINE, BITCH. YOU TAKE MY FLOWERS WITH A SMILE ON YOUR FACE, BUT SPEND YOUR TIME CRYING OVER SOME MOTHERFUCKER THAT ISN'T EVEN THERE. I HEARD YOU TODAY! YOU ARE MINE, DANIELLE! IF YOU THINK SOME OTHER MOTHERFUCK WILL HAVE YOU WHEN YOU BELONG TO ME—YOU ARE DEAD FUCKING WRONG.

My skin crawls in outrage and anger when I read the words. When I think about how Dani must have felt when she saw this, my heart starts to beat wildly. Fuck. I should have been here for this. I should have been here to protect her from harm and I wasn't. That is my burden to bear and one I'll work every day for a lifetime and then some to make up for.

"Is this the last of it?" I ask through clenched teeth.

"Not even close."

"Explain," I spit, my mind going into survival mode, and the *hunter* I've been trained to be fights for control.

"After the note, she passed out." He holds his hands up when I open my mouth to explode. "Stop and listen, Cohen. Don't go off half-cocked until you know all the facts. Now that you're home, you need to know what you're up against."

"Keep going," I rush out.

"The flowers didn't start up right away, but they didn't stop. We were able to intercept enough of them that Dani doesn't even know just how bad it continued to be. Axel was concerned about her being in the early stages of pregnancy and what the added stress could do to her and the baby. Understandable considering his and Izzy's past. We've tried, but thus far, we have been unsuccessful in tracking down the origin of the purchases."

I can feel myself becoming angrier and angrier. The need to protect what's mine is starting to manifest into a craving to kill whoever is threatening her safety.

"I promise you, Cohen. She was never alone. Either there was someone at the girls' house or she was at work. The few times she went out with everyone, there was always Liam, Nate, or Chance with her. As much as Axel hated it to begin with, her wanting to stay at your place so that she could be near you, whatever that means, gave us a little peace of mind because we all know that Chance is more than capable of protecting her. They've formed a friendship since you left and that's all it is—a friendship."

"I get that now. What else is there?"

"Today, she was at work and ordered some lunch. I think she had been there for about five hours before she placed the order. According to the surveillance cameras we have placed in the doorway and on the salon floor, there wasn't anyone alarming. Clients that Sway has confirmed are regulars and no new ones. The stylist and staff. The camera and production crew for that Sway All the Way show. That's it. Dani ordered Chinese, and when the order came, the delivery person brought in the food, had her sign, and left. We lost her when she went into the breakroom to eat, but I've seen what she found when she opened the bag . . . and what it did to her. You aren't going to like this," he warned.

"Just fucking tell me so I can get to her, Dad." My anger becomes a palpable thing.

"What you need to do is calm down, because as pissed as this is going to make you, you need to be there for her. I have no doubt that what you saw was a terrified woman being comforted. Sway sent someone over for help, but with Axel and Beck out of town and Maddox up to his elbows in case backlog, Chance and I were the ones who showed up. Chance took her out of there while I waited for the police and secured the scene."

"What. Did. She. Find?" I grind out forcefully.

He sighs and returns his attention to his computer. Within seconds, the monitor is turned my way and I have to fight the urge to throw up.

My God! What in the fuck?

"Someone has their sights on her, Cohen. This is one of the first times that she's actually dressed to show off her stomach. Normally, she wears baggy clothing, and honestly, I wouldn't have been able to tell until today. She dressed up—according to Megan, who rushed over to help Chance earlier—to show off her pregnancy because she knew the cameras would be back after a two-month break. Whoever this is, they honestly didn't know about the baby until today. That I'm almost positive about."

"They've been watching my woman, Dad. Watching her close enough that this was a clear threat. You read that first letter. We're dealing with a fucking lunatic. Someone who views her as theirs. What do you think is going to happen now that I'm home? Just by being with her, I'm placing her and my unborn child in danger."

He studies my face for a beat. "But your being gone is killing her. Plain and simple, Cohen. It's not been easy, despite the brave face she's kept. You can protect her. You *will* protect her. Don't let some stupid thought that she's better off without you even enter your brain, son. I raised you better than that shit."

I shouldn't be surprised that he so clearly read me.

"I need to go to her." I state.

"You need to go to her," he agrees.

I give him a quick hug and all but rush out the door.

With a renewed sense of confidence and the feelings of overwhelming fear for her and our child, I speed through the streets and make my way to the woman who I, just hours before, wronged.

I have a lot to make up for, but my parents are right. When you feel something as powerful as what Dani and I share, you don't ever stop fighting for that. I'll be damned if I let some crazy fuck threaten the future I will have with Danielle Reid.

Chapter 32

Dani

I DIDN'T EVEN CRY WHEN Cohen stormed out of the apartment. The shock from the day still held my tears at bay. I wanted to. God, how I wanted to. But I managed to keep my shit together. When that door slammed shut, I stepped away from Chance and, without a word, locked myself in Cohen's bedroom.

I should be angry. I should be so mad that I leave and never look back. I should be a lot of things, but what I am is numb.

Never did I think I would have that kind of reception from Cohen when he returned. I had envisioned it in my head over and over. The homecoming I would give him. How happy I would feel when I was able to tell him about our child. The love I would feel from him.

I don't know why I didn't even stop to consider that he would look at me with distrust and accusations. I guess I just believed him to be better than that.

I sigh and turn to my side, my nose burning with emotion but my eyes still dry. My hand carelessly rubs against the light kicking coming from my belly. I squeeze my eyes shut, willing the memories of this afternoon out of my head when I once again think about the terrible image that met me from the lunch sack.

When I open my eyes again, I realize that I must have fallen asleep. The sun, which was been dropping when I laid my head down, is long gone, and through the window, the moon is casting a soft glow around the room. I can hear Chance moving around outside of the room. I should go talk to him. Ask him to at least take me home. But even with the earlier events, I don't want to leave the one place where I've felt close to Cohen.

I hear the doorknob shake, and it's followed by some scratches. And then the light from the hall filters into the otherwise dark room.

Looks like Chance got sick of waiting for me to emerge.

I keep my body still, waiting to see what he'll do next. Chance isn't exactly a man of many words, so I'm guessing I'll get a quick, "Let's go."

I almost jump out of my skin when I feel the bed depress. I move to leap out of the bed when two steel bands carefully wrap themselves around my body and I'm pulled back against a hard, warm body. I struggle, panicking with the thoughts of Chance being in Cohen's bed with me. That is, until the familiar scent of Cohen invades my senses and my body instantly deflates. The tears I was doing such a damn good job at holding off rush to the surface when I feel his body—a body I've missed for so damn long—hold me even closer.

"Dani-girl," he groans.

His head drops to my neck, and I feel his lips against my skin before his arms let up slightly. But only long enough to travel from my chest and for his warm palms to stretch out against the small bump that holds our child within.

"God, Dani," he breaths out with a slight tremor.

That right there is all it takes for me to hiccup once, twice, and a third time before a huge sob vibrates through my body.

"Baby," he exhales. "I'm so fucking sorry, Dani. More sorry than you could ever imagine."

It takes me a second to calm down, but when I do, I shift and turn in his arms, instantly missing the feeling of his hands against my belly.

"You thought that I . . . that Chance and I . . . Cohen, you believed the worst in seconds. I haven't set eyes on you in months, and the second I do, you actually believed that I had been with another man—Chance of all people."

He drops his forehead to mine and doesn't speak for the longest time. He runs his fingertips through my hair, down my face, and over my lips. His eyes follow every movement his hand makes. He doesn't stop until his fingers are pushed into my hair and he's holding my head in his hand. I wait until he locks eyes with me, unwilling to back down about how his reaction made me feel.

"You have no idea what it's been like to be without you this long, Cohen. My heart felt like it was only beating half beats. I felt like I was missing a part of myself for so long. I craved the day that you would return and I would feel whole again. I had that feeling for one night—*one night, Cohen!* I knew within hours of being with you that I would stop Heaven and Earth if it meant that I could just have one more second. I didn't doubt in the power of that . . . the power of us. So please tell me how in the world you could take one look at me after all of that and think what you did."

His eyes close tight before he opens them and looks at me, his lids filling with unshed tears.

My mouth drops in shock. I have never seen him cry. Never. He's always been someone who holds his emotions close, but not in a way that keeps him closed off. It's just how he's wired. So seeing him let me in so effortlessly and letting me physically see how much this is costing him is huge.

"I can't justify how I felt away with excuses, Dani. That is all it would be—one giant, fucking stupid excuse. I've been running on fumes since I got word that there was trouble brewing at home. Running on fumes that would bring me home to you, baby. I lived the knowledge that, if I just hurried up and finished my shit, you would be in my arms—where I could keep you safe. It's been the only thing I could see for months. Months. The second I got back, I did what I needed to do so that I could get home to you. Drove through the night and into the day with one thought on my mind. You. When I walked in and saw you in Chance's arms, I didn't even see anything other than someone other than myself touching you when I haven't been able to for fucking months. My jealousy got the best of me, and I can't apologize enough for that."

I narrow my eyes at him. "I saw your face, Cohen. You looked at me and saw my belly and thought the worst. Don't even deny it. I got the same look from my own father, so trust me when I say that I know exactly what that looks like. I didn't even dream that I would get that from you."

His eyes flash, and I see the remorse dancing behind his sorrow. "I'm not proud of it, Dani. I'm fucking ashamed that I even let the thought, however brief, cross my mind. Nothing I say can make that up to you. Nothing. But I promise, baby, that I don't think that you were unfaithful to me."

"Yeah, Cohen, you do. Somewhere deep inside of you, you felt that."

He shakes his head. "No, baby. I don't. I promise you that. What I did feel was every single emotion and helpless feeling I've had crash into me at once. The pain of being away from you when I knew you needed me. The worry that I wouldn't be here when you needed me. Everything that has haunted me day to day and week to week. That and the crash of adrenaline I had been riding high on since I got back stateside just got the best of me. My jealousy got the best of me and turned me into someone I'm not proud of. I've never felt this way towards someone, Dani. It's all new to me, and I guarantee you I'll fuck up again, but I'll spend my life making it up to you. God, Dani . . . please fucking tell me that I didn't let my temper get the best of me and ruin us."

One tear escapes his eye, which is followed by another, and another. His breathing is picking up, and his chest is rising rapidly under where my palms are resting.

"You hurt me."

"I know, baby. I know," he sighs.

"I've been dreaming of the day you would return to me and I would feel whole again. Dreamed of it, Cohen. Every night that you've been away from me, I've pleaded with God to bring you home in one piece."

"Fuck, Dani-girl," he chokes out, his eyes closing and again tears leaking down his handsome face until they disappear in his stubble.

"It's been the only thing that's kept me from falling apart with the shit life has thrown at me. You and your love."

He doesn't look up, but his arms lock even tighter around me and he pulls me closer to his warmth.

"Even though you hurt me—and, God, did you hurt me—the

only thing I craved since seeing your face again was this feeling right here. This feeling of your arms around me, your heart beating strong and healthy against my palm, and the life we created moving between us. Through all that pain, the only thing I wanted was the one person who'd caused it."

"Stop, please, Dani," he begs.

"I've loved you for a lifetime, Cohen. A lifetime doesn't just give up when the other part of me makes a mistake. A lifetime takes that mistake and turns it into a building block for an even stronger foundation."

His eyes snap open and his hopeful gaze locks with mine. "Baby?"

"I love you, Cohen. That will never change. But don't ever hurt me like that again. I'm strong, baby, and I'll make as many building blocks as we need until the day my last breath leaves my body, but don't make me build them out of pain."

His eyes flash, and in seconds, his lips are against mine.

Hard and demanding.

He takes my mouth in a bruising need that steals the breath right out of my lungs.

"I love you, *my* Dani-girl. I promise you that I will never doubt what we have. Never again, baby," he mumbles against my swollen lips before he takes control of my mouth once again.

His hands trail down my back, grasping my hips, as he rolls onto his back while taking me with him. My skirt rides up instantly when my legs are spread to make room for his hips. I use my hands against his chest to push up so I'm straddling his lap and looking down at his brown eyes, which are so full of love.

I sit up straight and let out a slight moan when I feel his erection press against my panties. His eyes flash when I take his hands, which were resting on my hips, and move them around to the front of my belly.

"This," I stress, pressing his hands against the thumping our child is making against my belly. "This is our child, Cohen. One that was made with a love so powerful even I struggle to understand it. A love that was formed over a lifetime and solidified with one night that I will forever remember as one of the best of my life. We've been fated for this moment since before we were even born, baby, and I'm beyond fortunate with this unexpected fate that's been given to us."

His eyes darken with each word I speak. I notice the second that my words register and he realizes the words I used.

The same words he used in the letter he left me all those months ago.

"I love you, Cohen."

"And I love you, Dani-girl. And I you."

I drop my head and take his lips in a slow, deep kiss. Our tongues move together as our breaths mingle. We take the kiss as deep as we can without physically fusing together.

He flips us so that he's on top, and his hips rock gently against my core. He's careful not to put his full weight on my stomach, but he makes sure every inch that can touch is touching.

"Wrap your legs around me, baby," he demands, breaking from the kiss for just seconds until I do what he's asked. "Just like that," he says, and I feel him grow even harder against me.

He moves against me until I'm seconds away from coming undone. My whole body is feeling as if it's burning as my climax slowly starts to crawl up my spine. Right when I pull my lips from his to cry out in what promises to be a powerful climax, he stops.

"Oh, God! Don't stop. Please don't stop," I beg on a sob.

"Never," he declares.

His lips start leaving a trail of fire across my jaw and down my neck until he reaches the fabric of my blouse against my chest. He leans back onto his knees and trails both hands along my collarbone until they rest in the V of my cleavage. I catch his intentions only seconds before he takes a fist of silk in each hand, and with a firm pull, my blouse is ripped right down the center. His eyes darken even further when he takes his first glimpse of my bra-covered chest.

He doesn't speak a word. His fingers continue to light their fire along the cups of my bra and over the swells of each breast. He flicks the front clasp but doesn't move to unhook it. His fingers dance in twin caresses down my stomach until he's cradling my rounded stomach between his strong palms.

"This right here makes me the happiest man in the world, Dani.

Seeing you swollen with my child. Knowing that part of me is inside of you right now is one of the hottest things ever. God, I fucking love you," he groans.

His hands roll over my stomach before those sinful fingers move back up to my bra. In one deft move, the clasp is flicked and my breasts spill free.

"These tits. Fuck, Dani. I'm going to fuck these tits," he promises before he bends down to take one nipple between his teeth for a light nip before soothing the pain with his tongue. "I'm going to fuck them until I come all over your chest, baby. Then I'm going to eat you until your juices are running down my chin. And when you're begging me for it, I'll give you my cock." His mouth returns to my other nipple, and he flicks his tongue over it before pressing his lips around the tight bud and sucking it deep.

"Shit," I moan, feeling my pussy clench and literally weep for him. "I need you," I beg.

"Not yet," he says around my sensitive nipple. His breath causes me to shudder. "I'm gonna fuck these tits first."

He leans up and squeezes each globe together a few times, pressing them tightly together before letting them go, and he licks his lips when they bounce to the side. "Yeah, I'm going to fuck these tits."

I cry out when I feel his hips leave mine. My eyes widen when he jumps off the bed and all but rips his clothes off. When he moves his hands to his waist and pushes his jeans and boxer briefs off in one swift move, his cock springs out and bumps against his stomach. His long, thick length is swollen with need, and I can see the drop of semen rolling down the hoop through the head. He pumps his cock roughly as his eyes trail over me.

"You need to be naked, baby. The second I feel your body against mine, I won't be able to stop. And those"—he points to my skirt and panties—"will be in my way," he growls.

I yelp when he jumps onto the bed and causes me to jolt. His fingers go to my waist, and I feel him roughly pulling the fabric from my body. He gives my mound a quick kiss that leaves me begging harder before he straddles my body and starts to climb up. His cock is pointing angrily at my face as he carefully moves over my rounded belly, his hands bracing the headboard to ensure that no extra weight falls on me. I bend my head and lick the top of his cock, and he groans long and low.

"Yeah, I'm going to fuck the hell out of these beautiful tits," he says. "Squeeze them tight, baby."

I do as he requested and push them together so that his cock is nestled between them. He closes his eyes and drops his head forward. Beads of sweat roll down his face and drop from his chin onto my chest.

His hips start to rock, slowly at first, until he picks up his thrusting. "Squeeze your tits harder," he grinds out. "Fuck me. Been so long," he says on another groan.

I never imagined that being titty-fucked would be so hot, but with each thrust, the piercings through his hard cock rubbing against the inside of my tits and the tip of his cock just a breath away from my mouth, I find my mouth filling with saliva and just begging to take his length in deep. The quicker he moves, the more my fingers squeeze each nipple until I'm only seconds from coming.

"God damn," he breathes.

I lean my head down and open my mouth so that, with each thrust up, the head of his cock is inside my mouth. His movements start to falter after that, and with one powerful groan, he pulls back and takes his cock in his hand. After a few pumps, I feel his warm semen coating each tit and hitting my chin. I reach up, swipe at his come, and stick my finger deep in my mouth, watching his eyes burn as I lick away every drop.

"I want my come on your tits while I eat you, Dani," he demands before moving his body down and latching his mouth firmly against my swollen and weeping clit.

"Fuck me!" I scream.

"I will," he rumbles against my core. "I fucking will and you're going to be begging for it until your screams are shaking my windows, Dani."

"Now, please," I whine, not even ashamed at the pathetic tone my wanting has brought forth. "God, please . . . I need to be full of you."

"Fuck, that mouth. Now I want my cock in your mouth." He

moves his mouth from my sensitive clit and gives me a long lick before nibbling along my swollen lips. Each bite of his teeth has me whimpering louder.

"Give it to me . . . Give it to me . . . Please," I pant.

He ignores my begging, sucking along the seam and licking the wetness that leaks from my pussy. He feasts on my body like a starved man. When his tongue probes into my body, my walls clamp down, looking for anything to grab hold of.

"So tight," he murmurs on a groan. "I'm going to pound this pussy, Dani. Pound you until your ass is red from my balls slapping against them."

Oh, God. I'm going to die. If he doesn't fuck me now, I'm going to die. My body is strung tight, every muscle just waiting to snap, and the nerves are firing sporadically throughout my whole body. I whither against the mattress, my fist clutching the sheets as my body heats with arousal so powerful that my back lifts off the mattress and a whine-cry-scream noise shoots from my mouth. His fingers, which were holding my knees apart, trail down until he's grasping my thighs and his thumbs are rubbing on either side of my wet core. I can feel my wetness dripping down my crack and onto the mattress below. I should be ashamed of what my body is doing, but it just turns me on further.

"Please, God, please!" I shout.

He dips two thick fingers deep into my pussy and curls them, hitting me in a spot that has my eyes rolling back and a scream so loud bursting from my lips as I clamp down and come on his fingers. My body is locked tight as I cry out his name over and over again.

When I finally crash back down to Earth from the power of my orgasm, I look down my body and lock eyes with his. They're full of sinful promise, and my body quivers when he lifts his mouth slightly so I can see him roll his tongue over my clit, causing little quakes to shift through my limbs.

"You're going to give me another, Dani. You're going to come again and soak my chin. I want to feel your body cry out to mine." He bends, sucks, and looks back at me. "When I fuck you with that fucking wetness coating your virgin ass, you're going to beg me to take that too. Aren't you, baby?"

He doesn't give me time to answer him. He bends his head and gives making me orgasm again all of his focus until, just as he said I would, I cry and scream and claw at his neck and shoulders to get him to stop.

"I fucking need you . . . Need you so bad," I pant breathlessly. "I need your cock, Cohen. Please give me it, fill me, and fuck me hard. It's been so long, baby, please . . ." I trail off, mumbling who knows what about how desperately I need him.

He gives me another lick before he trails kisses up my body. When his mouth takes mine in a hungry kiss, the taste of myself on his mouth has me moaning deeply.

"Please," I mumble against his mouth, the word slurring.

"Are you ready for my cock?" he asks on a grunt as he reaches down to rub the head of his cock against my pussy.

The feel of his piercing rubbing against my fevered skin causes me to whimper.

"Do you want me here?" he asks, pushing just the tip into my weeping core. "Or do you want me here?" His hand leaves his cock, and I feel his fingertips against my asshole.

I tense, and his eyes heat until they're almost black.

"Does my girl want my cock in her ass?"

"Fuck, yes . . . anywhere. I need it, baby," I gasp when he rolls one finger in the wetness that is seeping from my body.

His soaked finger trails down from my pussy, and I feel him press against my ass again.

"Relax," he pants. "Relax and let me in," his says with an evil grin. "I'm so fucking hard for you. So hard that it hurts."

"Yes," I sigh and then yelp when his finger breaches my tight asshole. "Need it," I gasp.

"Fuck yeah, you do." He continues to push his finger in until I feel him stop, his knuckle-deep finger causing a delicious burn.

"More," I plead, not even sure what I'm asking for. My nails dig into his shoulders, and I almost pass out from the sensations that wash over my body when he pushes in deeper.

He shifts so that he is lying against my side, his rock-hard cock pushing against my thigh, and after pulling his finger from my tight hole, he returns to my soaked pussy, coating not one, but two fingers. When he trails down to my rim again, I'm ready for him and push out when his fingertips touch my tight opening.

"Fuck me. My girl is begging for it. Begging for my cock in her virgin ass. I want your pussy, baby, but I need this too. I need to take you here."

I nod my head, panting with need that is so great it has stolen my speech.

"As wet as you are, I would almost think you didn't need lube, but there is no fucking way I'm taking this ass without getting you ready. I want to hear you fucking scream, Dani. Beg. Me. For. It."

He doesn't wait for me to respond. He rolls to his side, I hear him rummage through his drawer, and then he's back. His wicked grin makes his handsome face flash with a dirty promise.

"Scream, Dani. Scream until my ears ring," he says, and without warning, he flips me so that my knees are on the mattress. He's mindful to keep my stomach off the bed, placing a pillow between my body and the soft sheets.

I hear a noise and then feel cool liquid rolling down from the top of my ass until it rolls onto the mattress. His fingers move from where he was holding my hips in place, and I feel him rub the lube until his fingers and my crack are slippery.

His fingers dip slowly and deep into my ass, scissoring and stretching my hole to take his cock. The feeling burns in pleasure and makes me feel a delicious fullness. His other hand squirts some more lube, this time gathering some on his fingers. I lean up on my hands and look over my shoulder to see his head thrown back, his teeth digging into his bottom lip, and his other arm—the one not thrusting two fingers into my ass—stroking his cock.

He looks down, locks eyes with me, and pulls his fingers from my dark hole. When I feel the steel of his piercing against my body, I tense and his eyes flash.

"Don't do that. Fucking beg me, Dani," he commands.

I take a deep breath, and before I can get the words out, I feel his palm against my ass, the feeling startling but not unpleasant. I moan and do as he said, begging him to take me.

"Yeah. That's what I want to hear. Louder, Dani." His words slur, and I feel him press harder against my body. "Make me believe you."

I do as he said, my body once again feeling like a coil that is being pulled too tight.

"Just. Like. That!" he roars before slowly pushing himself into my body. "Push out, baby. Push against me and take my cock."

The burn is almost too much. I can feel each of the piercings that line his cock until he's settled in as deep as he can go, and the one piercing that's left is pressed against my stretched hole. It hurts in a way that is so all consuming, and I scream out with the pleasure that his pain brings me.

"So fucking good," he pants, pulling out just an inch before rocking into my body again. "Made for my cock."

I cry out, scream just as he predicted, and hold on for dear life as he builds up his speed until he's pushing into my body in a pace that has me feeling like I can't breathe.

"So full of my cock, Dani-girl. Your ass is begging for it."

Thrust out and push in. Each time, gaining speed until I'm not sure if I'm even breathing anymore.

"God. Damn." His fingers dig into my hips before I feel his fingers circling my clit, and just like that—with that one simple touch—I explode in the most powerful orgasm my body has ever felt. My head is thrown back and his name is the last thing on my lips as my body milks his cock of every ounce of come he has left.

Chapter 33

Cohen

I'M NOT SURE WHAT'S GOTTEN into me.

One second, I was begging for my girl to forgive me. The next, I was demanding that she beg me for my cock.

I took my pregnant woman rough and hard. And I didn't just fuck her. No, I took one look at her body, ripe with the pregnancy of my child, and lost my fucking mind.

I move from behind her, careful that her spent body doesn't fall onto her stomach, and lay her on her side. After jumping off the bed, I walk to the bathroom to clean myself off. As I wash my cock with a warm washcloth, I look in the mirror at my flushed skin. Sweat is beading down my chest, and my cock is still impossibly hard even after having just come twice.

After making sure I cleaned myself off, I run a new washcloth under the warm water and walk back over to the bed. Her eyes are closed, and her chest is moving up and down in a slow rhythm. My eyes trail down her flushed neck, and when I see my come dry on her skin—all over her long neck and tits—my cock jumps. Fuck, that's hot.

I bring the washcloth to her skin and almost hate that I have to wipe myself off her body. She doesn't even flinch as I clean her chin, neck, and tits. Not even a twitch when I rub the warm cotton over the ass I just fucked hard. She does hum in her sleep, but other than that, nothing.

I use this time to take in her body. Her belly looks so large now that I'm getting a good look. Her slim body makes her look like she swallowed a ball. When I think again about our child growing inside her, I want to fuck her all over again. It's as if it wakes some primal desire to claim her that was dormant until now.

After tossing the dirty washcloth towards my hamper, I climb into the bed and pull the sheets over her body. My hand goes straight to her belly, and when I feel little bumps against my palm, my eyes go wide.

That. That right there is my child. A child I made with Dani.

That primal urge hits me again, reminding me that now she is connected to me forever. I know she loves me. There is no denying that. But this child? This child connects us in a way that will never change.

Our baby continues to make its presence known, and I close my eyes and let the peace that washes over me settle my heart.

"I'm going to marry you, Dani-girl," I vow to the silence around me.

"Okay, baby," she mumbles.

I thought she was asleep, so when I hear her sleepy voice answer me back, my eyes shoot to hers, and when I see her beautiful smile and bright-green eyes swimming with tears, I shake my head and move to kiss her deep.

"Why the tears?"

"I love you," she says, not answering me.

"Dani. The tears."

"I love you. That's why the tears. But if you plan on marrying me, you better ask me when you haven't just fucked me raw."

I laugh, kissing her again, "Noted."

"I missed you," she sighs.

"I know, Dani-girl. Never again. I won't leave you again, baby."

She shifts so that her eyes come to mine. "You can't promise that, Cohen. You don't know when they'll call you back." She doesn't say it, but I hear the fear in her voice, and I hate that it's there.

"Actually, I can promise that. I'm out, baby. I let them know that I was leaving the program two days ago. I still have some shit I need to tie up with them, but I won't be leaving."

Her eyes go wide, and she looks at me in shock before—much to my surprise—she lets out a pitiful noise and drops her head, wrapping her arms around my body and holding me as tight as she can while she loses her shit.

"Dani-girl, you need to calm yourself."

She doesn't stop, just sobs harder.

Helpless and unable to stop her from drowning us both with tears, I bring her body close and wait for her cries to end.

"You're not going to leave us?" she questions after a few minutes.

Us.

Her and our child.

"Never."

"My God," she cries. She looks up at me in awe, those eyes I love so much taking in every inch of my face. "You have no idea how happy that makes me."

"Yeah, the tears were a little questionable," I joke.

"You're going to be here . . . every day?"

"Every day from here on out."

She smiles and cuddles her body close, relaxing instantly in my arms.

"We need to talk about what happened today, Dani."

I probably could have timed it better, but the calm that was rolling down her body like a blanket evaporates the second I open my mouth.

"You don't have to repeat that shit, baby. I know everything, but we do need to talk about what you think. What you think and what your gut is telling you about these things happening. I don't fucking like it one bit, and until we figure out who's behind these threats, I don't want you leaving my sight."

She opens her mouth to complain—I'm sure—but I stop her before she has a chance.

"I won't waver on this, Dani. I just won't. Not when it comes to you and our child's safety. You can just think of it as us making up for lost time. Like it our not, I'm your new shadow, baby."

Her face scrunches up, and I wait for her to speak, my fingers trailing over the soft skin of her back.

"I hate this. I hate feeling powerless and terrified to even look out the window, Cohen."

"I know you do. But this shit will end. I won't stop until I find out who has been making you feel like you aren't safe. I won't let anyone take you from me."

We lie there in silence until she speaks again.

"Who do you think is doing this?" she whispers into the darkness.

"I'm not sure, but rest easy that I'll find out."

She nods her head against my shoulder and settles in deeper as if her body needs to get as close as possible to feel safe. I feel her stomach press against my side and smile into the darkness.

"A baby, huh?"

"Yeah," she breathes. "I know we didn't plan this, but I couldn't be happier. Knowing that a part of us is cooking away in there gives me the biggest sense of completion I've ever felt. It helped me fill the void that your being gone had left, but it wasn't until I had your arms around me again that I realized how right this feels."

"My Dani-girl is having my baby." I let that settle around us before another thought quickly takes its place. "Your father really is going to kick my ass."

Her giggles float around us, and with a smile, I fall asleep. And for the first time in almost seven long months, I sleep peacefully.

Chapter 34

Dani

COHEN DIDN'T LET ME OUT of his bed for two days. Of course, he kept me well fed and hydrated, but other than that, we spent the two days that followed his homecoming locked in his room with our bodies connected in every way possible.

The phone had long stopped ringing and it seemed that our family and friends were content to wait us out and give us the time we needed to become us after too long apart.

I asked him once between one of our long lovemaking sessions if he felt like it was weird that we came together so quickly. He laughed and told me that if we hadn't been dancing around it for so long, I would have been his years ago. There was no doubt in my mind that I was right where I was meant to be.

"Dani," I hear him call from the other side of his shower curtain. "I think they've given us as much space as we're going to get. Your brother called to give me a heads-up that our parents should be here in about twenty minutes."

Ugh. So much for staying wrapped up in each other.

"I'm surprised they lasted this long," I mumble and rinse the shampoo from my hair.

"Me too," he says, and I jump when I realize that he's stepped into the shower with me.

"You just took a shower," I say lamely.

"Yup," he responds and takes my conditioner from my hand.

"Turn."

I do what he says and spin, giving him my back. I hear him groan as his free hand palms my cheek. "I love this ass," he says and gives it a light slap.

"So I noticed."

"We have twenty minutes, baby."

I look over my shoulder at him and raise my brow in question, wondering where he's going with this.

"I wonder how many times I can make you scream my name in that time." He drops the conditioner, forgotten on the bottom of the tub, and pulls me against his hard, naked body.

Thirty minutes later, he has made me scream his name four times, and even while the front door is being pounded on by our expected visitors, he takes my body until I give him one more.

I glare at my father and continue to attempt to brush the tangles out of my wet hair. Since I didn't use conditioner, the long locks have become almost unmanageable. My father, having noticed that we were both wet when we opened the door, hasn't taken his eyes off Cohen.

Cohen, who I'll press, hasn't let me away from his side. When our parents filed in his doorway, I gave each of them a hug, and then he had his arm around my shoulders and my body pressed against his. I offered to get everyone something to drink and he just said no and pulled me onto his lap when he dropped down on the oversized chair in this living room.

Where I'm currently sitting, glaring at my father.

"Dani has agreed that it's best if she took some time off work," Cohen says to the room, and I snap my head to his.

"I did?"

"Sure you did," he says, looking at me like I've lost my mind.

"I don't remember that."

"That's because you've been busy," he says with a wink.

I snap my eyes over to the corner where my father is standing with his arms crossed over his chest when I hear him growl. "Did you really just do that?" I snap at him.

"Axel," Mom warns him.

Cohen brings his arm around my waist and rests his palm on my stomach, and I can't even enjoy *that,* because once again, my father is acting like a dog, growling and all but frothing at the mouth.

"Seriously, Daddy!" I exclaim. "That's a bit much."

"Axel," Mom tries again, walking over, placing her hands on either side of his face, and attempting to bring his gaze to hers.

He doesn't budge though; his eyes stay locked on Cohen.

"Seriously?" she huffs. "You're acting like a caveman, Axel Reid. Time to stop."

Cohen seems to have a death wish, because his other hand moves from where it was lying against the armrest and his long fingers curl around one of my jean-clad thighs.

Daddy moves like he's about to push off the wall only to stop when my mom pushes against his chest. I look over at Cohen's parents, and my eyes widen when I see his mom wink at me and giggle softly, which earns her a squeeze by Greg.

"As I was saying," Cohen continues. "Dani is going to be taking some time off work. I've already talked to Sway, and in light of the other day's events, he agrees that is the best move. I've already talked to Chance and let him know that, as soon as Dani finds a house she feels works for the baby and us, we'll be moving out. I say we because I don't plan on her going anywhere until said house is found. He also sees the wisdom in this plan."

"The fuck you say," Daddy says, finally having enough and snapping. He pushes past my mother so swiftly that she almost tumbles. His arm shoots out and he helps her steady her footing, never once removing his heated gaze off Cohen. "The fuck. You say!"

He prowls forward, and when he gets about halfway to us, Cohen pats my thigh and indicates that he wants me to shift so he can stand. I do so, mutely, and wait to see how this plays out, knowing that it has to play out for us to be able to move forward.

"You knock up *my* girl. Demand that she move in. And not even plan on making an honest woman out of her?" he fumes.

Cohen stands toe-to-toe with him, their eyes almost level, but even with Daddy having a few inches on Cohen, he doesn't back down. His chest heaves, but for the most part, he remains calm.

"I didn't say that, Axel. I plan on marrying your daughter the first chance I get, but *that* is something that is between the two of us. I respect you enough that I *had* planned on coming to you privately to ask for your blessing, but I have to be honest with you—I will be marrying *my girl* whether you give that to me or not. With all due respect, I love your daughter and I couldn't really give two shits if you want to bless that or not."

"What did you just say?" Daddy turns and looks over at my mom. "What did he just say to me?"

"You heard him, honey," she says with a smile. "I think it's time you took that alpha male down a few notches, big boy."

My gaze shoots from my mom to my dad to see his reaction, and then it lands on Melissa when she throws her head back and laughs loudly.

"Hush, beauty," Greg tells his wife. "Son, I think you need to tread carefully here. I like your head right where it is."

Melissa snickers even louder at that.

"You don't care for my blessing?" Daddy tosses back at Cohen, and there's no mistaking his body language—he's ready to kill. His hands are flexing and his face is beet red.

"Ax—" Mom tries.

"Don't you dare 'Axel' me, Izzy. Don't you dare. Did you hear him? He just said he didn't give *two shits!*" he roars. "You're walking a tight line here, Cohen."

This is getting out of hand. I know there won't be a good outcome if I let the two men I love the most fight over this. Standing carefully from my seat, I give Melissa a wobbly smile when she nods her head in encouragement before I go to stand in front of Cohen and face my father.

I feel Cohen move, and before I can speak, I'm behind him and he's once again between my father and me. My eyes go from his solid back to the only two people I can see—his parents. Cohen's move of dominance and protection is one I know didn't go unnoticed by my father because I see Greg nod and Melissa smile so huge that it looks unnatural. I grasp his shirt in my hand and try to get his attention.

"Cohen," I start.

"Not now, Dani. I get you think you need to protect me from your father, but this needs to happen and it needs to happen now."

I sigh, drop my hands from his shirt, and do the only thing left I can. I wrap my hands around his stomach and spread my palms wide against his abs. It's another move I know doesn't go unnoticed because Melissa's smile gets even larger, and when I move my eyes to Greg's, I see that his are shining bright and his smile matches Melissa's in size and happiness.

"Are you going to do anything?" I ask him.

"Nope. My boy knows what he's doing." He leans back and pulls his wife to his chest, and they just watch with those big, loopy-loo smiles as Cohen stands his ground with my father.

The father who I know could kill him with his bare hands.

I gulp.

"I'm going to tell you this once, Axel. I love your daughter. I've loved her before it was right to feel that way. I fought those feelings until she was ready for me, because I'll tell you this. It was never a question that I was ready for her. What we have is something I will never feel worthy of. Not of her love. Something she gives me without hesitation. I know she deserves the best that life can hand her. You do *not* have to remind me of that. But even though I don't think *I'm* good enough for *her*, I'll spend my life making sure that she knows she's the best thing I will ever have. Do you understand that? I will make sure there isn't a day that passes that she doesn't know how much I love her. I'll spend every second I have left on this Earth giving her everything I possibly can. I waited, out of respect for you and for her, until I couldn't wait a second longer, and I will not—not for you—give up even a sliver of time with her now that she is mine."

I hold my breath and wait. I keep my eyes on Cohen's parents for some sort of clue of what's happening beyond the wall of Cohen's body.

It feels like a lifetime passes before I hear my father's laughter boom through the room.

What in the hell?

"Well. Why didn't you just say that to begin with?"

I repeat; What in the hell?

"You didn't really give me a chance, Axel," Cohen says.

"Right. Well, now that that is out of the way, let's talk."

Jesus Christ. I've entered the Twilight Zone.

It doesn't take long for us to settle back down. Cohen turns and gives me a kiss, and when I hear my father's growl again, I pull back and look over at him. He throws his arms up and gives me a tired look back.

"What? You don't expect me to just flip a switch and turn it off, do you?"

"Crazy old man," I mutter.

Cohen takes his seat again and pulls me back onto his lap. One hand goes to my belly and the other is resting back on my thigh. Without a thought, I wrap my arms around his shoulders and settle in for what promises to be a long chat.

"My dad filled me in on everything that's happened between the letter, flowers, and . . . yesterday." He pauses to look down at me. "I want to be fully briefed so that I'm able to understand this from every angle that I'm sure you have worked. My gut tells me that it's someone she knows. Someone she trusts. But until I have all the intel, I'm not comfortable making that call. I've been told that the police also have run into nothing but dead ends?" He looks between my father and his and they all nod. "This bastard is slick, I'll give him that," Cohen mutters.

"Slick, but he'll fuck up. I heard from my contact at the department that there was a print lifted from the bag. Dani's has been ruled out, so they're running it through their database to see if they get a match."

Cohen nods his head at my father's words but doesn't speak.

"I agree with you, son. This is too personal of an attack for it to be someone that she hasn't come in contact with."

I shiver when Greg's words hit me. Someone I know? I can't even think about who it might be.

"You think it could be a client?" I ask. "I have plenty of male clients, but until yesterday, no one really knew about the pregnancy.

Until recently, I wasn't really showing much and I had been able to hide it well. I . . . well, yesterday, with the cameras back, I wanted to show my belly off."

"Client, or someone that you've been in contact with. However brief, it doesn't matter. They've latched on, and judging by everything that's been said with the two messages, they aren't happy that you're in a relationship with my son—well, anyone for that matter. You've always held back, Dani, and until Cohen, you didn't really date seriously. I don't think that this person saw a threat until Cohen."

I try to make sense of what Greg just said, but I just can't seem to wrap my mind around it.

"Little princess," my daddy says gruffly. "Think about this. The flowers started when Cohen left. I don't want to know details, but if this person has been watching you, it's reasonable to believe that he saw the connection between you, and when Cohen left, he pounced and attempted to make his feelings known with the flowers. When that didn't work, something triggered that first note. I've been over this with your mom, and she told me that you two had spent that afternoon discussing the seriousness of your relationship with Cohen. I have no doubt that, if he's that close, he didn't handle overhearing that very well."

I nod, following so far. Cohen's breathing has gone wild, and I look up into his eyes to see that he's having a hard time holding on to his cool after hearing all of this.

"After that, things calmed down, but the flowers continued," Greg adds.

"Right," Daddy starts and looks between Greg and Cohen. "Dani, you don't know this because, between all of us, your brother, and Liam, we were able to grab most of the deliveries before you even knew they had come . . . but they never stopped. I think they would have probably continued until Cohen came home and, once again, that threat against whatever he sees in his sick mind of you having with him is back. That is until you went out with your belly the focus and he realized that something he considered his had been touched by another."

"Oh my God," I gasp.

"I tell you, sweetheart, this motherfucker will pay. Not only has he threatened you, but as of yesterday, he's now threatening my grandbaby."

"Agreed," Greg says forcefully.

"I agree with what Cohen's said. You need to stop working for a little while. Stay home and enjoy the rest of your pregnancy. After the baby is born, then you can decide what to do about work, but until this fucker is caught, it would make everyone feel a lot better if we could limit the people you're around. Being at Sway's with everything going on with clients in and out as well as that show being filmed, just isn't safe."

I nod, seeing the reason in this.

"I'm not going to say that I agree with you two moving in together, but I know Cohen is trained well to take care of you and he's proven that he's willing to do whatever it takes to keep you safe in my eyes. Kills me, baby, to admit this, but you're better off staying put right here."

Oh wow. "That must have been hard to say," I say, trying to make light of how big this moment is.

"You have no idea." He smiles.

I look up at Cohen and give him a smile before I move to climb off his lap. He lets me go without argument, and I walk over, bend, and wrap my arms around my daddy's neck.

"You'll always be the first man I loved, Daddy."

"I know, little princess. I know."

I swallow the lump in my throat, kiss his tan cheek, and walk back over to Cohen. When I feel his arms wrap around my body again, I let their strength soak in, and I listen as the men in the room go about what the best course of action from here on out is.

I don't think I'll feel settled until the invisible threat around me is gone, but right here, in this moment, I feel as safe as I've ever felt in my life because I'm wrapped up in the arms of the man I love.

Chapter 35

Cohen

"DO YOU WANT MY COCK or my mouth, Dani?" I ask and trail my fingers down the center of her collarbone and between the valley of her tits.

"Your cock, baby," she pleads.

"Do you want my cock in your pussy or your ass?" I question, continuing my path down her body until my fingers dance over the smooth skin on her mound.

"My pussy?"

"You don't sound so sure about that, baby," I murmur and dip my finger into her body. "Although your cunt is begging for it. Is your ass going to milk my fingers if I dip them in deep?" I ask, pumping my fingers into her wet center.

"Ye-yes," she stutters.

"I'm sure it would, but right now, I want my cock right here," I say and curl my fingers until I hit that spot that has her juices running down my fingers and down her crack. "So responsive."

I pull my fingers out of her body, and she watches with heated eyes as I pop them in my mouth and hum.

"Fucking taste so good."

I push my fingers back in and give her a few hard pumps before I take them and offer them to her mouth, wiping her juices along the seam of her lips before she opens and sucks them clean.

"Fuck," I groan and move so that my cock is rubbing against her.

Her legs drop open and she starts to rock with my hips. My cock ring and other piercings make her cry out each time they roll over her clit.

"Do you want me hard or do you want me soft?" I ask, rocking even harder when those hot fucking mewling sounds start climbing up her throat.

"Soft . . . and hard," she pants.

"Yeah," I say and pull my hips back, and when I line up, I push home in one slow thrust. Her eyes go glossy and her moan is long. "Yeah, baby. Soft and hard."

I give her what she wants. Soft thrusts until my balls can't take it any longer. The second I feel her walls start to flutter and I know she's seconds away from coming apart in my arms, I start to slam into her hard enough that the headboard bangs against the wall. She takes every thrust I have, and right before I feel my balls tighten, she throws her head back and screams my name loud enough that the sound pierces my ears painfully. My climax tears through my body, and my cock is milked dry by her tight walls.

After a few more thrusts to feel her walls quivering against my sensitive cock, I pull out and lean back on my knees to watch our combined come drip out of her body.

"Fuck that's hot. I wish you could fucking see us falling out of your body," I tell her.

I bring my hand to her pussy and thrust my finger deep into her still-shuddering cunt. When I pull my finger out, it's gleaming with our joined come, and I look past her rapidly falling chest to meet her wide, turned-on eyes.

"You see how fucking hot we are together?"

She nods, and her eyes darken to the hunter-green color they always take when she's turned on.

"My girl likes that?" I ask and move my hand back down to her pussy. I rub my hand through her slit and rub our come into her skin. "Open," I demand and wait for her to understand my meaning.

My fingers, wet and dripping with *us,* start moving towards her head, and without question, she opens her mouth wide and waits for my fingers.

When her warm lips close around two of my wet fingers and suck me hard, I almost come again.

"Fucking hell," I groan.

"Mmmm," she moans in return, and I look down to see her rubbing her legs together.

"Already?" I question.

"Always," she retorts.

Fucking hell, indeed.

Hours later, with Dani passed out in my bed, I throw on some sweats and walk into the living room.

Chance sees me coming from his spot in the chair by the window and pulls off his Beats. "I take it I can remove these now?" he asks with a raised brow.

"She's asleep if that's what you're asking."

"She isn't screaming, so that's my answer."

"Did you find out anything?" I question, ignoring his comment.

"Nothing you're going to like."

"Well, fucking give it to me." I spit in his direction.

"Questioned each person who was in the salon when that package came. So far, I've been able to sit down with everyone except two people. Don W. Johnson—one personal assistant to Devon Westerfield—and one of their cameramen. That's as far as I've gotten. I looked into the background checks Axel had run when they first started coming around, but so far, nothing is sticking out. Devon, the producer, is being as helpful as he can. My gut tells me that he is no threat. His other assistant, Mark Seymour, has also been very forthcoming. He and Dani had struck up a friendship and he was very concerned about how she is fairing in light of all of this. He did mention that Don wasn't too happy about Dani being pregnant. Something about it putting a wrench into their filming."

"I see," I tell him, careful to calm myself before I snap about some douchebag being close with Dani.

"I'll keep digging."

"You do that," I tell him. "I'm taking Dani to look at houses next week. Are you sure you're cool with this?" I ask, knowing that, even though he's a loner as of late, that isn't something he deals with well. Chance has his own issues, but I know that the front he puts on for the world to see isn't the man I know.

"I'm not going to swallow a bottle of pills or cut my wrist because my buddy is moving out, Cohen. I'll be fine. Plus, I won't be around much anyway. We've picked up some big clients lately at CS and I'll be doing some bodyguard work until we can train more men."

"You'll let me know if the nightmares come back?" I ask.

"Fuck," he sighs and rubs the back of his neck. "Yeah, all right, I'll fucking let you know." He stands from his chair and walks over to the desk in the corner of the room, grabbing some papers and tossing them to me. "Printed the ones I felt would fit what you two need. Some I grabbed are a little more than you'll be needing right away, but with the way you two go at it, you'll need the space."

I look down, confused, and laugh when I see the handful of printouts of houses for sale he gave me. "Thanks, brother."

"Yeah," he mumbles and walks down the hall.

I wait until I hear his door click shut before I laugh to myself and toss them down on the coffee table before I pad back down the hall and climb back in bed with Dani in my arms.

Chapter 36

Dani

"I'M NOT SEEING HOW A house *this* big is something we need, Cohen." I look up at the large colonial house and my eyes hit every window—and there are many—and I look over to my left at the four-car garage that sits at an angle to the house. "Four cars seems like overkill."

"Nah," Cohen says and grabs my hand before pulling me up the front steps.

We've been house-hunting for the last three weeks and I'm over it. True to his word, he hasn't left me for a second. He came with me a few days after it was decided for me that I would move in with him and helped my brother and Lee move all of my stuff back out of the townhome I shared with the girls and into his apartment. Lee thought it was hilarious, and after Nate got over trying to act like our dad when it came to Cohen and me, he joined in and thought that my being basically kidnapped was the funniest thing he had ever seen.

Of course, that was after I kneed him in the balls.

Lyn and Lila were over the freaking moon about the new status in Cohen's and my relationship. Maddi was just happy I was happy. They thought that it was the best thing in the world.

Megan was the only voice of reason I had, but even that was short-lived when she witnessed firsthand how Cohen was around me. Her eyes got wet, and after I fussed, she told me that we reminded her of how her husband had been towards her when they'd first gotten together. Of course, that concerned me, but she was able to settle her emotions and, after that, was another cheerleader Cohen had in his corner.

After that, I just decided to say the hell with it and roll with what came.

We're about to be parents, so it makes sense.

Plus, there's that whole thing with my heart feeling like it's breaking in two when he isn't near.

All things considered, living with the man of my dreams and the love of my life isn't exactly a hardship.

Between looking for our future home, we've spent the last three weeks becoming closer than ever before. In between family dinners at either my parents' house or his, we've spent the majority of the time in bed either making love or talking about everything we can think of.

It's been some of the best times of my life.

"Come on, Dani-girl. There's something I want you to see," he says and gives my arm another tug.

"Okay, okay . . . Jeez," I laugh and follow him through the front door.

He leads me past the smiling real estate agent and up the huge staircase that dominates the front entry. He doesn't stop until we're both facing one of the many closed doors in the upstairs.

"Go ahead," he urges and nods to the door.

I give him a look but reach out and turn the nob. When my eyes settle around the room he's found, my lip quivers. "Oh, Cohen."

"It's perfect, hmm?" he says, coming up behind me and wrapping his arms around my body until he has his hands against my belly. His lips press against my temple. "I figured, with us deciding not to find out the gender, that this color would be perfect. You can match anything you want with a green like this. It reminded me of your eyes, and that made me think about our little one having the same green eyes as you, and it just seemed like a sign."

"It's perfect." And it is.

The large room has light-green walls and a dark hardwood finish. The back wall has a huge floor-to-ceiling window that overlooks the wooded backyard. I walk deeper into the room and notice the huge walk-in closet through one doorway. The other doorway leads into a connecting bathroom. I imagine where each item I have carefully planned on buying for our child would go, seeing the room come together instantly.

"This is it, Cohen," I tell him and watch his handsome face brighten with happiness.

"I hoped you would say that since I put an offer on this one last week."

"You did what?" I laugh. "Then why have we been looking at house after house since then?"

"Even on paper, it was perfect, Dani. There's more than enough room for us and our family to grow. I had no problem putting our future in writing. I wanted you to see your choices before I showed you mine. Had you liked something better, I would have pulled my offer and gotten you that one." He walks over and rubs my belly. "You, me, and baby against the world."

I nod my head and lean up on my tippy-toes to give him a kiss. "That's right, Superman." I giggle.

I'm not sure what kind of strings Cohen pulled to have us in our home so quickly, but not even a week after he showed me the beautiful home with our child's perfect nursery, we are moving our stuff in.

Against his better judgment and a lot of convincing from me that I would be perfectly fine at the apartment with Chance, Liam, and my brother—not to mention that my girls were all on their way to help—he left to meet with the realtor and the contractor we had hired to finish our basement and to wait for the furniture company to deliver ninety percent of our stuff. He had a busy day at the new house, and with all of us busy boxing up the rest of Cohen's and my stuff, it was best for him to leave me here to make sure it gets done.

"Chance!" I yell out Cohen's bedroom door. "Where is the packaging tape?"

When no one answers, I heave my almost eight-month-pregnant body off the floor and walk into the living room, where I left them arguing over which PlayStation games belong to Cohen and which ones he had stolen from them. Sometimes, I wonder if they're really grown children.

"Hey, where are you guys?" I ask, looking around.

"Danielle."

I jump and spin towards the familiar voice.

"I've been waiting for you."

My eyes widen when I see the blood staining the knife in his hands, and when I move my eyes back to his, I notice that they're wild.

Oh. My. God. This isn't happening. I quickly look around and search for the guys. The blood on his knife could only mean one thing, and my stomach drops when I realize what that is.

"Where are my friends?" I question. *Keep him talking* . . . I think that's what Dad said to do in a situation like this. Keep him talking until you can figure out a way to get help.

"Your *friends,*" he says as if the words taste bad against his lips. "Those men that you've been whoring yourself to aren't going to be a problem. The big one and your brother left a second ago, and I took care of that other motherfucker just like I took care of Don and Clint."

"Don and Clint? Clint the cameraman? What are you talking about, Mark?"

"I saw the way they looked at you. Always looking at you. And you let them. You shouldn't have done that, Danielle." He laughs, the sound making my skin crawl. "You shouldn't encourage that they had a chance with you. *YOU* are mine and I'm tired of watching you act like a slut when you know, YOU KNOW, what we have."

I gape at him, dumbfounded. "I have no idea what you're talking about, Mark." A sense of dread starts to take hold of my body, and I try to think of a way out of this mess.

Until he speaks again and I'm shocked to my core.

"I saw the way that you would look at me. I know you felt it. All of our dates we would have. When you would tell me what you loved about me as a boyfriend. I remember it all, Danielle. But you've been a naughty girl. It's time to take care of all of these . . . complications." He waves the knife around until the tip is pointing down. At my swollen belly.

"No," I gasp and clutch my stomach. "No!" My scream goes unnoticed by him as he takes a step forward. "Mark, those weren't dates. We had lunch—with about five other people—in the breakroom at Sway's. That was it. You were asking my advice for the girl you were dating. Mark, we aren't anything." My attempt at reasoning with him only angers him further.

"No!" he bellows, repeatedly jabbing the knife in my direction. "We're EVERYTHING!" his voice takes on a manic level of insanity, and he starts to advance on me.

"Please . . . I'm begging you. Don't hurt my baby. I'll do whatever you want, but please!"

"That," he says harshly. "That is an abomination and it must be removed from you. I won't stand for it."

I grip my stomach tighter and sob. The tears mix with the snot as they roll down my face. The hope I was holding on to that I would be able to talk him off the ledge starts to dwindle. I look around again, praying that I'll find something that will give me the answer on how to escape this impending doom.

This is it. I'm going to die right here where my future started. Right where it started, we're going to die, and I know there is no way Cohen will survive this kind of loss. That knowledge and my love for him are the only hope I have left. I spot the lamp just an inch away from my fist right when Mark makes his move and lunges forward. Given the fact that my belly has gotten huge in the last seven weeks since Cohen returned home, my movements are slower than normal, and right when I feel his knife pierce my left side, I heave the lamp with everything I have and clip him right on his temple.

Mark goes down hard, dazed but not out, so I bring my arm back—weakly now that my side is killing me—and swing at him again. His lifts and his knife digs into the top of my hip. Desperate to do what I can to protect my stomach, I twist and fight with everything I have in me. If this is the last moment I have on this Earth, I'm not going to be taken out easily.

"Stop fucking moving so I can get that thing out of you!" he bellows, and it isn't lost on me just how far gone he is on the sanity scale.

"You won't get my baby, you sick fuck!" I scream, and with a renewed strength, I start to kick my legs between driving the heavy lamp down onto his face. “You can’t have my baby,” I sob, my body growing weaker. “Never!” I scream out and never stop, my throat burning with the raw sounds coming out.

I feel it before my mind registers that there is nothing else I can do, and as my body is pulled down with nothing left to give, I use the last bit of my strength to twist so that, when I fall, my baby is protected.

Chapter 37

Liam

"HOW HARD WOULD IT HAVE been to carry this shit down when Cohen got here and could help us?" I ask Nate after dusting my hands off on my jeans.

We've just spent the better part of thirty minutes trying to get Cohen's big-ass seventy-inch television down three flights of stairs and attempted to get the damn thing loaded into the back of my truck without breaking it.

"It seemed easier than it was when I planned it out in my head. It's not my fault it's heavier than it looks. Damn thing looked like it would be easy."

Yeah. Famous last words of Nate Reid.

"Plus, if Chance wouldn't have been so fucking lazy, he could have helped out too."

"Chance"—I reach over and shove Nate as we start to walk back up the stairs—"is up there keeping an eye on Dani. Something that, I'll remind you, *we* should be doing as well."

"Seriously, Lee? She's right up there! What the hell is going to happen in the two seconds we took to take care of that shit?" He pulls his UGA ball cap off and scratches his thick, black hair before jamming it back down. "Fuck, it's hot out here."

Right when my booted foot touches the bottom step, I hear a sound that stops my heart. I look over at Nate to see if he heard it and see all the color drain from his face.

"Fuck!" I yell and start to bound up the steps in threes. "Call Cohen, Nate. Call Cohen and then call your dad." I keep running, letting my training take over and my instincts kick in.

For the last two months, I've been in training with the local police department, and for the first time, I'm thankful for every second of that training. I don't look behind me to see if Nate's coming. I grab my cell and dial 911 as I continue up the stairs. As I reach their landing, the operator picks up and I give her the short version of what I know. Which is nothing. After rattling off Cohen's address and telling her to send an ambulance as well as the police, I stop talking and ease up on the cracked door.

"Sir, is the intruder still on the scene?" the female voice says through the line.

I feel Nate coming up behind me and hand him the phone. I hardly register his response to the operator. When I don't hear anything from inside the apartment, I slowly toe open the door and ease inside.

What I see is a scene I will never forget. If I should live to be one hundred, this image will still be branded in my mind. The walls, floor, and tan couches are all stained red.

Blood red.

I can't see over the loveseat that blocks the view from the doorway into the living room, but I see Chance's crumpled form behind it, and I slowly move towards him and check for a pulse.

Strong and steady, thank Christ.

He has one hell of a bump forming on his forehead, and I check the knife wound he has to his left shoulder, but it's a clean cut that isn't bleeding heavily anymore.

I stand, move around the chair, and feel a sob bubble up my throat.

"Dani!" I yell and rush towards her. I step over the unrecognizable man that is lying—unmoving—in front of her.

"He has the knife," I hear Nate say weakly behind me. He rushes forward and kicks it away before checking the douchebag for a pulse. "Fuck! She fought, Lee. She fought while we were down there dicking around with a goddamn TV!" He stands and kicks the body behind me. “She fought hard enough that she killed a man threatening her with a knife with a damn lamp.”

I don’t move my eyes from Dani as I check for her pulse and find it weakly beating against my fingertips. “Help me stop the bleeding until the ambulance gets here, Nate!”

We both rush, careful of her pregnant stomach, and hold down the wounds we can, and I look into Nate’s eyes and see the same panic I feel.

That panic never leaves. Not while we soak through the towels we have held against her body and not when I notice that the pulse I keep checking is slowing down.

Not once—even when the paramedics rush through the door and take over care.

It doesn’t stop as we rush behind them as they carry an unmoving Dani on a stretcher.

And not when we’re speeding down the highway behind them on the way to the hospital.

That panic never leaves, and I know that, if Dani doesn’t make it, it’s a feeling I’ll never get over.

“Did you get Cohen?” I whisper towards Nate.

He’s rubbing his bloodstained hands together and doesn’t move his eyes from the back of the ambulance holding his sister.

“No.”

I look away from the road, shocked. “No?”

“He didn’t answer and I rushed after you before I called back. I’ll do that now,” he says with a monotone voice. His movements are robotic as he grabs my cell from the cupholder between us and presses the screen until I hear the ringing echoing throughout the cab.

“What’s up, Lee?” Cohen asks when the call connects. He sounds happy, I notice. “I should be back soon. I’ve—”

“Coh,” I say, my voice cracking.

He doesn’t say anything until I hear him roar through the phone. “Where is she?” he screams. “Where the fuck is she?!” I can hear the strain in his voice, and I imagine that he’s running towards his truck.

“We’re headed to Grady Memorial, Cohen. She’s in the ambulance in front of us.”

"Is she—"

"I don't know, brother. I honestly just don't know."

Cohen disconnects the call, but not before I hear the sob that tears out of his throat.

Another thing I'll never forget.

Never.

Chapter 38

Cohen

MY MIND GETS ME TO Grady on autopilot.

Every second it takes to get me there feels like eternity. Not knowing how she is, the status of her injuries, is like fuel to the fire of my misery.

After slamming the truck in park, I jump out and run towards the emergency entrance.

Fifteen minutes *after* the call from Lee.

Fifteen unknown minutes filled with thoughts of Dani and our child.

"Coh."

I look over when I hear Lee croak out my name, and when I take in his appearance, I drop to my knees and feel every second of those fifteen minutes weighing me down as I cry out for my family.

It isn't until I feel two strong hands press down on my shoulders that I look up and see both my father and Dani's standing on either side of my fallen body.

"Get up, son. Get up and pull yourself together and be there for Dani and the baby. Until you hear otherwise, you don't ever fucking give up hope," my dad says and holds his hand out to help me stand.

I nod and accept his hand, standing and turning towards Axel. His eyes are red and bright with emotion. He doesn't even try to stop the tears that are falling.

"Her mother will be here soon. She was at the salon when we got word. Melissa went to get her. Let's go get word on our girl so that I can give my wife something good to focus on, yeah?" He doesn't stick around to see if I follow.

I push down my despair and follow behind my girl's father, praying with every fiber in my being that we get that good news.

When Izzy came crashing through the emergency room doors with Melissa, Dee, and Sway hot on her heels, we were still waiting for word from the doctor. Shortly after they arrived, my sisters and brothers rushed in. Lyn and Lila rushed to my side and wrapped their arms around me. My brothers, never the ones to wear their emotions on their sleeves, went to Mom's side but looked at me with unmasked sympathy.

It didn't take long before we had overtaken the emergency room and were taken to a private room. Maddox and Asher showed up with their families in tow. Beck came in next, and after checking on Lee, he grabbed his wife and has held them both in his arms since. Megan was the last one to show, explaining that she got here as quickly as she could find a sitter for Molly.

Chance walked into the room last, and there wasn't an eye that didn't land on him. I untangled my body from the girls and walked over to him, grabbing his shoulder and pulling his body in toward mine, hugging him tight.

"I'm sorry," he rasps. "I'm so fucking sorry. I didn't even see him," His voice breaks, and I hold him as he loses it.

"Don't. He got the jump on you, Chance. You can't blame yourself for a crazy fuck getting the jump on you."

"It was my job to keep her safe, Cohen. My fucking job."

"No, it was my job. A job that, when she pulls through from this, I will never, not once, take a break from," I vow.

I can tell he doesn't believe me. His guilt and worry are getting the best of him. I shake my head, and after watching him walk over to the chairs on the other side of the room—away from everyone else, who's huddled together—I walk back over to where Lyn and Lila are sobbing softly to each other and take them in my arms.

And wait.

"Reid family?"

My eyes snap up from the floor, and I rush from my post against the wall.

"Yeah. That's me. Well, us. That's us."

"And you are?" the doctor asks.

"Her husband," I hear and look over my shoulder to see Axel stand next to me. "And I'm her father. How is my daughter?"

The doctor looks between Axel and me before he moves his eyes to the clipboard in his hands.

"Sir, your wife lost a good bit of blood, but we were able to replenish that quickly and she was very lucky that her wounds weren't deeper than they were. The blade missed two major arteries by a hair. She went into labor in transit, and after delivery, our major concern was blood loss and the wound that she had gotten to her side. I can't stress enough just how lucky your wife is."

"She's okay?" I question.

The doctor looks between us again, and for the first time, I notice the noise around us as the family realizes that she's alive and going to be fine.

"The baby?" Axel asks.

And just like that, the room is silenced.

"Ah . . ." He looks down at his notes. "You'll have to excuse me. I was in charge of your wife, and after delivery, she became my sole patient." He moves a few things before pausing to read some notes. "It says here that the baby is in the NICU at the moment being monitored, but for a thirty-two-week baby, his vitals are strong."

"His?" I choke out.

"Yes, his. Congratulations. You have a son."

And then I pass out.

Chapter 39

Dani

I OPEN MY EYES AND jerk when my last memories hit my like a tsunami.

Mark. The knife. The lamp. And my will to live—to fight.

"She's waking up, honey."

I move my head and look at my mom, who is standing on the left side of my bed. My daddy is standing right behind her with his arms wrapped tight around her, their eyes red and swollen. I move my eyes around the room and see Nate, his eyes dripping with tears. I give him a weak smile, and he turns his face from mine as he struggles to take control of his emotions.

I continue my rotation until I look down at the weight pressing against my hip. The dark-brown hair buzzed on the side and over-grown on the top. The strong shoulders heaving with emotion. And I feel his tears wetting my hand he's holding against his parted lips.

My heart breaks for the pain he's in, and I know there isn't any-thing I can do to ease it until he works out on his own whatever is running through his mind. I squeeze him, anxious to see those dark-brown eyes. I need him to see that I'm okay—I need to see that *he's* okay.

"Cohen—" I rasp and clear my throat. "Baby," I beg, feeling my own tears roll down my cheeks.

His shoulders start to heave when my voice hits his ears. I watch helplessly as the man I love falls apart. I look over to my parents and pray for answers, but I watch as my mom's own tears cascade down her porcelain skin. My dad has his head bowed and his forehead resting against her shoulder, his body hunched in a way I know can't be comfortable. I hear the door click and look over to see that Nate has left the room.

Without getting any help, I move my attention back to Cohen and try again. "Baby, please look at me. I need your eyes."

He struggles to control his emotions, and I watch with my eyes filling with tears as he lifts his head and I get a good look at my handsome man.

His chocolate eyes are filled with pain, and through the red-rimmed swelling around them, his tears continue to fall. His lips are dry from what I'm guessing is the sobbing I felt against my skin.

I reach up and run my fingers across his cheek. "It's you and me against the world, Cohen. Never goodbye, remember?"

He closes his eyes at my words and gives me a nod. I watch as he struggles again, but he wins against his pain, and when he opens his eyes again, I see *my* Cohen looking back at me.

"Just see you soon," he sighs.

"Every time I close my eyes."

He smiles. It's slightly wobbly, but it's a smile nonetheless, and I return it.

"We have a son," he says in reverence.

"He's okay?" I study his face for clues, and when the little sadness that was left in his eyes vanishes and he hits me with the full force of his smile, my heart bursts.

"He's perfect."

"Perfect," I cry. "Tell me more," I beg.

"He's big considering he was preterm. Just under five pounds, but he's a fighter, Dani-girl. They have him in NICU being monitored, but when I spoke to the nurse, she said she could see him coming home in a month at the most. He looks like me," he adds with his smile growing. "With your lips."

I soak it in, the fact that we have a son. Cohen and my baby together. Our little fighter.

Seems fitting that a love we've both been fighting to withstand, overcome, and, in the end, fight for would produce a little miracle that was a fighter in his own right.

"Our little fighter," I say, repeating the words I just thought.

He nods, and I swallow the lump in my throat.

"I thought I lost you," he says after studying my face for the longest time.

"Never, baby. Never."

"I thought I lost you, and that was one of the most terrifying experiences I have ever felt. I won't spend another second without you being mine. I mean it, Dani. When we get you and our boy home, I'll drag you right to the courthouse, but you will be mine."

I reach out, wrap my hand around the back of his neck, and pull him towards me. "When you learn how to ask me, then we'll talk."

His eyes flash, and his leans down to give me a deep kiss. I hear a growl from my side and smile against his lips.

"Hush, Axel."

I feel Cohen laughing softly against my mouth, and I join him only seconds after.

Four Weeks Later

"Cohen!" I yell up the stairs. "We don't need the diaper bag. Come on please. I need to get him home."

I smile when he comes bounding down the stairs and scoops me up in his arms, twirling me in a circle before placing me back on my feet.

"Our boy is coming home today!" he bellows through the room, the sound bouncing off each wall and echoing through our house.

"Stop acting crazy and take me to our son," I beg with a smile on my face.

For four long weeks—a solid month of going back and forth—we've been spending every second we had between the house and the hospital. With the help of our mothers, his sisters, and Megan, our house was fully decorated and the baby's nursery fully stocked before I even left the hospital. They kept me for four days to monitor my injuries as well as my recovery from my C-section, and since my emotions were so crazy when I got home, I cried for hours as I walked from room to room before finally settling in the nursery glider.

It was hard to come home without our baby, and I suffered from a bit of postpartum depression, so things amplified after that. I needed my son home and there just wasn't anything that would make that feeling better.

Cohen was my rock through it all. He held me when I needed to cry and then again when I needed to scream. He talked me through every second of pain I felt over the events that had happened and taught me that it wasn't right to feel guilt over a second of it.

Easier said than done. Because some crazy man had fixated on me, and I'd entertained that by thinking he was a friend. We'd almost lost our son—and Cohen had almost lost us both.

I know it's irrational, that guilt, but it's part of the healing process. Or so I'm told by my therapist. But it's a feeling I'm not alone in carrying. Nate had a hard time coping after the attack. He felt guilt worse than mine because he hadn't been in the room. Lee was dealing with similar issues, but he was able to rationalize his pain and focus on the positive—that he was able to save me. They have both joined me for more than a few of my therapy sessions, and I know they've been helping us all heal. Cohen is there for everyone. We've talked about how he felt and how he's coping with it all. I wasn't surprised in the least that he was still feeling a deep fear about losing me.

He's been working on his issues with letting me out of his sight. It took my father's sitting him down for him to finally come to terms with the fact that what had happened was a horrible, traumatic experience, and that, if we can't focus on moving forward and healing, then it will just drag us down until we're smothered in memories.

In the end, we were helpless and in a situation beyond our control. Had it not been for their swift response, I have no doubt that both the baby and I would have died in that apartment.

Chance is another part of the reason I've been struggling with so much pain. It kills me that he blamed himself—likely still does. But until he's ready to cope with that and work on healing, I'm afraid there isn't anything I can do.

It's been easier. He comes around, but I notice that his eyes never leave mine. Like he's afraid to look away for fear that someone might attack. He threw himself into the investigation of Mark Seymour like a man possessed.

We found out about two weeks after I was released from the hospital that Mark had been staying in the apartment directly under Cohen's. Not only had he been watching me for over a year, but he had also had a sick collection of photos of him and me that were horribly Photoshopped. He had created a whole fantasy life—albums after albums of us.

If that weren't bad enough, he had set up the apartment with items of mine that he had stolen throughout the year. Things I hadn't even known were missing. He had a whole life made up for us, and the only thing that was missing was . . . me.

After his death, the police were able to locate the bodies of the two men he had slain before he'd stormed us that day. He had left detailed notes about where he'd tossed their bodies. At least, with that, their families would get some closure.

It's been hard for everyone. We are struggling with just how insane the man who almost stole my life before it could truly begin was, but we're all slowly healing. Today will be a big step in that process.

"I can't wait to get him home, Cohen. To show him the house and have him under our roof."

Cohen reaches over and grabs my hand, the one he placed a ridiculously huge diamond on three weeks ago—without proposing. "Same here, Dani-girl. It's going to feel damn good to have my family together in our home." He kisses my knuckles, flicks my ring with his thumb, and looks out the windshield with a huge grin.

We make it to the hospital in record time and have our son discharged and strapped to his car seat as soon as the last form is signed. I hug all the nurses we had gotten to know over the last month, and we make quick work of leaving the hospital behind on our way back to our house.

It is past time to get our family home.

Owen—meaning little fighter—James Cage. Our gorgeous son. I

smile to myself and look over at his sleeping face from my spot in the back seat.

Just like Cohen said, Owen looks just like him. His dark hair, tan skin, and perfectly handsome face.

But those lips are all mine.

Chapter 40

Dani

IT'S BEEN TWO WEEKS SINCE we brought Owen home from the hospital, and leaving him today for my six-week checkup was harder than I ever imagined. Cohen and I had agreed that, since the visit would be a short one and I could pump any milk Cohen would need to feed him while I was gone, I would use this as a dry run to leave the baby.

In the last two weeks, I've struggled to do something as mundane as take a shower. The fear I've had over letting him out of my sight is unexplainable. I know Cohen is worried about me, so I agreed with him more or less to placate his concerns.

But sitting here, with the paper sheet over my naked bottom half while my ass sits on the cold chair, isn't making me feel like I've hit some big milestone. It makes me feel like I need to have my baby in my arms.

"I think it's time to stop freaking out, Dani."

I look up, meet my mom's eyes, and give her a small smile. I don't even try to hide my mild embarrassment.

"I understand how you feel, my darling girl, but leaving your son for a few hours isn't the end of the world. It's good for him to bond with his father alone—or his grandparents. I'm not saying you should start planning vacations, but sitting at home day in and day out while never letting him out of your sight isn't healthy."

I sigh. "I know." And I do. I know it isn't normal, but I can't seem to get my body to get with the program and physically leave him.

"If it would make you feel better, we can call Cohen. He can give you the reassurance that you need."

I shake my head, knowing that, if I call home thirty minutes after leaving to check on Owen, all it will do is make Cohen worry about me more. "No. I trust Cohen, and I know he won't let anything happen to Owen. I just need to get over my issues that something bad is going to happen. Ever since the whole . . . Mark thing, I keep thinking that something else is going to come and take away my happiness."

Mom sighs and walks over to me, grabbing my hand and looking me in the eyes. "There isn't one thing in this life that's a guarantee, Dani. Nothing. I've lived a life that I can say that with clarity. But if you continue to have yourself stuck in the past of worry and fear, there is no way you're going to be able to enjoy the life and future you hold in your hands."

I study her face, finding love in her eyes and the hope that I understand what she's saying.

"I need to get out of my head," I respond.

"Yeah, sweetheart. You need to get out of your head," she says with another big smile.

I felt a little better after my doctor's visit. The two hours I had been gone from the house didn't feel as stifling by the time Mom pulled us back up to the house and I rushed through the door, eager to see my boys.

I smile when I hear Cohen muttering to the television at whatever sports show he's watching. When I round the corner and see him sitting in our big, overstuffed chair with Owen laying on his naked chest, my heart swells. He has his thick hand resting under the baby's diaper-padded bum, and I smile when I see Owen's big, round—blue for the moment—eyes looking off at nothing. His fist is pulled up to his thick, Cupid-bowed lips, and he's sucking away while his father explains to him the finer points of football.

"You look cozy," I hum. Walking around the couch, I slide onto

Cohen's lap and run my fingers over Owen's silky-smooth skin. "How was he?"

"Fine, Dani-girl. Just like I told you he would be. You're looking at the extent of our day of fun."

"Oh, a little party animal, huh?" I joke.

"What did the doctor say?" Cohen asks, shifting his weight so that I can crawl into the chair next to him.

I place my head against his shoulder and look into Owen's eyes. I lay my hand against his back, and Cohen's rests over mine.

"Everything looks good on the healing end. He still wants me to wait a few more weeks before we resume any sexual activities or exercising. I think that, with everything that happened, he just wants to make sure my body has time to heal. Especially since I explained that our workouts tend to be a little . . . vigorous."

"Vigorous, huh?" Cohen laughs. "Everything else looked okay though?"

"Yeah." I pause and look up at him. "I talked to him about my separation anxiety, and he's given me some antidepressant medication to take for a while. Given everything we've been through, I think it's a good call. But I feel a lot better abut not being around Owen all of the time. Leaving today helped a lot."

"I'm glad, baby. I was worried."

"I know you were and I'm sorry."

"Don't be sorry. I love that you love our boy so much that you don't want to be without him, but you have to make sure that you're taking care of yourself too. I can't stand the thought of something happening to you, Dani-girl."

"I'm not going anywhere," I tell him—not for the first time.

"Yeah, baby, and neither is our boy."

I look up at him, and I think for the first time that I really get what he's trying to tell me and has been trying to impress upon me since we got home with Owen.

I nod my head and give him a smile before returning my head to his shoulder so that I can look into our boy's eyes. I let the love I feel for both of these people wrap around me, and I fall asleep while Cohen holds us both safe within his arms.

Chapter 41

Cohen

OWEN'S TAKEN TO THE CHANGE from hospital to home like a champ. Though I'm not shocked that my son is perfect. He's a calm baby who only fusses when he wants to eat. Or when he wants his mother's attention, but I can't fault him there. When I want his mother's attention, I get fussy too. The first month home was a slight challenge. Between Dani's not wanting and not feeling like she couldn't leave our son and our getting used to having a little human to care for, we were slow in adjusting to our new life. Now, though? Now, we're freaking pros.

Dani has gotten so much better about leaving Owen. It started small. The doctor visit, then a quick run to the store, and eventually, she was able to leave without thought. Of course, I think a lot of that had to do with her finally realizing that, by letting her fear consume her, she wasn't able to enjoy the life we had.

I walk down the hall in search of my woman. She took Owen to his room to get him dressed for the day out, and I haven't seen her in almost thirty minutes. Which usually means she's breastfeeding.

Not shockingly, the sight of her breastfeeding my son has been a major turn-on for me. Since she isn't clear for sex yet, the fact that I almost come in my pants when she pulls her swollen tits out and I see them leaking with milk . . . Yeah, she started leaving the room when Owen needed to eat after that. I have no clue why I find it so fucking hot, but when I see her tits leak, all I can think about is pushing them together and fucking her tits while her milk works as lube.

Goddamn, I need to go jerk off again. I press my hand against my cock—which is now standing at full attention—and continue my search for her. It's been eight weeks; if I don't have my wife soon, I might die. Literally die. From blue balls.

"Our mothers are on the way, Dani," I say when I find her rocking in the glider in Owen's nursery. I bend to kiss her before placing a kiss on Owen's soft head. "And from what my dad said, they have every bridal magazine known to man. I told you—the court house is just a second away, baby."

"I didn't get my proposal. I'm getting my wedding," she smarts.

"So I've been told. How much longer until you're done planning this damn thing, Dani? I need you to be mine."

She smiles but doesn't answer. I give her another kiss before standing and walking out of Owen's nursery. I've been summoned to the CS offices today, and it's been a request I've put off for the month since we brought home Owen. Time to suck it up and leave my house—even if the thought of leaving Dani and Owen has my stomach in knots.

Yeah. Hey, pot. Meet kettle. I harp on Dani about getting over her fears, but I'm just as bad.

I run down the stairs and into the kitchen to get breakfast ready for Dani. She's been running on fumes lately since Owen has been going through some growth spurt and feeding more than usual. Even though it isn't much, at least it's something I can do to help.

"Hey, baby?" Dani says, walking into the kitchen a short while later. "Mmm, that smells good." She walks by, Owen in her arms, and snags a piece of bacon off the plate. "My mom texted and asked if you could bring me over to her place on your way to the office. It would be easier since all of the wedding planning stuff they've been collecting is over there anyway."

I wave her off when she goes to nab another piece. "Yeah, baby."

"I can drive us over if you need to get down to CS," she offers, her head tilting slightly.

"No, Dani-girl. It's never a problem if I'm a little late because I'm taking care of my family." And it isn't. They are and forever will be my number-one priority.

"So," she starts, and something in her tone has me looking away from the eggs and waiting for her to finish. "My mom mentioned keeping Owen tonight. I think we should take advantage, baby. I can pump enough so that she has all the milk she needs and we can celebrate my eight-week mark."

I feel my brows pull in as I try to understand what she's saying. "I'm a little lost here?" I try to play it off, but the fact that she's talking about leaving him overnight is a huge milestone here.

"I noticed. Had you realized what I was talking about, I'm pretty sure breakfast would be forgotten and we would have Owen dropped off already. It's been two weeks since my appointment with the doctor, baby. He said eight weeks until all activities could return as normal. It's time to make love to your woman."

And then I switch off the burner, eggs forgotten, and rush up the stairs to pack Owen's bag.

Tonight, I fuck my woman.

Dani

"I thought you wouldn't ever get over here," Lyn complains and reaches out to take Owen from my arms. She doesn't even pay me any attention as she walks over to the couch and starts to make baby sounds in Owen's face.

Lila rolls her eyes and takes Owen's bag from me. "Come on. The makeup guru is waiting for you."

Following her lead, I walk into a kitchen full of insanity. My mom is running around with her hair in rollers, Melissa is barking at a Mexican man who looks terrified, and Maddi is standing with her hands on her hips, clearly not happy that I'm late.

"Sorry," I grumble and sit in the chair she's pointing to.

"How hard was it to stay on track, Dani? How hard, huh?" she snaps and starts to apply my makeup. I wisely decide to keep my mouth shut and let her do what she does best.

I feel my hair move, and I open my eyes.

Sway pops his head around and gives me a big smile. "Almost show time, little mama." He reaches over my shoulder, and I slap his hand away when I feel him trying to pop my top button.

"You crazy man!"

He laughs, straightens, and starts to work on my hair.

Almost an hour later, my hair is pulled back in a loose chignon and my makeup is done flawlessly in a natural way that highlights all of my features. My eyes are lined heavily to showcase my eyes, and Maddi decided to paint my lips a bright red.

I walk into my parents' bedroom, and with the help of Melissa, I step into my dress. She gives me a huge hug and quickly walks from the room, but not before I see the first tear fall from her eyes.

"Mom!" I call as I walk through the insanity.

Lyn is trying to step into her dress without letting her sister hold Owen. Maddi is finishing up Stella's makeup while doing hers as well. Sway's decided that Owen's little baby hair needs to be styled into some type of baby mohawk. Megan and Molly are laughing from the sidelines as Sway starts to make blowfish faces at the baby.

"Out here, baby."

I follow the sound of her voice out the back door and onto the back deck.

When my eyes take in the transformation their backyard has taken, I take a deep breath and will myself to believe that this moment is happening.

Today, I'm surprising the man of my dreams with the wedding he's been begging for. He's waited this long, and I know he would have waited longer, but I'm ready to be Dani Cage. For our family to become whole.

With our fathers' help, I had them enlist him in some case they needed help with at CS, and I got a promise from both of them that they wouldn't return him home until later that evening.

They have one job: get my man to the end of the dock before the sun sets on the lake. Well, I should say that Greg has one job since, as I look down at the backyard, I meet the very emotional eyes of Axel Reid, and I smile as my daddy visibly struggles to get a hold of his emotions.

"You look like a little princess," his awestruck voice whispers hoarsely. "I can't believe this day has come. My baby is getting married."

"Do you need a tissue, Daddy?" I joke.

"Very funny." He reaches over and carefully pulls me against his body.

I dust a piece of lint off of his tux-covered chest.

"No matter where you are in the world, you will always be *my* little princess, Dani. Married or not, you were my girl first. I love you, baby. I know I don't say it often, because we wouldn't want him to get a big head, but I'm thrilled with the man who won your heart."

I struggle with the lump in my throat and, in the end, settle for a nod of my head.

"I knew you would grow into a beautiful woman, and I'm damn proud of who you've become. I know, with Cohen by your side and Owen in your arms, that beauty is just going to blossom even further." He leans down and kisses my head before walking away.

I let him go, knowing that he needs the same moment with his thoughts that I do.

I keep my eyes on the family as they move around the tables set up on the back lawn and smile when I see the lights strung out along the railing on the deck. They light the way that will bring Cohen to me in just one short hour.

Cohen

Fucking pointless afternoon. My dad and Maddox kept me up to my elbows in old case files. Anything from the last ten years that had gone cold was suddenly something I needed to help them with right that second.

I finally had enough when I realized it was getting closer to dinnertime and the only thing I had on my mind was getting to my girl and getting her back home.

"I'm done. We can pick this up another day? Right now, I'm going to Axel's house and I'm taking my girl home for our first night alone."

"Alone?" Dad questions.

"Her parents offered to keep Owen tonight so we can have some alone time."

He gives me a knowing look. "Ah. It's all-clear time." He throws his head back and gives a booming laugh. "I completely understand, son."

"I hear you," Maddox adds in. "One of the best nights with Emmy was when the doctor finally cleared her after having our girls. I swear she turned into an animal."

My dad goes to open his mouth, but I stop him with my hand. "Don't even think about adding to that. I don't want to know about it and I damn sure don't want to think about it."

They laugh, and I narrow my eyes.

When I stand from the conference room table, Dad reaches his hand out and grabs my arm. "Go into the back bathroom There's something in there for you."

"What the hell?" I ask his back, and he and Maddox walk out of the room. "Crazy old man."

I walk toward the back bathroom, and when I walk in to see a perfectly pressed tux, I feel my eyes narrow in confusion. Seeing the note that's attached to the hanger, I snatch it off and read the words that bring a rush of overwhelming love through my body.

Today, I marry my best friend. I marry my lover. I marry my heart. I love you. I'll see you where it all began.

I turn the paper over and feel the lump in my throat grow when I look at the picture Dani wrote her message on. The picture she'd had blown up and placed over her bed when I was overseas.

The one of her in my arms at the end of her parents' dock when we were just children.

It takes me no time to shed my clothes and don the tux. The promise of marrying my girl is all I need to get to the Reids' house as quickly as possible.

Today, I'm marrying my girl.

Chapter 42

Cohen

I'M NOT SURE WHAT I expected to happen when I got to Axel and Izzy's house. I was prepared for anything. I think one part of me expected Axel to jump my ass the second I stepped foot on his property.

However, what I am met with almost brings me to my knees. My mom opens their door with tears streaming down her smiling face, and without a word, she hands me my son. I watch her walk away, her light-blue dress flowing behind her, before I look down at my wiggling boy.

Owen is dressed similarly to me, a little tux looking as out of place on my little baby's body as I feel like it does on mine.

"Hey, little man," I say softly and notice the piece of paper sticking out of his mini jacket. "What do you have for Daddy, baby boy?"

He looks me in the eye, his mouth puckering up with the cutest little pout. He's content to be held in his father's arms. He's filled out so much in the last two months that he's started to get the most adorable chubby cheeks.

God, my son is perfect.

Carefully, I adjust Owen in my arms and unfold the paper I pulled from his little jacket.

Mommy says that she's ready to be a family . . . officially.

I smile when I read the words and feel my heart beat wildly in my chest. With my son in my arms and a smile on my face, I take off in the direction my mom went—through their large living room, then through their kitchen, and out on the back deck. I still don't see anyone, so I keep walking until Owen and I are standing against the railing, looking down at every family member and friend we love.

My dad is standing with my mom, my sisters and brothers at his side, all of them beaming. Axel is next to him with Izzy between his arms and Nate at his side. Again, not one of them is missing a huge grin. I follow the lines of Maddox's family, Beck's, Asher's, and Sway's. I see Megan and Molly and Chance before my eyes follow the white flower trail that leads me to the end of the dock.

Where I see a vision in white that has my eyes stinging. There, waiting with a smile on her face and tears in her eyes, is *my* Dani-girl.

"Let's go get the girl, son." I whisper to Owen.

I walk down the stairs that bring me to the backyard and walk through the lines of our loved ones until I reach our parents. I look to my left and smile at my parents and siblings, handing Owen to Lyn when her arms come up.

"I love you, son." My dad says gruffly.

"We're so happy for you and Dani," Mom says. "I love you, handsome boy."

I give them each a kiss before facing Dani's parents.

Her mom wraps her arms around me, giving my cheek a quick

kiss. Her eyes are wet and shining with happiness. I give Nate a slap on the back and laugh when he puckers up. Then I look at Axel.

I am prepared for battle, but when I see his eyes—bright with happiness and not anger—I am momentarily struck dumb.

"You didn't think I would be able to do it, did you?" he asks me.

"Not for a second," I laugh.

"If you make her cry one tear that isn't out of happiness, I'll cut your balls off," he warns.

"Noted."

"I'm proud of you, Cohen. Of the man you've grown to be and for the love you have for my girl. I mean it when I say that I couldn't have picked a better man for her myself."

"Thank you for that," I tell him honestly. No matter what I said in the past, having his blessing was something I desired when it came to Dani becoming my wife. "She's my life," I remind him.

"I know the feeling," he says and looks down the dock. "Go on and stop keeping my daughter waiting."

I nod, taking a few measured breaths before I turn and let my eyes take her in.

She's wearing a simple, long, and flowing, white dress. It fits tight to her body while still rippling in the slight breeze around us. Her shoulders are bare, and with her hair swept away from her face, she looks so angelic with the sun setting behind her and casting a soft glow around her body.

I take the last remaining steps that take me to where she is standing with the man I assume is the minister.

"Surprised?" she asks.

"Yeah, baby."

"Are you ready to be my husband?"

I smile. "I was born ready, my Dani-girl."

And with the sun setting around us, our family surrounding us, I marry my unexpected fate.

By the time we were able to get away from the family and I was able to pull Dani away from Owen without having her melt down, the sun had long since set and my girl had become my wife. We danced and ate. Laughed and smiled. It was a magical night full of love. We danced our first dance together as man and wife to Brett Young's "Kiss by Kiss," and I held her in my arms while she softly cried. When my lips dropped to hers and I heard the all-familiar growl at my side, she threw her head back and her laughter rained down on me.

It was equal parts joyful and torture because all I could think about was getting her home. Since the second my lips touched hers after the minister pronounced us man and wife, I've been rock hard to take my wife and make her mine in every way that counts.

"Slow down, husband," she snickers when I pull her from the truck and up to our porch. Her squeal when I pull her up into my arms is like music to my ears.

"Are you ready for me to carry you over the threshold, wife?"

She smiles her radiant smile and nods her head.

I don't waste a second. The key hits the lock, and in a flash, I have her rushed through, slamming the door behind us. She reaches out and keys in the code to our alarm, and the second I hear her reactivate it, I bound up the stairs. Her pearls of laughter trail behind us and don't stop until I prowl into our bedroom and toss her in the air and onto the middle of our mattress.

She pushes up on her elbows and looks at me with heated eyes.

I watch her move until she's up on her knees and groan when she pulls her dress over her head and tosses it carelessly to the floor.

"If I had known you were naked under there, I wouldn't have made it as long as I did today," I tell her.

"I know." Her hands come up and cup her breasts.

I smile when her eyes follow my hands when I place them on my belt. It's a smile that doesn't last long because her next words have me fighting not come in my pants.

"I want your cock, husband. First, I want to lick you from your neck to your balls, and then I'm going to suck them deep until you're begging me to take your cock in my mouth." She pauses in her speech to lick one of her fingers before tracing her puckered nipple with it. "Then I'm going to fuck myself with your fingers. If you're a good boy,

I'll let you lick them clean. And when your balls feel like they're about to bust from the power that your orgasm promises, I'm going to ride you until you come deep inside me."

"Fuck yeah, you are," I growl and pounce.

She jumps back, laughing, and I swallow her happiness when I take her mouth in a bruising kiss.

"Fuck me, wife," I command and lie back in the bed.

Dani

"Fuck me, wife," he orders in a tone that is wild with desire.

"I'm going to lick and suck you first," I promise, climbing up until my legs are straddling his hips and my mouth is trailing kisses along his neck and collarbone.

I feel my pussy lips spread wide to accommodate the side of his hips, and his hard cock settles right between them. The second I feel his hot, velvet skin against my wet lips, I moan and start to rub myself against him. His hands go to my hips, and I feel him thrusting to meet each rotation of my hips.

I trace my mouth down his chest, and when I hit one of his nipples, I lightly bite it between my teeth. His hips jump off the bed, and I squeal when I feel the tip of his erection jab against my swollen clit.

"Do that again and you're going to get my cock in your pussy or your ass and you can forget your mouth having a turn."

I smile against his skin and keep moving my lips down his body. He moans and twitches every time I hit a sensitive spot—which, I'm learning, my husband has a lot of.

"I'm going to take your cock into my mouth until I choke on it," I huskily whisper.

"Fuck," he splutters when I wrap my lips around his swollen cock head.

I move slowly until I have the tip of his cock touching the back of my throat. Relaxing my throat, I breathe through my nose and take him into my throat.

"Fucking hell!" he exclaims and shoots off the bed.

His fingers go into my hair, his hips thrusting his cock into my mouth on their own accord. My eyes water with the force of his thrusting, but I take everything he has to give to me and love every second.

When his movements start to stall, I lean back on my knees and lick my lips. "Why did you make me stop, baby? Was that not good?"

"Any better and you would have killed me, but when I come for the first time as your husband, it's going to be while my cock is pounding that sweet, fucking tight pussy. Climb up here and ride me . . . hard." He adds the last as an afterthought, and I don't even hesitate.

I'm up, straddling his hips and resting my weight on his chest with one hand as I use the other to guide his thick cock into my wet core.

"Fuck yourself on my cock, Dani-girl," he moans when I start moving. "Fuck your husband," he continues.

I bounce as quickly as I can, and when my movements start to falter, he grabs my hips and starts thrusting like a piston into my body from his position on his back.

"That's right, baby. Fuck me hard."

"I can't. My legs," I whine, feeling my climax slipping away.

He flips me before I can even think and pushes my legs over his shoulders.

"I'm going to fill you with my come, Dani. Fill you with my come and fucking pray that another child takes root. I'm going to come so hard that it will leak from your pussy while my cock is still buried deep. You want to taste us when I finish, baby?"

When he stops talking, I swallow thickly, already craving the taste of *us*.

"My girl—my wife—wants my come?"

I nod.

"Fuck, I love you," he says through clenched teeth.

His hips start to power against my body, and it only takes a few more thrusts until I'm screaming out his name, following it with a bunch of gibberish.

"Love this cunt. Fuck me, Dani. I love it when you come all over my cock. Hold on, baby. Going to take you harder."

My eyes widen because I never imagined that he could take me harder than he already was. His balls slap so loudly against my ass that it sounds like hands clapping. He curls my body so that my knees are pressing into my tits, and the first mighty thrust he takes into my body has me screaming. The second has me coming. And every one that follows after has me sobbing and coming and coming and sobbing. And a weird mix of the two.

"Fucking love this pussy."

"Fucking love this cock."

He looks down at me, his eyes ablaze before he throws his head back and rumbles out his release in one loud thundering roar.

After he pulls his spent cock from my pussy, he makes true on his promise to give me a taste of *us.*

When it's all said and done, we don't make it four hours—another long session of him taking his wife—before we're throwing our clothes on and driving to my parents to get our boy.

Epilogue

Dani

Five years later

"DO YOU KNOW WHERE YOUR brother is?" I ask Lyn.

"He said he was running to the grocery store," she says over her shoulder and turns her attention back to her computer.

"What? I just went the other day."

"Yeah—well, in case you didn't notice the last time you were pregnant, you tend to eat a lot when you're knocked up." She laughs and goes back to her computer browsing.

"Well, where is your sister?" I ask.

"She has Evan with her at my parents.' Something about giving you some time to rest before your husband got home and kept you up all night. I think she's still scared from the last time she spent the night and you two kept her up all night moaning."

I throw my head back and laugh because she isn't wrong.

In the five years Cohen and I have been married, the desire we crave for each other hasn't changed one bit. Which explains why I'm pregnant again. I swear he's made it his life's mission to see me pregnant forever. I got pregnant with Evan almost right after our wedding. Cohen was pretty proud of himself and convinced that it was our wedding night that did the deed.

I managed to keep him away from me long enough to not get

pregnant for six months after I had Evan. Unfortunately, that pregnancy ended in a miscarriage that we both took hard. We waited a while before we tried again, and now here I am, pregnant again.

Cohen took a job at Corps Security shortly after Owen was born. He said that his dad was thinking about retiring soon and it was time that he learned the business. This was something I supported one hundred percent. I loved knowing that he was going to never leave us for any more deployments.

"What do you think about this one?" Lyn asks and spins her computer. I laugh when I see the tiny newborn dress she has pulled up on Baby Gap.

"You do realize that it's probably going to be another boy, right?"

"No way, Dani! I'm going to get my girl, dammit. You hear that, baby? You better be a girl."

"I'm pretty sure it doesn't work that way, Lyn," I laugh.

She gives me a hard look and turns back to her computer. I roll my eyes and stand up, walking around until I find my phone and dial Cohen's number.

He picks up almost immediately. "Hey, Dani-girl."

"Where are you?"

"Owen wanted to go find ninjas, so we're in the back lot—looking for ninjas." He explains it like that should make all the sense in the world.

"And why are you looking for ninjas?"

"Because he wanted to fight them," Cohen says.

"Is that supposed to make any sense to me, baby?"

"Nope, probably not. But it makes sense to us and that's all that matters. Plus, he started asking about the earring in my cock again today and there is only so much I can take, Dani-girl. It was mission 'divert and distract' this morning."

The second he stops talking, I throw my head back and laugh.

Since the day Owen walked in on a naked Cohen and got a good look at his hardware, he hasn't stopped for a second. All he talks about is those damn earrings in his daddy's cock. Which is something Cohen's parents think is hilarious. Cohen, not so much.

"Hurry home, baby. I miss you."

"You just saw me an hour ago." He laughs.

"So? I miss you."

"See you soon, my heart."

"Every time I close my eyes." I smile.

An hour later, I'm sitting on the back deck with Lyn, who is still looking up baby clothes, when I hear a rustling in the leaves. I stand and move to the railing, and when I see my two big boys walking towards the house, my smile goes from normal to wonky.

Cohen has Owen on his shoulder, Owen's little fist holding tight to his father's hair, and behind both of them flaps their matching capes.

My heroes.

My unexpected beautiful fate.

Cohen looks up, gives me a wink, and taps Owen's knee with the hand that's resting there. Owen looks up and gives me the biggest toothy grin.

"Mama! We faught awel does bad guys!"

"All of the bad guys? I'm so proud of you, my handsome man."

"I wuv you!" he yells.

I look down at his face and smile. "And I you, son."

They climb the stairs, and Owen drops from his father's shoulders and rushes to his aunt's side. I walk over to my husband, wrap my arms around him, and give him a deep kiss.

"I love you," I tell him.

"And I you, my Dani-girl."

Wedding Morning

Oh, God.

Jesus.

It should be illegal what he can do with his tongue.

... and other things.

"Please, baby," I mewl, not even ashamed of the begging tone of my voice.

He makes me feel like I'm about to combust. Every inch of my skin feels alive—like the blood moving through my system is hyper-charged and zooming at lightning speed.

"Hush." He grunts against my core, the vibrations shooting up and throughout my whole body.

I shamelessly whine again and grind myself against his mouth. I can hear the wet sounds of my desire echo around the room when he pulls his cheeks in and vigorously licks my clit. My back bows, and my hands reach out to curl around his ears, pulling him even tighter against my body.

"Please," I pant, tingles crawling up my spine with a blaze of red-hot fire.

"Hush, Dani-girl," he commands, flattening his tongue and licking me where I want him the most all the way back up to my clit—giving me another hard flick before settling back in with a growl.

I know it's pointless to beg. Cohen doesn't like to be rushed when he's where he wants to be. He's made that clear many times over the years, but it still doesn't stop me. I get off harder when I know I've pushed him to the point of snapping that carefully crafted control.

My eyes roll back when I feel him push his tongue into my body, his nose pressing against me in a way that has me panting, unable to catch my breath. His hands curl around my thighs, fingers digging in deep—bruising—and he hums in pleasure when my body shows him just how much I love this.

"Cohen!" I scream, my inner muscles clamping down and trying to pull his tongue in deeper—needing to be filled in a way that only he can fill me. My fingers, now clutching the sheets tightly, cramp as the power of my orgasm washes over my body. My throat burns and I pull in a deep breath when I realize I held it through the powerful rush his touch brings me.

When I open my eyes again, I'm looking into Cohen's expressive dark chocolate blaze. The desire he has for me makes his gaze seem molten as he covers my body with his hard heat. His cock sliding between my wet lips causes me to moan, and my body jerks slightly when I feel him glide against my oversensitive parts.

"You want my cock?" he questions with a knowing smirk on his handsome face.

"I always want your cock," I respond smartly.

"Greedy."

"For my *husband*? Always."

His eyes darken even more until they look almost black in the muted light around our room.

Husband. My God, that sounds amazing.

"Say it again," he tells me, his voice a brittle mix of desire and happiness, the same mixture of emotions I've felt since we said 'I Do' earlier today in my parents' backyard.

"Husband," I hum. "My husband."

"Wife," he whispers, sliding his hard length into my body. "*My wife*," he continues, his voice darker and hypnotizing. "My Dani-girl."

"Yes," I hiss. My arms go around his body as my fingers dig into the muscles on his back, searching for purchase when he starts to pull out of my body. My need to have him filling me turns desperate when I feel the metal of his piercings at my opening, his cock just a breath away from falling from my body.

"You're making it hard for me to go slow and make love to my wife," he grunts when I use my legs to try to force him back inside my body.

"If I wanted you to make love to me, maybe I would care, but I want my *husband* to fuck me."

Before I'm even done talking, his body is vibrating. His control's slipping with my hungry words and desperate actions to try to force his power. Lifting my head off the pillow, I bring my lips to his jaw and nip with my teeth.

"Dani," he warns.

"Fuck me, Cohen. Fuck me so hard that I can't sit without remembering our wedding night tomorrow."

"Jesus Christ." He drops his face into my neck, and I feel his mouth kiss my skin. "I fucked you hard last night, baby," he reminds me—not that I would ever forget. The first time he took me was wild and totally unforgettable. I imagine we would have spent the whole night like that had we not missed our boy so much we went and picked him up from my parents' house not even a few hours after leaving.

"Please," I beg, still trying to force him back inside my body, the thick tip of his cock kissing my entrance.

"If I fuck you like you're begging me to, you're going to wake up Owen," he tells me with cocky confidence, thrusting his hips slightly and giving me another inch of him.

"I can be quiet," I pant, still trying to get him to do what I want.

"You can't ever be quiet." Again, pure ego.

That's it. Seriously, a woman can only take so much when her body is craving the one thing being dangled—literally, mouth-wateringly, with the promise of toe-curling pleasure—right between her legs. Of course, Cohen underestimates my need for him because the second my feet dig into the mattress and my hips come up with rapid speed, he doesn't even have time to register before I'm the one taking every inch of him. My body welcomes his length at the same time I lift my body and force him to his back with a roll.

His breath comes out with a whoosh when I land on top of him. My legs spread as his length goes impossibly deep, and my hands land on his hard pecs for support.

"Oh, God," I gasp, rocking my hips against his before rolling them in a wide arch. He twitches inside me at the same time his hands reach out and clamp around my waist.

"You've got me where you want me; now, show me how much you want my cock."

"Was there any doubt of how much I want it?" I ask while rocking forward, only to pause when he hits that spot inside me that makes me feel like I'm about to lose my mind in the most delicious of ways.

"Not when your cunt sucks up my cock in that greedy grip and your come soaks my balls. No, baby, there is never a doubt."

"You want me just as much as I want you," I moan, lifting up on my knees and bending so that I'm nose to nose with him—his cock half inside my body. "Help me take you," I order him, moving my hands from his chest, to where he has a tight hold on my hips, and squeezing the tops of his hands.

I hold his gaze, loving how they're so dark and stormy with his need for me, before lifting my body up and kissing his nose. My hands go back to his chest, and with a long, slow roll, I sink back down on him. He makes a noise deep in his throat but doesn't otherwise react.

When I start to lift my body again, dragging him out of me slowly, I feel him let go of the hold he has on his control. His fingers spasm at the same time that he speeds up my movements before slamming me back down onto his cock. It's hard to tell who is really fucking whom here. I move, but he helps, making each push and pull of our bodies turn into a synchronized dance of sweat and sin—beautiful sin.

It doesn't take long before I feel the rush of wetness leave my body. The sounds of my wetness start to mingle with the moans slipping from my mouth—something I have to consciously remind myself to keep down so we don't wake Owen. His grunts and groans each time I slam down on him are something he clearly has no control over, though, because he is by far louder than I am right now.

"Fuuuuck," he drawls out when I reach behind me and brace my body on his knees, giving his cock a whole new angle to tap when he lifts his hips off the bed to force himself even deeper—deeper than I've felt him before. I almost feel faint with the enormity of pleasure that this new position gives me. I drop my chin to my chest and look down my naked body at my husband, expecting to see his eyes burning up at mine, but his focus is solidly on our hips. He's pulled his full bottom lip and caught it between his white teeth as he watches my body rock against his cock.

"I'm going to come," I gasp, the look of pure rapture on his face coupling with the unbelievable pleasure he gives me making the ribbons of desire start to unravel inside me. I can feel them fluttering uncontrollably inside my body before starting to wind back up tightly. "I'm going to … ohhhh, God!"

I would have screamed the house down had it not been for Cohen's rapid movements. His body curling up, his mouth capturing mine, and my scream being lost in a kiss so hot I feel like my orgasm is a twisting wave that is unbreakable. It just continues to swirl and crash inside me. I feel like I can't catch my breath; I'm unable to focus my eyes, and the only feeling I have is my body exploding as he takes hold of my hips and helps me continue to move against him. The only thing I can feel is the powerful thrusts of my husband's cock as he fucks me through my orgasm.

"Goddamn," he moans as I cry his name into his mouth, our tongues still swirling together in a tangle of wet glides. "Fuck it," he grunts, and I squeak when he slams my hips down and rolls us so that my back is once again on the mattress. One brow cocks and he bends so that his mouth is just a breath from mine, my inner muscles still clamping and pulsing in the aftermath of my release.

"I can flip you over, and you can use the pillow, or you can have my mouth to hold in your screams if you don't want to use your hand. But tell me now because I'm about to fuck you raw, baby."

"Your mouth," I gasp. "Don't want to lose your eyes," I rush when he starts to drop down to give me what I want.

His eyes flash, but he gives me what I want—his mouth drops to mine, and his eyes stay open as he pushes into me in a rough and hard thrust. His balls slap against my ass as I scream, coming again just as quickly as I did the last time. The sound muffles as his kiss deepens. Each hard thrust into my body has us moving farther and farther up the mattress until he has to use his hands to block the hardwood of our headboard from slamming into my head. It doesn't take long before he slams into me and doesn't retreat, the hot splash of his release mixing with mine and running down between our joined bodies.

We lay there and come down together, his big body covering mine and the sun just starting to rise behind our curtains. His mouth trailing soft kisses from my neck to my shoulder, but he doesn't move aside from that. His cock still inside me.

He lifts up, slipping from my body, and smiles when a sound of complaint slips from my parted lips.

"Good morning, wife."

"Good morning, husband."

I smile, his gaze dropping to my mouth, and I know that if our beautiful son decides to sleep just a little longer, I'm about to get another soul combusting good morning from my husband.

"You're Pretty ... I'll Keep You"

Cohen

"Sir?"

I turn, the nervous flutter going insane in my gut picks up speed when I see the nurse who's been in charge of Dani since we got here last night.

"Anne, was it?"

She nods. "Your wife … well, she requests your presence."

I hear a bark of laughter leave my father, who's still standing behind me, followed by a bellow of hilarity that I know is coming from Dani's brother. I turn my head to give him a pointed look before addressing Anne.

"Is that your polite way of telling me she demanded my return?" I ask with a smile in my voice.

Anne blushes, and I have a good idea that my beautiful wife was rather colorful in her request. Her blush intensifies as she looks behind me at the room full of family gathered. "Well, Mr. Cage, you left the room, and she told us that no matter what you said, she didn't want an epidural. The doctor decided to give her some pain medication to help with her pain management, but … well, we were unaware of her reaction to pain medication."

Nate's laughter increases. I have a feeling if I were to turn around and look at him, he would be halfway out of his chair, unable to hold himself up with that god-awful cackling he's doing.

"It wasn't in her chart?" I ask, knowing damn well it should have been.

I feel my father's hand on my shoulder, and I turn to give him my attention, smiling at Owen still passed out on his shoulder.

"Worry about that later, son. Go take care of you wife and we'll be waiting for news when the baby is born."

Bending, I kiss Owen's temple then give my father a look of gratitude. Without regarding the nervous nurse Anne, I turn and walk down the hallway to where I can hear the off-key singing of my wife belting out Tom Cochrane's "Life is a Highway." Jesus Christ, they must have given her some good stuff. Rounding the corner, I walk through the doorway just in time to see my very pregnant wife dancing around her hospital room, IV pole in hand, and shaking her naked ass between her open hospital gown. Not willing to miss the show, I close the door silently behind me and lean against the wall.

"I know you're there, handsome," I hear before she turns around. "If this pole would stop moving, I could give you a good show."

My chest moves as I try to keep my laughter in.

She moves toward me, still dragging the pole behind her, and my eyes move to her swollen belly that not even the boxy hospital gown can hide. Seeing her pregnant with my children is something that I can't explain—pride, sure, but it almost makes my heart hurt with how much love I have for my wife. Fuck, she hasn't even had this baby, and I'm already thinking about how soon I can get her pregnant again. She would probably shove that pole up my ass if she knew where my thoughts had gone.

"You sure are pretty," she hums, reaching out with her free hand to pet my cheek—yes, pet me.

"I am?" I ask, playing along.

"Don't tell my husband. He doesn't like it when other men are near me. But you're too pretty to keep away."

"Not sure being called pretty is a good thing, Dani-girl."

Her head tilts to the side, and she studies my face. "My husband calls me that. Do you know him? He's a big man. You should probably hide if he comes in here. I wouldn't want him to hurt your pretty face."

"I think I'll take my chances, sweetheart."

"I'd like to take a chance with you," she hums, dragging her hand down from my cheek to rest on my chest. "Oh, you're so hard!" She flexes her fingers into my pec, and I have to remind my cock to stand down. Moving closer, she juts her belly into my lower abdomen. "So hard," she continues, letting go of the IV pole now to start rubbing my chest and shoulders with both of her hands.

"How about we get you back in the bed, Dani," I suggest, hoping that she won't fight me on that—but I should have known better.

"Oh! That's a great idea, pretty."

"To rest," I add, causing her to frown.

"I don't want to rest. I want to play with my pretty man."

"Your pretty man will still be here after you rest."

She lets me help her to the bed, easing her back onto the pillows before pulling the sheet over her belly. I page the nurse and let her know that Dani is back in the bed if they need to reattach the monitors to her stomach. The whole time, Dani just lays back and smiles at me, the haze of the painkillers making her look drunk.

I try to back up when Anne comes in to reattach the monitors, but Dani's hand slips out and grabs my forearm. "Where are you going, pretty? You said you would still be here, and mister, you'd better be. Don't tell my husband, but I think I'll keep you."

I just shake my head and pat her hand; it's easier just to let her say what she will. Dani and pain meds never mix well. She always talks like a crazy person.

"I'll leave you guys to it. I checked her just before I came to get you, and she was at four centimeters. Hopefully, she can get some rest before we check her again."

I hear Dani grunt softly and look over at her. Her eyes are closed, and her nose wrinkled.

"You okay, Dani-girl?"

She takes a few deep breaths before opening her eyes and focusing on me again.

"Yup," she says, popping her p. "Just had a strong one for a second. Hey, pretty, have you ever heard of fuggling?" She pats the side of her hospital bed and wags her brows at me. "If this nice lady could shut the door on her way out, I bet we can fit some of that fun in real quick."

It takes me a second to get over the shock of my high-on-pain-meds wife propositioning me during labor, but after a few seconds, I throw my head back and bellow out a laugh.

"I'll tell you what, sweetheart, as soon as you bring that little miracle into the world, we can set a date for some fuggling."

"Promise?"

"Oh, yeah."

"Yes, pretty. I think I will keep you."

She gives me a droopy smile and then turns to her side and falls asleep. I laugh to myself, pull the chair to the other side of her bed so I can see her face, and wait. I know from her labor with Owen that things will get crazy the closer she gets to have to push, so I'm glad she can rest now.

With a deep breath and a heart full of love for my wife, I lean back and watch her sleep.

Almost nine hours later, with no memory of her pain med high, my beautiful girl brings our little Evan into the world. I swear I feel like my heart might burst right out of my chest when she looks up at me, tears in her eyes, and thanks me for giving her the world.

If she only knew—she gave me the world, not the other way around.

Acknowledgments

TO MY FAMILY—for putting up with me when I get insane and jump into my head for weeks at a time. For putting up with me leaving for Starbucks for HOURS and then not going to bed at night. And to my husband for making sure the kids are still alive when I come out of my head and rejoin you guys. ☺

To my amazing readers.
For your endless support and love for the worlds I bring you.
And the men that dominate them.
For loving my females just as much as you love those sexy alpha males.
And of course, for just being you and putting a smile on my face.
Love that can last a lifetime on carefully placed building blocks.

To my amazing support system, friends, daily motivators . . . you get the point. Ella, Rochelle, Crystal, and Tessa. I would probably die without you ladies. Well, I might not die—but I would be lonely as hell. A HUGE thank you to Ro and Ella for reading UF while I was writing and for all the feedback.

Kelly, Andee, and Felicia. You ladies have become three of my bestestestest friends in the world. I am so blessed for everything you guys do and continue to do.

Ellie—YOU, my dear, rock my world. Not only did you bring me the beautifully perfect models that are 100% Cohen and Dani, but you are an editing queen and I'm so thankful that you took on my world. I can't wait for many more books to come with you!

Sommer—I'm really not sure what I can say here that means more than thank you. You gave me Cohen and Dani in a way that made me think you were in my head. I adore you.

Stacey—My books would be terribly plain without you. Every little detail and touch that you put into them to makes them shine is phenomenal. I'm so thankful to you and all that you do for me (and my books.)

NEW YORK TIMES & USA TODAY BESTSELLING AUTHOR
HARPER SLOAN
Bleeding
LOVE

Speakers by Sam Hunt
Bright by Echosmith
Dead in the Water by Ellie Goulding
Nothing Left to Lose by Kari Kimmel
Jealous by Labrinth
Love Me Like You Do by Ellie Goulding
Get Me Some of That by Thomas Rhett
Home to Mama by Justin Bieber
Make You Miss Me by Sam Hunt
Brown Eyed Girl by Van Morrison
Human by Jon McLaughlin
Photograph by Ed Sheeran
Everything by Lifehouse
Must Be Doin' Somethin' Right by Billy Currington
Marry Me by Train
I Choose You by Sara Bareilles
Silent Shouts by Adna
Hold My Hand by Jess Glynne
Capri by Cobie Caillat
Like I'm Gonna Lose You by Meghan Trainor

A Thousand Years by Christina Perri
To follow the Bleeding Love playlist, https://open.spotify.com/user/1293550968/playlist/2dLpvRylcnJS4fX522BTQY

Dedication

To everyone who has ever needed a helping hand and those still searching for theirs.
Never give up.
And know, you are never alone.
Even when you think that 'next step' is the hardest one to take–
it's often the most beautiful.
Just . . . take my hand.
-Liam Beckett

A woman who opens her heart to love you,
when it's already broken,
is braver than any person you'll meet.
-Steven Benson

Prologue

Megan

Holy shit.

What am I doing?

"Oh, God! Right there . . . I'm coming . . . Don't stop!"

Is that me screaming like that?

Holy shit.

I didn't even know that noises like that could come out of my mouth!

"You like that?" he asks with his lips pressed against my neck—the vibrations shooting straight to my core.

I focus, my now alcohol free vision, on the man thrusting above me. His dark hair is blending in with the shadows that are dancing around the room. His face is a mask of ecstasy as he thrusts into my waiting body. It's a look of pure desire that I will never forget.

What the hell am I doing?

"You feel so good. Your body so greedy for my cock. You want it harder, darlin'?"

I moan shamelessly and feel my body get even wetter with his huskily whispered words.

Screw it—this feels way too good to stop now.

I reach down, dig my fingers in the firm globes of his ass, tip my head back and beg. Beg with incoherent cries for him to take me harder. To take everything he can.

Two Hours Earlier

"You look beauuuutiful," I sing as Dani Reid—No, Dani Cage—walks over to sit next to me at one of the tables scattered around the backyard wedding.

She looks at me, her stunning green eyes bright with love and happiness.

"And you sound a little drunk, my friend," she laughs.

I just smile at her, running my fingers through the lace on her wedding gown. "This is soft."

She just laughs and leans back and looks across the yard to where her new husband, Cohen, is standing by the dock talking to some of his friends. This is another one of those moments when I'm reminded that this group doesn't have a single unattractive person in it. I take a second to look at all the well-built, good-looking men standing around him. When my eyes meet Liam Beckett's, I look away quickly. For months now Liam has made no secret that he would love nothing more than my undivided attention.

"They're all so unfairly hot. No men should be *that* attractive," I whisper in awe, gaining me another chuckle from Dani. I blush when I realize that my thoughts aren't staying in my head, where they belong. When I look back over to where the group of men are standing, my eyes hit the familiar pair of deep brown ones again, eyes that always seem to know each and every time I'm looking their way. I quickly look away, feeling that blush get even brighter. I'm not ready to deal with *him* right now. At least not when I'm this tipsy.

Picking up my wine glass, I take another healthy swallow as I do a quick scan, taking in all that is the Reid Family property. They've done a beautiful job transforming the backyard of Dani's family home for Cohen and Dani's wedding. I still can't believe that Dani managed to pull off a surprise wedding without Cohen even catching the smallest hint of her plans.

"Are you sure you're okay with Molly spending the night with my parents, Megs? I know it's hard for you to leave her overnight, but they just love your daughter to pieces. And I know Owen loves having her around." Dani reaches out and takes the hand I had resting against the table while she speaks.

"Yup," I smack and nod my head.

"You're drunk," she says, repeating her earlier observation.

"I'm not drunk, I'm tipsy. There's a huge difference there. If I was drunk I wouldn't be able to walk. Watch!"

I jump up from my chair with a little more power than I mean and quickly stumble when the narrow heel of my five-inch shoes sinks into the soft grass beneath me.

"Whoa, there darlin."

I feel it, those words, every single syllable deep down in my gut. Each rumbled word vibrating through my body creating a slow burn until they end with a sharp pulse between my legs. His arms locked at my elbows and my back solidly against his front—where my graceless stumble caused me to end up. I jerk my body tight and feel his laughter reverberate through my body once again.

I attempt to pull my arms from his loose but strong hold, only to give up when it becomes clear that he isn't going to let go. Shifting until my face is turned, he lets one arm go and helps me spin until I'm facing him, and moves his hands from my elbows to my hips.

"Hey," he says with a smile, the dimple in his cheek popping out.

"Liam," I sigh and then curse myself for not being able to hide my reaction to him.

His smile turns knowing and his eyes darken before dropping to my lips.

I gulp.

"You should be more careful, Megs."

"It's Megan," I snap.

"I know, babe, you don't have to keep reminding me."

"Then why can't you seem to actually remember it?" I squeak and try to pull my body away from his grip—and fail, again.

"Someone doesn't sound *drunk* anymore." I hear Dani speak but I don't take my gaze off Liam. "She does look it though." She muses on a laugh, which finally gets my eyes to snap to hers.

"I'm fine! I just had a few glasses of wine and I haven't eaten much. But, I most definitely am not drunk. I think I would know if I was drunk."

Okay, so that's a lie. I might not be drunk, but I am definitely slightly past tipsy. Dealing with Liam—or rather my attraction to Liam—is hard enough for me on a good day, when I'm completely sober. But with this amount of wine flowing through my body, I just can't trust myself.

It's taken everything I have to keep him, and his obvious interest, at bay for the last couple months. When he's around he goes out of his way to get me alone and lay it out. He wants me.

"You look stunning when those shadows aren't rolling around your shoulders," Liam whispers, his lips press close enough to my ear that I can feel his words one by one against my skin.

I shiver, his words hitting me close to home, but the tone causing me to forget I should be pushing him away. Especially when he's talking about things that he has no business speaking about.

"I'm fine," I stammer.

"Yeah, darlin', I know you are."

His eyes keep their hypnotizing hold on my own. I hear Dani excuse herself. I don't turn to watch her disappear in the lingering crowd of party-goers that are still left milling around. The music is still floating in the air around us. As I look into his eyes everything around me feels like it's . . . alive. It's a feeling that I've been missing for the last few years. A feeling that only comes to visit when I'm with my daughter, or until recently, when Liam Beckett is in the same room. It's a feeling that, even though I shouldn't, I feel guilty for allowing myself to enjoy.

Whether it's the wine, the fact that Molly left a few hours ago with Dani's parents, or the man standing in front of me, all I know is if I don't hold on to this feeling for as long as I can right now, I'll regret it for years to come.

"Megs," he says on a sigh, his fingertips digging in and his eyes swirling with a rich hopefulness that turns those golden flecks you can normally see swimming in his brown eyes into a burning fire lighting his gaze.

Hungry eyes.

I don't think. If I had given myself just a second to process my next move, I'm sure I would have backed out of his hold and run as fast as I could to my car. But, I didn't think, so my next move was pure, one-hundred-percent Megan. But not the Megan I've been for the last couple years since my husband died. No, this Megan feels like I've finally dug myself out of those ashes I've been living in since my life burned up around me. The cloak of depression that normally lingers loosely around my shoulders, dropping to my feet with the feel of Liam pressed tight. I know this feeling won't last, but I suddenly want to hold on to every second I can of this experience, until it leaves me.

I reach out and curl my fingers around his forearms. My eyes growing wide when his brow lifts. With a quick push I rock up and close the distance that is left between our mouths. When my lips touch his, that feeling of being alive burns so bright every nerve in my body feels it, each inch of skin boiling and cooling so quickly it's as if I can't make up my mind if I want to be hot or cold. My hairs stand on end, my skin pebbles—going cold before rushing heat fills my veins, and the very thump of my heart seems to skip a beat the second our lips touch.

One thing I know for sure. I want this. I want this and Liam's going to give it to me.

He doesn't pause. His groan vibrating against my chest only lights the feeling that is firing through my skin. My hands move from his forearms and I run my hands up his chest until both hands curl around his neck and I use the hold to pull my body even closer to his.

His hands move from my hips and he curls them around my bottom, pulling me tightly against his body. When I feel the very obvious sign of his attraction, I moan deeply, and shiver when he answers with one of his own.

I can't tell you how long this kiss lasts. When his tongue moves to swipe against my lips, I open without reservation. We continue, our tongues dancing together while each of our moans are swallowed by the other, until I have to pull away to gulp a breath of air before I pass out—however, the way I feel right now, passing out might very well be a possibility.

"This is finally happening," he snarls in a tone that should scare me, but all it does is act as kerosene to our already uncontrollable fire of lust.

"It is," I agree without question.

"Now," he says.

"Okay," I agree on a sigh and sway toward his hard body.

With the encouragement he needs, his hands finally leave my body. He turns me, wraps one thick arm around my shoulder, and turns to walk toward the front of the house.

"We're leaving?" I question lamely.

"Darlin' I didn't stutter. This is happening," he says, pausing when he reaches the side of the house and the shadows that will give us the privacy we need. His body turns, moving me to stand before him once again. "I need to know you're with me, Megan. I've wanted this since the day I met you, but I knew you weren't ready for me. I've been trying to keep my distance, just waiting for those clouds to leave your eyes. If you don't want me to take you back to my house, strip you naked and fuck you until you can't walk for weeks, then say so now, because the second I have you I won't be letting go."

"Oh, boy," I whisper.

"I prefer *oh God,* but I'll make that the first item on my to-do list."

"You'll make what?"

"My to-do list, Megs. The list of things I've wanted *to do* to you for months now. Making you scream *oh God* will be number one, followed by my name, of course."

"Oh, God," I repeat, my mind swilling with the promise his words inflict.

"Yeah, you're getting it."

His mouth crashes down on mine for a hard but quick kiss before pulling back and giving me another one of those knee-melting smirks. "Last chance, Megan," he whispers while his hands are framing my heated face.

Whatever he sees in my eyes is enough, he gives me a light kiss, takes his hands from my face and curls one around my left hand and pulls me toward his truck.

Liam

Fuck.

I thrust in again, feeling her tight walls squeeze my cock, and roll my hips while I take her mouth with my own. Her moan turns into a high-pitched scream that I swallow. I can feel her release wet my balls when I bury myself deep, again rolling my hips. Her small hands grab hold of my ass and I groan when I feel her nails bite into my skin.

"Next time you come against my cock, you scream my name," I demand, looking her in the eyes. Her eyes widen briefly before they roll back when I thrust deep again. I don't give her time to respond before I power my hips back and take her in a bruising speed. "My name, Megs," I rasp. "Don't you come without screaming *my* name."

She whines.

I groan.

She gives me a small whisper of breath against my lips when I lean closer to her, moving my hips faster.

"Do you want it harder, darlin'?" I question.

"Yes," she whimpers.

"Do you want me deeper?" I continue, pausing when the tip of my cock is about to fall from her body, smiling wickedly when she makes a cry of protest. "Do you want to feel my cock even when you aren't with me? Want me to take everything you have to give me? So greedy. So fucking greedy." Without giving her a chance to answer, I bend forward and crush my lips to hers. She opens immediately and our tongues meet, causing a fire to race down my spine and curl around my balls.

Damn she feels good.

"Tell me, Megs. Give me the words."

"Take me, Liam. Give me everything. Make me *feel*. God, please make me feel!"

Her eyes bore into my own. With one gaze she is telling me everything her words don't. This means more to her too, I can see it, and fuck me—my body locks tight when I see the depth of her plea.

"Yeah, darlin'. Everything."

She doesn't know it, but with that one word I silently vow to stop at nothing until I make this woman mine.

With one powerful thrust, roll, and push, I give her everything I have—over and over. When she throws her head back, it's my name she's screaming loud enough to cause my ears to ring long after her breath grows slow and her face relaxes with sleep.

I lay there looking at her after my cock softens and falls from her body. I remember the first time I saw her, I knew that she would one day be in this position. Naked in my bed and spent from taking my cock for hours. Over the months since that first meeting, the feeling, the craving, to make her mine had only grown. I've tried, tried to reach her, but it was clear she wasn't ready. So I waited and fuck me was it worth the wait. Now, having confirmed what I knew then, I know I won't let her go without a fight.

And it will be a fight. That I'm sure of.

But it's also one that I know I'm ready to take on. I know what I want. I know *who* I want.

I also know in order to have those things, I will be fighting the hardest fight I've ever fought.

Because not only am I fighting for someone that can't see through the shadows to find the rope I'm holding to pull herself off rock bottom, but I'm also fighting the ghosts of her past that I'm not sure will let her go long enough to make that climb.

After rolling away from her warm body, I walk to the bathroom and clean myself off, not wasting any time before I move back to my bed. Quietly I lie back down and pull her into my arms. Even in her sleep she curls into me, her head hitting my shoulder, arm curling around my stomach and her legs tangling with my own. I reach down and hike her thigh over my hips and smile to myself while fighting another erection when her wetness hits my hip.

Sitting there, looking into the darkness I know I've finally found her. I've been searching for *her* for as long as I can remember. That person that would make my heart beat faster.

When you grow up with parents like mine, you know without a shadow of a doubt that a love worth fighting for is a love worth keeping. The fight—that drive—the desire to have the person you love,

love you back just as fiercely? That's all it's about. They showed me that when you want something, you don't stop until it's yours.

I think I was about eight when I first realized the relationship my parents shared was something . . . different. I was about sixteen when I realized that different was something I wanted. They had some sort of magical power to their love. Nothing that you would ever be able to describe, but when you saw them together there was no denying it. They would look at each other and it was as if there was some invisible cord that connected them completely. Mom would give Dad a smile and he would laugh softly under his breath, always causing her face to redden. He would walk into the room and her whole body would jolt like it had been struck by lightning. Her skin would pebble with goosebumps and she would always snap her eyes to wherever he was. Of course it took me years to understand what that look meant.

They felt each other.

They knew each other past a feeling that could be physically felt.

They had a love that went past anything explainable.

And just like I knew when I first met Megan, she was the person that I would have that with. I knew when I was younger when my person stepped into my path, there would be nothing that could stop me from making her mine. I wanted what my parents had and now there isn't a damn thing that will stop me from getting that.

Megan isn't going to know what hit her.

With that final thought, my lips tip up and I let my body drift off to sleep, while I hold *my* future in my arms.

Chapter 1

Megan

Two Months Later

"Tell me about your husband," Dani asks softly.

I look over to where she's sitting in my living room, reclined back against the love seat, her legs propped up in the seat next to her, and her baby boy, Owen, sleeping against her chest.

I don't answer right away; instead I watch her hand rubbing his small back. The diamonds in her wedding ring glittering against the sun that shines through the window.

Jack.

She wants to know about Jack.

It shouldn't be this hard to talk about him, but even after almost three years it still feels like yesterday sometimes.

"He was my best friend," I tell her honestly.

"Like Cohen and me?"

"Nothing like you two," I laugh humorlessly. "God, Dani, it feels almost like a betrayal to his memory to even admit that out loud. What you and Cohen have . . . that's a love story for the record books. Jack and me . . . well, we kind of fell into love in the most unconventional ways. No, that's not right. We fell in love with each other all because of Molly."

"What do you mean?" she says, her voice just over a whisper.

I sigh, "We grew up together, Jack and I. It sounds so much more glamorous when I say it that way, like we were kids that would run on perfectly paved sidewalks and in each other's backyards until we were called for dinner. But that couldn't be further from the truth. We lived in the backwoods, wrong side of the tracks, trailer park from hell, in a small town in nowhere Georgia with one blinking caution light and the only store for miles was a mom and pop grocery store that, most of the time, only had expired goods for sale. It was hell on earth, really. But Jack, God Jack, he was always seeing the brighter side of life. He had these huge dreams. He was going to get a scholarship to the best football playing college, play for a few years until he was drafted—early of course, or so he would say. He wanted to play with the big boys, Dani, and he could have. He really could have. He was that good."

Dani doesn't talk, but her silence encourages me to finish.

"I wasn't a wild child. Not by a long shot. I was the silent one that flew under the radar and hid in the shadows. Jack was one of my only friends and by far the closest. Had we not grown up next door to each other, I'm sure we wouldn't have even been friends. I was that much of a wallflower. But Jack, despite where we lived and how we grew up, was destined for greatness. The most popular boy in school, captain of the football team, class president, you name it and that was Jack." I smile and look over at Dani, meeting her sympathetic eyes. "My parents were shit, Dani. Not like yours. Nothing like yours. Home wasn't a safe place for me. I'll spare you the details of that because really, you don't want to know. When I got pregnant with Molly, Jack left all those huge dreams he had and joined the Marines, married me, and gave me the promise of a safe and happy love. He knew that he had nothing to offer me with just a pocket full of dreams and by enlisting, we might not have a future he had imagined for his life, but he did what he felt he had to do to protect me. Having Molly turned a love we had as friends and it grew into one that we had as husband and wife."

"I don't know what to say, Megan. I know a bunch of 'I'm so sorry's' aren't going to make it better, but I'm glad that you were able to get out—make a better life out of a bad start. Did he . . . um, did he regret it? Not following his football dreams?" I can tell she doesn't mean this in a nosy way, but just to better understand what Jack and I had.

"Never. Jack wasn't built in a way to ever regret the path his life took. He believed that everything happens for a reason. Although, I'm not sure he would feel the same way now seeing as he died jumping on that new path he dug for his life."

"You miss him," she states without any doubts in her tone.

She would understand, as a wife of an ex-marine she knows what it feels like to live without someone, even though her husband came home, you still feel that emptiness when they're gone. The physical void, as well as the cold hard fear that they may never make it back.

And Jack . . . he never made it back.

"Every day."

And I do. Not just because the physical loneliness, but losing him—someone that I had had by my side every day since I was in preschool—was one hell of a hit to take mentally too.

She nods, reaches her hand over the table separating the love seat from the couch and takes my hand. She doesn't speak, just gives me a gentle squeeze and looks back at the television. I'm sure neither one of us are even watching the reality show rerun that's playing on the screen. I'm lost in my thoughts and I'm sure she is too.

It's hard to believe just how much my life has changed in the course of six years. I went from being a single teenager without much care to what happened in my future, to married with a newborn in what felt like seconds. Don't get me wrong, I wouldn't change having Molly in my life for a second, but losing Jack has changed me. At first I struggled with the will to live, sinking into a depression so deep that I'm shocked I made it out. Molly helped with that. She was my will to live. But even now, after all of these years, I still have days that I sink right back into that dark place. I'm sure a lot of that has to do with the fact that I've never had to be alone, aside from him. Now it's like I've had to learn how to not only live without him, but to live essentially alone.

For the last three years I've been in some sort of limbo. I've come so far from where I was when he first died. Instead of thinking I would never have good days, now I know the bad days come few and far between. His birthday, our wedding anniversary and the date he died are still, and probably always will be, dark days. Moving forward, one foot in front of the other, in the process of moving on. Even though the thought of 'moving on' is still, to this day, laughable. To move on, I would need something to move toward, and it's really hard to focus on the beauty in life when you're stuck living a haunted one with the memory of someone who has been dead for years. Back in the shadows. All those moments that once brought a smile to my face and gave my heart a reason to beat a little quicker, gone. I was reminded, while Dani and Cohen completed that fairy tale for the record books that is their love, how beautiful life can be and as I watched them dance on their wedding night, I found myself wanting that. Craving for a love that deep that I physically ached for it.

And for one night I let myself forget the weights that have held me down.

For one night I lived in the now. I allowed myself to open up and feel all of those things that I have always been convinced I would never have.

For one night I felt the promise of *more* and it scared the crap out of me with the power of those emotions.

Those are the moments that all feel like lead in my gut now. The ones that make it hard for me to push myself past drowning when I dwell on them too long.

Before Jack died we had created a beautiful life. It was a life that held so much promise.

I was, after we were married and left our old lives behind, a phoenix being reborn from the ashes we had left from all the burning pain of our old lives.

All that fire and all that pain, washing away memories we never wanted to have again.

We had been married for two years before he died. It took us a while in that time, to find our way. To feel that promise of a beautiful life. And in that two years I held something beautiful in the palms of my hands. I felt alive.

Reborn.

I didn't live in the shadows around me, meekly praying that no one would notice me.

We were alive and gloriously happy.

I believed with my whole heart that every hardship I ever felt served a purpose because it brought me a happiness that was out of this world perfect.

Until it was gone.

And in its place I was left with a pain that burned so bright I just knew there would be no ashes left for me to be reborn again.

Once again I was stuck in those shadows—that cold place where I was just existing and not living—Molly being the only bright spot in my darkness. It's a painful place to be and it wasn't until Dani and her gang of friends came along that I was able to start clawing myself out of that depression I had sunk into.

So, yeah—it was hard after all that to even think for a second that I would ever feel that promise again. We had come so far and lost so much.

But one night with Liam, I felt it instantly.

That is something I've been struggling with since.

I shiver with the thought and look at Dani, focusing my mind back on our conversation.

"I don't want to be that person I was when we first met, Dani."

She looks back up, her hand jolting against mine, and shock etched in her face. We haven't talked about how I used to be. How bad I was when we first met.

"When I first saw you, at Cohen's going away party, even when I knew what happened to you, all I could see was the sadness. It brought it all back, that night I mean? Made you remember Jack?"

I nod, "It was hard sometimes. I wasn't in a good place back then."

She doesn't speak at first, her thoughts clearly something she is struggling to piece together.

"You're still struggling, I know, Megan. I see it. It hurts me as your friend to not know how to make it better for you."

I smile softly, "I have my bad days, but they're coming far less frequently than they used to. Jack was a huge part of my life and even if we didn't have the same kind of love that most couples do, I loved him more than life. Maybe because he was all I had in mine besides Molly. There isn't a single memory from growing up that doesn't have him in it. I think that's what makes it so hard, when I think about life without him in it now, it's painful to know that the new memories will never have him in them."

"Is that why you won't date? Because of that love you both shared?"

I laugh, this time with humor. "No. Jack isn't why I won't date."

She clears her throat, adjusting herself so that she's more comfortable, and looks down at Owen. "I couldn't imagine my life without Cohen in it. It hurts to just think about it. Even having Owen as a reminder of him would be painful, but a pain I would be happy to have if it meant I held just a small part of him."

Her words rip through me, each one searing me deeply and I fight the gasp that almost escapes. She has no idea how painful her words just were. And of course she wouldn't because even if she is the closest person in my life right now, that doesn't mean I've let her all the way in. God if she only knew.

"But," she continues and I focus back on her, "I know Cohen would never want me to be alone. He would want me to find love again, even if just the thought makes me sick, I know deep down he would be right. You, Megan—you have so much love to give."

"And I give it . . . to Molly." My tone comes out harsher than I meant it to and I can tell that Dani felt the sting of my snapped words.

"You deserve happiness, babe." She smiles, but it doesn't even come close to hitting her eyes. My pulse picks up with the look she gives me next and I know where she's going. Where she's been dying to go since her wedding reception. "I thought for a second you could have found that with Lee."

This time the gasp I held back slips out and I slap my hand over my mouth, my eyes going wide. I shake my head and she looks at me with kindness in her eyes.

"I understand best friends more than you can imagine, Megan. I'm the same way with Lee, well, minus the whole falling in love part." She smiles, the kindness still there, but this time there's something else in her beautiful green eyes. Something that I'm not sure I want to hear. "I see the way he looks at you."

I shake my head and she returns my denial with a bigger smile and another nod.

"Oh, I see it. And I see the way that you look at him when you don't think anyone is paying attention. You two have been dancing around it for almost a year now, Megan."

"All you see is two people that happened to have shared one night of drunken sex and that's it," I fume, finally finding my voice.

"Bullshit." She moves, sliding her legs off the cushion and adjusting her sleeping son while turning to look at me. "You're afraid. I didn't get it. Not until you explained all of that just now. I thought you were playing games, but now I get it."

"Get what?" I ask impatiently.

"The fear."

I look at her. My eyes blinking a few times while my breathing comes in quick bursts.

"You lost your husband and honey, I feel you. I hate that you lost that and although I will never understand what you feel physically, I do know what the thought of a life without my husband would feel like. But you didn't die with Jack and I know he would want you to move on. Do you think he would want Molly to be alone too? You lost your husband, but baby, she lost her father."

Her words wash over me like someone had just thrown an ice bucket over my head. Then as they replay in my mind I feel the blow just as hard as if it was physically thrown.

"Please leave."

Her eyes widen and a soft gasp comes out of her full lips.

"Now."

"Megan," she starts.

"No." I shake my head and will the tears back. "I'm going to go get ready to go get my daughter from school. When I come back out here, please be gone."

I get up from the couch and walk on wooden legs to my bedroom, her words slamming around in my head.

I know I'm being unfair to Dani. She doesn't know how hard the slap of those words hit.

You lost your husband, but baby, she lost her father.

You lost your husband, but baby, she lost her father.

She lost her father.

I stop at the mirror in my bathroom and look at my pale skinned face reflecting back at me.

She lost her father.

I take a deep breath.

You lost your husband.

I squeeze my eyes closed and clamp them tight.

She lost her father.

My pulse speeds up and my skin goes from ice cold to burning hot.

You lost your husband.

My fingers dig into the counter at my hips and I feel one lone tear sneak past my tightly closed lids.

She lost her father.

I open my eyes, look back at my face and feel nothing but rage. Picking up the closest item I can, my hairbrush, I rear my arm back and hurl it at the mirror. When the brush strikes the surface, the mirror splinters and I turn just as the pieces shatter from the force of my throw.

I did lose my husband and when he took his dying breath, I lost every single piece of the only person that ever loved me.

But she's wrong. It isn't the fear from losing Jack that keeps me from opening up. It isn't that I don't *want* to fill the loneliness that I have lived with every day since Jack left—until that night in Liam's arms. No, the part that I struggle with and have struggled with every day since, is the feelings that he brought back into my cold life are so much more powerful than what I ever felt before. Even with Jack. The images of Liam—Liam and me, Molly and us—that had filtered through my mind while I slept in his arms, *they* scared me. I loved my husband, but I was never in love with my husband, and the feelings that Liam Beckett created in my gut have been a burning guilt of that fact since I snuck out of his bed before the sun came up.

She lost her father.

God, if she even knew.

Chapter 2

Megan

I hit save on the document I've been working on for the past few hours and turn to smile at my daughter, her eyes still tired since she just woke up.

"Can I go play with Mr. Axel again?"

I smile, reach up and hold her soft cheek in my palm. She smiles bigger, her dark brown eyes sparkle with happiness.

"Please," she whispers loudly.

"Little bird, I think Mr. Axel has other things to do than play with your adorable self."

Her smile grows and I wait to see what her brilliant little five-year-old mind comes up with.

"He told me the other day I was the prettiest princess in the whole world and I could come have tea parties with him all the time!"

Something about the image of Axel Reid telling my daughter she could come over and have a tea party was just so ludicrous that I burst out laughing, causing Molly to join in and laugh as well. That's my daughter, always smiling and always laughing, even if she is clueless to why.

"Molly, Mrs. Izzy watched you the other night for mommy while I got some work done. I don't think it would be nice for me to ask her to watch you when I don't have anything to do for work right now."

"Sure you do," she states in the most adorable voice and points to my computer.

"Sure I do what?"

She smiles brightly, "Have work to do. I saw you working just now."

Well, I can't very well argue with that.

"Molly, I always have work to do, but that's why I have a schedule so that I can have tons of little bird time and still make my deadlines."

"Deadline doesn't sound like a fun word." Her nose scrunches up and she sticks her tongue out.

"Deadline is Mommy's least favorite word in the whole world. I like peas more than I like deadlines."

Molly grabs her tiny stomach and throws her head back to giggle. And giggle loud. Her blonde ringlets jumping up and down with the force of her hilarity.

"But you hate peas, mommy!" she giggles even harder.

"I know, little bird," I smile and tap her nose.

She doesn't say anything else but just continues to look at me with a big smile.

I smile back.

Waiting.

"So . . . Can I go see Mr. Axel?"

And there it was.

"How about this? How about I call Mrs. Izzy and see if maybe she is free for a few hours and I'll work those nasty pea deadlines I hate so much. But, Mr. Axel might be at work, okay baby?"

She nods her head, those beautiful ringlets dancing again, jumps off my lap and runs back to her room. I can hear her moving around and the sounds of her making what I'm sure will be a huge mess, echoing down the hall. With a deep sigh, I pick up the phone and call the Reid house to see if my darling daughter can spend some time with the two people she has adopted as hers.

Growing up without grandparents myself I know what it's like to want that familiar closeness, so it shouldn't be a shock to me that she's grown so close to them. Axel and Izzy Reid have treated Molly like she's their blood grandchild since before Dani's wedding. If it isn't Molly asking to go spend time with them, it's them calling to see if I need some time to work. It's been a blessing I'm happy to have in my life, but it still feels weird to rely on someone else when it comes to Molly.

But I also wasn't lying when I said that deadlines are something that I hate more than peas, and I hate peas a lot. A whole hell of a lot. With my newest novel due to my publisher in just weeks, it's something that has been stressing me out and affecting my writing. A bad combination for an author. Maybe Molly knows what I need more than I do.

For as long as I can remember, I've loved writing. When I was growing up, I used writing as a way to escape. Now, as an adult, it's much the same—but now I also write for pleasure and not just for companionship.

I published my first book when Jack was deployed the first time. I never, not in a million years, expected my first romance novel to be a success, but here I am five years later with multiple bestseller titles. Writing kept me from being pulled under by the grief I felt when Jack died. It kept me warm when the loneliness became too much to handle. It was, in a sense, the therapy that I needed to begin to heal.

My books got a little dark during the first year after losing Jack, but it's the books that I hit publish on during that time that are some of the most raw feelings I ever, to this day, have put into my pages.

It's not hard to write about fear, loneliness, pain and heartbreak when you're living it. It was through those characters that I was able to start rebuilding my life.

I place the phone to my ear and wait for it to connect.

"You've reached the Reid house, where we can put the plea in pleasure in seconds."

My eyes round and I burst out laughing when I hear Nate's answering voice.

"Give me the phone, boy! Sometimes I wonder if you were dropped on your head," I hear Axel gruff in the background.

"Oh come on, I knew it was Megan!"

There's a sound of shuffling through the line before I hear the phone clatter against the floor.

"You crazy old man!" Nate laughs.

The phone clatters again and I laugh listening to the two Reid men acting like children.

"You two take it outside! Overgrown apes. Hello? I'm so sorry," Izzy's sweet voice comes over the line and I laugh again when I hear the men clearly have not taken things outside.

"Hey. It's Megan," I say between giggles.

"Hey honey. How are you? How is that sweet little princess?"

"I'm good. However, Molly has basically insisted I call because she says Mr. Axel promised her he would be willing to play tea party every second of her life."

Izzy laughs, the sound bringing a smile to my lips. I've been so lucky to have formed such a close relationship with Dani's parents. In the last year they've become family to Molly and me.

"Like you even have to ask," Izzy says.

"You know I do. Plus I know she loves you to pieces, but she was very specific that she wants that tea party and she wants it with Mr. Axel. I swear that kid could talk the heavens into rain."

"If I tell Axel that I turned that princess away he would wring my neck. I swear the older he gets the more insane he is. Molly is a sweetheart, Megan. Bring her over, I'm sure you could use the time to write. Hey, why don't you pack her an overnight bag and we can have a sleepover. I'll have Dani bring Owen over. Maybe a little girl's night is just what you need."

I laugh, "I don't need anything, Izzy. I couldn't ask you to keep Molly overnight!"

"Darling girl, you need more things than you can see." She oddly tells me. "Bring her and bring a bag or I'll lock you out, take her shopping for clothes, and not give her back until tomorrow afternoon. See you soon!"

I pull the phone back when I hear her disconnect and stare blindly at my cell. What the hell?

"Mommy!"

I shake my head and turn from my desk to where Molly is standing. All thoughts of Izzy's strange comment gone when I see she has turned herself into a real life Disney princess. She's wearing head to toe dress-up gear consisting of about five different princess costumes.

My girl, never a dull moment.

"Come on, let's go get you packed. Mrs. Izzy said she wants you all night and just won't take no for an answer."

"Yay!" Molly screams and smiles a huge smile up at me.

Looks like I'm going to have a night to myself whether I want one or not.

DING.

I stop mid-step and turn my head to my front door. I've been back from dropping off Molly for about two hours and in that time I had managed to clean the house and catch up on about two weeks of emails.

DING.

I narrow my eyes and walk to the door. As long as we've lived here, we still don't know our neighbors. They're all older and don't want to be bothered to meet the widow and her kid, which is fine, we've gotten used to it. Since Cohen pulled me into his group of friends it isn't odd that one of them pops over. Usually it's Cohen or Chance checking on things around the house, but with Chance gone I know it's not him. Cohen, since getting married, doesn't stop by as often. I know he's busy, but he makes a habit of coming by and making sure we don't need anything.

He's done that every few weeks since we lost Jack. He and Jack were good friends and I know Cohen uses those visits to make sure Jack's family is okay. I wish I had the heart to let him know how much those visits hurt more than help, but it's on those rare bad days that I slip into that depression that never seems to go away all the way, his visits are just what I need.

And now, having grown into an amazing friendship with Dani and her group of girlfriends, my life is almost bursting with people when before there was no one but Molly.

DING.

"I'm coming," I mumble to no one and hurry to pull the door open.

I pull the door open with a smile and quickly frown when Dani pushes her way in, brown bag in hand and dressed for the club.

"What in the hell?"

"Don't give me any lip. You've been avoiding me and I get it, I over stepped, but it's been two weeks. Mom called, said bring Owen over because you need a girl's night but won't ask for a girl's night because—her words—that girl is stronger than she has a right to be—not sure what the hell that means, other than I'm pretty sure my mom is calling you stubborn. Either way, time to get ready for a night out." She ends her rambling and turns to face me in a huff.

"Uh," I stutter.

"Nope. No timid or unsure Megan now. The girls are on the way so it's time to get your ass ready!"

She holds up the brown bag and my brow lifts in question when I hear the glass clink.

"Liquid courage, my friend."

I laugh, because really what can I do. Dani's going to get her way here or she will just bring the party to my house and I'm pretty sure old Ms. Timmons will shit in her diaper if a party hosted by Dani Cage starts next door.

"Where are we going?" I ask, turning my back to walk toward my bedroom, knowing she will follow.

"Don't know. I guess we'll figure it out when we get there. There's a new club downtown that I've been told is a great place. Ember dragged Maddi out there last week and Mads said it was pretty chill."

"Maddi and I have a different interpretation of chill." I remind Dani.

Maddi—or Maddisyn Locke—is another friend that I met through Dani and I swear that girl is always working some hidden angle. If she's in on this little impromptu party then I know something's up.

"Whatever. It'll be fun. Plus, I haven't had a night without Owen in a few weeks. I love my boy, but mommy needs some girlfriend time."

I glance away from her with a roll of my eyes and head to my closet to try and find something appropriate for going out with the girls to some club downtown.

“That one,” Dani says absentmindedly after watching me flick some hangers around and then turns to sit on my bed.

I look over at Dani to judge her outfit before I even dare follow her barked order. She’s dressed for a night out, but I’m shocked Cohen let her leave the house like that. She’s got on a tight black dress that hits right above her knees with a slit in the middle giving her boobs a highlighted ‘v.’ The dress is long sleeved so really she isn’t showing much, but I know Cohen is the type of man that doesn’t like his woman’s assets showing and with her still nursing their son, there is plenty of boobage to show.

“Where is Cohen tonight? I find it hard to believe he saw you leave the house in that.”

“Of course he did. He’s in tonight. Something about a game on television or something.”

Had I not been flipping through my clothes I might have caught the look she gave me when she finished talking, but because I was too focused on the fact that I have nothing to wear to a club, I missed it. Probably just as well, because if I had caught Dani Cage in her lie about where her husband is, there is no way she would have been able to drag me out of the house.

Chapter 3

Megan

I pull the hem of my dress down. Again. And look over at Dani from under my lashes while I take another sip of my drink. A large sip this time.

"Smile," Maddi says loudly in my ear, causing me to jump and rattle the whole table when I bump into it.

Maddi laughs, throws her hands up, and walks around to the other side of the table. She gives Zac a hug before walking to Nate and giving him one as well. Well, what I'm sure started out as a hug but ended up with her jamming her elbow into his stomach when he pinches her butt. She throws a look over her shoulder at her sister before walking back over to me and picking up her drink.

Maddi—like me—is wearing a form fitting dress. Hers is a light purple color that looks amazing on her tan skin. Her long, black hair is up in a high ponytail and her make up is done to perfection. But unlike me, she doesn't have to struggle to keep her dress from riding up her ass. Mainly because even though she has a great ass, she doesn't have the hips that I do. Which is a major reason why I have avoided wearing anything this . . . tight.

The dress that Dani insisted I wear, ended up being one of the ones that she had her best friend Lyn drag over. Something that they claim they just had, but being that I'm the only one of them that has hips for days, I know they're full of shit. Which was confirmed when Lila, Lyn's twin sister, apologized for being late because they took too long at the mall.

The deep blue dress fit me perfectly. I have to admit it's stunning, there's a thin layer of lace that covers the blue material of the dress and takes it from looking like a cheap bar dress to something a little classier. I should be happy because it covers all the important places, but the low neckline makes me boobs stand out. Then there's the whole back of the dress issue . . . or I should say lack of the back. The blue material stops at my butt and the lace continues about two inches and then it's nothing but skin except for a thin line of blue that crosses mid back, holding it together. A thin and tight chain connecting each side that I'm convinced is going to snap. A very stupid thin line that prevented me from wearing a bra, so with the added joy of being free, I've been praying that my nipples just keep the fun under control.

I tug the hem down again and pull the straw from my drink, toss it on the table, and down the rest of my Long Island Ice Tea.

"Ha! Chug it babe!" Nate yells across the table with a smile. "Wanna see who can drink more?" He challenges.

"Uh, no? Why are you here, anyway?"

"Someone isn't so sure. I'm here because I know you want to play with Nate Dog?" He wags his eyebrows and I cough out a laugh.

"Did you seriously just call yourself Nate Dog?" I hear Stella yell from the corner.

"Sure I did." Nate says and puffs out his chest. "Don't you know how much dogs love to play with cats?"

"What the hell are you talking about?" I inquire.

"Cats, babe. You know, pussy. If there's one thing that a dog can chase, it's pussy. Wanna play?"

"You're such a child," Dani groans and slaps him on the back of his head.

Despite the fact that he has the maturity of a teenager sometimes, he does look hilarious pouting at his sister. He reaches up, pulls his shoulder length hair from his topknot and fixes the man bun that his sister knocked loose. Looking at him, strong bone structure, handsome features and green eyes just as stunning as his sister's, I have to admit he's without a doubt one good-looking man.

When he catches me studying him, I get a wink and he thrust his hips, earning him another smack from his sister.

"Leave her alone," she yells.

"Whatever, sis." He holds up his hands and looks back at me with a wicked smile. "So, wanna drink meow?"

I laugh and walk around the table and loop my arm through his. "Sure, big boy, let's go get some drinks. Right, meow," I jest.

I push my arm through his offered elbow, and start to walk toward the bar. I feel like I have to stand on my toes even with my heels to keep our height even as we walk through the crowded dance floor.

An hour later, I'm pretty sure I've lost the ability to stand up straight. Not because I'm drunk, well . . . I might be a little, but watching Nate work the room with what has to be the worst pick-up lines in the world has me laughing so hard that I've almost fallen over more times than I can count.

"And then he said to her, 'You sure are beautiful. Almost as beautiful as my sister, but you know that's illegal.' And you should have seen her face. She looked like she swallowed a fly. Didn't even take a second for her to turn and run."

Everyone laughs when I finish telling them about one of Nate's attempts at picking up one of the chicks he walked into after our third trip to the bar. Well, everyone except Dani.

"You are so disgusting. I swear Mom and Dad picked you up on the side of the road." Dani turns her head and rolls her eyes at me.

"What? Hey, I called you beautiful. Doesn't that give me brownie points?" Nate holds his hands up and actually looks confused by why we find his failed pick-up lines hilarious.

"Dude, you basically told her that your sister is hotter but you can't do her because she. Is. Your. Sister." Zac says, holding his sides as he laughs as hard as I am.

"That wasn't even the best one!" I yell. "He looked at that one," I pointed across the room to a tall, stunning blonde before looking at Nate and laughing so hard I almost fall off my stool again. Thankfully two strong hands grab my hips before I can move too far off. I look up at Zac and smile my thanks for him catching me before I fell on my ass. "Then he says to her 'Taco Bell isn't the only thing that's open late and I love tacos' and she," I pause to laugh harder when he narrows his eyes at me, "And then, she said 'baby I've been waiting to have someone offer to play with my taco since I had my sex change!'"

After that, there was no way my laughter could have been stopped. Everyone around us starts laughing and Nate just rolls his eyes and takes a pull of his drink.

"Hey, I love this song."

I jump from my seat and run around the table and into the mass of bodies dancing on the dance floor. I turn and see Dani, Maddi and Stella have joined me as we dance and laugh as each song starts to blur into the next.

We had been dancing for a while now, each of us laughing and having a great time. Nate and Zac seem to be on watchdog duty, because each time someone tries to get too close, they step in. I have a good feeling that they both only showed up for girl's night to keep an eye on us. Or at least they had been until Mr. Cowboy started to get too grabby.

I had just turned to straighten my body after spinning around in a few circles and wiped my hair out of my face with a smile that died instantly. The stranger that we had been fending off for the last five or so songs gives me a sinister looking smile before pulling me into his arms. I look around, frantic, before I realize my spin dancing must have separated me from the group. I can just see the top of Nate's head standing a good distance away from me. At six and a half feet, the fact that I can only see the tip top of his head has me swallowing a hard lump of fear. Being this far away, I know he can't hear me if I call out for him.

I watch Nate's head disappear as Mr. Cowboy starts to pull me further away.

"Hey! Let go, jerk!"

Pulling me against him, he drops his head and puts his mouth against my ear. The feeling of his breath making my skin crawl instantly. When his mouth opens and he pulls my earlobe into his mouth I start to struggle against him with renewed vigor. My fear turns to panic when his teeth bite down on my ear, causing me to scream out—only to have the sound be swallowed up by the loud beats of the music around us.

"I've been waiting for you to come to me," he slurs and pulls me against his hips. I want to vomit when I feel his erection poke me in the stomach. Memories long since suppressed, start to float to the surface and I start struggling harder. I can feel his frustration as his grip on my arms tightens. My arms burn with the strength of his hold and I just know I'll have two nasty bruises.

"I could tell you wanted some of Big Daddy," he moans when I stumble as he pulls me toward the back hall and my stumble does nothing but push me closer to his body. "Yeah, baby. I knew you wanted some of this."

"Let me go," I whisper, the panic starting to close in on me. "Please," I squeak out.

He lifts one hand from my bicep and takes my jaw roughly, his thumb digging into my flesh and he jerks my head up. My eyes water and I let out a whimper.

"You want me. I'll show you what all that teasing your dancing has been doing gets you." He grinds his hips one more time and I almost lose the contents of my stomach.

"What the fuck!"

Before I can even process the move, a fist comes out of nowhere and crunches into Mr. Cowboy's nose. The sickening sound of his bones breaking takes that battle I've been fighting against my stomach to a whole new level. Mr. Cowboy goes back but doesn't remove his hold on my arm so I'm jerked like a rag doll.

"You think about taking my toy and I'm not going to be very happy, pretty boy," Mr. Cowboy says through the blood pouring from his nose and into his mouth.

My stomach heaves.

"Get your fucking hands off her," I hear Nate growl and his warm hand gently goes to the arm that isn't being held. In my mind I picture some sick game of tug of war beginning.

"Fuck you," he spits and in a move quicker than I can process he lunges forward and clocks Nate right in the left side of his face, jerking my body again so hard that my head snaps back and I feel a sting against my back as the chain on my dress snaps.

He doesn't even flinch. I can see Nate torn and not wanting to fight while I'm in the middle of them like some convoluted game of monkey in the middle. Well, that is until the jerk that is *still* holding on to me moves to punch Nate and gets me right in the back of my head.

Luckily for me, he had been drinking enough that the power in his punch was dulled down quite a bit, regardless, my vision swam and between the fear and pain—the battle with my stomach was instantly lost. I lurched forward and spewed every ounce of Long Island Ice Tea I had consumed tonight, along with my dinner, all over that stupid cowboy.

Shock held him still and even though he was covered in my vomit, Zac, coming from behind, grabs a hold of him and started pulling him through the room. I lost sight of them when Nate stepped in front of me and gently tipped my head up. He gives me a quick look, his face stone-cold serious. An expression rarely seen on his carefree face. Seeing this version of Nate jumpstarts the reality of just how serious this situation could have become.

"Come on, Megan, let's go get you cleaned up before the cops get here."

"Cops?" I ask, confused.

"Yeah, babe. You're going to have to give them a few minutes. No way is that douchebag going to get away with trying to force his hand with you."

"What?"

"Megan, are you okay? Jesus Nate, give her your shirt or something." Dani rushes around her brother and I feel her messing with my dress. When I look down I almost throw up again. The whole top of my dress is torn and hanging by my hips. "Your back is red. Did he touch your back?"

I shake my head to tell her it was just when the chain snapped but no words come out. I'm too mortified that my dress malfunction had me exposed during my struggle.

"I saw him pull against the top of her dress. When the back ripped I think it snapped against her," Nate snaps, his tone hard. He's holding on to his anger by a thread.

"What?" she questions.

They stop talking and I feel fabric being pulled over my head.

"Megan, he was taking you to the exit."

I blanch at Nate's words and his eyes widen as I bend forward and lose the rest of my stomach across his shoes.

Between Nate, Zac and Dani, they have me cleaned up and sitting on the couch in the owner's office. Dani hasn't let go of my hand since she sat down next to me. Zac has been off and on the phone since we got in here, standing over in the far corner I can't hear his words, but given that he keeps looking at Dani I think it's safe to bet there will be a very unhappy husband on his way.

I look around the room and try to take my mind off the officer's voice as he questions Nate. It's a nice, clean office, but my skin is still crawling thinking about what could have happened if that man had gotten me out the back door.

I feel dirty.

Not to mention my head is pounding.

"Are you sure she doesn't need EMS to take a look at her?" The officer asks Nate for the tenth time.

I shake my head and hold even tighter to Dani's hand. Nate looks over and gives me a small smile.

"She says no and I'm not about to give her more stress than she needs by forcing it. We'll make sure she's okay."

I glance up and smile weakly at Nate. He gives me a small nod before looking back at the officer. They continue to talk for a few minutes and I zone out. It's been a long time since I felt that helpless rush of fear like I did earlier. The memories that his touch had brought forth are still sticking to my skin. As I think about his hands against my arms, my breathing starts to come rapidly and I feel Dani squeeze my hand.

"It's okay, Megs. It's okay."

I'm not sure who she is reassuring, me or her but I can't form words to respond.

"Where the fuck is my wife?"

I look up at Dani when I hear Cohen's voice thick with rage coming from the hallway. She gives me a small smile and waves at Nate to sit down. I watch as she climbs off the couch and walks over to the office door. When she throws it open Cohen comes rushing through and doesn't stop as his body plows right into Dani. She wraps her arms around him and holds tight as he picks her right off the floor and keeps walking into the room. His head dips into her neck and I can hear him mumbling to her. I tear my eyes away from the intimacy of their connection and turn my head back to the door.

Or I would have looked at the door had there not been a pair of thick thighs covered in dark pants blocking my view. I follow the path of the perfectly pressed material, over the belt—carefully skimming over the gun held at the owner of those thighs and hips—up the trail of buttons on his uniform shirt, until I get to the lightly tan skin on his neck. When I continue my journey I'm met with the dark brown, angry and deeply concerned eyes of Liam Beckett.

He turns his head—his eyes never leaving mine—and says something to Nate. I hear them talk, but I understand not one word out of their mouths. Shock holding me stupid at the sight of Liam. Until the other officer we had been dealing with sticks his ass into their conversation. I lose Liam's eyes when his head snaps over to where the officer is standing.

"Excuse me?"

"Real lucky we got him, Lee. This guy has got a hell of a lot of people looking for him. Nasty guy. Usually he uses drugs to get his women, but he grabbed her right off the floor. Pretty sure he would have—"

Liam's growl shuts him up, "I would stop talking now, McKnight. Remember where you are when you start speaking freely." He looks back down at me, his dark eyes going from every inch of my face before he takes me in sitting there wearing Nate's huge shirt. "Are you hurt?"

I go to speak, but again no words come out.

"Where the fuck is that bitch? She fucking wanted it. Was all over my dick." I hear coming from the hallway and look up right in time to see the jerk from earlier push off two cops standing inside the office and lunge forward, toward me.

Liam moves, stepping in front of me. Mr. Cowboy doesn't make it far, but his words come flying back and that panic from earlier rushes back to the surface.

"Shit, Megan!"

I hear Dani, but my fear is all-consuming and before I can beat it back, my vision starts to blacken and I sway on the couch.

Chapter 4

Liam

"Shit, Megan!"

I whip my head around and watch as all the color drains from her face. I bark at my partner, Daniels, and don't even wait to make sure they have the douchebag secured. I dip, push one arm under Megan's legs and one behind her back, pulling her into my arms and turning to walk toward the door in the back corner of the office. We've been called to this club enough that we're familiar with the layout of the place. Nate jumps and follows my lead, opening the door to the large bathroom.

"Shut the door," I tell him and wait to hear the click of the door.

"Okay, it's shut," Nate says.

I turn toward him and give him a look that would cause most men to piss themselves. Nate just holds his hands up.

"Well, fucking excuse me. It's been a long night. You could have said shut the door *behind* you. And maybe said please," he adds as an afterthought.

"Get. The fuck. Out." I snarl in a deadly serious voice.

Once again, Nate tosses his hands up, the white shirt he had under the one Megan's wearing, stretching against his broad shoulders.

I don't turn my gaze from the door until long after Nate had pulled it closed, this time with him on the other side of it. I can feel my breathing coming rapidly and despite the fact that I know I need to calm down before I take care of Megan, I can't seem to ease the fear that I have had since I got the call from Zac. When her small hand reaches up and presses lightly against my chest, I take a deep breath, and let the calm of her touch seep through my skin. Even through my vest, I can feel her touch like a branding burn to my skin.

Turning I look deep into her eyes, careful to keep my anxiety from being seen. She looks up at me, her brown eyes assessing and roaming over my face. I can tell she's trying to place my emotions and it's not something I want to add to her plate. She doesn't need my shit to add to what she must be feeling after almost being taken by a known rapist.

"You okay, Megs?"

"It's Megan," she mumbles.

I close my eyes and drop my head until my forehead is resting against hers. "You're okay," I breathe out in a rush, my body relaxing instantly.

Her body jerks in my arms, but I don't move. When I open my eyes and meet her gaze, her gasp tells me that I'm doing a shit job at hiding my feelings right now.

"Not a call I like getting, darlin'. Scared me to my core."

She pushes at my chest with my words and I wait a beat before dropping her slowly to her feet. I don't move my body away from hers; instead I wrap my arms around her and pull her as close as I can get her with my belt in the way. She struggles, not against my hold, but with where to put her arms. Finally settling with just letting them hang at her sides. I hate that she won't take some strength from me. Dipping my head, I press my mouth against her neck, smiling when I feel her shudder. I don't speak, but when I take a deep breath, pushing the air out in a rush, she shivers again in my hold.

"You've been avoiding me, Megs. I don't like it."

"It's Megan."

I laugh softly, "Yeah, baby."

I don't speak again, just continue to hold her while she shifts awkwardly. Finally with no other option, her arms come up from hanging limply at her sides and wrap loosely around me. My belt digs into her abdomen and I curse the fucking thing for keeping us apart. We don't speak and it takes a few seconds before she pushes against my hold, giving her the space she needs to drop her arms back down to her sides.

I take another deep breath and allow her to fully pull away. Her arms instantly shoot up and wrap around herself in a protective stance that makes my relief from just seconds before vanish instantly.

“This ends now,” I state.

“What does?”

“The games, baby. No more avoiding me.”

I bend, pressing my lips against hers, but don't move to deepen the kiss. When I back away, I move my hand and lightly caress the marks that asshole left against her pale skin. They aren't going to bruise, but they're fresh enough that I can still see the impression of his fucking thumb and just that mark alone has me wanting to charge through the club to put a bullet through his skull.

“He touched you.”

“I'm okay, Liam.”

Dipping my head, I move until my eyes are level with hers.

“Not yet, but you will be,” I tell her.

I give her another kiss, this time I linger, letting her feel what I wish I could say without spooking her further. When I pull back, I study her eyes before turning and walking to the door. I give her another glance over my shoulder, her eyes wide and her body soft, no longer holding herself in a protective move. With a wink, I turn the knob and walk through the door.

Chapter 5

Megan

"Molly, baby?" I call down the hall toward her room, sighing when I don't get a response. "Molly?"

"Yeah!" she screams, running around the corner and crashing into me with a giggle. I wince when her arms reach up and touch the soreness on my arms. Luckily she misses it and with a bounce jumps back to smile up at me.

"What have you been doing in there, baby?" I ask and run my hand through her soft blonde curls.

"Playing," she says with a smile.

"Playing what?"

"G.I Joes. Mr. Reid told me all the tough guys are Joes. He said so. He wouldn't play with my Barbie's, only with the Joes."

I laugh at the thought of big bad Axel Reid playing with anything close to dolls. "Did he, now?"

"Yup! I gotta go!" She turns and runs back to her room before I can even form another word, let alone ask her if she wants pizza for dinner. It's our Sunday night ritual to have a pizza and a movie date, but after her sleepover with the Reid's, I'm sure she's going to be ready to crash early.

After the night I had last night—the one I still feel with every move I make—I'm just too tired to think about cooking. Dani and Cohen dropped me off in the wee hours this morning after we finished up at the club. I waved off their concern and they left worried, but I needed to be alone. The first thing I did was take the hottest shower that I could stand. Then after a few pain pills, I crashed and the only thoughts that had filtered through my mind were ones of Liam.

I walk back to the kitchen and allow a smile to form when I think about this morning when I went to pick up Molly, despite her whines to stay with Mr. Reid.

I wasn't the only one that thought it was hilarious that my five-year-old daughter had wrapped him around her small finger. Izzy couldn't stop laughing. She answered the door with a small giggle and told me to follow her. When I found Molly running a brush through Axel's hair, I joined Izzy in her laughter. Apparently, my daughter had been giving him a make-over for a good hour before I got there. When he turned, red lips and pink blush were all over his face, and he gave me a wink.

"If you think that's funny, wait until you see Nate," Izzy laughed in a hushed whisper.

"Where's Owen?" I question, looking past my smiling daughter.

"Oh, Dani and Cohen were back before the sun was even up to pick him up. I'm shocked they lasted as long as they did," Izzy says with a smile.

"I didn't even have the door all the way open before Cohen was pushing his way in and snatching my boy back," Axel adds on a grumble from the floor.

"This way," Molly sings before putting each of her tiny hands on both of Axel's cheeks and turning his head back toward her. "Do this," she demands and smacks her lips together. "It's not big enough," she mumbles and I laugh when she picks up the lipstick tube.

"Baby, I'm not so sure Mr. Reid will think that is his color."

My face reddens when I think about the burden she's been on them. Molly has always been a child that loves easily and loves big, but usually she's shy around men. She had just turned two when Jack passed away and it's always been just the occasional babysitter until Dani's parents started keeping her. Of course, she knows and loves Cohen and Chance, but even that took her months to warm up to them. It shouldn't be a shock that she instantly connected to Dani's father, the older she gets the more curious she has become, and she has recently been asking more and more about Jack. My heart squeezes when I think about all the things she's missed out on.

"Of course it is, right Molly-wolly?" Axel booms. His voice literally vibrates through the room.

"Get ready for it," Izzy strangely says and I turn to look at her only to have my confusion intensify when she just smirks.

"Where, oh where, is the Princess of Pretty? Oh, Princess! I'm in the need of your magic for I have lost my way! There's no time to waste! The ball is in minutes, no seconds!"

My jaw drops. Eyes widen. And I have to work to keep the hilarity of this moment from bubbling out.

If I thought Axel boomed earlier I was wrong. Because skipping—*skipping on his toes*—comes Dani's older brother, Nate Reid, his voice vibrating through their large living room. All six-foot-something of his muscular frame with a sheet wrapped around his hips as a makeshift dress, and tank top flipped up and folded between his huge pecs to make some sort of weird bra. His make-up is even heavier than his father's, his green eyes even brighter with the amount of shadow my daughter has painted, in what I can only guess is her best impression of raccoon eyes. His lips look like he was stung by hundreds of bees, the red circle of lipstick going from mid chin to the bottom of his nose. But it's his hair that makes me lose the fight to keep the laughter in. He has what has to be twenty ponytails pulling his shoulder length hair up in a million different directions.

He skips toward me, stops and my laughter gets to a level of insanity when he gives me a crooked grin and curtsies before spinning on his feet and falling dramatically onto the floor next to Molly—who is smiling a crooked grin of her own at him.

"Princess, please stop trying to make that ugly troll pretty and tell me where I go to get to the ball! I have to meet the prince before midnight!" Nate takes one thick hand and throws it over his forehead in a dramatic fashion that would give the best actors a run for their money.

"Troll!" Axel yells and kicks out his foot to jab his son in the hip. "I'll show you a troll!"

I watch in fascination as the two very manly men wrestle on the floor, not for one second caring that they're both dressed for a day of drag.

I'm shaken from my thoughts of the morning madness when the doorbell rings. My brow furrows and I switch gears from the kitchen to go answer the door. The only people that would be coming over would be Dani, Cohen, Chance or maybe Nate—after last night he's called a few times to make sure I'm okay. Given that I just got off the phone with Dani, I'm sure it isn't her. Chance would call first and since I know he's going through some personal stuff after the issues Dani had before Owen was born, I know it isn't him. Chance only comes over when he needs someone to talk to, and lately he hasn't been happy when I push for him to go see someone over the depression he's fallen into.

I pull the door open and stop dead.

Liam.

"Miss me, Megs?"

My jaw drops when he shoulders his way into my house and I turn to snap at him when I catch a whiff of pizza.

"What—"

My words die when he leans down and gives me a hasty kiss.

"Pizza."

That's all he says. He holds up the *five* boxes of pizza in his hands and turns to walk through the house. He knows where the kitchen is; he came with Dani, Cohen and the rest of the crew when Molly had her fifth birthday party a few months ago. He didn't say much, but I felt his eyes on me every second that he was there.

"You can't be here," I snap.

He looks over from where he's putting the pizzas down on the counter and rolls his eyes. "Baby, I've been inside you."

He did not just say that.

"You did not just say that, Liam Beckett." My face heats, but not with embarrassment, oh no, he's got me about as angry as I've ever been.

"It's the truth," he says raising one dark brow in a manner that makes me think he's just daring me to give him a fight.

"My daughter is here, Liam."

"You don't call me Lee like everyone else, why?" He questions, while ignoring me.

"You can't be here," I say again, my voice wavering with panic. Molly has never seen me with a man. Well, she has, but never one on one like this. Alone in her home. Mainly because I've never been on a date much less slept with someone since Jack died. She isn't ready for this.

"I told you last night no more games. Knew you wouldn't make it easy for me, baby, but this right here," he stopped to point between him and me, "this is me not letting go. I'll give you last night, even though I don't like it, I was on shift and you needed some time, space. You didn't need me breathing down your neck making sure you were okay. Nate did the calling, kept me in the loop. Cost me, staying away from you when every inch of my body was screaming to come and make sure you were okay. Gave you the day and now I'm here. With pizza," he adds as almost an afterthought.

"With pizza," I parrot.

He nods his head and my anger grows.

"*With pizza!*" I shriek.

"Pizza!" I hear screamed from the other side of my small ranch house and close my eyes in prayer.

Please, *please.*

Maybe she'll forget she heard that and not come in here.

Maybe . . .

Not.

"Pizza! Yay!" Molly comes bounding in the room and skids to a halt when she sees Liam standing with one hip against the island. "Hi," she says with a huge smile.

Liam smiles his knee-melting smile and pushes off the counter. I hold my breath when he walks the few steps over to Molly and drops to her level and holds out his hand. "Hi," he says softly, his smile getting even bigger and even more knee-melting when Molly places her small hand in his.

"You came Lee," she sighs. Even my daughter is easily charmed by that smile.

Wait. What? He came?

"Yeah, little lady, I did. Told you I would," he strangely responds.

She giggles, much to my shock, and pumps her small arm up and down to shake his hand.

"Yup! I'm five. See," she yells in her youthful glee and pulls her hand from his and holds it inches from his face to show him all of her pink tipped fingers. "Want me to give you a make-up-ver?" She asks with a big smile.

Liam looks up at me with a smile and a question in his eyes.

"Baby, Liam doesn't want you to give him a make-over. He's got to go." I give him a hard glare and hope he gets a hint.

"Go where?" Molly asks.

"Yeah, babe, where?" Liam adds with a smile. That damn knee-melting smile.

"Home."

"Nope. I don't have to go home."

I narrow my eyes at him.

"See! He said he doesn't got to go, Mommy! Wanna do a tea party now?" Molly jumps and spins around the room.

"A word, Liam?" I say through a clenched jaw as I watch Molly turn and grab the doll she dropped when she saw Liam. Making sure she isn't paying attention to us before I return my focus to the man standing in front of me.

"No."

"No?" I gasp.

"Megs, let me be clear here. The only word you want to have is the one that has me leaving and we both know that isn't what you really want. Listen to me and hear it this time. I'm not leaving. I'm not letting you have weeks and weeks of avoiding me. I'm not giving up. And I'm not stopping until you admit to yourself that you see what we could have between us."

"What . . . what we could have?" I whisper and shake my head.

"You need some time to come to terms with it, that's okay, I'll give you that, but you're going to have it with me doing everything I can to remind you what this is."

"What this is? We had one night."

He looks at me. His eyes burn brighter and his smirk turning devilish. "Yeah, I'll give you that one too. But we've also been doing the foreplay dance long before that one night that solidified everything I needed to know, baby. What did that *one night* show you?"

I open my mouth and snap it shut. What am I supposed to say to that? Logically I can argue that we don't know each other, well past the biblical sense, but I know him. Just because I've done everything I can to avoid him because of what he made me feel during the night I lost myself in his bed.

Over and over.

"You have to go," I breathe, my words coming out a hushed whisper that if it wasn't for his eyes going soft, I would have sworn he couldn't hear me.

"Yeah, that's the last thing I need to do. Come on, Megs, come pick out some pizza and let's eat."

With that, he turns, smiles down at Molly and proceeds to charm my daughter with pizza and that damn knee-melting smile.

Chapter 6

Megan

"Will Lee be here when I wake up, Mommy?" Her lyrical voice is tired with sleep but I can't miss the hopefulness in her eyes.

"No, baby," I sigh.

It's been Lee this and Lee that for the last three hours. One of which I spent throwing daggers at him across the table while him and Molly chatted about everything and anything and the other two while we watched *Frozen,* while he held her in his arms and watched every second. I, however, spent the entire movie freaking out while I watched my daughter become enamored with him.

"But—"

"Goodnight, my princess. Tomorrow I'll make blueberry pancakes, okay?"

She smiles, all thoughts of Liam forgotten with the mention of her favorite breakfast.

"Love you, Mommy."

"Love you back, baby, to the moon and beyond."

I give her another kiss and turn to leave the room, shutting off the light and closing the door. I rest my head against her closed door for a few seconds before I turn to walk down the hall. Stopping short when I see Liam leaning against the wall at the end of the hall.

"You need to leave," I tell him, ignoring the fact that he watched me and my little silent moment of freaking out.

He doesn't give me a chance to pass him, his hand sweeping out in front of me and curling around my body before pulling me toward him. My traitorous body sings its joy when his skin touches mine.

"We need to talk."

I shake my head and narrow my eyes, which just earns me a laugh.

"Yeah, I can see we need to talk."

"I don't see what we need to talk about, Liam. We had a night, one night, and I'll admit it was good . . . what?" I question when his brow shoots up.

"Good? Baby, that's all you have for me?"

"Well it was."

"Good wasn't when you came against my mouth the first or third time. Good wasn't when your thighs squeezed me so hard I might even have bruises months later. *GOOD* wasn't when you screamed my name, and baby you did, so damn loud my ears felt that for days. Good doesn't even come close."

"Well, it was good."

"No, Megs. It was fucking unbelievable."

His words stop me and I—for the first time—really look at him. His nostrils are flaring and his eyes have turned into that gold flecked burning that brought me to my knees, literally. Good lord, he's serious.

"It's Megan," I say weakly.

"You felt it," he presses, ignoring me.

I shake my head, refusing to give him what he wants.

He tips his head back and I can see his lips moving.

"Are you . . . counting?" I question.

He doesn't answer right away, but his lips continue to move and he is definitely counting.

"Why are you counting?"

His breath comes out and his lips thin. Then to my ever growing frustration, he continues to count.

"Why are you counting?" I ask, again.

He continues before looking back down. His eyes hold mine for a few beats before he looks down at my lips before meeting my eyes again. My breath stalls in my throat with the intensity I see in his eyes.

"I'm counting, *Megan*, because if I don't, I'll take you right here in the fucking hallway. Your baby is right down the hall so that would be a bad idea. I'm counting because I'm trying to have enough patience for the both of us. I'm counting because my damn cock is so hard, I'm not sure how there is any more blood flowing through my body. I'm counting, *Megan*, because I want you more than I've wanted anything in my life and *that* frustrates the shit out of me because you either can't or won't see it. I need you to see it, baby. I really need you to see. I'm counting because since last night, leaving you when I wanted nothing more than to drag you home where I can keep you safe, I've been filled with nothing but worry about how you're handling everything. I guess you could say I'm counting so I don't lose my shit."

I'm shaking my head before he even stops talking and he just sighs deeply.

"Why?" I ask, ignoring the vast majority of what he just said.

I'm not even sure what I'm asking, but clearly he does, because without letting go he turns and leads me to the living room. He stops at the worn leather loveseat letting me go long enough to settle his body before he reaches out with both hands on my hips and drags me down. My knees hit the seat and my bottom presses against his hard thighs. He moves around until he's leaning back and pulls both my hands forward. I watch in fascination as he pulls one of my clammy hands toward his chest. My right hand right above his heart. I try to pull my hand away, but he holds strong.

"Let me tell you something. I've been watching you, Megan. You came into our group kicking and screaming, even if you didn't do it physically, you were resisting all the same. Dani, being all that is Dani, pulled you in and refused to let you go. She has that way about her, always seeing what people need even if they can't see it for themselves. Months. It took months before I saw you even smile. But I still watched. Watched and waited."

"Waited for what?" I ask, the words coming out as shaky as I feel. His heart beating strong and steady under my palm.

"For you to see."

I cock my head to the side and wait for him to continue.

"You saw it that night, baby. And you saw it last night when you went from shivering in fear to a comforting calm just with my hands on your body. I wasn't alone in that bed, Megan, and I damn sure wasn't alone last night."

"It was dark," I say lamely thinking about our night together.

"Yeah and what I'm talking about is something you don't need light to see, baby."

Well, now I'm even more confused.

"You won't get it right away. Hell, you might not even see it, but you will eventually. I've been waiting, Megan and after last night, I'm done waiting. It's time for me to help you *see*."

"See what!" I snap.

"Everything."

That's it. That's all he says. He gives me a smirk, his dimple coming out with his knee-melting smile and his eyes burning bright. I sit there like a dead weight on his lap with my hands still against his chest, his heart beating steady under my palm and try to understand his words.

"Everything? What is that even supposed to mean?"

His smirk grows into a smile. One that has my fingers curling into his skin and my thighs involuntarily pressing against his legs to try and ease the pressure building.

"You'll see."

"Look, Liam. You're a nice guy and all that, but I just don't think you and I are on the same page here."

"Same book, different chapters, baby. Don't worry, you'll learn to read fast."

"Ugh! I don't think you get it. I mean, I tried to be nice about it. It was sex, Liam. Just sex. I needed it, you gave it, and we both got something out of it. Why can't you just leave it at that?"

He throws his head back and laughs. I literally stop breathing at the sound. That burn in my gut coming back tenfold.

A burn that I haven't felt in so long.

Feelings.

He turns his eyes back to mine and smiles when he sees my expression. "Ah, I see you're starting to understand."

Okay, now I'm getting pissed. I rip my hands from his grasp, instantly missing the warmth of his chest against my palms. I want to kiss him and I want to slap him all in the same breath.

"You don't understand, Liam. I can't . . . I just . . . I can't do this." My nose burns and I can feel the emotion start to climb up my throat, but I beat it down. I try to get up but his hands quickly grab my hips and he pulls me tighter against his lap. "I can't," I choke out, once again fighting the emotions from bubbling out.

"Wrong, Megan. You can, you're just afraid."

"You're fucking right, I'm afraid." My eyes widen when I realize what I've given away. I shake my head and struggle against his hold. His face softens and his eyes don't leave mine when he lifts his hands from my hips. I scramble off his lap so quick that I lose my balance and crash to the floor. He moves quickly to help me, I hold my hand up and give him the back of my head. "No. Don't."

"Megs."

"It's Megan, dammit!" I scream before clamping my lips tight. "Please, it's Megan. I haven't been Megs in three years, Liam. I need you to get *that* if you don't get anything else."

He doesn't say anything and when I get the courage, I turn and look him in the eyes from my position on the floor. He's pulled his body to the edge of the seat and his arm is still outstretched to help me off the floor. His eyes, they're telling me everything his silence isn't. He gets it and to my shock it looks as if it hurts him just as much as it hurts me.

"I can't be Megs,"

"All right, darlin'. I understand," he says softly. "I need you to be honest with me, sweetheart. Please. I get that this is new, sudden and scary for you. You get me when I say I've been waiting?"

I shake my head.

He sighs, "Can you please let me help you off the floor?"

I shake my head again and use the coffee table to pull myself to my feet, going to sit on the couch opposite from him instead of the chair next to where he's sitting on the loveseat.

His eyes get hard, but as quickly as his frustration was shown, it's gone.

"Yeah, I'll let you have that play, baby. You need to be as far from me as you can to think that will put some distance between us, that's fine. Won't work, but I'll give you that."

"You drive me nuts." I tell him honestly.

"Probably. But I want you to think about it and really think about it and tell me that it's a feeling you don't like."

I narrow my eyes, "Who in their right mind would like being driven nuts?" I ask him, my voice growing higher.

His lip turns up, just the side with that damn dimple, and I harden my gaze. All that earns me is the other side curling up until he is giving me the full force of that smile. Thank God I'm sitting or I would melt in a pile of goo. He smiles at me for a few more seconds before his face grows serious. My chest starts to rise and fall with each breath as he sits there and just looks at me. His dark eyes seemingly see right through me. I curl my arms around my chest and wait. It isn't until he opens his mouth that I lose every ounce of air in my lungs.

"You like it because it makes you feel, Megan."

I gasp.

How? How can he know? How can he have a clue that I, for the first time in three years, felt something other than my love for Molly and I only did that because of him?

"You're getting it. I'm a patient man, Megan. I've waited for you. Waiting for that person that would make *me* feel and, baby, I'm ready. You aren't, but you will be. I just have to make you remember how good feeling is."

"You don't know me," I evade, ignoring his all too accurate nail on the head.

"I know you, Megan. You've been around this group for over a year now. A year of you being in a fog while everyone around you was living. You've forgotten what it's like to live and I'm going to remind you. And while I'm reminding you, all you have to do is feel. Then you'll get it."

"Get what," I say softly.

"Everything."

I open my mouth but close it when he shakes his head.

"It's sudden. You don't get this now, but you will, what feels sudden to you, feels just right to me. I'm not going away, Megan." He pushes off the loveseat and walks over to where I'm sitting in shock, and kneels in front of me. "You were *going to be* mine long before you tripped into my arms at the reception, Megan. You moaned my name as your body greedily sucked my cock dry and I knew you would *be* mine. And you *became* mine last night as I held you trembling in my arms. I've got all the time in the world to make sure that happens. Sleep tight, I'll see you in the morning." He lifts up, gives me a long look until he sees whatever he's looking for and before he's completely standing gives me a kiss on my forehead. "Lock up behind me."

And with that, Liam walks out the front door.

I rush forward when the door closes and turn both the locks before I turn my back to the door and slide down until my ass hits the floor. Looking across the entryway, my eyes take in the pictures that are sitting on a small table across from the door. Right there is a picture of Jack holding a newborn Molly. I look into his handsome face, his bright blue eyes and black hair shaved close to his head, and let the sob that had threatened earlier bubble up.

It's time, Megs.

I close my eyes tight when I hear his voice filter through my mind. Shaking my head back and forth as the tears fall rapidly.

He's right. You need to feel again, Megs.

My eyes clamp tighter.

I miss him. My Jack. My best friend.

It's time, Megs.

The voice repeats.

I pull my legs up and wrap my arms around them.

It feels wrong, after everything that Jack had done for me, to feel this way for Liam. It shouldn't feel like guilt, but it does. I'm still here when Jack is gone. I'm still breathing when he gave his life for me.

He's right. It's time. I need to take this final step and open myself up to live again.

I stayed on the floor until my face was stiff with dried tears. My bottom was asleep and my chest hurt with the force of my sobs. But I finally got up. Instead of going to my bed though, I went to my daughter's room and pulled her into my arms.

My daughter who looks everything like her father even though I wish she looked like Jack.

Chapter 7

Liam

Last night I stood at the other side of her door and fought every instinct I have in my body to not break that door down while I listened to her sob. I waited until I heard her tears stop. Then I waited even longer while the lights through her house turned off one by one. It wasn't until I could uncoil my body from its position outside her front door that I was able to leave. Pulling each of the palms that I had resting against the wood of her front door to stand up straight and force my legs to take me to my truck.

Even then it was another ten or so minutes before I was able to turn the key and pull out of her drive. Leaving her tonight, knowing she was in pain, is even harder than it was to walk away from her in the club owner's private bathroom.

I make a mental note before pulling out of her drive that her grass is about a week past the point of really needing to be cut.

When I turn out of her neighborhood I press the button on my steering wheel that will allow me to make a phone call. Wincing slightly when I see it's almost past ten.

"Call Dani home," I say into the silence around me.

"Calling Dani home," I hear before the sound of ringing comes from the speakers.

"Hey," she says softly into the phone.

"That . . . God, Dani," I say in lieu of a greeting.

I don't need to say anything else. Dani has been my best friend since before we were out of diapers. She knows me better than I know myself sometimes. There isn't anything that I wouldn't do for her and the same goes with her.

"That bad?" she asks.

"I knew I would be in for a fight. I knew it, but it still doesn't make it easier to leave when I know she needs me. Do you know how hard it was to wait a full fucking day to come over here?"

"Lee."

"Don't Dani. Don't tell me I might not be the one she needs. I didn't give you that shit when you were fighting for Cohen to see you."

"That's not fair," she gasps.

"How is it not?"

"Cohen and me are completely different and you know it, Lee. Megs is . . . she's been through a lot."

"It's Megan." I say harshly. The look in her face coming back like a physical slap when I saw how much pain that nickname brings her. The nickname her dead husband called her.

"What?" Dani demands, clearly confused with my anger.

"I used to think it was cute how she always corrected me when I called her that. Well, it wasn't cute tonight, Dani. Jack called her that. I have enough against me here, I don't need to be bringing that pain to her every time I call her that. So just don't okay?"

She doesn't say anything for a second. "I didn't know." I can hear her shifting through the line and she tells Cohen she'll be right back before I hear her moving through her house. "She never told me Jack called her Megs, Lee. Hell, I call her that all the time. She's never once corrected me."

"That's because she's locked up tight, Dani. She doesn't tell anyone anything that might cause her to feel a thing."

"She's been through a lot, Lee. Do you think . . . I don't know, maybe this won't end how you are hoping it will."

My fingers curl around the wheel and I let out a deep breath. "That isn't something I can accept, Dani."

"I've never seen you like this Lee. I don't know how to help you when I'm not sure that this is best for you."

"What did you feel when you were without Cohen? When he went overseas that last time? What did you really feel like?" I ask, clearly confusing her yet again with my change of subject because she's silent for a few minutes.

"I felt nothing, Lee. You know that. I felt nothing but pain."

"Yeah? And you knew he was coming back. You were scared for him, understandably, but you knew he would be back. Take that feeling out of the equation and then add three years of locking yourself tight, then tell me what you have left."

She lets out a shaky breath. I hate bringing up when Cohen was gone. I know it was the hardest time Dani ever had. But in order to understand Megan, to understand my fight *for* Megan, she has to go back there.

"I felt nothing, Lee," she sighs, her breath choppy. "I felt like I was living half a life with him gone. Half a life that I knew wouldn't get better without him."

"Yeah, and thank fuck it didn't happen, but if he hadn't come back to you? Then what would you have felt?"

"Nothing, Lee." She stops and I know this is costing her. "I wouldn't have felt alive."

"Bingo, Dani. Bingo."

"She feels, Lee. She has Molly."

"She feels, but she's forgotten what it feels like to be alive."

Dani gasps and I hear Cohen ask her if she's okay in the background. "I'm fine, baby, I'll be just another second, okay?"

"Yeah, Dani-girl. You tell Lee if you're still crying in five minutes I'm going to come kick his ass though."

"Noted, Dani." I tell her and she laughs softly and I hear her give Cohen a kiss.

"What can I do?" she asks after a beat.

"Help me show her that she's alive."

"I'm not sure that's something that can be shown so easily, Lee."

"That's where you're wrong," I tell her and feel that flicker of hope start to burn a little brighter when my plan starts to take form. "Tomorrow, meet me at the house for lunch? I've got something I need to take care of in the morning, then . . . then we plan."

She laughs and agrees, not before telling me I'm crazy. When we get off the phone I take a deep breath and let the surge of excitement that this plan gives me, to douse that flicker of hope until it's a full on burning inferno.

Luckily I have the day off. Last night I had been coming off a two-day run of ten-hour shifts, giving me the next two days free. When I pull up to my house at eleven thirty, Dani's SUV was sitting in the drive. My sweaty skin sticks to the leather seat when I pull my body out of my truck. I reach in and grab my sweat-drenched shirt that I had tossed on the floor earlier and make my way up the walkway to the front door.

"Dani?" I yell into the house.

"Back here in the kitchen. I think something's dead in here."

I smile at her words and make my way toward her voice.

"Yeah, might be last week's Chinese. Or maybe that was two weeks ago."

I turn the corner into my kitchen and see her with half her body in the fridge and two full garbage bags at her feet.

"Christ, how long have you been here?"

"You're lucky I'm not your mom. She would kick your ass for letting things get this gross."

She pulls herself out of the fridge and turns toward me right when I'm about to give her a hug. "Don't you dare come near me when you're wet with sweat, Liam Beckett!" She backs up when I smile and go to do just that. "Hell no, you nasty pig!" She laughs and jumps over the trash bag she had been working on filling up and holds her hands up. "Do it and I tell Cohen you touched my boob!"

That stops me in my tracks.

"First, uh no. Second, not funny. The last time you pulled that shit I had a black eye for two weeks. And I'll add that I didn't even touch your tit, my shoulder brushed against it when we were stuck playing drunk twister."

"Whatever," she smiles.

"Yeah, whatever my ass. You didn't get the black eye AND you spent an hour after it laughing your ass off."

I reach past her and grab a bottle of water out of the fridge. Turning to look at her again.

"Why is there only water in here?"

"You should be thankful I considered that was safe enough to stay. I figured with them being in sealed bottles they could stick around. I thought about calling the CDC in to make sure there wasn't something dangerous living in that fridge!" She throws the towel she had been wiping the fridge out with and I just barely move out of the way.

"So, I've been busy."

"You work too much," she says, changing the subject and grabbing a water of her own before heading to the sink to wash her hands.

"So you've told me, *Mom.*" I sigh.

She sticks her tongue out at me, same old Dani, when she can't think of an insult back, out comes the tongue.

"I have my mom's lasagna cooking and it should be ready by the time you hose your nasty smelling ass off. Then you can clue me in to why I left my family to come over here." She smiles and I know she doesn't mean it, but I feel guilty for pulling her away.

"Sorry, Dani. I could have waited a day or two."

"Don't be sorry, Lee. You know I'm joking. Plus, when I left my boys were watching a baseball game. They probably won't even notice that I'm gone."

I tip up the water and down the whole bottle in one go. I should have thought to bring water with me earlier, but I was in a hurry to get everything done.

"Where have you been anyway?" Dani asks before lifting her own water to her lips.

"Megan's. Mowed her yard, weeded the flowerbeds and fixed up a few boards that had started to warp on her fence. Stuff like that."

I turn and walk out of the room leaving a shocked face Dani with water dribbling out of her open mouth.

"Jumping in the shower!" I call over my shoulder and head off to get cleaned up.

Twenty minutes later I walk back in to my now sparkling kitchen to find Dani impatiently tapping her foot with her arms crossed over her chest.

"Tell me all of it. Now." She demands with a smile.

"What do you want to know?" I ask, pretending I have no idea what she wants.

"You can't drop a bomb like that and just walk away, Lee!"

"I told you everything. I went to her house this morning, did some work and came home."

"Uh uh," she nods, her smile growing. "And? Did you see Megan? Talk to her? Anything?!"

"Good Christ, calm down." I shake my head and walk over to the table and sit down. "Where's my mail?" I look up and see Dani hasn't moved and now she looks like she's about to come out of her skin if I don't give her something.

"Junks in the trash, bills are over there," she says with a point over her shoulder, "Now speak."

"Impatient much?"

"Lee!"

"You act like I've never been interested in a woman before, Dani."

"Well, you haven't. Not like this."

I pause and think, God she might be right. I dated through high school and college. I had a few serious girlfriends, but no one that I've had to work for it with. And definitely no one that I could see myself bringing home to meet my parents. Megan on the other hand, I can't wait to bring her and Molly home.

"She's different, Dani." I wait for her to sit down before I continue. "You know how it is, you have it with Cohen. It's not something I can describe, I just know. I felt the same way back when she first started coming around. Every time she walks into a room it's like I can feel her. Fuck, I sound like a sappy Lifetime movie."

She sighs and rests her cheek on her hand. I just shake my head and laugh under my breath.

"It is pretty fucking sappy."

"It's beautiful."

"Remember when we got drunk a few years ago and I went on and on about how one day I would find *her*? Well, I did. I found that person that is worth fighting for. The one that makes me excited to just be around her."

"Damn, Lee. How long have you felt this way?"

"I'm not sure. A few months before Owen was born. But I don't think I really understood what I was feeling until your accident." I stop to make sure she isn't having any issues at the mention of the accident that almost took her and Owen from us. "I remember when she got to the hospital she was exhausted from running around all day with Molly with the added panic of rushing to find a sitter. She was a mess. Emotionally holding on by a thread. She sat in the corner and wouldn't move her eyes from Cohen. The whole time she just looked at him with nothing but fear and worry."

I look over from where I had been looking off in the distance of the back yard when I hear Dani sniff.

"She was so alone, Dani. I couldn't just see it, I felt it. I could *feel* her pain and even then it killed me. After Mom and Dad got there, I moved from them to sit with Megan. She didn't speak, hell I'm not even sure she knew it was me she was holding on to, but I held her hand until they came out to tell us what was going on. When the doctor was talking to Cohen I thought she was going to break my hand, she held on so tight. That woman has so much love in her, she's just afraid to give it."

"God, you're gonna make me cry, Lee."

"Anyway, I felt the attraction to her before then, but sitting there in the hospital with her, I just knew. I've spoken to her a bunch of times before then, but at that moment, when I wanted nothing more than to reach inside her and pull her pain away, I knew there was more to it. I've tried to take it further a few times since then. Made my attraction known. Waited for her to take the bait. I didn't have my chance until your reception."

She opens her mouth and her eyes get huge. "You took advantage of her when she was drunk?" she screams.

"Are you serious?" Of all the reactions, didn't think I would get that one from my closest friend. "Tell me you aren't fucking serious."

"Lee, I was there, she had been drinking."

"Yeah, drinking, she wasn't drunk. I see drunk almost daily at work. I know the difference between enjoying the party with a few drinks with a good buzz and shit faced. She was one hundred percent herself when I was with her."

"With her?"

Jesus, this girl.

"What is it that you think would happen, Dani? I practically fucked her on your parents' back lawn!" I boom, getting frustrated.

"Oh, well that was hard to miss." She rolls her eyes and leans back in her seat. "So, you guys went somewhere and hooked up, got it. Have you not seen her since then?"

"She's been avoiding me."

She laughs and I give her a hard look.

"Well, okay."

"I told her last night I was done with the games."

She slaps my arm. "You did that after everything she went through?" she asks shocked.

"No. I did that when I could tell she needed a distraction to keep her mind from going into self-preservation mode. I did that because when I got that call, I thought that I was going to go out of my mind with worry. I pulled that shit because I'll be fucking God dammed if I let a day go past that I'm not there to make sure shit like that doesn't happen again."

I take a deep breath and remind myself that my anger shouldn't be directed toward Dani.

"Oh. Well. Okay. Now what?"

"Now I figure out how many hoops I have to jump through before she can see past her fear. I understand, she lost her husband and I'm not looking to take his place, but I'm fighting to win here, Dani. I want her."

She doesn't say anything, but I know Dani. She's working out what she wants to say. I stand from the table and grab another water, waiting her out.

"Okay. I think I get it. I mean, I know all about finding that one person and having to fight for it, but I guess I'm worried. Not just for you getting hurt, because as much as I hate to say it, there is a lot of room for you to get hurt here. But, I'm also worried for her and I'm worried for Molly. What happens if Molly gets attached to you,

Lee? She's already lost her father and I know Megan hasn't dated since Jack."

"I know. Fuck, Dani, I know. The last thing I want to do is hurt either one of them."

"Then it's time to plan. Let me call Cohen and let him know I'm going to be awhile." She stands up and walks to her purse. I laugh when she gets on the phone and starts to tell Cohen why his wife isn't going to be home until after dinner. I have a feeling the next time I hit the gym with Cohen he's going to try to kick my ass for this unintentional cock block.

"Dani, you should go home." I tell her when she hangs up with a smirk.

"Nope. Trust me, he got what he wanted out of that."

I laugh and try not think about how Cohen is going to win here.

"So . . . what's the first plan?" she all but screams when she sits back down, rubbing her hands together with a weird grin on her face.

"You're way too excited about this."

"It's not every day your best friend—the all but confirmed bachelor—falls in love."

"Do what?" I question.

"Huh? Where are you confused?"

"The love part."

"Such a guy," she gripes. "What the hell do you think is happening here? Awe, I'm so proud. My big boy is growing up! Wait until your mom hears about this."

That gets my attention real quick. "You will not tell my mom anything about Megan and me until there is a Megan and me, got it?"

"Whatever, Lee. Let's go. Come on. Time to plan."

"I'm not in love, Dani." Fuck. It *is* love.

She gets that stupidly weird grin back on her face and nods her head, "All right, Lee. Not in love, got it. So, let's talk game plan."

Choosing it's better to ignore her than continue fighting her on something she's made her mind up about, I move on, but now that she's mentioned it, I know deep down that the feelings I have for Megan are teetering on the edge of love. One thing is for sure; I wouldn't admit it to Dani first. When I say those words out loud, Megan will be the first one to hear them. Love? It's close, so fucking close.

With a big smile on my face, I spend the next thirty minutes explaining everything I know about Megan, how she's been living half a life, and how she is consumed with fear to let more people in. In the end, I think Dani is more confused than she was when we started.

"Dani, she's afraid to feel. Don't you get it? She lost her husband and you and I both know that's the biggest issue here. She was alone long before Cohen and Chance dragged her into our group and even then she was alone until she let you in. Tell me, has she let any of the other girls in?" I wait until Dani gives me a sad smile. "I didn't think so. She might talk to the girls, but you're the only one that she's let in."

"That doesn't mean much, Lee. She might have let me in, but she still won't really talk to me. Not about anything major. I've tried. I know her and Jack were close, like we are close, they had a friendship long before they got married, but past that she doesn't talk about him. I know she didn't have a good childhood—or hell, life before her and Jack got married. No details though. Nothing past the basics."

Jesus, this is going to be harder than I thought.

"One step at a time. First things first, she has to remember what it feels like to be alive, Dani."

"What? What the hell does that mean?"

I smile and I know Dani can see my determination because she gives me one of her own. "Now I bring her back to life. One day at a time."

"You're crazy."

"Nah, more like determined."

"Well, what's this grand plan entail?"

"What's the best way to feel alive?"

"Lee, I don't think you can just have sex with her every time you see her. Things might get sticky . . . no wait, that's a bad word for it. Gross." She makes a gagging noise and wrinkles her nose up.

"Shut it," I laugh. "Not quite, however when that comes she definitely will remember how alive she is. No, I'm thinking more like doing things that make her heart pound. She needs to *feel* and as much as I can't wait to have her in my bed again, that's going to have to wait. Unfortunately."

"You won't last a week."

"Dani, I'll last a lot longer than a week. I had her one night, I know it's worth the wait."

She just smiles before pulling a piece of paper from her purse and a pen before turning back to me. I watch as she writes in her neat handwriting, *Feeling Alive,* and draws a line under it. "Let's go, big boy. Let's make a list of all the ways you can make Megan feel alive."

I laugh and before I know it, we've filled up the whole damn sheet and Dani stands to leave. I look down at our list and smile.

"You're going to have one hell of a fight on your hands here, Lee," she says and wraps her arms around me in a hug of support.

"Yeah, but it's one worth fighting."

She gives me a squeeze and mumbles, "I'm here if you need me."

"Thanks for today, Dani. Go get home to your boys before Cohen comes kicking my door in."

After walking Dani out, I head over to my cell and pull up an empty text screen. I send what I need and with a smile I head to the living room to catch up on Sports Center before bed.

Chapter 8

Megan

I saved the document I had been working on when my phone chimes. Molly crashed early, so I had been working for a little while before bed. It wasn't often that I got to work before the late hours, so I was soaking it up while I could. One plus about being an author, I set my own hours. Of course the flip side of that, with each release, it was a little bittersweet because I didn't have anyone to share those moments with.

My phone chimes again and I'm reminded of the text that came through earlier.

Unknown: Your house. Tomorrow. Noon.

What in the world?

I run through my mind who could possibly be texting me when my phone goes off again.

Unknown: Don't ignore me. I'll find you.

A shiver runs through me.

Me: Who is this?

Unknown: Lee, baby.

I drop my phone and listen as it clatters against my desk. Liam. My God, he doesn't give up. I pick up my phone and without much thought, program him into my phone.

Me: I'm busy.

Liam: Don't lie, darlin', we both know you aren't busy. Molly will be in school so don't use her as an excuse either. It's my last off day and WE have plans. Night, doll.

Me: I won't be here.

Liam: Then I'll find you.

Me: Liam . . .

Liam: Megan . . .

I ignore him. If I continue with this bazaar game he seems to be playing then I'll just encourage him. I turn my attention back to my computer when my phone chimes again. I spend a few seconds telling myself not to look. Just ignore it. My willpower lasts all of five of those seconds and when a reminder chime goes off, I snatch the phone up and I can't help the smile that slowly tugs my lips up.

Liam: Sweet dreams, darlin'.

I don't respond. I don't acknowledge the warm feeling that covers me like a blanket either. But I also don't stop smiling until long after those sweet dreams he told me to have had taken over.

Each and every one of them included Liam Beckett.

"Mommy! I want to wear the white ones," Molly whines and points to her dress shoes.

"Baby, not today. Let's wear those when you get home from school. The last time you wore them you had blisters. Remember how bad you said your feet hurt?"

She wrinkles her little button nose and her smile drops.

"How about when you get home we can put on a fashion show? We can both wear our pretty shoes."

Just as quickly her mood changes and a big smile takes over her adorable face.

"Kay!" she screams and leaps up to wrap her arms around my neck, causing me to lose my balance from where I had been hunched down to pull her shoes out of the hall closet.

We both land and laugh before I climb up and finish getting her ready for school. By the time we leave the house we're already running ten minutes behind. I try not to pay too much attention to how beautiful my yard looks now that Liam spent yesterday morning giving it some much needed attention. I definitely don't look at the fence on the side of the house that now doesn't look like it is about to fall apart. I most definitely don't look at my now weedless flowerbed and its addition of a wide variety of new flowers he planted yesterday in a rainbow of colors. Nope. I don't notice any of that. And I for sure don't have a huge grin on my face as I drive away from my now perfect yard.

After I drop Molly off at school, I head to the grocery store to get a good shop in while I don't have an energetic five year old with me. The last time she was with me at the store, she very loudly told me and everyone around the freezer section how her 'gina'—what she calls her vagina—got cold when I opened the door to get some ice cream. That's my Molly. No filter at all.

By the time I finish up my shop it's only nine so I rush home and unload before heading back out to run some errands. Errands I really don't need to run.

My plan is to stay as busy as possible. I have to pick up Molly at two thirty, so I have a lot of time to kill. So I do what every woman does when you need to kill a few hours, just walk into a Target. You could probably lose a decade of your life in one shopping trip, not to mention spend enough money to need a second mortgage. That store, it's my crack.

The last time I looked at my watch, while browsing through their book section and peeking for my own—and finding it—it was almost eleven. Two hours so far spent shopping for stuff I don't need, but now don't know how we got along without them. I mean everyone needs wine sippy cups, right? Well, probably not, but they were cute. I just need one more hour and I can start my ride home. Surely Liam will know I'm serious when he shows up and I'm not there.

I turned the corner to take me to the movies and stop dead. Leaning against the new release section with that damn knee-melting smile lighting up his face, is Liam.

I don't move. My full to bursting cart acting as my lifeline and guard against him. He shoves off and starts toward me, but I back up and move the cart toward him to stop his progress. His smile grows.

"Hey, darlin'."

My mouth waters as his deep voice hits my ears. Not to mention I can feel my sex clenching in want.

"You see, I'm not a stupid man, Megan. I didn't think you would continue to play games though, but that's okay—I've always loved to play. Especially when I can take my time and make sure every single move counts."

Surely he didn't mean that as dirty as it sounded? Right? Something tells me that he knows exactly what his words made me think though, because that smile of his hits a level that is just downright sinful. My knees don't just melt, my whole body does.

"Do you want to play games, darlin'?" he asks, sidestepping the cart and pulling my hands from the handle. "I think you would love the kind of games I have in mind." He whispers and leans down. His hands come up and his warm palms frame my face, his fingertips pushing into my hair and he tilts my head up so I'm looking at him. "I would love to show you some of my games, baby. I guarantee you'll be screaming my name again before the day's over." My mouth drops open and I gape at him as he gives me a wink. His eyes never leave mine as he lowers his head and gives me a bruising kiss.

I don't say a word when he pulls away, all sense of thinking has dried up with that kiss.

"Come on, let's get you checked out. Game time, baby."

Games? Oh. Shit.

Of course, Liam doesn't allow me to pay. Which causes a good five minute standoff in the checkout lane that ends, with him snatching my card right out of my hand with a wink before swiping his own.

He grabs my hand and pushes the overflowing cart with his other, and drags me to the parking lot.

"I'm parked over there, Liam." I snap, pointing in the direction of my car.

"I know where you're parked. As soon as we get to your house I'll have Nate meet me there to get your keys. Don't worry, darlin', when we get done, your car will be safe in your driveway."

"What?" I fume.

"You heard me, Megan. Help me out here without throwing too much of that sexy attitude and let's get these bags in the cab."

The shock of his actions only adds to the fury his determination has sparked in me. I can't remember the last time I wanted to choke someone at the same time wanting them to take me against their truck. I don't think I've ever felt this much raw energy.

"You make me so angry." I tell him and he oddly smiles at my words.

"Good."

"Good? You want to make me angry?"

He turns and looks at me. My feet braced apart like I'm gearing up for a fight and my hands fisted at my hips. I'm sure my face is the mirror image of a raging bull.

"Darlin', angry is the last thing I want you to be. But, as far as I can see I'm doing something right because you, babe, are feeling something."

"Huh?"

"You'll get it soon and once those light bulbs click on I hope to fuck you'll let me show you how beautiful being alive can feel."

He leans over and gives me a kiss against my cheek and with a smack to my rear, he turns and continues to throw my bags in his truck.

With no other choice, I climb into the passenger seat and ignore him while he finishes up. He takes the quickest route back to my house and as I'm slamming the door he laughs before speaking again.

"Darlin' go put on something old. Something you don't care to get a little dirty."

I look over at him and roll my eyes before stomping up the path to my front door. Before I open the door, I notice the perfectly pruned rose bush and my anger dissolves a few notches. Not completely, but hey he did spend four hours working on my yard yesterday, he can't be all that bad.

Tossing my purse on the kitchen counter, I spin and have every intention in ignoring his request, but as he walks in the door, dropping the bags softly on the kitchen table, he turns and gives me a wink.

"Come on, Megan. Unless you want me to get you undressed myself. Something tells me we wouldn't make it out the door if that happens and I would hate to lose our appointment time."

I sigh, "I have things to do, Liam."

"Like what?"

"Work." That should work. You can't argue with someone that needs to work.

"Babe that can wait."

"No it can't." I argue.

He steps forward.

I back up.

His smile grows.

My frown deepens.

"What do you need to work on that can't wait a few hours?"

"Stuff."

He throws his head back and booms out a laugh. I notice my mistake the second his eyes look behind me into the formal dining room. I woke up this morning before Molly to get some paperbacks signed from online orders. I had them all lined up with their invoices neatly tucked into each book. There were, if I remember correctly, twenty-seven individual books lined up on the dining room table, eight more piles of series book orders and that doesn't even count the piles that I had yet to personalize and tag with their shipping information.

All my books. The secret life that I've been able to keep from everyone since Jack had passed away. The part of me that I didn't share with anyone anymore—exposed.

I close my eyes and wait for the questions. I wait and wait, my eyes clamping tighter with each passing second. When he doesn't speak I lift my eyes and look where he was standing, only to come up blank. My heart speeds up and a cold like fear seeps through my veins.

Oh, God.

With a deep breath, I turn, and watch in horror as he lifts one of the unsigned books out of a box I had sitting on the floor in the corner. His eyes take in the cover, a simple dark shaded cover with a heart broken in two with ashes falling from the center. *Bleeding Love* imprinted in a beautiful font that doesn't quite match the darkness of the cover.

And my pen name, Megan Sands, like a freaking neon sign right there on the front.

He still doesn't speak, running his fingers over the cover before turning the book and reading the back. I know what he's reading. I wrote that book when I was at my darkest point. It was the one and only book that I wrote the year that Jack died. In a way, it was the only thing, besides Molly, that kept my head above the water. It was through that book that I was able to find some sort of healing peace with the loss of my husband.

I let my love for Jack bleed out between the loss and redeeming love that the main character, Mia, found when she was faced with a tragic loss of her own husband. I let my mind drift over the plot of *Bleeding Love* and it isn't until I think of the name of the hero that my gaze snaps up to Liam's. How could I have forgotten? Someone up there must be having a field day with my life today.

Mia found her peace with her white knight . . . Liam.

God, shoot me dead now.

Liam, still holding the book, opens his mouth to speak but closes it before his words are formed. I wait, knowing they have to be coming.

I watch in shock as he gently places the book back in the box, letting his fingers linger over where my name is printed, before he walks over to me. His eyes are swirling with questions but he doesn't voice a single one. He takes my face—his fingers lingering over where I had been held by that douchebag last night—between his hands and bends to place a light kiss against my lips. When he pulls back, his eyes haven't lost a single ounce of intensity.

"Liam," I whisper.

"Yeah, baby. We're going to get there."

I frown and he leans forward to kiss the crease between my brows.

"A love worth having, is worth fighting for."

I gasp when I recognize the quote from the back of *Bleeding Love* and I feel my eyes grow wet.

"Go get changed, darlin'," he whispers.

As raw as I feel right now, I don't even fight him. I turn, walk down the hall to my room, and grab an old pair of jeans to pull on with one of my paint tank tops.

Liam doesn't say anything when I return to where he's standing. He takes a look at my outfit before giving me a small nod. "Nate's waiting outside for your keys, grab them for me, babe."

I mutely dig in my bag and hand over my keys. Liam doesn't say anything just turns and walks out the front door. I stand there and look around the room and take in all of my books lining the small area. There is no way he doesn't know they're my books. How can he not have questions?

"Here, throw this on." He tosses a Hope Town Police Department hoodie at me and waits for me to listen.

"Isn't it a little warm for this?" I ask, looking down at the big HTPD block letters across the front.

"You can thank me later," he oddly responds.

"Uh, right." I jam my head into the hoodie and feel my pulse race when his scent floods my senses.

After I'm dressed, he waits for me to set the alarm and lock up, leading me back to his truck, opening my door before making his way to the driver's side.

"Can I get a clue?" I ask meekly.

"Just go with it. Promise me though; if for one second you aren't having fun, tell me. And darlin'," he pauses waiting for me to give him my full attention. "Just feel," he oddly says.

I don't respond. I keep quiet until we pull into the local paint ball center. He parks in the lot and kills the engine. I take in the building, surrounded by a tall fence and look back to Liam.

"Step one, even when you feel pain you can be having the time of your life. You don't have to let that pain be the only thing you feel. The fun in paintball is all in the game. Take that pain and remember, it's only temporary and when you get to the end, the only thing that's left is some colors on your skin that help you learn how to play the game better."

"What game?"

"The game of life, darlin'."

"You make no sense."

"Like I said, it will make sense soon darlin', and I can't wait for you to get it."

He drops out of the truck and walks around to my door. I wait for him and we walk into the center, his hand never leaving mine for a second.

After the longest hour of my life while the owner runs us through the rules and safety procedures, I'm being suited up with more protective gear than the swat team probably wears. I'm not sure how I'm expected to move around like this.

Liam looks over after he adjusts the strap on his own helmet, and gives me a grin. "How do you feel?" he asks me.

"Hot. And stiff."

He laughs and hands over my paint ball gun. I look at it and then back up to him. His grin grows and he walks over to show me how it works.

"I think you got it, darlin', just point and shoot. Just don't shoot anyone on our team."

"How do I know they're on our team?" I ask lamely.

He taps my yellow helmet and then points to his own. "Avoid the yellow."

"Right, avoid the yellow," I gulp.

I kept chanting that as we make our way out the door into the back of the center. The whole thing looks like some weird obstacle course. There are different areas clearly meant to shield and some that look like my worst physical education nightmare come to life.

"Ready?" the owner asks when we make it to the group of ten or so other people all geared up in yellow and blue helmets.

Avoid the yellow. Avoid the yellow.

"When you hear the buzzer, go."

Shit, I missed everything else he said. Liam looks over and gives me a wink through his goggles and when I hear the buzzer sound I watch as everyone scatters. Liam grabs my hand and pulls me toward one of the bunker like shielded areas. It takes me a few seconds to get my head in the game, but when I hear Liam laugh, I watch as he pops his head around the side before pulling his gun up to pop off a few shots. I hear a grunt and then a muted curse before Liam turns with an even bigger smile.

My blood is pulsing through my veins so hard that I can hear it roaring in my ears. I can't figure out if I'm feeling pure fear or excitement. My mind is telling me to run, but the look of joy on Liam's face, transforming him from handsome to panty-soaking gorgeous, makes me want to keep it there.

My hands shake as I pull myself up and peer around the side. I see a few yellow helmets, but my gaze zeros in on one lone blue one with her back to me. With a ridiculous amount of jittering, I bring my own gun up and let off a few pops. When I hit her clear in the back with one of my yellow paint balls the adrenaline rushing through my body spikes, and I feel like my body might explode with excitement.

I can't explain the feelings running through my system. When I drop back down to where Liam is waiting and turn to look at him, the smile on my face can't be stopped.

I'm having fun. So much fun that I don't even think. I drop my gun and grab his padded shoulders and give him a huge hug.

When I pull back, his smile matches my own.

"Let's do this!" I exclaim.

He gives me a nod and for the next thirty minutes I *feel,* just like he asked, and for the first time in a long time, while the adrenaline is rushing around and my heart is about to beat out of my chest, I'm looking forward to every second that is to come.

Chapter 9

Megan

"Let me put ice on it, please," Liam asks for the tenth time since we pulled up at my house.

I look over at him with a smile, the same smile that hasn't left since my first hit during the paintball game. Not even when one of the last blue players got me right in the back of my thigh and the burning pain caused me to face plant in the middle of the field. Of course, the pain was easily forgotten when I watched Liam stop and turn sharply and pelt the guy with one try before he dropped down to make sure I was okay.

That smile was shining bright when I watched Liam hand his phone over to the owner, grab me by my middle and position me in front of him. It was still shining huge when his phone came up, flash went off, and I know that had I looked when Liam did, I would see one big wonky smile on my face in that picture.

If the look on his face was any indication, he liked seeing that big wonky smile. He liked it a lot.

I still haven't come down from my high. I look up, smiling at him and shake my head.

"It's going to hurt more if we don't put ice on it."

"I feel fine," I tell him and honestly I am. It's sore, but it doesn't hurt. Well, it doesn't hurt that much.

He looks up from where he's been studying my thigh and gives me a long accessing look.

"What?" I ask him.

"Nothing, darlin', nothing at all."

He doesn't take his gaze from mine. I look down at where he's kneeling against the floor and just drink him in. Today has been the most fun that I've had in a long time. All because of Liam.

"You feel it yet?" he asks after a few minutes.

"Huh?"

He opens his mouth to respond but snaps it shut when the front door opens and I hear my precious daughter laughing at the top of her lungs.

"Mommy! I got to ride in a monster truck!"

My eyes widen and I look at Liam in shock. I had called Dani earlier when it became apparent that my kidnapper wasn't going to give up, and asked her if she could get Molly from school. I know Dani doesn't own a monster truck. The thought of my daughter in a monster truck scares the crap out of me.

"Breathe," Liam says softly.

"Right." I take a deep breath and nod my head, looking deep into his eyes.

Molly rounds the corner that separates the front hall and the living room, her infectious smile causing me to give her one of my own. When Nate comes into the room, my smile slips slightly.

"You aren't Dani," I tell him.

"Nope. I'm prettier. Right, Mols?"

She giggles and gives him a hug. "Yup! Hi, Lee! Mommy, look, Lee's here!" She turns from where Nate is standing and bounces toward Liam. I hold my breath and wait to see what she'll do next. It seems, if her leaping into his lap is any indication, that my girl is getting attached to all of these men in her life.

I ignore the slight pain in my chest when Jack's face crosses my mind and will myself to not think about the things that he's missing in her life.

"Hey, little lady."

I look away when I see the look of reverence in her eyes. Yeah, my girl sure is hooked.

"Where is Dani?" I ask Nate, avoiding the look on Liam's face as he gazes at my precious daughter.

"She's in time out," Nate tells me, ignoring my shocked face and dropping down to hold his arms out. "What? I'm prettier than that troll, Mols! Has my beauty let you down?" He throws his hand over his forehead and drops to the ground in a dramatic faint.

Molly claps her little hands and giggles at Nate's antics. I swear, this girl.

I look over when Liam laughs and scoops Molly up in his arms.

"Be gone you ugly ogre! Princess Molly has no time for the likes of you!"

My eyes widen and I watch in fascination as the two huge alpha males play with Molly effortlessly. Of course my daughter is eating up every second of this. I sit there, watching and in the middle of her beautiful laughter I feel like the walls are closing in on me. Not in a bad way, necessarily, but it hits me that this is something that I've been keeping from her. By closing myself off and making it so nothing and no one can come close enough to form bonds that can break, I've also kept Molly locked up.

I've kept my innocent daughter from experiencing relationships of others. Sure, I can justify it away that I'm keeping her from the pain if we were to lose someone else, but what is that teaching her?

My God, I'm teaching her fear.

Fear for the unknown and that fear will keep her from having the beautiful life that I so wish she will have.

With wooden legs, I stand. They don't notice, the three of them having too much fun chasing each other around my living room. Their laughter trails after me as I walk down the hall, into my bedroom, and finally my bathroom. This is the safest room for me to hide away and let the guilt of what my own fear has pressed upon my daughter.

I want to move past this. I know deep down that this is the unhealthiest way of living. I should move on. Jack is gone and there isn't anything that can bring him back. Logically I know that, but mentally I don't know if I can handle jumping over that last hurdle.

It really is time to move on.

Right there in my bathroom, I let the last of my grief over losing Jack bleed out. Knowing that I've been so wrong to stay locked tight for this long. But, just because I've accepted that, doesn't mean it doesn't kill me to let those last bits of fear start to leave my body.

I lean against the counter and focus my thoughts. Looking up at where the mirror used to be, I suddenly can't keep it locked up anymore. But instead of tears, a manic hysterical bubble of laughter comes shooting out.

And then another.

Before I know what happened, seconds pass and I slide to my ass in the middle of my bathroom, hands held over my stomach as the cramps my laughter has caused sink in. Tears blur my vision, and a pain so blinding that makes my breath come in rushed gasps, rips through me.

That's where Liam finds me, of course, the poster child of sanity rocking back and forth on her bathroom floor. If he had any doubts of my mental status before now, I'm sure they're all confirmed now.

He doesn't say a word and as the laughter turns to sobs, he shifts around me and lowers his body to the floor. His legs frame around my rocking body and his strong arms wrap around me tightly. His silence continues as he tightens his hold. He doesn't speak, just lets me lose it in his arms. When I finally calm, he moves us both so that I'm sitting across his lap. His arms come back around me, one going around my middle and pulling me in close. His other arm comes up, hand moving to cradle my face and press me against his chest.

Turning my head, I take a deep choppy breath and let his scent fill my senses. That warm intoxicating blend of wooded pines and leather. All Liam. It fills my head and when I let the air back out, I feel a small sliver of control come back over me.

Almost as if his hold alone gave me some of his strength.

"Molly?"

"Nate's got her, baby," he mutters.

"I'm sorry," I exhale.

"Far as I can tell Megan, that was a long time coming."

"Yeah," I confirm.

"Want to tell me what brought that on?"

I don't want to, but after today—him giving me a day of carefree fun—I feel like I owe him something. Maybe, just maybe, if I let him in just a little he will understand why I'm absolutely no good for him.

"I've . . . I . . . God. I thought that if Molly just had me she would be safe."

His arms jerk, but he doesn't speak.

Pushing my head closer to his body, I take that strength, that safety that his body gives me, and continue, "I never wanted her to know what it feels like to miss someone. Know the pain that comes when part of you dies. That's what Jack was, part of me, of us. She was too young to understand or feel that loss. I guess I've been living in a bubble. Keeping her wrapped tight with me so that we would never have to depend on someone else for *our* happiness."

"Darlin' you aren't living."

"We are," I sigh, "We have each other. But yeah, we—no, I—haven't been."

"And how well is that going, Megan?"

I pull my head up and look at him, *really* look at him. His eyes hold no sympathy, just empathy. He isn't judging me. As I look into his handsome face, all I see is his understanding, but also his searching gaze boring into my own as if he's trying to communicate something without words.

He's letting me lead.

And if the way his heart is racing against my body is any indication, his holding back right now is costing him.

"She needs this," I confess.

"Yeah, baby, she does, but so do you."

I nod my head and his eyes go soft. His hand moves from where it fell when I shifted to look at him and his other comes from between our bodies. His warm hands take my face and his reverent hold and the tender look in his eyes, causes me to close my eyes.

"Look at me, Megan."

I shake my head.

"Darlin," he says as his breath dances across my lips. "You need to *look at me.*"

"Why?" I murmur.

"So you can *see.*"

His thumb moves, the pad of his finger running along my jaw. He waits, giving me a few breaths. My eyes slowly open and when I look into his face, just inches from my own, his eyes are burning with an emotion I've never seen directed at me.

I've seen it before and the knowledge of what he's trying to communicate with just that searing gaze, makes my heart leap in my chest before beating so violently it feels like it might break right out of my body. This is a look of complete affection. Tenderness that I've seen a million times since Cohen pulled me into his world. It's one that Cohen is often giving Dani. But right now, coming from Liam, it's mixed with the hunger that is simmering just beneath the surface, his simple look has turned into something I've never experienced, but always wanted and made me yearn to see it a million times over.

A look that no matter how much Jack loved me—it was only a love of friendship and never, not once, a look that made me feel like I was the only person he ever saw.

I gasp, my thoughts feeling like nothing short of a betrayal to his memory.

"You feel it."

My eyes widen and I don't move. Not confirming physically, but giving him that regardless with my silence.

"Yeah, baby." His forehead drops against mine and his eyes stay locked with my own. "You've given that angel everything she needs, Megan. She doesn't lack love, but she has so much to give. She doesn't understand loss, but she will. You can't keep that from her no matter how hard you try. It's part of life. All you can do is be there for her when it inevitably happens. And as hard as this is for you, you have to know that she needs to experience all of the ups and all of the downs that life has. She. Needs. To. Live."

He stops, brings one of his hands from where it was resting lightly against my neck and wipes the tear that had rolled from my wide eyes.

"There is no doubt in my mind that you have been doing the best you can. You protected her while you have been protecting yourself, but it's time to step out of that bubble and let yourself *feel.* Live. You both need this, not just her. You've watched her this past year, Megan. When everyone is around, that little girl lights up. So much love to give. She gives it freely and eagerly. Not one person she comes around isn't affected by that smile."

"I've kept her from this, Liam."

"No, baby. You haven't kept anything from her. You've been too busy guarding yourself that you've missed it. She already has it. Do you really think Nate would have fought his own sister off and volunteered to bring her home from school if he didn't want to? He told me he locked Dani in her own house and brought Molly home, just so he could spend some time with her. Half the time when Izzy is watching her, Molly is watching Nate. Did it seem odd to you that she didn't even bat an eye when I was here the other night? Darlin', those times Dani has had her while you were working? You know Dani and I are close?"

I nod and his smile deepens.

"I look real good in Dani's makeup baby."

My jaw drops and the image of Liam—all very male Liam—the subject of one of Molly's makeovers.

"I'm there, often, and I'll be the first to admit that she has me wrapped around her finger as tight as I can get."

He finishes and gives me a second while my mouth flounders.

"She never told me." My voice comes out harsher than I meant and I can tell he doesn't like it.

"You've been scared of your own shadow for a while now, Megan. She might not have told you outright, but she wasn't keeping it from you."

"Molly never told me," I continue.

"She didn't tell you? Or you didn't want to hear it?"

My brow wrinkles and I think about what he's saying. Had I been purposely been ignoring things I don't want to see? All those times that Dani had watched her for a few hours, she had come home on cloud nine. Her chatter had been nonstop and most of the time so rapid that I couldn't keep up. But—my God! What kind of mother am I?

"Tea parties," I say hoarsely. "I always thought that Leelee was . . . well, not you. That night you came with pizza—" My voice trails off as I remember how my daughter so oddly spoke to Liam like she had been waiting for him. Like she had anticipated his arrival at her home.

"It's not hard to love her, Megan. I would never hurt either of you, but you have to know had I refused the innocent love she so freely throws to everyone around her, that it would have left a mark."

"Why didn't *you* tell me?"

I try to shift, but he doesn't allow me to move from his lap.

"I've been trying to."

"You're so confusing. You haven't been trying to do anything but get back in my pants."

His eyes go hard and he moves so that I can't do anything but look right at him. His eyes burning, but this time without giving me any kind of warm feelings.

"Make no doubt that I would love to be back in those pants, Megan. I guarantee you that the next time I'm right back in those fucking pants it's going to be because you want me there. But don't ever accuse me of using your daughter to get there. The only thing confused here is you. You're too busy trying to keep yourself from seeing what's right in front of you. You've got yourself so twisted in knots to keep everyone out, that you can't see a damn thing."

He stops talking and moves to stand, leaving me with no choice but to follow him up. He straightens, helps me finish my climb from the floor, and drops his hand instantly.

"If I didn't know with all that I fucking am that you're worth the trouble, I would leave and never look back."

I step back a foot at his words.

"So fucking stubborn, Megan. So stubborn. What happened out there," he says, pointing in the direction that Molly and Nate can be heard laughing. "What happened is you finally seeing past the goddamn guilt and fear that has been eating you for years. The fear I can understand, baby, I get it. But the guilt, I don't see it. I've tried to wrap my head around it for months now, and I still can't get it. You aren't living and until you get your head out of your ass you're going to continue living this lonely life. What happened out there was you seeing that, even with you trying to keep her from experiencing anything that may one day cause her a second of pain, she's breaking free of those tangled webs and *living*. Take a page from her book Megan and maybe we can finally be on the same chapter. I was wrong before, we aren't just on different ones, you're still ten books behind me."

He turns, looks to where my mirror used to be and even without knowing, I'm sure he's smart enough to put the pieces together. Especially since bits of the shattered mirror are still stuck to the wall.

"Open your eyes, Megan. It's time to grab the rope," he so strangely says before turning and walking through the door.

As I watch his wide shoulders walk through my bedroom I let his words sink in. He's right. I know it. He knows it. The only problem is, I'm not sure I know how to clear a path to the road he wants me to travel on.

He's right. I feel guilt. Probably not for the reasons he suspects, but it's guilt nonetheless. I had a man who gave up everything for me. Hopes, dreams, a career, and eventually his life. A man who gave up everything so that I could escape a nightmare I was living. A best friend who turned into a husband of safety and then eventually one of friendly love. I was content with that, and I know Jack was too.

The part I struggle with the most is the feelings Liam brings into my cold, painful life. They are so much more powerful than what I ever felt for the husband that saved me. The battle I feel within is that Liam, with all his annoying determination, is showing me a promise of something that I know deep down, if I were to lose it, would take me to my knees with a pain I know I could never shake free of.

That . . . that is a terrifying feeling.

But one that I know I need to be brave enough to take that step toward and that hand he's been offering me.

Chapter 10

Liam

I give Molly a hug and ignore the pain her begging me to stay causes. That little girl could shake me to my core with just one little pout.

"Stay until she comes out?" I ask Nate.

"Yup. I've got a date with the prettiest girl in the world." He looks down at Molly and she smiles huge. Her brown eyes crinkle at the corner and her crooked grin shining bright. "Isn't that right, Molly-Wolly?"

She giggles and I hate that it isn't me she's giving that look to. Fuck me, I'm in deep here.

"Next date's mine, little lady," I tell her and she nods her head, her curls bouncing around her face.

I turn and right when I make it to the door I hear her yell my name, her little voice ringing out and echoing against the walls. I turn just in time to catch her small body before it comes crashing into my legs, reaching down I pull her up and her small arms wrap around my neck.

"I'll miss you, Leelee," she whispers.

I hold her tight and when I look up, I see Megan standing in the hallway with her hand pressed against her chest and her eyes wide.

"I'll miss you too, little lady, so much."

My eyes never leave Megan's. Her pained face the last thing I see before I drop Molly softly to her feet, ruffle her curls and turn to leave them behind. Ignoring every instinct I have to charge in there and demand Megan see what I see.

That together, if she would just grab that damn rope I'm struggling to hold on to and climb, that we—us and Molly—would have *everything.*

It isn't until I pull my truck into my parent's driveway that I realize it wasn't just pain in her gaze right before I left her house. If I'm not mistaken . . . there was also hope.

I climb down from the cab and make my way up the walk to the front door, my thoughts running a million miles a minute. If I'm right, if that was hope, then maybe—fucking maybe—I've finally started to break through the wall that's been separating us.

"Whoa, baby boy!"

Pushing my thoughts aside, I look up and smile at my mom. Her dark hair streaked with gray, her brown eyes holding strong laugh lines, but right now looking at me and seeing right through the smile I've plastered on my face.

"Do you need your mom or your dad right now, honey?"

I reach out, pull her into my arms and give her a tight hug. Her arms come up and hold me close.

As my hug pulls her off her feet, she laughs. "My guess is my boy needs me." She guesses correctly.

"A little of both, Mom. Definitely a little of both."

After I place her back down on her heels, she reaches up and pats my cheek. I look down and give her a weak smile.

"Well, come on. Let's not let any flies in the house. Your dad is out back mowing the lawn. Let's me and you have a chat before he comes and hogs all your attention."

I follow her in, going straight to the kitchen and pulling one of the chairs from the table before dropping down.

"Water, coke or beer?" she asks from the open fridge door.

"Vodka?"

"Ah, I figured this chat would be coming sooner or later."

I look at her, questions clear in my eyes because she just smiles. She doesn't speak as she bends to the cabinet that holds the strong liquor. I watch—and wait—as she fixes my drink before rounding the island and joining me at the table.

"It's Megan, right?"

I narrow my eyes and take a healthy pull, enjoying the way the burn feels down my throat.

"Should I ask how you know this?"

"You could, but I won't give away my secrets. One day, when you're in my shoes you'll understand me when I tell you that a mother always knows."

I shake my head and look down into the glass. Not really seeing anything except the way that Megan looked when I walked out of her door.

"I have no idea if I'm doing this right," I tell her honestly.

"Oh, baby," she starts. "There isn't a right or wrong way to do anything when it comes to what the heart wants. Everyone has to learn that the hard way. Your father and I had to, just like everyone else."

I look up at her words and I feel my brows pull in.

"Don't look at me like that." She reaches up and pushes against the skin between my eyes until I relax my gaze. "I talked to Izzy the other night, that's your freebie." She winks, letting me in on her secret to knowing why I'm here before I could tell her. "Dani fills her in often on how Megan is doing. I don't think it's lost on you that Izzy and Axel have a soft spot for Megan and Molly. They call them their M&M's," she smiles.

M&M's, I smile. So fitting.

"Every step of the way, baby boy. What I haven't seen for myself, is when you two are in a room together, I've heard bits and pieces through Izzy—who got them from Dani."

I look back down to my glass. Damn Dani and her big mouth.

"You know your father had his hands full when he met me," she says and I look back up, meeting her sad eyes.

What is this?

"I didn't make it easy, honey. I could kick myself now for all the trouble I was in the beginning. Really made him work for it and all because I was scared. I don't know what's holding her back, but it wouldn't be a stretch to guess. Fear is a powerful thing, but honey she's also got a lot of loss on her shoulders. All I can tell you is that you're one hundred and fifty percent your father's son and I have no doubt in my mind that you feeling this way, means you know what you want. Nothing and I mean nothing, honey, stands in the way of a Beckett man when he's found that."

I laugh, the sound coming out flat.

"Not sure that she wants that Beckett determination barking at her door, Mom."

"Then I have no doubt in my mind that you, being your father's son, will make her change her way of thinking there."

"I'm trying. God, I'm trying."

She smiles, reaches out and pulls my hand from my glass. "Tell me what's going on. Let's talk game plan, honey."

I give her a smile, matching the one on her face, and proceed to tell her everything that's been going on for the last year. Starting with the feelings I had when I first met Megan. When I started spending time with Molly. How I knew she would be mine long before I confirmed that feeling. And finally how I've been trying to bring Megan back to herself. When I finish talking she has tears in her eyes.

"You've always felt deeply, son. I have to say, hearing how you talk about her and her daughter makes me feel nothing but pride."

I open my mouth, but before I can get a word out, I hear the back door open.

"Wildcat, get your man some water. Damn it's hot out there. I haven't been this sweaty since—" My dad's words die on his lips when he turns to see me sitting with my mom. His gaze, never missing a thing, takes in the serious vibes floating around before he—thankfully—can finish his sentence. "What's wrong?"

"The apple doesn't fall far from the tree, Beck baby." She gives my hand a squeeze, drawing my attention from my father, back to her. "You never give up, baby boy. Never. What you're feeling, that's all going to be worth it in the end. If you need me you know I'm here. I love you."

She stands, gives me a kiss on the top of my head and moves to my father. His head tips down but his knowing eyes never leave mine. He gives her a kiss, turning his eyes to hers. I watch just as fascinated as I was when I was a kid and they would have one of their silent moments. They don't speak, words never needed with them. Her hand comes up and caresses his cheek and he turns his head to kiss her palm. Her skin instantly filling with goose bumps and I know, if I could see her face, she would have that soft look and her eyes would be full of love.

He waits for her to fill a glass of water, taking it from her offering hand, before giving her another kiss and walking the few steps that separated the doorway and the kitchen table.

"Call me later, baby," she tells me and I give her a nod.

I watch her walk through the arch that takes her from the kitchen and to the stairs that lead up to the second floor before I turn and look at my father.

"I knew this day would come."

"Did you now?" I ask, pulling my glass up and draining the last of my drink.

"Always knew it would, I just hope I know how to steer you right, son."

"At this point, I'm not sure there's a right or wrong way to go."

He smiles, his brown eyes so similar to my own give nothing away as he settles into his chair, leaning back and taking another sip of his water.

"Mom fill you in?"

"She filled me in enough. What does she mean about the apple not falling far from the tree?"

He laughs, "Liam, God son," he takes a deep breath. "My guess, you've got a fight on your hands?"

I tip my head, rolling his words around and trying to form an answer. Before I can speak, he opens his mouth and continues.

"I always knew, with how badly I had to fight just to get your mom to give us a chance, that it would come easy once we finally got there. She has and always will be worth every fight and every struggle. I knew the second she came into my life that she was it. One look in a smoky, crowded bar, and I was knocked so hard on my ass I'm sure that I still have the bruise to show for it even now two decades and then some years later."

With nothing but an empty glass, I lean back and wait for him to continue.

"When you were playing ball in high school, what did I tell you?"

Clearing my throat, I say, "That anything worth having is worth fighting for."

"Exactly that. I don't listen much when your mother is yammering on the phone with the girls. I sit back and let her do her thing knowing if she needs to clue me in, she will. So, son, tell me about her."

"Tell you about?" I hedge.

"Megan."

"You sure you don't listen in, old man?" I laugh.

He winks and I laugh. Then, just like Mom, I tell my father everything about Megan and Molly. As I speak, his knowing eyes get bright and I watch as, through my story, my father loses himself in his own memories. When I finish speaking, he clears his throat and drains his glass dry.

"It's like history repeating itself, Lee," he oddly adds when I finish speaking. "Not the exact same, but the foundation built on the same rocky ground."

"Riddles don't suit you," I quip.

"I suppose not when you've got more on your mind than you can keep up with." He studies me before speaking again, "One look, you said?" At my nod, his smile grows. "Buckle up, son, it's going to be a bumpy road."

"I've got four wheel drive," I laugh.

"Liam, I'm really not sure I can add anything here that will help you. As far as I can tell from what you've just told me, you're about ten steps ahead of where I was when I was wearing your shoes. Half the battle is already won. You're in and breaking down that wall, you just need to make sure you're ready to catch her when she falls from that prison she's been living in."

"And if she doesn't ever get to that point? Because I've got to say, I have a hard time seeing the end game through all of this right now."

His hand comes out and grips my shoulder, hard. "That is not an option you give yourself, bud. You don't give up and you damn sure don't allow her to give up on you *or* herself. Your plan's a good one. Hell, it's a great one. But I promise you, it's one that is going to have her hurting before she can heal. From what I know about Megan, she's been given a lot of pain in her life. It's up to you to show her that in pain there is always beauty to be found."

"I don't want to give up on her."

"Then don't. Honestly, son, this isn't about you right now. Sure, in a way it is, but until you get her to . . . what did you call that list?"

"Feeling Alive," I tell him.

"Yeah, until you get her to remember how to live past that pain she's been clutching tight to, then you need to hold on and gear up. What's the next step?"

"Number two on the list was karaoke."

His brows furrow. "What in the hell is there about karaoke that put it on the list at number two?"

I smile, feeling that determination that I had started to lose come back.

"You have to learn to laugh when you feel so scared that you just want to run and hide. You have to hike those big girl pants up and even though you want nothing more than to run back to your little bubble of safety, and push through the fear to let yourself dance to the music."

He smiles and I look into my father's eyes and give him a big grin of my own.

"Proud of you, son. She isn't going to know what hit her with my boy working that Beckett magic."

I laugh, "I hope she doesn't. Thanks for the chat, Dad. Love you."

"Love you too, bud. Now tell me how much you hate those ten-hour shifts."

We spend the next hour talking about how my shifts at work are going now that I'm on patrol. He tells me how things are going down where he works at Corps Security and as always reminds me that he wishes I had decided to come and work for him and not joined the force.

By the time my mom joins us we'd moved into the living room, beers in each hand, and the television on the sports channel. I don't leave until long after my mom had filled my stomach with a meal fit for a king and a calming sense of purpose to get my girls.

Chapter 11

Megan

It's been a week since Liam stood at my front door and hugged my daughter goodbye.

A week of silence from him.

A week of me missing him fiercely.

A week of realizing that continuing to push him away will be fruitless, because in this week I've craved him with an unhealthy degree.

It baffles me that he could be under my skin, so deeply imbedded this soon. While we've known each other for almost two years—or at least that's how long it's been since I was first introduced to everyone at Cohen's going away party. In that two years we've been thrown together at various parties, group nights out, and basically whenever Dani pulled me out of the house when I would get too consumed with work. For the last six months of those two years though he hadn't hidden his attraction. Little touches here and there, the casual brush of his skin when he would walk by, or most recently—after Dani and Cohen's wedding—our shared night of the hottest sex I've ever had.

I think it was during the paintball game that I realized he had started to burrow under my skin. When I looked at him, his knee-melting smile shining bright, and felt my gut get tight . . . that's when I knew how much trouble I was in.

Then he held me in his arms while I completely lost my shit and ever since I felt his arms wrapped tight around me in comfort,

I've been craving that feeling for every second of every day since he walked out my door.

"What are you thinking about that has that frown making an appearance?" Dani questions.

"Just thinking," I tell her.

I look up from where I had been signing the last of my book orders and look around my dining room table. She isn't focused on me, instead on packaging the last book that I had slid her way. I watch as she handles the paperback with so much care, her eyes rolling over her fingertips as she touches the glossy cover. Moving my gaze from hers, I look over at Maddi and Stella, who have been helping me get together my weekly mail outs.

This—having them in this part of my life—was a huge step for me this week. It was part one of my plan to let those walls crumble and what better way than finally letting them see *all* of me. Dani, of course, knew but it was news to the other girls.

"Thinking about Lee?" Maddi probes.

I take a deep breath, "Yes."

Dani stops what she's doing and snaps her eyes to me, causing me to laugh.

"Shocked I admitted to it?" I jokingly ask.

"Well, uh . . . yeah."

"She's played stupid long enough, figured one of these times she would open up," Stella mumbles.

"Do you want to talk about it?" Dani continues, ignoring Stella's comment.

"Yes," I breathe.

Her eyes widen a fraction because she carefully closes her shock down. Or maybe it's excitement. Either one, what my friend is not hiding is her happiness that the subject isn't being dropped.

"So, all right. Let's do this," Maddi exclaims, rubbing her hands together.

I laugh, letting some of the nerves leave my body. These are my friends. I'm safe here. They won't judge me and they won't think badly of me. I keep reminding myself that there is nothing to be afraid of as each of them sit back and wait for me to speak.

"Uh," I stammer. "So you know he's been . . . persistent?"

Maddi laughs, "Is that what we're going to call it?

"Okay, maybe adorably annoying with his determination would be better?"

They all laugh at me and my nerves ease instantly.

"Don't keep us waiting, Megan! What is going on up there?" Maddi asks on a laugh, reaching over the table to tap me lightly against my temple.

I swat her hand, enjoying the easy banter between us. Sobering slightly, allowing the serious thoughts I had been having minutes earlier to come back, I look at each of these girls that have come to mean so much to me.

"Things got a little intense last week," I start. Each of them lose a little of their smiles. "I guess. . . . well, I—damn this was so much easier to word in my thoughts."

"Just start from the beginning, babe, can't see a better way to clue us in on what's weighing heavy on your mind."

I give Dani a small nod and a weak smile when she stops talking.

"The beginning, right." I look over at Maddi and Stella. "Do you two know about . . . did you hear that we, uh, had a little sleepover?"

They look at me and I can tell they're both struggling to hold onto their laughter. Did I just really call it a sleepover?

"I hope it wasn't little," Maddi belts out, causing Dani and Stella to erupt in giggles as my face heats to a roaring burn.

"Oh, God!" I clasp my hand over my mouth and shake my head.

"Is that a no? It wasn't little?" Stella giggles.

I look at her and narrow my eyes. "For your information, not that it's any of your business, he is far from little. In fact, he was so, uh, well endowed, he had to really work at it!"

Shit. Dammit. Did I really just admit that?

"Explain," Stella says, leaning forward, her face the picture of seriousness.

"No, please don't," Dani gripes.

"Ignore her. Finish. Explain."

"Jesus, Stell . . . that's Lee you're talking about."

"Lee has a dick, right. He's always been selective with who he dates and you know just as well as I do that he didn't bring anyone into our group so I never got to grill anyone. I'm curious, screw me. I bet he's hung. He's hung, right?"

"Do you want a tissue for that drool?" Maddi mumbles and rolls her eyes.

"Maybe, I don't know yet. Finish!"

"This is so embarrassing," I tell Stella, then look to the other two girls. "If you don't want to hear it, cover your ears or leave the room."

Dani instantly pulls her hands to her ears and starts humming, loudly. Maddi makes not one move to shield her hearing; she just cocks her brow and waits.

Looking back at Stella with burning cheeks, I give her what she wants. "He was so large that he had to work me over twice with his mouth, then again with his fingers. By the time he finally gave me every single thick inch of himself I should have been embarrassed with how wet I was. Happy?"

Stella throws her head back, her recently dyed purple hair falling in a thick wave of curls as she laughs at the top of her voice. Maddi on the other hand is just smiling and nodding her head. When I look over at Dani she looks like she might puke, obviously she wasn't humming loud enough.

Pulling her hands away, she looks at Stella. "You are sick, my friend. God, I'm never going to be able to look at him the same again."

My face flames even brighter.

"There isn't a thing you should be getting so worked up about over there. Jesus, Megan, you would think you were a virgin with all the blushing you're doing."

I narrow my eyes at Stella.

"I told you what you wanted to know, no need to be rude now."

"I'm not," she says in an offended tone. "I swear. I just want you to feel comfortable with us. Promise."

Maddi reaches out, all traces of joking gone from not only her supportive gesture, but also her expression holding nothing but understanding. "He was—please don't think I'm being insensitive here—the first? Since Jack?"

I nod.

"There isn't one thing that you can't talk to us about, you know that?" she continues and waits for my confirmation that I understand before opening her mouth again. "What was Jack like?"

Given the subject of our chat, her meaning can't be missed.

Step two in knocking those walls down, here I come.

Time to stop holding back when it comes to telling people about my past.

"Timid," I tell them truthfully. "The first time we had sex it was so awkward. We had been nothing but friends, but with where we were at that point in our relationship, it was the next logical step."

True enough, I tell myself.

"And after that first time?" Maddi requests, clearly deciding she's the self-appointed leader of questions since I opened up to her first.

"A little less timid, but still awkward." Instantly I feel my stomach start to cramp. Admitting how our relationship had been to myself had been hard enough, but letting others know is a whole new level of painful. Not to mention it feels like I'm stomping on his grave mentioning how unfulfilling our sex life was. "I loved him, but we were probably the most dysfunctional couple in the history of ever inside the bedroom." My words come out quickly. Just like ripping off a BandAid.

I can tell they don't understand. Of course they don't, *they* only know half the story.

"Okay," Maddi coughs. "So, I'm going to go out on a limb and say that those times you were together were few and far between? I mean no disrespect, I promise, I'm just trying to understand."

I give her a small smile.

Give them more, Megs. It's okay.

I shiver when I hear Jack's voice in my mind. Well, not his voice, I'm sure. If my mind wants to play tricks on me so that I keep going, fine. I can't go back to the old Megan.

Baby steps.

"He was deployed during most of my pregnancy and was only home for two weeks after her birth. He shipped back out again and the only other time he was home was for a few months when she was one. He died during that tour shortly after Molly turned eighteen months. Needless to say, he was gone a lot, but even when he was home . . ."

I trail off and remember those times he was home. Those times had been all about Molly. He loved her so ferociously. We did things as a family and when Molly had been asleep for hours, we did what we had always done best, spent long hours just enjoying the other's companionship. Hours spent reading to each other, him enjoying some of my books or whatever project I was working on, sometimes just helping me hash out some plot point I had been stuck on. He was huge on board games. We would spend so many hours just laughing over whichever game we had picked up.

What we didn't do often was have sex.

"We slept together the night before he shipped off . . . that last time, and that was almost four years ago."

Dani reaches up and brushes a tear off her cheek.

"I loved him," I meekly say in Jack's defense. And I did.

"We know you did, babe. No one here thinks differently," Maddi speaks first and the others nod in agreement.

I take a huge breath. Then another. Then I speak again. "That night, with Liam, I felt the earth move."

Stella snorts when Dani gags and just like that, the heavy mood is lifted.

"Go on," Maddi encourages.

"The way he touched me. The way that felt. The way *he* felt. All of him. His strong body covering mine made me feel delicate . . . fragile. And the way he talked to me, my God the way his words alone worked me up should be illegal."

"Okay, so Lee is good in bed, can we *please* move on!?" Dani snaps.

"Figured he would be," Stella laughs and sticks her tongue out when Dani huffs.

"So then what happened?"

I look over at Maddi and smile. "Paintball happened."

She gives me a look, not following. Stella gives a 'huh' and Dani oddly smiles all wonky.

"Did you say, paintball?" Stella questions.

I smile, mine feeling just as wonky as Dani's is.

"Well, I guess the bar night happened first. He showed up and laid it out that he was done with me avoiding him—which I had done since that night—and thus began the annoying persistence."

My smile, which had started out smallish on the wonky scale, was full out cheek hurting now.

"The next day he had told me he would be around my house at noon. I, of course, made it my mission to be gone. He tracked me down at Target an hour before noon and, well . . . then paintball."

Maddi tilts her head. "Paintball?"

"It was the most fun I had had in years, Maddi. It's like Liam knew just what I needed. The rush, that feeling of adrenaline tipping over until you're so full of it that you might explode, it was incredible."

"All right, so paintball," Stella stammers. "So weird."

"Then what happened?" Dani says a little too excited.

My cheek-burning smile slips. Then Dani's follows.

"Then I proceeded to flip out after he brought me home. Well, after Nate had brought Molly home."

Dani's shoulders drop. "I know, I told you I was sorry about that, but you try fighting off a man over a foot taller than you when he locks you in your son's bedroom and yells through the door that he's taking the cutest girl in the world on a date. I swear, he kidnapped her right from my house." She crosses her arms over her chest and leans back in a huff.

She had explained to me earlier in the week that her 'time out' had been more like Nate imposed jail time while he stole my kid. I can't be mad about it. I know Molly is safe with him and he took her carseat out of Dani's car so that she would be safe in his truck.

I give her a smile, "It's okay, really. Molly loves Nate and honestly it was the best thing that could have happened."

"Now explain *that!*" Stella gasps.

With my eyes never leaving Dani's so that she knows I mean what I'm saying, I continue. "Seeing Molly, so innocent and happy while playing around with Liam and Nate, I realized that by keeping myself closed off from everyone, that I was keeping her locked away from those relationships too. I was, in a sense, keeping her in that limbo I was in. Long story short, she brought it all to light while two grown men acted like my house was a wrestling mat. It was time for me to move on. So, yeah . . . I broke down and Liam found me losing my mind on my bathroom floor. He wouldn't give up either. I may have come to the self-realization that I was teaching my daughter to fear life, but he hammered the nail home when he helped me see she was breaking free no matter how hard I held her back. I was just too far in my head to see it."

They don't speak but I can tell the room had lost all traces of earlier hopefulness. It dawns on me, in that moment, that they haven't just wanted me to hook up with Liam, they *really* want me *with* him. They've been rooting for us long before they let on to it.

"It's okay," I tell them. "I'm okay."

"Sorry, babe, but all that doesn't really give me the reassurance that you're okay. We worry about you," Dani states.

"I really am, Dani. It hurt, God it hurt, but it needed to happen. Things got a little heated between us, and not in the good kind of heated. I said some things I didn't mean and he once again was all Liam. Fully honest and didn't hold back. He gave me the words I needed to help me take the final step."

Dani's brows curl in, her beautiful face turning from worried to confused. "Final step to what?"

I hear Liam's parting words filter through my mind and with a smile I tell them, "Grab the rope."

Chapter 12

Megan

After the heaviness of our conversation earlier, the girls all agree that we need to lighten things up. Mainly, Dani decides that we need to have some time to just relax and laugh.

So that leads us to now. Another attempt at girl's night, this time it's more like girl's night plus chaperones.

We decided to head to a local bar that caters to more of a mature crowd and not so many college kids looking to get drunk.

Mike's, has been one of the places that we've often spent a Friday or Saturday night. The music is always good and the bar is big enough that a group our size has enough room to lounge. The bar opened about four years ago, from what I understand, and since its opening night, has been one of the top karaoke joints north of Atlanta.

I never joined in on the actual singing, but it really was too much fun to watch some of our crew get up there and belt it out like they didn't have a care in the world.

Dani called Lyn and Lila to see if they wanted to come before we left my house to head over to the Reid's to drop Molly off with their parents. Lyn was all in, but Lila had plans already and promised to come next time. When we got to Dani's parents, Cohen was already there and after we said goodbye to the kids, we headed out. When we got to Mike's, Zac, Zac's little brother Jax and his girlfriend, Ivie, had been waiting in the huge back corner. It was blocked off like some kind of VIP area, holding two couches and four chairs that formed a closed off square.

Zac, always ready to have a good time, was surprisingly quiet without his sidekick, Nate. We got a chin lift from Jax, but otherwise he was too busy keeping the blush on Ivie's face. She gave us a wave, but was distracted when Jax shoved his hand up her shirt. They were sickly cute, high school sweethearts that everyone was convinced would be married before they graduated college.

I used to see them and just hurt with how close they were. Same with Dani and Cohen, but now—it's so much easier to see their love and not feel a pang of depression wrap tightly around my neck. The fact that I can see them now and feel nothing but happiness that they've found that person that makes them whole, is a testament for how far I've come in the last year.

I look around our little corner, sip my third heavy-handed drink, and let myself enjoy this newfound sense of life. One where I'm able to laugh a little easier and sit a little straighter without that damn cloak of pain holding me back. I can't explain the way that feeling makes me feel. It's like I'm reaching for something and I'm just a touch away from it. Like my glass is just a breath away from being full. I guess that's part of healing the gap, in a sense. I'm almost there—so close—and I've never felt better.

Well, that's a lie.

I close my eyes when Liam's face pops in my head. His eyes bright with happiness and that smile that makes me weak at the knees blinding me with his power. I let my lips tip up with the thought and slowly let my lids open.

And gasp.

"Boo, darlin'."

I look down at my almost full glass, trying to figure out if I had enough drinks that I'm starting to hallucinate. Surely I'm not drunk enough to be conjuring up Liam's face just a breath away from my own.

The couch dips and I move my eyes from my drink to the large body that joined me. My view is blocked temporarily by a tan arm that is corded with muscle as it comes up slowly. My eyes follow the limb as it moves up and over before I lose it and feel it's warmth like a burn when the weight settles against my shoulders. When I move my gaze down from where the arm had been, I see Liam's handsome face so close to my own.

He doesn't say a word before his handsome face moves and his lips touch mine lightly. "Hi," he breathes against my lips.

"Hey." My voice comes out on a wisp of air. I know with the music floating around us that there's no way he could hear me, but his smile grows all the same and I have to shift in my seat when the throbbing starts between my legs.

"Don't you two look all cozy like? Any room for this stud?"

My eyes don't leave Liam as he turns and flips off Nate. I study his strong jaw, stubbled with hair. My eyes roam over his skin drinking him in with every inch. When he swallows, his jaw clenches and I can feel my body responding to just that small movement. His hair is stylized in that sexy way, the thickness tamed with whatever product he shoves in it, slightly longer at the top and I just know he effortlessly must run his hands through it, almost as an afterthought while getting ready.

His head turns and those dark eyes of his meet mine. He studies my face for a beat before one brow arches, and if I didn't know better I would swear he could hear my thoughts. He knows, with just one small look, how badly I want him.

My hunger spiked so high, I'm mad with my cravings for his body.

When a shiver runs through my body, one corner of his thick lips tip up and he gives me a small nod before turning his head back to the group.

Mutely I turn and stare at Dani across from me on the other couch, where she's settled on Cohen's lap. She gives me a wink and I watch as her hands come up, thumbs sticking high, and relax slightly as a laugh bubbles up from deep in my belly. Liam's hand, the one resting against my shoulder, curls into my skin and my eyes widen, as my panties get wet with my arousal.

It's going to be a long night.

With no choice but to run with it, I give the new Megan a mental shake and vow to take each moment as it comes.

Fifteen minutes later, a new drink in my hand, and I'm faced with the first test to my newfound resolve of living in the moment. The old Megan, the one living in fear, would have bolted the second that Liam was called to the stage. But the new Megan, the one that's determined to climb the rope and leave rock bottom for good—that new version of *me* is shocked still.

Never, in all the times that we've been here, has Liam taken the stage. And I knew before I started coming out with them, that he hadn't done it before me either. Nate said once, after spending an hour trying to convince him to sing *Baby Got Back* with him, that he never goes up there because he is as tone deaf as it gets. I remember the moment like it was yesterday. Liam just nodded and turned his gaze back to the stage. But I also know from being around this group long enough that despite his over confident demeanor, Liam Beckett has a mean phobia when it comes to being in front of a crowd. Something that Dani has had way too much fun with in the past.

That knowledge is what holds me to my seat. When he stood from the couch, I instantly felt his loss and my body moved to the edge of my seat, almost as if it was trying to stay connected when I lost his weight against my side.

When the opening to Van Morrison's, Brown Eyed Girl fills the air, I gasp. Liam, with all the confidence in the world, takes the mic and opens his mouth. His voice ringing out around us, booming through the speakers, hits every note as if the song was written just for him.

Perfect pitch.

His body moves with the beat and even with a song like Brown Eyed Girl, Liam's movements look nothing short of sexual to me.

My heart speeds up and I know, without a doubt, that he's planned this moment just for me.

You're my brown-eyed girl.

As I watch him work the crowd like a pro I feel like I'm about to jump out of my skin. The need to have those hands, the ones that are holding the mic to his lips, on my body is burning me alive.

He keeps singing as he jumps off the small stage and makes his way over to our area. I can see our group eating this up. Clapping and singing along with him as he takes the final steps until he's standing right in front of me.

"Hell yeah," Nate yells and grabs the mic when Liam hands it off before the song finishes and I hear him belt out the end of the song as the crowded bar gets even louder.

"Darlin'," he pants and reaches out a hand for me to take. I don't move. I can't imagine what my face looks like right now, but whatever he sees brings a smile to his lips the likes of which I've never seen before. "Take it, baby. *Take my hand.*"

With a trembling arm, I reach up and finally take his hand.

Chapter 13

Liam

I might puke.

If the churning in my gut is any clue, it might be soon.

Fuck, this better work.

When I hear my name called out, I shove that feeling aside and make my way to the stage, tagging the mic from Todd, the announcer, and waiting for the music to start.

Never once taking my eyes from where Megan is sitting.

Fuck, this better work.

She's moved since I stood, her ass just about to fall off the edge of the couch. Her lips parted slightly and her eyes holding me captive.

Yeah, baby, I'm sure you didn't see that coming.

When the song starts, I instantly forget my hatred for being on display like this and look at Megan as if she is the only woman in this room. She might as well be. As I jump from the stage and make my way to her, making my intentions clear as I keep my eyes locked to hers, I'm rewarded with seeing her eyes light a fire and that desire I've been waiting to see, start an inferno. Her chest is moving rapidly when I take the mic from my mouth and shove it blindly toward Nate.

This is it.

Moment of truth.

I know, from Dani, that Megan has been living a little lighter since I left last week. I also know, from her help conspiring to get Megan here tonight, that it's a green light, full steam ahead for number two on our list.

The rush that's flying through my body from my little moment in the spotlight is making my breath come out in pants, but I keep on, eyes on the prize as I reach out and hold my hand out for her.

"Darlin."

Her eyes go from my hand to my face. I wait for the panic to wash her features, but when I see a hunger that could rival my own take over, I feel my body relax and with a grin stretches my lips.

Thank Christ.

"Take it, baby. *Take my hand.*"

To anyone watching I'm sure it looks like the simplest of gestures. But I know, I fucking know, if her hand hits mine that she finally sees what I've been waiting for. That she is ready. Ready for me to give her everything.

I hold my breath. The magnitude of what this moment means hitting me like a tsunami.

This. This is it.

When her soft skin comes up and even through her trembling movements I know, my girl is ready.

Time for number three.

"Time to go," I tell her and she nods. It's small, but she nods. I bend down, grab her purse and turn without saying a single goodbye to our friends and walk out the door. Not with Megan behind me, nervous or scared, but with her matching me step for step as we head through the bar and out into the warm Georgia night.

When we reach my truck, I unlock the door and help her into the cab, handing her her purse after she clicks her belt. She looks in my eyes and gives me a smile, not timid at all. Her smile is strong and sure.

"Ready?" I question.

She closes her eyes, clears her throat and her smile grows, "Yeah, Liam. I'm ready."

"That's my girl."

I lean forward, hands pushing into the soft hair around her face and I curl my fingers, giving her the slightest pressure before I press my lips to hers in a kiss that demands her compliance. It's a kiss that shows her without words what's to come.

Breaking the kiss, I press my forehead to hers and pray I can get through the next step without my rock hard cock taking control.

Soon. But not yet.

I round the hood and jump into the driver's seat, turning to look at her as her fingers run along her swollen lips. She moves her head and when her eyes hit mine, those lips tip up and a carefree excitement takes hold of her nerves and I breathe easy knowing I've finally broken through.

"Where are we going?" she asks as my truck bounces through the dirt path we turned off of just seconds before.

"A little late to ask, darlin'," I joke.

"Well, I don't think I was able to form a sentence that would make sense until just now."

"Yeah?"

"You, Liam, kiss me stupid."

My laugh comes out quick and I turn to look at her for a second before returning my eyes back toward the dirt road before us. I know this road like the back of my hand, but in the dark I know better than to take my attention away for too long.

"Stupid isn't how I want you."

"How—how do you want me?" Her question is just above a whisper and the quiver attached to each word works my cock so well, she might as well have wrapped her lips around my shaft.

I can see the clearing just ahead and I wait until the truck's parked before I answer. Turning slightly, I reach out and with one finger pop her seatbelt free. Her eyes follow my hand and as the fabric of her seatbelt moves across her chest she pulls her arm free and lets it clang against the side of the truck.

"How do you want me, Liam?" she repeats, her body moving slightly so that she can see me better.

Reaching out with both hands I grab her hips, curl my fingers into the soft skin and pull her toward me. She helps, just as eager as

I am to be closer. Her legs move, straddling my lap, and when the weight of her body settles against my lap, we both moan. My hands, still at her hips, pull her toward me in a rocking motion that has the heat of her pussy warming my erection to the point that I'm questioning if I just came a little.

Her small hands come up and wrap around my neck. "How do you want me?" she says with her lips moving against my own.

My tongue comes out and I trace the curve of her bottom lip. When her mouth opens slightly, causing her lip to move closer to my mouth, I nip it with my teeth, pulling it slightly before letting go. Her eyes hood and her hips rock forward against my hold, causing my fingers to dig in tighter.

"Tell me, Liam. How do you want me?"

Rocking her against me again, I watch as her head rolls back and I bring my head toward her exposed neck. Running my tongue over the soft skin from her collarbone until I reach her jaw, where I once again give her a soft nip.

"Do you feel it, darlin'?" I ask, ignoring her repeated question.

Her head tips forward and she nods.

"No, baby. Do you *feel* it?"

She takes a few stuttered breaths and as I wait, I run my hands from her hips, up the tight material of her black tee and when my hand passes right under her pits, my thumbs roll over her erect nipples before I continue my path, until my hands curl around her neck and I pull her head forward until she has no choice but to look at me and only me.

"I want you, darlin', to feel. That feeling your body gets when it's sparking at every nerve. When your skin feels tight and your stomach drops. When you don't know if your heart is beating in your chest or coming through your throat. I want you to feel that wind in your hair, pulse racing, wild, free as a bird, stomach-dropping rush. I want you to feel," I pause, bringing my lips to hers in a soft, eyes-open, kiss, "*everything.*" I finish and close the distance again.

Her mouth opens instantly and when I push my tongue inside and meet hers, the kiss goes from wild to electric. Her hands slide into my hair and she grabs hold and pulls me as close as I can get while her hips move without reservation. A kiss that is dangerously close to having me rip her clothes from her body and taking what I've been craving.

I pull back when I feel my balls start to pull tight, ripping my mouth from hers as we both pant rapidly.

"Fuck me," I groan, tilting my head back and fight back the orgasm that almost had me coming just from dry humping.

"I want that," she whispers.

"Words, Megan. You want what?"

"Everything."

"Well, thank fuck."

Chapter 14

Megan

"This way, darlin'," Liam tells me as he walks us from his truck and into the darkness.

I know we're in the middle of nowhere. As his truck pushed through the dirt path and into the clearing you could just tell there wasn't anyone around for miles. When his headlights shut off and you could see millions of stars light up the sky like little gas filled flashlights, it was confirmed. No way you would see something that beautiful, a sky so clear, there wasn't one single spot you couldn't see for miles, if there was even a town close. I would guess, seeing as we didn't pass a single house for at least five miles, that there isn't much of anything out here.

"Uh, Liam?"

He stops and I almost slam into his back.

Turning, his hand comes up to hold my cheek against his palm and I search through the shadows around his face to find his eyes.

"Trust me?"

"Yes," I tell him instantly.

His fingers spasm against my skin.

"Finally."

That one word warms my belly and I roll onto my toes and touch my lips to his.

"I wasn't ready yet, before I mean."

I don't know where all this newfound strength is coming from.

If I had to guess, it's all because of the man standing in front of me.

"Yeah, darlin', I know you weren't. You took my hand. That told me everything I needed to know, but that doesn't mean it isn't good to hear you tell me."

"I'm sorry."

Time for me to take that step. The last one I need to climb from my old life and on to the new path full of hope and promise.

Letting the darkness be my shield, one I know I don't need against Liam, but one I'm going to hold on to as a safety blanket regardless, I take a deep breath and knock some more of that damn wall down.

"The way you make me feel, it scares me. It's a good feeling. A different kind of fear. More of an unknown. Never, not once in my twenty-three years have I ever felt a connection as strong as I do when I'm with you."

He drops the hand he had been holding onto and moves to wrap both of his arms around me. His chin rests against the top of my head and he doesn't speak until my arms circle his waist.

"The last thing I want to do is scare you, Megan. That's the last feeling I want you to have when I'm here. What scares you?"

"That's a long story, Liam."

"Lucky for you I've got all the time in the world when it comes to you."

I tighten my grasp on him and soak up the way his embrace fills me whole.

"Every time you're around me I just know I'm that much closer to falling way too quick. It's something that I know if I let happen, I'll tip over the edge in a free fall that I wouldn't be able to pick myself up from if I lost it."

His arms go tight, his body solid, and I take a second before continuing.

"You, everything that is you and the promise of you, is something I'm terrified to take because you hold the power to crush me. You hold all of the power here."

I feel his head move as he shakes it lightly.

"Yeah, you do. And it isn't just me, Liam. You wouldn't just be crushing me, but Molly too. I let you in and it isn't just me I'm giving you. I'm giving you a little girl who I've known for a while now, but only just come to terms with, is so desperate to give *her* heart to someone to hold."

"Darlin', you give me that and there is no way I would throw the world away when I hold everything I want in my hands."

"You say that now, but—"

He pulls back and I silence immediately.

"I say that now because I have no doubts. Megan, I'm not just some stranger you just met. You know me. I've gotten to know you as much as I can. You opened yourself up to me for one night and I knew with no fucking doubts that I would fight until I was blue in the face for this chance. I've watched as you've come alive, baby. You had me hooked before I even said one word and everything I've discovered about you over the last year and a half just dug that hook deeper. These few weeks, seeing you grow and *heal* took that hook and dug it so deep it hit bone. That was all you. All I did was give you a little push."

He pauses, but I know he isn't done when his finger comes up and silences my words before they can leave my lips.

"You spend one second with Molly and you're in love. Doesn't matter if you're a stranger on the street or a man with his own desperate need to give *his* heart to someone to hold. Wouldn't be a hardship to take what she so willingly gives, darlin'. I want that. I want this. I want you both. Please tell me you can see that."

"I see it," I utter as my vision clouds with tears.

"You see *what,*" he implores his tone just a hint away from begging.

"Everything," I choke out.

He doesn't say another word. His body relaxes instantly against mine and before I can blink, I'm pulled flush against him and his mouth is against mine. I gasp, breathing him in as he uses my shock to deepen the kiss further until I'm not sure where I end and he begins.

Our hands roam over each other's bodies in a frantic pace. I slip my hands under his shirt and moan when I feel his warm, soft skin against my fingers. It's an odd mix of silk and steel as I move my hand over the ripped muscles of his back and sides. My fingers dig in and try to find purchase when he bends slightly and with his hands flexing against my bottom, he pulls me up and my legs leave the ground to wrap around his hips.

"I had plans, Megan," he moans against my lips. "Have a list of things I need to check off, but right now that has to wait."

"Wait for what," I breathe, kissing a path from behind his ear and down his neck.

"For me to make you mine."

He starts walking, back the way that we just walked. I continue to let my lips learn his skin as he moves to open his truck. When he drops me lightly into the passenger seat, I whine from the loss of his body. Bending forward, his lips find mine again and when he pulls back, the dome light above our heads illuminates his face.

"Last chance," he tells me with a wicked grin. "And this time I mean last one, darlin'. We take this step and make no doubt about it, you will be mine. You give me this and I fucking promise you that I will never make you regret taking that step. You ready to jump from that chapter you've been skimming through and skip into mine?"

I give him a smile, one that is full of confidence and not the least bit unsure as the words that he had told me weeks before come back between us.

"I'm ready."

"Fuck," he groans. "Buckle up, baby."

My smile doesn't slip for a second. Not when I pull my belt across my chest. Not when he slams the door and races to his own. It grows wider when he slams the truck in drive and fishtails back onto the path that will take us back toward town. It isn't until his big hand reaches out and takes my leg in his strong hold that my smile slips slightly, but it only slips because my head falls back and I whimper and try to rub my legs together to ease the ache between them. I lose the smile completely when my mouth drops open and that whimper turns into a loud whine as his long fingers dance up my legs until he slips beneath the hem on my shorts and pushes my panties to the side, pressing against my clit in sure movements that have me panting in seconds.

"Fucking drenched," he grounds out through his tightly clamped teeth.

I roll my head against the headrest and look across the cab at his face. His finger dips from my swollen clit and as he drops his hand lower, his wrist twists slightly so that when he gets there his finger slides deep inside me.

My legs spread instantly when his thick finger fills me and I hear his rumbled groan fill the space around us as he slides his finger as deep as his position allows before pulling it back, then repeating his movements until I can feel myself soaking his hand. If he keeps this up, I won't last. He adds a second finger and my hand digs into the door and I reach out, wrapping my other around his forearm and choke on shattered breaths when he thrusts his fingers so deep, I feel like I've been electrocuted as he hits *that* spot that has me panting, whimpering and begging incoherently.

"Please, Lee, please," I pant. How I formed those words, I'll never know.

"Fuck," he snarls, the sound making my arousal spike even higher. "You'll call me that when I'm so deep inside you my balls will be soaked with this sweetness."

His fingers curl and I pant, my hand cramping around the force of my grip.

"Please, oh God. Not without you, please."

I pray he understands my plea and when he curses, I know he gets me. His hand leaves my pants and I cry out, causing him to spit out a string of curses that would make a sailor blush. His leg slams down and I feel the truck pick up speed as I watch him take his fingers to his mouth and lick every drop of my wetness from his skin.

"Holy shit," I exhale.

"You're getting my mouth first, darlin'. That wasn't enough of a taste and fuck me, I'm starved."

I say nothing, just continue to feel like my heart is about to slam from my chest as I continue to shift my legs back and forth in attempt to ease the burn he's lit between my legs.

Chapter 15

Megan

Liam pulls the truck up his short drive and doesn't waste a second turning the key and ripping it out. His door is thrown open and I watch immobile as he stomps around to my door, my head tracking his every movement.

When my eyes meet his through the window, I shiver with the intensity that is written all over his face. My door opens and his hand snakes out, unbuckling my belt and pulling me from my seat with strong gentleness.

Of course, that gentleness is gone the second my feet hit the ground. He hands me his keys and without a word, I'm in his arms and he is prowling toward the door.

"Let us in, darlin'," he grumbles and I falter when his mouth starts to lick and nibble down my neck. When I don't move, he pulls his mouth from my neck and grunts, "Need you to open that door before I fuck you in the yard, Megan."

"Oh, okay," I sputter.

He dips his head again and I feel his body shake with silent laughter. "Only you could make me laugh when I'm so hard it hurts."

"Oh."

"Yeah, oh. Let us in. Now."

His mouth takes control of my neck again and with a shiver down my spine, I reach out with his keys and unlock his door, turning the knob to let us in. The sounds of his alarm beeping hits my ears and he steps through, kicking the door shut behind him before moving us toward where the waiting alarm panel is.

"Two-Nine-Six-Two," he grumbles against my skin.

My hand is shaking so violently, I almost don't hit the right combination. The second his alarm is settled, he turns and takes the stairs two at a time. His hold never falters as he then stomps through his hallway and into the darkness of his bedroom. Walking right up to the edge of his huge bed, he places me against the mattress, and shifts his body as his hands come out to grab my hips and spin my body until my legs are dangling off the edge.

I watch as he lifts his arm, grabs a fistful of his shirt and pulls it over his head. Each inch of his golden skin making my mouth water as the moonlight through his open window hits his muscular torso. I reach out, running my hand down his abs and lick my lips.

"You can play later," he tells me as his hands then move to push mine out of the way and toward his buckle.

The second he releases the leather and his deft fingers start to pull each button from their secure hold, I have to fight the itch I have to rip the material from his body. I can see his thick shaft pushing against the denim as he works to free himself.

His hands leave their mission and I watch as he stands, thumbs hooking his briefs and jeans before he gives me a crooked grin and bends to push them both down, before straightening once again. Then he gives me a blink to take him—all of him—in before kneeling on the floor in front of me. I look down my body at him and he licks his lips.

"Now. Now you get my mouth."

Oh, God. The rush of arousal overpowering my already overloaded system.

His hands reach out and I jump when he palms the skin right above my knees, earning me a smirk. He takes his time, killing me with the slowness that his hands take as they travel up my thighs. Right when he reaches the top, his thumbs brush against the crotch of my shorts and I almost come unglued, my hips jolting off the bed. He moves quickly then, moving his hands to my hips and pressing me back down before curling his fingers into my skin.

"The smell of you, God damn. I thought I was starving for you before. I'm going to eat you until you can't breathe, Megan. Fucking drown in you."

"Oh, God."

"Hold on, darlin'," he tells me and then my shorts and panties are flying over his shoulder, his hands back at my hips and he pulls me against his mouth—hard.

My head falls back and I lose the strength to hold my body up. When my back falls to the mattress, his hold gets tighter until I'm being pulled to the very edge, with my ass hanging half off. One of his strong hands leaving my hips and curls under my leg to throw it over his shoulder, fitting his mouth even tighter to my core.

When his tongue starts to twist and push against my clit, I cry out and he grabs my other leg to pull it over his other shoulder. Then in a move that would make a porn star proud, his mouth opens wide and his cheeks pull in as he sucks hard while his tongue drops down and pushes inside of me.

That's all it takes for the burn to catch fire and sear through my body in an explosion that puts stars in my vision, and my breath to stall in my throat. My back arches and my fingers ache as I fist his sheets between them.

He hums his approval against me just when my climax starts to ebb and I jump right into a second spike of pleasure, screaming until my throat burns. His head twists and his stubble burns against the sensitive skin on my thighs. My hand moves from its hold on the sheets and I push my fingers through his thick hair and try to move his mouth from its delicious torture against my swollen skin.

He growls against me and shakes his head, making me whimper when I feel the movement shoot up my spine.

"Please," I gasp.

He doesn't move, only intensifies his movements.

True to his words, he doesn't let up until I've come another time against his talented mouth and only when he's licked every inch of my oversensitive skin, does he start to move up my body. Licking, sucking and biting his way as his hands pull the material of my shirt up. His hands wrap around my back and lift me slightly as he fingers the clasp on my bra. When it gives, he makes quick work of continuing his journey of hands and mouth until his teeth bite down on my right nipple.

The feeling of pleasurable pain makes me jolt and he gruffs out a laugh against my skin.

He takes his time rolling each of my nipples against his tongue. Nibbling softly and biting down hard as I arch and writhe under his touch.

"Thought about nothing but this for months, Megan. Since the last time I had your pussy choking my cock, this has been running through my mind. I wanted to take my time, go slow, make it good, but there will be nothing slow about this time, darlin'," he says against my breast.

I say nothing, but squeak when his hands push under my pits and push me further back in his bed, allowing him the room to drop his knee between us.

"I need to fuck you, hard."

"Please," I answer.

"When you come, you scream my name. When you called me Lee, fuck baby, felt it squeeze my balls so tight I could have come in my pants. Dig those heels in my spine, your nails in my shoulder, and you. Call. Me. Lee."

I gasp and try to nod. His eyes search mine for a beat and then he lifts, reaches over to the side of his bed and I watch as he rips a condom open and rolls the latex down his shaft.

When he's done, his hands move until he's holding me with his fingers wrapped around my neck and his thumbs resting against my throat.

"I didn't want to give you an angry come, but it's been building for months. Building so high until that's all I can give you. Next time, you ride me until you take what you need. Put me in you, darlin'," he grunts.

I reach with an unsteady hand, between our bodies, and take his cock in my hand, running my fingers over the condom-covered skin until he groans.

"Now," he demands and I stop teasing and move the tip of him where my body is weeping to be filled.

"Fuck," he grinds out, his eyes never leaving mine.

His hands tighten slightly, not in a painful way, but the pressure against my throat makes me whimper just the same. The feeling of him holding me there while his body is heavy against mine works to have me climbing the high as my orgasm threatens again. And as he fills me in a bruising thrust that has the sound of his balls hitting my wet skin echoing out around us, my mouth drops and I cry out.

"You're soaking me, Megan. You want it harder?" he grunts against my lips.

I push my head up, his hands tighten against my throat and I feel another gush leave my body.

"Fucking love it when I'm rough? God, your pussy is so greedy for me. Just me," he rambles and then crashes his mouth to mine.

His hips pound against mine and his mouth swallows each and every cry that leaves my mouth. He continues his bruising pace as his hands leave my neck, I instantly miss the pressure and let it be known with a low whine. He sucks my tongue in his mouth and dips one elbow in the mattress as his other hand glides down my body and up the leg that is wrapped tight around his back.

His mouth leaves mine and with his hand still on my leg, he demands, "Dig your heels in deep, baby."

I give him what he wants, but not because he told me to. I give him what he wants because when his hand leaves my leg and pushes into the mattress, bringing his body up he goes even deeper into my body and those heels push hard.

Just as he demanded earlier, my hands go to his shoulders on my own accord and as he takes my body hard, my nails dig in with my heels still pushing hard against the small of his back. Our eyes never leave each other's probing gaze. Never once do I take my eyes away from his, so full of lust that I know there isn't an ounce of control left in his body.

He drops his head and I lift up to meet him in a kiss so sweet it doesn't match the powerful way that he's taking my body. A kiss that gives me more than words ever could at this moment. His hips slow and as his tongue rolls against mine, his hips start to take me in slow, deep rolls. He doesn't pull back, just rocks his hips against mine.

I push up and cry out when he slips even deeper.

His lips come from mine and his hooded eyes open a sliver. "Feels like heaven," he says softly. "Everything, darlin'. Feels like everything."

He drops his head, his forehead, wet with sweat, and hits mine softly. Then he starts to move, slowly dragging his cock from my body before pushing back in even slower. Each thrust he takes, every pull back of his hips, bringing me closer to breaking into a million pieces.

My breath comes quickly, matching his pants above me. It's building so high that I know the power of my release is going to tear me in two.

"I feel it," I gasp. "I feel it, Lee."

"God, yes." His eyes close and he drops his body down so that he's resting on his elbows, arms pushed under my shoulders, and my head in his palms. "Finally."

I feel tears leak from my eyes at the beauty of this moment and while I'm wide open for him in every way that counts, I push back against his hold and when I come, it isn't Liam that I scream . . . it's Lee. And the reward of this moment is when this big beautiful man, closes his eyes on a hard exhale and whispers *my* name like it's the most precious thing he has ever experienced.

Chapter 16

Liam

I watch as Megan moves from my bathroom and walks through the dim lighting of my bedroom before her knee hits the mattress and she crawls up my body, before settling half on top of me and half on the bed. Her head hits my shoulder, her arm wrapping around my torso and her legs tangling with mine. She doesn't speak and I give her the silence she needs. Her body is completely relaxed against mine. I take a deep breath as her fingers start to move against my chest in small circles.

Each circle her fingers take has me wondering where her thoughts are running to. I don't worry because after what we just shared, I know there is no way she's going to pull away this time. She let me in and fuck if it wasn't the most beautiful thing I've ever experienced.

"My . . . Jack. Jack didn't love me. I know he didn't, but I was happy with him. He gave us a happy life."

My body goes solid at her words. The hand that had been resting lightly against her back jolting and pulling her tighter against me.

"He cared for me and he cared deeply, but it wasn't love. The only love we ever shared was what we had as friends. Best friends all our lives." She takes a shuddered breath before her hand continues the circles against my skin. "He protected me. Made my life safe. Gave up everything he had, even his life, for that safety. Even knowing all of that, looking at what we had, it feels like the lie that it was now. I remember the happiness. I remember never regretting the path our lives took. But, looking back, all I can focus on is how I didn't feel and a big part of that is the love we lacked as lovers. I hate feeling that. Hate it. It feels like I cheapened his life somehow."

"Darlin,'" I start and try to move her so I can see her eyes.

"No. No, Lee. I need this," she says and pushes her body even closer.

I keep my mouth shut and wait. I know she's about to speak when those circles pick back up.

"I was seventeen when he managed to drag me to one of the parties the football team was famous for. He was my best friend and it hurt him that I was living a life full of nightmares. He wanted me to have fun. Get out of the house where my crackhead mom was passed out and my drunk of a father was doing his best job at drowning in a bottle. So I went, because I wanted to see what the big deal was. Why he had been begging me for so long to go with him. I figured what the hell, school was over the next week and we would finally be graduating. He would always say, 'Megs, it's a big world past this park.' Or 'Megs, you just need to live a little.' He always saw the best in everything. He could see past the crappy trailer park we lived. Past the terrible parents, through the poor status of our financial lives, over the glooming fact that no one in either of our families had made anything of themselves. So, for him, I went and tried to see what he saw."

My body feels like it has cement flowing through my veins. Turning me into stone as each muscle pulls tight, bracing for her words but not daring to move while she is finally giving me the rest of her.

"We had been there for a few hours before he left me to run and pee. He hadn't left my side once. Not because he felt like he had to stay, but because that's just the type of friends we were. He wanted to share his excitement with everything he did with me. He was the life of the party and I was not. But for those few hours I had actually had fun. I got him. When he left me, he told me not to move, but the second he mentioned the bathroom it was like the floodgates opened and I needed to go right that second. He went through the back door and straight into the woods behind the house, and I . . . and I went down the dark hall like the stupid little girl I was."

Her hand stops and I know she's lost in her memories.

I can see what's coming even without the words. In my line of work this is a scene we see. Not a lot but too often to sit right. But even knowing what's coming and being ready to hear it is two different things. I give her the only thing I can while I wait for those circles to continue against my skin. I tighten my hold and pull her as close against me as I can get.

And wait.

"Two guys I had never seen in my life got to me before I even got close to the bathroom. They were older, which wasn't rare with those parties, for some of the college kids from the local community college to show. Twenty minutes later what little innocence I had left was gone as they took turns stripping it from me. They were smart, took me down to the basement where there was one of those soundproof rooms. Apparently the kid who lived there, his dad was some hot shot in the record business. Had his own recording studio, locked so tight it didn't matter how hard I yelled for someone to save me. Jack found me. He missed them by seconds. I will never forget the look in his eyes as he picked me up and helped me leave the house without anyone seeing me. I know that cost him, taking care of me and not going after *them*. It cost him even more to keep that secret. One that no one, besides you now, him and those two men know."

"Darlin', please," I beg as a feeling of helplessness so strong takes hold.

"You need to know. I wish I could keep this from you, but I don't want to start this with my ghost pulling me down anymore."

I nod, my chin rolling softly against her head.

She shifts and her body moves from my side until she's draped across me completely. Her forearms rest against my chest and her tiny hands land on my face, her thumbs tracing my lips as she looks into my eyes.

"Molly isn't Jack's." Her voice, so small with those three words and I hold her eyes and wait for her to finish.

Giving her what she needs. It kills me to keep quiet and let her voice her pain. Fucking guts me. She needs this and all I can do is wrap my arms around her and wait it out.

"I have no clue who her father is, Lee. No clue," she continues.

She closes her eyes and two tears roll down her cheeks. I bring my arms around from the hold I had on her and wipe them away, causing her to open her eyes again. I search her gaze and make sure she is holding strong. She gives me a small nod.

"After I was raped, I didn't even consider the possibility. I wasn't stupid, but I had been too busy healing the wounds they left on my soul that it didn't even filter through. When I found out I was pregnant, Jack took charge. He wouldn't listen to a word I said. He enlisted the next day and a week later we were married. He knew, God he knew, if he left me there I would rot. And, Lee, I would have. He gave up everything for me. He had a full ride playing football and he was so good. He gave it all up to marry his best friend because he felt responsible for what happened to me."

"Baby, he loved you," I tell her honestly.

She shakes her head and it kills me that she really believes that.

"Megan, look at me. *See me, darlin'*." I plead. I wait for her to collect herself before I continue. "You know I love Dani like she's my sister. You and Jack are just like Dani and me. Best friends with a bond that can't be shaken. He didn't give up anything for you that he wasn't okay with losing. But he was not okay with losing you. He did what he did because he loved you. Have you been living with that guilt this whole time?"

"Since the day he told me he enlisted. He did it all for me, Lee and in the end he died for it. I've felt that every day for the last six years. He gave me a happy life, you have to understand that, we were so blissfully happy that I didn't mind that we had the most unconventional marriage. But I have always felt the guilt of his decision since the day when he made it. I didn't show him. Never let him see that cloud hanging over us, but it was there and I felt the bone-crippling pain of that guilt when they told me he was killed."

"You need to let that go, darlin'. Let go of that thought that he didn't love you and forget it. I'm telling you, as a man cut from the same cloth, if Dani had been in your shoes, I wouldn't have married her, baby. Not because I wouldn't have wanted her safe, but because I don't love her past a sibling-like bond. I would have made her safe, but not by marrying her. Your husband, baby, he loved you."

Her eyes widen and I watch, helplessly, as her lids fill and when the first sob hits her body, I take her in my arms and hold her as she not only relives her pain, but comes to terms with the realization that she's had it all wrong for six very long and very agonizing years.

"I didn't love him like that, Lee." She says a long while after the tears had dried and her body had stilled. "What kind of person does that make me, that I never loved him like that? He was my best friend and I loved him, but I was never ever in love with him. Not when he saved me, made it safe, or even after we had Molly and we fell into a real marriage. It always felt so forced when we tried to be more than just friends."

I tighten my arms and close my eyes. I run my fingers through her hair before resting my hand against her head as it rests against my chest.

"Makes you human, Megan. You two made the best out of a shit situation. He died serving his country, baby. He died a hero. He died knowing he was a father of a beautiful girl that has her mother's smile and the fighting spirit of the only real father she will ever know—your husband. He loved a good woman and if I had my guess, with all of that, he died happy. Darlin', it's time to let it go. Give it to me and let me take your pain, but you never forget that despite everything that happened before, he loved you and Molly, and he died a happy man that had the world."

"How do you know that?" she sobs, her tears picking back up. Tears she needs to finally heal from her pain. Tears that, as they soak through my naked skin, heal because I take her pain.

"Because, there is no way he could have you and Molly in his life and not know what kind of beauty he held in his hands. Darlin' trust me. He didn't regret a second of it. Bet my life on it."

"Oh, God," she sobs. "Lee."

My name comes out of her mouth and I know that I will never forget the sound. Her agony laced so deep into that one word that long into the night I hold her to me, tight, as she slips in and out of sleep. The tears don't leave for long and even when she managed to drift off to sleep, those sobs never stop shaking her body.

My hold never wavers as I make true to my promise and take

every single pain filled tear, every ghost of her past that comes shaking from the force of her cries, and I pull that pain deep inside and lock it tight so that it can never hurt her again.

Chapter 17

Megan

"Good mornin,' darlin.'"

I shake my head against his voice and burrow deeper into his warm skin.

"I would let you sleep the day away if I could. No place I would rather have you than right here naked in my arms, but we need to talk and I want some time to enjoy my woman, soft from sleep, before we have to get going."

Lifting my head, I look through the blonde mess of hair that is currently more in my face than his now. His eyes look tired, but alert. The stubble from last night has darkened his jaw even more, framing that knee-melting smile to perfection.

"You need to use the restroom before we have that talk?" he asks, that smile deepening until his dimple pops.

I nod and before he unwraps his arms from my body, his head tips up from the pillow it was resting on and his lips touch mine. So soft it was just a breath of his skin before he pulled away.

"Hurry back to me, darlin.'"

Without too much fanfare, I untangle my body from his, instantly missing the warmth of his touch. I hear him laugh as I pull the sheet with me as I stand and I turn to glare at him, but stumble on my feet instantly. My glare vanishes and my jaw drops.

I should have considered, possibly, that it wasn't the best idea to take the only sheet we had with me. All I thought was that there was no way I wanted to parade through his very bright bedroom with all my jiggly bits on display. But, I didn't think because in nabbing that sheet, I left him—all of him—on display and he's loving every second of this. Very obviously.

My eyes go from his erection to his face a few times, not stopping to enjoy the deliciousness in between. Just like a tennis match, crotch to head and back again. My eyes widen when his laughter picks up and that beautifully huge erection of his bobs up and down. Just jumping around like a Mexican jumping bean or something. There wasn't any going back to his eyes after that. My gaze was trapped on his cock and it would take an act of God to change that.

"Keep looking at me like that and we're going to have issues," his voice grumbles.

I lick my lips and all his laughter stops. But my eyes never leave his crotch. Jesus, is he getting harder?

"Megan," he warns.

I don't move. My hands itch where I have the sheet clamped tight against my chest and I have to shift from foot to foot with the building pressure between my legs. He *is* getting harder.

"Lick your lips like that again and I won't be able to hold back."

His voice sounds strained. Well, hell, judging by how angry his cock looks, I would guess strained is a pretty fair assumption.

"Megan," he barks and I jump slightly. "Bathroom. Now. We need to talk before I fuck you and if you keep this shit up there won't be any of the former. Just a lot of fucking."

I nod then lick my lips. When I hear him make some kind of animalistic noise deep in his throat, I jump, spin and run to the bathroom.

I make quick work of the toilet, wash my hands and attempt to do something with my wild hair. When I look at myself in the mirror I want to puke. My eyes are swollen from crying most of the night; little, puffy red bags making them look small and beady. My nose is red and my lips are slightly chapped.

I look like a hot mess.

And Liam—no Lee—still wanted me. A lot.

I smile to myself when I think about what calling him Lee does to him. The second I used his nickname, something I have never done because I felt like by not using it I could keep some more distance between us, he came alive and the reward was so great that there is no way I'm going back to Liam.

My gaze falls from my face and I look around the counter. I see his toothbrush resting in a cup next to the sink. The toothpaste on the other side, neatly capped and not a mess like some people leave theirs. A girly looking bottle of hand soap, that I know deep down either came from his mom or Dani. No way he would have something like that. Lee strikes me as the kind of man that would have a bar of off brand soap, but not high-end girly stuff.

Shifting on my feet, I worry my lip and try to figure out the whole smelly breath, yucky teeth, situation I have myself in right now.

"Megan," Lee barks from the other side of the door. "Did you fall in?"

I take a deep breath, hike the sheet tighter and turn to open the door. He hasn't moved from his bed, his hands folded behind his head and that gloriously hard cock still standing at full attention.

"Stop," he warns and my eyes shoot to his. He studies my face for a second before speaking. "What's bothering you, darlin'?" His tone is soft, comforting.

He starts to come up, his elbow digging into the mattress as his feet uncross and he starts to swing his frame from where he had been resting. I hold my hand up and he pauses.

"I, uh, well . . . okay. I know you're a single guy living alone and all, but sometimes single guys stock up and like to be prepared. I mean, I'm prepared, but I have Molly so it makes sense to have, like, ten of everything—"

I snap my mouth shut when he lifts off the bed and prowls toward me. He moved so quickly that one second he was in the bed, and the next he was standing in front of me with his hands resting right where my back meets the swell of my ass.

"Breathe,"

I do and he smiles.

"Not single," he states and I feel my brow wrinkle. "Darlin', wasn't alone in that bed last night. I. Am not. Single."

"Oh," I say on a sigh.

"Darlin." He dips his neck down and moves his face level with mine. "Seriously?"

I shiver with the look in his eyes. Soft and hard, all at the same time. But not for a second holding back his happy adoration.

"Seriously?" he questions again.

Coming out of my fog, I shake my head and when he pulls back I hurry to find my voice.

"I know," I gasp. "I know. I mean, I think I know. I, you, uh . . . we . . . what I mean is, shit. I just wanted to know if you have a spare toothbrush."

I look up when I feel his body start to move slightly and his knee-melting smile hits me at full force, dimple and all.

"It isn't funny, Lee."

His eyes drop with my words and those hands at my lower back move down and hit my bottom. With each hand, his fingers flex and he pulls me closer. I stumble when the sheet tangles with my feet, but move to fall into his body. My eyes losing his as my vision fills with his tan chest.

"You aren't single either, Megan."

"I just need a toothbrush," I mumble against his skin and pull back enough to place a kiss against his pec.

"And you know you aren't single."

"I know," I whisper.

"You know that because last night, you felt it. You felt *everything* that I've seen since day one."

I nod, but don't speak.

"You felt it all."

"I did," I confirm and with my words, I take the last bit of the wall I had around me for years and kick the shit out of it. "Lee, I just need a toothbrush."

His body shakes, hard this time, and I pull my head back just in time to see him tip his head back and laugh. The sound, rich and like velvet to my skin, brings a smile to my face and a feeling of completeness settles in, taking the void I have felt for so long and filling it so full, it's spilling over the edge.

"Had my mouth on you just hours ago. All over you, darlin'. My mouth was inside of you. As deep as I could go. I think it's safe to say, my toothbrush, is your toothbrush."

I narrow my eyes and his smile grows.

"You just ruined the moment, bucko!" I snap and pull from his body then stomp into the bathroom.

His laughter trailing behind me.

And when I look in the mirror for the second time this morning, I don't see that lingering sadness. I pick up his toothbrush and as I stand there and brush my teeth, all I see is happiness.

Finally.

I unloaded on him last night and I know he wants to talk about that, I just don't know what to say. It was so much easier in the darkness. I used his strength and that helped to get the courage to open up. He deserves me giving it all to him and in order to do that I need to give him the light too.

With a deep breath of courage, I rinse off his brush and open the door. He walks over from the spot just in front of the door where I left him, the second I step out of the bathroom. His head comes down and I get a quick kiss.

"Don't get dressed, darlin'. I like your skin on mine."

And then he's gone, with the bathroom shutting to a crack behind him.

Well.

I might not get dressed, but the sheet stays.

My ass had just hit the bed when he came back into the room. Not even giving one thought to the fact that he is *still* very naked and very aroused. I hear his laugh and snap my eyes up from where I had, once again, been staring at his erection.

"Darlin' I really need you to focus. You'll get my cock when we finish, okay?"

"I am focusing," I retort.

He laughs, "Yeah, focusing on my cock isn't going to help us right now."

He reaches out and his large hand wraps around the base of his shaft. His long fingers curling to pull his sac up. He moves his hand, fingers dropping his sac, and he gives himself a few lazy pulls. I close my eyes and drop my body to fall to the mattress with a groan.

I feel the mattress dip with his weight and when my eyes open his face is right there, so close that our noses are just a breath away.

"Good morning, darlin'," he says, repeating those words he rumbled earlier.

So carefree and confident. He's changing me. Every second that I'm with him, I feel myself changing into a person that feels the lightness of happiness. *He* is making me a better person.

"Hey," I smile.

His hand moves up my side and when he reaches the top of the sheet, it's pulled and thrown away from our bodies and out of my grasp in seconds.

"I told you, I like your skin on mine."

My pulse speeds up and I look into his amused eyes.

"You have nothing to hide from me, Megan. Not your body and not your thoughts."

"Okay," I gulp.

"We need to talk, darlin'," he tells me softly, his eyes searching.

"I know."

"Do you want me to start?"

I nod and he gives me a quick kiss before adjusting our bodies. When he's done, my back is to the mattress and his large body is covering mine. He keeps his weight off, but still manages to make me feel like I'm covered head to toe in his strength. Our legs are tangled together, his body turned slightly so that, even with me fully in his arms, his hips are on the bed next to me. One of his arms goes under my body at my shoulders and the other hits right under my chest, his long fingers wrapping around the base of my breast. His face dips into my neck and he gives me a kiss before pulling back and looking into my eyes.

"You gave me a lot of heaviness last night. Pain that you've carried for a long time, darlin', and I know that has to leave you hurting. Honesty here, complete honesty, it cut me to the bone to hear what's been weighing you down for years, Megan. It's a pain I don't mind, if it means you've unloaded some of that weight for me to carry. What I need is to know where your head is."

He waits, his unwavering patience with me so clear in this moment.

"It's gone," I whisper, my eyes never leaving his.

"What is, baby?"

"The pain."

His eyes close and the arms holding me go tight.

"I have a lot of years thinking one way, that won't go away over night, but what you said, about Jack, hearing that and letting those thoughts roll through my head all night . . . you're right. Every memory I have of him, before and after Molly, there isn't one that he isn't over the moon happy. Even though we didn't share a love that was built conventionally, I can see it now. He was my best friend and he made my life a better place as a child and as my husband."

"He held the world, darlin', no doubt in my mind about how he felt."

"He would love you."

"Yeah?"

He settles and I roll slightly so that I'm about to look into his eyes, our bodies now facing each other.

"It's hard, because I will always miss him and I would never wish Molly away, but had my life taken a different turn and I met you . . . he would have been our biggest cheerleader." Reaching up, my hand cups his jaw. "He always wanted me to live a life better than what we were born into. He saw it for himself, but I couldn't, not for the life of me, see beauty coming from that. He would joke that one day I would walk right into a new life and I would be too busy living in my head that I would miss it until my ass hit the ground. Lee, you pack a mean punch and I think my ass still feels the sting of the ground."

"You see it now, huh?" He looks deep into my eyes and blinds me with that smile.

"Yeah, baby, I see it. I see everything that I couldn't see before. Everything."

"I won't let you go, Megan. I waited and I knew the second that I saw you that this was it for me. Do you know how hard it was to keep my distance and wait for you to be ready?"

"I'm still scared," I tell him honestly.

His body moves closer and I move into his body until my arms wrap around us and I feel him completely.

"You get that what I had with Jack was something that, when I lost him, almost destroyed me?" He nods and I continue in hushed tones. "That almost destroyed me and the way I feel toward you, even this early, I know it's so much more powerful."

"It's not early, Megan. I've been here, picking away at your walls for almost two years." He laughs but it holds no humor. "If it hadn't been Dani and Cohen's wedding, it would have happened not long after. You were weakening around me every time I was near and it was only a matter of time. We've spent enough time together that you know what you feel. It's never too soon when you're sure. We didn't just meet on the streets. We've been building this for a long while, darlin'."

"That doesn't mean I'm not scared, Lee."

"I know, but we'll get there. Together. You just have to take my hand and let me take care of your heart."

I nod, not trusting my voice right now.

"Almost done. Can you handle more?"

"I'm okay, Lee. I really am. Last night was hard, but I feel free of that pain. It just stings a little."

"First, before we finish this up. You need to know that you never have to keep Jack from me. You shared a life with him and he's a part of you and a part of Molly. I want you to be able to come to me and know that I will never, not once, turn you away. He gave you a good life, baby, and he should never be kept in the dark."

My eyes fill with tears and I nod, my hands flexing against the skin on his chest. I move them around his back and hug myself to his body.

"Thank you for that," I tell him.

"You don't have to thank me, darlin'," his voice rumbles against my ear. "I don't want to bring this back up. It kills me, but I have to know so that I don't fuck something up unintentionally. Is Jack on Molly's birth certificate?"

"Uh, yeah." I tell him, confusion with the path this conversation has turned.

"I assume that means that you two decided before she was born there would be a certain amount of care when it comes to Molly's knowledge of how she was conceived?"

"She will never know. Never, Lee. I don't ever want that to darken her life. Ever."

He must have read the panic in my tone because his body moves until he's sitting, back to the headboard, my legs spread wide framing his thighs, until he's settled his arms back around me. His hands squeeze my hips before moving up to curl around my neck.

"She can't know," I gasp.

"And she won't, Megan. You trusted me with that last night and I will never betray that. I needed to know so that I could proceed with a full deck. She was and will always be Jack's, okay?"

I study his face. Those eyes giving me nothing but understanding and I nod.

"You're mine now, darlin', and with that comes Molly. It's a package deal that I want more than you'll ever know. This is up to you on how we play this, but she knows me. That little girl stole my heart the first time she put hot pink lipstick on me, so it isn't going to be a hardship for me here, but I need to know how you want to introduce *us* to her."

This is it. This step will be me giving myself over to him completely and with a newfound strength, I give it to him.

"She's young, but not stupid. I'll talk to her when I pick her up. Give her some time to hear it from me before. I saw her with you, Lee, I know this will not be news that isn't exciting for her. But I don't want to throw us in her face. We start with dinner. Then we take it as it comes. Together."

"I like that, darlin'."

His lips hit mine in a deep kiss that holds the promise of more before he pulls back.

"Thank you," he tells me.

"For what?"

"Everything."

Then I get his lips.

And then he gives *me* everything.

Chapter 18

Liam

I look over at Megan as we drive toward her house. She called to check on Molly right before we left, letting Izzy know that she would be there to get her shortly after lunch. That gave us two hours to fill and I used every second of our time until we had to leave. After last night I've been worried that she would be having a hard time, but she's shown no signs that the pain she held onto for so long is haunting her.

She's lighter.

Her laughter coming easier and her lips have been curved up since I pulled her from the bed and into the shower.

I can tell she's holding back a little, that fear of starting something new won't go away overnight, but she's ready.

And she's finally mine.

"How do you think this is going to go?"

She turns her gaze from the window and gives me her eyes. I get a smile before turning my focus back to the road ahead of us.

"Molly?" she asks.

"Yeah, darlin'."

That smile grows. I can't see it fully, but even while my eyes are on the road I can hear it in her voice.

"She won't even blink."

I laugh, "Meaning?"

"Molly loves easy and hard. She is happy when I'm happy. She enjoys life with a full speed ahead attitude. My guess is that she's going to be riding the high of me telling her you're going to be around, a lot, for a long while to come."

"She's a great kid," I voice honestly.

"Yeah," she sighs.

I reach over and pull her hand over the console and hold it against my lap.

"I won't make you regret this, giving us a chance. I promise you that I will do everything in my power to drive the three of us on this new path."

Her hand squeezes mine.

"I know, Lee. For the first time in a really, really long time I'm excited to see what happens next."

We continue the drive in silence as I hold her hand in my lap.

When I pull up to her house and I watch as she hesitates to leave my truck, I grin and climb out to walk over to her door. She gets down and I laugh to myself as she visibly has to force herself to leave me.

When we get to her door, I pull her into my arms. She doesn't hesitate to wrap her arms tightly around my back.

"I'll be back tonight, darlin'. If you think that Molly isn't ready for that, you call and we will try tomorrow."

"Okay."

"You're going to have to walk through that door, baby. If I had my way I wouldn't let you go, but one step at a time."

"Okay," she says into my chest.

"Give me a kiss," I demand.

Her head comes up, "Okay, Lee."

When her lips touch mine, that smile never slips.

"See you tonight."

She nods and I wait for her to unlock her door, getting another grin before she shuts the door. I stand there for a second before I walk back to my truck and pull out of her driveway.

I've been ready for this moment for what seems like a lifetime and now that I have it, I'm nervous as hell. Not for what I'm building with Megan, but with the unknown that Molly is. She's been through so much in her short life that I don't want to rush my presence in her life. I don't want her to feel like I'm taking her father's place either. In all the times that I've been around her while Dani was watching her, she didn't even blink around the men that came around. Nate and Zac had often sat in on our tea parties and she ate that attention up.

But, there's a big difference between playtime while she's with Dani and a man being in her everyday life.

In all my plans to make Megan mine, I never doubted a single step. I never feared that it wouldn't work and I was never nervous.

Funny that all it takes is one five-year-old girl to have me breaking out in a sweat.

My thoughts are interrupted when my phone's ringer starts coming through the truck speakers. Looking at the display in my dash, I see Dani's name come up.

"Hey," I answer.

"She just called Mom to tell her she would be there in thirty minutes to get Molly. Mom called me to let me know that. Now I know she isn't with you . . . so spill!"

"You get that I have a dick and gossip sessions don't apply to me, right?"

"Shut the hell up and tell me!" she huffs.

I flick my blinker and head toward my house while I process my thoughts and for the first time, I don't tell Dani everything. My promise to Megan and the relationship we're building means more to me than anything else in my life. Even the best friend that knows every single thing about me.

"I'm having dinner with her and Molly tonight."

"Uh," she falters. "Is that it?"

"That's all you're going to get."

"Seriously?" she gasps.

"Love you, Dani, but last night Megan finally, thank Christ, broke through the chains that have been holding her captive and those moments are for her and me alone."

"Oh my God," she wheezes. "That is so beautiful."

I roll my eyes.

"If she lets you in, then good. I'll be happy with the outcome either way because right now I know she's moving on and we're going to do that together. It's good, Dani. Really good."

"I'm so happy for you, Lee."

"Thanks, babe."

"How do you feel about tonight? Nervous? You are, aren't you?"

"Dani, I'm out of my mind, could puke, nervous."

She laughs and proceeds to spend the rest of my ride home talking my nerves down.

Chapter 19

Megan

I'm going to puke.

Maybe.

Probably.

"Is he here yet, Mommy?"

"Not yet, little bird," I tell Molly and laugh when her little lips pull into a frown.

To say my daughter is excited would be a great understatement.

"Come here, baby. He'll be here soon and then you can tell him all about our day."

She climbs into my lap and settles in to wait. Sofia the First fills the room and I settle back with her curled against me and think about how the morning went.

It wasn't the same madness that had met me the last time I picked her up from the Reid's. Since I didn't arrive until well after lunch—thanks to a very long shower with Lee—Axel had already left for work, dragging Nate with him to 'learn the ropes,' according to a laughing Izzy. I think Izzy could tell my nerves were sparked bright. Her knowing eyes spoke volumes. Of course, she also knew that I spent the night with Lee since the first words I stuttered were just that.

"I think Lee is my boyfriend," I told her with my cheeks flaming.

Izzy had barked out a laugh and pulled me into a tight hug.

"That's just their way, honey. His father was the same way with Dee. Axel the same with me. Greg and Melissa. Maddox and Emmy.

Asher and Chelcie. My sweet Dani with Cohen. Heck, even Davey had his moment with Sway. These men, it's just how they are. When they set their minds to something there is nothing and no one that will hold them back. And sweetheart, before you even let this thought take root in your mind, when they know, they know and they know in a way that sticks forever."

Of course *that* did nothing but make me freak out even further, causing Izzy to laugh harder, and Molly to join in while dancing in circles around us. I came down from my freak out . . . until I got my little bird home and while I watched her pick and peck at her snack, my nerves climbed once again.

I should have known better. With Molly, there needed to be no doubt.

Leaning my head back, I settle in for our wait and playback my conversation with Molly.

"Mommy, what did Mrs. Izzy mean? About being sticky forever?"

I turn my head from the counter I had been wiping—the same spot for the last five minutes—while staring off into space. Her brown eyes full of curiosity smile up at me from the table.

"Not sticky forever, little bird. She was talking about a feeling, kind of. She meant it like how I love you will be a feeling that sticks to me like yummy, chewed up bubble gum."

Her nose crinkles and her lips twist in a way that I know she's holding in a giggle. "That's gross, Mommy!" she tells me seconds before peals of laughter come bubbling out of her mouth. "I don't want to stick to you with chewy bubblegum!"

Smiling, I move from the counter and over to sit next to my sweet, full-of-love, daughter.

"It's a little different than that, sweets, that's just the best way to explain it."

She stops laughing out loud, but those eyes of hers are still burning with amusement. I watch her expressive face as she thinks about what Izzy told me *and what I just told* her. *And then I watch as all of it plugs into the right plugs and the connection is made.*

"Who do you want to stick to with chewy bubblegum, Mommy?"

Ah, my smart little bird. She's always been so wise beyond her five small years.

"I don't want to stick to anyone with yucky, chewy bubblegum," I laugh.

Her small hand comes out and falls on top of where I have mine placed on the table. Small thumb rubbing and little pink tipped nails going up and down in a thoughtful wave as she looks at me.

"Yes you do."

"No, baby. Just you."

"You're silly, mommy bird!"

"And you're sillier, little bird."

Her fingers continue their light thumping against my skin and I watch her eyes get soft and full of love, all for me.

"You told Mrs. Izzy that Leelee is your boyfriend. Is he the one you want to stick to with chewy bubblegum?"

Ah.

There it is.

My opening to tell her.

And my opening for a spiked up, nerve filled, freak out.

I went over this a million times since Lee left and I picked up Molly. How much to tell her. How to tell her. Is it too soon? How she would feel. Every possible thought of fear, followed by excitement, and then back to fear mixed with worry.

But my little bird is smart. Smart and knowing. And more importantly, I owe it to her to be honest about our future.

A future that I hope to God will be filled with Lee.

"I wouldn't want to be stuck to him with chewy bubblegum, but yes, sweets, I would very much love to be stuck with him."

"Like that time my arms got stuck in my swim wings? When you couldn't get them off?"

My smile grew as some of those nerves let go of their strong hold. "Something like that, little bird."

"Will Leelee come over for tea parties now?"

"Yeah, baby, I think so."

"Will Leelee make you smile all the time?"

Oh. My. God.

"You make me smile all the time."

Her head tilts and she smiles a smile that is so small you almost can't tell it's there. It's a sad smile. One that I know—and hate—that I've put on her face.

"Not all the time. You don't smile all the time."

"Oh, baby. Come here."

She makes quick work of pulling out from the table and into my lap. I wrap my arms around her and hold her as tight as she's holding me.

"Mommy was sad for a long time, little bird. I'm so sorry for that. For not smiling all the time. I missed your daddy a lot and for a long time my missing him was too hard to smile."

"You smile a lot now," she mumbles into my chest.

"Yeah, sweets, I do."

"Does that mean you don't miss Daddy?"

I tighten my embrace before moving my hands under her arms and moving her body so that she can see my eyes.

"No, honey. I miss your daddy a lot and I always will, but the way I miss him is different than it was then. When he went to heaven, I missed him so much that all I could see was how much I missed him. I got lost for a while, baby, and I couldn't remember the way. You gave me my smiles, smiles so bright that you helped me light up the way then and you still do, but for a long time all I could see was your smiles but not the way they wanted me to go. Those smiles made me happy even though I missed your daddy and because I missed your daddy so much, I thought a lot of sad things for a long time. But, now Mommy can see again. I can see my way that I had lost for a little while and, little bird, it's a beautiful path, so full of beautiful flowers, rainbows, and blue skies forever and ever. Now I can hold your hand and we can run through the flowers together. But, even while we run we can still miss Daddy. We just miss him in a different way."

"That sounds nice, Mommy."

"Yeah, honey, really nice."

"Will Leelee be with us when we run through flowers?"

My smile grows and I look into her very hopeful gaze and with a lightness I haven't ever felt in all of my years, I tell her, "Yes, Molly. He's going to come and run with us through the flowers and we're going to chew bubblegum and be stuck forever."

Her eyes light up and her face is the picture of joy.

"And we can have lots and lots of tea parties and makeupovers when we run in the flowers!"

After our talk, she went back to her snack and talked about Lee all afternoon. I let her know that he would be over for dinner later and I didn't think she would ever come down from that high.

Which brings us to now. My daughter, so full of eagerness over the night, that even with her favorite show on television, her eyes are glued to the hallway that leads to the front door.

I look at the clock, for the hundredth time in seconds, just as the front door thumps and the bell echoes through the house.

Molly's head snaps up and with wide, happy, eyes whispers, "He's here," before scampering off my lap, elbowing me—twice—in the ribs, and running as fast as her little legs will take her to the door.

"Molly, don't open that door until I'm there!" I yell, coming off the couch quickly.

"Too late," I hear and my nerves flutter like a million butterflies in my gut, rooting me in place.

"Mommy! Mommy! Leelee is here . . . and, and . . . and HE HAS FLOWERS!"

A head to toe tingle starts taking over my body. My lips curve and I move forward with the largest beaming grin on my face.

I walk forward and around the wall that separates the living room from the front door and stop dead at the sight that meets me.

Lee is holding my daughter in his strong arms while her face—bright with the happiness she is feeling—is stuffed into a small bundle of light pink roses. I look from her with wonderment to Lee's arm that isn't holding her tight to see another bundle—this one much larger—of more roses.

I don't move.

His brow tips up and I know he's wondering if he overstepped. This big, confident man that has gone after me with steadfast determination, is actually unsure and that has my feet moving before I can even process a single move I make. When my body hits his, the force of which I clearly didn't process, he rocks back slightly before his arm comes up and wraps around my shoulders. I reach out and pull my arms around both him and Molly, then shove my head into his neck.

"If you brought bubblegum, I swear I'll cry right now," I mumble into his skin before both Molly and I laugh so hard he has no choice but to hold onto us both a little tighter.

Chapter 20

Liam

"She asleep?"

Megan drops down to the couch and curls into my side. "Yes, finally. However I'm pretty sure she isn't sleeping heavy since she is still riding her Lee high."

I laugh, "Lee high?"

She comes up with her elbow pressed to the back of the couch and her hand against my chest, "Yes! Apparently the 'Lee high' is just as intoxicating to her as it is to me. This isn't funny," she snaps when my head goes back and I laugh. Hard.

"Darlin' that's the funniest thing I've heard. Lee high," I chuckle.

"Whatever," she gripes, moving her body to rest against mine again.

"Give me your mouth, Megan. I've missed it."

She shivers against my side. Her head snaps up and without giving her a second to think, my mouth comes down and I take her lips.

Just like I've been craving to do since she turned the corner earlier and stopped dead. But I wasn't worried because she had an expression on her face that I've been waiting to see.

The pain wasn't there anymore.

Not a single sliver of it had a hold on her beautiful body.

The weight of the world, off her shoulders, and even through her shock I could tell that she was . . . happy.

Bringing my hand up, I push my fingers into the silky hair on her nape and turn her head slightly so that I can deepen the kiss. Her tongue comes out, slowly, and slides against mine. Her head tilts and even though she doesn't move past her hands curling into my side and chest, with just one swipe of her tongue against mine, the hunger in that kiss grows. My cock swells against my pants and I know I'm in serious danger of this kiss becoming out of control when I feel her scissor her legs together.

Fuck me.

My girl can kiss.

Pulling back slightly, not removing my lips from hers, I give her a few light pecks. Not only to bring her back down from the rush I hope to fuck is burning through her body too, but pray it's enough to squash the urge scorching my blood, to sink my cock deep into her body.

Fuck me.

"I can smell you and, darlin', I've never thought it would be possible to want you more than I already do. Fuck, I crave you, Megan."

"Oh, God," she sighs and those damn legs start moving against each other again.

"I want nothing more than to lay you down, strip you bare, and worship every delicious inch, but that isn't happening tonight. I have no doubt this will cost me huge, but not tonight."

Her head comes down and crashes into my neck and I feel her nod.

"When Molly is used to me being around. When the excitement isn't so new and we know she's handling us, handling the knowledge that I will *not* be going anywhere, then we play. But until then, we wait until she isn't just a room away."

She nods again and her fingers curl even tighter, letting me know that I'm not the only one that is suffering right now.

"I need you to stop rubbing your thighs together, darlin'. Fuck me."

Her body shakes and when she pulls her head from my neck, her lips pulled in and I can tell she's about to lose her hold on her laughter.

"You have no idea how bad I want to fuck you, Megan," I tell her in a tone that came out harsher than I meant.

"I'm sorry," she says, laughter leaving her face.

Pulling her tighter to me, I press my lips to her temple. "Don't be sorry for wanting me. Don't ever be sorry for that, darlin'. You just have no idea how small that thread of my control is right now and as much as I crave your sweet body, we both know it can't happen."

"I know, Lee."

And fuck me if that doesn't go straight to my cock too.

Trying to think of a way to distract my need to fuck her, I ask, "Want to tell me why you and Molly both about lost your mind at the mention of gum earlier? I swear I thought I was going to go down, you two were laughing so hard."

"You're our gum," she bizarrely tells me.

"I'm not real good at understanding code, darlin'."

I move my arm when she pushes up and wait for her to settle. Instead of doing that at my side, one long leg comes up and settles at the opposite hip of her other. Her ass lands mid-thigh and both of her hands come up to my neck, curling around and then she leans in. Her face just inches from my own. I reach out and settle my hands to her hips and wait for her to speak. Enjoying the way she feels in my arms like this a little too much and vow to have her riding my cock like this real soon.

Her voice brings me out of my thoughts and I look into her eyes as she speaks.

"You, Lee. You are the chewy, icky, sticky, bubblegum that will never come off."

"Still not following, baby," I mutter against her lips.

"Well, I guess you aren't the gum. More like the one I want to stick the gum to. Or whatever. It makes a lot more sense when it comes from a five-year-old."

"Yeah, I'm guessing it does," I laugh. "Care to add on to that a little?"

Her head tilts in the most adorable way.

"Please," I try, earning me a curl of her small nose.

"It's really nothing. Actually it is nothing. It's silly. Just something that Izzy had said and Molly heard, then of course I explained in kid terms. So, I don't think it really makes sense, you know, to a man and all, if I explain it like I did to Molly."

If I thought her actions were cute before, this stuttering and rambling version of her takes the cake.

"It's kind of embarrassing," she tells me.

"I've been inside you. What I mean," I rush to finish when her eyes narrow, "Is that I've seen every inch. Touched, licked and kissed those inches. There is not one thing you should ever feel embarrassed about with me, Megan."

"Oh," she breathes.

"Yeah. Give it to me, baby."

And she does. God, does she. And in that moment I make a note to make sure Izzy Reid gets one hell of a thank you delivery of flowers.

"I might have been a little nervous this morning and blurted out to Izzy that I thought . . . that maybe you had . . . shit, okay, it just slipped out that you were maybe my boyfriend. Or had made me your girlfriend. But now, saying that out loud and to your face makes it sound kind of silly. Boyfriend and girlfriend, I mean. The label, that is."

I smile and she drops her head to mine.

"I told you it was embarrassing," she exhales.

"No, it isn't. The rambling you do when you're nervous is cute, darlin', that's all. So cute that it hits me right between my legs, so I would say that isn't embarrassing at all. I'm not huge on labels, but if that's what you need to know you're mine and I'm yours, then they work for me."

"Oh, okay," she says with red cheeks.

"God, you're cute."

Her lips curl and I pull my head from the back of the couch to give her a kiss, not deep, but I still feel it just the same and I'm fighting the urge once again to take her.

"And when did bubblegum come into play?" I ask.

"Right," she breathes. "So Izzy may have told me that you guys—all of you guys—have a history of this."

I feel my brows pull in and wait, not sure about where this is going.

"I mean . . . this is kind of hard to explain, but she kind of said that all of the guys, your dad, Axel, and all the way down to Cohen, have a way about making someone yours. A way that, when it happens, sticks forever. Molly was curious, having heard that, but not understanding everything else, and asked what it meant to be stuck together forever. So, I told her it was like bubblegum."

I nod, loving everything she's said, but still not getting the damn gum.

"Right. So, the best way to explain it to her was to tell her how being stuck together or wanting to be stuck together is a feeling and not really being stuck, but if it wasn't just a feeling, it would be like wanting to have someone as close as possible and that feeling is like being stuck with chewy, sticky bubblegum."

"Bubblegum," I mumble and she closes her eyes.

"Bubblegum," she echoes.

"Open your eyes, Megan."

She doesn't move.

"Darlin', see me."

And those brown eyes hit mine.

"I've got a brand new pack of spearmint in the truck. Happy as fuck that you would gladly use it to stick yourself to me, but you don't need the gum. I'm happily stuck and have no plans to become unstuck."

Her eyes shine and then her head goes back and her laughter hits me like a punch in the gut.

Perfection.

Her happy in my arms, her daughter safe and warm—also happy—in her bed, having the chance at something I've known would feel like this, has my hands pushed into her hair and her mouth on mine in seconds.

Only now I have a hard time reminding myself why I need to pull back before I get too lost in her.

Bubblegum, I think to myself as her tongue slides against mine and the mint taste I tasted earlier invades. One that only a slice of gum can leave behind.

I've never loved bubblegum more.

Chapter 21

Megan

My body is going to burn up from the inside if he keeps this up. These slow kisses that I know will not go a step further with Molly home, boiling my arousal so bright that my veins are on fire.

"You taste good," he mumbles against my neck.

"Bubblegum," I wheeze out when his teeth bite down on the sensitive skin between my neck and shoulder.

Then my brain catches up to my mouth when I lose his mouth and I feel his body move in amusement. My eyes open wide and I watch him attempt to stop his laughter, and fail.

"I'm never going to live that down."

His laughter dies down to a chuckle at my pouting tone.

"I'll probably never even be able to chew a piece again," I continue.

His chuckle stops, but his smile stays. His perfectly straight teeth bright against his tan skin.

"You probably think I'm nuts."

His smile doesn't slip as he shakes his head.

"I think I'm nuts."

His body starts to shake again and without a word, his mouth is back on mine. His tongue darting out to rub slowly against my closed lips until I give him the access he wants. Then he slides in and kisses me hard. So hard that all my thoughts of stupid bubblegum leave instantly.

A while later, still in his arms watching *Pitch Perfect,* my choice not his, he breaks the comfortable silence we had slipped into after my bubblegum meltdown.

"I'm working tomorrow, pulling a double for another officer that needs the day to take his daughter on a school trip. That means I won't see you for a few days. The last double I pulled had me sleeping almost twenty-four hours straight. But, we need to finish the plans that got cut short—not that I mind one second of how they were cut short—but I still need to finish."

"Okay, Lee. You don't need to explain that to me."

"You get that we're together now?" he harshly asks.

"Uh, yeah."

"Then I need to explain that to you."

"I think, maybe, I should give you a little history of my life," I tell him, trying to not get annoyed with myself or more specifically the lack of experience I have when it comes to relationships. "I've been in a relationship with one man, Lee. And while I was married to him, what we shared wasn't a typical relationship. We were both faithful and while yes, we were intimate, it wasn't often. That being said, he didn't explain his plans for days to come with me. If he needed to do something, he would give us a kiss goodbye and go about his business. Before Jack, I didn't date. Not once. So, I think it would be a good guess that I'm about as stupid as it comes, when it comes to this," I point between him and myself. "I don't expect you to report to me."

His eyes go hard during my little speech and when I finish talking, I wait, bracing for him to realize what a mess I am and leave.

"It might not be tomorrow, or hell even a month from now, but you're going to fall into this relationship effortlessly. I know that because in the two days that we've established a togetherness, you've come out of your shell and without one doubt taken each step forward. I'm not telling you my plans for any other reason but for you to know while I may have to be somewhere else, I want to be here. I'm letting you know where I'll be because I *can't* be here, and trust me, I would rather be here than sitting in a patrol car for two ten-hour shifts. Give and take, darlin'. I'm giving you my plans so that when I don't, I can take."

"Take?" I question.

"The other night, when I took you to the clearing, I had planned for a night of four wheeling. Had my ATV out there waiting. No way in hell that I'm going to complain about how the night progressed, but I still have plans and those plans include that clearing, us and my ATV."

"Four wheeling"?

"Muddin', darlin'. We need to find another night after some rain though. It was a perfect night to take the trails, but the second it rains we get a sitter for Molly and go."

"Okay, why would I want to do that?"

He laughs. "You'll see."

"That makes no sense, Lee. I've never been, but I know you end up dirty as all hell and I can't imagine the fun in riding around getting mud up my nose."

Small lie. I've heard Dani and the girls talk about all the times they've been off-roading. Sometimes they go in trucks, but often on ATVs. Each time they talk about them, I've stayed silent. Even though I'm curious, the thought of riding one of them without fear seems impossible to me. I've heard horror stories about people getting hurt and sometimes killed.

"It's a rush, Megan. It isn't about just driving around and splashing mud all over the place. You pick the right trail, hitting those climbs and knowing but not seeing what's coming has your body on one hell of a high. After a good rain, those trails are slippery and when you come over the climbs then race down to the waiting mud—it's all part of the rush. When that water and mud flies all over the place, I promise the last thing you will think about is that you're dirty and may or may not have mud in your nose."

"I still don't see the appeal here."

His face gets soft and I watch something move behind his eyes, gone too quickly for me to pinpoint. "How about you look at it this way. You'll be on the back of my machine while it rushes through the trails back on old man Sampson's property, your arms will be wrapped around my body. You will be pressed so tight to me that when the motor is rumbling and your hips move against mine, you will have to work real fucking hard not to think about how hard that is going to make me. And, darlin', when we're done, dirty and wet, I'm going to have a lot of fun cleaning you up."

"Oh. Well. I guess I could partake in a little off-road fun," I say, my voice hoarse with arousal.

Lee keeps his eyes on mine, the brown depths not hiding how turned on he is, and when a few minutes pass, he pulls me back into his arms and while looking at the television I hear, just barely, him mumble how 'cute' I am.

Lee's double shift ended up taking a lot more of his time than planned. He worked Monday for his shift and then the one he was covering, however he ended up having to take another one—with only two hours of sleep—when they called him back on. Apparently being understaffed is a huge issue for the HTPD. So huge of an issue that when two officers are down with a massive stomach virus, they have to call in one that's just come off a double.

Lee doesn't complain. He actually said he didn't mind going in, but was pissed that meant he would need to crash the second he finished his shift and wouldn't get to come over.

That was over a week ago and things have just been too crazy for us to get together. Between his work, my deadline, and Molly, there just hasn't been time to go out. That being said, our late night phone calls have kept me plenty entertained. If I thought Lee talking dirty in bed was hot, hearing his deep voice rumble over the phone, telling me everything he can't wait to do to my body, is unbelievable. Add to that the sounds of him coming when I return promises of my own has kept me aroused for eight very long days.

I pick up my cell and smile when I see Lee's text, reminding me that he'll be over tonight to pick me up for dinner. Actually, his reminder was that he was taking 'his' girls out and the mention of me and Molly being his girls has created a smile on my face that I'm pretty sure won't be slipping for a while.

Scrolling through my texts, I bring up Dani's and type out a new message.

Me: I need your help.

Dani: Shoot!

Me: Tonight is my first night out with Lee. I need to change some things up. It's time.

Dani: I've got a block empty around nine if you can get here in the next fifteen. I take it this is going to be more than just a cut?

I take a second and think about her question. I've been thinking about this since my quest to move on started. It's time, for me to let go of the old Megan and get a new look. Nothing crazy, but since I've had the same long blonde hair cut at regularly since I was a teen, yeah . . . it's time.

Me: It's for the new me.

Dani: Well, right on, babe! Sway is going to eat this up. That man lives for makeovers.

Me: Uh.

Dani: Don't worry. This is going to be a blast! See you in fifteen.

Okay. So I guess I'm getting a makeover.

Chapter 22

Megan

Shock holds me in place as I'm being circled by Sway—the short, but fit, owner of the salon that Dani works at. He's probably a good three inches or so shorter than my five-foot-nine, however the five inch heels that he's rocking make him taller than I am. Not to mention, the man makes skinny jeans look better than I ever could. Of course, he doesn't have my hips. I've heard, but never seen, that he also rocks his long blond wig better than most women can.

Yeah, Sway is a force that you will only understand if you know him. He's flamboyant and over-dramatic, loves glitter to the degree that it is probably unhealthy, and isn't afraid to tell you exactly how it is.

He's also Stella's dad.

But even though I love Stella and even though Dani seems to think this is a brilliant idea, having Sway circle me while muttering, is freaking me way out.

"Those hips, child! God, only the lucky ones have hips like that. I've tried, trust me. I had hips when I was a sexy plump man, but they never looked as good as yours. I bet that gorgeous man just grabs hold and goes to town!"

My cheeks heat and I hear Stella, who also works at the salon, yell at her dad to stop embarrassing me.

"Nothing to be embarrassed about. I've told you before, child, I don't bat for the kitties but I still think like a man. Well, sometimes. And those hips. Yes, honey . . . oh yes! Now come sit in Sway's chair and tell me all about that hunk Liam Beckett."

Then my hand is in his and I'm being pulled past Dani and into Sway's chair.

"You do realize she is my client, right?" she huffs.

"No. She was. Now she's mine."

I watch through the mirror as Dani puts her hands on her slim hips and snaps, "You can't just steal my appointment. She's my friend, you weird old man. I swear, if I didn't love you I would quit."

He laughs, throwing his head back and his arms in the air. "You," he points to her and then reaches out to unbutton the top button on her black blouse, "Will never learn to let those babies free. Can you believe her?" he asks, looking at me through the mirror. "She has those great girls now that she's turned into a human milker. Never shows them off. I tell her, time and time again, now that she has the man doesn't mean she should put them away. And you," he snaps, turning back to Dani. "Leave me to this sweet child. She needs Sway. You need to go tug up the girls and go give your man a nooner before he calls here, again, and yells at *me* for keeping you away from the house."

"He did not yell at you," she yells. "He just asked if I could take a longer lunch and then got a little upset when I had to leave before we finished."

"Oh yeah, and what didn't you finish? Huh? You think he was happy with me because you have too many clients? No, not Cohen Cage. Just like his daddy. Wants to lock you up in the bedroom and never let you go. I bet you have another little Cage in that belly before too long."

Her face reddens. "I was talking about lunch, you perv! We didn't finish lunch!"

"Hmmm," he mumbles and starts running his hands through my hair. "And what, honey child, was he eating?"

My jaw drops when hers snaps shut and I watch, fascinated, when she turns her eyes to me and with a shrug says, "Sorry. Looks like you're his now." Then stomps off to the back room.

"Uh," I start.

"You need to ignore her, sweetheart. I figured out she was pregnant two weeks ago, mind you she has not a clue, but she will. She always gets snappy in the beginning. So, while I love that I get to get my hands on all this hair, I also get her off her feet while she's back in the breakroom having a snit. So I win, but she wins bigger," he whispers close to my ear and then pulls back.

"Pregnant? Again?"

"I swear it must be a Cage thing. Runs in the family. Super swimmers, both of them."

"Uh," I mumble.

"She'll find out soon enough. If her losing her breakfast this morning was any help, if not, she will when she stops focusing on her best friend's love life long enough to remember she hasn't had her lady time yet."

"Oh my God," I say, still low and soft. Shocked.

"You, sweet girl, are ready for the new you?"

I nod, still thinking about how Sway could know that Dani is pregnant before she does.

"Then sit back and relax, time for me to work my magic."

I nod again, because really what can you do when a man who does heels, skinny jeans and a loose blouse better than you ever could, starts waving his hands around with scissors attached? You sit back and shut the hell up. That's what you do.

"You've had a hard life, honey," he tells me some time later, while painting some high or low or whatever he called them lights. I have no idea; he just said it was time to make my blonde hair come to life.

He looks up from my head and gives me soft, kind eyes. "It takes an old wounded soul to recognize another."

"You?" I don't finish because his eyes get even softer and he nods.

"It isn't easy growing up in the south as a gay man that loves women's clothing. I wouldn't say I'm a cross dresser, but I love what I love and that happens to be heels and tight clothes. It wasn't popular then and it still isn't now. I'm a lucky man though. I have a wonderful husband and a daughter that is my whole entire world. But, all my life until I moved to Hope Town, I felt the pain of my life choices. People think I'm crazy and that's okay with me. I can laugh about it now, but I surround myself with things that make me happy and far as I can see, you're starting to do the same."

"The glitter," I laugh, looking around his station at everything that shines in the lights around the salon.

"Oh yes. Started at church camp. My parents sent me there in hope that I could be saved from the devil that lives inside of me. That, well that backfired when I found art inside that camp. Sitting there during arts and crafts time while the glitter fell through my fingers, I was able to find a little happiness that, as you can see, I keep with me at all times."

I chuckle to myself. He isn't kidding. He really does keep it with him at all times.

"My light in the darkness. We all have that light, honey. Some people, it's an object like glitter. Other people, it's a person that takes their hand and takes the lead."

I look into his eyes. "Is there anything you don't see?" I ask.

"Not often. Plus, I cut Lee's hair the last four times that fine man came in because pregnant patty was too busy taking 'lunch breaks' with her husband."

My laughter comes quick and when Sway starts to freak out because I won't stop moving my head, my laughter climbs. Soon enough, he's joined in and we don't stop joking and laughing until he flips off his blow dryer and turns my chair.

"He isn't going to know what hit him, honey child!" Sway says as my eyes take in the 'new' Megan.

My blonde hair is still blonde, but now there are strips of dark and light blonde, all looks so natural that you would never guess I just spent the last two hours in Sway's hands. I never would have thought that my natural light blonde was a bad look, but now seeing this, I feel like I've been brought to life. My eyes look brighter and my skin looks darker against the softer color.

"You deserve to keep the happiness close to you," he tells me.

"I'm trying," I reply. "Still scares me to pieces."

Which is true. Giving myself to someone, giving them the power over not just my heart, but my daughter's as well and all of it being so new, is scary. It isn't that I don't trust Lee, but when you have had a lot of nothing, then a lot of loss, believing that you can have something beautiful takes time.

"I imagine it does. I'll admit, knowing what you've lost and honey I am sorry for your loss, but knowing that you lost your husband overseas, I was a little shocked you ended up with another man with a dangerous job. You're going to be just—what? What did I say?"

"What's wrong with Megan?" Stella asks and I turn my shocked eyes from Sway to hers and then I look at myself.

Pale skin, wide eyes, and a look of fear.

"What the hell?" My eyes snap to Dani.

"I never even thought about his job," I mumble, my fear taking hold and the roots digging in. "Never once crossed my mind that he . . . good God, he wears a gun . . . and a vest! How could I never even realize how dangerous his job is? Oh my God!"

"Oh, shit," Stella mumbles.

"Oh, no," Sway sighs.

"You, come with me," Dani says softly and pulls me from the chair. "You stay," she tells Sway. "Let's go." Her hand grabs mine and she starts to walk me toward the room she stomped toward earlier.

I don't resist, too shocked and too busy thinking about all the things that could happen to Lee while on duty to even process anything else.

Dani pushes me down to the couch when we walk into the break room and kneels down in front of me. My panicked eyes not focusing on a thing until she taps me on the cheek. Lightly, but with enough force that the shock of it has my eyes focusing on hers.

"I didn't like that. You made me slap you and that's not something I like. But I really don't like watching you fall back to where you were a year ago. Let me tell you something, honey. Sure, Lee has a job that deals with dangerous situations, but he's a smart man and he's trained. He carries a gun and wears a vest because there may come a time when that's needed, but you cannot let that ruin what you two are starting."

I don't speak.

"Megan. You can't give up on him because his job is a little dangerous. It is nothing like Jack. Nothing. Jack was in a war-torn country and you know without me having to detail it that the types of danger over there are nothing that Lee will have to face."

"I could lose him," I tell her.

"You won't," she states strongly. "You need to talk to him about this."

I nod my head, but know I most likely will not.

"Promise?"

I nod, but don't give her the words. If I don't give her the words then I can keep this to myself until I figure out what to do with it.

Chapter 23

Liam

"You okay?" I ask Megan for the tenth time tonight.

She looks up from where she had been watching Molly color on her children's menu and gives me a weak smile. Not answering verbally, but telling me without a doubt that she is far from okay with just one look.

I glance at Molly, seated in between us at the half circle table before turning back to Megan. "We're going to talk, darlin'."

Her eyes close and she nods, but again no words.

"Leelee! Look, I made you!"

I continue to look at Megan and try not to let the worry that she's holding something back show on my face when I look at Molly.

Molly turns her menu and when I see what she's drawn, I pull her close and give her a hug.

"Tell me about it?" I ask her.

"Okay! That right there is you," she says pointing to the blue stick figure. "This is Mommy," she continues, pointing to the red one. "This is me," her finger goes to the yellow one. "And this is going to be my baby brother or sister," she finishes, pointing to the little green dot that I didn't even notice before.

I fight to keep my body loose and look over at Megan. Her eyes are wet, but she's holding it back.

"Oh yeah?" I ask Molly, not moving my eyes from Megan.

"Oh yeah," she says in wonderment her melodious voice sparkling with awe. "Can I have a baby now?" Her eyes don't leave mine and I have to work even harder now to push down the emotion that threatens my own chest.

"Little bird," Megan whispers.

"I really want a baby now," Molly returns her own voice now as hushed as her mother's.

"That's not how it works, sweets," Megan continues.

"But, why?"

I clear my throat and move my eyes from Megan's pleading ones to Molly's hopeful ones.

"But you said Leelee is going to stick like gum. You said it. That means if he's my new daddy, that you and Leelee can give me a baby!"

"Hey," I butt in when I see how much this is costing Megan. "I'm already stuck like bubblegum, little lady. Stuck so sticky and gooey that I'll happily be stuck forever. One day, but not now, okay? And Molly, I love you and your mommy, and if one day I'm lucky enough for you to call me daddy, it will stick some more happiness right to my heart with a huge big piece of bubblegum, but I won't be your new daddy. I'll be your other daddy."

"Why?" she asks, her voice still small but her smile big.

"Because you, little lady, already have a daddy and even though he's not here anymore doesn't mean he isn't always with you."

I look up when I hear Megan sniffle and reach out to grab her hand over the table. Molly lets the subject drop, but even through her continuous chatter throughout dinner, Megan remains quiet and I know whatever was weighing on her mind hasn't been made any easier.

"Talk to me, Megan," I demand.

She walks around the couch and sits. I notice, but don't call her out on it, that she purposely placed her body out of arm's length.

Ever since Molly's bomb dropped at dinner, the dark mood she's carried with her since I arrived at the house has continued. I've waited, not wanting to press while Molly was awake, and put on a smile for her sake. But now, Molly is in bed and I'm not putting up with this shit.

"I won't ask again, darlin'. I haven't seen you in over a week, a long week with your goodnight calls being the only thing pushing me through, but now that I finally have you where I want you, you're a million miles away. What gives?"

"Dani's pregnant," she says.

"Good for Dani. Good for Cohen. Not that I'm shocked seeing as they can't keep their hands off each other. Now I know that isn't what has you walking around with the weight of the world on your shoulders, so what. Is. The. Problem?" I push, my frustration clear as can be in my voice.

"You wear a gun," she oddly says.

"Not when I'm off duty. I don't have one on me right now."

"You wear a gun," she repeats, her voice growing louder. Panicked.

"Yeah, Megan. I wear a gun. I'm a cop. We wear guns."

"You wear a vest."

"Yeah. Again, I'm a cop."

"You wear a gun and a vest, Lee!" she shrieks and I draw back at her tone.

"Darlin'," I call, my frustration bleeding out the instant I realized what this is about. "They're to keep me safe."

"You . . . you wear a gun and a vest, Lee," She quivers and wraps her arms around her body.

I don't respond, but I do move so that I can pull her into my arms.

"I thought we were past this, baby. I wear them because for one it's part of my uniform, but they're also there to keep me safe. I know how to work a gun, Megan. I've known how to work one since I was five. I also know what to do if something happens and I need my gun. I'm not going anywhere."

Her body shakes in my hold and her tears wet my shirt.

"Megan, please, darlin', hold onto me and don't let this pull you under."

"Just the thought of something happening to you kills me, Lee. What if something happens for real? What if I lose you too?" she mumbles against my chest after her cries die.

It tears me to my core to see her hurting. I've wondered if something like this would come up, but I never considered her fearing my career. Putting myself in her shoes though, it makes sense, and I kick myself for not seeing it sooner. Preparing for it.

"I'm not going anywhere, Megan. Stuck like gum, remember?"

Her body curls closer and she doesn't speak.

"I love you, Megan. Do you really think, for one second, that now that I have you I wouldn't take every care in the world to make sure I never lose you? That includes my own safety. Things happen, every day things happen, and God willing I hope they never happen to us. If I was ever in the need of my gun or my vest, you have no fears in the knowledge that I will use both to make sure I always come back to you."

Her head comes up and her tear filled eyes blink a few times before she whispers, "You love me?"

"Head over heels, in fucking love, darlin'," I utter back.

"You're in love with me?"

"I'll say it as many times as you need it, but it won't change. I'm in love with you. I love you. I love *you,* Megan—you and Molly. So fucking in love with you that I knew it even before you said your first word to me."

Her tears pick up, this time silent, and her eyes continue to search mine.

"I didn't even pause when your daughter asked me if I was going to be her daddy, not when she asked for a baby, and not when I made it clear to her that should I get that honor—and it would be an honor, Megan—that I would love every second of it. Because I can tell you right now, what we've been building, that's the plan. You, Molly and whatever children you give me will never, for a second, doubt how much I love them."

"Your job is scary dangerous to me, Lee."

"I understand, darlin'. I'm not saying that fear is going to go away, but we will work to make sure you can and know how to handle it, okay?"

She nods her head, the motion making some of the wetness in her eyes roll over and down her cheek.

"You love me?" she probes.

"Fuck, you're cute."

"I love you, Lee. I'm so in love with you that it's terrifying, but what's the most scary is I've never felt like this before. I don't know if I'm doing it right."

My chest swells, my heart speeds up and I swear with the way I feel right now, I might as well be Superman. Fuck, hearing her say that. Knowing that it's costing her to admit, not only to herself but out loud, that she feels love for me that she never felt for her husband.

"There isn't a wrong way to love someone, Megan. You keep giving me you and I swear that you will never regret giving me that."

"I'm still scared, Lee."

"We'll work on that too, darlin'. One step at a time."

She nods.

I close the distance between our mouths and kiss her deep. Deep and full of unspoken promise. "Go check to make sure Molly is sleeping, baby."

She doesn't move. Her eyes still half mast and if I had to guess, she hasn't come out of the fog that kiss put over her.

"Megan. Go make sure Molly is sleeping. And do it quick before I strip you down and fuck you right here."

She almost trips over her feet when she hurries off the couch and back down the hall. I take my time, making sure the door is locked and the house is shut down, because I have no intention of leaving after tonight.

Chapter 24

Liam

"She's asleep. Out cold," She tells me and steps toward where I've been waiting. I moved to the hallway outside of Molly's room after turning all the lights off in the house and checking the lock on both front and back doors.

"I know we said we wouldn't do this until Molly had time to adjust, but baby she asked us for a baby tonight, I'm pretty sure that's as adjusted as it gets. I need to get you naked and my mouth on you so I can remind you why you love me so much."

I started stalking toward her before I finished speaking and without waiting for her to speak, I pull her into my arms and drop my mouth to hers. My body pushes hers into the wall next to her bedroom door and my hands grab her hips to pull her closer.

"I'm not leaving, Megan."

One hand goes up and I take her full breast in my hand, giving her a squeeze and then thumbing her nipple. Her head falls back against the wall and she moans.

"I don't want you to leave, Lee," she pants against my mouth.

"I'm not talking about tonight, Megan, even though I'm not leaving tonight either. I mean, I'm not going anywhere, darlin'."

She pushes up on her toes and I bend, helping her get my mouth. Letting her take the lead, I open my mouth when her tongue presses against my lips. The second my mouth opens, the kiss turns hungry and her hands claw at my arms. I bend and place her ass in my hands. She doesn't hesitate to give a little jump and as I lift, her legs wrap around my waist. She deepens the kiss and as our tongues swirl together she starts rocking her pussy against my hard cock. She's got on another pair of short shorts and through the thin material I can feel the heat of her, making me groan, and then rock my hips forward when she answers me with one of her own.

I fumble slightly, but make my way into her bedroom without breaking our connection once. Turning before I sit on her bed, I move us until my back is against her wooden headboard and her legs are wide on either side of my hips.

"I don't have any condoms here," she blurts after pulling her lips from mine.

I take a deep breath and give her a reassuring smile.

"Are you clean?" I ask, knowing her answer.

"Of course, yes."

"I'm checked, often, for work. But even if I wasn't, I haven't had anyone but you in over a year. It's your call, but darlin', I would love to feel you with nothing between us."

"I'm on the pill. Regulates me, I mean . . . we're good."

"Then no more condoms, baby," I tell her with a grin and move my lips back to hers as she blushes.

My hands move from her ass, under her shirt and up her sides. When I hit her bra, it takes one flip of my wrist to open the clasps. She pushes herself from my mouth with a gasp, moves back so my hands fall to the sides and while looking me in the eye, pulls both her shirt and bra off. Not a second later, her mouth is back on mine and her small hands are pulling at my shirt.

"Darlin', what's the hurry?" I ask when I pull back to remove the shirt that she has been so desperately trying to claw to shreds.

Her breathing is coming rapidly and she lets her head roll back as her hips continue to rock against mine. I'm not even sure she heard me.

"I need to feel you." Her voice is wild, anxious, and I know in that moment that this is something more than sex.

More than making love.

More than just *us*.

It hits me, that after everything that's been running through her head today, that she really does need this. She needs to feel me and know that I'm still here.

"Then take me, darlin'," I tell her and look deep in her eyes, hoping that with that look I'm showing her how much I love her. "Take me. Take everything, Megan."

She makes a noise. It's a heartbreaking mix between a cry and a moan before her hands come forward and she starts to desperately claw at my belt, needing it out of the way with a fever that has her crying out when it doesn't unhook right away. I give her what she needs; helping her undo my belt and I push her hands aside when she goes to my jeans, knowing that she will just get frustrated again.

She scurries off my lap and I watch, while pulling the buttons on my jeans apart, as the rest of her clothes come off. Before I can push my jeans any further than down my hips and around my ass, she's back in my lap, her lips on mine the second that her ass hits my lap. This time, I help build the kiss and pray that some of that desperation will be healed when she takes me.

Her small hands come up and she takes my face between them, slowing her kiss down until her tongue is making lazy sweeps.

"Darlin'," I moan when she starts to rock against me. "What do you need?"

"You. Just you," she answers.

"Then. Take. Me."

She doesn't. She looks into my eyes, hers still holding onto her fear, but she does not take me.

"Megan. I'm here. Fuck, baby, I'm close to coming with just feeling your wet pussy against my cock. Please, take me."

Again, she doesn't move.

"Megan."

Nothing.

"Darlin'," I murmur, my hands coming up to curl around her neck.

At my touch, her eyes drop and my heart clenches when I see a tear roll out.

"Baby," Kiss. "Please, take me."

She opens her eyes and shakes her head.

"Megan," I start, my own worry starting to climb, causing me to hold my breath when she interrupts me.

"Help me," she whimpers.

I give her a squeeze with my hands resting on her hips and cock my brow, letting her know without words that she never has to doubt. She pushes up with her thighs as I help lift her weight and one hand comes off my shoulders to wrap around my cock. I moan the second her fingers close around me and my hips jerk. Fuck me, it's going to take an act of God to last longer than a second.

With her eyes locked on mine, she drops down until her ass is flush to my thighs and my cock is deep inside her wet pussy. She doesn't move past the slow rocking of her hips.

"Megan, take me. Take what you need to know I'm right here," I beg and relax the bruising hold my fingers have on her hips.

It's fascinating to watch, the way that she is healing with just a connection to my body, but as she slowly rocks, the fear that had been prominent in her gaze weakens until it's all but gone. In its place, hope and love start to burn bright. The worry lines around her eyes, fade, and the tight pinch of her lips relaxes until her mouth is parted with gasping pants. Finally, the tiny furrow of her brows pulls back and when her eyes fill with tears this time I know they aren't anywhere close to the ones that wept out earlier.

These are tears that recognize what we're doing.

Feeling tears.

Tears that don't just feel a little—they feel everything.

Her hands roam over my chest, until she pushes them up to curl around my shoulders. Mine move from her hips and up her torso until both of her full breasts are in my hands. I roll her nipples between my fingers. Her breathing hitches and I release her nipples and run my fingertips down her body, lightly grazing. My eyes follow the path as goosebumps spark all over her body, followed by a quiver that lightly jolts her body.

When my hands move back to her hips, I give her a squeeze.

"Take it."

Her eyes close at my demand. And then, she takes it.

The hands at my shoulders dig deep, until I know I'll have her nails indenting the skin when we finish, and those thighs start moving. Up slowly, just to slam her body down before rocking forward. She repeats her movements, each time building in speed. It takes every ounce of willpower to keep my body still and let her take what she needs when all I want to do is flip her to her back and pound into her. My cock is aching from the force of my desire.

"Take it, Megan. Fuck me, take it, darlin."

She moans and speeds up again, this time her movements jerky and I know she's close.

"God, you feel so fucking good taking my cock."

"Lee," she moans.

"Take it."

Her head moves and those nails dig deeper. Then her lips are on mine and with her tongue dancing with mine, I swallow her screams.

I pull back when I feel the last spasm against my cock and look into her heavy eyes. "You need me to take over baby? Rock hard and the way you're coating my balls with your come is only making me harder."

She hums and nods her head before taking my mouth again. When I flip her to her back, her head is hanging off the bottom of her bed. Thankfully she has a bed with just a headboard, giving me more room to play. I lift up on my knees until I'm kneeling with her pussy still clamped tight around me then I lift her hips a little more until just her shoulders are resting against the bed.

"You need something to hold on to?"

I feel her walls give a squeeze and her head rolls.

Pushing in while I lift off from kneeling has my cock hitting her deeper than I have before. Her hands come up from fisting the sheets next to us and wrap around my wrists. When I sink back in, rocking her body with the force of my thrust, her head comes up and her eyes shoot to where my cock is gliding in and out of her body. Wet with her juices.

We both moan.

"Please," she begs.

Sweat drops down my back and I lean forward, panting. I lose the hold I had on her hips and move my hands to the bed, hovering just above her while my cock is still deep.

"Please what, darlin'. Tell me what you need."

"I need to feel all of you," she says softly. "Cover me and take me, but I have to feel you."

Understanding hits and my heart pounds even quicker. God, my sweet girl. She might understand that while my job holds a fraction of the danger that her husband's did, but she needs to rid herself of those ghosts today's spell brought back, by reminding herself that I am very much alive.

And to do that, she needs to feel.

Feel alive.

I close my eyes and drop my head to hers. My body follows until I've given her as much weight as I can. Her legs come up and wrap tightly around my hips. I feel her arms at my side and then around my back. Then, her head comes up and her mouth fuses with mine.

Only then, when she's completely wrapped herself around me, do I continue to move inside her. My arms against the mattress, elbows digging in, and hands in her hair. There isn't an inch of our bodies that doesn't feel the other. Even though my body is screaming for it, I rock slowly, and give her everything that she needs.

With each thrust, I pray that she feels what she needs. Our lips never part and when I feel her walls tighten and her wetness coat my cock, only then do I push deep and come harder than I've ever felt before.

"I love you," she whispers in my ear, her breathing coming in choked pants.

"I love you, too, Megan. So much, darlin'."

Chapter 25

Megan

It's been a month since I lost my mind over Lee's job. A month of him handling me with care, but also a month that's been full of healing. It's been hard at times, but he's been there for every stumble to help pick me back up. At his urging I started seeing a grief counselor. I'll admit now that it's a step I should have taken on my own years ago, but with both of their help, I've been able to let go of almost all of my pain. Lee started coming to my twice a week meetings at the counselor's urging. It started about three weeks after I started going and I'm glad I made that step. Having him with me, his hand in mine, was a strength I needed to get through some hard memories.

It was also through those meetings that he made it clear, sometimes with and sometimes without words that a huge part of him fell in love with me because of my strength. I didn't understand it, because I've felt nothing but weakness, but Lee told me, in those meetings, that only a person with a strength of an army would keep fighting to live. I couldn't see it, living in pain, but he's right—something I can see now—I've been fighting my whole life. Losing Jack was a hard blow and even though it took me a long time to battle the depression his death set upon me, I never gave up.

Another milestone that we made as our new threesome, was Lee's relationship with Molly. I haven't been shocked that she fell into her love for him easily, that's just who Molly is. She doesn't doubt her feelings.

Needless to say, they have been inseparable. Regardless of if we're at our house, his, or out, my daughter is always as close as she can get to him. Lee and I talked about it and we both agree that it is just the way Molly is. She wants him to know how much he means to her, but because she's so young she doesn't know how to verbalize it, instead she gives him what she can. Herself.

Seeing them together was a big part in my healing. Seeing that she loves him as much as I do, gives me the reassurance that we're where we're meant to be.

Lee showed me again how big his heart was when he fell into his new role as a father figure with effortless ease. His protective nature only adding to the power in which his bond formed with her. You can tell, there is nothing but love that he feels for his girls.

And that's what we've become—gladly—to him. We're his girls and he . . . he is our man.

Today is my last step in letting go. One that I've been putting off, but now I know needs to happen for us all to move on completely pain free. I don't think I was putting it off because I wasn't ready, but more that I didn't know how to do it or what to say.

How do you tell your dead husband that you've moved on?

I look up and see Lee walking with Molly as I trail behind them. When we got to the graveyard he had asked for me to give him a second and then took off in the direction I had told him when he asked where Jack was. When he reached his hand out for Molly's my reaction couldn't be stopped. I gasped, but Lee being his confident self, just gave me soft eyes.

Which leads me to now, as I watch them strolling through the headstones hand in hand. I move to a bench about ten paces from Jack's spot and wait. I used to only come every month, sometimes when the pain was too much, I wouldn't come until it eased up a little. Now, for the last year, I've been coming with Molly every two weeks. This, however, is the first time we've asked Lee to come.

Lee stops and I see him reading over the headstone, then he kneels and pulls Molly closer. Her little arms hug his back and her head turns to rest against his shoulder.

When his lips start moving, facing Jack, my heart speeds up and deep down I know he isn't talking to Molly. She doesn't move, but her arm pulls his shirt as her fist grabs hold of the material.

Call it an invasion of his privacy, whatever you want, but nothing in that moment could have kept me from walking over. My eyes don't leave where they're at, his head turns but his words don't stop and he turns back, acknowledging that I'm coming regardless, but he doesn't stop.

Then his words hit my ears.

And if I had any fears left in my body about this new path for Molly and me, they vanished in a heartbeat.

"Like I said, you don't know me, but I like to think we would have gotten along. Hell, we might have played golf on my off days, had beers while watching the game, who knows. I hate thinking it, because it isn't fair that you lost your way, but when you did, it made it possible for me to find mine. It gave me my girls and I wouldn't be the man I am right now without their love. Rest easy knowing that not a day will pass that I won't make sure they know how grateful I am that I've been given that gift. Not a day will pass that I don't show them how much I love them in return. I'll fight to keep them safe. I would give my own life to make that promise a reality if need be. And one day, if Molly decides it so, I hope to share the title you had while in her world, but if that day never comes, I'll still love her as if she was my own. I owe you my thanks and so much more for loving Megan and bringing her everything she needed while you were here. You have no worries now, brother, knowing that I'll do everything in my power to give them the world. They've both given me everything I've dreamt of just by handing over their love and I'll never take that for granted."

My God.

This man.

I move forward and take the last two steps that take me to his side. My hand comes out and I run my fingers through his hair.

"Hey, Jack," I say and continue my sweep of his thick hair. "I guess you met Lee."

I hear both Lee and Molly laugh, but I keep my eyes pinned to the stone in front of me.

"I miss you, Jack." I tell the stone. "I miss you, but that's okay. It doesn't hurt anymore." Lee's hand moves and I feel him reach out to grab the hand that isn't playing with his hair. I can't stop my movements. Touching Lee, having that, is keeping me grounded right now. "Molly is so big. The top of her head hits Lee right at his belt. She does this really cute thing when she sees him in uniform—he's a cop, you know—and thinks it's hilarious that she can't give him a hug with his belt on because all of his special police stuff whomps her in the head." I take a deep breath, calming my racing heart and hopefully stopping my rambling. "Anyway. I'm happy, Jack. So happy that sometimes I think my heart is going to burst right out of my body. I get these waves in my stomach when Lee's around and sometimes I feel like I might puke," I stop when I feel Lee's body moving as he laughs. "What?"

"Darlin', not sure it's a good thing I make you want to puke," he laughs.

"Mommy that's icky," Molly chimes in.

I roll my eyes at the stone and continue. "Anyway. I feel, Jack, I feel so much and for a long while I didn't feel anything. You left and I just felt emptiness and pain. Now it's like I feel everything, but those feelings are amplified. It's so beautiful."

The headstone doesn't reply. The breeze around us picks up and I smile into the wind.

"I love you, Jack. You gave me and Molly a beautiful life and even though you had to leave us, that beautiful life turned into a beautiful forever."

Lee's hand gives me another squeeze and I lose my hold on his hair when he stands, taking Molly up with him. His arm goes around my shoulders and when I'm pulled into his side, I wrap my arms around him. In the end, both Molly and I have Lee in the circle of our arms as he holds us tight.

"You gave me the world, Jack. I can never thank you enough for that kind of gift. Rest easy."

Molly looks away from Lee when he finishes and whispers toward the stone, "I love you, Daddy."

And with dry eyes watching the wind quiet, I tell my husband goodbye. "We love you, forever, Jack. We'll miss you just as long. I know somewhere up there you're smiling huge and loving the fact that I'm living a life that's full and I promise you that I will take each day head on looking forward to that beauty."

When we turn to walk back to Lee's truck, not once do any one of us let our hold slip.

Chapter 26

Megan

"Don't be nervous," Lee tells me, tightening his hold on my clammy hand.

"What's that mean?" Molly asks from her perch in Lee's other arm.

"Your mommy has so many butterflies in her belly she's about to squeeze off my fingers, her hand's holding mine so tight. So many little ticklish butterflies in her belly," Lee's deep voice rumbles in response.

"Why did you put butterflies in there, Mommy?" her melodious voice chirps, easing some of my nerves.

I turn my head, looking away from the front door of Lee's family home, and before looking at my beautiful daughter; I stare at the strong man holding her. His warm gaze bringing a deep breath to my lungs that washes over me like a calming touch.

"Lee," my voice sounds in hushed tones.

"I asked you a while ago to just take my hand, darlin', I wasn't just asking you to do the action. It was my nonverbal promise to you that I wouldn't let go. Each step forward, we do together. I'm here and I'm not letting go. You've got not one thing to be nervous about, but I understand why you are. They're going to love you and they're going to love Molly. Not just because I love you both, but also because if anyone knows what it feels like to overcome from pain to find beauty, it's my parents. Trust me, okay?"

His hand gives me a squeeze and even though I still feel some of those nerves, he's right. I've never been given a reason to question that.

"She's got princess shoes," Molly whispers in Lee's ear loud enough that I move my eyes from his, up to hers and then follow them forward to see his mom standing in the doorway, wringing her own hands in front of her nervously.

Of course I know who his parents are. In the last two years of me being pulled into the fold, I've been to a few gatherings where all the parents were also in attendance. I also know that she's Dani's mom's best friend and has been for years and years before they had Dani and Lee, thus the reason that Dani and Lee were destined to be best friends even before birth.

But besides the small smile in passing, I've never spoken to either of them.

Add to that the small fact that their son has fallen in love with a woman with baggage of a widowed mom.

A woman, that until about five months ago, hasn't been able to see the beauty in life past her guilt filled grief.

A woman that they very well may see as someone not good enough for their son.

And that's what's been keeping me so full of nerves that I've been on the edge of puking all day.

"She always has princess shoes on, little lady. Even when she's cleaning the house or doing laundry. My mom, she's a silly girl."

Lee's voice pulls me back from my scared thoughts and I steady my breathing, give him a squeeze and when his feet start carrying us up the driveway, toward his waiting mother, I follow and pray that I don't make a fool of myself.

And that his mother won't see Molly and me as the wrong choice for her son's future.

"Hey, Mom," he greets when we reach the front porch. "Meet my girls, Molly and Megan."

I gulp and give her what I hope is a welcoming smile. She looks at her son with love in her eyes before they turn to me.

"Megan," she breathes. "It's so good to finally, formally, meet you. We've been waiting for this."

"Uh, hi," I squeak and Molly laughs.

"Mommy has butterflies all inside her belly. Leelee told me so."

I feel my face heat and my hand gets a gentle tug. I look up and meet Lee's gaze. He gives me a wink and then his face washes with love and compassion. His expression filling my heart instantly with his love and effectively kicking the crap out of those butterflies.

Turning back to his mom, I reach out my hand, and blurt, "I did. They were crazy butterflies that fluttered their wings so much I couldn't take a deep breath. So, hi, I'm Megan and I'm absolutely terrified that you won't like me."

I feel Lee shaking with his amusement, but my eyes are transfixed on his mom as I watch, with fascination, as her eyes, so much like Lee's, fill with understanding before my hand is knocked to the side as her body moves forward. Her arms reach out and wrap around my middle and then she gives me a hug that knocks the wind out of my chest with her strength.

"Oh, honey. I was in love with you before I even knew who had stolen my son's heart. Have no worries about that. You keep doing whatever has that smile on my boy's face. I swear, it's been like watching his father all over again these last few months."

I don't know what to say. Or do. So I follow my gut, drop Lee's hand, and hug his mom back just as tight.

"He's easy to love," I tell her honestly.

"I know," she whispers. "It's a Beckett thing."

I laugh, but don't let go.

"Uh, Mom. You think I could have my woman back now?" Lee laughs.

"No, you can't," she snaps and continues to hug me tight.

"Dee, baby, let go of Lee's woman and let them come inside."

I open my eyes at the new voice and look up into Lee's father's eyes. If I thought he looked like his mom, I was wrong. Lee is the spitting image of his father and I have no doubt that when Lee gets older, his good looks will only become richer. John Beckett, or Beck as I've heard so many call him, has the same thick dark brown hair as his son. His strong bone structure a mirror to his son's. You can tell that he laughs hard, and often, because the smile lines on his tan face are deep, even when he's just smirking.

Lee's dad is smoking hot.

Of course, his mom is downright stunning too, so it isn't a shock to me that Lee is as handsome as he is.

"You look like my Leelee," Molly states in awe.

"Hey, sweet girl, I sure do. Want to know why?" Lee's dad asks her.

"Yup!" she shouts.

Lee's dad chuckles deep in his throat, "That's because he's my Lee too. We're his mom and dad. He looks like us just like you look like your mom."

When Dee lets go of my body, I turn and watch Molly move her eyes from Lee's smiling face, back to his father's. Then in typical Molly fashion, she gives out more of her love.

"Yay! That means you're mine too. I get to keep you and I'm never, ever, ever going to give you away! Do you want a makeupover?" she exclaims in rushed excitement. "Mommy, yay!" she finishes at a whisper. "We get more."

And just like that, a sense of calm I never thought possible earlier today rushes over me and I smile at my daughter. "We sure do, little bird. So much so, that we have everything."

Lee reaches out and grabs my hand, this time not to give reassurance in the face of my nerves, but to confirm that we do, in fact, have everything.

"Right," Lee's mom speaks, but pauses to clear her throat. When I look back to her, her eyes are misty and she gives me a smile. "Well, now that that's settled. Molly, do you want to come and help me make the table?"

Molly gives Lee a hug around his neck, kisses his check, and then asks, "Can I go play with your mommy, Leelee?"

"Call me, Dee, baby. I have a feeling that will change soon though," she oddly adds, making her husband laugh low in his throat

"Leelee, can I go play with mommy Dee?"

God, my girl.

Lee gives her a nod and with a smile, sets her on her feet. She doesn't waste a second taking Dee's offered hand and following her into the house.

"Nice to finally meet you, Megan. You've made our boy real happy," his dad says when Molly and his wife move out of sight.

Turning back to him, I take his offered hand. "It's a pleasure to meet you, Mr. Beckett," I respond and stiffen when he starts to laugh. The lines around his eyes deepening with his mirth.

"Call me Beck, honey, everyone does."

"All right, Mr. Beck," I confirm.

He laughs harder. This time Lee annoyingly joins in.

"Just Beck, drop the mister. We're family here and Megan . . . welcome to the family."

Family. I nod, not trusting my voice. Just like that his parents have openly accepted both Molly and me, giving us the family I always wanted for my daughter. One that loves without reservations and opens their arms immediately, no questions asked, to give that love freely.

When Jack and I were married, we knew that we would never be able to give Molly this. My parents, being the drunken, drug filled messes they were, have been long since forgotten. Jack's parents were just as bad. His mom died when he was younger and his dad; never able to put the bottle down before that, never fell into his role as a parent. Thus, Jack was just Jack. We learned his father had passed away a few months after we married and left town. Knowing all that, we were okay that Molly would have only us. It wasn't until recently that I realized how much it had bothered me that she wouldn't have a large family full of love.

I look up at Lee and smile, brightly, thankful for yet another gift this man made a reality, when his unwavering determination to make us an "us" has paid off. It was through his strength and love that we have a future so bright it burns.

This time, that burn, one I had felt differently before, was welcome. Before I had no ashes left to be reborn from, because the pain burned too strong. But now, because of the burn of his love on our life, taking away the ashes left from my guilt and suffering, I just know the new life born from the last will be overrun with love and happiness.

It's our future.

"And this one, well, our Liam went through a stage that lasted almost six months. In that time he was naked every time we turned around. Beck thought this was hilarious, which is why there are so many pictures. I, however, did not. Do you know how embarrassing it is when your son gets buck naked in the middle of the supermarket?"

I shake my head and laugh even harder than I had in the last hour of Dee showing me old pictures of Lee. Once I got over my nerves, it was like I had been a part of this family forever. Molly has been on cloud nine too. Going from helping his mom set out the takeout—because according to Dee, she does not cook—then talking Beck's ear off about all the things we do as a threesome, to which Beck's handsome smile grew even larger, and those lines got even deeper.

"But I got him back, his father I mean. He didn't think it was funny when our little nudist stopped being a nudist and started wearing my heels all over the house. Oh, he didn't think that was funny one bit, but I did. God didn't see it fit for us to have a girl, but he did give me a boy that had no problems walking in four-inch heels," she laughs.

"He didn't," I gasp, shocked at the picture before me of Lee. He looks to be Molly's age, huge smile, dimple sticking out and his mother's bright red heels on his feet. "Oh my God, he did!" My giggles turn into deep belly laughs at this point.

"What are you two in here cackling about?" Beck asks, rounding the couch and settling in next to his wife. "Oh Dee, your son is going to kill you," he gruffs with a smile.

"Oh hush, old man. He isn't going to do anything of the sort."

"If you don't stop showing his woman all those embarrassing pictures of him, he will."

She turns and narrows her eyes at her husband. "I've been waiting his whole life for this moment. When my little man would bring home his future. All my life, John Beckett. You do not spoil this for me."

I wouldn't have guessed, because she seems so soft-spoken and sweet, that his mom would have a backbone that would snap tight, but I was wrong. She may look the part of quiet and motherly, but right in this moment, I can tell where Lee got a lot of his stubborn grit.

Beck's eyes soften and he gazes at his wife with love written all over his body. "Pull those claws back, wildcat," he hums, his voice sounding deeper, rawer, and I instantly feel like I'm intruding on something a little too intimate.

"Would you two stop?" Lee laughs and drops down next to me. His eyes hit the open photo album seconds before shooting back to his mom. "You didn't," he groans.

"I did. Don't you start on me either, Liam. I'm your mother and it's my mother duty to share all of your embarrassing moments with your girlfriend. You haven't given me the chance before and if I'm judging right, I won't need another, so I'm taking it and you can just deal."

Lee puts his hands up, surrendering to his mom, and pulls me back to his chest.

"Molly, come here, little lady! Old grandma Dee has some funny pictures to show you."

Dee's eyes narrow at his reference to her age, but when Molly comes skipping into the room, her face goes soft. "Just Grandma, honey or nanny works too. Don't listen to that grumpy man. He's just mad he doesn't fit in my shoes anymore," Dee tells her and we all laugh when Lee starts to sputter.

We continue looking through the photo albums, laughing when Lee gets embarrassed, but true to her word, his mom doesn't stop until the last book is finished.

"That was a terrible thing to do to your only son," he grumbles and leans back crossing his arms over his chest.

"Mommy, Leelee is having a fit," Molly snickers.

"He sure is, little bird," I tease.

"You just wait, Liam," Dee starts. "You just wait." She looks over at me, "You make sure and take lots of pictures of Molly and any more children you're blessed with. You'll love this moment just as much as I have. I don't have a daughter, but I'm sure if I did, this lump here would be doing the same thing I just did," she says and points to Beck before laughing when he pulls her to his side.

"The hell I would," he rumbles, giving her a soft kiss before looking at me. "But I would be cleaning every gun I own at the approximate time that any man was due to arrive," he tells me in all seriousness.

"That's not a bad idea," Lee mutters to himself and I look over at him. "What?" he questions, throwing his hands up. "It's a good idea. When Molly starts dating it's also one I won't forget."

"What?" I ask lamely.

"Darlin', she looks like your twin now at five. Add ten years to that and I'm going to go out of my mind when boys start coming around."

His parents laugh and Molly joins in, but I just look at him. Right when I'm about to respond he opens his mouth and shocks me again.

"You give me more girls and I'll have to buy more guns though. You give me some boys and I'll make sure they know how to help me clean those guns. I figure though, with me being a cop, there isn't going to be a single knucklehead that messes with my girl."

"What's a knucklehead," Molly questions, breaking into my thoughts.

"Boys are knuckleheads," Lee tells her. "And I don't want knuckleheads near my girl."

His parent's laughter grows.

"That's me, right?" Molly inquires.

"That's right, little lady. You're all mine forever and ever."

She twitters a laugh that sounds like a happier version of her chirpy bird giggles.

"Mommy, I love being Leelee's girl."

I don't hear his parents laughing now. My eyes don't leave Molly's when I nod and tell her how much I love that too. But I don't need to see his parents to know how happy they are for their son.

When Molly's arms reach out and wrap around both mine and Lee's neck, I hug her back and close my eyes, loving every second of our little threesome. But my thoughts are confirmed when I hear his dad, gruff voice that is thick with emotion, tell his son four words that make my throat thick with emotion.

"Proud of you, son."

Chapter 27

Megan

As promised, Lee's work schedule and the rain finally synced up. Last night, while watching Lee and Molly have the cutest tea party I've ever seen, it started to rain. Not just any rain, this one shook the whole house with its power. Lee stops, teapot in hand mid pour, looks at me across the room. His smile was no less knee-melting, but it held a youthful excitement to it that had me pausing.

I've seen a lot of Lee smiles in the past. The ones when I first started coming around, before we came together, held mischief. After our first night together, they held promise of his determination. Then, while I was busy ignoring and avoiding, even though his smile still held that determination, there was also a small hint to what my avoidance was doing to him. A little dip on the left side that prevented his dimple from coming all the way out, a little dip that showed me it cost him to keep his distance. Now, the only smile he gives us is one that expresses his love toward Molly and me.

Until this one.

This new one that I've never seen.

And mixed with the love on his face, this exuberance toward something as simple as rain, gives my heart pause before picking back up as if it's in the race of a lifetime.

It's feels freaking amazing.

"It's raining, darlin'," he told me.

"Cats and dogs," Molly jokes.

He looks across the expanse of the tea party covered table. "Yeah, little lady, huge dogs and fat cats. Do you hear how loud they are?"

She giggles, "You're silly, Leelee!"

He puts the teapot down and runs his hand over her ringlets, nodding, before standing from his spot and walks around the coffee table until he's standing just feet in front of me.

"It's raining," he repeats.

I nod.

"And I'm off tomorrow," he oddly states.

I nod again because really, he's telling me something I already know.

"Change of plans. Can you lose a day of writing and it not affect your deadline?"

"Uh, yeah?"

"Can you really? Or are you just telling me what I want to hear? There isn't a right answer, baby, if you can't take the time, we won't. You told me last week that you were stressed about your deadline with your editor pushing into the time you needed to have it to formatting."

Okay, so to be honest, I can't really give up a day. I've been working on my first self-published title I've released in three years. A title that means the freaking world to me because the plot mirrors mine and Lee's relationship closely. A second chance love story that holds so much of me between those pages that even if I wasn't on deadline panic mode, I would still be in panic mode.

The Healing Hand, with the urging of my grief counselor, was what I needed to take the last pieces of my pain, guilt, and grief into a tangible form that would help me heal. It's been an emotional journey the last eight weeks that I've been working on it, but Lee's been by my side every step of the way. He held me when the scenes became too much that I had to stop. The tears that I shed during those chapters, cathartic in the sense that each warm drop felt like it leaked the pain straight from my soul.

However, seeing Lee so excited over whatever he's plotting, has me saying, "Of course I can take the day off," with no doubt in my mind that it will be worth the extra hours of late night typing.

His face goes soft, but he doesn't lose an ounce of excitement. He sees right through me, but doesn't call me out.

"I'll call Dani, make sure she's off to watch the little lady. If not, I know Izzy is around. But, baby, my mom has been itching for some Molly time."

I give him a smile, "Then, honey, call your mom."

His dimple comes out and I can tell how much that answer means to him. In the last six weeks since our first dinner at his parent's house, we've had dinner there every Sunday since. Molly has dropped the first names and they are now Nanna and Pops. It's rare that Dani watches her when Lee wants to go on a date night. Now Molly has two grandmother figures, Izzy and Dee that seem to take great joy in fighting over her.

I lose his eyes when he moves his gaze to his phone, but hear him when he so oddly says. "Got it. Get ready for your feel trip." Then his thumb starts moving over his phone and when he looks up, all I get is a wink before his call is connected.

Did he say feel trip? I listen, distractedly, as he talks to his mom. Not that I'm surprised, but she immediately asked for Molly to spend the night, to which Lee agreed after checking with me.

"I'm not sure why you asked my permission, honey," I tell him after he disconnects the call. "What?" I question when he looks at me like I've lost my mind.

"Darlin', nothing would make me happier if Molly was mine, but until the day we make that official, I'm not the one that has the power to make that call."

"Yes you do," I tell him, not understanding completely.

"No, Megan. I do not."

I look over at Molly to make sure she isn't listening and grab his hand, pulling him into the kitchen. "Where is this coming from?"

He sighs, "You know I love you? Both of you?" he asks.

"Of course I do."

"One day, God I hope I'm lucky enough, when I put my ring on your finger and you become my wife, then I hope Molly gives me the blessing of being a man she calls daddy. One day, when we take that step, then yeah I would feel like I have the go to make a call on whether she stays with my mom or Dani. But bottom line, I don't yet and I have enough respect for you to ask."

I close the distance between us and smile up at him. "You have no clue how much that little girl loves you, honey, but I understand. I don't agree with you, but that's because in my eyes, you already hold that right. And one day, if *I'm* lucky enough, I'll enjoy those rings on my finger." I lean up on my toes and give his slack jaw a kiss, loving the way that my lips tickle against his stubble. "I'm going to put *our* girl to sleep, you want to come tuck her in with me?"

He seems to visibly shake himself from the shock that held him still, then with a small smirk on his lips, follows me to get Molly ready for bed.

"Are you sure about this?" I ask Lee.

"Darlin'," he replies but gives me nothing more.

"You're so annoying sometimes."

He laughs and the vibrations tickle my palms, matching the vibrations that are doing nothing to squelch the arousal that having his body pressed close to my front gives me.

"Ready?" He asks, turning his head slightly, giving me his dimple.

"Uh," I sputter and look away from his dimple and across the rain-soaked, mud-filled, expanse of earth in front of us.

"You're ready," he laughs. "Just hold on, Megan. Hold on and feel."

"Again with this?" I retort then snap my mouth shut when he hits the gas.

My fingers dig into his shirt and my thighs tighten around his strong body. I feel the wind whipping against my face, my hair flying behind us as we speed up, and then . . . my stomach comes flying up to my throat and all I feel is cold before my eyes shut tight and wetness coats my skin.

"Holy shit," I breathe.

When I finally feel like my stomach might have returned back to my gut, I open my eyes and watch as the trees blur by us. Lee holds the handles with his usual confidence and I know, even though I'm scared out of my mind, that he won't let anything happen to us.

I lean forward, the helmet he insisted I wear even though he isn't wearing one, tapping his on the side of his head, and do as he instructed. I hold on and feel.

He takes the winding trails for what feels like hours. The roar of his ATV trailing behind us with his speed. He doesn't shy away from those big, mud-filled puddles, nope. Not my Lee. He spots one and it's full fury of his speed powering through them. The first time that the muddy water coated us both, I almost had a heart attack. Mainly because I thought it would be like the first puddle we hit that was full of just rain water, splashing us and then just leaving wet marks behind. No. Not these monster baby lakes filled with muddy water. Okay, slight exaggeration, but that's sure what it felt like.

He moved down from the trail we had just been climbing and started to take the steep dirt path downward. Not paying a bit of attention to the trail because I was too focused on wondering how hard it would be to get myself off using his body and the vibrations, when his nose end hit the mud first, a huge wave of brown wetness covered us. And of course, because I was too busy trying to work at getting myself off, my back was arched. I had, in my mind, the best plan to arch my back and rub my core against the seat and his hard body. But when that mud wave came up and then back down, it shot straight down the back of my pants.

"Oh, my God, Lee!"

He doesn't answer, just laughs harder. So hard, in fact, that he has to stop the four-wheeler.

"This isn't funny! I have mud . . . oh my God . . . I have mud in my ass!"

His laughter picks up until he is forced to hold his sides.

"Holy crap. I can feel it. It's all in my panties, Lee!"

Again, the big jerk just keeps on laughing until he has to pull his shirt up, flip it to the inside and wipe the tears his laughing has caused, rolling down his face.

"I swear, Liam Beckett. I was this close, this freaking close," I scream, holding my pointer finger just an inch from my thumb, "To having one hell of an orgasm. It was building so high, I was too busy wondering if I would fall off the back when I went off. This freaking close and now . . . now I have mud in my ASS!"

Too busy flipping out, I didn't even notice when Lee stopped laughing. That is, until he moved and jumped from the seat. He reached out, grabbed my hips and in a move I still can't process, his ass was back in the seat with me facing him. Our muddy covered chests pressed tight and his mouth on mine in a bruising kiss.

All of the mud is forgotten as his lips plunder mine. My fingers curl into his shoulders and I moan deep into his mouth.

He pulls back and searches my eyes.

"How was that feel trip, Megan?" he says in a growl, the soft look in his eyes betrayed by how forceful he spoke.

"Huh?" I ask in a daze.

"Fuck me," he says hoarsely. "Fucking, fuck me."

"That . . . uh, would be nice, but seeing as I have mud in places mud shouldn't be, I would be worried about infection." I tell him in all seriousness.

"Fuck."

"Yup."

"I didn't want to stop so soon, but I take it by the fact that you laughed so hard before that last puddle that I have no doubt you felt and all that you were feeling was nothing but excitement. You took something you were dead set wouldn't be a bit of fun, braved it, and had fun. That is until I ruined your orgasm, so as far as I can see my job here is done and I should make up for that lost release."

"Uh, baby, I'm not following," I tell him.

"I imagine you aren't. Feel trip over, darlin'. We get back home, I show you my list and then I fuck you hard."

"Your list?"

"Yeah. My list is about to change. My girl feels, freely and happily, with no small amount of brave courage. Time to take that list and turn it into a bucket."

"You make no sense."

He just smiles and nods. When we situate ourselves back on the seat, he takes the trails at a slower speed, but none less exciting, until we reach his truck. He loads his ATV back up in the bed of his truck, and then walks over to me.

"Get naked," he orders with a wave of his brow.

I look around, seeing nothing but trees and sky, and then because I'm too busy wondering about his list and bucket riddles, I pull my mud soaked shirt over my head. His eyes shoot straight to my chest and I smirk to myself when he groans.

"Towel," he barks after I wrestle my wet jeans down. He wraps a clean towel around my body, then folds at the knees to help me step out of my pants. "Leave your panties on. I know it isn't comfortable with the mud and all, but if you take them off I wouldn't even care if it was a dirty fuck, I would take you so hard."

"Ohhh kay, so they stay on," I sarcastically draw out.

"While I get ready. Pull the glove box open and grab my list. Mark off number three, and then take a look. Pick which ones you want to experience together, then cross off the ones you don't. Then our list becomes a bucket."

"Do you mean bucket list? What? Did you have one before? I don't think they work like that, Lee. You can't take your bucket list for yourself and make it a couples project."

He doesn't respond; too busy peeling his mud-soaked clothes off before wrapping a towel around his hips. I roll my eyes and move to climb into his truck, pressing the latch on his glove box and reaching in to grab the solo piece of paper on top of his owner's manual.

I recognize the handwriting as Dani's and my brow pulls tight. I do a quick scan to see it's a good size list, full of activates. On the top, Feeling Alive, is written boldly and underlined. Two items already crossed off, reading them both brings tears instantly to my eyes. Paintball and Karaoke. It hits me then that this isn't *his* bucket list, it's the one he created as mine. Or better yet, going by the title, he created this as a map for his plan. My hand shakes when I see the third line has "muddin'" written in Dani's neat script.

"I had this brilliant plan that if I did enough things that made you feel, it'd cause your body to spike in adrenaline and your heart to go out of control, that you would remember how much fun being alive is. You'd been living in a dark place and I just knew you were keeping yourself from feeling in order to protect yourself. I understood it, darlin', every bit of it, but in order to make you see how much I care, I had to remind you that feeling alive is worth the fight."

"Oh, God," I mutter.

"I figured I could have stopped the list when you became mine, but then I remembered how beautiful it is to see you experiencing the beauty of living. So, instead of Feeling Alive, we make a new list, Feeling Together. You pick from there, or we pick together, but we make a list of things to do. Once a month, Molly goes to Mom's and we live our lives, together, and never stop feeling."

I look back at the list, smiling when I see 'sex' made the list at number ten. My voice coming unstuck and I look back at Lee. He's studying my reaction and I notice, to my shock, that he seems nervous.

"Sex wasn't until number ten?" I ask and his shoulders relax and his dimple comes out.

"Well, yes and no. I didn't tell Dani when she helped me write that list, but *that* sex was public sex and not just sex, sex. I hadn't planned it out yet, but I figured that one could move around when we found a bathroom with a sturdy lock on it."

I laugh, place the list down in my lap and reach out to grab his hand.

"Could we maybe add some things that Molly can do with us?" I ask.

"Yeah, darlin', I would love that."

"Then as far as I can tell, we've got a good list to keep us busy for a while. But, Lee . . . there is no way in hell you're going to get my to jump out of a plane or off a bridge. No way."

He throws his head back and roars with laughter. My hand tightens on his and I watch as his abs flex with his rumbles and when his eyes meet mine again there is nothing but love in them.

"You're going to enjoy every step of us feeling together, darlin'," he vows.

"I already do, Liam. I already do."

Chapter 28

Megan

"Oh, God!" I scream when Lee tightens his hold on my hips and pulls my body back forcefully to meet his thrusting hips. When he pulls back just a breath and then slams back inside my body, I clamp down.

"So tight. Fuck, the way you squeeze my cock, darlin'." His voice is strained and when he pulls back, my pussy clamps tight in response, not wanting him to leave me.

"Please, Lee," I beg with no idea of what I need except for him to make it happen.

"Fuck," he growls and his hands leave my hips when he pulls completely from my body, causing me to whine instantly, before I'm flipped and his body is covering mine.

"You'll get my cock, Megan. Fuck, when you make that noise I swear to Christ I can feel it in my balls. Pulling tight until I have no doubt I could come from you making that sexy as fuck whine from losing my cock."

Instantly, I mewl and whine, the sound making him close his eyes.

My hips rock against his and I watch as his jaw clenches, making those sexy flexes pop out near his ear. Of course, since I find that ridiculously hot, my hips pick up speed and his cock, already wet with my excitement, slides between my folds. He doesn't open his eyes, but his hands come and frame my face, his palms holding my head by my ears and his long fingers curling around the top of my head.

"Come inside me, baby," I beg, wanting him to fill me so badly that I'm panting for it.

His eyes hold mine and he groans when, again, I rock my hips. "I love you, Megan."

My heart thumps, "I love you, Lee."

His hips move this time, slowly. "So much, darlin'," he murmurs and then closes his eyes.

"Yes," I breathe. "So much."

He pulls back his hips, but doesn't move the rest of his body, keeping us connected from hips to head when his lips brush lightly over mine.

"You've given me the world," he says, still whispering.

I nod and then gasp when he moves his hips back in, my legs coming up, and his cock filling me without aide.

"I'll love you until I take my last breath," he pants, his hips thrusting in a torturously slow speed. "Forever, Megan."

"Yes. God, yes, Lcc. Forever."

His eyes never leave mine. His thrusts never speed up. When we both come, together, I watch as one small tear leaks out of his eye and falls onto my face. He doesn't speak or acknowledge the sign of how deep his love is rooted that still burns an invisible trail down until his tear is lost in my hair. When we both come down from our climb, he doesn't leave my body, just wraps his arms tighter and pulls us to his side.

We fall asleep like that and while in the safety of his arms I feel the peace I've been working for. All the pain of the past vanishing as I let go of the last hold it had on me and while I drift off to sleep, thank God that Lee brought me back to life.

Liam

I felt it.

When she finally let go and gave me all of her.

It was a moment that rocked me straight to my core.

When she gave me her body, I watched that last tiny bit of fear bleed from her face, and the realization that she can trust in our love enough to let go.

I don't know what I did in my life to deserve her love but whatever it was I'll spend the rest of my life making sure I'm worthy of that gift.

Her body goes slack and I know she's asleep, but I still can't get my arms to let go. I hold on, all through the night, and not once do my arms slip.

"Darlin," I call down the hall, grabbing my keys off the table by the door before walking down the hall, "Megan?"

"In here," she grumbles from the closet.

"What the hell?" I question when I walk into her room. "Did your closet throw up?"

"Funny." She moves back from her closet and almost trips on the shoes that are scattered on the floor. "I was looking for my black boots, but I think they've vanished to the same mysterious land that my socks always go missing to."

"Mysterious land?"

Her hands come up and plant on her hips. "I'll have you know that place is real. How else do you explain how hundreds of socks a year just vanish? Poof. Gone and never to be seen again."

"My guess? They probably just fall behind or under the dryer."

Her eyes narrow.

"Or maybe they vanish to a mysterious land," I add with a smile.

Her eyes soften and she smirks. "Okay, so I'll admit that maybe I'm losing my mind because I have to finish this book and I know that, I do, but I can't seem to figure out how to end it. It's like the ending is right there, and I know it's going to be so beautiful, I just can't find the right words."

I reach out and lightly tug at her biceps until she shuffles forward, wrapping her arms around my waist and dropping her forehead against my chest.

"It's right there, Lee."

I fold her in my arms and bend to kiss the top of her head. "Maybe, darlin', you can't find the words because the story isn't finished."

Her head tips up and rests against my chest with her chin. "Meaning?"

"I'm not going to pretend to understand what goes on in your head when you're writing those brilliant books of yours, but baby, you've told me enough about this book that I see all the parallels with our own story. Maybe you can't find the end because it's not ready to be written."

Her nose crinkles and she bites her lip.

"I love you, darlin'. Take the time you need to work it out. I'll go pick up Molly from Mom and we'll go out to lunch. That should give you a few hours to figure out what you need."

"Okay, I can do that," she says, but I can tell she isn't paying attention. I've already lost her to her words.

I love watching her work. I could have a full conversation with her and she wouldn't hear a word of it because her mind is still playing chess with her characters.

I also wasn't kidding when I told her why I think she's held up on ending her newest book. She's let me read the beginning of *The Helping Hand,* a book she told me was titled after me. Or better yet, my urging in the beginning of our relationship to take my hand. It wasn't a shock after hearing that that the book she's working on might as well be a biography of her life.

Which is exactly why I think she can't finish it.

Yet.

But that should all change soon.

As long as my lunch date with my favorite five-year-old goes as planned, that is.

"I'll be home later," I tell her and kiss her forehead again.

"Buckle up, little lady," I tell Molly before shutting the door of my truck and turning back to my mom.

"She's a sweetheart, Liam."

"I know, Mom. Best girl in the world," I tell her, making her smile grow.

"I'm guessing you already know this, if I'm judging your plans today correctly, but you don't have to worry. That little girl already thinks the world of you."

I close my eyes and nod.

"In fact, I think you'll be happy with what you find out if you just ask her."

"Ask her what, Mom?"

"To be her daddy," she leans forward and whispers, looking behind me where Molly is singing along to the radio.

"She's already got a daddy, Mom. I would love to hear those words from her one day, but I don't want to take her father's place. I'd gladly share the role, but not take it when it's already been taken. God, I'm a nervous mess."

She reaches forward and pats my cheek, "I know you are. It's a big step, but one I know you're ready for. I've told you over and over how much of your father I see in you, but watching you fall in love with Megan really brought that home. Don't second guess yourself, son. I understand what you're saying about Molly and her daddy, but just because she has a father that she lost, doesn't mean you would be replacing him by stepping into those shoes. That girl has more love to give then she could ever figure out how to give out."

"As far as I'm concerned she's already my daughter."

My mother's wise eyes look into mine and she smiles, "And as far as your father and I are concerned she's already our granddaughter, so . . . I suspect it's up to you to make that official."

I laugh, say my goodbye and then hug my mom before jumping into the driver's seat.

"You and me have a date today," I tell a smiling Molly.

Her eyes grow huge and she looks over at me like I hold all the secrets in the world. "A date?"

"Yeah. You're my favorite little girl in the whole entire universe. It's time for me to show you off. Let everyone know that you're mine."

Her eyes don't lose their wide wonderment, but she gives me a small grin. "I'm yours?" she questions.

"Forever and ever, stuck with the biggest, stickiest, gooiest piece of bubblegum in the whole world."

She laughs, loud, and smiles at me with her crooked smile.

Molly chatters off and on about everything she did at my parent's house the night before. I don't hear much, my nerves too busy holding my attention, but I slip in responses here and there, each time her big smile grows a little more.

God, I love that kid.

When we get to the Italian restaurant that she loves so much, I make a big production of walking around to her side of the truck, pulling the back door of the duel cab open, and offering her my arm after helping her climb down. The whole time she just giggles.

Her snickers don't stop until we've placed our order and our drinks are delivered.

"Leelee?"

"Yes, sweetheart?"

"I love you more than the moon," she says softly with an undertone of unsureness that has me moving from the seat in front of her, to the one next to her.

"Molly, look at me baby," I demand and wait for her to move her light brown eyes from her water. "You want to know a secret?"

Her small head nods and she continues to study my face.

"I had another reason, other than showing the prettiest five-year-old in the whole universe off, to take you out on a date, just me and you. You see, I have big huge plans that I need to make with you. Plans I need to be kept a super-secret, secret. Can you do that?"

She gives me another nod, a small smile coming over her face, and I can tell she's losing some of that uncertainty that had come when telling me that she loved me. This little girl, having gone through so much in her little life, who loves bigger than anyone I know, is actually afraid I would turn her love away.

"You need to know, without a single doubt that I love you back, sweetheart. I love you just as much as I love your mommy, and that, Molly, is huge."

"How huge?" she whispers.

"All the way to the sun. All the way to the moon. All the way to the farthest star away from us. And then back again."

"That's really, really far away," she gasps.

"It sure is. I told you. I love you huge, sweetheart."

She's silent for a few seconds and I sit back. When her small hand reaches out and lands on the one I have resting just besides her water glass, I look back up and see questions in her eyes.

"What's on your mind, Molly?"

"If you love me huge and I love you huge, does that mean that you'll be my second daddy now?"

And my heart, when I didn't think it could get any bigger, grows so large my chest burns with it.

"There isn't anything I would love more, Molly."

"Yay," she says, her tone soft and her eyes bright.

"Yay," I answer in my own hushed tone.

"One more thing, baby, and then we can have the best spaghetti in town. Are you ready for that big, huge secret? You can't tell anyone."

Her head bobs, each long blonde ringlet dancing against her skin.

"In a few days, I'm going to take your mommy somewhere, somewhere special to us because the last time we were there she took my hand and never let it go. This time, sweetheart, this time I'm hoping that she takes my hand again. The only difference is, when she takes it this time, it means the three of us become a family."

"That sounds fun, Le—Daddy," she whispers.

And there goes that sharpness in my chest. Again.

"I have to ask you something first though, Molly. Something that's a huge secret so you can't tell your mommy, but I have to ask *you* because in order to have your mommy give me her hand, I want to know you will too."

She pats my hand and laughs. "I already gave you my hand, silly."

I smile and nod. "You sure have, sweetheart. But what I mean is, I'm going to ask your mommy for her hand so that I can give her a ring. A beautiful ring that only queens and princesses get. And if she tells me yes, I get to take her hand and put that big beautiful ring on there. That way everyone knows that your mommy took my hand forever and ever."

I reach down into my jeans and pull out a bracelet that I had picked up last weekend. It's a simple silver bracelet with one charm hanging on it. The charm is a single teapot with a base made of three diamonds. One for her, one for her mom and one, for me.

"I don't have a ring for you, little lady, but I do have this. I want to give you this so that everyone knows that you gave me your hand forever and ever. I put a teapot on there so you will always remember how much fun we have when we have our tea parties."

Her eyes move from the charm, to my face and back to the charm. Her little chin wobbles and for a second I fear that I've made a mistake. Maybe she isn't ready for this.

Those thoughts vanish instantly when she jumps from her seat and throws her arms around my neck. I lose sight of the table when her curls hit me in the face and my arms go around her tiny body.

"You're going to be the bestest second daddy in the whole entire world," she whispers in my ear.

Chapter 29

Liam

I have no clue how Molly has kept our secret this long, but one week turned in to two, and then two went into three. Before I knew it, work had kept me from executing my plan for a month. Somehow I had gotten roped into working every weekend for the last four straight. When Barnes, one of the other HTPD officers, asked me to work tonight for him, I gave him not just a no, but a hell no.

With our schedules being as crazy as they are, by the time I would get to Megan's, Molly would either be going to bed, or already asleep. What little time I've had with her, has been rushed.

I had been hesitant to start spending the night more than every once in a while, but it wasn't Megan who had put an end to my reluctance. Two weeks ago, it was Molly.

"Never leave us, Daddy! Never, never, never, ever! Please don't go. Stop going. We need you." Molly sobbed against my chest, where she had launched herself when I tried to leave the house two weeks ago.

Megan gasped, her hand going to her mouth and her eyes filling with tears. She had heard Molly call me Daddy a few times, but they had been infrequent as if she was testing the waters. There was nothing unsure about the way it came out of her mouth this time. Unable to do anything else with a small human attached to my body like she was trying to fuse herself to me, I sat back down on the couch I had just climbed up from and wrapped her in my arms.

It was very rare for Molly to have any sort of temper tantrums. Even more unusual for her to cry. I've only seen her cry a handful of times. She fell off her bike a month ago and tore her knees to shreds, not one tear. But what's coming from her right now is rivers of tears.

"Sweetheart, what's going on?" I ask and rub her small back, willing her to calm down.

"You can't leave us. Please don't go. We want you forever," she pleads.

Hearing her little voice while it begs me to never let go, killed. I look over to Megan to see her shake her head, her eyes red with the strength she's putting out just to keep her tears locked tight.

"Molly, look at me, honey," I request, feeling her body shake with sobs. "Baby, look at me."

Her head comes up, brown eyes red rimmed and her nose and cheeks reddened. I reach over, grab a tissue off the side table next to the couch, and help her dry her face. She sniffles a few times and I give her what I hope is a reassuring smile.

"I'm not going anywhere, baby. I was just going to go back to my house tonight. I wasn't leaving you. I'll never leave you."

"Wh . . . why can't you stay?" she demands, her voice shaking with the sadness leftover. "Why can't you just live here?"

I look back up to Megan, waiting for her help guiding this conversation. With a nod, she sits down next to us, taking my hand in one of hers and placing the other against Molly's back.

"Little bird, it isn't that he doesn't want to stay with us, that's just a big step that when adults decide to make it, they talk about it first."

Molly's eyes look between the two of us a few times and then with all the wisdom of a small child says, "Then talk about it."

"Uh," Megan stutters.

"Mommy, do you want Daddy to live with us forever and ever and always?" she asks, Megan, her small voice strong and sure.

Megan looks at me, her eyes wide, and I watch as she has a million emotions filter across her face, until finally settling on love.

"Yeah, little bird, I would love it."

Molly looks from her mom over to me and smiles a little bigger.

"Daddy, do you want to live with your girls forever and ever and always?"

With nothing left but to accept that a five-year-old has just put two adults in their place, I tighten my hold on Molly, reach out and pull Megan into our embrace and after moving my head close, I tell her without a shadow of doubt, "Yes, baby. I would love nothing more."

We waited until Molly had gone to bed that night before we finished the conversation. In the end, I moved what I needed and settled into their home. We both decided that selling the only house that Molly has known was a step that would come later, for now, all three of us wanted to be together and together we were.

Now, a month later from when I had originally planned it, I was coming off a shift and meeting Megan with the rest of our friends at Mike's.

After folding my body into the truck, I was about to call Megan when my phone rang.

"Hey, darlin'," I answered.

"Hey you. We're at Mike's now. Are you on the way?"

"Just left the station. Did Molly do okay tonight when you left her?"

Megan laughs, "Yes, honey. Her fever is gone and she's jumping around all over the place. I told you the doctor said it was just a little virus and it would run its course."

"That was five days ago," I complain. "Five days of her running a fever doesn't make me happy."

Megan lets out a small laugh, "You'll get used to it, Lee. She's a kid. They sometimes get sick like that."

"Doesn't mean I have to like it."

"All right. Let's take the over-protective mode down a few degrees. She's fine and need I remind you that she's with your parents? Parents that have raised a son perfectly, I might add."

"My mom let me wear her heels, baby. I'm not sure we can say perfectly."

Megan laughs and I hear the noise of Mike's start getting louder.

"You going in now?" I ask.

"Yeah, I think everyone else is here. Cohen and Dani are waiting by the door for me."

My chest swells when I think about all of our friends being there for this. It wasn't hard, talking everyone in to my plans. Hell, they didn't need a bit of urging. When I mentioned the ring, the girls would never have been able to stay away. The guys don't care about that like the girls, but I know my friends are just happy that Megan and I have found this together.

"Right, darlin'. Go inside and grab a drink. I'll be there soon."

I get her sweet voice telling me she loves me and any nerves that I had earlier evaporated instantly.

It's time to go get the girl.

The bar is crowded when I walk in. I look over to our usual corner and see that Dani had followed through, making sure that Megan was in the chair with her back to the stage. Nate and Cohen see me the second I walk in, clearly being tasked with lookout duty. I watch as dumb and dumber smile huge. Cohen knocks his knee over and it hits Dani, who snaps her head up and looks toward the door. Her eyes connect with mine and I watch as they start to get misty.

Jesus, that girl.

Nate coughs so loud that I can hear him across the room and over the music. I shake my head at his obvious move to clue the rest of our friends in that I've arrived. Lyn and Lila make a slow circle, looking around the room until they see me. I get a wink from both of them, which always freaks me out when they do twin things. Stella stands and stretches, looking behind her and I get a smile before she turns back toward the group and drops back down on the couch next to the twins.

Maddi and her sister, Ember, are less obvious. They're facing me on the other couch and they don't react, just give me their eyes as both of them tip their lips up slightly.

The only one that doesn't move or react is Zac, but with him sitting next to Megan, there isn't a way he could do that without her catching on. But I see his hand come out and rest on the back of Megan's chair. She laughs as he continues whatever they've been talking about and without missing a beat, his thumb comes up on the hand resting behind her.

With a light step, I make my way over to the side of the stage and wait for my turn. I called ahead, so they know what's going on, but because I got held up at work I wasn't there right on time.

I nod at Bennett, the guy in charge of handling the karaoke end of Mike's, and let him know I'm ready when he is. I wait as two drunken idiots butcher *Friends in Low Places* and then it's my turn. Bennett doesn't announce me, or the song, he just hands the mic over and starts up the only song I requested.

The first cords of Train's *Marry Me* fill the room and I walk to the center of the stage, not feeling a lick of my stage fright as I clear my throat and open my mouth.

My eyes don't leave Megan's back, so I don't miss her jolting when I sing the first line. She doesn't turn until I start the chorus. The second those two words are out of my mouth, I watch Zac snag her glass right before it goes crashing to the ground.

Then I move.

I jump off the stage and ignore the crowded bar full of people screaming and cheering. I only have eyes for the beautiful blonde staring at me with huge tears rolling down her face. I take the long path, going around all the tables before I even get close to her. I give everything I have while singing that song to her. Smile on my face and a love so strong for this woman that I feel the emotion of this moment filling my body.

My feet take me to her and I reach out to grab her hand before I drop to my knee. Singing the last word out clearly until the last note in the song plays.

"Well, darlin'? Make me the happiest man in the whole world. Marry me and give *me* everything this time?"

She nods, her head bobbing swiftly and her tears picking up speed.

"God, yes!" she screams.

I reach my hand out, not caring who takes it, passing off the mic. Before I move from the floor, I grab the ring that had been burning a hole in my pocket, and slip it onto her waiting hand.

Then I grab my woman, ignoring the catcalls that follow as I place an arm under her knees and another around her waist until I have her in my arms. She throws her head back, laughing through her tears and I carry her out the door.

To our future.

Epilogue

Megan

"Hey," I whisper into the wind. "It's a beautiful day. You would hate it though. We had a cold front come in last week and it's been so amazingly cold."

Silence greets me. It always does, but it doesn't hurt anymore.

"I miss you," I sigh, leaning forward and dusting some of the dead leaves off the headstone. "Molly has her first boyfriend. Well, she says boyfriend, but they're eight. Lee's having a hard time with that, but you would love how protective he is of her. He actually asked me if he could lock her up." I laugh, thinking about how adamant he had been about his grand plan of keeping his girl from any boys. "Anyway, she talked him down from that. I swear that girl could talk him into anything."

The wind picks up and I pull my coat a little tighter against my body before adjusting my scarf.

"She's growing so fast, Jack. I look at her and I see so much of myself. You used to always say that. Even when she was a tiny baby you would pick out parts of her that were all me. But she acts like you. Sees beauty in everything. So full of happiness, that girl. I'm glad. I know that in my heart, regardless of the truth, that she got that from her father—you."

I watch some leaves fall from the huge trees that surround the area around me. Each one twirling and swirling on the way to the ground before settling.

"Jack will be six months this weekend. He's such a good baby. And Molly is loving that her baby brother is finally big enough, mobile enough, that she can play with him more."

Looking back at the headstone, I smile, and start to climb from my kneeling position, careful of my slightly rounded stomach.

"Of course, it's harder for me now with another one on the way. We haven't found out the sex yet, but something tells me I've got another boy coming. Lee thinks you've played a part in making sure I have a little army surrounding me. I've got to say, he's probably not wrong."

I look around once more, seeing the fall weather settling around us and before I tell him goodbye, I look over at Lee leaning against our SUV waiting patiently with his long legs crossed at the ankles and his back against the door, while I have my chat with Jack.

"I haven't told you in a while, but thank you. For everything you did to make sure that Molly and I were safe. For getting us out and bringing us to Hope Town. I wish you were still with us, but even in passing you set us up for a future of everything bright. I'm so happy, Jack. Not a day goes by that I don't miss you, but Lee has brought something so special into our lives and I know somewhere you're resting easy knowing that."

The wind picks up and I turn my head when I hear heavy footsteps fall in behind me. Lee gives me his knee-melting smile that hasn't gotten any less brilliant in three years.

"You ready?" he questions.

"Always, Lee."

Lee turns his head and glances at Jack's headstone. He doesn't speak, but every time we come out here he takes a few seconds to just look.

"Are *you* ready?" I ask, smiling up at my husband.

His arm goes around my waist and I feel his hand over my pregnant stomach.

"Always. Just telling Jack thanks for handing me the world again."

His head dips and I get a soft kiss before we turn and walk toward the SUV. Lee's hand moves from my waist and his warm fingers close around my hand.

"I love you, darlin," he tells me his eyes full of love and his dimple flashing.

"I love you back."

The End

Feeling Alive

1. Paintball
2. Karaoke
3. 4-Wheeling
4. Six Flags (roller coasters)
5. Bungee Jumping (really, Lee?)
6. Sky Diving (Ha! Good luck with that)
7. Zip lining
8. Tattoo (a little overkill, I think)
9. White Water Rafting
10. Sex ;)
11. Rock Concert
12. Playing in the rain
13. Surfing
14. Rock Climbing
15. Swim with dolphins
16. Road trip to anywhere
17. Making her fall in love (Had to)

Say It with a Song

I might be sick.

Or pass out.

Maybe I'll be sick and *then* I'll pass out.

I look down at Molly. Her excitement makes me smile, but the nervous flutter in my stomach still doesn't die. She keeps peeking out from behind our hiding place to see if the man we're waiting for has arrived yet. She's been eating this up since we arrived. Partially because she gets to play a part in tonight, but also because my girl loves her daddy. Lee might not be her father by blood, but that doesn't change the fact that she sees him as her everything.

Since we got married a little over a year ago, things have been crazy busy, but we try to make time to go out with our friends a few times a month. It's not always easy, especially with his schedule and my deadlines, but we make it work.

It's 'guys' night' tonight.

Or so he thought when he left the house earlier. It was almost impossible to get him to leave. He's been pushing for a date night, but I played the deadline card *and* the lack of a sitter card and got his butt out the door.

Of course, when he found out the guys had been infiltrated by all our female friends, he sent me a text complaining that we should have gotten a sitter so I could be there too. I reminded him, again, that I had a deadline that couldn't be ignored. It pacified him but not by much.

Little does he know that was the plan from the start. Had it not been for him thinking I was unable to get a sitter, I doubt I would have been able to get this surprise past him. The downside of being married to a cop is they can see a surprise a mile away.

Everything has gone off without a hitch. According to the last text I got from Dani, Cohen hasn't had a single issue in convincing Lee to continue on to Mike's instead of going home to his girls, something she said Lee has already complained that he would rather do. All it took was a few good-natured ribs from Nate and Cohen, and Lee's stubborn ass would have stayed out all night.

I smile to myself thinking about how the night will go. I might be nervous, but I know this surprise is going to be something that rocks him to the ground—in the best way possible, that is.

"They're here," Molly whispers, turning to look at me with a huge smile.

My nerves amp up, and I smile at her, noticing not for the first time just how grown she looks at seven years old.

Moving to her side, we peek around the wall we're hiding behind to see our group of family walk in. Dani and Cohen lead the charge, laughing at something that Nate and Ember are saying behind them. Cam and Colt are next with Jax and his current girlfriend following. Stella, the twins, and Lee are next, with Zac heading up the rear.

Everyone that we call family.

I love them all, and I think God every day that I was brought into this fold. That Molly has this.

A new feeling of confidence rushes through my body as I watch them move through the crowded karaoke bar to the same table we sat at when Lee proposed to me with a song. Cohen moves to the side and lets everyone file into the booth before getting in himself and pulling his wife to his side. Lee sits at the edge of the booth, looking like he would rather be anywhere but here.

"Why does Daddy look like he swallowed the whole box of Sour Patch Kids?" Molly asks with a giggle, turning around and looking up at me.

"Probably because your daddy would rather be at home with his girls than here." I laugh back.

"But he's going to be so happy, right, Mommy?"

"Little bird, he's going to be so happy he's not going to know what to do with himself."

"You girls ready?" I hear and look away from Molly to the man in charge of the karaoke. Bennett's been a big part of our lives since the night Lee proposed. Of course, it doesn't hurt that our group of crazy is here every couple of weeks.

Ignoring the nerves, I look down to give Molly a big smile—one she returns—before directing that smile at the man in front of me. "You betcha."

He doesn't talk for a second, just looks back and forth between us with a weird smile on his face. "You know, it isn't often I get to be a part of two people's life-changing moments. I still remember the day that Liam asked me to help him propose to his girl. Just wanted to say, before you go out there, that I'm happy for your family."

He walks off before I can respond, which is probably best because I would have burst into emotional tears. When he gets to the steps that lead up to his DJ booth, he turns and points at the stage.

It's time.

I glance once more at our table of family. Once I'm satisfied he isn't paying attention to what is going on over on the stage area, I take Molly's hand and we walk out onto the brightly lit stage, stopping at the two mics that have been placed in the center. I keep my eyes forward. Lee is laughing at something Stella is saying, still oblivious to the two of us standing here.

I might not have his attention, but I have the attention of the majority of our table. Nate and Dani are both wearing smiles so big they look wonky. Cohen is doing a better job of hiding his, but still, one side of his mouth is tipped up in happiness. Stella is still talking to Lee, so she isn't able to be obvious about it, but I can see the joy on her face clear as day. The rest of our group—especially Maddi, Lyn, and Lila—are smiling like fools with tears shimmering in their eyes.

The song starts, and I look down at Molly. We've practiced this so many times that I shouldn't worry, but we have never practiced it in front of an audience. But my girl is a rock star, and I shouldn't have worried because she opens her mouth and, like an angel, sings the first line of Colbie Caillat's "Capri," and the room goes silent.

Did I mention that even at seven, my girl has a voice that will make her a star?

My heart bursts, and I feel my eyes get wet when she continues, and only when she finishes the first part of the song do I look to where Lee is.

His strong jaw is slack, beer halfway to his mouth but frozen in shock as our daughter continues to sing in her melodious voice. I can tell the second that the words register with him, and my guess is Cohen did, as well, because he reaches out and nabs his full beer glass at the same time that Lee's fingers go slack and he stands in a rush. He doesn't leave the table, and judging by the white-knuckle grip that he has on the back of the booth, I'm not even sure he could walk if he tried.

Molly continues to sing, and I smile when I hear her sing the line about an angel growing peacefully. Lee looks from my face down to where I'm holding a hand over my still flat stomach. He studies my hand for a beat before looking at Molly, his smile growing and his eyes getting soft for our girl. He gives her all of his attention while she continues to sing the song we picked. The song that will tell him that our family is growing, knowing that Molly singing this to him is just as important as I feel it is.

When the song finishes, you could hear a pin drop in the whole bar. Bennett hasn't spoken to the crowd, even though it's something he normally does to keep the hype up. Instead, he's waiting—just like the rest of the bar—to see how this moment plays out. To watch the man who got the girl in this same bar come full circle to get the girl, her girl, and now, their growing family.

Lee doesn't disappoint either. He rushes the stage area, leaping over the edge and dropping to his knees with a slide that brings him right between the mics and to our bodies. His arms go out, wrapping around us both, before burying his face against my stomach and Molly's shoulder. She looks up, and her smile is huge.

"I think Daddy is happy that we're growing a baby." She laughs, her voice carrying through the whole bar and causing everyone watching to laugh.

Lee looks up before I can answer, tears shining brightly in his eyes. He presses a soft kiss to my stomach before looking at our girl. “Happiest daddy in the world. Thank you, my sweet girl, for giving me that gift. I bubblegum you to the moon,” he tells her, something they started saying years ago.

“I love you too, Daddy,” she responds with a smile.

He stands, his arm going around Molly before facing me. “Surprise,” I wheeze through my tears.

His smile grows. “You’re carrying my baby?” he asks softly, and I watch his jaw tense as he struggles to hold back his own emotion.

I nod.

“God, I love you,” he breaths. One hand comes up to cup my cheek and he pulls me to him, stealing my breath away with a deep kiss. I hear Molly giggling, and my smile grows against his lips.

“How did I do for my first feel trip?” I ask when he pulls away.

He looks at me, blinks, and then throws his head back in a deep belly laugh.

“I’ll show you later,” he promises.

And show me he did. Over and over again.

Acknowledgments

After 8 books this part gets harder and harder. To every single person that helped me build this book from the ground up. My brilliant editors, Ellie and Emma, for making sure I don't look like an idiot. My extremely talented cover designer Sommer for knowing each time exactly what is in my head. Brilliant gifted eye behind the lens, Lauren. My models, Taylor and Laura, you guys . . . seriously, thank you for bringing Liam and Megan to life. My formatter, Stacey, whom I love, for always making my pages beautiful . . . putting up with my insanity. The ladies at The Rock Stars of Romance for hosting my tour and release blitz. You guys always take such good care of my 'babies' and me. Each and every member of my Alpha Babes group. You guys keep me going, help me when I need it, and never fail to let me know how much you love these characters.

To my amazing, incredible, kickass readers. Your love for not only me, but also my characters, fuels my soul like you would never believe. When I need my own 'helping hand' you never let me down. I can't even tell you all how much each and every one of you mean to me. Thank YOU, for always believing in me. Thank YOU, for opening your hearts and letting my characters feel YOUR love.

To my family . . . you guys deal with me at my worst and my best. You put up with my insanity and my (somewhat) sanity. I am who I am because of you. And my girls, M, T, and A . . . you make mommy want to be the best she can be. You push me to dig deep and never give up. But, you still can never read my books.

And to Felicia Lynn. You're crazy, but a good crazy. Not the kind of crazy that makes me worried you know my alarm code, but the kind that makes me fucking thrilled to call you my BFF. You don't judge me silently, or behind my back, but you tell me to my face how insane I am. That, and that there is no one I know that I could sit next to for hours a day and say so much without speaking one word. You get me. Wait for it . . . but I still won't fucking cuddle you, you weirdo.

NEW YORK TIMES & *USA TODAY* BESTSELLING AUTHOR

HARPER SLOAN

When I'm With

YOU

"Hollow" by Tori Kelly
"In Case You Didn't Know" by Brett Young
"Hold Back the River" by James Bay
"Ride" by SoMo
"Reverse Cowgirl" by T-Pain
"Sleep without You" by Brett Young
"Oh, Tonight" by Josh Abbott Band
"Talking Body" by Tove Lo
"Stitches" by Shawn Mendes
"T-Shirt" by Thomas Rhett
"PILLOWTALK" by Zayn
"Pony" by Ginuwine
"Wasn't That Drunk" by Josh Abbott Band
"Anywhere" by 112
"SexyBack" by Justin Timberlake
"Rock Your Body" by Justin Timberlake
"Lollipop" by Framing Henley
"Turn Down for What" by DJ Snake
"History" by One Direction

To follow the *When I'm with You* playlist: https://open.spotify.com/user/1293550968/playlist/1Cca7XUYvNUWxoeK29n7Aj

To Felicia Lynn.
Everyone should have a weird best friend like you in his or her lives.
Well, not ***you*** because you are mine and I don't share.
They should also have the right to refuse cuddles when said best friend breaks the 5.2 second skin contact rule and/or that best friend has proven themselves to be quite handsie when sleeping.
(Spoiler alert : I'm talking about you, Felicia!)
I'm pretty sure no one will ever love me as fiercely as you do or support me as brilliantly as you do. I've been one hell of a lucky chick to have you by my side day in and day out.
Plus, no one could spend hours and hours sitting together writing, never speaking a word, and even a writing session feeling as if we had just spent every second of those hours talking about any and every thing.
Best friend. Best writing partner. Best don't-touch-me sleeping buddy.
Best YOU.
I love your weird ass.
Also…Nate Reid is yours.

Graduation Night

"I love you," I whisper, my voice coming out in a weak wheeze. Holy crap, I can't believe I just said that. It has to be the beer. Or as my best friend, Nikki, calls it—liquid courage.

I force my hands to stop twisting the bottom of my sundress and look up at the man before me. Not a boy, no … he is all man.

His green eyes, the ones that always make me think of sunrises and dew-covered grass, are wide with shock. The thick lips I've spent way too much time dreaming about are parted in shock.

In all the time I've put into thinking about this moment, I never thought that shock would be present. I've built this moment up to be perfect in my head. Nothing but innocent dreams and naïve wishes clouded this moment because of course shock is what I should have expected. But no, all I've longed to hear when it came to me admitting my feelings for him are much deeper than 'just friends' is him repeating those three words right back to me.

Oh, God … what have I done? He doesn't feel the same. I mean I was so sure … so stupidly sure that he felt the same. That he saw me as more than a friend.

Thick panic fills me, and I know before my mouth even starts moving that I'm about to nervously ramble a string of verbal vomit that I'm powerless to stop. It never fails when I'm uncomfortable; the words come and come until I'm stopped or I slam a hand over my mouth.

Sure enough, the words rush past my dry lips as I silently scream inside my head for the earth to open up and swallow me whole. You know when the voice in your head takes over so loudly that you can't even hear the crazy nonsense that is coming out of your mouth anymore.

"I mean … I'm in love with you. You know I love you, of course, you're like one of my best friends, but I'm *in* love with *you.* I wasn't going to say anything; in fact, maybe I shouldn't have. I didn't … I mean I don't want this to mess things up between us. I would probably die if that happened. Well, not die, die … but I would probably feel close to death emotionally. I just wanted you … no, I needed you to know how I feel." I finally get my mouth to stop moving long enough to take a deep breath. I feel my heart speed up and force myself to continue to hold his gaze. "Please say I didn't just screw up big time?"

"Em," he starts before clearing his throat. His voice is thick and deeper than normal. The plangent tones vibrating from his chest wrap around my senses, and I shiver. "Ember, where is this coming from?"

I blink. Actually, I'm pretty sure if there were such a thing as slow-motion blinking, I would be doing that right now.

How could I have been so wrong?

"It's just … I'm making a huge mess of things, aren't I? God, I'm so stupid."

I'm not normally a crier. Then again, I'm also not normally a drinker. I've had a few mixed drinks with Nikki this past summer, but for some reason, I decided I needed to take up the art of drinking for courage. Of course, with my luck, I would end up being one of those people who get overemotional when drinking. My sister, Maddi, warned me about those annoying girls when she brought the beer over tonight.

My nose prickles with what feels like a thousand needles being pushed through the bridge. I can feel that thick bubble of emotion crawling and scraping up my throat, and I know I'm just seconds away from my eyes tearing up. I take a huge gulp of air, and it rushes out in a wobbled wave of emotion.

His normally carefree expression is nowhere to be seen. His eyes look troubled and his mouth pursed, making his lips look like two thin lines. When he moves from where he had been leaning against the porch railing, my gaze follows him closely as he takes a seat next to me on the swing. He lifts his arm and places it on my shoulders, pulling me into his stronghold. I go willingly, but I stiffen when my body encounters the heat of his.

The hardness of his muscles starts a slow burn in my gut. I couldn't explain the feeling, but I've felt it for the last four months.

It started with a crush from afar. Then my crush turned into a pact with Nikki to try to get him to notice me. It was time. So I did what I needed to do, and for the last few months, he's been helping me get my stupid calculus grade up.

We've always been 'friends.' With a makeshift family like we have, it would have been impossible not to be. But I've always been the baby of the group and getting the man I've crushed on to notice me always seemed impossible. That is until he started coming around twice a week, every week, for the last few months. During that time, our friendship grew stronger, naturally, because we had more time with just the two of us. Well, I guess we were never alone since we could always hear my parents from where we studied in the basement.

Many people don't take Nate seriously. Mainly due to his carefree, jokester persona, but also because he has never flaunted the fact he's insanely smart. Which he probably should—maybe then I wouldn't have had to convince my dad he was the best person to help me get my grades up.

Regardless of how it happened, my crush bloomed like a well-watered flower. During my tutoring, we shared lots of laughter and teasing moments. A few times, I even caught him just looking at me in silence. Little things added up in my head until I was sure this moment was worth the leap.

Clearly, I was mistaken. I thought things would be different, that this would be different, for us. But this *something different* is nothing like I had dreamed it would be.

"Em," he says softly, breaking me from my thoughts. "You know I love you, but I don't love you like that. We've known each other forever, and you know I would do anything for you, but I love you as a friend. What you're saying, suggesting, would change a lot more than our friendship."

Oh, God. There it is.

"I'm sorry." I sigh, feeling every second of those mistaken dreams about some big love between us crumble around me.

"There's no need to be sorry, firecracker." I close my eyes when he says the nickname he had given me. "We've spent a lot of time together lately; it's normal to get some wires crossed when you're around someone so often. Maybe when you're a little older, you'll understand better."

My eyes pop open, and I turn sharply. My body jerks, and I'm seconds away from jumping from the bench seat and pacing. His arm falls off my shoulders and hits the back of the swing. "When I'm a little older?"

His brow furrows; clearly, my Jekyll and Hyde move has confused him. I went from sullen to pissed off in two point five seconds. Like a firecracker. He always said my temper would light up and take off like an out of control firecracker, thus the reason for the nickname.

"Uh … yeah?"

"I'm eighteen. I'm not a two-year-old who doesn't know right from wrong."

He nods. "I know how old you are, Emberlyn."

"I'm old enough to know my own feelings, Nathaniel." He's never liked being called his full name—but neither have I—something we both are clearly using against each other in the heat of the moment.

"Jesus," he mumbles.

His eyes leave mine when he stands and starts to pace in front of me on the porch. The music I hadn't even noticed being so loud before vibrates through the wall of my parents' house, but thankfully, the large group of my friends and other random kids from our graduating class have stayed inside during this conversation.

I force myself to watch him. His large body moves in choppy

agitation and annoyed steps, so different from his normal fluid movements. He's always moved in a way that looked almost like he floated. His large body always moves with a graceful silence that reminded me of a ballet dancer. Which in turn would cause me to giggle uncontrollably because just thinking of the manly man in front of me in tights is too much to imagine.

"You *just* turned eighteen, Em. Just. Turned. You might not understand what I'm saying, but dammit, you don't even understand what you're saying. It's a crush. That's it. All I'm saying is that you're going to be able to make sense of that better when you're older. Not to mention, I'm six years older than you are. Six years is a huge deal. Not just to everyone else, but our families would shit themselves. Not to mention, what your dad would do? Do you even have any idea what people would say?"

"I'm not a baby," I snap, at a loss of what else to say, as I ease back down onto the swing's seat.

He stops his pacing and turns to face me. One hand pushes through his thick dark hair in frustration. I watch in fascination as his overly long hair moves in a thick wave before falling back into the mess it's always been since he decided to start growing it out. When he stops, his hand rests at the base of his skull and the end of his hair falls over a few fingers.

Finally, his words reach my lust-filled brain and a new burst of anger fills me. Making me feel even more the fool.

"I'm not a baby!" I repeat on a yell into the still night, my voice shrill, and I cringe at the emotional hit his words cause me.

"I didn't say you were. You just don't understand what you're saying."

"I assure you, I do."

He shakes his head, his hand still resting on the back of his neck. I notice briefly that his grip has tightened to the point of his fingertips turning white. When he starts to move forward, closing the distance from where he's standing and where I'm perched at the edge of the swing's seat, I jerk back, making the chains holding the swing up rattle loudly. He narrows his eyes and lets out a long breath. Dropping to his knees in front of me, he pulls my hands from their death grip on the wood next to my bare thighs. He doesn't speak for the longest time, and I foolishly let that flicker of hope light, thinking he must have realized he's wrong.

"I'm sorry, Em, but I don't feel that way toward you. I don't want to hurt you or lose your friendship. You might hate me for it, but we just can't be what you're saying. You loving me would do nothing but cause your heart ruin."

"You're wrong." I force the words past that damned lump in my throat.

"I'm not," he says softly, a sad smile ghosting over his lips, gone just as quickly as it appeared. "We're friends and always will be. One day, you'll see that."

Pulling my hands from his, I instantly miss the warmth of his skin as I stand and move around him. He doesn't move from his crouched position, nor does he turn to look when I move around him.

"I know what I feel, and you're going to be the one who has some grand understanding one day when you realize what you're denying. Sure, I might be young, but I'm not a baby and I know what I feel. I also know that you're using our families as an excuse. Especially my father because he also knows that I'm smart enough to know my own feelings and follow my heart. I thought you were someone different, Nate, I really did. I …" I sigh deeply, the one sound full of so much emotion. "You know what? Just forget I even said anything. We can chalk it up to me having some foolish, *childish*, drunk admission. After all, I'm just a kid … what do I know?"

It takes every ounce of strength I can muster to turn and walk away from him. Leaving pieces of my heart smashed on the deck at his feet while he just sits there and lets me go. The tiny sliver of my heart that had held on praying he would change his mind and stop me dies and joins the rest of the pieces on the ground.

Unfortunately for me, I'm so lost in my own pity party that I miss it. I walk away without knowing that the second my back was turned, he had silently moved, jumping to his feet. One arm started to reach out to me, only to drop heavily at his side after I moved out of his reach. I was so blinded by my own heart breaking that I missed the visible pain on his face as he felt the same pain with each step I took away from him.

Had I looked back, even stopped for just one second, maybe I would have heard his whisper, but instead, his words just floated away with my dying hope.

"I love you, too, Ember."

Chapter 1

Nate

I press my forehead against the wall, ignoring the bite against my fevered skin. My lips dance across the shoulder held captive between the hard surface and my body, as my head spins faster from the amount of alcohol I consumed tonight. With each pass my hands make over the silky smooth skin underneath my fingertips, I trail more wet kisses and bites across her neck. The rasped breath that escapes from the mouth pressed close to my ear only fuels the desire raging through my body.

Fuck. Have I ever been this powerless against the need to take someone?

Blindly moving my hands down the slim torso, my fingers dig in when I hit her hips, giving her a firm squeeze in warning before I pull her body closer to mine. Her legs wrap around my hips easily as her dress rides up and my dick instantly finds a home. Or the warm home he wants to go inside of, that is.

Fuck. I can feel how wet she is, the thin barrier of her underwear doing nothing to shield that from me.

I'm drunk enough to know I should stop, but even though the rational thought keeps crossing over the intoxicated waves rolling in my head, I would never be able to step away from this feeling. I justify that decision with the mental reminder that I'm not *that* drunk.

Drunk or not, even I have a few reservations about taking her when I don't even know her name. I might have been fucking my way through life the last few years, but even I have some morals.

The smell, taste, and *feel* of her are like nothing I've ever felt before. If I weren't already flying on a beer high, I would swear it was this little firecracker doing it to me.

Firecracker.

Even with another woman warm and willingly wrapped around my body, the vision of Emberlyn Locke hits me hard with just that one word. It's been years, years of fantasies and forbidden desire, and it never changes. I try my hardest to shake the image that is holding my mind hostage, using my body's desires for the willing woman in my arms to try to replace it as I move against her.

"Take me," she whispers on a moan when I thrust my hips harder against her pliant body.

I know from experience that now that I see *her* in my mind, I'll never be able to see the reality in front of me, so I'm not sure why I'm even trying so hard. This chick is just another faceless woman who will wear the mask of Ember's face. Like many before her have.

I push my cock rougher against her while reaching behind me for my wallet, hoping I remembered to stuff a condom in there earlier. She loosens her grip on my hips as I struggle to free the damn thing, and I feel one of her legs drop from my body. The sounds of music and people enjoying themselves float in the air around us, reminding me that I need to hurry this along before someone finds us. The last thing I need to get caught doing at my sister's wedding reception is fucking some chick.

Her hands roam all over my body as I make quick work of protecting myself, touching every inch she can reach. I go to lift my mouth from her neck, but she just tightens her grip on my neck, not allowing me to leave the spot I've been feasting on for the last ten minutes. If she's so dead set on me not looking at her, that's all the green light I need to hurry this along.

Finally, I grab the leg that dropped from me with a firm hold against her smooth thigh while pushing her back against the wall a little harder in order to stabilize our bodies. With one of her legs tight around my back, the other being held in my hand, I reach my free hand between us and curl my fingers into the crotch of her lace panties. In one powerful jerk, they're on the ground at our feet.

Turning my mouth from her neck, I bite the skin under her ear before lifting my rock hard cock from her body, feeling like my balls are about to fall off they're so tight. "Going to fuck you now. Fuck you so goddamn hard, babe."

"Oh, God," I hear, just barely, over the heavy panting coming from the two of us. Her voice so low I almost miss her next word. "Finally."

I laugh, the sound coming out more animalistic now that I have her wet heat kissing the tip of my cock. "Yeah, babe … finally. I wish I could wait to get you somewhere more accommodating, but I'll make it worth it." Remembering my earlier thoughts, I rush out the next words in a hiss as I start to push inside her. "Tell me your name, babe," I ask, moaning loudly when the tip of my cock enters her and is surrounded by the tight, scorching wet heat of her cunt. I might be an ass, but I'll, at least, let her think I care about who I'm fucking by recalling to ask her what her fucking name is.

Her legs lock and her body goes from soft and pliable to rock hard instantly. Confusion makes me pause in my movements, not pushing any farther into her tight as fuck little body. I can feel sweat beading on my forehead. I've never fucked a woman who felt this good around me, and I'm only an inch inside her snug pussy. The painful gasp that comes from her makes me jerk my head up from where I had been nibbling from the back of her ear down to her shoulder. I knew I should have waited until I could get her off this wall before fucking her.

With a gasp, I open my eyes for the first time. Confusion holds me in its grip for a beat before I realize I had been dreaming. *What the fuck?* The same one had haunted my dreams for longer than I care to admit and it never fails. I wake up with my cock hard, seconds away from coming, but never getting past that one fucking moment.

I search through the darkness of my room as I try to grab hold of the dredges of the dream that I never get to see the end of. No matter how hard I try, I never see her. I never get anything past that breathy gasp. Well, that's a lie … I did get a bed of my own come once when I decided just the thought of that tight cunt was worth letting a load out.

"Goddamn," I bark, the sound echoing off the empty room around me.

Lifting off the mattress, I toss back the covers and move to stand. My whole body is alive with the dream that never seems to leave. The location changes, as it always has over the years, but lately, it's been the same.

Me taking a woman I mask as Ember in some drunken haze fuck against the side of my parents' house during my sister's wedding reception. The hell if I can remember when it turned into that, though. I only recently started picturing and hearing the sounds of everyone partying around us.

The dreams started shortly after her graduation party, but they have never, not once, felt this real. Reaching down as I walk, I wrap my hand around my balls, feeling for the wetness that had been falling from her body in my dream, only to come up empty. Well, not fucking empty since I can feel just how real my mind thought that dream was.

Walking through my bedroom, I keep my hand on my balls as the discomfort from each step I take seems to hit me right between the legs. A painful reminder my cock needs attention now.

As I walk past my open bedroom door, I'm thankful that I live alone now. Not bothering with the light, I walk into the bathroom, opening the glass door of the shower, and turn the water on. I don't wait for the water to heat; I don't even feel the cold blast when I step in and under the spray. I'm too busy still trying to continue the dream.

With a sigh of resignation, I realize it's a fruitless endeavor even to try. Might as well give me a memory I would love to have had a chance at making a reality. My hand goes for the body wash as my mind brings up the most recent picture of Ember in my mind. Squeezing blindly, I fill my palm before soaping up my body, trailing my hand down my abs before moving back to my balls. I give them a little attention before my fist wraps around my painfully hard cock, stroking slowly as the vision fills my mind like a motion picture.

She hasn't changed much in almost three years. Her small body, big tits, and face that would tempt a saint have only matured. She was beautiful at eighteen, but now, just shy of twenty-one, she's breathtaking.

The last time I saw her feels like a lifetime ago, but it was maybe six or so months ago standing outside my parents' house during one of the monthly dinners we all have. Our parents have been a tight-knit group of friends since way before we were all born, and ever since they started adding kids to the group, monthly dinners have become a must for all to attend.

Everyone was there that night since it was her father's birthday. Thinking back, that was probably the only reason she was there, since she's made it a point to make herself scarce. Even before that night, she hadn't come but every other or so month.

The vision of her fills my mind, and I moan deep in my throat when the hand not busy with my cock rubs over my hard nipples; twisting the metal piercing through them causes the hard cock in my hand to jerk.

She'd pulled her dark auburn hair back in a high ponytail that day, highlighting her long neck. I remember wondering what it would be like to wrap her thick, long hair around my fist as I took her from behind with just that hold on her hair. She never took off her sunglasses, which, at the time, pissed me off because I could always tell what she was thinking with one look in those dark brown eyes. She kept herself distant from me, which also pissed me the fuck off, but I remember a breeze bringing the intoxicating scent of her to my nostrils.

Lemon and wildflowers.

Licking my lips, I stroke myself a little faster and let my mind continue with the thoughts of her.

I watched her all night; the vision in my mind as clear as it was that day. Every step she took highlighted every tan inch of her bare legs in her cut-off shorts as she walked around the backyard. Her legs, long and toned despite the fact that she's so short, moved gracefully with each step. But that's when I stop thinking about that night. Instead, I use that vision of her as a mold to place her in the dream that had woke me up. Now, in my dream, she's wrapping those legs around my body as I finally feel what the reality of fucking her is like.

I have to reach out to stabilize myself at the thought and I place one palm against the cool tile in front of me before dropping my head and feeling the water run down my back. My breathing speeds up until grunts of pleasure start to fall from my open mouth. I tighten my fist and work the straining flesh with a renewed fervor as thoughts of me taking Ember overwhelm me.

"Ah, fuuuuck," I moan, moving quickly so that my back takes the place of where my palm had just rested against the tile. The bite of the cold against my skin doesn't even register because the second my body is stable and braced against the wall, I bring my other hand down to join the one frantically pumping the top half of my cock. I squeeze my balls before moving up to fist the bottom of my cock as I tighten the hold I have over the tip, using both hands as I begin to fuck my tightly clamped fists, pretending with each thrust that I'm taking her.

My arms burn as I continue to fuck myself, my cock getting even harder under my wet hands until my orgasm rips through me. The thick jets of my come shoot forward, falling with the steady stream of the shower, as I ride out my pleasure.

My legs start to shake with the force of my orgasm, and I almost lose my footing. Releasing the firm hold I have on myself, my cock falls, still heavy with leftover desire, against my body.

I hate this feeling. No matter how great the pleasure my body gets from picturing her, I always feel empty after. A big giant reminder I'll never know what having her feels like. Like it or not, this is all I'll ever have. A hollow pit inside me that I've only ever felt was filling up when her smiles came at me without pause. A pit that's taken up residence inside me since the night she admitted to having the same feelings I've been feeling for a long time. Fighting with myself, I evaded the magnitude of fear those feelings brought with them.

"Fuck, it's going to be a long day," I say to the emptiness around me, stopping myself from continuing the depressing thoughts rolling through my mind.

I finish showering before I get out and start to get ready for the day, unable to shake the feeling of loneliness that I've had plaguing me lately.

Chapter 2

Nate

After my middle of the night shower, I had given up any hopes of returning to sleep. If I was honest with myself, it was more about self-preservation than actually not being able to sleep. I worried I would be haunted with more thoughts of Ember in my arms, and I just don't have the energy to deal with that shit right now.

Three hours later, just when the clock in my truck's dash turns over to seven in the morning, I'm pulling into the parking lot of the security business my dad owns with some of his old Marine buddies. No matter who you ask, they all say Corps Security was what brought all of our families together. I think after the parents of our group started having us kids, there was always a hope that we would all, in some way, join the business. Unfortunately, like our parents, we had our own dreams and many of them didn't include anything CS related.

Cohen Cage, my best friend and brother-in-law, started working here after he left the Marines himself, right before he married my sister, Dani. He followed his own father's footsteps into the 'family business,' which was probably the catalysis for my dad's desire to get me here.

Cohen's dad, Greg, was one of the men my dad had served with before they both joined the two security businesses they separately owned to form CS. My dad brought along John 'Beck' Beckett and Zeke Cooper when he moved to Georgia from California. Uncle Zeke passed away a few years later, but now, his brother, Asher, works for

CS. Ember's dad, Maddox Locke, was also part of their brotherhood and the man I currently work side by side with.

I respect the hell out of my dad and the men who work here, but I'll never be the man he wants me to be. I've been here for about a year and a half, but it wasn't until six months ago when I finally put my foot down and told them it wasn't for me. It only took one long-as-fuck stakeout with him before I realized watching cheating spouses will never be something I want for my future. Sure, they do a lot of other shit, but none of the cloak-and-dagger shit will ever be for me. Nah, not me. I've just been biding my time until I could do what I really wanted.

The second my dad realized how much I hated just about every aspect of CS, he decided to put my computer knowledge to work, and I've been doing the IT shit that no one but Maddox has ever been able to do since. Of course, when you can hack into just about anything, even Maddox couldn't keep up with me. It's never been more than a hobby out of boredom, or stinginess to get free porn. No matter how much fun I find the challenge of a good hack, the last thing I want is to spend my hours locked inside some dark room staring at computer screens. The plus side, though, is that the pay is ridiculous, and because of my time here, I was finally able to save enough to start living my own dream. So for the last six months that I've been working here, I've gone down to part time. Eventually, I'll be too busy for even that and only come in when they need my skills for a special case.

Unlocking the front door, I walk through the doors of CS. I look over at the picture of my Uncle Coop front and center when you walk in before moving to disarm the security system. The lights flick on after I punch the codes into the high-tech monitor. It takes a few seconds of my fingers flying over the screen to rearm the system and make sure the screen registers me as 'in,' so the alarms don't start blaring the second I move farther into the building. With a sigh, I walk around the empty reception desk to the thick closed door that separates the lobby from the offices. I press my thumb on the panel, waiting for the multiple locks to disengage as they recognize me before pushing the heavy door open. I repeat the same process when I get to my 'office' door; only, this time, I tip my head up and look into the camera above the door as it registers my facial imprint before disengaging the door lock and allowing me to walk into the dungeon. Or IT central, rather, but dungeon fits.

Not a single window exists in here and they painted the walls black for a reason I will never fucking understand. Being that it houses about twenty computers and enough technical crap to give the biggest nerd a wet dream, the air in here is kept cold as shit to prevent anything from overheating.

We monitor numerous residential and business properties around the clock, so this room is always humming, but since we don't currently have any active cases that require constant monitoring, things have been quiet in here. I hate when we get those cases. Maddox and I tend to switch off duty with a few other guys since it becomes tedious to stare at that shit for hours on end.

I move around the hub in the middle of the room that houses the bulk of our monitors and slide into my chair. My desk is pushed up against Maddox's, forming a square of sorts in the back corner of the room. It's easier this way, and our own personal computer monitors are designed so that, when we need to, we are able to swing them around to face the other person when another eye is needed. It's easy enough for me to get lost in my coding, surfing the dark corners of the internet looking for all the things that people think they've hidden forever. However, when he's sitting in his chair, I always feel like he's studying me more than he's studying his own monitors.

Secretly, I don't mind his dark looks or attitude since his frustration usually warrants it. I'm usually easily fifteen steps ahead of him on cases he's been stumbling through for days. Normally, anyone at the receiving end of his death glares would probably shit themselves but not me. No, I love it because while he focuses on being pissed at me, I can focus on things he doesn't need to notice me taking in. Sitting on the left side of his desk, butted up to the wall and turned slightly so I have it perfectly in my line of sight when I jot something down, is a picture of his girls.

Maddi and Ember.

But I only have eyes for Ember.

I do my best to ignore the taunting frame to my right as I quickly power on the computer. I grab the file I had been working on yesterday before I closed up, and it doesn't take long before I lose track of the things around me. I'm finally able to let go of the tense feelings I've been carrying around all morning.

I had been working steady for an hour or so when I hear the steady beep of the security system, alerting me to someone else showing up for the day, but I've been so close to closing this case that I don't budge. They'll see me show up on the security panel when they shut that shit off. I designed that brilliant system, knocking the old shit Maddox had installed out of the water. The iPad-size panel I had fiddled with when I came in the doors this morning not only works for the boring alarm functions of arming and disarming, but this one also keeps a running tally of the bodies in the whole office.

After an incident that ended with the death of Uncle Coop, they had installed some safeguards. But none of them had made this place as secure as my program. Now, you need to go through a few steps just to get in the front door when no one is manning the desk, but also, thumbprint and facial recognition is needed once you get deeper into the bowels of the building.

Which brought me to my favorite feature of the system. The second you step foot in the front door, the system recognizes you by a series of body and facial scans, leaving a small icon of your face on the bottom of the screen. It's helpful for everyone at CS to know who is in the building at all times. New clients sometimes act like they have a giant stick up their ass when we require them to be put into the system, but it beats the alarm going off all day during consultations because it doesn't recognize someone who's been past the main lobby longer than the registered safe period, which it's designed to do for our well-being.

"Son." I hear in the way of a greeting from the front of the dungeon.

"Morning to you, too, old man," I reply. I don't look away from the monitor, nor do I stop the rapid speed in which my fingers are dancing over the keys in front of me.

"Yeah, Nate, mornin'. Want to tell me why you're here, again, hours before any other of these sorry bastards even got out of bed?"

I let out a laugh. “You know you’re not just talking about yourself since I beat you here, but also the golden boy who shares a bed with your little princess?”

I don’t need to look to know my dad has a scowl on his face. He still can’t handle the fact that his little girl is grown up and married with two kids of her own. It’s way too much fun to remind him just how his grandsons got here.

Just the thought of Owen and Evan is enough to lighten a little of the dark mood that has followed me around since the dream that woke me up way too fucking early this morning.

“Don’t be a punk, Nate.”

I laugh, making sure to write down where I was in my coding before I drop the pen next to my log sheet and turn to where my father is now sulking.

“What’s up?”

“Not what’s up with me, Nate. What’s up with you?”

“Yeah, not following you. Old age making you go nuts already?” I lift my hand and point at the top of my head. “A lot more gray in there these days. You’re starting to lose the whole salt and pepper look and become more salt only.”

He shakes his head, not falling for my taunt, and pushes off where he had been leaning against one of the large floor-to-ceiling columns that hold our storage drive systems, or what I like to call ‘mother ships.’ He might ignore it, but I watch as he rubs a hand over his head while pulling one of the chairs around the hub monitors. I bite back the laugh as the few streaks of gray shine in the light of my computer screen when he pulls his seat toward my desk, settling his six-foot-six frame down with a grunt. I have to force my silence when the urge to take a jab at his struggled grunt when he sat hits my mind.

“Your mother is worried. When she’s worried, she isn’t happy. And, Nate, I hate it when she isn’t happy.”

And … there went the playful mood.

“Why do you automatically assume that I’m the reason she is worried?”

“Because she’s been like this since she found out you’ve been working yourself to the ground here, showing up before the sun, and then staying at that club until who knows when at night."

At the mention of *that club,* I feel my temper rise. It doesn't help that he still can't seem to mask his disapproval when it comes up. It's been a constant fight between my father and me since I bought *that club*.

"I'm fine. It's taking longer to finish the renovations, which is the only reason I'm there late. I don't know why she's worried. I'm a grown man, Dad."

He laughs, his deep booming chuckles breaking through the silence harshly. "Grown in age, maybe."

I flip him off, brushing off how annoyed I get when people assume that I'm not mature simply because I enjoy joking around. Especially since I've done nothing to substantiate that assumption. Sure, I like having fun and living the kind of life where laughter comes easy, but that doesn't mean I don't have a brain in my head.

He slaps my hand away, still laughing. "She won't ever stop worrying about you, son, and a mother knows when her kids are hurting."

Not liking how serious this little chat has turned, I can feel my hackles rising. "Well, this kid is just fine. Just stressed with getting everything finished over at *that club*," I snap.

"Nathaniel," he starts, and I take a deep breath so I don't blow up on him. One thing I've learned the hard way is no one blows up on Axel Reid without being burned in the process.

"Honestly, Dad, I'm fine. Stressed a little, but that's normal since I'm in the middle of trying to get shit finished with Dirty Dog, you know *that club,* and keep up with shit here. I promised you when I bought the place that I would stay on here so you wouldn't feel the weight of my absence. I'm allowed to feel stretched a little thin."

"You wouldn't feel that way if you wouldn't have bought that place."

"With all due respect, I'm trying really hard to remember you're my parent and that you're coming from a good place. I'm old enough to know what I want with my life. Too old to sit on my ass and not go after what I want, and what I want doesn't involve me sitting in this room for the rest of my life."

He's silent, his green eyes bright, while he processes his words.

Finally, he lets out a long breath. "I'm sorry, Nate. It's just hard for me not to be concerned that you're throwing away a fuck load of money on that place. Club Carnal's been closed for a long time and that place needed a lot more work than what it's worth. I just hate to think that you're setting yourself up for failure."

"Well, shit. Once again, thanks for the vote of confidence."

"I don't mean it like that, Nate. I'm just worried. You've been so closemouthed about this whole club thing. This is new for us, and we're allowed to be concerned. Your sister always had a clear path, no guessing games, so we're just trying to figure it out with you."

"Did you think that maybe that's because I've been looking forward to showing it off a little? Fuck! This is getting so old; the constant assumption that I'm going to fuck it all up because I'm not as driven as Dani."

"That's not what I mean, and you know it."

I do, which sucks, but I can't help but get pissed that we always seem to have this fight. "I'm sorry. What can I tell you so that you can stop worrying that I'm going to go off the deep end and end up homeless?"

"Don't be a smartass."

Throwing my hands up, I lean back in my chair and scowl at him, measuring my words so that maybe, hopefully, he will get it. "How's this," I start. "I've saved up enough money to buy the old club outright as well as the two units that were on either side. I've been able to get all of the renovations finished on the budget that I set, without having to get a loan, and I did that by being hands-on and doing most of the work myself. My business plan is solid. Regardless of the fact that I didn't actually finish school to get my degree, I did remember the shit I learned. I've already hired a complete staff as well as worked out a plan to ensure that if I don't start turning an immediate profit, I'll be fine. I have entertainment booked so far in advance I could sit on my ass and drink at the bar instead of actually work once I open. All permits and licenses are in my possession and the interest for opening night was so heavy that I've had to sell tickets, and those sold out in four minutes and sixteen seconds. You think that's enough to stop worrying about me? I'm already in the black on Dirty Dog and the doors aren't even open."

I know I've shocked him because, by the time I finish talking, his mouth is wide open. Yeah, guess there wasn't too much faith in his little boy, after all.

"You're in the black?"

Taking another calming breath, I relax in my seat. "I've saved every dime I've ever gotten or made for almost twenty-eight years. Aside from buying my truck and the house, I haven't touched a dime. Further, when my trust was released, I didn't touch that either. Instead, I invested all of that and it grew. It grew a lot. Everything I've ever had or made has been building for this, Dad. Just because I didn't talk about my future dreams like Dani didn't mean I didn't have them."

He doesn't speak, but I can see the pride in his eyes. As good as it is to finally see, it's annoying that I had to prove myself in order to have it.

"I'm not sure what to say, son."

"How about start with I'm sorry and end with how you're going to let Mom know she can stop losing sleep."

"Smartass." He laughs, easing some of the tension in the room. "I'm sorry, Nate. I worry about you just as your mom does, and that's never going to change. We don't compare you to your sister, but it's hard for us not to have concerns when you two are traveling on completely different roads."

"One of these days, you're going to realize that I like being on my own road."

He laughs again. "You always have, son, always have."

Chapter 3

Nate

After my talk with my dad, I finished what I needed to on the case I was working there. It's a simple, well … not-so-simple hack and monitor of a large corporation out of Atlanta that suspects one of their chief financial operators to be laundering money. Tedious but easy, since the owner had given me full access to their secure network, camera systems, as well as the cameras in the CFO's penthouse paid for by the company. It's taken me spending two months deep in cyberspace, but I've finally uncovered almost all of the fucker's dirty secrets.

Maddox hadn't come in by the time I finished up, and I needed to get over to Dirty Dog, so I saved my shit and left. I avoided stopping by my dad's office. Instead, I pulled out my phone to call Shane—my soon-to-be club manager—in order to be too busy to talk to anyone I passed.

"Headed to Dirty, want to meet me there?" I ask when he picks up.

"Already there." And he disconnects.

I laugh to myself and toss my phone over on the passenger seat of my truck before pulling myself in.

Shane's been a damn good friend since we met during my short attendance at the University of Georgia. I say short because I was more interested in partying than I was going to class. How we met was unconventional, at best, but he's been around for almost a decade and proven his loyalty to me more than once.

By the time I make the half-hour drive to what used to be Club Carnal, I'm about to come out of my skin with excitement about today. When I told my dad I had enough entertainment booked, I wasn't kidding, but a large part of that is because about seventy-five percent of that entertainment is in-house.

Dirty Dog is, in a sense, my play on Coyote Ugly. Only, because I know where the money is from experience, we won't have smoking hot chicks dancing on the bar. We've split the old club into two sections, which is the main reason I bought both surrounding units and knocked down some walls.

The entrance is on the side now, going into the first building on the side of the old club. When you walk in, there is now a large 'holding area.' Our hope is that we're so popular that there will always be a line, but by creating the holding area, no one will ever have to stand in the elements. It was a bitch getting that set up with fire codes and all, but we eventually decided that unit would stay intact with just a single black door added inside to lead to Dirty Dog. Our way of saying fuck you to building code and the fire marshal's rules; even if we're the most popular club in the southeast, the holding area will never fuck with the club's max out capacity since it's a large area in its own right.

Once through the door separating the two, you hit the sanctuary. In the center of the room is a large square bar with a thick wooden finish built to withhold the heavy bodies spotlighted throughout the night.

When I first decided to play off Coyote Ugly, Shane was the first to jump on board. All I told him was that we would have dudes dancing and not chicks. That was enough for him. When I told Cohen about it, his first assumption was that Shane was gay, but he couldn't be further from the truth.

It's simple really. Girls flock to clubs. Girls love seeing men who know how to work their bodies. When the girls get one look at the talent at Dirty, it won't be long until they're going to be rushing us. Any man with a brain would be able to look past anything when you basically guarantee massive amounts of horny women. Which, if everything goes as planned, will be the reason that we don't just succeed in having a successful club but we fly through the top of all the popular ones around.

I shouldn't have been shocked with Cohen's concerns about Dirty. Unlike my dad, he didn't voice them because he doubted me; he just couldn't see the big picture like I could. To him, he thought we would turn into a gay club with little success because we aren't exactly a town with a need for one. I wasn't going to let him know the reason why I was so sure we had this.

The idea for this place came to me back in college when it became crystal clear that sex, men dancing, and booze were all you needed to build an empire on a party life. No one knows about the six months I worked at a strip club out of pure boredom and a sex drive that was borderline sex addiction levels bad. Pussy just fell in my lap when I danced at the club in Athens.

Since Shane had spent the last five years stripping, continuing well after I left town, he knew more than anyone the untapped market I was about to break into. Women loved men. Plain and simple. They went stupid over half-naked ones, and when you threw in some carefully placed hip thrusts, well … you might as well be a fucking god.

And that's where Dirty Dog turned from just a small, fleeting dream to what is already turning out to be the next best thing to hit the South.

I pull up behind the bar and park next to Shane's BMW. The smile on my face grows as I walk from my truck and through the back of the building. I really should stop calling it a bar because this place is a monster too big for such a small word. We're so much more than just a bar. We're a nightclub formed with the bar atmosphere in mind. I guess the reason I always fall back on calling it 'the bar' is because each of the five bars that fill up the vast space work to form the whole basis to our appeal.

The old converted warehouse used to be on its last leg, but almost a year after buying it, the transformation is like night and day. The hallway that the back door feeds into leads to our storage units, coolers, and locker rooms for staff, as well as the large break room for some downtime between shifts. I even went as far as to add a gym so that the guys wouldn't have to keep paying for memberships elsewhere. After all, our bodies are the main attraction here.

The center of the main room for Dirty holds the central and biggest bar. Each side of the building has two smaller, but no less impressive, ones with a huge open area between all of them for dancing. One back corner holds the DJ booth, stage, and electrical area for all the music. Then you have the second-level VIP area that runs the whole length above the holding area. Two staircases lead to that level with ten separate VIP areas.

My office takes up the other side building, running half the length, and the other half houses the gym. The only thing you can see from where I'm standing in the main room is a wall of black windows that runs from each side flanked by stairs like on the VIP end. Under that area, we have one more bar in the center surrounded by multiple booths and such.

After taking in all that is Dirty Dog, I walk farther into the main room to find Shane talking to six of the bartenders I had hired. I give a nod to Travis and Garrett, the Hanks brothers who used to dance with Shane. Brent, Logan, and Matt are standing behind them, and I get the same greeting back from them.

Denton, the sixth to round out our main bartenders, is already on top of the bar with his shirt off, showing them what he wants them to do. He's taken on the role of resident dance coordinator, a job both Shane and myself were happy to pass on to him.

We lucked out picking up Denton. Not only does he have the look that will guarantee him being a crowd favorite with his background in modeling, but he also recently tried out for the show *So You Think You Can Dance*. He didn't make it to the very end, but he got far enough to be our own little celebrity here at Dirty.

"You plan on just standing there, Dent? Or are you going to show us how it's done?" I deadpan, only to laugh when he flips me off.

"Have you decided how you want the first showcase to go?" Shane asks when I drop down onto one of the barstools he had pulled over from one of the tables scattered around the room. I look the few feet that separate us from where Denton is now standing with his hands on his hips.

"Fuck yeah, I did," I say with a smile. Just thinking about the ingenious idea I had around not only the first spotlight, but also what will be the signature drink. "How do you feel about lollipops, gentlemen?" I ask.

"What the hell are you talking about, Nate?" Denton calls down before bending at the waist and sitting on the edge of the wooden bar top.

"Lollipops, how do you like them?" I ask, again.

Seven sets of eyes just blink at me, clearly not following my train of thought. Nothing new there.

"Fine." I sigh with fake exasperation. "How about I show you what I'm talking about?"

"Might be a good idea since you lost us when you started talking about candy," Shane jokes, earning a laugh from the others.

"Where is everyone else?" I ask, getting up and walking across the large open space toward the platform in the corner where the DJ booth and sound system are set up.

"All the girls are in the holding room finishing up their uniform fittings with Hilary. She was finishing up the last as I went in there, though, so you should be good."

I give Shane a nod while looking through the extensive list of songs we have on our playlist software—another program I created. Finding the song I need, I set the timer before turning up the volume, making sure to engage all the speakers and subwoofers before making my way behind the main bar.

"Do me a favor, Trav, and go get the girls. Get off my bar, Dent."

I look up and see Shane's mouth form a smile knowing where I'm going with this. None of these guys, besides him, have ever seen me dance. I don't give a shit how big of a dancer Denton is, either. He's about to learn just how to make a girl melt in seconds.

Making sure I have what I need: coconut rum, clear apple juice, and one of the thousands of cotton candy flavor lollipops I ordered in bulk, it takes me no time to get the drink measured out, sugar around the rim, and the lollipop wrapper off. I check my watch to see how much time I have left before the song will start then drop the candy into the glass so just the stick is popping out and push it forward.

The girls start walking in just as I rest my hands on the bar top. A few of them are new faces that I haven't gotten to know as well as the others. I look over and let my gaze hit all twenty faces of our floor girls, stopping when I see the one that will work for what I need.

"Come here, Julie," I demand. One blond brow goes up, but she doesn't miss a beat, and just when she steps up to the bar, the first notes of Framing Henley's "Lollipop" blasts through the room. Some of the girls jump but not Julie. She takes the glass sitting on the bar, then pulls out the lollipop and lifts it to her red stained lips.

The second she finishes the last drop and places the lollipop into her mouth, I use both hands still resting on the bar to push my body up and leap onto the sleek wooden surface.

Then I get the reaction I want.

I have only a second to appreciate the way the uniform of choice—black shorts that might as well be a pair of those sexy boy short underwear chicks wear and a black corset—fits her body before looking around her to make sure I have everyone else's attention.

My eyes settle back on Julie just in time to see her own widen as she steps back slightly, wobbling on her tall-as-fuck blood-red heels, another Dirty Dog requirement.

I grab the bar that hangs down from the ceiling above the bar, parallel with each length of wood and pull myself up, using one of the rotating hooks to spin myself in a quick but powerful circle before slamming my feet back down on the wood.

She stands there as I lean down and take the stick from her red lips. Holding the stem to my crotch, I pull her from behind the neck until her lips are touching the wet candy. She gasps when I run the wet candy over her open mouth by thrusting and rolling my hips before I release her head and stick the lollipop back in her mouth. I give her a wink before I finish moving on top of the bar. Continuing to move my body with the heavy thumps of the music, I run my hands up my tee shirt, starting at the hem, and pull the fabric up until it's over my head and tossed to the floor at her feet.

I don't put my all into the dance, but regardless, before the song is over, there's no question in anyone's mind that had there been a woman up there with me, I would have been fucking her right there on the bar.

"Wow," she pants when the song ends and silence once again fills the room around our group.

"Thanks, ladies. What do you think of our spotlight dance and the new signature drink here at Dirty Dog?" I ask the room before jumping off the bar and letting my heart rate settle back to normal. They all give different variations of the same nod and breathy praise.

Just what I was hoping for.

"Well, I guess that's one way of doing it." Denton laughs.

"Someone's been practicing," Shane grunts, slapping me on my sweaty shoulder. "And here I thought you would have lost some of those moves over the years."

"Do you see this," I ask him while gesturing down my body. "No need to practice when you're working with perfection."

He rolls his eyes. I open my mouth to say something to the guys but stop when Julie walks into my space.

Rolling onto her toes so that she can get closer to my ear, she says, "Call me later?" She drops back down so that her heels are back against the concrete floor before giving me a devious smile. I should have known it was a mistake to bring her on; we hooked up once, a long fucking time ago, but now that she's working for me, it won't happen again.

I don't respond. Instead, I pick up my shirt and pull it back over my head.

"Opening night is Friday," I tell the room, instantly feeling the energy go from aroused to electric with excitement. "Has everyone got their schedules for the next month?"

"Went over those before they had their fitting with Hilary. We're set, no issues, and we've already gone over the girls' responsibilities for working the floor." Shane grabs a clipboard from behind the bar. "We've got these three ugly bastards working opening night and the next three nights after." He points at Travis, Garrett, and Denton before looking back at his paperwork. "After that, it's a rotation between them. Some nights all six, though, especially weekends, working the main bar. Then we have the other guys working the three other bars, but they won't be in until tomorrow."

I nod. I know without adding that he's made a note to have Denton fill them in on "Lollipop" before looking over to where the girls are standing. "You ladies ready for opening night?" They all smile and nod. "Things might be a little intense, but you're all aware of where the bouncers are stationed and there won't be a second when you girls aren't covered. But if you don't feel safe, find one of them or us and let it be known."

"And let's not forget that we're expecting close to five hundred bodies opening night. That's just ticket holders, so I'm sure we're going to have our share in the holding room. For those who aren't assigned the VIP area, don't forget to make the rounds out there, too. None of the VIP assigned girls should be handling anything but the people in your area up there. Everyone else remember—just because they're not in the hot zone and stuck out in the holding room doesn't mean they shouldn't have fun. Plus, allowing them to drink in there means they're going to be ready to party once they get in the door. They're carded before they even get that far, so no worries there." Shane looks over at me when he's done talking and we both get the same giddy-as-fuck smile on our faces.

"Most importantly, have fucking fun and remember we're the best of the fucking best," I boom. Everyone laughs, and with the excitement of opening night giving us all one hell of a high, I walk around the bar and start making enough of my go-to drinks for everyone. "Grab yourself a drink and let's toast to Dirty Dog!"

Chapter 4

Ember

"Family dinner," I hear my sister bark through my phone, and I pull it away from my ear with her sharp tone. Bam, my five-year-old English mastiff, looks up from his bed in the corner but loses interest quickly. With a huff, he drops his big head back down. "That means the whole damn family, Em. What part of that is confusing to you? You've skipped the last eight! Eight months you haven't been there and don't think that hasn't gone unnoticed."

Dropping my brush into the water next to my canvas, I walk over to the couch in the corner and look out the window of my back room. When I moved out on my own, this room sold me on the small house. Huge picture windows cover every inch of the back wall, giving me a breathtaking view of the woods that surround my property. I've been here a year now, and I still get chills when I'm in my painting room.

"I'm busy," I tell her, which isn't a lie, just not the full truth. "And it wasn't eight. I came a few months back." Six actually, but who's counting.

"You're *always* busy. I know for a fact that you finished up the last piece you had to do for your exhibition next month, so don't give me that busy shit."

I sigh. "Just because I finished all of that doesn't mean I don't have other pieces that need my attention."

Maddi's humorless laugh comes through the line. "You could knock out any of your beautiful paintings in no time. What is going on with you? You've been like this for a while now."

I watch a bird fly around one of my birdfeeders before leaning back on the couch. "I'm just busy, Maddi." Bam's head settles on my leg, and I move my hand to scratch him behind his ears like he loves.

"Dad said if you aren't there, he's going to come toss you over his shoulder and force your ass to—and I quote—make time for your goddamn family."

"No doubt he will too." I laugh.

"Don't you know it," she responds, her tone less heated than just moments before.

"I'll be there, okay?"

"Perfect. Don't forget we have plans this weekend too!"

My brow furrows, and I try to remember what plans we could possibly have.

"What plans?"

"I swear, Emberlyn Locke! You're the only girl I know who couldn't care less that her twenty-first birthday is coming up. We have plans! All the girls. Even Dani's in. Her parents are watching the boys, and you had better believe she's ready to turn it up now that Evan's finally off the tit."

"You're so crass," I interrupt.

"No, I'm not. She's the one who said it. The second he hit six months and tried to take off her nip with his tooth, she was done. Off the tit, she said. Time to party, she threatened. So Cohen is all-in for a girls' night out getting his wife drunk off her ass because he says he will reap the benefits when she gets home."

"That should be interesting," I comment, not really listening to her.

"You bet your ass. She hasn't had a lick to drink since right after the honeymoon when she found out he knocked her up again. She might just be all the entertainment of the evening we need."

"Who else is coming? And what are we doing?" I ask, picking at some of the dog hair and lint on my leggings.

"Everyone," she responds but doesn't elaborate and doesn't answer my other question. That could mean so many things, but since I sadly don't have many friends outside of Nikki and the close-knit group of kids that make up our 'family,' I figure everyone isn't that big of a bunch. I know it's pointless to try to get my stubborn sister to spill the beans when she clearly doesn't want me to know the plans, so I just let it go.

"Sounds like a blast." I dryly sigh.

"Yup. I also heard from Dani that Nate's new club is opening this weekend. I can't wait to check it out! He hasn't said much, but just by the hype he's gaining on social media alone, it's supposed to be a club like no other."

At the mention of Nate, my throat closes and I forget about the lint picking.

Of course, she doesn't understand that Nate is the main reason I've been skipping our monthly family dinners at the Reid house, a tradition started before I was even born. No one knows that he's the reason I've backed away and now spend so much time focusing on my paintings that I eat, sleep, and breathe brushstrokes.

And humiliatingly enough, not even Nate seems to know what he did to cause me to pull back.

"We aren't going there? Right?" I ask.

"I'm not telling you what we have planned. Plus, I heard it's sold out, tickets only, for opening weekend. Oh! I already talked to Nikki, and she's also in. I think that *friend* of yours is coming too since Seth is going."

I don't even waste my breath to respond. My sister had made no bones about letting me know she didn't approve of the man I've been seeing for the last two months. She loves Nikki, even gets along with her boyfriend, Seth, but Levi … no, she hated him on the spot. It's been a constant bone of contention between us. She does nothing to hide the fact that she doesn't like him—even to his face—while I'm helplessly stuck trying to keep the both of them happy.

Of course, Levi only gets frustrated when Maddi starts her crap, so it's made me pull back from her more to keep him happy; another thing that hasn't escaped her notice.

Just another reason I've felt like breaking things off with Levi is the best move. I hate that I've even let him come between my sister and me.

"No worries about Levi; he's working this weekend. Please drop it, Maddi. I don't have the patience to deal with it right now. I'll be there tonight, okay? We can talk more about this stupid birthday celebration then."

We make small talk for a minute before I drop the phone on the couch next to me and look back over at the portrait I had been working on. One of the many I have of the very man who's caused me more pain than I thought possible. No matter how many times it happens, I'm still shocked when I see a picture-perfect likeness of Nate Reid filling a once-blank canvas. What's sad is I don't even realize I'm doing it. I just zone out and hours later … there he is.

Leaving everything where it is and ignoring the huge canvas of Nate, I walk from the back room and through the house so I can start getting ready for tonight. Bam's nails click on the hardwood behind me as he follows. It's been childish for me to skip these monthly dinners, I know that, but that doesn't matter. The hurt he caused me years ago holds nothing on the pain he inflicted more recently. He was right that night I professed my true feelings for him when he said he would ruin me, but stupidly, I was too naïve to believe him then.

Pushing back the same hurt that ruin caused, I do what I have been doing for the last year and pretend it never happened.

When I pull up to the Reid's house later that night, I curse myself for procrastinating leaving my house for so long. I spend so much time lost in my head that I'm almost always late, but since Maddi made such a big deal about me showing up tonight, I can only imagine that they've assumed I wasn't coming again.

I park my car behind the many others that line their driveway and groan when I see my dad leaning against his truck. True to Maddi's word, it looks like he was prepared to follow through with his threat.

Turning off the ignition, I fiddle with my phone and shoot Nikki a quick text to let her know I'm at a family dinner and I'll call her later. We've made a habit recently by turning Wednesdays into our wine night, so if I don't let her know I'm not home, she's going to freak out.

I'm always home, so it would be about as abnormal as it gets for me.

The second I reach the handle to open my door, it's swung open and I let out a startled scream. My phone clatters to the driveway with a sickening sound that has me saying a prayer I didn't just crack the screen.

"Cutting it close," my dad says, bending over to pick up my phone and handing it over before stepping back so I can get out.

"Sorry," I say with a shrug and lean up to give him a hug. He bends, meeting me halfway, and I instantly feel settled when he wraps his arms around me. Just like coming home. "I lost track of time. You know how it goes when I'm working."

He leans back, giving me a kiss on my temple, and I get one of the rare smiles that he reserves just for 'his girls.' Eyes so like my own crinkle at the corners, and he just shakes his head.

"I'm here?" I continue, hoping to get off the hook from what I'm sure would end up being the third degree of questioning if he had his way.

"Yeah, sweetheart, you are. I've missed you," he says, and I instantly feel guilty for not being around. It's not his fault this is the last place I want to be.

"I missed you too, Dad."

He turns, favoring his bad leg, and I frown. He just shakes his head. "Don't even start, Emberlyn. Your mom's already been on my ass for overdoing it this weekend."

"Then maybe you should start listening to her before your ass is on the ground."

"Sass," he warns. "Just like your mom. Just like your sister. I'm surrounded by fucking sass."

"Whatever." I laugh, wrapping my arm around his waist as he pulls me to his side with one arm over my shoulders. "What did you do this time?"

"And still she sasses me."

I look over and up, way up, and stick my tongue out at him. His soft laughter vibrates against me, and I smile at him.

God, I love my dad.

"Went head to head with Asher at Crossfit the other day. Little shit still can't handle the fact that I can kick his ass with one leg."

"I swear you two act like kids sometimes," I joke.

We walk the rest of the way together, and I selfishly soak up the comfort his nearness brings me before we walk into the madness of family dinner night. As usual, the Reid's house is full to bursting and the echoes of two dozen or so voices carry from the back deck. When we round the corner to where their back family room is, I stop short at the sight in front of me.

"I think the little fucker has some cross-dressing tendencies if you ask me," I hear and take my eyes off the scene in front of me to look over and meet Cohen's laughing eyes.

"I'm starting to agree," my dad jokes, releasing me and walking through the open patio door that leads to where the rest of our huge family is.

"Molly!" I look up when Megan walks in from the porch and give her a smile.

"Yes, Mommy," Molly sings from her spot in the middle of the living room.

"Would you leave Nate alone and come on out?"

"I can't. He isn't a princess yet," she continues with her singsong voice, the smile in her tone matching the huge toothless one on her face.

"Yeah, definitely has some cross-dressing tendencies," Cohen repeats, taking a huge pull from his beer. "Hey, Em," he says and walks over from the kitchen island to give me a hug.

"Hey," I softly respond, looking back at Nate.

"The girls are asking about you. They're down at the dock acting like little schoolgirls. All you hear is giggles coming every few minutes. They've been like that for the last half hour, ever since Dani got out of time-out."

"Time-out?" I laugh, my eyes moving back to Nate again.

He looks up after Molly stops brushing the god-awful electric blue shadow on his lids and gives me a smile. My stupid body starts to burn with just that little bit of attention from him, and I hate myself for it. Why can't I get over him? Even now, when he is as far from appealing as it gets, I crave him.

His shoulder-length hair is pulled in every direction with little butterfly clips of every color of the rainbow. Aside from the eye shadow, he has bright pink lipstick on, what I'm assuming is blush making huge circles on his cheeks, and as if that wasn't enough, he has a bright pink tutu on.

And still, he's the most beautiful man I've ever laid eyes on.

If anything, the horrendous makeup just accentuates the hard chiseled lines of his face. He looks just like Cohen said, like a cross-dresser, only a cross-dressing Adonis.

"She needs to learn to listen. She tried to tell my Molly-Wolly that blue wasn't my color, so she had to go to time-out until she thought about her actions. Right, Molly-Wolly?" Nate answers my question with a smile.

I ignore his smile and turn my back to him, just as I've done every time I've seen him over the past year. I can feel his eyes on me as I make my way out back. Maybe a year ago, I would have laughed with him and asked him why he continues to put the women in his life in time-out, but not now.

Cohen continues down the steps when I pause at the railing and look around at everyone spread out over the large backyard. Megan is walking away from her husband, smile on her face, and heading down toward the dock. Lee, her husband, is standing with Cohen's brothers, Cam and Colt, following his wife's retreating back. That is until Cohen steps up and gives him a good-natured shove. Zac, Jaxon, and their dad, Asher, are tossing the football around with Beck and Greg. Axel and my dad are standing around the grill while Izzy, Dee, and Chelcie move around the huge farm table that takes up one side of their outdoor dining area.

Spotting my mom with Melissa, Sway, and his partner, Davey, I make my way to where they're playing with Dani's boys. I stop to give my mom a hug, saying hello to everyone else I pass as I make my way down to the dock.

Just as Cohen said, all the girls are there. All six of them indeed giggling in their little makeshift huddle. My sister looks up when my feet hit the wooden planks and gives me what I couldn't mistake as anything but a relieved smile.

Being the baby of the girl side of our group—hell, the baby of the whole group—I don't spend as much time with them as she does, but it doesn't mean our bond isn't strong. All of our parents have been friends for so long that even though I only share blood with one of them, we are very much a family.

Dani breaks away and gives me a hug before pulling me forward. Megan smiles and gives me a hug as I walk by, and then Stella, Lyn, and Lila are next before my sister gives me one of her bear hugs that I swear cracks a rib every time.

"About time you got here!" she yells after backing away.

"Don't start. Dad was in the driveway when I pulled up."

She laughs, and the others follow suit. "I told you. Over the shoulder threats are never made lightly by him."

"Yeah, yeah … what did I miss?"

"Oh, nothing," she says sweetly, a little too sweetly.

"We're planning Saturday night," Dani says, earning a scowl from my sister.

"And that would be the party I didn't ask for?"

She nods, and I see the others' smiles grow. Shit … this can't be good.

"Would anyone care to fill me in?"

Each of them barks out a 'no' at the same time, and I narrow my eyes. No one moves to speak, but Stella starts laughing so hard that I worry she might fall into the lake.

"I'm not sure I like the way this is going right now," I admit, feeling even more uneasy about the weekend plans I don't want.

"Well, you don't even need to worry about a thing. We've got it covered from your makeup and hair, all the way down to what underwear you're wearing under the dress we've already bought. All you have to do is show up at Dani's house to get ready around dinnertime Saturday."

I narrow my eyes at my sister, but before I can speak, Axel bellows out that it's time to eat. "This conversation isn't done," I threaten, but they all wave me off as they start to walk up to where the food is being set out on one of the custom-made buffet-style bars that line the Reid's outdoor kitchen of sorts.

I do my best to ignore the huge six-foot-four man wearing a tutu as I fix my plate and wedge myself between Cam and Colt at the large table. I swear this thing is big enough to fit a whole football team, but even with all that space, I feel like nowhere is far enough away with Nate here.

My eyes never leave my plate, but I see him sit down across from me next to his sister and Cohen. I can see him out of the corner of my eye bend down to kiss his nephew, Owen, before looking back in my direction.

Conversation flows easily when we're all together. Typical catching up on what everyone has been doing. When Melissa, Greg's wife and Cohen's mom, asks about my art exhibition coming up, I finally look up.

"It's already looking to be pretty big. From what the owner of the gallery has said, there are already whispers of a few pieces that she anticipates will sell quickly."

"That's wonderful, Ember!" she praises. "You know we're all going to be there."

"Hell yeah, we are," my sister yells from the other end of the long table.

"Maddisyn Locke," I hear my mom scold. "Children at the table."

I watch Maddi raise one perfect brow at her, and I know she's about to throw some of what my dad calls sass. "Need I point out that these children have heard much worse from every person in attendance, especially all you elders?"

I hear a grumbled 'sass' from the end my father is sitting at, and my mother just laughs.

"Nate, how are things going at the club?" Asher's wife, Chelcie, asks.

I look back at my plate but listen for his answer. Truth be told, I've been curious about this new project of his. But not enough to ask anyone openly about it. I've followed the news on social media, which it seems like you see something everywhere. Every local radio station is plugging the opening of Dirty Dog, but no one knows much besides it being billed as the biggest thing to happen to the Atlanta area club scene in decades. All everyone sees are the pictures of the old Club Carnal, what used to be a popular club years and years ago, transformed into a huge and breathtaking mix of class and rustic flair. Everything on the outside has been pictured everywhere. The huge warehouse covered in brick is now painted black with steel accents. When the Dirty Dog logo went up, in all its bright red glory, it popped so brightly it demanded attention.

"Sold out every weekend for the next three months. We didn't do tickets for the weekday nights, but I'm pretty confident that it will be crowded. Or hopeful, at least."

"Well, isn't that lovely," she says, looking over at where Nate's mom, Izzy, is sitting across from her. I don't miss the look that passes between them, but it shocks me to see the worry on his mother's face.

Worry? Anyone with eyes and ears can see the hype surrounding his grand opening is going to carry for a damn long time. If I let myself, I would feel so much pride for him.

"Yeah, I guess."

"You going to dress up like a fairy on opening night too, little princess?" His sister laughs at him but snaps her mouth shut when he turns slowly to face her.

Cohen, not ever one to miss anything, takes his son from Dani's arms just as Nate stands from the table. He bends his tutu-covered waist and pulls his sister from the table before tossing her over his shoulder.

"You big jerk! Let me down, Nate! Daddy, tell Nate to leave me alone!"

"Nate, leave your sister alone." He complies, stuffing another piece of steak in his mouth and not even looking in their direction.

Dani continues to smack his back and kick her feet, but he just walks over to the back corner of the covered dining area and drops her to her feet. He silently spins her so that she's facing the corner and points at the stone covered wall in front of her.

"Two-minute time-out for insulting the princess," he tells her, then silently walks back the way he just came. He stops to give Molly's beaming face a kiss on the cheek before taking his seat and picking up his fork.

"Maybe we'll check it out," I hear his father say, continuing like nothing happened as his daughter stomps back to the table, shocking me enough that my eyes automatically shoot from Nate's face to his before looking back at Nate.

He looks ridiculous, but he puts his fork back down and turns to look at his dad, the makeup on his face making him look anything but serious. "Afraid you're going to be out of luck there, old man. Unless you get lucky and find a scalper out front, we're sold out."

"Nathaniel." His mom gasps on a laugh. "Not even for your parents?"

I watch him shake his head at her before looking over and meeting my eyes, holding them captive with the intensity brewing in his emerald gaze. With my heart in my throat, I look down at my plate and busy myself with moving some food around while listening intently to his words.

"I'm not sure it's your scene, Ma. Definitely not something for the faint of heart, and to be honest, I'm not really sure I want my parents to see me in action."

"In action?" I hear someone ask from the end of the table.

"Ha!" Cohen burst out laughing. "Trust me on this, Izzy, the last thing you want to do is see your boy here in action."

"You make it sound like he's running a brothel," someone else jokes making Cohen laugh even harder.

What in the world?

"Well, I'm going, and you can't stop me. Even if I have to buy a ticket because my own son won't let me in."

"We've got ten!" I hear my sister yell, making Cohen laugh even harder.

"Ten? What the hell," Nate calls her way.

"Oh yeah, we've got *bigggg* plans this weekend, don't we, girls?"

Shit, kill me now. They're taking me to Nate's place? No … no way.

"Would you stop laughing," Dani tells her husband, only causing him to start a new wave of hilarity.

"Uh … big plans for what?" Nate continues, ignoring his sister and brother-in-law.

"It's Ember's big twenty-first. What better way to celebrate than doing it Dirty style, right Nate-*Dog*?"

At that point, Cohen is laughing so hard I fear he might break something. The only thing I can do at this point is to pray this is all a joke, but when I look up and meet Nate's eyes again, I know if it is, then the joke's on me.

His lips are tipped up in what can only be described as a shit-eating grin sinful enough to melt panties, pink lips and all. I don't even try to figure out what he's thinking because all I can focus on is trying not to throw up.

Chapter 5

Nate

Ember's tan skin has held a blush on her cheeks for the last two hours. Dinner continued as normal after the announcement of the big plans for her birthday, but other than that moment when she looked at me in shock, she hasn't given me those eyes once more. I've tried because I can't understand for the life of me why there was pain dancing in them when she found out she would be spending her birthday at my club.

How have things gotten so strained between us?

Sure, we had a moment when things were awkward years ago, but we had settled into our friendship easy enough after some time passed. Things were never the same— fuck, far from it—after she admitted her feelings toward me. Feelings I had been fighting for her for a damn long time surfaced and obviously haven't gone away, but they have never put this kind of tension on our friendship.

It's been bothering me for months, but I still can't figure out what I fucking did to make her look at me like she wishes she had a knife to stab into my back. Hell, up until Dani and Cohen got married a year and a half ago, things had been fine. Then she started skipping out anytime everyone was together. When she did show, she avoided me like I had the plague. I can't even remember the last time we had a conversation, let alone a time that I was on the receiving end of a genuine smile from her.

Plates pushed aside, everyone continues to talk and catch up. I look back across the table as Evan pulls on my hair, ignoring the pain in my scalp as he tries to pull my hair from my head, and kick my leg out in her direction. She jumps but doesn't move her attention from Cohen's brother, Cam. She listens to whatever the fuck he's carrying on about and ignores me as usual.

Fuck this shit.

"Ember, mind giving me a hand getting this shit off my face?" I ask, knowing she has too good of manners to ignore me when I've spoken directly to her. Especially as I did it loudly enough that those around us look over and laugh at what Molly did to me earlier.

I watch her take a deep breath before looking away from Cam and fucking finally giving me those eyes.

"I'm pretty sure you can handle it," she says softly, and once again, I see that pain just below the surface.

"Might be so, still asking for your help."

One way or another, I'm getting to the bottom of this shit. I finally have everything in my life going on the right track, full speed ahead, and I want my little firecracker along for the ride with me.

Her lips thin for just a second before she catches herself. Right when she's about to open her mouth, I assume to give me another line of bullshit, my mom interrupts her. "You can use my bathroom, honey. Ember, the makeup remover is in the second drawer on the left."

I raise one of my eyebrows at Ember, daring her to fucking say no now. Panic briefly crosses her face, so fleeting I question if that's what I saw, before she stands from the table and starts to walk up the deck stairs and into the house. Not even saying a word.

"Come here, little prince," my sister coos and takes her youngest from my arms. "Be nice," she whispers at me when I move to stand. I look at her with confusion, but she just gives me a sad smile.

What in the fucking hell? I swear all the women in my life are insane.

I unsnap the tutu I had made for myself when Molly told me she wished I had one just like hers as I walk up the deck stairs, dropping it on the couch when I enter the house. The silence around me is so thick I want to knock something off the wall just to ease the trepidation it's creating. Shaking off the ridiculous feelings, I walk through the house, up the stairs, and into my parents' bedroom at the end of the hall. I find Ember in their bathroom pulling out some girly shit, and I stop in the doorway to wait for her to acknowledge that I'm there.

"How long are you planning to stand there?" she asks a minute later, not looking away from what she's doing.

"Depends. How long are you planning to ignore me, babe?" I shoot back, my confusion growing when her shoulders pull tight.

"Don't call me that," she seethes, only pausing briefly in her task.

"What the fuck, Em?"

"Just don't. Do not call me babe. I'm not your fucking *babe*," she says with so much hate in that one word I'm struck dumb.

"Right," I stutter, finding my feet and walking into the room. Maybe it's her lady time? I sit on the chair in front of my mom's vanity and look up at her. Her eyes are pinched tight and her chest is moving rapidly with her rushed breaths. "It's just a word, Em. I didn't realize it was offensive."

Her eyes snap open, and she looks down at me, the pain not even masked in the slightest.

"What's going on here?" I cluelessly question.

She picks up one of the square cotton looking things in one hand and a bottle in the other, back to ignoring me, but her face is saying enough. I search my mind trying to figure out what's happening right now, but fuck if I have a single light bulb going off.

I close my eyes out of instinct when she moves toward my face with that shit, her movements angry as she roughly wipes my face.

"Keep your head still," she snaps.

"Kind of hard to do that when you're dead set on removing a layer of skin, babe."

She stops instantly, and I curse myself.

"Do *not* call me *that*!" she screams.

I open my eyes, blinking when whatever the fuck she had been wiping on me gets in my eyes and burns. I stand quickly, knocking over the chair and stick my head down, turning on the water in the sink and grabbing the towel off the hook. I scrub quickly before standing and looking down at her. She hasn't moved an inch, but now, her hands are gripping the counter so hard, it's as if it's the only thing keeping her standing.

The water falling from my face is soaking my shirt, but I turn and look in the mirror to make sure I got all that damn makeup off, and frown at the clips still in my hair. I pull at them angrily, throwing them down onto the floor. When my hair is free, I pull it up in a knot on the top of my head and bring my attention back to Ember.

"Tell me what is going on, Em. What have I done?"

She's silent but turns to look at me.

"What did I do to get this kind of reaction from you?" I continue.

Still nothing.

"Fucking tell me, Emberlyn! What made you look at me with hate in those beautiful eyes? I can't stand it anymore."

She jerks back with so much force that I know there is no way she didn't feel the snap all the way down her spine.

"What did you do?" she weakly questions.

I nod. "Yeah, what did I do because, for the fucking life of me, I can't figure it out."

"What did you *do*?" she repeats, her tone getting harsh.

I don't say a damn thing. Growing up with a sister, I know when a woman is on the edge of crazy.

"You really have no fucking clue, do you?"

I shake my head, but clearly, even that was the wrong move because she again jerks but this time with her whole body.

"You're unbelievable, Nate."

The silence continues after that, more because I'm afraid if I so much as breathe, she is going to stab me with my mom's cuticle scissors.

Just when I think it's safe, her eyes narrow and she leans up. Because I have a foot plus on her, that doesn't do much, but still, I don't move. Even pissed as hell, she's still beautiful.

"What's your name, *babe*?" she oddly asks, before walking around me and slamming the bathroom door in her wake.

I look around the large bathroom, trying to figure out what just happened before looking at my reflection. "What in the fuck just happened in here?" I ask my reflection, stupidly wishing it could throw me a bone here.

I hear another door slam, and I throw the door open and move to the window in my parents' room just in time to see Ember running to her car and jumping in. It's gotten darker out, but her dome light is illuminating her, and the second I see her swipe at her eyes, I kick my own ass.

If I could just get her to talk to me, without it turning into whatever just happened in the bathroom, I could fix this. We could go back to the way things were. With my mind made up, I rush out of the room and down the stairs, taking them two at a time. I open the front door just as she turns the engine over.

"Ember!" I yell and race down the driveway.

Before I can reach her car, she's backing out so fast that her tires protest against the speed.

"Ember!" I bellow, running down the driveway trying to catch her. A feeling of pure helplessness starts to crawl up my throat when she looks over at me with tear-filled eyes before gunning the gas and taking off. "Em," I whisper, pleading with her taillights for what, I have no idea.

"Figure it out yet?" I hear behind me but don't look until the glow of her taillights is completely gone.

When I turn, Maddox is standing at the end of the driveway, arms crossed over his chest, stoic mask in place.

"Not even a little," I tell him honestly, hoping that he's going to be more of a voice of reason and not a pissed off father right now.

"You aren't a stupid man, Nathaniel, so it really shouldn't be this hard. I'll help you out because I love my little girl and her happiness means more to me than kicking your fucking ass right now, but you best believe that moment is coming and I'll be nice enough to give you time to prepare for it."

A normal man would probably shit himself right now, but I match Maddox in size, and if anything, I'm bigger than he is, so if I'm looking at a beating to come, I'm fairly sure I could hold my own. I think.

"You know I respect the hell out of you, Maddox, but I'm not sure what I've done to earn that anger from you."

"You aren't now, but you will be and I suspect that you'll come willingly when I tell you it's time for that fight."

Cryptic motherfucker.

"My little girl's had a crush on you for way too long. I didn't mind when she was younger because I knew you had too much respect for her—and me—to cross that line, even though you wanted to. However, my baby isn't a baby anymore and those feelings she has for you still run deep."

I open my mouth to say something, fuck if I know, but close it when his eyes narrow.

"Don't insult my intelligence by denying that, Nate. You might act like a little shit, but you have a good head on your shoulders. You fucked up, so what are you going to do about it?"

"Can I talk now?" I ask him after a moment of silence, my head spinning.

He doesn't speak. I watch as his jaw ticks and his eyes grow harder.

"I'm pretty sure she doesn't, um … have those kind of feelings for me," I hedge.

"I told you not to insult me."

"Right." I sigh, dropping my head and looking down at my booted feet. "Are you saying you don't have an issue with your twenty, almost twenty-one-year-old daughter crushing on a man who is almost thirty?"

"Didn't say that, did I?" he growls at me. He uncrosses his arms and steps up until he's in my face, and I brace, thinking he's changed his mind about that ass kicking. "What I said was my little girl's happiness means more to me than kicking your ass. Seeing her smile is the reason I fucking live, so when I see the reason for her smile runs hand in hand with her feelings toward you, I'm willing to put my own feelings aside, for now, to get that back on her face where it belongs."

"I respect you there, Maddox, I do, but what I'm asking you isn't about her smile."

"You want my little girl."

His response is enough to shock me stupid. The venom in his voice says enough. He knows my 'want' is a fucking lot more complicated than that. I fucking crave her.

"I'm going to ask you again because I would really like to not have any surprises here. You do understand what you're saying … right?"

Again, he doesn't talk. His eyes don't even blink as he continues to level me with those black orbs of intimidation.

"I've been in love with her since before it was legal to feel that way," I tell him honestly, voicing my feelings for her for the first time out loud.

One eye twitches, and on the opposite side of his face, I see his jaw tick.

"She hates me."

That gets him, and he steps up until we're chest to chest. "She doesn't hate you, you clueless fuck. She's hurt because you fucked up major. That's my baby girl, so I really don't like talking about this shit, but she's a woman and I'm not stupid. Remember. Think really fucking hard, Nate, and remember your sister's reception. Fix this shit and bring back that smile, but I warn you … the next time you call my daughter *babe*, you're going to know how she felt that night before she ran off and her smile died."

What. The. Fuck.

No. That's not possible.

My breath stills in my throat when his implication hits the mark. Vivid images of that night—that dream night—hit my brain, only this time I know the same thing that's kept me up night after night has also been keeping her up, but for different reasons.

And as if that wasn't enough, I know now that her very overprotective father knows I fucked his baby girl without realizing whom I had in my arms.

"Oh fuck," I grumble.

"Yeah, oh fuck is right. You fix this and me and you … we aren't done with this shit," he tells me with another intimidating look before turning and walking back into my parents' house.

Chapter 6
Ember

Placing the last brush back in its designated drawer, I look over at the sunrise landscape that I had been working on for the last two days. I study it with a critical eye and a deep exhale.

It's beautiful, stunning even, but looking at it just causes me to feel nothing but sadness when it should inflict the exact opposite.

I started with the tall maple trees lining each side of the canvas and the center focusing on the rising sun. The sun is and should be the spotlight, but for me, the grassy field that takes up the whole bottom half is. The sun's rays hitting the empty field cast an entrancing effect, as each blade appears to be glowing.

I've always had a talent at making my work look as if it was a picture rather than a painting, and this one is no different. My fingers itch to reach out and see if I could feel the light sheen of dew covering the valley between the trees.

The bright green blades look just like Nate Reid's eyes.

I know exactly why I escaped to my art after the family dinner two nights ago. Painting has always been the only thing, other than being near him, that made me feel like I was complete. An outlet that I can channel to express the feelings I never know how to separate in my jumbled thoughts. I've never been the type of girl who wants to go out every night and party.

To me, art is something I can understand when people never have been. I don't need to pretend to be someone else to get some sort of approval when I get lost in an introvert's heaven. But because of that, a loneliness I just can't shake always lingers.

I hate the knowledge that the only other time I've felt safe enough to be me outside of my painting was when things were normal between Nate and me. I never had the feeling of judgment from him. He never looked at me as if he had no clue how to deal with the shy, quiet, awkward girl.

Some people might think I'm insecure, but I'm not, even though it has taken me a while to realize that. Getting past the fear of being accepted as the weird artsy girl will probably always be with me, but I'm ready. I'm just lonesome. A little lost maybe, but I know something needs to change. I need to learn not to care what people think and live my life for me, no one else.

It doesn't take me long to tidy up my workspace now that my brushes are clean and stored in the large wooden storage chest that my dad had made for me. I'm meticulous in the order of that chest. Each paint pot, tube, and brush is stored in its labeled spot before I leave the room. When I push the last drawer closed, I run my hand across the bright teal of my name inscribed on the top of the white painted box. It's the only purposely-placed color in this whole room, aside from my canvases that is.

Of course, that chest is the only thing that's neat and tidy in this room. I deliberately decorated this room in all whites from the ceiling to the floor including every piece of furniture in here; that way, if paint spilled or transferred from me as I moved around, the room would take on a life of its own. My own little piece of living art. Little smudges on the couch, chair, and table. Splatters dance across the floor in random successions. Even a huge smear of bright red graces the center of my ceiling courtesy of a very overeager new tube of paint exploding when I tried to open a jammed top.

I can't wait until the day that this whole room is a collage of my career.

With a smile on my face, I move over to the sink and wash my hands before picking up my phone and turning it on. A few notifications start popping on the screen as the signal wakes up. I give them a quick glance, reminding myself to open the Uno with Friends app

I've been obsessed with lately so I don't lose my daily accumulative rewards.

A few messages from Levi come, letting me know what time he's picking up Nikki and Seth before coming for me, but before I can open his message to reply, another one pops up.

Nate: Call me, Ember. I've been trying to get in touch with you, but I need you to work with me. Call me, text me, just do something other than continue to ignore me. Please.

Yeah, no.

After the family dinner and a pity party I'm not proud of, I decided no more stupid thoughts of something that will never be. I should have moved on and I had done a good job of that after my graduation night … until his sister's wedding and one too many drinks.

Inhibitions and fears went out the window as old feelings and dreams started trying to mend my broken heart that night. I had been coming around the side of the house, laughing to myself about getting lost on the way back from the bathroom, when I found myself colliding with a hard body. I'm still not really sure how things progressed from there; all I knew was that my panties were on the ground and I was burning from the inside out.

Then, of course, there was the figurative bath of cold water when I realized Nate had no idea who he was pushing his hard dick inside. The next thing I knew, I was no longer in his arms as I rushed from the darkened corner blindly.

Not even wanting to think about everything that followed, I ignore his message and go to Levi's text.

Ember: Sounds good. ;) I'll be ready in an hour. See you soon!

I don't get a reply, but I didn't think I would since Levi is the worst at responding. I shoot Nikki a similar message while walking to the back door and letting an overexcited Bam in from his run in the backyard. I leave my back room to head to my bedroom and get ready for a double date night.

I look across the table at Levi and try to focus on the conversation around me. He and Seth have been going on and on about some new training program they've been on to 'bulk up.' Whatever the hell that means. Something about their muscles getting bigger … or was it sharper? More defined? I don't know.

Nikki nudges my foot under the table, taking a sip of her beer, and rolls her eyes.

"I hit the gym twice yesterday, man. My veins looked like they were going to pop through my skin by the time I finished."

"So, Levi," Nikki interrupts him and turns her attention to the man next to me. "How are things at the fire department?"

"Good," he says, giving her a small glance before looking back across the table to Seth. "So I told Allen I would be there at six in the morning tomorrow to work my legs some more. Since I'm working a double this weekend, no gym time until Monday."

Nikki gives me a shrug, not really caring that she was dismissed, and we both continue to eat.

The look of displeasure that I got from Levi when I ordered pasta almost made me regret my decision, but I've never been one to shy away from a hearty Italian dish. Just because he's a health nut doesn't mean I have to be. I should be annoyed that he tries to control what I eat, but I don't really care. I'm not going to become someone else just to make him happy, even if my knee-jerk reaction is to do just that. I'm not a skinny girl, but I'm also not big. I'm just me, soft in all the right places.

"Are you sure you can't get someone to take your shift?" I ask him before taking another big bite and smiling at him when he frowns at me. He gives me one of his devastatingly handsome grins when the noodle slurps loudly, just shaking his head at me. After two months, I might still get the looks and a few comments, but he knows I'll be the last one who starts to worry about what goes in my mouth.

"Sorry, babe," he responds, and I succeed in hiding my grimace at the pet name. "I tried to get Trenton to switch, but his little sister is getting married so it was a no go."

"I can't believe you're letting her go party on her twenty-first," Seth chimes in.

"Letting her go?" Nikki questions with a harsh tone.

"Yeah, letting, Nic. I remember how wild things got at mine. Fuck, dude, there were strippers that—"

"I probably wouldn't finish that sentence." Levi laughs.

"No, please … tell me all about the strippers, Seth," Nikki sarcastically drawls, leaning back in her seat after placing her fork down and crossing her arms over her chest.

"Seriously? What's the big deal?" Seth looks clueless as to why his girlfriend is pissed, which is sad.

"The big deal is that you probably shouldn't be talking about the strippers you had that night when your very pissed girlfriend, the same girlfriend you had three years ago during said birthday full of skank happened, is sitting next to you."

Levi and I burst out laughing at Nikki's smartass response. They continue to fight and I soak up Levi's attention as he gives me a soft, chaste kiss before returning to his meal.

Nikki pushed me toward Levi almost two months ago. I'm not sure what made me say yes, but I knew it was largely in part to the loneliness I was sick of feeling. Our first date was great. We had dinner at a local Mexican place before following that up with a movie. He left me a few hours later with my first front porch kiss experience. He was easy to be with and the relationship progressed from there.

I say relationship loosely because lately, he's been acting so weird. I think the only thing that Levi really cares about having a relationship with is his gym membership. A few other little things lately have also been making me question if being with him is the best thing for me.

Nikki and Seth continue to bicker, and I look over at Levi as my thoughts darken. He doesn't notice my attention, which is also something I've noticed a lot of lately.

He looks like such the boy next door. All-American type with the looks that could probably put him as the front cover model for J. Crew or something, but underneath is a simmering anger I've only recently been privy to. He wasn't always like this. When we first met, he was amazing, and I really had high hopes that he would be someone worth exploring a relationship with. But I'm not sure what to do with this new easily angered and controlling side of him.

"Are you excited to hit up Nate's place?" Nikki asks me, clearly done fighting with her boyfriend since she's now taking a big forkful of her own pasta with a look of pure pleasure. She doesn't notice that her question has now caused a dark cloud to settle over my side of the table.

"Who is Nate?" Levi asks her in a hard tone. His question might be directed at Nikki, but the anger is all for me.

"A friend," I tell him, ignoring him much like he's been ignoring me for most of the evening.

"What kind of friend?" His words come out sharp and forcefully.

I shrug and keep chewing. I look up when I see Nikki stop her fork's upward path to her mouth; the utensil paused halfway to her mouth as she looks at him with wide eyes, not used to seeing this side of him.

I take a fortifying breath for patience and turn so that I'm looking at him. He's so handsome, even when he's pissed. His blond hair is cut short, but long on the top. His blue eyes are narrowed, but that just makes the sharp edges of his facial features stand out more. Add the tan that I'm pretty sure he gets with the help of a tanning bed, and he really should be making my heart beat with desire.

But it doesn't.

Because it only does that for the man I can't have.

Yet another reason I can't keep dragging this on with him. It's very clear that I'm just not feeling like a girl should when she's in a relationship with one man, but still in love with another.

A cold flash of rage flickers in his eyes when I continue my silence and I shake off the chill that skirts down my spine.

What the hell was that?

"I grew up with him," I finally say, feeling the goose bumps pebble across my skin. "He's a childhood friend and nothing more," I assure him.

"Let's hope so," he says through thin lips. "How come I haven't met this friend before?" he adds.

I look back at Nikki, her fork still in the middle of its journey to her mouth; only now, half of her fettuccini is hanging off. Her eyes say it all, but then she mouths *creepy,* and I can't even deny it.

"We aren't that close anymore, Lev. I see him once a month during the family dinner."

"If he's close enough to attend the infamous family dinner, I would say he's someone I should have met by now," he growls through clenched teeth.

I give him what I hope is a reassuring smile, not interested in having to deal with one of his 'dark moods' when we're in public.

"Don't be like that. I told you, I grew up with him and his parents are good friends with mine. He's just a friend." *A friend I'm in love with*, I silently add.

"Maybe it's finally time you took me to a family dinner then, babe. You've kept me from your *family* long enough, and it's time they meet the new man in your life."

I can tell he's seconds away from the rage in his voice becoming a scene, so I do the only thing I can to stop the train wreck from happening. I lie through my teeth.

"Of course, it is. Next time, I promise," I placate him.

Yeah, I'm thinking it's definitely past time I call a stop to things between Levi and myself.

Things didn't get any better from there. He returned to his meal after a good two minutes of just looking at me and breathing hard. He only talked to Seth and even that was with short and impatient responses. If Seth noticed, he didn't care. By the time I had finished my food, my head was throbbing with what promised to be one hell of a migraine, but it wasn't until the bill came that the pain exploded in a burst so painful I thought I might throw up.

"I forgot my wallet, babe, you got this," Levi tells me instead of asking, not even a small amount of shame present. He doesn't wait to hear my response before tossing his napkin on the table and standing.

He looks down at Seth before jerking his chin toward the front of the restaurant.

"Here," Seth says to Nikki, handing her his wallet and standing, following behind Levi as they make their way out the door.

"Stupid son of a nutcracker," she mumbles under her breath, opening Seth's wallet and pulling out enough cash to cover both of our tabs. "Serves him right for being friends with that tool."

"Need I remind you, that tool is the same guy that you told me was my soul mate just a few months ago?"

She leans back in her seat, and I feel bad when I see her face get soft. "I know, I know. That was crazy intense, Em." She places Seth's wallet in her purse before looking back at me. "I knew he could be a jerk sometimes, what guy isn't, but I've never seen something like what just happened. That was creepy as hell. More creepy than the weirdness he's been oozing lately."

"I know." I sigh, rubbing my pounding temples. "He's been doing stuff like that more and more. Getting excessively controlling and possessive the last few weeks, but ever since we slept together, he's become … well, that," I say and point toward the door.

"Has he ever—"

I stop her with a shake of my head, knowing where she's going with this. "No, Nikki. I wouldn't still be here if he had put his hands on me. I'm smarter than that," I tell her. Even though I'm reasonably sure that's the case, I know now the loneliness I had felt for so long was the only reason I had allowed things to get this far between us. Instead of me breaking things off when I first noticed how over-the-top he would get when it came to me.

"He got really mad when I brought up Nate. I figured he'd met him already. I didn't know you hadn't brought him around anyone. I mean he wasn't just mad … he was *mad*. He bent his fork," she says and points at where his discarded fork is lying on the table. Sure enough, the metal is bent slightly in the middle. "Are you okay?"

"I'm okay. I don't know why you assumed he had been around Nate when I've been avoiding him for the better part of the last year. After Maddi had taken an instant dislike to him, I figured I would hold off on my parents. Look, I'm going to talk to him after this weekend.

Since he's covering for someone else, he's working a double and we won't see each other until Monday."

She doesn't look happy, but she gives me a weak nod before we move from the table and walk together outside. Not surprising, Levi and Seth are already in the SUV. I can see them talking as we walk around and get in the back of his Tahoe, Levi's eyes never leaving mine until he was forced to in order to keep facing forward.

We continue our silence as we drive through town, and I'm thankful my house is on the way to Nikki's apartment, so I can avoid being alone with Levi. How I have allowed myself to get this deep in our relationship is beyond me.

No. That's a lie. It isn't just on me. He did a damn good job of hiding his true colors from me for weeks. It's just my fault that I let it go on as long as I have. The signs have been there for a while now, and I would rather be single with an occasional case of the lonelies than have to deal with this.

"You missed my street," I whisper from my seat, the blinding pain slamming around my skull and making me feel weak.

"I didn't," he responds.

I lean my head against the window and try to argue, but Nikki takes my hand with a gentle squeeze.

"I think Ember needs to get home, Levi. She isn't feeling well."

"And she'll get there when she gets there, Nikki."

"Which should be sooner than later. Seriously, Levi, turn around."

I squeak when the brakes compress harshly. I had been resting my head against the window, but the second the seat belt cuts into my stomach, I lose the battle with my nausea and hurry to open the door before losing my dinner on the street.

"Like I said, she isn't feeling well," Nikki snaps, unbuckling her seat belt and shifting to the middle seat to help me hold my hair back.

I had just finished heaving, feeling another wave of vomit fighting its way up my throat, when he slams on the gas. The door, not able to stay open with the power of his acceleration, bangs into my already pounding head. I have to choke down the vomit as the pain becomes something of the likes I've never experienced.

"It's okay," Nikki tries to reassure me, scooting back over on the seat and pulling me until my head is in her lap. I focus on the feeling of her fingers running through my hair, and it isn't long until the hypnotizing movements have me asleep in her lap. Just as the pain dulls enough for slumber to take hold, I hear her mumble under her breath. "You're a fucking motherfucker, Levi Kyle."

I have no idea if he responds; my last thought is that she couldn't be more right.

Chapter 7
Ember

I wake up in a fog.

It takes me a second to realize that I'm no longer in Levi's backseat but instead laying in the middle of my bedroom floor. The revolting taste in my mouth is enough to make me want to vomit all over again. My head is still pounding, but not like it was when a monster migraine rushed through my skull.

I've always had trouble with migraines. They don't hit me as often as they did when I was in high school, but high-stress situations always have been a big trigger for me.

Pulling myself from the floor, I notice how weak I really feel as I move to the bathroom.

The second I'm upright, blackness tugs at the corners of my vision.

Well, that's new. I can't remember a migraine ever doing that.

I stumble with my first step, and I fight with the exhaustion that washes from the top of my head all the way to my toes.

"Jesus, what is wrong with me," I mumble to the empty room. I look for Bam, but I don't see him anywhere. "Bam-A-Ram," I weakly call out but still nothing. He's probably pissed at me for not giving him the rest of my lunch yesterday.

Ignoring the fact that I'm becoming overwhelmingly more exhausted with each moment I'm up and moving around, I turn the shower on. It takes me forever to get my jeans off, pulling my underwear with them and kicking them to the side. My arms get caught in my shirt as I pull it over my head, and for a second, I wonder if my arms had turned to Jell-O at some point while I slept.

The second I step into the steaming hot shower, I take a deep breath and try to remember how the hell I got home. The last thing I can recall is getting sick, then Nikki's soothing touch helping to ease the pain enough for me to fall asleep.

Then nothing.

I don't spend much time washing, just putting in the good old college try of hitting the hot spots with the bar of soap. It falls from my hand in a loud clatter the second I finish. I had the fleeting thought to ignore my hair, but the memory of puking in it last night is all the motivation I need to push through my exhaustion and reach for the shampoo.

I cry out in pain when my fingers push against a huge goose egg on the side of my head. The shampoo from my hands running down my face and into my eyes as I rinse it off just makes me cry out again.

"Shit, shit!"

I raise up, opening the shower door and jump out to grab a towel. When I'm standing in front of the mirror, I turn my head and move my thick hair out of the way. When I part my hair, I see the painful bump I had felt in the shower as well as a small cut in my scalp. That explains the headache, I guess.

I rush out of the bathroom and start searching for my phone. It takes me a few failed attempts, but I finally find it tossed behind the couch, just inside the front door. I fumble with the stupid thing before pressing the right prompts and holding it to the uninjured side of my face.

"Someone had better be dead," Nikki grumbles in greeting.

"How did I get home last night?" I breathlessly ask.

"Ember?"

"Nikki!" I yell, closing my eyes when a pain shoots through my head. "How. Did. I. Get. Home."

"Uh, you're freaking me out, Em."

"I'm freaking *myself* out!" I scream. This time, my head doesn't just give a burst of pain. Now, I feel a joining wave of nausea.

"Levi dropped you off. Well, we dropped you off. After you got sick and passed out, I kind of went a little nuts and threatened to cut off his balls if he didn't take you right home. I figured he was over it when we got to your house. Seth was pissed about how Levi was acting, but he got your door unlocked and Levi carried you in."

"I don't remember any of this," I tell her. "Did you come in too? Or just Levi and Seth?"

"Seth made me stay in the car. I think he was worried about Levi going off the handle because I got a little lippy and wanted to keep me away from him. He just unlocked the door and came back to wait for Levi. You scared the shit out of me, though. I know you need your migraine meds and your bed when they get that bad. I just had to make him listen."

"Did you take Bam with you?" I ask, still trying to figure out how I'm missing a huge chunk of last night.

"No, why would I take that beast with me?"

"I can't find him. I can't find him, and I don't remember anything. On top of all that, I've done something to my head and I CAN'T FIND BAM!"

I hear her move around, the groaning of Seth complaining before she speaks. "I'm on the way."

I hang up, drop to the couch, and look around my living room.

"What the hell is going on?" I ask the empty room.

I must have zoned out, or passed out is more like it, because the next thing I know, I have a frantic Nikki banging on the front door and screaming my name. By the time I was able to pull myself from the couch, she must have remembered she had a spare key and she was bursting into the door.

"Joe Jonas on a stick!" she screams, bringing a smile to my face. She loves using Jonas's name in vain. "You scared the ever-loving shit out of me, Emberlyn Locke!"

I look up at her, hair wild and frizzy just sticking out in a million different directions, as she stares down at me. My head is still spinning, but I managed to sit and lean forward on the couch. My elbows propped on my knees and my head hanging between my legs.

"I found Bam," she tells me, bending down so that she's at eye level with me. "He's limping a little but seems fine. He was tied to the back fence. Why would you tie him to the fence?"

"This makes no sense, Nik. You know I would never do that. I just woke up, and it's like a whole chunk of my night is gone."

She looks at me, worry flashing in her eyes. "What's the last thing you remember?"

"The ride home. I remember the ride home, throwing up, the car door hitting me ..." I trail off and reach behind my head and feel another, smaller knot on the back of my head from where the door slammed me. "I have a bump from when he took off after I was sick, but where did I get this one?" I question her, feeling my eyes go wild as I push my head up, grabbing her hand and pushing it gently into my hair so she can feel the larger bump.

"Holy Madonna." She gasps, reaching forward and poking around the injured skin. My head jerks away from her touch instantly. "Em, that didn't happen when you were with me."

I just look at her, and I can tell by the scared look in her eyes that we're both thinking the same thing.

Levi.

Levi had something to do with this.

Bam nudges my knee, and I look down at my beautiful beast. He whines when I rub his furry head, and I know without a doubt that if Levi is responsible for my new aches and pains, he most definitely had a part in Bam's.

"Let's go get you checked out, Em. I would feel a lot better if you went to the hospital."

I shake my head and look up from Bam's brown eyes. Nikki, clearly thinking her suggestion is a done deal, is gathering some more clothing out of the neat laundry stacks I had made earlier yesterday before running out of time to put them away. I look down and realize that I'm still wearing just my huge bath towel knotted at my chest. Luckily, it's large enough that even sitting as I am, I'm covering everything important.

Bam whines again when Nikki almost steps on him, moving away with a limp that makes my heart hurt.

"Here," she starts. "Let's get you changed."

"I'm not going to the doctor, Nik. I can tell you right now that

I most likely have one hell of a concussion. Whether that's from the door or whatever happened to me when I got home, I'll never know. But if I show up at the emergency room, this will get back to my dad, and I just can't deal with his overprotectiveness right now."

She frowns. "I don't think that's a good idea."

"Maybe not, but it's not going to change anything."

Sighing, she drops the clothes on the couch next to me. I look over at the yoga pants and tank top and move to stand before dropping the towel. Nikki ignores me as I cover up my nakedness. We've been friends for so long that we lost our shyness a long time ago.

"I'm not leaving," she tells me with determination so I don't try to persuade her otherwise.

"Good. You can drive me to the vet when they open later this morning so I can have Bam checked out."

She makes a sound of annoyance and throws up her hands. "So you'll check on your dog but not yourself?"

I nod, pulling my top down and looking back at where Bam is licking his back leg with slow swipes of his tongue. He looks up, his eyes trusting, and I give him a smile.

"Yup."

Chapter 8
Ember

As much as I love Nikki, I'm going to kill her in about three seconds. She's refused to leave my side, being a constant shadow since my early morning phone call a day and a half ago.

Annoying, smothering, and overwhelming with her mothering.

"Nik, you need to go home. I need to get started on my final piece for the exhibit before everyone comes over for the big secret plans tonight."

She looks at me with determination and maybe even a little uncertainty concerning leaving me alone. Even though I've been fine, save the little headache that is just finally receding.

"I'm fine, Nik!"

Bam barks at my outburst, and I smile at him. He's still limping slightly when he moves around, but the vet assured me that he just had a nasty bruise.

"You aren't fine, Emberlyn. You hardly have any energy."

I huff out a growl type noise and place both my hands on my hips before giving her a look that clearly shows my losing battle with patience. "I would have plenty of damn energy if you weren't still here waking me up every hour to make me recite my name, alphabet, and the presidents' names in order of office term!"

She has the decency to look sheepish, but before she can voice some sort of comeback, I continue.

"And I should add I wouldn't ever be able to tell you the presidents' names in order of office term without freaking Google! So your argument that I must surely have brain damage because I couldn't complete your asinine tasks is just ludicrous. I'm fine, but I need a nap to make up for my lack of sleep, Nik. Especially since you guys are still set on me going out to party tonight."

"They weren't asinine! You know damn well that I know what I'm talking about. You don't just forget first-aid training."

I narrow my eyes. "First-aid training that you got when you were twelve in 4-H!" I scream.

"Well, it still makes me more qualified than you are to make that decision, now doesn't it."

"I'm going to kick your ass if you don't go home."

She smirks before picking up the nail file she had been using and continued to shape her nails. "No, you won't."

My hands fly in the air, and I toss my head back to let out another groan.

"I'm going to go back and work. You need to go home so that I can finish in peace, get a nap for a few hours without you waking me up, and come back tonight with everyone else."

I turn from where she is sitting at the kitchen table and walk to my studio. The second my feet touch down on the white floor, I let out a calming breath, instantly feeling at home.

Looking at the clock hanging over the doorway, I make a note of how much time I have before I need to stop. Since the sun has just now touched the top of the trees, I know I have a good five hours before I need to stop. My sister told me earlier, through text, that they would now be over to my house around six tonight with dinner before starting our prep to go out.

I turn on my music before setting my timer for just after lunch. I go about getting all my paint and brushes set out in front of the huge canvas that is bigger than I am tall. The curator of the gallery where my exhibit is being housed didn't even bat an eye when I asked her if I could change the featured piece at the last minute. The idea came to me last night during one of the rare moments Nikki let me sleep, and I hadn't been able to stop thinking about it since.

The first thing I did, before calling her, was go through the blank canvases that are stored in my guest room to find *the one*. I remember when I bought the six-foot-by-four-foot canvas; I never thought I would find something to put on it, until last night.

Placing the canvas so that it's horizontal on my easel, having to adjust the custom-made brackets in order to hold the monster, I instantly pick up my brush and drop it into the gray paint.

It isn't long before the music, my mind, and my arm against the canvas are synced together in a beautiful dance. Each stroke is made without thought; each dip into the paint is made without looking away from the swirling arches and twists of black, gray, and white paint.

Never have I created something that wasn't full of color, full of life. All of my paintings are known for being vibrant and as lifelike as a picture. But not this one. This one is as abstract as it gets.

My timer goes off, and I step back to look at the work that has held me captive for the last five hours. I take a deep breath and move from one side of the canvas to the other, taking in the unfinished work. I'm surprised that I managed to get as much as I had done today, but really, I shouldn't be. It's been a long time since I was that captive in my zone.

I make quick work of cleaning up my supplies and moving the unused paint mixtures to the pods that will keep them fresh until I can return to my work tomorrow. I ignore the grumble in my stomach as I drop down on the couch with a heavy sigh and give in to the exhaustion that I've been pushing off.

My dreams are full of the black, gray, and white world I just knew would be my best piece of art to date.

"What?" I ask around a mouthful of pizza.

My sister just continues to look at me with narrowed eyes.

"Seriously, what is your problem?" I snap, dropping the crust after tearing off the last delicious bite.

"Dad is going to shit his pants when he sees your head," she tells me, crossing her arms over her chest.

"Yeah? And how is he going to find out unless someone opens her big fat mouth to tell him?"

"You two annoy the shit out of me," Stella bluntly states, causing my sister to snap her eyes over to where she is finishing Dani's hair. "I'm so happy that my dad didn't have more kids. I could never handle that crap."

Dani laughs, earning a scowl from Stella when her head moves too much. "Just imagine having to deal with a miniature version of my dad as a brother!"

"Yeah, no. No way in hell I could handle that shit," Stella continues, curling another long piece of Dani's hair around her flat iron.

"You have it all wrong, Stel." Lyn laughs. "There is no way a sibling could have handled *you*!"

Everyone laughs, and Stella just shrugs, sprays another lock of Dani's hair with hairspray, and continues without disagreeing.

"He's going to find out," my sister continues as if she hadn't just been interrupted.

"Shut up." I groan and move to walk into my living room where the rest of the girls are hanging out in various forms of readiness.

Dani and Stella had been doing everyone's hair since the moment they all arrived two hours ago; now, the only two left are the both of them. My hair had been first and the beginning of my sister's annoying chatter about my dad potentially freaking out. The second Dani moved the shorter hair that always brushes over the side of my forehead and got a look at the now yellow and green bruising, she hadn't stopped.

I can hear her muttering under her breath as she moves around the kitchen to clean up the last of our group's dinner mess, but she wisely stops giving me a bunch of what my dad refers to as our 'sass.'

Megan and Lila are talking softly on my loveseat, and judging by the way she keeps turning her phone in Lila's direction, I'm assuming she is showing off pictures of her newborn son, Jack.

They're both wearing black dresses, but where Lila's is on the shorter end of slutty, Megan's is not. Megan's is a beautiful shirtsleeve dress that hits her right in the middle of her thighs. Loose in the skirt and hiding what she refers to as her stubborn baby weight.

Lila's is sleeveless, but with thick straps and a deep neckline that shows off her cleavage impressively. And where Megan's is loose, Lila's is skintight and hits her just under her bottom.

Nikki, Lyn, Dani, and Stella are in similar dresses as Lila's, each a little different from the other but all black.

"We look like we're going to a funeral," I mumble before attempting to sit on the couch next to Nikki. But before my bottom hits the cushion, she is pushing against my back and shoving me forward. "What the hell, Nik!"

"You need to go get dressed!" she snaps.

"She's right," my sister says, coming in the room. "You're the last one!"

She pulls me forward and down to my bedroom. When the light snaps on, illuminating what has been laid out on the bed waiting for me like a snake ready to strike, I feel my stomach start flipping nervously.

"Uh," I start.

"Nope. No. No way in hell," my sister starts to fuss. "You will put that on and freaking like it."

"That," I say, pointing to the blood-red fabric on my bed, my voice getting a little manic as I continue, "is not a dress. That looks like something a toddler would wear."

"It's stretchy," she tells me as if that's all that matters. She starts to unbutton the shirt that I had put on over my strapless bra earlier and I slap her hands away.

"I'm not wearing that," I screech.

"Yes, you are," I hear behind me and turn toward the doorway to see Stella. "My pops spent a ridiculous amount of time hunting for the perfect birthday outfit for you for as he says *hours and hours, darlin' girl*," she says, mocking her pop's voice perfectly. "You know what happens when you ignore the advice of that man." She stands up straight, tosses her long curled hair over her shoulder before continuing in Sway's voice. "There's certain times in a woman's life when she needs to make sure to work the goodness God gave her with no hesitation whatsoever, darling girl. Just flaunt all that beauty and make every man you pass die a little inside because he will just not live another second if he can't have you. For little Miss Emberlyn, that moment will be tonight, and Sway demands pictures and pictures before you hit the town." She relaxes her posture instantly and shrugs. "So let's do this."

Chapter 9
Nate

Opening night is in full swing.

I'm sweaty and hotter than fucking hell, but the smile on my face hasn't left for a second since we opened the doors three hours ago. Even before the six o'clock opening time, the line had been so out of control to get in the door that we went ahead and opened up the holding room at almost four in the afternoon. The girls and guys had been working together in perfectly synchronized movements ever since.

I see Shane the second he starts to climb the stairs to my office, where I've been observing the insanity while I cooled off some.

"Fucking madhouse," he rumbles with a smile on his face.

"We did it," I tell him, not looking away from the packed floor below us. Even the areas that hold the tall tables and beyond are packed with bodies undulating with the pounding bass flowing through the speakers. The house DJ, Thorn, changes the song to another fast-paced tune and throws one arm up and down with the beat. The bodies surrounding his staged-off area begin to move together a little closer. You can tell without being down there that things are getting heated, which isn't a surprise since each bar has been passing drinks in rapid speed.

"We didn't do shit, brother. This is all you."

I move to deny his claim, but a flash of color by the entryway into the madness stills the words before they could even leave my lips. I squint my eyes and try to see through the dim lights and smoky air, but the vision was gone so quick I'm almost positive it was just a trick of the lights.

"Did you see the crowd during the bar dances?" Shane asks, moving to my side and watching the floor.

"Insanity." I laugh, and it had been. Complete insanity. The second the DJ had dropped the bass and cranked up the volume, our boys had sprung into action. The patrons didn't know what to think at first. All drink orders had been stalled, and instantly, they had their heavily booted feet up on the glossy wood. They pulled back their drinks and the surface was cleared for them. Even I could appreciate the show knowing that it was my brainchild that had held the masses captive and hypnotized as the guys moved like whatever was in front of them was a naked woman ready and willing to be fucked … hard.

"I think they're starting to anticipate them now. Every time we inch closer to the top of another hour, drinks start being pulled off the bar before Thorn even has a chance to drop the beat."

I nod. "You going to get out there tonight?" I ask him.

"No clue. Are you?"

I turn my back to the crowd beyond my window and lean back against the glass. "Depends, my friend. If the mood strikes, maybe. Not sure I see anyone worth getting up there and shaking my ass for anyway."

Shane laughs, dropping his hand heavy on my back. "Yeah, something tells me that motivation isn't going to be an issue for you," he oddly says and walks back to the doorway. "Let's go join the party, brother."

The second he opens the heavy steel door, the music thumps and pounds through the once silent space. A familiar rush of adrenaline fills my body as we both stalk down the stairs together and onto the overheated floor. I see, but ignore, the females around us as they turn and attempt to gain our attention. I continue through the pulsing bodies that litter the massive open space and walk toward the bar.

"Yo, Nate," Dent yells over the music, and when I turn my head toward him, he slides a shot down the sleek wooden surface.

My hand shoots out and grabs the glass right when I hear Logan yell, "Bottoms up." Without thought, I bring the liquor to my lips. The burn travels down my throat, and when I settle the shot glass back on the bar, Travis is already there with the bottle of tequila in his hand, refilling it instantly.

I ignore the chick to my right and turn to look around the room. The small smile that had been playing on my lips drops when I see the woman dancing just a few feet in front of me.

"What the fuck," I mumble, dropping the once again empty glass down and stalking forward.

I look around when I lose her in the crowd, but continue to stomp through the crowd to the other side of the club where the other dance floor is moving like one giant wave to the music.

I see her again and instantly fume.

"You want to tell me what the fuck you're doing here," I rumble low in my throat when my head dips down until my mouth is right next to her ear and grab her by her forearm.

The thin arm is pulled from my grasp when she turns around. I stand back and cross my arms over my chest and wait for her to talk.

"What is your problem," she yells over the music.

"My problem?" I yell at her and bend down so that I don't have to scream over the noise. "My problem, dear sister, is that you're in my club dressed like … that," I tell her and point my finger at her dress. "Does your husband know you're here?"

She narrows her eyes and stops dancing to stand up on her toes and get in my fucking face.

"He sure does and I'll have you know that he will be here later."

I drop my head back and look up at the ceiling. I should have known they wouldn't stay away. It's not that I don't want them here, I do, but not if I have to look out for her while he's not here.

"Plus, we're celebrating," she yells before dropping down on her impossibly tall heels and dancing again.

"Celebrating what?"

Her smile goes all wonky and shit. She looks downright fucking evil.

"Ember's birthday, big brother," she tells me with a pat against my chest before spinning around and vanishing through the thick crowd.

Ember's birthday.

And then it hits me.

Ember's *twenty-first* birthday.

Fucking shit.

And if I know my sister and her gang of misfits, she's up to something a lot bigger than just celebrating. Of all the places they could have ended up tonight, they picked my fucking club knowing damn well that things between Ember and me are one giant mess. Dani isn't stupid, and since she was the first person I ran into after my chat with Locke the other night, she knows exactly what's going on between us.

With a single-minded determination, I start to scan the room for Dani, Ember, or any of the other girls that I'm sure are tagging along for the showdown they're hoping for.

Each pass my eyes makes around the room just coils the tension in my gut tighter until I'm determined to find them and kick them out. If I were smart, I would find Shane and make him take care of it … but clearly, I'm not of sound mind because the second my eyes lock on Ember, I know the last thing I'm going to do is let her walk away from me again.

I feel my cock jump when I see past the group dancing between where I'm standing and she is laughing with the girls around one of the tables just off the dance floor. Then I get my first good look when the definition of living sin meets my eyes.

"Holy fucking shit," I breathe out in a rush of words, feeling like I've just been punched in the stomach.

The possessiveness that fires through my body at the vision before me is nothing like I've ever felt before. The anger that anyone else in this room is free to look at her slams into my body with a force so strong I almost reach out to steady my footing … almost.

My feet are moving just as rapidly as my racing heart as I move toward her. Dani, facing my direction, drops her jaw as her eyes widen. I see Stella roll her eyes in a bored way before giving Maddi a nudge and nod in my direction. I don't look at Ember's sister long, but I don't for a second miss the small smile that hits her face when she sees me fuming behind Ember. I pay no attention to the rest of the girls in their group but reach out to spin the little devil in front of me around gently.

She teeters on her feet, and I glance down with a frown. Each bare inch of her tan legs has me clenching my jaw, but when I see the tall-as-fuck heels on her dainty feet, whatever blood I had left in my brain blasts to my cock. I groan when my eyes travel back up to a dress that shouldn't be allowed past the bedroom as my balls grow painfully tight.

"What the fuck are you doing here?" I growl.

Fucking growl. Like a goddamn bear.

She doesn't respond, but she also does a shit job at hiding the hurt that flashes in her eyes.

Shit.

"Don't be a jerk," I hear my sister yell.

I lift my gaze and narrow them on her. "You had better watch it before your nose is in the corner for a much-needed time the fuck out, Danielle Cage."

She rolls her eyes, and I make a mental note to deal with her later, looking back down into Ember's pissed face.

"You shouldn't be here." The second the words are out of my mouth, I feel regret slamming into me. *Fuck yeah, she should be here*, my mind keeps screaming over and over. "You don't belong here," I continue to speak. I can't stop the words coming out of my mouth, and I know the second my heart starts to pound at an unnatural speed that I'm fucking up major here.

"You're a son of a Bieber's biscuit!" I hear a drunken screech from my side and look over to see Ember's best friend, Nikki, reach out to poke me. "Son of a Backstreet Boy," she oddly screams next and brings her offending finger to her chest to cradle it as her brow furrows in pain.

Weird girl, that one.

I take a deep breath to fill my chest with the smoky, raw air around me, before doing what I should have done in the first place. I bend, and before Ember can react, she is over my shoulder and I'm stalking back to the stairs that will lead to my office. My hand splays out against her backside so that the short-as-shit dress she's wearing doesn't give a view to the room that should be for my eyes only.

My eyes only? Where the hell did that thought come from?

I feel her small fists beating on my back, but I ignore her as I climb the stairs, trying my best not to think about the heat of her pussy against the palm of my hand. The second I slam my office door shut, closing us in the room, she launches herself off my shoulder. Luckily for her, I was near the couch, so when she stumbled on those heels, she landed on the soft leather with an oomph.

"What the hell is your problem, Nathaniel!" she screams, launching herself up to stand and pushing me with both hands against my chest. "You have no right!"

Taking her tiny wrists in my hands, I bring them down and trap them behind her back. She struggles and my eyes drop to her chest as each heaving breath makes the material drop a little lower.

"How the fuck is this even staying up," I fume. Switching my hold so I have both wrists in one hand, I bring up one finger to pick at the thin fabric strap going over her shoulder. My eyes roaming over the exposed skin of her neck as I trail my finger down the thin strap until I hit the deep V exposing the silky smooth skin between her tits. All it would take is one real deep breath and her nipple would be on display.

"N-nate," she stutters, and I lift my gaze from the valley of tan skin to look into her eyes. The anger is still there but it has dimmed, and in its place is pure fucking lust.

"No one should see this much of you. Not one fucking person but me."

"I'm not yours," she fumes, and I can see that the fury is winning over the lust.

"You're fucking wrong, babe," I respond without thought.

She snaps back and pulls one hand from my hold before I can even process her movement. In the next blink, that same freed hand cracks against my cheek and I feel a red-hot burn.

"I *am not* your fucking *babe!*" she shouts.

"I'll give you that one, but only that fucking one, Ember."

"I'm not yours, Nate. You had that chance, and you didn't want it."

Bending down so my eyes are level with hers, I give in to the possessive need to claim her. "You were fucking born to be mine, little firecracker, and mine you will fucking be." My words coming out in a thick rumble, and I watch in satisfaction as her pupils dilate.

Check. Fucking. Mate.

Her shocked gasp works in my favor, and in the next breath, my lips are on hers as my tongue slides into her mouth and caresses the slick heat of her own. My hands hit her hips, and with a flex of my fingers, I pull her against me roughly.

The body that had been rigid in my hands goes weak the second our bodies press tightly together, and she kisses me back with a fervor that surpasses my own. Her arms, no longer hanging limp at her side, move up until her hand is pushing into my hair and the tie that had been holding it up behind my head is ripped out as she pulls me closer to her mouth by my now loose locks.

This kiss is all about domination, and at the moment, I'm not fucking sure I want to be the one to win this war. Our moans are mingling together and the wet sounds of our mouths feasting drown out the dull thump of the music. Letting her own silky lips take the lead, I hum deep in my throat. My erection rubs against her belly as my hands slide down to the point where the fabric meets burning smooth skin.

The second my fingertips curl around her dress and begin to lift the fabric, she jerks in my hold. The hands that had been tugging through my hair drop to my chest, and with a strangled sound, she pushes me away.

We stare at each other, chests heaving.

When I move to take her back in my arms and give us both what we clearly want, her arm comes up and stops my movement with one palm against the center of my chest. I look down at the offending hand with a tilt of my head, trying my fucking hardest to get my brain to turn back on. Or at least, will some of the blood that is currently lacking from my head to leave my hard-as-shit cock.

"No," she whispers hoarsely.

"Yes," I demand, my eyes snapping back to hers.

"This will not happen."

Again, I'm struck dumb and I just tilt my head again like a confused puppy that just wants his bone.

"Nate." She sighs with a small shake of her head. "This won't happen. I have a boyfriend."

I feel one of my brows go up as I continue to look at her.

"Not only that, but you had your chance … twice … and both of those times ended disastrously for me. I'm not willing to put myself through that again."

Shaking my head, finally getting some sense back in my system, I clear my throat before speaking. "You *had* a boyfriend, Ember. But that's going to change real quick. You've ignored me since dropping that bomb on me the other day, and trust me, firecracker, we will be talking about *that*. One thing you need to get through that pretty little head of yours, though, is that this will be fucking happening."

She's silent but not for long. She comes up on the balls of her feet the best she can in order to level her eyes with mine, but she just ends up with the top of her head getting there before dropping back down with a huff.

"I handed myself to you years ago, Nate, and the only thing that was missing was the silver fucking platter. You rejected me. Like a stupid little girl, I thought my crush on you was this big grand love, but you proved me wrong, and I was *crushed*. You get that? Then, when I had finally put that behind me, you treat me like a faceless slut *YOU DIDN'T SEE* as you almost took my virginity against a fucking wall. So, no … this will *not* be happening."

"You're mine," I grunt deeply. "Fucking mine."

"I'm no one's but my own, and I'm definitely not yours. I'll never be *yours*."

She storms past me and wrenches my door open before disappearing down the stairs.

"We'll just see about that," I mumble to the empty room as the door slams in her wake.

Chapter 10
Ember

The fucking nerve.

My lips burn and I can feel the wetness between my legs with each step that pulls my underwear against my bare sex.

My core throbs with the climax I had in his arms from that kiss alone.

I should feel terrible that I just came apart in a man's arms that didn't belong to my boyfriend, but I don't. That could be because my mind had already put Levi in the ex category, the actual breakup just being a formality.

The crowd seems to part as I push through the room and back to where the girls are still drinking and laughing as if Nate hadn't just carted me off over his shoulder.

How embarrassing.

Not a word is spoken as I snatch my purse from the table and reach in to grab some cash before spinning on my heels and making quick work of getting to the bar.

I don't look around, too afraid of what I'll see on the faces I pass. My eyes go up to the black glass above me, and I know without being able to see him that those eyes are tracking my every move.

"What'll it be, babe," I hear, bringing my focus away from the wall of windows.

Babe.

I'm so sick of people calling me babe. I feel like that word alone is going to drive me to the edge of sanity.

"I don't care. Just make it strong," I yell, slapping the bill down on the bar.

The shirtless man just nods as he turns around to grab one of the bottles of liquor behind him and a shot glass. He slides it forward, but when I push the money toward him, he shakes his head and walks away.

With a shrug, I lift the cool glass to my lips and take it down with one swallow. My eyes sting as the liquid burns down my throat and into my belly. I blink a few times to clear my vision as I slam the glass down and wave the same man over.

This time, he takes my money, and I wave him off when he goes to get change. I shoot the drink back before pointing at the glass again, silently demanding another.

He leans against the bar and just tips the bottle over the glass again.

Three more shots and no more cash, I'm finally able to handle the burn without wanting to gag.

Of course, that would be when I open my eyes expecting to see my new best friend the bartender's brown eyes, but instead, I see the emerald fury of Nate Reid.

Maybe it's the shots or maybe it's just the hold he's always had on me, but I don't move. Not even when I see him moving his arms as my old friend, brown-eyed bartender, hands him a cup and a few bottles. He does something with them, but I couldn't tell you what because my eyes never leave his face.

When a body collides with mine from behind, pushing me against the bar painfully, the trance he had me stuck in is broken, and I look away to watch some drunken man stumble after a group of girls. Before I look back at Nate, I peek over at the table our group of girls is occupying. Gazes locked on us, they all wear expressions with slack jaws.

Well, everyone except Nikki. She looks like she just discovered Santa was real and won the lotto in the same sweep.

I feel something cold hit the hand I have resting on the bar, and I turn back around, glancing down to where Nate is pushing a drink into my hand. I look at the colorful drink instead of the man pushing it toward me. He's swirling the drink around with a stick, mixing the colors inside the glass for a second before he pulls his hand up. I watch as the stick becomes a lollipop, then follow its path up until Nate's smirking lips open to suck the candy in his mouth once before popping it out and dropping it back down into my glass.

My gaze doesn't look at the drink this time, nope … no sir, this time, I study his mouth as his tongue dips out and wets those thick lips that had me coming undone just minutes ago. I feel my breath pull in a choppy inhale and look up to meet his eyes. I'm not sure what to make of the expression on his face, and if I'm honest, fear and self-preservation are what keeps me from trying to figure it out.

At that moment, all rational thoughts die a shocked death.

Nate reaches forward, tags the lollipop from my drink again, and before I realize what's happening, he begins to paint my lips with the wet, sticky candy of the lollipop, and the music changes from some Justin Timberlake song to something I haven't ever heard before. His features morph into a sadistic grin and an equally wicked gleam shines in his eyes before pulling the candy away and dropping it back into the glass.

Call it intuition, but the second I see both his palms press against the bar's surface, I reach out and tag the glass in my hand, pulling it toward my chest just as he literally jumps from where he had been standing on the ground to a crouched position with his feet on the bar.

I hear the whole club go electric and notice just out of the corner of my eye that my brown-eyed friend is also standing on the bar as the song's lyrics hit my brain. Something about lollipops.

Holy shit.

Nate stands, his body moving with the music, and I back up to see him a little better. A small step, but that's all that is needed. He reaches up, his eyes never leaving mine, and grabs some handle thing that is hanging above him.

You know that scene in *Magic Mike* when Mike is spinning and all that on the stage … well, that's the only way I can describe what Nate does next. One large fist around the handle holds his huge body up while spinning him in quick circles. I gasp when he lets go and slams his feet back down on the bar. He doesn't even look the slightest bit dizzy when he drops down to his hands and knees against the wooden surface.

He flips his loose hair from his face and turns his head to look directly into my eyes, pulling his thick bottom lip into his mouth as he starts to fuck the wood under his body. I have to squeeze my legs together with the vision before me because I know, I just *know,* if I were under him with my legs spread, his dick would be drilling into my body, deep and hard.

When he pushes up and spins on his knees to face me, his crotch eye level with my face, he slowly starts to move his shirt up. As he reveals each deliciously hard ab, I can hear the screams around us getting louder.

I hear the music increase in tempo as he leans forward, dropping his shirt and covering his beautiful body. I stand there in shock as he pulls the lollipop back up from my drink and presses the cold, wet candy against my lips. They part without conscious thought to take the lollipop inside my mouth.

The song ends and he gives me a wink as he pulls the candy from my mouth and into his own before he jumps from the bar to the space in front of me. I feel lightheaded when he leans down and runs his nose against the shell of my ear, making me gasp.

"You.Are.*Mine*," he growls before taking my earlobe between his lips and biting my flesh roughly between his teeth. A moan rumbles from deep in his chest and his breath echoes in my ear.

And what do I do?

I stand there and come, again, from just the simplest of touches.

Well, fuck me.

Chapter 11

Ember

"Stop moving," I groan and pull my covers over my head as I pray for my stomach to stop swirling.

"I'm not moving, the world is," Nikki rasps from behind me and rips the covers from my face to cocoon herself in some weird blanket burrito.

She wiggles some more and the movement makes my stomach instantly revolt. I jump from the bed, almost tripping over where Bam is laying on the floor. I'm sure if I could see the weird dance I make to keep from stumbling to the ground, I would laugh, but instead, my eyes start to water as I run through my dark bedroom and into to the bathroom. My knees slam on the ground so hard it feels like my teeth rattle in my mouth. Ignoring the pain, I lift the lid and vomit violently.

"Oh, God!" I hear Nikki scream and the sounds of her rushing from the bedroom. I can hear her own sounds of being sick echo through my house and hope she, at least, made it to the guest bathroom before losing the contents of her stomach.

Long, agonizing minutes later, I finally feel like I can move my head from the toilet. I drop to my butt and lean against the wall as I test my ability to move without getting sick again.

Slowly, I crawl on my hands and knees until I reach the bed. Bam gives me a sniff before ignoring me to go back to sleep. Lifting my arm, I glance at the clock next to my bed and see that it's just past four in the morning. With a groan, I reach up and pull my comforter down from the bed before curling up next to Bam's furry body as the world continues to spin.

I fall back to sleep just as I hear Nikki stumble back to the bed. She mumbles about having no covers, but then her snores fill the air, and I join her a beat later.

I hear my phone vibrating against my nightstand. Peeling open my eyes, I see that the sunlight is now shining through the slats in my blinds. Feeling marginally better, I reach up and grab my phone without moving much of my body.

"'Lo?" I utter into the phone.

"Be quiet," Nikki grumbles.

"Well, don't you two sound pleasant this morning," my sister practically sings in my ear.

"Do you have to be so loud?" I question.

She laughs and I pull the phone from my ear. "Get up and drink tons of water, brat. Take some Advil and trust me when I tell you that you'll feel better with something bland in your stomach."

"There is no way in hell I'm putting anything in my stomach," I force out when just the thought makes my stomach revolt.

"I'm on the way." She sighs and hangs up.

I drop the phone and curl back up with Bam.

This time, instead of getting a little peaceful sleep, my visions are full of Nate. That kiss. That *dance*. And his words.

By the time my sister is poking me with her foot, I was so worked up I was seconds away from shoving my hand down my sleep shorts and taking care of my arousal.

He's put some voodoo curse on me.

My body seems to be stuck in some sort of Nate-induced provocation of lust and need.

"Time to get up, Em!"

I jump at Maddi's outburst and glare up at her.

"Here," she says and thrusts a huge bottle of water in my face.

I take it with greed-fueled need, as the dryness in my mouth seems to intensify at the sight of water.

"Slow down," she says when I take huge pulls and gulps of water, the excess running from the sides of my mouth and onto the top of my shirt. "You're going to get sick if you drink that fast. Slow down and take these," she stresses, pulling the bottle away from me and pushing two pills into my mouth before pressing the water back to my lips.

She continues to stand over me until I've drunk almost half of the bottle before giving me a piece of toast. I give her a look of disbelief—doubting I'll be able to actually keep that down—but I take it and slowly nibble. By the time I had finished the second piece, I was feeling less zombie-like and closer to a lukewarm human.

"Better?" she asks knowingly.

"Don't be a bragger."

She just laughs at me and helps pull me up from the floor. I look over at Nikki with a smile when I see her finishing some toast of her own.

"Don't worry, she got to me too. She's like the hangover Nazi."

"Go clean yourself up, then meet me in the living room so we can chat," Maddi says before leaving the room.

"Well," Nikki says with a mouth full of toast. "You heard the tyrant. Get your ass in gear before she comes back in here with more demands."

"I heard that," my sister calls from further in the house.

"I meant for you to!" Nikki yells back.

Rolling my eyes, I drag myself into the bathroom and go about 'cleaning myself up.'

"So …"

I groan, pulling the brush through my hair, and ignore my sister.

"Yeah, I second that so," Nikki adds when I don't make a move to speak.

I finish brushing my hair before dropping the brush down on the coffee table. I curl my legs up and wrap my arms around them before looking at the two of them sitting on the loveseat together, waiting none too patiently for me to give them what they want.

"So he just danced a little. What more do you want?"

"Uh … no. I want you to start with when he pulled you over his shoulder like Tarzan and you disappeared up those stairs. *Then* you can end with what happened when he 'just danced a little,' which in turn caused you to put so much alcohol into your body that you had to be carried out to the car and put to bed without so much as moving a muscle."

I gasp at my sister in shock. "I had to be carried out? I don't remember that."

She laughs. "Well, I would think not since you were basically comatose when Cohen helped you in the back of his truck. You didn't even move once. Which, bravo on taking your twenty-first down like a beast."

"I'm never drinking again," I vow.

"Sure … that's what everyone says." She laughs.

"Would you two shut up and get to the good stuff."

I roll my eyes at Nikki, look down at my toes, and make a mental note to repaint them later.

"I'm not even sure I understand what happened," I tell them honestly.

"How about you start at the beginning, and we can help you figure that out," Maddi says compassionately.

With a sigh, I do just that and start from the beginning. Well, more like the middle since both of them know what started all of this—that being my humiliating graduation night.

I gloss over the night of Dani and Cohen's wedding. I'm not sure why, but deep down, I know that moment should be left between Nate and me. "We had a run-in almost two years ago. It wasn't pretty, and no, I'm not going to give you more than that. It's been … hard, you could say, for me to be around him since."

"I knew it," Maddi exclaims. "I knew there was a lot more to why you weren't coming around when the family was all together."

I narrow my eyes. "Are you going to let me finish?"

She holds up her hands. "Sorry, proceed."

"Anyway, I reminded him earlier this week why things had been strained and he's been trying to get a hold of me since. I ignored him because I really wasn't ready to face that stuff yet. Hell, I'm not sure I am now. Then … well, then last night happened."

"I'm not really sure where to go with that, Em. That's pretty vague."

I drop my head to my knees at my sister's words and try to organize my thoughts.

"He threw my love for him in my face years ago, Maddi. Then hurt me even worse a few years later. Then, without memory of even doing that, he hurt me again a few days ago. Until last night, he's never even hinted at feeling anything more than a friendship type bond toward me. Now, my mind is running wild because last night he dragged me to his office, kissed me to the point of death, and then ended it with that dance. Then he left me standing there stunned stupid as he said to me, and I quote, 'you are mine.' So … where you might not be sure where to go with that, I can assure you that *I* most definitely feel even more lost than you do right now."

Looking up, I stop avoiding them and take in two very stunned faces.

"He did *what?*" Maddi gasps.

"Well, way to go Nate-Dog!" Nikki yells.

"What about Levi?" my sister continues with a bitter look on her face, ignoring Nikki's outburst completely.

"I know it doesn't make it better, I mean I did kiss another man last night. Well, he kissed me, but I didn't push him away immediately, so I'm at just as much fault, but for what it's worth, I was breaking up with him tomorrow. It's been a long time coming, but I've just been putting it off to avoid the confrontation."

Maddi tries, but she does a crap job at hiding the happiness in her expression.

"You didn't do anything wrong," Nikki says softly, her face a mask of understanding as she nods gently. Of course, she understands. She knows everything that's happened between Levi and me that has led up to that decision.

"When did you decide this?" Maddi asks hopefully.

"A few days ago, for sure. But I've been thinking about it for a few weeks. I would have already broken it off, but he's been working all weekend. He got off this morning and went right to bed. Hell, maybe the gym, but regardless, we don't have plans to see each other until later tonight or tomorrow."

She nods, looking over at a still nodding Nikki before her nod turns into a shake of her head at my weird friend's theatrics.

"Okay," she starts, and I hold my breath. I would hate it if she were disappointed in me for the way I'm handling the men in my life. Shit, men in my life? When did I become one of those girls? "I'm going to have to agree with Nikki, Em. You aren't exactly an angel in this situation, but you didn't instigate things between you and Nate. And if I'm being honest, if I were in your shoes, I'm not sure I would have been able to resist the kind of sexual tension you two have going on."

"But?"

Her face goes soft before she stands and walks over to the couch, sitting down next to me and pulling me into her arms. "No buts, little sister. You're in one hell of a complicated situation, and the only advice I can give you is to follow your heart."

"My heart needs to stop and ask for directions," I mumble against her chest.

I feel her laugh before she speaks. "Then you know what I think?"

Lifting my head with a sniffle to keep my emotions in check, I wait for her to continue.

"It's time to call Mom."

Chapter 12

Nate

My cock is going to fall off.

I grab the shirt I had thrown off last night and wipe my come off my abs before tossing it in the general direction of my laundry hamper.

I look down at my still hard cock in disgust and wonder if this is one of those moments I should call my doctor because my erection has lasted longer than four hours.

Hell, it's lasted longer than twelve.

I frown when I watch it grow even harder at the memory of why I've been in this predicament for so long.

Ember.

My little firecracker.

She lit up like the Fourth of July just from my kiss.

She might think I didn't notice, but when her body got tight in my arms just seconds before those sweet fucking tremors took hold of her, I knew.

I reach out and grab my lube, again, and get ready to fuck my fist when I would give just about anything to have Ember here in my bed. Just when I'm wrapping my fist around my cock, my phone goes off and I sigh, looking sadly at my crotch.

"Dude, you're going to have to just stay hard," I moan before placing my cell to my ear.

"Son?"

"What's up?"

"Do I even want to know what you were just saying?"

"Probably not, but hey … how long do I wait for my dick to go soft before I need to worry?"

Silence meets my question, and I pull the phone from my ear, checking to see if the call was dropped.

"Uh," my dad starts, and I drop back on the bed, feeling my cock bounce against my stomach.

"Not something I'm exactly excited to have to ask, but I would rather ask you than call the doctor."

I hear my mom say something in the background. My dad's voice sounds muffled when he says something in return, then I hear him moving around the house before responding. "Nate, did you take something?"

I laugh without humor. "Fuck, no. I wish that were the problem."

"If you didn't take something, do you want to tell me why you're having this little issue?"

"It's not a little issue," I mumble looking down at my cock again to see just how far from little my issue really is.

"Smartass."

"Let's just say, I had a run-in with a woman who started this problem, and I haven't been able to get soft since."

"And you didn't take anything?"

"Jesus fucking Christ, I don't do drugs!"

He chuckles softly, and I try not to be annoyed that he thinks this is a time to be cracking jokes.

"I remember when I first met your mother," he starts, and I quickly shut that shit down.

"I'm going to need your advice to be void of anything that starts with a sentence like that," I boom into the phone.

His laughter rumbles louder.

"Not even that took care of your problem, huh?"

I look down, my cock still angry fucking red, the tip wet with pre-come when I shouldn't have anything left in me, and groan.

"Hate to break it to you, son, but you're going to be walking around like that until you can run back into the woman who started the problem."

"That's what I was worried you were going to say," I groan.

He's silent, but I know it's more about him weighing his words than not having anything to say.

"Care to fill me in a little? I might be your dad, but I could also be able to help even if it's uncomfortable as shit for both of us to be talking about your dick."

"I'm not really sure this conversation would get any easier if I filled you in a little more, old man."

Ignoring the pain in my crotch, I pull myself from the bed and grab a pair of sweats, carefully tucking my hard buddy in and walking to the kitchen to make a protein shake.

"Try me," he says.

"It's Ember."

This time, I know the silence is a lot more than weighing his words. "Ember as in Emberlyn Locke, Maddox Locke's baby girl?" he grumbles deeply through the line.

"One and the same," I respond, before taking a long swallow of my shake.

"Shit," he murmurs under his breath.

"Yeah … that about sums it up. Oh, I think the kicker would be that Maddox is very aware of what is going on between Ember and me."

His humorless laugh comes first. "Of course, he knows, Nate. There isn't much that has ever gotten past that man."

"He's going to kick my fucking ass," I tell him.

"Without a fucking doubt," he confirms. "How's that help your problem?" he adds with a laugh.

"Not even slightly better."

He laughs even harder, and I just roll my eyes, grabbing a banana and taking half down with one bite.

"Ignore your dick, Nate," he says after a minute of solid belly laughs. "Ignore that shit no matter what until you know what you want to do when it comes to Ember. If you don't intend to start something solid with her, well … then your dick should be the last thing that you give attention to."

"I don't think it matters what I want with Ember," I complain.

"And that would be why?"

"Because I fucked up when I thought I was doing the right thing. I fucked up even more a while ago without even realizing it, and I'm not sure which one was worse, but I'm pretty sure them both together means my wants pertaining to Ember mean jack shit."

"Tell me," he says with seriousness. "When you fucked up the first time, did you do it to protect her or because you would rather be a little punk?"

"Nice," I grunt, finishing my second banana. "I pushed her away because not only was she way too fucking young, but also because I wasn't ready to see what was right in front of my face."

"And now?"

"And now, I'm not just ready to see it, I want it more than I want my next fucking breath."

"Well, son, if you ask me, I think you have everything you need to know right there. We're men, we're going to fuck up, but the beauty of finding that one woman meant for you is that no matter how much you fuck up, she will always be there to help make it right. So it's up to you to do what you can in order to right the wrong turns you made and then spend the rest of your days doing everything in your power to only make right turns."

"What the hell does that mean?"

He laughs some more. *Fucking asshole*. "Let me make it simple for you. Find out what you want from Ember. Look in your future, picture her completely out of it, and ask yourself if you can live with that. If not, work your ass off to prove to her that no matter how badly you fucked up, you'll do anything to make it up to her."

"Easier said than done."

"It's pretty fucking easy when all a good woman ever really wants is the unconditional love of her man."

I stare blindly out my front window, looking into the woods that surround my property while rolling his words around in my head. "Her dad is going to kill me."

"Nah, he knows that would hurt his girl too much. He'll make sure he doesn't leave any marks that can't be covered up."

"Not helping," I grind out through clenched teeth.

"Learned my lessons a long time ago, Nate. Lessons that hurt with so much vicious pain that sometimes I still feel the tug of them. But one thing I will never take for granted is that love, true love, is always worth fighting for even if you're fighting the one person who holds the key to taking all that pain away because, in the end, love conquers all, Nate."

"No one said anything about love, old man," I respond without conviction because it would just be a lie. I've loved that girl since I lied to her face and broke her heart.

"You didn't have to," he softly says. "I'm here if you need me, son. It won't be easy, but don't give up until you've won."

"Never," I say, this time having no trouble with the conviction in my tone.

I hear the call disconnect and I drop my phone down before collapsing on the couch with a deep sigh. With one more sad look toward my crotch and tented sweats, I start to plan.

Chapter 13
Ember

Maddi hasn't stopped smiling at me since she called my mom and asked her to come to my house and bring lunch for us. Nikki, sensing this moment should be between a mom and her daughters, left shortly after that call.

While waiting for her to show up, I busy myself in the bathroom to brush my teeth again and go about freshening up in the attempt to feel just a little more human before I bare my soul for not just my sister, but my mother as well.

Hell, it could be worse … it could be my father too.

"Sweetie?" my mom calls into my bedroom with a soft knock on the door.

"Come on in, Mom," I respond with a smile that only grows when she pops her blond head through the crack in my door.

You would never guess that she's in her mid-fifties. My mom still doesn't even look a day over forty, if that. Her blond hair doesn't hold a single gray, and her freckled skin is wrinkle free. She's the most beautiful woman I know.

"You okay?" she asks, walking into the room and shutting the door. I'm silently thankful for the privacy, something she clearly sees judging by her next words. "I sent your sister home, honey. Now, give me all your worries and let me make them better."

A sob bubbles up before I can stop it, and I step into my mom's arms. She holds me while I get it out, maneuvering us until she is leaning against my headboard and she has her loving arms wrapped around me.

Sometimes, no matter how old you are, the only thing that makes you feel like you can manage all the things spinning around you helplessly is to have your mother's arms wrapped around you.

"Is this about Levi?" she hedges.

"No … yes. God, I have no idea how to even answer that."

"Well," she says and pulls back to look into my eyes. Her light brown eyes full of love and understanding. "Give me everything and we can pick it apart and figure out what needs to happen next."

"Directions … I need directions," I mumble through my sniffles.

Her blond brows pull in slightly and a small frown hits her lips. "Directions to what, baby?"

"How to follow my heart." I hiccup.

Her frown disappears instantly replaced with a wide smile. "Then directions we'll find."

I drop back into her arms and give her everything, not leaving a single detail of it out, and when I finish, I don't feel any less confused.

"Oh, my sweet girl. You always, even when you were a tiny baby, overthink any and every challenge placed in front of you. That is something I'm afraid you came by honestly. Your father was the same way. Overthought everything and let his fears and insecurities overrule what his heart was screaming."

I lift up and move to cross my legs, facing my mom as she mirrors my position.

"What changed?" I ask, searching her eyes, having a hard time picturing the strong and confident man I know like that.

"Your father did." She laughs. "Well, I think it might have been a little of my stubborn will mixed with his and his steadfast determination mixed with both our fears and endless love, but in the end, it was the same result."

"I'm not sure I follow," I return.

She laughs again, the sound like little bells ringing, and my heart lightens some.

"You know that your dad and I didn't have an easy start. I was insecure and feared many things because of the way I was raised.

Your father, well, he had many similar feelings, but also had some stupid, misguided beliefs that I was too good for him and he would ruin me. Silly man."

I gasp, thinking about just how similar that sounds to Nate's and my situation. "And … what changed?" I ask again.

"He woke up. I didn't give up. He didn't give up. A lot of the same, but it was just our love being too big to ever ignore."

I look down at my nails, picking at my polish, but I don't speak.

"And a lot of sass," she continues.

I throw back my head and laugh, feeling lighter.

"So this isn't about Levi, exactly, but more about you and Nate?"

I nod, still not looking up.

"Sweetheart, look at your mama."

Instantly, I give her my eyes. She's still smiling. "Nate's a good boy. He has a huge heart and isn't afraid to laugh. He's one of those live big and live loud people. I've watched him grow up from a baby into the man he is today, so I can say with certainty that he is a man worthy of your love. But I can also see how Nate, being the man he is, took the youthful, innocent love of a just turned eighteen-year-old young lady and panicked. His age difference doesn't seem like a big deal right now when you're both in your twenties, but then, that difference was a bigger deal to a lot of people."

"He said he would ruin me."

"Baby." She sighs. "Nate's seen a lot of bad things happen to people who loved each other completely. He might have been young, but he was still around while each and every one of your father's friends fell and fought for their love. He's seen his sister go through terrible things for love. Watched Lee and Megan fight for what they have. If I had to guess, that boy is afraid of what could happen if he was to give in to what his heart is saying."

I frown and think about what she's saying. It makes sense. No one in our 'family' has had an easy go at falling in love, but they all took on that beautiful war and won.

"So what do I do now? How am I supposed to listen to my heart when it's been broken to bits by the one and only man who holds the power to fix it."

"That depends. He hurt you, and I understand it, baby, I do, but in order for you to follow your heart, you have to forgive him. You just said it yourself; he's the only man who holds the power to fix the hurt."

"And what if this is just a game to him? What if I am just some conquest?"

She reaches out and takes one of my fidgeting hands in her own, rubbing my knuckle with her soft thumb.

"Make him prove to you that isn't the case. Open your heart, cracks and all, and give him a chance to validate what you feel. Don't give up on him, even when it hurts, because you could be throwing away something truly beautiful."

"God, that's terrifying."

"That's because love is never easy, sweetheart. But it's worth every single bump, scratch, and crack in the end. Now, sit back here and tell your mama all about this lollipop dance."

I toss my head back and laugh.

By the end of our chat, my heart feels a little less heavy, and I know that I need to give Nate a chance. If anything, we need to sit down and talk.

But first things first—I need to break things off officially with Levi. There is no way, even if I hadn't been thinking and working toward this moment for weeks, that I would feel good about waiting another day when it is clear we have no future.

After the heavy conversation in my bed, I pulled my mom to the kitchen and settled in to catch up with her over the lunch she had brought.

Chicken salad sandwiches, my favorite.

The rest of our early afternoon time is spent with her curled up on the couch in my studio, watching me get lost in the heartbreaking canvas I had started the day before. I was so tuned in to what I was doing that I had completely forgotten she was still there until her soft voice broke through my tunnel vision.

"Okay, sweetie, give me a hug. It makes me feel good to see that dark cloud hanging over your head starting to clear away. Promise me that the next time you need me, you'll pick up the phone?"

I don't hesitate to wrap my arms around her and agree.

"I love you, Mama."

"I love you, my sweet Ember."

Chapter 14
Ember

My phone has been going off for the last few hours, annoying, but easily something I can tune out when I've hit that sweet spot in my painting. I hit that magic spot while my mom was still here, and I haven't stopped since, even with the lingering hangover that still haunts my body.

More often than not, when I've hit that spot, not a single thing can tear my focus away. Everything is falling together like magic and the once blank canvas is now beginning to look exactly how I envisioned.

I was right yesterday when I thought this might be my best piece yet.

So much haunting beauty in this large glory.

Heartbreakingly sad, but alight with a hopefulness for something 'more' swirling between the brushstrokes.

Today, I had concentrated on the two outstretched arms meeting in the center of the canvas as the focus. Each finger on the opposing hand extended, trying desperately to reach the other, but never getting close enough. Being as close as I am to the piece now, I can see the outline of the man and woman starting to take shape beyond those two hands.

When I'm finished, the abstract piece will be more blur and fade around the edges, the two bodies becoming clearer the closer you get to those two perfectly painted and in focus hands.

This is me.

This is Nate.

It's us.

So much beauty and pain in one huge piece that I can't help but think it is eventually my soul stripped bare and splattered against the canvas.

"A Beautiful War," I declare to myself with a smile, knowing instantly that the title for my piece has been born.

Bam bumps my leg, and I look down, smile still in place. "What's wrong, handsome man?"

He whines before moving to the door of my house. With a laugh, I clean off my brush and close the tops of my paint before moving around my easel.

"Come on, beast." I snicker when he starts to wag his tail in excitement.

When I push open the door that leads into my kitchen from my studio, he rushes through the house and I hear him barking at the front.

"I'm coming, I'm coming," I complain, almost tripping over the chew toys that he had strewn all over the kitchen floor. "You're worse than a child, Bam," I chide with a chuckle, picking up the few toys on my way to the living room.

I can hear him whining as I turn the corner into the living room from the small hallway and come to an abrupt halt when I see the imposing figure sitting in the middle of my couch. His arms are over the back in a relaxed manner, but his face betrays him. I can tell by the tick in his jaw that the calm he is portraying is a mask, but why he's looking at me with eyes cold and calculating is beyond me.

"Ember," he drawls, his deep voice thick, the way it always is when he's angry.

"Levi, hey … I thought you were going to call me later tonight?"

He doesn't speak, but I watch his jaw clench now as his lips thin. The unease that I had felt when walking in the room grows to a burning ball of anxiety in my gut.

"How was work?" I hedge nervously.

"Fine."

"Would you like something to drink?" I continue, moving to settle in on the loveseat opposite from him.

He leans forward, dropping his arms from the back of the couch and placing his elbows on his knees, never dropping his eyes from mine. "No."

"Okay." I gulp, not understanding his mood today. Hell, I haven't seen him since the other night, and even though we didn't leave on good terms, the brief texts that we've had since haven't given me a clue to why this is happening now.

Unless he knows you're about to break it off.

I ignore the inner voice and will my hands not to start fidgeting as I shift in my seat.

"How was your *party*?" he questions, deadly calm as he continues to leer at me.

"Good," I respond. "Well, good until I figured out that the hangovers are never worth the buzz," I clarify in an attempt to lighten the mood.

"That's nice. I didn't hear from you after you told me you would be going to that new club in town," he accuses.

Losing the battle with my nervous fidgeting, I twist my fingers together in my lap. His eyes cast a quick glance at them before they flit back to my face. "Yeah, sorry about that. After the girls got here, things just kind of went crazy. They had me busy from the second they opened the pizza boxes until I got home last night."

"Hmm," he remarks.

"Anyway, how was your night?"

"Interesting," he discloses ominously.

"Did you have a lot of call outs?" I ask, trying to ease the alarm I feel over his calm anger.

"Not really. Just one."

"Are you okay?"

He studies me for the longest breath before leaning back with one side of his mouth tipped up. Instead of looking like a smile, it only makes his face look like an evil sneer.

"Levi?" I coax when he doesn't speak.

"Tell me, Ember," he starts. "Would you think for one second that I would be okay with my fucking woman dressed like a slut while some man had his hands on her?"

"What?" I gasp in shock. I don't take my eyes off him, but I have a bad feeling things are about to get ugly.

"Did you fuck him?"

"Levi! No, of course not. You know I'm not that type of girl." Except, I'm not really sure what would have happened if rational thought hadn't returned after the touch of Nate's lips to mine last night. If I'm honest with myself, we were, in fact, seconds away from becoming a tangle of naked flesh.

"I'm not sure I believe you, Ember. Imagine my shock when we get a call to come check on that new fucking club because of the crowd size, and I walk in to see my girlfriend in the middle of some weird bar lap dance. I have two goddamn eyes, and I would be a fool not to believe what was right in front of my face."

Shit.

Damn.

Well, this wasn't exactly how I had pictured this going, but I might as well get it over with. Rip off the Band-Aid and finally make the long overdue move to end things between us.

"Nothing like that happened, Levi. I'm sure that Nate was just putting on a show because he knows the girls would think it was hilarious to embarrass me."

His eyes flare at the mention of Nate's name, and I feel my heart pick up speed and my skin flush cold with chills.

"Nate?" he bursts out, the sound like a deep rumble of thunder, making Bam bark. Levi's head swivels toward where Bam is sitting, and I hear my poor baby whine, which is so unlike my sweet-natured pup. He loves everyone.

My mind goes back to the other morning when I found out he had been tied to the fence, and I know, somehow, deep in my gut, that Levi was responsible.

"Look, Lev. I had hoped that we would be able to go out to dinner tonight to have this talk, but clearly, this just needs to happen now. I've felt this way for a while now, but we're just not working. I think it would be best if we broke things off."

There. I said it and the world is still spinning away.

His head twists from Bam, and he studies me with his stoic and quite frankly terrifyingly calm mask still in place. I wait with bated breath as he continues his silence. The clock on the wall behind me ticks away. Bam's panting echoes against the walls. My heart is in my stomach as trepidation climbs up my throat.

I watch as something dark dances across his face, briefly, before he gives me a nod and stands. I lean back in my seat at his sudden movement.

"If that's what you want. I'm not going to stick around if you would rather whore yourself out around town and look like a fool."

He stomps toward the door before stopping when his body is in front of the small entryway table I have next to it. His hand comes up from where he had been clenching his fist at his sides, and I watch as he picks up one of the many frames that decorate the surface. I try to visualize the order of my framed memories but can't seem to recall what could have possibly drawn his attention.

The muscles in his back ripple with tension, pulsing through the tight fabric of his dark tee shirt, before he turns to lock his evil gaze on me. I don't have time to comprehend his movement before the picture is sailing through the air and crashing into the wall, just barely missing my head.

"Family friend, my fucking ass. Have a nice life, bitch," he seethes before opening the door so hard that the doorknob sticks in the drywall.

My breaths come in rushed gasps as I stare in fear at the open doorway. Bam rushes to my side and lays his head in my lap with a gentle whine meant to soothe me. I hear the sound of Levi's truck start up, but it isn't until the sound of his engine had long since faded away that I rushed from my spot and muscled the door out of the wall before slamming it and throwing back the locks.

I scramble around my vacated seat and bend to grab the broken and shattered photo from the ground, gasping when I see which one it was.

I don't even remember who took the picture, but I had never been able to take it down and put it away. It's been one of my favorite images and cherished memories for so long that I should have realized it was the one Levi had seen.

It was a few months after Nate had started tutoring me. Everyone had been enjoying a long day at the Reid's. My skin was pink from being out in the sun for hours, but I didn't mind a second of that sunburn later that night.

I had been standing at the edge of the lake; you could see the out-of-focus people peppered in and out of the water, but at that moment, the camera caught me laughing at something Nate had said to me. My head was thrown back, hair down my back; my bikini had been a new purchase that I got in so much trouble with from my dad. I looked beyond happy and carefree.

And Nate … he was standing next to me, his board shorts low on his hips in the most delicious way. But I loved his face the most in this picture. He wasn't laughing with me. Instead, he was looking at me as if I was the most precious thing he had ever seen.

That look helped to convince me months later to take a chance and tell him how I felt. I was desperate to see that look again with my own eyes, but it wasn't until last night that he ever gave me a chance to see it once more.

There is no doubt in my mind that Levi saw the same thing I had built all my hopes on when he saw Nate's face, and as twisted as it is to feel this way, the only thing his outburst has done is given me the verification needed to see the direction my heart wants me to follow.

Chapter 15

Nate

Night after night for the last week, Dirty has been insane. A good insane. The kind that solidifies the fact I knew in my bones for a long time coming that this place would be a success.

But it's also been somewhat of a double-edged sword.

The madness kept me there for the past seven days while I've had to fight with myself every second of that time not to say fuck it and rush off to find Ember. I hadn't even had time to jump over to CS until now to finish the cases I still had to close.

I spent the first day after my chat with my dad still struggling to get my cock under control. The day after that, I kept going over and over what he had said. Picturing my future without Ember in it. Visualizing her meeting someone, getting married, having his kids … and in the end, I felt like I would be sick. Hell, I almost was.

There was no doubt about it; the thought of her with someone other than me was unfathomable. At that moment, I knew that my old man was right. I had to work my ass off to make up for the shit I had done that not only hurt her and pushed her away, but also get to the bottom of that night at my sister's wedding.

My memories still start and end with the dream that had haunted me for months, but until I hear it from Ember, I'm not sure how to make up for that.

The only thing I know for sure is that I'm going to fucking do it.

I hear the door open but don't look away from the monitor in front of me. I had neglected my responsibilities here at CS for a week now, and regardless of my responsibility to be at Dirty, I can't let my dad down.

"What's wrong with your face?"

I look up from my computer at the sound of Maddox entering the room.

"Shit," I mumble under my breath.

"I can hear you," he says, walking around to drop down on the chair at his desk. I look up in time to see him scowl at the picture of his girls, the same picture that I had turned slightly so I could see Ember better earlier, and wince when he grumbles low in his throat before shifting it back—only this time so I can't see shit.

"You want a picture on your desk of my girl, you need to earn the right to have it there."

"Yes, sir," I smart.

"Nate," he calls, and I pause my typing to focus on him. There's no way in hell I'm going to do anything that could piss him off when he knows I'm after making his baby girl mine, so I wisely give him one hundred percent of my attention. "Did you fix things with her?"

A lesser man would have looked away when Maddox Locke turned his penetrating black eyes on them. He's a hard man; rarely smiling unless it's at one of the three women in his life, but that silent dominating hold his very presence commands hits hard. He has a dark side; a side you don't ever want focused on you.

"Working on it," I respond, my voice strong and true.

"Work harder. I don't like seeing her upset, Nate."

My brow furrows. "I wasn't aware that she was upset," I add.

This time, his expression darkens, and I know I fucked up, even if I didn't mean it in the way it sounded.

He opens his mouth to speak, but I stop him with a sigh and one hand in the air. "Don't. I understand that you mean well right now, and I respect the hell out of that, but from now on, what happens between Ember and me will stay that way—between us. Before you assume that I didn't know she was upset because I had been avoiding her, let me set that straight. I've been working at Dirty from noon until almost four in the morning for seven days straight, and I finally pulled myself away from that to give up some much-needed sleep in order to close these cases out. I already told Shane, my manager, that I wouldn't be in tonight because I needed to take care of something. Now, it isn't any of your business, but I had planned to go see her tonight. I'll also share that I've talked to her briefly during the week, and she understands that I couldn't get away until tonight. So if she is upset still, respect *me* enough to know I'm working on it."

"You done?" he probes when I stop talking, an odd look crossing his features.

"I think so."

He nods, looking down at the frame before reaching out with one tan finger and pushing the corner of it until it is—once again—facing in a way that I can see Ember's beautiful face.

I take a deep breath, slowly, so he doesn't see I might have been seconds away from shitting my pants.

We continue to work on our respective cases in silence, the hours passing quickly. I look down at my work, making sure to finish my notes up in as much detail as possible before hitting the enter key with so much force that it echoes around us.

I lean back with a satisfied smile when I think about the hell storm that is about to rain down on the CFO I had been investigating. Now, with that strike against the keyboard, not only will our client know the depths of his employee's deceit, but the FBI will as well.

Now that my work is done, the rest is up to them.

And that officially ended my work at CS for the foreseeable future.

I look back at the turned frame and let myself relax knowing that even if she puts up a fight, now that I'm finished here, I can go there and then, I'm one step closer to getting my girl.

"Nathaniel."

I look up at Maddox and pray he isn't about to kick my ass now. I would rather not have to explain to Ember that her father tried to kill me before I even had a chance to win her.

"Sir?"

"I'm proud of you," he declares, causing me to pause cleaning up my files. "I'm not an easy person to stand up to and the fact that you had no problem putting me in my place shows me just what kind of man you've become. You might play the part of the carefree clown, but you have a strength about you that shows me if my baby girl decides to give you her heart, you're worth holding on to it."

I almost lose control of my body and drop dead in shock at his words. Fuck me, but I never thought I would get his *blessing*. I figured winning Ember would be the easy part—winning her father's approval being the fight.

"Thank you, Maddox," I reply, pretty damn proud that I'm able to keep myself from pumping my fist up in victory.

"That being said," he continues, his voice taking on a threatening tone. "If you hurt her in any way, remember that I know how to kill you and make it look like an accident. Don't make me have to kill one of my best friends' boys, Nate."

"Uh," I hesitate, my eyes widening.

"Nothing to say. I know where you stand and you know where I stand. You have my blessing to make her happy, but with that comes the promise of what I'll do if you fuck that up."

I nod, swallowing the pool of saliva that had gathered in my mouth.

I place the last folder of my closed cases in the tray on the side of my desk and grab my phone off the charging dock before turning to leave, only to stop in my tracks when Maddox calls my name.

"Coming from me as a man and not a father, know I speak from firsthand knowledge that women don't take kindly to being pressed against a wall unless you actually remember doing it to her too."

Fuck me. He did not just say that.

"And," he continues, looking down at his monitor. "My daughter deserves better than being pushed up against a dirty wall. Don't do that shit."

Without knowing what in the fucking hell I'm supposed to say to that shit, I give him a gruff sound of acknowledgment before turning and walking with just a little more speed than normal out of the dungeon.

Chapter 16
Ember

Nate: I'm on the way.

I look down at my phone but decide to finish my task before responding.

I pull the latex glove down onto my hand and grimace when I reach out to pick up one of the two dead birds right outside my back door. I had already cleaned up the broken bird feeder that had been hanging on the overhang leading into my house. My heart broke thinking that I had been responsible for two little birds dying because I hadn't secured their feeder well enough.

This week has been full of me cleaning crap up, it seems.

Five days ago, a branch had fallen off one of the oak trees outside my bedroom window, shattering the window above my bed before landing in the middle of my mattress with enough force to puncture the damn thing. That, fortunately, had happened when I had been up late finishing my last piece for my show, trying to make up for the two days I missed after my birthday and subsequent hangover. Still, I made a point to have the men delivering my new mattress help me move my bed to the other side of the room—the one without a window near it.

Three days ago, in what would appear to be one hell of a night for some bored kids, my house and two surrounding it had met the sun with a yard full of toilet paper. Enough toilet paper it almost looked as if we had a snow day.

Not wanting to even deal with that for a second, I hired someone to come clean up the mess. I had enough going on with getting my painting done in half the time I would normally spend on a piece.

Yesterday, my mailman had apparently decided to try his hand at crash test dummies. I got home from the grocery store to find my mailbox trampled in a vibrant display of shattered wood and crushed metal.

And now, the damn bird feeder is murdering my feathered friends.

I swear nothing is going my way this week. I can only hope that with Nate coming over now, I'm not about to have another wave of bad luck.

After grabbing the second bird and carrying it to the trashcan with my arm completely outstretched, I snap off my glove and throw that in as well. Bam trails behind me the whole time, his thick head looking all over the yard as his tongue hangs lazily out of the side of his mouth. The big beast has been attached to my side since Levi almost took my head off last week. I've almost broken my neck more times than I can count because he decided to move his bed in the corner of my studio and drag it directly behind where I stand. I've even woken up to him in my bed four times this week, which is something the big pup had never done before. You would think that when a two-hundred-pound dog clambers up to your bed at night, you would wake up, but not me.

"Ember?" I hear called from the front yard, and I look down when Bam takes off with a bark around the side of the house.

So much for being my big shadow, I guess.

I follow his path, going around the house instead of inside. When I find Nate crouched down, Bam is happily soaking up the attention as he scratches him from head to tail.

"Bam, here," I call sharply, but just roll my eyes when he flops his huge mass down on the grass and sticks all four legs up waiting for Nate to give his belly the same attention.

Nate laughs but gives Bam what he wants for a minute before standing and brushing his hands against his jeans. Jeans that I should note are molded to his thighs and highlight the bulge in his crotch.

I watch, my eyes almost crossing, when the bulge in question visibly twitches beneath the denim.

"Em, please don't. I can't handle another reminder that my cock doesn't know how to behave."

I snap my eyes to his, wide with shock at his words. "Uh … I'm sorry?" Really, what else could I say right now?

"Long story, but please don't be offended if I end up walking funny soon."

I can feel my cheeks heat the second I visualize him having to walk funny because of an erection.

"Did you want to go get a bite to eat?" he asks, making me stop thinking about his dick and try to form big girl sentences.

"I cocked. I mean I'm cocking. *Fuck*." I bet my face is bright red now. How embarrassing.

"Right, so you're making dinner?" he questions, moving his hand to adjust himself. I watch his long fingers work the raised denim with a groan deep in his throat. "Let's go inside, Em, and please let me go first. I'm not sure I can handle seeing those shorts going up the stairs."

I follow mutely, not really sure what just happened.

Nate walks in and follows Bam as he excitedly rushes through the house and into the kitchen, his nails tinkering across the wooden floors as he leaps and jumps in front of Nate.

I watch his ass.

He freely admitted he would have done it to me, so it's only fair.

And what an ass it is.

He moves around my space as if he's spent every day here. He grabs Bam's food bowl, filling it up, and then repeating the process with his water. He moves to the stove and lifts the lids, stirring the pasta sauce before grabbing the spaghetti noodles I had been waiting to put in until the water boiled. I just stand there mutely as he makes himself at home.

He turns after the putting the noodles in and leans against the counter with a sigh. My eyes move from the stove, to Bam, and back to the huge man making my kitchen seem like it had shrunk in size.

"I'm guessing spaghetti is good with you?" I question.

"I love spaghetti."

And he does. He especially loves my mom's sauce, something I had spent the whole day cooking at a low simmer.

"That's good."

My fingers twist together as my nerves get the best of me, and I look down at the floor. I've always wanted to see him moving in my space with me, but I never in a million years thought it would actually happen. It's one thing for us to be together for family dinners or even when the gang got together to go out as a big group but never have we been alone in our own homes.

"Why are you nervous?" he inquires, pushing off the counter with a shove and walking forward until his booted feet meet my vision.

"You're here," I weakly exhale.

"I am."

"I'm just trying to figure out why. Why now." And it's the truth. Even with the knowledge that I would open my heart to whatever was happening between us, I would be an idiot not to have a little bubble of nerves about it.

I close my eyes when I feel his fingers brush my hair behind my ear. His warm palm slides down from my cheek until he's cupping my neck with his thumb resting just under my chin. My head is pushed up gently and his fingers tense and flex where they rest at the back of my neck.

"I'm a smart man, but not always a bright one. I have a lot to prove to you, but I'm here because it's where you are."

I shake my head while he speaks, but he smiles, and without saying another word, he bends down to kiss my lips soft and quick.

"Dinner first, then we get to the heavy stuff, okay?"

I nod, not really trusting my voice, and move around him to stir the noodles. We work together as if we've been doing it forever, and in no time, everything is done and we're sitting at the table with huge plates full of spaghetti.

"God, I forgot how much I loved this sauce," he moans, with his mouth full of his first big bite.

"It's just store sauce," I lie, twisting my fork in the sauce coated noodles. Inside, I love that he realized, with his first bite, that it wasn't just any sauce.

"Store bought, my ass. I would recognize this sauce anywhere. I used to beg your mom to come over and make it for my mom, but she would just smile and give me another huge helping. I think she thought I was joking, but let me tell you, my mom could never get it right."

I feel my nerves recede some and smile at him. "It's a tricky one. You have to cook it for hours, but I loved smelling it all day when I was living there, so it's nice when I cook it myself and have a little of my childhood memories filling my own home."

He drops his fork, his mouth red from the sauce, and just gapes at me. "You made this?"

I tilt my head, chuckling to myself as I swallow my bite. "Of course, I did. How else would it have gotten here?"

He mumbles something about a ring before shoving another huge forkful between his lips. I watch him chew, his eyes closed in bliss and his moans deep. I mutely hand him a napkin before the sauce that had been trailing down his chin could fall.

"I figured you had just heated up some frozen shit you had from your mom."

I gasp. "Uh, no. The first thing my mom did when I was old enough to walk was pull a chair to the counter while she cooked to teach me everything she knew. I can make her chicken fried steak and mashed potatoes better than she can."

His fork falls on his plate and he looks at me with awe.

"What?"

"Good God, woman, don't tease me."

"Promise, even my dad says so. I'll make it for you tomorrow, er … I mean some other time. If you want, that is."

He reaches out his hand, his face going soft and his smile growing big. "Tomorrow sounds good, baby, but you'll have to bring it by Dirty. I need to get some paperwork done, and Shane won't be there to cover for the night."

Baby?

Oh.My.God.

"I can do that," I squeak.

"Good, it's a date."

"A d-date," I stutter.

He just continues to smile, and even when he picks up his fork and continues to eat, that smile never leaves his lips.

Of course, the one on my own never left either.

Chapter 17
Nate

After the last pot was dried, I grab Ember's hand and pull her into the living room. She stumbles at first, and I hate that she is looking at everything I do and trying to figure out what game I'm playing. I saw it in her eyes earlier when I told her we would make a date out of dinner at Dirty tomorrow. It was written all over her face when I started the pasta, and then again, when she admitted she didn't understand why I was there.

She was justified in her thoughts, I muse as I drop down on the couch and pull her down to sit on my lap. I fucked up and I'm just now beginning to see just how much.

"Ask me," I stress, shifting her so that she is sitting sideways with her back leaning against the armrest and put one arm over her shoulder to twist one of her long locks of hair around my fingers, while my other hand comes up and rests over her fiddling hands, halting her movements.

"Ask you what?" Her eyes widen, and I watch as her chest starts to rise and fall faster with each breath.

"Ask me what I was thinking when you told me that you loved me the first time."

She jerks in my arms, and I fight back the groan when her weight rubs against my swollen cock. I tighten my hold on her with a squeeze of the hand that is holding her two captive and pull her closer to my chest.

"I can just tell you, but I need to know that you actually want to hear it."

She sighs, and I know she would rather be saying anything else right now, but she does it. "What were you thinking?" There's a slight tremor in her soft melodic voice, and I say a silent prayer that she doesn't start crying. I'm not sure I could handle her tears.

"I was terrified out of my mind. I had been fighting my feelings for you well before you turned legal. It didn't matter in my mind that you were finally eighteen; there was still a gap between us that wouldn't have been easy for us to overcome right then. You were still finding yourself, and we both know that I needed to stop being a punk and grow up. I had been drifting, content in life, even though I had dreams that no one knew about. Dreams that I've only now made a reality."

She continues to search my face as I speak. I pause to collect my thoughts, pulling her hands apart and clasping one of her tiny hands in my larger one. She sighs and I take a deep breath before continuing.

"That wasn't the only reason, Em. I had some stupid fear in my head that pain always comes with love. I watched some fucked-up shit happen to Dani only months before, and seeing how lust, love, and all the feelings in between can turn sour real fast, I let that fear rule me. But I also knew, even if you didn't see it, that there was no way us being together wouldn't cause issues within our families."

"It wouldn't have," she rushes out quietly.

"Yeah, it would have. I wasn't the same man I am today three years ago. I needed to wake the hell up and make something of myself. I can tell you, the man I was then wasn't worthy of you."

"You're so wrong." She sighs sadly.

"Yeah, well … I see things differently now, but I still think it would have been a damn hard road for us then, and I'm not sure I would have been strong enough to make sure it was one we traveled with no trouble."

"You hurt me, Nate."

I take a deep breath and give her the rest of it. "Yeah … I hurt me too."

She jerks in my arms, visibly shocked at my admission.

"Denying what I felt. Hurting you to push you away. Knowing

deep down that I would regret that moment for a long time coming. *Being without you* for the last three years, yeah … that hurt me too."

She pulls her hand from my hold and shifts in my lap until she is facing me with her knees on either side of my thighs. "You never acted like it," she accuses, her hands coming up to rest on my chest as she searches my eyes, running her gaze down my face and over my features.

"Because it was easier to act like I didn't have a care in the world than to admit that I was wrong and risk you rejecting me like I did you."

And that's the truth of it, something that I didn't even realize until recently when I forced myself to really think back to why I pushed her away. The reasons behind denying us what we both wanted.

"I never—" she starts, but I stop her with a shake of my head.

"It's in the past, Em. A wise man once told me that looking back wouldn't do anything but make the hurt grow a little bigger."

"I'm not sure I agree with that," she tells me.

I smile. "Yeah, maybe not, but my dad's got some years on him and he's been through enough shit that I'm going to take his word for it. If we're going to make anything of our future, Em, we're going to have to stop looking in the past. All that's going to do is stop us from creating our forever."

Her face is comical when I finish. Her beautiful brown eyes round and huge in disbelief. Her lips parted slightly and I don't even need to look down to know that her tits were heaving beneath her tank top. A thought that I should have tried to ignore because, not even a second later, I watched her face flush when my cock jumped against her core.

She shifts, and it jumps again. I quickly take hold of her thin hips with one hand grasped tightly on each side of her waist. "Don't you move," I demand through clenched teeth.

Her eyes leave mine, and she drops her head. A submissive move that I don't miss in the least. My cock pulses violently at the thought of taking control of her while I fuck her in this position. Not letting her top from the bottom while I show her who holds the reins.

"Look at me," I command in a hard tone, fucking thrilled when she instantly gives me those eyes again. "You need to let that go. For us to move on and forward, we can't do that successfully if you're holding that against me. I can't change it, but I can promise you that I will never willingly hurt you again. Understand?"

She nods, swallowing audibly, and I know the controlling and dominating side of me that I normally only let out when I'm in the bedroom is turning her the fuck on. I always thought that Ember might be a sexual submissive but to have that confirmed feels damn good.

"Time to move on?" I probe while looking into her eyes and caressing the soft skin at her hips where her shirt had ridden up. "This next part isn't going to be better, but we need to clear the whole table, and in order to do that, I need you to fill in a whole bunch of blanks I have right now."

She goes wooden in my arms, and I fucking know she understands where I'm going with this.

"Nate," she whimpers.

"I know, Ember, but I need to explain myself and I need you to be honest with not only me but yourself after I do. Got it?"

She relaxes her body but only marginally.

"For months and fucking months, I've woken up from the same dream. I'm with a soft and willing woman hot for me against a wall. My eyes never open in the dream, but even then, your face and scent filled my senses. I had never pictured anyone but you. I would wake up with the scent of lemon and wildflowers so strong in my nose that I was convinced it was real, but it always ended the same. Me opening my mouth and asking that woman's name."

With every word that leaves my lips, I watch as she struggles, and loses, the fight to control her emotions. When the first tear slips over her lids, I want to kick my own ass. Hell, by the time the second one spills over, I was ready to call her dad myself and tell him I was ready to take what he had to give me.

"When you," she starts but has to pause when a giant hiccupping breath steals her words. "You didn't even see me, Nate."

"Baby, I was so drunk, I didn't even see *me*. Even in that damn dream, I'm aware of how drunk I am."

"When you pulled my arm as I was coming back from the

restroom, I was startled at first because I didn't know who it was. It was so dark on that side of the house, but the shadows you pulled me into made it almost impossible to see. But then you grumbled something about not being able to wait any longer. I thought you knew, Nate. You said you couldn't wait to have me, and I thought you knew!" she screams and drops her head down on my shoulder. She turns, resting her forehead against my neck before she continues to speak. "The second you said those words and pushed me up against the wall, I didn't even care that I was about to have sex for the first time with my family and closest friends around me in the middle of the shadows. None of that mattered because it was *you,* and I knew that I would be safe. Then …" She sucks in a stuttered breath. "Then in the same second I thought I would die of happiness, you pushing your thickness inside me just a bit—a place no man had ever been—you asked me *who I was.* There I was experiencing the best moment of my life with the man I had loved *forever,* and he didn't even know who he was about to fuck. That. Killed. Me."

"God, baby." I exhale through the pain her words inflict on me.

"Then after I pushed you away, you just fell to the ground like nothing had happened. I can't tell you what you did after that because I was too busy running away as fast as I could. Which, awkwardly for me, just happened to put me on a collision course with my own father. It was the worst moment of my life, Nate."

Her breathing continues to come in choppy gasps as I hold her tightly to me with my arms wrapped around her back. I never would have believed that damn dream was just a drunken memory. Had I known, fuck, I would never have let this much time go—the hurt fester—without making it right. Now, I'm not even sure how to fix this.

"I understand now," she says with a hitch to her breath. "It doesn't take away all of the pain it caused, but it goes a long way in dulling it."

"I'm so sorry," I lament. "It sounds like a weak thing to say, I know that, but fuck, I am … so sorry."

She pushes off my chest and lifts herself until her face is level with mine. You would never know she had even shed one tear. Most chicks I know turn a hundred different shades of swollen red when they're crying but not Ember. Her face is just slightly flushed, but other than her wet eyelashes, you would never know.

"I'm terrified, Nate, honestly terrified. If what you say is true and looking back on painful memories only makes that hurt grow, then I need to get over it. But I don't know how. In my head, I'm convinced that you're just going to drop me if I blink too long. My heart, though, is telling me to wrap myself around you and never let go. I feel like I'm being torn in two different directions."

She is silently begging me with an expression mixed with fear and hope to provide her with all the answers, but I know nothing I can say will give her what she needs.

This is something I need to show her.

Prove to her.

Fight for her.

I frame her face in my hands, feeling her pulse beat wildly at the base of her neck as I lean forward and press my lips against hers. I don't deepen the kiss, but when I take a deep breath through my nose and my senses are full of everything that is her, this kiss feels more intimate than anything I had ever felt before.

"Keep following your heart, Ember. Follow it—*me*—and let me worry about guiding the way. Allow me to prove to you that I'm worthy of you giving me your love back. How does that sound?"

Chapter 18
Ember

I'm a bundle of nerves.

I called Nate about an hour ago and told him I would be there around eight and he told me just to pull up out back and he would meet me there.

When I drove up, passing the entrance, I was shocked to see so many people lined up outside. There were so many people; it looked like they were pouring out of the club. I never thought that Tuesday would be a popular club night, but apparently, it is.

When I was here for my birthday and first witnessed what they called the holding room, I thought it was a brilliant idea to have a whole building designated for the people waiting to get into the actual club. But seeing all the people lined up outside, I feel an instant sense of pride that Nate's club is so popular that they can't even make room for everyone, and that's just in its second week of operation.

Pulling my car beside Nate's huge truck, I turn the key and take a huge gulp of air in an attempt to calm the butterflies swirling around my stomach like a tornado. Stepping out, I walk to the trunk and pull out my picnic basket. Before I can shut the trunk, though, the basket is being taken from my hands and Nate's scent hits my nose.

Whatever cologne he uses is so distinctively *him* that I've caught myself over the years following the trail when I would catch a whiff of it in random places. If I knew the name, I'm pretty sure I would buy a bottle just to spray on my sheets.

With that thought, coupled with those damn butterflies, my

mouth opens and I speak without turning. "What cologne do you wear?"

His low chuckle rumbles against my back as he kisses me on my temple before leaning in and breathing right next to my ear. His scent becomes stronger instantly.

"Acqua Di Gio," he hums against my ear, the reverberations washing over me, and I shiver instantly.

"Who makes that?" I ask breathlessly.

"Giorgio Armani."

I'm definitely buying a bottle and spraying every inch of my house.

"Give me some time, baby, and I'll transfer it on every inch myself. Just need you to help."

"Shit," I hiss when I realize I spoke that out loud.

His free hand comes up and turns me gently before pulling me to his side. "Hey." He laughs.

Embarrassment forgotten, I look up into his handsome face and echo his greeting in a whisper. He shakes his head, his hair moving around his angular face, making my palms itch to run my fingers through the silky strands. I'm so used to seeing him with it up in one of those sexy man buns that the rare sight of it falling free makes my mouth water and my core clench.

Damn, he is so sexy.

His lips twitch, and I know I did it again.

"Come on. I've been starving for you, and it hasn't even been twenty-four hours since I left your house."

He grabs my hand, the other holding the basket full of our dinner, and pulls me toward the door that I just now notice the bartender who served me shots on my birthday is holding open.

"Dent, meet my girl, Ember. Ember, my friend, Denton."

I go to reach out my hand to take the one Denton is offering in greeting, but jerk it back when I feel Nate growl low and deep. Denton's head goes back, and he booms out a thundering laugh.

"Did you just growl like a dog?" I ask Nate in shock and turn to look up at his face.

He keeps his narrowed eyes on a still laughing Denton, not

answering me.

"That's a little much, don't you think?" I continue.

Nate looks down at me like I'm the crazy one for even asking him that, and I ignore him by returning what I hope is a hard look of my own. He shrugs and pulls me through the door and into a dark hallway.

"It's nice to formally meet you, Denton!" I call over my shoulder while still being pulled behind Nate. I hear another animalistic sound from him and just roll my eyes.

He's crazy.

When we reach the end of the hallway, I can see that the club is just as packed as it was the last time I was here. I continue looking around while keeping up with Nate's huge steps as he leads me to the stairs that I know will lead me to his office, only letting go of my hand long enough to wave me ahead of him.

I look down at my outfit, a short summer dress that I picked after an hour of throwing almost everything out of my closet, and wonder if I miscalculated when settling on this one. I hadn't thought about the long climb up. He probably wants me ahead of him so I don't flash anyone.

When I look back up at him and see the mischievous twinkle in his eyes, I know that I was wrong. He wants me ahead of him so that *he* can catch a flash of what is under my skirt.

Well, he's in for a shock. I wink and laugh when I see him frown in confusion before moving around him and starting my climb. The hissed breath that I hear over the music at my back gives me a rush of power and confidence. I put a little extra swirl in my hips with each step, and by the time I'm halfway up, my lips are curled in a smile so wonky and big that it hurts my cheeks.

Just when his warm palm hits the inside of legs, I reach out and push the handle on his office, about to come out of my skin when the tip of his thumb touches my bare sex.

"Oh my God," I gasp and stop just inside the door of his office.

He hits my back, and I hear the contents of my picnic basket shift. "What the hell?" he explodes behind me when he finally sees what stopped me in the first place.

Oh, how I wish it were just because of his hand.

The skirt of my dress had ridden up from the jerk of his arm when I stopped abruptly, and I hastily pull it down. Lord knows, one half-naked woman in his office is enough.

"Oops," the sickly high voice says from his couch and she stands slowly. Her naked breasts sway as she bends to pick up the black corset top.

I look back at Nate and see him just barely keeping a leash on his anger. I know whatever we just walked in on isn't something welcomed by him, even if I wasn't here. He moves into the room and tenderly—despite his very raw anger—moves me out of the way so he can shut the door and silence the music that is pounding up from the club below.

"You want to tell me what the fuck you're doing in my office, Julie? Without your top on, no less."

He walks over to his desk, unfortunately placing him closer to her, and puts the basket down with utmost care. His hand runs across the top in an almost reverent caress, and I can't even describe what seeing him do that does to me.

Even though she's tainted our moment … whatever this is, he is still almost disbelieving that I'm here, with him. Well, he's not the only one, and I'm not letting this woman ruin a moment I've only dreamed possible.

She steps closer to him, her top still not on, and reaches out to touch him.

I don't even think. I move to stand in front of him, my wedges almost tripping me up in my haste to get between them, and I cross my arms over my chest with a growl low in my throat.

I feel Nate bend, his mouth going to my ear as one strong hand curls around my hips and pulls me flush to his body. "Did you just growl like a dog?" he mockingly breathes so low I only hear him before nipping the sensitive flesh behind my ear.

"Back up now," I fume when she has the nerve to look at me as if I'm the one intruding.

"Who the hell are you?" the woman—Julie—snaps at me.

"His."

"Mine."

We both speak at the same time, and her eyes dart back and forth between the two of us before narrowing and she addresses Nate. "That's not what you told me last night." One very thin blond brow attempts to go up, but judging by the way it just kind of twitches, she's got a little too much Botox going on. Her red lips tip up and what could have been a smothery look just makes her look like a devil.

A she-devil.

"Nice try, but you're going to have to work a little harder if you're going to try that kind of garbage with me because he never left my side last night."

I see my words hit her when some of that malevolent spitefulness dims. She doesn't know I'm lying, but I know she is.

"That was a nice try, *babe*," I tell her before reaching over and picking one of her blond hairs off her breast, my finger grazing her hard nipple and I curl my lip up in disgust. "Honey," I call over my shoulder, not giving her the satisfaction of looking away first.

"Hmm?"

"Do you think bleach would ruin your couch?" I ask, my brow arching high.

His laughter bellows from his chest, the richness fills the room instantly. The hand still holding my hip flexes and he pulls me closer, the other arm going around my chest to hold me to his body. Whether he's doing that to keep me closer or to keep me from *her*, I don't really care. The second every hard inch of him presses against me from top to toe, the woman before us might as well have been invisible.

He is finally able to calm down his hilarity to just a few bursts of air that I feel tickle the top of my head a few moments later. The woman is still topless and still fuming in front of us.

"You're fired. If I see you back inside or near Dirty, I'll make sure you're in the back of a cop car in seconds, got me?" His deadly calm tone causes a shiver of arousal to stream down my spine. He's doing it to intimidate her, show her he's serious and in control, I'm sure … but hearing him take a tone full of domination flips a switch inside me that makes me shift uncomfortably when I feel the wetness between my legs.

"What?!" she screeches and throws her hands in the air. "A few weeks ago, you were on the bar dancing for me, and now, you're throwing me out when we both know this is what you want."

Instead of allowing her words to cut me, I reach back and push my hand between our bodies until my palm rests against the bulge in his pants. He's not hard, thankfully, but he's obviously a sizable man if the heavy weight of his cock beneath my palm is anything to go by. He hisses out a breath when I squeeze my hand. I want him to know that her words aren't affecting me in the least and the only way I can think of is to remind him that I meant what I said yesterday. I still want him even with this clusterfuck in front of us. The old Ember, the one that let her past rule her, would have run the second I stepped into his office, but not the new me. I intend to live up to the nickname he gave me a long time ago.

His length hardens with my touch, but he just flexes the hold his hands have on me and lets me continue to play.

"You know damn well that I was giving a demonstration that day. Not for one goddamn second was I dancing for *you*. I don't know what sick fantasy you've built up in your head, but I promise you that it will never come to fruition. Get the fuck out of my club."

She hesitates.

"Now!" he roars, and she hastily covers herself with her top before running toward the door and down the stairs.

I feel him breathing rapidly against my back, my hand still holding his now very hard cock. I give him a squeeze, and it's almost as if someone stuck him with a cattle prod. He jerks back, his hands going to my shoulders, and he spins me around roughly. I would have fallen, but the second I was facing him, he bent, grabbed me at the back of both thighs, and had me up in his arms before I could blink. His mouth crashes against mine roughly before turning us. I feel my back press against the cold, hard surface of his windows before all rational thought flies out the window.

"I won't take you here," he rumbles against my mouth before turning his head and deepening the kiss. I try to roll my hips, desperate to ease the ache between my legs, but he pushes me harder against the glass. "No." The unwavering authority in his voice stops me instantly.

He steps back, gradually helping me to my feet until he is sure that I have steady footing. Stepping back and running his hand through his hair, I lick my lips when his brown hair falls back in a shiny curtain against his face. At the moan I must have let slip, he jerks and turns to face me.

"No, Ember. We're going to set the table," he commands, pointing at the table I hadn't noticed on the other side of the room. One single rose sits in the center of the black surface. "You're going to go over there and get everything set up before sitting down like a good girl. You aren't ready for the kind of time-out I have planned for you, but know that if you disobey me, I'm going to start adding that shit up. I'm going to the bathroom to take care of this problem you've created, and you're going to set the table, sit down, and wait for me so I can give you a proper first date you will remember for the rest of our lives."

The shock of his words is still slamming into my overheated body when I hear his door slam. *The kind of time-out he has planned for me?* Something tells me it will be a whole hell of a lot more fun than the kind of time-out that always ends with his sister having her nose shoved in a corner.

He wants a first date to remember for the rest of our lives? Something tells me that isn't going to be a problem at all.

Chapter 19

Nate

I have the only woman my cock has been craving just outside this door, and here I am in my office bathroom fucking my fists roughly so that—hopefully—the bite of pain I'm giving with each thrust of my hips and twist of my wrists will be enough to calm me down.

I had my cock in my hand before the bathroom door had even slammed behind me, and here I am, not even minutes later, with my balls tightening and the tight coils of pleasure starting to unravel.

I move over to the sink, continuing to work myself with both fists, as I line myself up to empty my come into the basin. I feel my balls pull up and the blinding pleasure that shoots up my spine and wraps around my brain makes my vision go black as I roar out with each thick rope of come that shoots from the tip of my cock.

"Fucking goddamn," I moan deeply, feeling my knees lock. I look down, blinking against the gray still clouding my vision to see that I'm still pulsing heavily. Relaxing the hold my hands have on my cock, I take one hand and slowly stroke my oversensitive skin, watching as the last few spurts hit the basin.

I swipe my thumb over the tip before letting my—thankfully—soft cock drop heavily against my undone jeans. Washing my hands first and ignoring the ridiculous amount of come painting the inside of the basin, I carefully tuck my cock and shirt in then zip my jeans and push my belt through the loops.

If what just happened is anything to go by, it might just kill me when I finally sink into Ember.

Looking in the mirror, I see the wild look in my eyes and I say a silent prayer that I'm able to keep the promise to myself that I won't take her until I know I've proven myself to her.

When I open the door and see her sitting demurely at the set table, I groan and almost stumble when the tip of my cock—still sensitive as hell from my release—brushes against the denim of my jeans.

Ignoring my needs, I walk around the table and stop directly behind her. I smile when I hear her suck in a breath only to let it out in a moan. My girl enjoys my smell. I reach up, pulling my hair back and holding it in my fists, and I bend. The side of my stubbled cheek rubs against the smoothness of hers on my descent. She shivers, and when I reach her tan, bare shoulder, I turn my head slightly before opening my mouth and sinking my teeth into the tender flesh where her neck meets her shoulder, sucking lightly. She whimpers and shifts her body the best she can since my teeth are still pressing against her skin.

"Good girl," I rumble low against her skin, kissing the teeth marks and pink bruise my mouth left behind. "It pleases me that you listen when I tell you to do something."

She doesn't respond; she just tips the right side of her lip up and looks at me with lust-filled eyes.

Taking my seat, I look down at the plate before me and wonder if I could come again just from the mouthwatering aromas swirling up from the hot food.

"To a first date to remember." She breaks the comfortable silence around us, picking up the Coke she must have brought with her and waiting for me to do the same with the one in front of me.

"And many more to follow," I add, touching the top of her can with mine before placing it back down and picking up my fork and knife.

"Better than Mom's," she smarts with a wink.

"We'll see."

She waits while I cut into the meat, dip it in the mashed potatoes, and bring it to my mouth. I couldn't hold back my moan if I tried because the second the flavor hits my taste buds, my mouth waters, and I close my eyes. I see her starting to cut into her own food, still smiling, but I'm incapable of talking at the moment. Not while I'm eating the best damn thing I've ever tasted.

"You're right," I mumble around the mouthful of food. "Better than your mom's, baby."

That damn smile just gets bigger, and she silently continues to eat.

It doesn't take long before I'm about to lick my plate clean, but she just reaches out and places the rest of her dinner in front of me with a knowing look.

"Next time, I'll make sure to bring more than one helping for you, honey."

My chest warms when she calls me that, something that I just vaguely recall her using when Julie was in the room, but now that I know she wasn't saying that for her benefit, I let the pleasure of it fill me.

"You know I didn't want her here, right?"

She nods, taking a sip of her drink and leaning back in her seat. "I'm not upset about it. I'm just glad I was here to let her know you aren't on the market anymore."

I give her a sly smile before asking, "Yeah? I got myself a woman?"

One of her shoulders comes up in a shrug and she laughs softly. "We'll see."

Oh, we sure will, Emberlyn Locke. We sure as fuck will. Knowing I'm not sure I can last much longer without hearing her agree that I do, in fact, have a woman, I mentally give myself two weeks tops to make it happen.

"Come with me?" I request.

We had finished our dinner about an hour ago and instead of pulling her to the couch as I would have liked, I sat in my desk chair, pulled her on my lap, and swiveled the seat so we could look down at the club below.

She turns her head and looks over her shoulder at me before

giving me her smile and a small nod.

I help her to her feet before climbing to my own and pulling her toward the door, down the stairs, and into the madness. The crowd parts without trouble, and I make sure she settles safely at an empty spot I found for her at the main bar before jumping over the surface and behind the counter.

I hear the sound of her laughter over the music when my feet land. I look over my shoulder with a wink before grabbing a shot and pint glass. I place them both down in front of her before reaching around and grabbing the amaretto and filling the shot glass about three-fourths full before getting the 151 proof rum and filling it the rest of the way. Then I place the now full shot inside the pint glass. I feel Dent move to my side and hand me a beer, smirking a knowing smile when he watches me fill the pint glass up until it's level with the already full shot glass.

Her eyes follow my hand as I reach out and hold my palm up, knowing that Dent will be ready for the next step, and he doesn't disappoint.

Both of her dark brows shoot up the second I flick the lighter and hold it to the shot glass in the center of the pint, the flame sparking instantly as the liquor burns brightly in front of her.

While it burns between us, I catch her gaze, and with one finger, I point at the brightly lit sign above me.

I had one installed at each of the bars around the club last night. Luckily, I know enough people around town that when I want something done, it's done right away. Some sort of glowing backlight design illuminates the simple wording centered on both sides of the solid black sign.

Dirty Dog's Pleasure Elixir :: Ember Firecracker

I watch her jaw drop, knowing without words what I mean by that display. I'm claiming her as mine for everyone to see the second they step up to any of the bars inside Dirty. Well, I'm sure the majority of people who order Ember's drink will have no fucking clue except for those who know us personally. And honestly, it's more about making a statement to her anyway.

One that screams I, Dirty Dog himself, only find my pleasure from *my* Ember.

My firecracker.

Chapter 20
Ember

"Come on, Bam!" I yell across the expanse of my backyard as I wait for him to bring back the nasty, slobber-filled tennis ball that he loves more than life. I watch him frolic around; tossing his huge body up in the air before running in circles to chase whatever imaginary thing he's found.

Giving up on getting him to come inside so I can get some cleaning done before finding something to eat for dinner, I flop down on one of my outdoor chairs and give in to the thoughts that have held my mind captive for the last week.

After the night at Dirty when I brought him dinner, I've been burning for him, and it had nothing to do with the drink that he had created for me. A drink that I know in my bones was his way of letting me see just how serious he is about this newly created us.

I stuck around for another hour after his grand reveal of Ember's Firecracker, but I had a feeling that, by me being there, Nate was having a hard time focusing on what he needed to do, which was run his club. I made my excuses, even if I wanted to stick around, and after another explosive make-out session next to my car, I headed home.

That night, even with the shocking start we had with his office surprise, had been one of the best of my life. Unfortunately for us, the timing just hasn't been on our side for the last week. Not since he has to deal with everything that comes with having the most popular club around two weeks after opening their doors.

Over the week since, we've been able to steal a few phone calls here and there and texts when calls weren't a possibility, but I've had enough. I know he's busy, and it had almost been a blessing since I've spent almost eighteen hours a day working nonstop on *A Beautiful War.* I never dreamed a painting that scale would only take a little over two weeks, but if I keep up my pace, I'll be finished middle of next week. Just over a week before my show.

This afternoon, though, I hit my breaking point. All those calls and texts were officially not enough. I'm desperate to see him face-to-face. To feel his arms around me again and his lips against mine. Which is probably why I currently feel nothing but pent-up sexual frustration and eagerness for him to return my text … or plea, rather.

I bend forward to reach behind me to pull my phone from my back pocket and check it—again—to see if Nate had texted back, but not before seeing the message that I sent him an hour ago. My desperation for him had hit a peak so high I thought I needed to take a break with my vibrator.

Ember: Come over when you're done at Dirty. I need you. No matter the time. Key is under the mat.

Would he think I was crazy? Probably not. Would he come? Probably. Would he wonder what I'm really asking for? Absolutely.

"Come on, Bam. Time to get your tail inside." I laugh when he leaps again, this time chasing after a bug.

He turns, his tongue wagging, as he runs toward me.

When I open the back door, he charges into the house, and I hear him rushing into the kitchen seconds before he greedily starts lapping up his water.

Just when I shut and lock the back door, my phone vibrates in my hand, causing my heart to pick up speed. When I look and see Nikki's name on the screen, I can't help but feel a little disappointed.

"Hey," I answer.

"Hey, you. White or red?" she oddly asks.

"Uh, white or red, what?"

"Wine, Ember. Really? We skip a few wine nights, and it's like you forgot what we do once a week."

"It's Tuesday." At least, I'm pretty sure it's Tuesday. The downside to not having a conventional job is that time has no meaning most days.

"Oh," she murmurs. "Really?"

"I'm pretty sure. At least, that's what my planner said this morning when I was checking my deadline for the last piece I need to get over to Annabelle at the gallery."

"Well, son of a Bieber," she complains. "Well, we might as well just have wine night anyway. I'm in desperate need of it since I've been two seconds away from killing Seth since last week."

I laugh, not surprised that they've been fighting … they're always fighting. And honestly, she isn't the only one who is in the mood for a much-needed wine night with her best friend.

"How about get one of each and we will just play it by ear. I could use a good night of relaxing with a glass."

"Or ten," she mumbles.

"I wouldn't go that far." I snicker. "I'll start dinner in an hour, so come over whenever."

"'Kay. Love ya, bye!"

"So did he ever text you back?" Nikki all but wheezes, her eyes wide as her mouth hangs open with shocked anticipation.

I had just finished catching her up on everything that's going on between Nate and me. Needless to say, she's been about to fall off the couch with every word I've spoken.

"Nothing, which is weird for him. Even when he's been busy, he doesn't usually take this long to respond to me."

She nods her head but doesn't speak.

"Should I try again?" I ask, taking another sip of the nasty red she picked out.

"Nope. No way. Don't look desperate."

"I *am* desperate!"

"No, you aren't. You're horny."

"And that's different?"

"Sure, it is," she muses. "You want some of his dick, which I bet is *huge* if I'm being honest right now. But I digress; you're horny for what he can give you, not desperate in the sense that you're going to die if it doesn't happen right this second. Plus, judging by what you've told me, I think you still have some doubts about his motives, which is stupid as hell."

I turn my head from where I had been looking out the front window, staring mindlessly into the dark night, and narrow my eyes at her.

"And you think I shouldn't?"

"I didn't say that. You've been hung up on that for a while now, so it makes sense you have reservations, but now that I've heard his side of things, I think it's time to at least take his advice and try to put the past in the past to stay. He makes a good point; the longer you hang on to that pain—remembering how much it hurt—you feed it the fuel it needs to grow bigger. Also, you were just out of high school, Em. Then and now are like night and day. I'm not saying you should just jump in head first without thought, but I don't think he would even be pursuing anything if he wasn't serious about you."

I mull over her words before responding. "You're right," I agree with a sigh of acceptance. "But we've had one, technically two, dates. If you call them that. How can I know he's serious in that short period of time? What if he finds something about me that he doesn't like? Hell, we haven't even done anything past kissing. He might not like what he gets if we take it past that. He's *a lot* more experienced than I am, and every time I've been with a guy, there wasn't even a spark, let alone fireworks. He could figure out on the next date that I'm not worth the trouble or risks."

She snorts, almost spilling her drink. "Yeah, no. First of all, you have known him your whole life. I doubt he's going to find something he doesn't like about you. Knowing someone that long means you know all their faults and just choose to look past them. Second of all," she continues, jabbing the air with her finger. "How does every other happily committed couple know anything after two dates? They don't, I'll tell you! They just take a chance and enjoy the hell out of it. You can't rush *that*. THIRD!" she screams, again stabbing the air between us. "You got Fourth of July-worthy fireworks from a kiss, Ember. You don't have those kinds of sparks only to find out that sex gives you something like a sparkler."

I open my mouth to respond, but Nikki is on a roll because before I can open my mouth, she jumps from her seat and throws her hands up in the air.

"AND! Let me tell you something, missy! He told you what 'risks' were holding him back before. Risks that I might add he is finding no trouble accepting *are* worth it to take now. He knows how close you are with your sister. He also knows Maddi can't hold a secret to save her life. The second he made that play, he was accepting those risks with the confidence that he *wanted* to make that trouble worth it when y'all's relationship went further."

She lifts her wine glass and downs the contents of the half-full glass before wiping her mouth with the back of her hand. Only then does she flop down on the couch and lean her head back with a sigh.

"Ohhhkay," I droll, my heart pounding as her words take root and the understanding and acceptance blooms.

Her head rolls on the back of the couch, and she narrows one eye at me, looking ridiculous instead of intimidating. "You know I'm right. But I also know that you overthink everything. It's time to stop that shit. If you need a little more time, then take it, but don't question him or his motives until he gives you a reason to. A current reason to, I should add. Forget the rest of it and just give him a chance."

"You're right," I begin, but I'm forced to stop talking when her finger hits my lips to silence me.

"Of course, I am. And now that you've listened to reason, I think you should sleep with him and get that silly thought it won't be explosive out of your head. Since you've already established you're horny for his dick AND you know damn well that you're holding on to your crazy excuses about his motives as a shield of protection, drop it and be the one willing to take risks this time."

"You don't think it's too soon?" I wonder out loud; it's something that's been on the back of my mind since I did just get out of a relationship, even if that relationship had been very short-lived.

"Too soon?" She snorts and starts to cackle loudly, slapping my thigh as she cracks herself up. "You've been in love with the guy for *forever*. You've known him *forever* and you've been dreaming of having him—in every way possible—*FOREVER*. Too soon? More like it's about time!"

I roll my eyes.

"Don't be a brat. You know I'm right … again. If he doesn't text you back today, call him tomorrow or go see him at Dirty. Make the move. No one says you have to wait on him to do it."

"Okay. You're right," I say with a slight shake to my voice. I take another sip. "If he doesn't text me by tomorrow night, I'm going to him."

"That's my girl!" she screams, and we both start giggling.

God, I love my best friend.

Chapter 21

Nate

I drag my feet after softly closing my truck door and try to keep my eyes open. I've been on my last ounce of energy for the last two days, not that I'm complaining, but things have been so busy at Dirty that I hardly had time to even eat. Not to mention, I've been spending every second either at Dirty or passed out after I finally manage to drag myself home. Now that things are starting to move along, I'm confident that Shane is ready to handle the nightly operations himself, especially since we've already promoted Denton to give Shane the coverage he needs to have time off himself. I can't fucking wait to be able to go in during daylight hours to handle office shit and only have to stay a few hours at night.

If it hadn't been for a text earlier from a certain woman that has plagued my every thought for a week, I might have passed out behind the bar hours ago.

I need you, she had said. Well, she had said a bunch of other shit too, but nothing stood out more to me than seeing her say she needed me.

Those three words had lit a fire under my ass, and I had been busting tail in order to get out of there before closing. Thankfully, Shane was there to close because if I had to wait a second longer, I was going to come out of my skin.

I lift the mat in front of the door, and sure enough, a shiny silver key catches the moonlight. I snatch it up with the mental note to spank her ass for leaving a key there. She might as well put a big neon sign telling every lowlife motherfucker to come on in.

I enter the house silently, only briefly looking at the woman sprawled half on and half off the couch, the TV muted as some late-night infomercial plays on the screen. Nikki looks about as uncomfortable as can be, but judging by the drool pooling under her cheek, the girl is out cold.

Bam meets me at the mouth of the hallway, but after a sniff, he walks over to where Nikki is now snoring and climbs on top of her. Well, on top of the one leg that is still on the couch, but she doesn't even flinch when his head drops onto her ass.

Weird girl.

My booted feet are silent as I make my way down the hallway toward the doorway that is open at the end. When I step into Ember's room, I'm confused for a second since her bed isn't where I know it used to be. The same place it was when all the guys in our little family—at the demand of her dad—helped move her stuff in here two years ago. Looking away from that spot, I see it now on the opposing wall. The moonlight doesn't touch the bundle in the middle of the mattress, but I can see clear enough and what I see makes my mouth water and dick twitch.

Her covers must have slid down at some point, tangling with her bare legs. My eyes trail up those legs and I almost choke on my tongue when I see what is on display for me. The shirt that she's wearing twists around her stomach, and with the way she's lying on her side, you can clearly see one very naked ass check.

That's all it takes for me to silently start pulling layers of clothes from my body. I bend, making quick work of my boots before placing them against the wall near her bedroom door. I unhook my belt, pull the button at my waist, and slowly drag my zipper down. Wisely, I leave my boxer briefs on because if I allowed my painful cock the freedom he wants, I would be inside her in record speed. My shirt comes next and after pulling my hair free of the band, like I know she loves, I close her bedroom door. The only sound breaking the silence comes from the soft snick of her lock.

Nikki might have looked passed the hell out, but I'm not taking a chance that she comes to when I'm about to finally have my girl in my arms.

The first step I take toward Ember's sleeping form has me taking my swollen cock in my hand and squeezing through the cotton of my briefs as I look down at her. If she were to turn just a little, I would be able to see her pussy clearly and that thought alone makes a little spurt of pre-come leak from the tip of my cock.

Fuck me.

The second I lie down next to her, I'm going to be hanging by a very frayed thread. I know without a doubt that if she gives me what I need, by the time the sun is coming up in just a few hours, I'm going to be coming inside her body.

With one last squeeze to my very confused cock, I place my knee on the mattress and move to climb into her bed. When my weight makes her roll slightly, she turns. The one leg that's covering her up shifts and she moans. I still, waiting to see if she's awake, but when her soft breathing continues, I move and lie down next to her. This close, her legs open slightly, I can smell her—all of her, but I ignore the cravings that scent brings and turn to the side before reaching over her and pulling her closer.

The second her ass settles against my crotch, I jump. The soft flesh of her lush ass rubs once as she tries to get comfortable without waking. I should feel guilty about my next move—I should—but I don't because she isn't the only one who needed someone tonight.

With our bodies pressed tightly, my front to her back, I spread my hand open against the smooth skin of her stomach, the tip of my pinky hitting the soft, short hairs on her mound. I shift until my nose is in the crook of her neck and I take a deep inhale, my cock pulsing again when her scent fills my senses. My hand travels up, moving under the bunched up shirt, and I rest my palm just under her full tit as her heart beats steady beneath.

It took fifteen soft kisses to the silky skin on her exposed shoulder and neck before she started to moan. I counted. When I ran the tip of my tongue from the edge of her shoulder all the way up to the back of her ear, I felt her shiver in my arms. When I pressed my cotton-covered erection against her hot naked ass, she arched her back and rubbed herself against me with a deep groan of desire.

But the second that I lightly bit her neck, she vaulted out of my arms and with lightning speed, had me on my back with her straddling my lap.

"You came," she pants.

"Not yet, but if you keep rocking against my cock, I will."

"You never responded. I didn't think you would come." She continues to speak, ignoring my smartass response, but she also doesn't stop grinding her core against me, the heat of her making me clench my jaw.

"Ember, you need to stop."

"Nate, you need to *start*," she stresses with a moan.

It's taking every bit of control I have not to flip her off me and show her who is in charge in here.

"Em," I moan, my head pressing against the pillow when she gives a hard jerk of her hips.

"I need you," she pleads.

"You don't know what you're saying."

"Make me yours," she whines.

My heart thumps erratically. "Yours?"

"God, yes," she moans, rocking even faster.

Reaching out blindly, I find the lamp next to her bed and click it on. Her flushed face and unfocused eyes don't hide from me when the harsh brightness fills the room.

I curl my abs and lean up, forcing her with our new position to stop her movements. She pants, her chest heaving, and I know she was just seconds away from coming.

"Make you mine?"

She nods.

"You ready for that?"

She nods again.

"I take you, baby, and I'm never fucking letting go. You ready for *that*?"

She nods, but I don't miss the small hesitation. She wants this, us, but she still has some lingering fears.

"That's okay, my little firecracker, I'll have fun making you believe that."

Her hands move from where they had been resting against her spread thighs and she places each of them on my chest, pushing me back down to explore my body. She twists each of my nipple rings and her pupils dilate.

"I'm ready to be yours, if … if you're ready to be mine."

I feel my chest rumble, having a hard time hearing over the roaring in my ears, but I'm sure whatever sound I'm making right now sounds more animal than man.

"Yeah, Emberlyn Locke, I'm beyond fucking ready to be yours."

Chapter 22
Ember

The sleepy drunk feeling was just starting to recede when Nate spoke the words I've longed to hear for such a long time. Words that I had given up on ever hearing. Words that, if I lived to be a hundred, I would never forget how I felt when I heard them, finally, for the first time.

"Yeah, Emberlyn Locke, I'm beyond fucking ready to be yours."

His eyes drop to my mouth as I feel my lips spread into a wide, toothy smile. I watch in fascination as his green eyes seem to darken and the color on his cheeks gets just a little flushed when his attention comes back from my mouth. His expression, so open and easy to read, is void of the playful mask he usually wears.

The realization that he's been hiding his feelings, acting and trying to make everyone believe he is so unaffected by *anything*, hits me hard. How have I missed that? Probably because I've had my head up my ass licking my own wounded pride for the last couple of years.

I push back the thought that I could have changed things a long time ago and focus on here and now. His stare still holds me captive, just as the hands gripping my hips roughly are, but I have a feeling deep down that what I see in his eyes is love, not lust.

My thighs, still spread with his body between them, try to close when the enormity of the moment mixed with the adoration in his eyes hits me. All rational thought flies out the window and I know, I just know, if I don't have him right now, I might just die from the need overtaking my body.

"I want you so bad," I mumble through the arousal rushing and flowing over every inch of my body, tingling up every nerve and swimming around inside me in overdrive. "I've dreamed of this for so long," I continue, my words coming out in a pant as I rock my hips.

"Ember," he warns when I jerk my hips out of his unforgiving hold, giving us both the friction we're in need of when my wet and swollen lips slide against his erection. "Stop," he barks in a deep rumble, his neck straining as he takes my hips again between his hands.

"Never." I let my head roll back and start to pick up my movements, each thrust up getting the attention to my clit. The burn in my core starts to fire up my spine, wrapping around me as it climbs through my body, gearing up to explode.

"Fuck!" he roars.

Before I realize what's happening, he's flipping us. My head lands in my pillows, just a breath away from the headboard in the center of my bed. It takes me a second, still clinging to the climax that had been just seconds away from taking over, and I push my hair off my face with both hands. When I look down my body, I almost retreat when I see the feral expression on the man kneeling between my spread legs.

He takes huge body rocking gulps of air, his chest heaving with their power. His hair is a loose mess hanging free to dance at his shoulders, a few pieces falling into his face that he either doesn't notice or just doesn't care about.

And his eyes are focused downward.

If I didn't believe he was fighting the same all-consuming feelings as I was, I would have thought that his downcast gaze was for another reason, but seeing those brilliant emerald eyes locked on my very exposed and wet sex, I know that *I'm* the reason he's being slammed with a hungered need.

The power I feel seeing his reaction to my excitement is a high I never want to live without. Something that I will wake up thinking about and fantasize every second we're apart, trying to think of new ways to make him come alive like this. That uncontrollable, feverishly strong emotion he's wearing can only be an aftereffect of our chemistry. Until it burns so bright that it's exploding around us like a brilliantly beautiful display of fireworks.

And with that thought, he makes a sound low in his throat, pushing forward in the next breath to cover my body with his as his mouth takes mine in a deep, bruising kiss. His underwear still keeping him from me completely, but that doesn't stop him from thrusting against my body as if he were already inside me. Each time he slams against me, the headboard slaps against the wall and my eyes roll back in my head.

It was foolish of me to think I would ever be able to control this man once I saw the fierceness burning in his scrutiny break free of his careful control. When I try to push my hands into his hair, he breaks our kiss with a hiss and narrows his eyes at me.

"You're not to touch me, Ember. Not at all. I'm so worked up right now because of you. I'm about to fucking come all over myself and the only place that's going to feel my fucking come will be the inside of *your* pussy. Do not test me by putting those wicked little hands on my body until I can take my time to show you what it's really like to *take* while *giving*."

"Please," I rasp past my dry throat, needing that so desperately.

"No, not *please*. From this point on, the only word I want to hear from your lips is my name. Moan, groan, scream out your pleasure, but you say no other word than my name. I want to hear you scream *that*, Ember," he stresses with a hard thrust. "You don't come until I tell you to," he rumbles deep in his throat. I lose his eyes as he bends to trace my ear with the tip of his tongue before whispering against it. "And when you do, you had better do it loud enough to feel pain in your throat from the pleasure I'll give your pussy."

"Take me," I beg, trying to rock against him, but his weight on me restricts my movements.

"Nate," he grunts in my ear. "No more fucking words but my name. Know who is claiming you. Let the whole fucking world hear who is taking you and making you his."

He runs his hands up each of my arms, stretching them out until I can almost feel the edge of my mattress and his hands are curling around my fingers.

"Hold on," he commands with a wink.

My shirt is instantly pushed up until he's forced to stop because of the position he has put my arms in. I can tell he's trying to figure out if making me move from my position is worth removing the shirt completely. Then he looks up into my eyes before jumping off the bed and walking over to the desk in the corner.

He searches the top, looking through each pen-filled coffee mug, before pulling the drawers open. My eyes widen when I see him turn holding a pair of scissors. I open my mouth to protest, but at the hard look he shoots my way, I snap my jaw shut.

He stalks back to the bed, but when I thought he would climb back on top of me, he just places the scissors on the bed and hooks a thumb under his underwear before pushing the tight black material down his powerful thighs. His cock springs free, his red, angry tip wet with his pre-come, and I lick my lips.

One of his hands grabs the scissors and the other starts to stroke the hard flesh between his legs.

"I want to see you wearing my marks, Ember. Your hips already have my handprint and just seeing that on you makes the animal you've awoken inside me fucking pleased. But it's not enough. I *need* you to wear my marks." He starts to mumble some more under his breath, but I can't make out his words with my loud and harsh breathing echoing throughout the room. When he brings the scissors up and starts to cut my shirt up the center of my breasts, I cry out. Not in pain but in anticipated pleasure. He walks to the foot of the bed when he's done and looks up my body before placing his hands down and slowly making his way back to me. "I'm going to eat you now. With my hands holding your legs captive at the back of your spread thighs, digging my fingers in each time you try to deny me what I'm going to take. My tongue will make you so crazy you might come, but you had better not. Not until I've marked enough of this perfect tan skin."

Then, true to his warning, his hands are pushing between my legs and the mattress as he lifts and pushes until he's holding me to his mouth by the bruising grip he has on the back of my thighs. I can feel the wetness of our combined fluids running down the crack of my ass. My legs being pushed until I can feel the top of my thighs touching my belly as my toes touch the top of the headboard.

If I could find a way to open my eyes, I might find it funny that

I can look at my toes at this moment, but when he opens his mouth and closes his wide lips over my core with a hard suck, I'm pretty sure I died.

I scream, pant, and almost black out as he moves his mouth against the slick wetness he's causing. My fingers cramp up as I hold on to the mattress for dear life. The only thing keeping me from coming right now is the look in his eyes that I see when I finally open my own. He's looking up my body with burning eyes. Eyes that are daring me to disobey his demand. For a brief second, I consider giving in to the need my body has to come, just to see what he will do, but when I open my mouth, his eyes narrow and his growls vibrate against my pussy. I almost lose my control, almost come against his mouth, and he knows it since his tongue is feeling the fluttering of my inner walls as I fight to hold on.

And just when I think I can't take anymore, he releases me with a pop. His tongue coming out to give one thick flat swipe before his hold on my thighs eases and my legs are tenderly placed on the bed once again.

"You ready for me to make you mine?" he asks, his voice thick and deeper than normal.

I nod, not willing to take the chance that he denies me if I speak.

"Ember, I want you to answer me with words this time and only this time. Are you on birth control?"

I have to clear my throat to get a sound out, the scream of my release just waiting in a giant lump. "Y-yeah. The pill."

"Thank fuck," he rumbles, dropping down to one hand placed next to my head as he leans to press the tip of his nose against mine. I can feel him running the hot tip of his dick up and down between the lips of my sex, and I open my mouth with a silent gasp each time he presses it against my swollen clit. "You've been a good girl, keeping yourself from coming even though I know you were close a few times. You quivered against my tongue, and I thought I was going to have to stop to put my mark on your ass for not being able to hold yourself back."

I hum low in my throat, and his pupils widen as he mirrors my noise.

"You like that?" he asks, and I nod. "Next time. You'll get my hands on your ass before I let you put your lips on my cock."

Another sound comes from me, and I almost lift my hips off the mattress when his thick, blunt head pushes into my pussy just a breath before he swipes it back up to my clit.

"Next time, I want your hands in my hair when I cover my chin with your wetness," he muses and rubs the tip of his nose against mine while I feel him enter me again, this time almost an inch of him. My eyes widen and I gasp, earning a brief kiss from him when I'm able to keep my silence. "Hold on, Ember. I'm going to claim this pussy, and when you scream my name like a good girl, know that you're giving me all of you when you take my come deep inside your body."

He lifts up and looks down our bodies. After lining himself up and pushing the tip of him inside me, he brings the hand that had been holding his cock up, resting it on my collarbone. His eyes watch his hand as he trails it down until he is cupping the underside of my breast, his palm on top of my heart.

Then he looks up.

His fingertips press and flex before he lifts his hand and puts one finger right above my heart. "All of you," he vows and thrusts himself inside me in one rough push. His thickness makes me see stars as the pain of his size mixes and swirls into the most intense pleasure I've ever felt. He doesn't move, allowing me the needed time to get used to him, all the while holding me captive with eyes that are almost glowing with intensity.

When he pulls out, almost falling completely from my body, I mewl and whine, needing him back inside. The feeling is short-lived because, in the next breath, he is slamming back inside so hard that my bed slamming against the wall is louder than the scream that bursts from my throat. One side of his mouth tips up at my cry and then his lips are on mine as he continues to pound his cock inside my body. The bed protests with each and every thrust. He lifts up when another raw scream comes out of my mouth and cocks his head at me. I whine, not even ashamed of it, because the need to come has so much intensity driving its power that I know it won't be long. My searching eyes plead with him.

"My fucking name, Ember. Come on my cock and *scream!*" he bellows before lifting up and taking hold of my hips. While kneeling between my legs, he starts to fuck me even harder. So hard that I'm not even sure I *can* scream; the force of my climax raging through my body is too powerful. My eyes water, not from pain, but because of the feelings he is bringing forth.

I want to declare that I'm his.

I want to demand that he is mine.

I want to scream for him to never stop.

I want to sob that *I love him*.

Instead, when I feel myself detonate into a million pieces, I open my mouth and do what I was told to do.

"NATE!" My voice breaks at the end, and I sob as I come, and come, and come. "Nate, Nate, Naaate," I continue, unable to even think about saying anything *but* his name.

Just when the intensity almost becomes too much, I feel his rhythm falter before he gives one final thrust forward. His fingers dig into the tender flesh at my sides, but all that is forgotten when I feel him pulse inside me as the heat of his come enters my body.

My vision clears to a hazy fog when he falls and covers me with his weight. The feeling welcome and wanted. I look up and search his face, unsure what to say after that, but words aren't needed, not when our bodies said everything for us. He adjusts his weight until he's leaning on one elbow and turns my head to look at him with a gentle touch of his hand cupping my face.

"Ember," he whispers, ghosting a kiss over my lips. "My Ember. I'm never letting go, baby. Not now. Not ever. And pretty soon, your head is going to catch up with your heart and you're going to understand that. I meant it; I want *all of you*. I'm going to make it my mission to show you, prove to you, that I'm worthy of getting that gift from you again." I open my mouth, not even sure what I'm going to say, but he just bends and gives me a slow, wet, and beautiful kiss.

A long while later, after he had switched us so that his back was to the bed and I was in his arms, I rested my head against his chest as he breathed slow and deep. Even in his sleep, he held me tightly, and at that moment, I knew he didn't have anything to prove to me because my head had already caught up with my heart.

He's had it since I was seventeen years old. Even when I thought it would never heal when he turned me away a year later, he still held it. He will *always* have all of me.

Always.

Chapter 23
Ember

Monday

"I wish you didn't have to go," I whisper against his chest, my body still coming down from the fourth climax he's given me. We haven't been able to get enough of each other since the first time he took me a week ago.

His arms tighten around me, and I feel him press his lips against the top of my head. He had just shown up a few hours earlier, right as I had been making my way out to the studio, and he took me roughly against the front door the first time until I was screaming out one hell of a hello.

The second time was when my back was on the couch; he held my legs apart as he kneeled on the floor between them.

The third was against my own hand as I swallowed every drop of him as he pulsed in my mouth.

And the last, we had finally made it to where we are now, a tangle of sweaty limbs in my bed.

"I wish I didn't have to go," he agrees. "I thought it would be easier to spend less time at Dirty now that we have Dent on as a manager, but things have just been crazy. I shouldn't complain, but fuck, I would rather be here with you than doing a bunch of paperwork."

"We've had plenty of time together, Nate." We haven't, but I don't want to make him feel bad when I know he's stressed about finding a balance between being the owner of a very popular club and my boyfriend.

Boyfriend? Is that what he is? I mean he's said that he was mine and I was his, but he's never spoken the words.

"Slipping into your bed in the middle of the night does not equal plenty of time. I haven't even taken you on a date, Em."

I push up on the hand that had been resting against his chest and look down at him. "Did I complain?"

I feel the rumbles of his silent laughter against the palm. "It's been a week since I promised I would prove to you that I deserved the gift of you. Two weeks since we decided to be together, and so far, the only thing I've been able to do is have dinner at the club between the little time I had to take a break. You are worth more than a rushed dinner, Ember. It's frustrating the hell out of me."

"Nate, you don't have to prove anything to me." My belly flops, and I shift to lean up a little more, giving him a brush of my hand against his hair. "Don't be so hard on yourself. I understand and don't hold it against you that you're needed at the club."

"That might be the case, Ember, but you deserve better."

"I deserve you," I whisper.

His eyes fire, the reaction to my words so strong that I can feel his heart pick up speed under my hand.

"Yeah? And it's my job to make sure you never forget that, baby."

I shake my head, knowing that I'm not going to get him to realize that I don't care if all we've had time for the last six days is a few hours here and there that he's made to come to my house. Before I can speak, though, his head comes up and he flips us while taking my mouth in a deep, slow, kiss.

Then he makes me come for the fifth time.

Tuesday

I hear my doorbell just as I had finished signing my name to the bottom right corner of *A Beautiful War*. Bam starts barking at the chime, and I drop my brush to go answer it.

After Nate left last night, I haven't left my studio. The sun set and rose while I worked feverishly to finish. I feel like I'm about to drop, the exhaustion so strong, but every bit of my sluggishness is worth it after the signature I just penned on the canvas.

"Flowers for an Emberlyn Locke," the gruff voice greets when I open the door. "Here," he continues and thrusts a clipboard at me, just giving me enough time to take it before turning and walking toward his truck.

"Oh, okay," I mumble and sign my name next to the huge X he had scribbled.

"Here. There's more," he huffs and thrusts a huge vase of roses into my hands.

"More?"

"Yeah, lady. More. As in eight more."

I look at the roses in my hand, judging there to be about two dozen bright red buds before snapping my head back up. "Are you sure?"

"Been doing this for twenty years. I don't get my orders wrong. Nine vases, twenty-four roses in each, to an Emberlyn Locke at this address. The only way I'm wrong is if you're not really Emberlyn Locke."

"I am, but this is a lot."

He gives me a weird look, holding out the second vase impatiently. "I'm just doing my job."

I struggle to hold both, so while he stomps back to his van, I turn to place them down on the table next to my door. I wisely stop questioning him and hope there's, at least, a note on one of these.

His surly demeanor doesn't slip until the last vase is in my hands. Then I get a smile from him before he turns to leave. "See you tomorrow," he oddly says over his shoulder before slamming his door.

Tomorrow?

Wednesday

Sal, my new florist best friend, showed up just as I was returning from dropping my last painting off at the gallery. When his van had pulled in, I had been juggling my keys and the bag of fast food I had grabbed on my way home after I realized it was past noon and I hadn't eaten yet. Since he had to wait for me to put that down before I could sign and take the next enormous floral display, I had asked and gotten a very impatient '*Sal, as in Sal's Flower's*' before he pointed with a weathered finger toward his van.

I just shrugged and took the flowers.

Since his order yesterday, I was quickly running out of space. I figured it was wiser to just place them on the floor until Sal left, then find somewhere for them.

When he handed me the last one, number nine, I got the same grumpy wave as he trudged to his van. "See you tomorrow."

Uh? He can't be serious.

I look down at my feet, seeing just the top of each rose. A sea of red that only two hundred and sixteen roses can make. The scent of roses has already overtaken my house, but all I can do is smile.

I don't look for the card right away, knowing it's here, but walk around my house trying to find a home for each vase. With the last one in hand—and no other option—I place the last four in the middle of my kitchen table before plucking the card I see off one of them.

Your smell is more intoxicating than any flower.

- Yours, Nate.

His handwriting is rough and slanted, just as it was on yesterday's card. Of course, the one yesterday had just said, 'Yours, Nate.' Today's corny line makes me smile when the first made me melt. I drop the card on the table before pulling my phone from the back pocket of my shorts.

"Hey," he hums in my ear as the sound of shuffling papers comes over the line.

"You know, pretty soon I'm going to be sleeping on roses."

He laughs.

"Thank you, honey."

"You sound happy," he muses softly.

"And you sound tired. Do you need anything?"

He's quiet for a second, more paperwork shifting around. "Just you, Em. I'll be over later, but don't wait up."

"It's wine night with Nikki, so there's a good chance I'll still be up when you leave Dirty."

"I hope so. I miss my girl."

I laugh. "It's been two days, Nate."

"Two long-as-fuck days."

I don't respond because he's right. Instead, I change the subject.

"My mom asked if I would be at family dinner tonight. I told her no, but … uh," I trail off, not sure how to word what I really want to ask. Something I've been wondering, but not willing to ask and add to his stress.

"I got the same call from my mom. Not a surprise, but her question was actually whether *we* would be at family dinner."

"Uh …"

He chuckles deeply. "Em, what did you think was going to happen? You're not just some new girlfriend she's gotten wind of."

"Girlfriend," I echo on a squeak.

His hilarity grows, but I sense it's more sarcastic at this point. "Yeah, Ember. Figured that was clear."

"You just hadn't said and I … well, I didn't want to assume any titles had been placed."

"Yeah, I have, and now, I'm working on showing. Titles were placed the second you came on my cock, Ember. See you later, baby."

His disconnect is instant, and I pull the phone away wondering if I just screwed up by being all nervous and unsure.

My next call was to Nikki.

"So let me get this straight … he sent you almost five hundred roses this week?"

I take a sip of my third glass of wine and look over at Nikki. She's about to fall off the couch as she leans forward with wide, excited eyes.

"Actually, it was four hundred and thirty-two. Not that I counted or anything."

"Holy shit." She gasps.

"I know. What does that even mean?"

"That's so romantic!" she screams, ignoring me.

I thought Nikki would be able to help me figure out what my mind couldn't, her experience with men being a lot more than the few short-term boyfriends I've had since high school, but I didn't think she would turn into a squealing and screaming freak fest.

"Yeah, but *what does it mean?!*"

She stops bouncing and narrows her eyes. "What does it mean? Oh my God, Em! If that isn't the grandest of gestures to show someone you love them, I don't know what is!"

"Love?"

Her expression gets a little crazy at that. Her eyes turn into angry little slits, as her head tilts to the side, and I can picture the wheels churning in her head. "Are you blind! Hell, I shouldn't be shocked you're confused when just last week I had to remind you of what the chemistry between the two of you would be like. Something, I might add, I was right about if the sounds that woke me up that night are anything to go by. Stop questioning his actions and just see them for what they are. He's trying to make up for the past by showing you how he feels first. My guess is that *he's* now the one worried about saying he loves you."

"Nikki, we haven't even been together for a month."

"And you've loved him for years. He made it very clear that he has had feelings for you just as long. Stop overthinking it and just enjoy the ride. You guys are being forced to date a little unconventionally with him being the uber-busy owner of the brand new most popular club around and all. If this were a normal beginning to a relationship, you guys would have been on a bunch of dates and you would be able to see how right I am."

I let her words sink in, and I have to admit she's right. It's been almost three weeks and had he not been so busy, my reservations wouldn't be warranted.

"Maybe he's waiting for me to say it?"

"So say it."

"You make it sound so easy." I laugh.

"What are you really all worked up about because I know it isn't the fact that he's sent you a ridiculous amount of roses."

"God, Nik. When he mentioned his mom asking about both of us, I freaked. I mean I know it's going to happen with us what we are now, but he had made it such a big deal when he rejected me. He said they wouldn't understand. How is it any different now?"

"Yeah, well, when he said it, he was probably right. A lot has changed in three years. You're not just a teenager fresh out of high school. You've been to art school, finishing well ahead of time. You have one hell of a career as an established artist now. You're an adult and even if your parents or even his thought something of you two being together, they have no say in it."

"Oh, I'm sure they'll have a say in it." I can picture my dad having a lot to say about it, actually. "I guess I'm really worried that he's going to cut and run when it comes down to standing up together in front of them."

She gives me a soft look of compassion. "I think you're underestimating him. The only thing I can tell you is to ride it out and let him do what he said he was going to do. Prove that he's worth giving your heart to."

We continue to talk about a whole lot of nothing after that, and by the time I felt him climb into my bed and pull me into his arms, my head was a lot clearer. I'm still a little nervous about what's to come, but seeing things through her eyes makes me look at them from another perspective.

One where he really might be the one afraid of getting hurt this time.

Saturday

By the time I realized that my daily deliveries weren't going to stop anytime soon, I started looking up places where I could share the happiness Nate was literally raining upon me. Sal showed up, surly as ever, and instead of taking today's nine vases inside, I had him help me load them in my car. It was a tight fit with all twenty-seven vases total that I had received since Wednesday, but we made it work. I think he actually cracked a smile when I told him I had planned to drop them off at the local nursing homes, but it was short-lived and he left with another promise to see me tomorrow. I didn't mention anything about it being Sunday and I would most likely not see him.

At this point, I wasn't sure when they would stop, but Nate was determined to make a point and I was loving every second of it. Which is why I decided to pass them out at nursing homes. Seeing the look on some of the elderly patients was the best feeling in the world, but hearing that I was the only one who had visited the vast majority of them in years solidified my decision to share Nate's love. Of course, I planned to talk to him tonight when he came over for dinner now that I had given the majority of them away. I probably would have kept each one, but after almost breaking my neck on one of them earlier, I realized that I couldn't keep the overwhelming amount I had.

I hear his truck pull into my driveway right when I pulled dinner out of the oven, and I felt giddy with happiness that he was here. I continue getting dinner ready as I dish out the lasagna onto our plates and the sounds of him greeting Bam reach my ears.

Just when I had put them down on the table, I feel him.

His arms go around my middle and his mouth presses against my exposed neck, making me shiver. I straighten and wrap my arms over his as he continues to kiss up my neck until he has his lips at my ear. "You smell good enough to eat."

"I think that's dinner," I joke.

"No, definitely not dinner," he rumbles and presses his erection against my back. "I love food, but food doesn't make me hard."

"You're a man. Food is like number one on the makes you hard list."

"Not true," he groans when I push against him. "You're number one through fifty on that list."

"And what's fifty-one?"

"Probably porn, but I haven't tested that since I haven't watched a single one in weeks."

I throw my head back against his shoulder and laugh.

"Damn, it's good to have you in my arms."

Still laughing, I turn to look up into his eyes with a smile. "You've been in my bed every night. Me in your arms. You're good for my ego when you act like you haven't seen me in years."

His lips are smiling as he gives me a brief kiss—one that had dinner not been ready, I'm sure we would have gotten lost in—before resting his forehead against mine.

"Hi," he whispers.

"Hi." I sigh.

"Thanks for making me lasagna. I've been craving that for days."

I shrug as if it's no big deal. The last thing I'm going to admit is that I hate cooking the dish and only did it for him. Hell, no. Not when he's looking at me like I'm the answer to his prayers.

"Come on; let me let you feed your man before I forget about dinner and demand dessert first."

He has to turn and literally push me into my seat after that comment because the thought alone is enough to make me want to forget all about dinner myself.

"Are you ready for your show next weekend?" he asks a little while later, after he's devoured his third huge plate of lasagna.

"As ready as I'll ever be, I guess. I'm nervous, but Annabelle seems confident that I shouldn't be."

"It's normal to be nervous, Em. This is your first solo show? Right?"

I finish swallowing my bite before wiping my mouth. "Kind of. I had one when I had just finished school, but it wasn't this big. Things kind of got a little crazy when Annabelle discovered me. She's featured my paintings for the last two years, and they sell within an hour of going on display, so I know I shouldn't be worried, but it's a lot different when you're the only artist on display. More pressure somehow,

I guess."

"She's the one?"

I tilt my head in confusion. "The one?"

"The one who went to one of your art school's showcases and freaked out about you right in the middle of it, right?"

"How did you know about that?"

"Uh, I probably shouldn't admit this at the risk of sounding pathetic, but I was there."

I can feel the shock on my face. He was there? I knew that the majority of our group had been there, but I didn't remember seeing him. Then again, I had been about as close to freaking out as it got when the Annabelle Kingston, the owner of the largest gallery in Atlanta, had started dancing and screaming in front of one of my pieces. She had taken me under her wing before I even finished school, each of my paintings turning in a higher and higher profit. Here I am, two years later, debt free, in my own home, and my own show proving that I am—in fact—a successful artist.

Finally able to find my words, I open my mouth. "How come I didn't see you?"

He wipes his mouth before dropping his napkin over his plate and leaning back. "I didn't want you to see me."

"I see." The hurt I feel from his answer is not something I'm proud of.

"Stop whatever you're thinking, Ember. I went because I wanted to support you, but I knew things were still weird between us and I didn't want you to look back on that show and remember me making it awkward for you. I went and celebrated for you in the shadows."

"I wish you would have been at my side." I think out loud.

"Yeah, I wish I would have been too, but the time wasn't right."

"You're coming next weekend, though?"

He stands and offers me his hand. Once I'm upright, he bends to look into my eyes. "I'll be by your side every second. I'm so damn proud of you, and I want everyone to know that I'm the man in your life." I shiver—something he doesn't miss. "Clean up in here first or dessert?"

"Dessert. You could burn the kitchen down for all I care, just as long as I get dessert now."

He bends and with a squeal, I'm in his arms as he walks to my bedroom.

Chapter 24

Nate

"I want your come in my mouth," I tell her, feeling her hum against my cock. All fantasies I had over spanking her ass before she had me in her mouth vanished when I first felt her mouth take all of me. Her head moves up and down quicker, but I don't miss her hand moving between her legs. "You touch *my* pussy, and I'm going to spank your ass, Ember."

My cock touches the back of her throat before I feel her relax her neck and take me so far down that I feel the breaths from her nose on my skin. My head slams against her headboard when she swallows my cock. The sensation of her wet mouth sucking hard on me, her hand playing with my balls, and the hum of her enjoying the fuck out of this was becoming way too much.

"Jesus fuck. That's right, baby, take all of me."

She continues bobbing her head and hollowing her cheeks until I fist her hair in my hand and thrust into her mouth. She whimpers against the bite of pain I'm sure my hold brings her, but just sucks a little harder before she pauses in her sucking to lick against the sensitive flesh she's consuming.

Through the narrow slit in my eyes, I catch her free arm moving, and I know she's ignored my warning. With a noise of protest from her, I pull her up off my cock, ignoring my own jolt of displeasure when I lose the heat of her mouth, and lean forward so that she is looking directly at me from her kneeled position between my legs in the center of her bed.

"I told you not to touch yourself. You don't come unless I tell you, and you damn sure don't get to take your sweetness from me by coming against your own hand." She doesn't speak, but her eyes spark with the knowledge of something, although it's a mystery to me what that something is.

"You're going to wear my mark on your ass now," I promise her darkly.

She shifts and I watch as she rubs her thighs together. Then, to my utter disbelief and fucking pleasure, she turns so her head faces the end of her bed, and bends so she is on her elbows with her knees still kneeling on the mattress. That ass I just promised to mark is up in the air, presented to me like a goddamn gift. The wetness coating her pussy makes my mouth water, and for a brief second, I forget why she is getting her ass pinked.

"You're going to remember what I said about taking your sweetness from me tomorrow when you can't sit without the burn of my touch heating your flesh, aren't you," I vow, my voice low and controlled even though I feel seconds away from losing my shit. The sight of her offering herself to me, ass up with her wetness begging to be filled, is unmanning me.

Shifting until I'm up next to her, my knees next to her legs and my cock pointing at her hips, I rub my palm softly against each of her smooth cheeks. I go back and forth as my free hand trails up her spine. I can feel the heat of her with each pass I take down her left globe, but I ignore her whines when I get close enough, and continue to caress her skin.

Just when I know she had started to relax into my touch, I bring my hand back and quickly slap one and then the other cheek before rubbing the sting. Her scream, of pleasure and not pain, hits my ears, and I give her another two quick cracks of my palm. It isn't long before she has the red imprints of my hands on her skin. I keep rubbing her flesh with my hand as I lean to the side and see that her arousal is now starting to drip down her thighs. She could come from my hand alone and that thought pleases the fuck out of me, but it won't be tonight. After another solid slap, I keep my hand in place, loving the way that her ass shakes.

My eyes never leave her red ass as I straddle her calves and take her hips in my hands. I lift her up with my hold and dig my fingers in while lining up my cock. The second I push into her, she lifts up her head and screams. Her cunt sucks me in even deeper before it clamps down tightly. I grunt, deep in my throat, and rock forward even though she has every fucking inch of me. That's all it takes for her to scream my name and coat my fucking balls as her juices leak from her body.

"God, yes," she continues as I pound into her.

I let go of her ass when I push in again, using my own hips to hold her up and bring my palm down on her ass, loving when she clamps down on my cock again. "You're going to come again, Ember," I order before returning my hand to her hip and picking up my speed.

By the time I feel her start to tighten against me, I know she's close and I tilt her again so I'm hitting that sweet fucking spot inside her. The words coming out of her mouth don't even make sense, but the second I feel my come shooting deep inside her, she jerks in my hold and gives me what I want.

I slowly drag my spent cock from her wetness, loving the way that her cream coats it, and help move her so that we're lying on the mattress. She doesn't say a word as her fingers trace my abs. I place my hand on hers when I feel my cock twitch and hold it against my stomach, kissing her head, and tightening the arm around her back. She pulls one leg over my thigh and tilts her head up. Pressing my chin down, I look into her sated eyes with a smile.

"Thank you," she slurs, drunk from the pleasure I've given her.

"Thank you for what, baby?"

"For giving me you. For taking me. For giving us … us. I think my head is ready to catch up to my heart now, Nate."

And with that, she tucks her head back down and drifts off to sleep.

If only she knew.

The sound of my phone hits my ears before I could register Ember shifting in my arms, our bodies still on top of the covers where we had fallen asleep after 'dessert.' Not willing to let go of the soft woman in my arms, I ignore it and pull her closer.

"That's the third time it's rung, Nate," she sleepily mutters.

Shit. "Okay, baby. Let me grab it."

She moves so that I can slide out of bed, and I almost ignore the phone when I see the look in her eye when she sees my hard cock.

"Hold that thought." I laugh, bend, and grab my jeans and search the pockets for my still ringing cell.

"Nate Reid," I answer, annoyance in my tone when I see Shane's name on the screen.

"I need you to come close. I got a call from Lacey and I need to go home."

Fuck. Me.

"Does she really need you to come home or is she just pulling some more of her shit because she doesn't like you working at Dirty?" I question, knowing damn well his girl would do that shit. I can't stand the bitch, but I'm not going to tell him how to live his life.

He sighs. "I don't know, man. She claims she fell and hurt herself, but she didn't sound like she was in pain. I need to go check it out, and if she's pulling another stunt, I'll be back. I don't know what the hell her problem is lately."

"Dent?" I ask, hoping that I don't have to leave Ember on the one night that was supposed to be just for us.

"Still in LA. Won't be back until next week. Fuck, man, I hate calling you for this shit, but I don't know what to do."

I sigh, turning to look at Ember, expecting to see anger. However, she gives me a nod and smile, understanding that I need to go without even hearing the reasons. Supporting me and my responsibilities to Dirty without thought. Something that Shane's woman clearly doesn't understand. "I need to say good-bye to my woman. Give me thirty and I'm there."

I hang up, and when she stands from the bed and walks into my arms, I pull her naked body close.

"I hate leaving."

"I know you do, but you can't help the reason why."

"I wouldn't go if I wasn't needed, but Shane is the only one there and he has to run home."

She leans back and looks up with a smile. "You don't have to explain things to me, Nate. I'm not upset."

"How can it not bother you? We haven't had time to do anything but eat, sleep, or fuck when we're together."

Her eyes narrow. "Way to make it sound so meaningless," she snaps.

I open my mouth to soothe my comment over, but she shakes her head.

"First of all, I support you and Dirty because I know how much it means to you. Does it take you from me? Sure. But it also just opened and you guys are all still just getting your footing. It won't be like this forever. Hell, it might not even be like this next week. You will all find your stride. If you feel like it's taking too much from you personally in a few months, I'll still be here, and you can find another person to help hold the reins. Second, we have spent plenty of time together, and if anything, it's been better than if you were to take me out to dinner or whatever. We've had time to ourselves alone, sharing who we are now and getting to know each other as a couple and not friends. Third, if you would kindly find another way to express what we do when we're in bed and not sleeping, I would appreciate it."

Her gaze travels to my mouth when I feel my lips curve.

"I'll work on that, baby."

"That would be splendid."

I toss my head back and laugh, but when I feel her small hand smack my naked ass, my head drops forward and all laughter stops when I see the wicked look in her eyes.

"You're going to pay for that later," I threaten.

"That's what I'm hoping for," she smarts and pulls from my arms, grabbing her robe and walking out her door.

"Fucking Shane," I mumble under my breath and start to dress. I would kick his ass for pulling me from my time with Ember, but regardless of how I feel about his girlfriend, I know I would be doing the same thing if I were in his place.

Chapter 25
Ember

The high scream of my smoke detector is the first thing that I hear.

Confusion fills my sleep-fogged brain, but when I feel Bam jump on the bed and whine in my ear, I wake with a start.

He starts leaping from the bed to the floor while the alarm continues to blast and I almost fall on my ass in my hurry. Luckily, when Nate left, I had pulled on some yoga pants and an old tee shirt, so it didn't take me long to leave my bedroom. As I cautiously walked down the hallway, the first thing that hit me was the smell of smoke. Panic started pulsing through me when I get to the living room and see the flames dancing around my kitchen.

I can't tell how bad it is from where I'm standing, but I don't dare go look. My house is newly remodeled, but it's an older construction and I'm not going to take the chance that something snaps and I'm trapped.

I turn on my heels and rush back to my room, where my cell is, before I sprint back to the front of the house and to the front door. I press a few keys before putting my phone between my shoulder and ear. Just when I reach the entryway, I hear the emergency operator asking me a question. I rattle off my address, telling her that there is a fire as I grab my purse off the entryway table and pull the door open. Right when I'm about to run out, I turn and grab the only other thing besides Bam that I care about.

She continues to ask me questions and I answer when needed,

but the second I walk to the side yard and see the back half of my home blazing, I want to scream in pain.

Flames completely engulf the kitchen and my studio.

I drop to my knees as I watch the inferno continue to destroy everything it touches.

I distractedly think about the painting that I had just delivered to the gallery earlier that day, but knowing that everything else is most likely going to be gone is still crippling.

Sirens echo through the night, and I hear the operator tell me that they're almost at my location, but I don't respond. I feel the tears and roughness in my throat only after I register that I'm crying. When the lights of the firetruck, ambulance, and police car surround me, I climb to my feet and back from the house.

"Ember!"

I turn, phone to my ear and tears running down my face, and see Liam, Megan's husband, jump from his patrol car and rush toward me. I keep pulling air deep in my throat, feeling my vision start to blur as more tears come. He pulls the phone from my ear and speaks to the operator before hanging up.

"Are you okay? Hurt anywhere?"

I shake my head, still clutching my belongings to my chest and just look up at him.

"Come on, sweetheart. Why don't you come and sit in my car while I go get some information? Do you want me to call your dad?"

I shake my head frantically, grabbing for the phone that's still in his hands, and pull up Nate's name before handing it back to him.

He looks at the screen, his expression slipping slightly in shock, but just nods before walking away. I keep my feet on the ground next to Bam, the door open, and I watch as people rush around to put out the fire. Liam is moving around as he talks, and when I feel someone rush to my side, I look away from him.

"Holy shit, Ember! Are you okay? I just heard about the fire and came right over."

I jump when Levi pulls one of my hands away from my body, Bam making a noise deep in his throat. The simple touch is enough to knock the shock out of me, and I jerk back, dropping the contents

I had been clutching for dear life on the ground.

He bends, ignoring my outburst, and picks up my purse, followed by the frame. The same frame I had just replaced when he had shattered it a few weeks before. He looks at the image, the one of Nate and me, and I see his jaw tick.

"Can I help you?" I hear Liam question, his voice full of authority as he walks back over, handing me my phone.

Levi stands and turns to look at Liam. "You can't. I'm checking on Ember here."

"It's okay, Lee," I interject before things get weird. "Levi is just an old … friend of mine. He works with the Hope Town Fire Department and was just checking on me."

"Is that so? That's mighty nice and all, *Larry*," Liam sweetly says. "You just happen to be driving by?"

At Liam's question, I look over at Levi and notice that he isn't wearing his uniform. Instead, he has on a nice polo shirt and jeans.

"It's Levi." His nostrils flare and he stands a little straighter. "I had stopped by the station, actually, on my way home and was there when the call came in. Not that it's any of your business." He adds the last part under his breath, but I know Lee hears him because he gets a cold look in his eyes.

"Actually, *Levi*, it is my business. Not only because I carry this," he stresses while pointing to his badge, "but also because Ember is a close friend."

I ignore them, not interested in their macho bullshit, and look over at my house. They almost have the flames under control, and it looks like it didn't move far from the back half of my house. I take a deep breath and try to calm my frazzled nerves, but that all goes to shit when I hear the sharp scream of tires protesting. I look up and see my father jumping from his truck and rushing over, my mom not far behind him, and jerk my eyes to Liam.

"That wasn't the call I asked you to make," I accuse.

He holds his hands up, ignoring the man still standing next to the open doorway. "Don't look at me like that. I'm not going to get my ass handed to me because I picked the wrong order when it comes to the men in your life. Your father is scary as fuck, and I know he can kick my ass."

"He isn't who I wanted here," I hiss.

"Yeah, well the one you wanted here I imagine isn't far behind."

I narrow my eyes, and he just rolls his. "I have a wife, Em. You can't intimidate me with that look. Not to mention, Molly puts you to shame."

At the mention of his daughter, I feel some of my anxiety ebb, just in time for my father to take my shoulders and spin me until my nose is pressed against his chest.

"Are you okay," he huffs.

"Oh my God, baby!" my mom screams in my ear when she joins the huddle.

"Shit, Emmy, not so loud," my father scolds before pulling me back and looking down at me. "You're okay?"

"I'm okay, Dad. Just … in shock, I think. Bam got me out of the house before the smoke had even hit my bedroom."

He continues to look at me, his dark eyes probing as he makes sure my words are true. I can feel my mom fidget nervously as she watches them work to put the remaining flames out. He looks down, assessing me for injury, I'm sure, before pulling me back into his hold.

"Who the fuck are you?" he snaps, the sound grumbled against the ear he has pressed close to his chest.

"Levi Kyle, Ember's boyfriend."

"No, he isn't! Ex! *EX*-boyfriend. We broke up almost a month ago!" I yell, my mouth muffled against my dad's chest. I try to turn around, but my father just holds me tighter against him.

"You're mistaken."

I shiver, the malicious tone in my dad's voice something that I don't often hear, but it never fails to cause me to tremble in fear. I've never had that tone directed *at* me either, and it's still scary as hell.

"Excuse me, I misspoke," Levi tries again. "We recently had a separation that I had been hoping to rectify."

"Oh boy," I hear coming from my mom, and I see her head pop in my line of sight, giving me a wink. She's loving this. Which shouldn't be a shock since she's married to my father and has taken great pleasure my whole life in 'throwing her sass' to get a reaction from him.

I finally push from my dad and turn to look at Levi. "At the risk of embarrassing you by doing this in front of an audience, I'm going to go ahead and say what I need to in the hopes that you'll hear me. I think it's nice that you came when you heard the call, but as you can see, I have most of my support here already. That being said, I think it was shitty for you to even say that during this," I stress and point behind his shoulder to where my house had been burning just minutes before. "But even if you had waited to do it somewhere else, the answer would be the same. I have no plan to rectify anything when it comes to us. Not now and not ever."

He makes a move to step toward me, but stops with a glance behind our little huddle, his eyes getting hard. I'm sure my dad is about to come out of his skin right now.

"You've had a rough night," Levi says, still not looking at me right away. "How about we talk about this in a week or so? Take all the time you want, but just promise we can talk. I miss you." He looks back at me with a smile.

"Are you stupid, boy?" my father snaps.

"Stop, it Maddox," my mom worries.

"I don't want a week, Levi. I don't want a day. Hell, I don't want even a minute. I really was trying to be nice, but I don't want you!"

"Damn fucking right you don't," I hear harshly barked and feel the instant rush of safety and relief rush over me at those words.

I turn to see that my father is still standing behind me with his arms now crossed over his chest, and I almost stumble with emotion when I look next to him and see the man mirroring his pose. Right down to the thin lips and narrowed eyes.

"Nate," I whisper on a sob, afraid to move without losing my shit and crumpling onto the sidewalk.

His eyes leave Levi's direction immediately, and he looks right at me. The anger that had been radiating from him dissipates the second he locks his eyes on mine. He takes a step forward and bends to pull me into his embrace. His head going to my neck and his mouth against the tender flesh as he lifts me with his hands on my ass until my legs wrap around his hips.

He doesn't move for a second, giving me all of him while my

body shakes. Now that he's here, I finally let the enormity of tonight sink in; the fire could have been so much worse had Bam not woken me from my deep sleep. I feel the frame that I had been holding digging into our abdomens, but I don't dare ease up on my hold.

Soft kisses against my neck are the only warning that I get before he lifts his head and starts talking. "I know who you are, but you don't know who I am. This girl in my arms is mine, and buddy, you're one stupid motherfucker for letting her go. But you did and I promise you I'm not going to be that damn dumb. She said it nicely, but you didn't listen, so now hear it from me." I tighten my arms around his neck and press my nose into his neck, smelling his familiar cologne mixed with the scent of cigarette smoke from Dirty. A combination that I've become addicted to and it instantly makes me feel like all is right in the world. "You have no place in her life, and as nice as you think it was to come rushing over to make sure she was fine, as you can see … she is. You can leave now knowing that she's right where she needs to be. And, one more time, since you seem to need it really dumbed down—Ember is mine now and for the rest of our days on this earth, so you can fuck right off knowing that in no way will there ever be a break in that for the likes of you."

And at that, Nate turns with me in his arms and starts walking away from them.

He stops and turns his body until he's sitting. I lift my head up and see the back of an open ambulance before looking at him in question.

"You're going to stay right here in my arms and let them look at you. When we're done here, we'll see what else needs your attention before I pack up your and Bam's shit and take you home. And baby, do not argue with me because I've been holding on by the thinnest of fucking threads since Lee called me."

I just nod because really what else can I do?

Chapter 26

Nate

I watched earlier as she was checked out while her dad was saying a few things to that sorry piece of shit before he stomped off, got into his SUV, and left in a rush.

I could have fucking killed him earlier. The fear that I had for Ember morphed into a rage like I had never felt when I walked up to them talking around Liam's patrol car. He saw me, that fucking fuck, but he didn't let me being there stop him from running his mouth.

Not even the happiness I felt from Ember's response to him was enough to dull the rage that I felt. When I moved to step in, Maddox had stopped me with a hand to my arm, warning me without words to stand fucking back and let Ember speak her mind. So I did the only thing that made sense; I copied his stance in hopes that I looked even half as scary as he did, and that slimy fuck got the hint.

She shifts, her head almost falling off my shoulder, but I adjust her before it can. Her movement jolts me into the present and my mind away from the dark thoughts swirling in my head. Not for the first time since we sat down on a chair Liam had moved over from her front porch did I feel something dig into my gut. I move my hand between us and pull out whatever I've felt for the last thirty minutes but hadn't dared move to get it until I knew she was good and asleep in my arms.

I'm not sure what I expected her to have been clutching as if her life depended on it, but seeing a framed picture of us wasn't it. I hadn't ever seen this one, but to be honest, I hadn't really paid much attention to the shit she had around her house when she was the only thing I cared about looking at.

I remember the day this was taken like it was yesterday. I had been tutoring her for a few weeks, hell, maybe a few months, I don't know. The struggle to keep myself from her was getting to me, and when she showed up in that bikini, I almost forgot all the reasons to stay away. My eyes kept finding her throughout the day, and I kept finding reasons to be near her. I didn't know this picture was even taken, though. How had her dad not killed me before now? Because I know damn well if he had seen this picture, he had seen something between us long before I did.

I study the picture some more, overwhelmed that this was one of the things she had left the house with. Keeping it in my hand, I wrap my arms back around her and look up. Maddox has his wife in his arms, standing next to where Lee is talking to him at his patrol car, but his focus is on me and the woman sleeping wrapped around me. He looks at her, and even in the darkness, I can see the struggle he's having with himself not to come and take her from me, but when he looks up, I get the briefest of nods before he looks away.

It's one thing for me to have had his verbal blessing to pursue his daughter, but when she had picked *me* over *him* earlier, I had been a little worried. There is no doubt in my mind that he's been struggling with that since, but I have a feeling that the nod I just got from him was his way of letting me know that I now had his acceptance and happiness when it came to our relationship.

"I just got the okay to go in," Lee says, crouching down next to my seat.

"How bad is it?"

"Not as bad as it could be. There's some smoke and water damage to her living room, but from what I heard, nothing touched her bedroom and the guest room. The kitchen and the sunroom are completely gone, though."

"Studio," I grunt, hating that I'm going to have to tell her that.

"Pardon?"

"Not a sunroom, Lee. That was her art studio. The one room in the house that she basically lived in and one that I know means a whole hell of a lot to her."

"Shit, sorry, brother."

"Nothing to be sorry about. My woman is safe and the rest can be replaced."

He gives me a funny look. "Your woman, huh?"

I knew it was coming, so I just raise a brow, twisting my head to make sure she's still sleeping before responding. "More than that, Lee, if you know what I mean. She's my everything."

He smiles and gives me a nod. He's a happily married man who knows what it's like to find your everything. "Happy to hear that, Nate. She's good for you."

"Yeah." I sigh. "You took ten years off my life earlier with that call."

"I imagine, but she's okay and that's the only thing that matters. I'm going to go with her mom to pack up some of her stuff. I'm going to just go on and guess that she's going home with you? Or should I send her home with Maddox?"

At the middle finger he gets in response, he climbs to his feet with a laugh.

Her dad takes care of talking to the official looking people while I wait for her mom and Lee to get some shit packed. For that, I'm thankful. I don't want to let her go, needing her against me to remind me that she's fine.

"I'll check in with them tomorrow," he says, walking to stand in front of me and looking down at his daughter. "I suspect, had this not been the first time I had seen her in a few weeks, that I would have seen she had gotten her happiness back?"

"That would be right."

"You going to fight me on where she goes tonight?"

"With everything I have."

He smiles, a ghost of one that is almost not even noticeable. "I wouldn't expect anything less. Remember what I said, Nate. Accidents happen."

I nod, lifting the frame I still have in my hands and hold it out to him. He takes it as I wait for him to see what I'm hoping he does. His throat works as his eyes roam over every inch of the picture. I wait and hope that he sees it.

"Even back then." Not a question because even a fool would know the answer to that.

"Even back then," I parrot.

"I see. Take my advice then. Don't wait to tell her that you love her."

He continues to hold the frame when I see Emmy and Lee walking from the front door with three suitcases and two huge duffle bags between the two of them. I'm not sure which one of them I need to thank for making sure she was heavily packed because if I have things my way, she won't be back here even when the repairs are done.

"He really didn't say anything to you?"

I laugh at Ember's question, something she's been asking since we got out of our shared shower and climbed into my bed.

"He didn't, baby. He's a smart man, and he knew it was time to let you go."

"Oh, wow."

"You expected something different?"

She lifts her head from my shoulder and studies my face for a while, not giving anything away with her expression.

"Well, yeah. I mean it was one of the reasons that you said we could never be together. I just assumed that you could see something in him that I couldn't. I've been worried about how he would handle us now because of that."

Well, shit. I feel like she just kicked me in the balls.

"Damn, baby."

"Don't say you're sorry, Nate. I didn't bring it up to make you feel bad, just pointing out that is what I had worried about when it came to us coming out, so to speak, and what his reaction might be. I understand why you said it back then, and I even agree."

"You do?" I ask, shocked.

"Yeah, and it doesn't matter now. We came out on top in the end."

"Yeah, I reckon we did."

She settles back down and starts to rub her hand on my torso. "Do you think my flowers will make it?"

I smile into the darkness around us. "Not sure, Em. Doesn't matter, though. I need to call in the morning and get your last couple of deliveries moved here."

She jerks in my arms. "There's more?" She gasps.

"Two more."

"Two more," she breathily repeats.

"Yeah, baby. One thousand five hundred and twelve in total. That's roughly one rose for every day I've missed since the night you graduated."

Her silence stretches out so long I wonder if she fell asleep, but when her breath hitches violently in her throat, I adjust our bodies so I can see her tear-streaked face.

"Ember?"

"That's the most romantic thing I've ever heard," she sobs.

Without a clue as to how to calm her down, I frame her face and just kiss her deeply.

Chapter 27
Ember

I hang up my phone feeling like, if he were in the same room as I was, I would physically hurt my father. When I showed up at my house two days after the fire—one that had been ruled an accident by faulty wiring—to find him directing a cleaning crew and movers, I snapped. Well, actually, I just gave him a hard look and got into my car to head back to Nate's without a word. With my show only a few days away, I need to focus on making sure everything is in order with Annabelle and the gallery.

But now, hearing that he's already hired contractors and the likes, without talking to me, I'm about to blow a fuse.

"You okay?" Nate asks, coming behind me and wrapping his arms around my chest. The scent of his deliciousness distracts me from why I was in a mood to begin with.

"Fine," I breathe, trying to take more of his scent in.

"You know, I learned really fast with a sister that when a woman says that word, she means the opposite, but at the risk of making you more upset, I'm just going to leave it at that."

I sigh. "It's my dad. He's taken over the rebuild at my house and even went as far as to move everything I own into storage."

He hums but doesn't respond. Instead, I feel his hand start to push up my shirt.

"Nate," I groan, pushing his hand when I realize something. "Nate!" I try again when he doesn't stop.

"What?" he says against my neck, biting the flesh between his teeth.

"Stop trying to distract me," I attempt but only end up moaning shamelessly when he cups my sex through my leggings and starts to move his fingers around through the fabric.

"You like it."

"Stop," I pant, shoving out of his wicked hands and turning.

His eyes are burning and his chest is rapidly moving when I look up at him. My eyes move from his chest to the sweatpants that are riding low on his hips, the erection tenting the fabric jerks when my eyes hit it, and I feel a noise deep in my throat in response.

"You're trying to distract me with your talented fingers and huge penis, aren't you?"

His face doesn't lose its intensity, but his lips twitch at my words.

"Do you know why my father moved everything I own into storage?"

He sighs. "I don't know for sure, but I can only assume."

"And your assumption would be what?"

"That he's doing what he would have done in my shoes, taking a guess at what I want, and doing it correctly."

"You're talking in riddles," I whine, tossing my hands up with a huff.

"Actually, I'm not. But I'll expand on that. He hasn't asked me how I feel about that fire or how I felt knowing that you could have been taken from me had you not got out. He does, however, know how serious I am about you, and with that being said, he decided to act as if he knew what I wanted to happen and make sure it's done."

"Seriously, Nate! How is that any clearer?"

He laughs, low and not with much humor. More like a sound that one would make if they knew something that the other person didn't. Which, duh, he does.

"In his shoes, if it had been your mother, he would have packed up her shit, repaired the house, sold it, and never let her out of his sight again. Her shit would stay in storage until she decided what to keep or donate, but her ass would stay in his house … forever."

I gasp, his meaning starting to become clear.

"Are you saying my father is preparing me to move in with you?"

"Like I said, he's acting as if he knows what I want."

My heart in my throat, I ask, "And what do you want?"

"Exactly what he would in my shoes, baby. The exact thing."

"It's been a month!"

He steps closer. "One month or one day, I would still feel the same about us."

And then his mouth is on mine, and I lose all ability to even form a thought, let alone another word.

"Come on," he says against my lips, taking my hand and pulling me from his living room and up the stairs to his bedroom. "I have you for another two hours before you need to head over to the gallery. How about we make good use of that time?"

And good use he does.

Over and over again.

"I think I like this one in here," Annabelle says, looking away from the series of landscape paintings to the few still-life ones that I have.

"Are you sure? I thought you wanted to mix them up some?"

She hums but keeps looking at the pictures she had cataloged of my artwork, placing a few against each wall in preparation to hang the respective canvases.

The way that her gallery is set up, it is essentially one large room with different 'walls' erected to hold various pieces. Normally, she has a good mix of art, even some freestanding displays for other mediums, but for my show, she has cleared off the whole floor.

We've already placed half of my collection, starting with the vivid colors of my nature scenes and ending now where we have the landscapes and still-life paintings scattered to make way for the huge abstract piece that will be the big focus of the event. The black wall that holds the picture solely takes my breath away; just seeing it up there with the spotlights on it and the tiny plaque that she had attached to the right corner.

It's a showstopper, and she knows it. When she told me that she was putting a fifteen thousand dollar price tag on it, I almost choked on my tongue. It's normal for some of my larger pieces to go for a couple of grand but never *that* much. However, now that I see it up there in all its huge glory, I now can see what Annabelle sees in those brushstrokes that make it worth that kind of price tag.

Hell, if she sells my whole collection, I could make almost seventy-five thousand dollars. And if this show goes off as she is saying it will, it's going to push my art to a whole new level when it comes to pricing. I've been waiting for this show. No longer selling five to ten paintings a month but selling that in a week. It will mean that I no longer have as much free time as I have now, but I'll be doing what I love, and since I already paint for fun seven days a week, this will mean that my 'fun' will now be sold instead of sitting in closet.

It's an overwhelming thought, but one that I'm ready for.

"I think we've pretty much got it all settled, Ember. We just need Daniel and his crew to come and hang the rest of your pieces. I can take care of placing the plaques tomorrow. You just need to spend the day focusing on getting ready for our big night. I'm so excited for you, honey."

"Are you sure you don't want more help?"

She laughs and places her hand on my arm. "You've done more than I ever would have asked. It's time you go on and enjoy some relaxing before tomorrow night."

"If you're sure." I look around one more time, seeing everything start to come together, and smile. "If you change your mind, just call."

She nods and walks away, dismissing me as her mind starts to wander with tasks, something she has a bad habit of doing.

When I first met her, I wondered how such a beautiful woman had never settled down with a family of her own, but I realized really fast that Annabelle Kingston is married to her work, and at fifty-two, she is perfectly content with her clients being the children she never had.

I grab my bag, pulling out my phone as I walk to the door and checking my messages as I climb into my car and start the engine. When I left Nate's house earlier this afternoon, he had said he was going to stop by Dirty but would be home for dinner. Seeing that it's now five, he's either finishing up there or already back at the house. Either way, the state of his fridge is scary, so my first stop will have to be the grocery store.

After the night of my house fire last week, Nate had been spending less time at Dirty, something that seemed to just happen naturally, even though it had been a big stressor in his life. He still goes in every day, but it is rare that he's there past midnight.

"Hello?" I answer, not looking at the display when my phone starts ringing through the speakers.

"Hey," Nikki says, her voice low and a little wobbly.

"Hey, you. What's wrong?"

She sniffs and I frown. Nikki isn't a crier. I often joke with her that her tear ducts are broken, but she just says it's a side effect of her black soul.

"I broke up with Seth." She sniffs again before blowing her nose loudly into the receiver. "Found that jerk in bed with some chick from his gym."

"Oh, Nik. I'm on the way to Nate's. Meet me there in ten, okay?"

She sniffs again, it coming out more like a snorted wheeze, but agrees before hanging up.

Pulling up to a light, I grab my phone and press Nate's name before placing it back down on the seat next to me. While I wait for the light to change, the phone rings a few times.

"Is it time for phone sex already," he drawls in a sexy rumble over the line, and I hear some deep masculine laughter break out around him.

"One of these days you're going to answer the phone like that and I'm going to make sure I had been playing with myself for long enough to just come in your ear as a response," I smart with a smirk when he grumbles a complaint.

"Get the fuck out of my office," he barks, and I hear his heavy breathing as footsteps echo and the sound of his door closing. "You've been told not to take my sweetness, Ember. Do you need me to remind you who that pussy belongs to?"

"Yeah, yeah, promises and all that. Listen, big man, Nikki's upset so she's coming over. Is that okay?"

"I told you that you don't have to ask permission to do shit. I want you to feel at home."

I roll my eyes. The same argument we've had since I all but moved in. "I'm still asking. It's your house, Nate."

He mumbles something, but his words are too low for me to make them out.

"I just wanted to warn you that you might be coming home to some pretty high estrogen levels and all that."

"What's wrong with Nikki?"

"All I know is that Seth cheated and they broke up. I told her to meet me there. I figured I could feed her ice cream and wine, the normal post-breakup comfort foods, and then see what else I could get out of her."

"Sounds good, baby. I'll stop by the grocery store when I leave here in ten. I have your back."

I laugh. "I'm pretty sure you're going to regret encroaching on a scorned woman's emotional breakdown time."

"Pfft. Don't doubt me, woman!"

He hangs up as my laughter booms around the cab, and by the time I pull up to his house, I'm actually looking forward to helping my friend if only for the reason that I know Nate has no idea what he's getting into.

Chapter 28

Nate

"And then she just kept bouncing around on his dick like it was the next best thing to sliced bread. Just bounced and bounced. I really was worried that one of her fake freaking boobs was going to pop!"

"What did Seth do?" Ember asks, her voice low and comforting. My eyes keep pinging back and forth between them, trying not to focus too long on Nikki for fear of my life when she gives me one scary ass look.

Nikki doesn't even notice Ember, though. She's too far gone remembering walking in on her man fucking some chick. I shift when she gives me another squinty-eyed look of contempt just because I have a dick.

"He didn't do jack crap because his hands were tied to the bed!" she screams, still looking at me as if she would carve my eyes out with the spoon she's eating her ice cream with.

You would think that she would be thankful; I mean I did stop by the grocery store and buy them ten different flavors of ice cream, but nope. The second I walked into the house, she looked like she wanted to murder me along with her ex.

"So," I start, attempting to make my excuses and escape into my bedroom with some SportsCenter, but I snap my mouth shut when she stabs the air with her spoon. I watch Bam follow the utensil helplessly hoping that something, *anything*, will fall to the ground for him before looking over at Ember and praying she has the answers as to how I can get out of here.

"Would *you* let some hoochie tie you to the bed?" Nikki questions me with an evil tone.

Again, I look at Ember. I'm not really sure the truth right now will help my chances of getting out of here alive. She just winks and I know I'm on my own.

"Uh …" I clear my throat. "No. I would not. I'm more of the one doing the tying in this situation."

Ember stifles a giggle before Nikki can notice, but I don't miss it. She's going to pay for that later.

"You would tie up some hoochie?! You son of a Cher!"

"Huh?" Son of a Cher? Good God, this girl is strange.

"Ember! Did you hear him? He's just like all the other ones. Just thinking about his dick and some hoochie."

"Actually," I interrupt, and she jerks her eyes from Ember to where I'm sitting. I briefly consider all my points of exit options that I have and figure no matter what, my legs are longer, and if it comes to it, I have no problem running like a little titty baby from this spoon wheedling woman. "I never said I would tie up some 'hoochie.' I just meant that when it came to being tied up or doing the tying, I would be doing not receiving. And the only woman I'm going to tie to my bed is here," I finish in a rush and point over at Ember.

She gives me a big smile, distracting me for a second, but a second is all that was needed. I feel the spoon hit my forehead before falling to the hardwood in a loud clatter.

"Oops." Ember giggles.

"What the hell was that for?" I ask, rubbing my head.

"That was for having a penis."

"Why am I being punished because I have a dick?"

"Because you're breathing and thinking about using it. That's where it all begins," she sobs, and I watch as she drops her head to her hands as her hair falls into the almost melted container of chocolate ice cream.

"I'm just going to go … uh, somewhere, anywhere."

Ember's chest moves as she silently giggles, but she just waves me off as she moves from the chair she had been sitting on to the couch where Nikki is wailing and pulls her hair out of the ice cream. I see her look at her wrists for a hair tie and not wanting to stick around longer than necessary, I rip the one holding my hair in a bun and toss it in her lap on my way out of the room.

What a fucking mess.

With nothing on TV, I decided to pick up one of the books Ember is always reading. I used to make fun of Dani for reading 'mom porn,' but this shit is shockingly good. I've already made some mental notes of shit I plan to do to Ember. If she enjoys reading it so much, she's had to have thought about reenacting some of the scenes.

I had been thoroughly enjoying some bum fun when the door opened and a very tired looking Ember walked into the bedroom. Her white tee shirt was streaked with what I'm hoping is chocolate ice cream. Her bare feet are silent as she turns to pull her shorts down her legs, giving me a great view of her ass.

"How is she?" I break the silence, and she jumps a good foot in the air.

"I thought you would be sleeping," she says tiredly.

"I decided to do some light reading instead." I hold up the book, and she just shakes her head with a small laugh. "I thought about getting a highlighter but didn't want to piss you off by marking your book up."

"Thank you for that," she sarcastically drones.

I put the book down, making sure to mark the page I'm on, and pat the bed. "Come on, you look tired."

"I'm exhausted. Things just got worse when you left and she's been crying between mouthfuls of ice cream for the last two hours. I finally had enough and crushed up a Benadryl in her wine. She passed out thirty minutes ago."

"Is that safe?"

"Yeah. I called the twenty-four-hour pharmacist and asked if it was okay to take a Benadryl after a few glasses of wine. She's just going to take a good, much-needed nap."

She climbs into bed, one of her arms going over my stomach and her head dropping to my shoulder. She shifts a few times, bringing one leg up and over mine until I can feel the heat of her knee near my balls.

"I don't know this ex of hers, but is this something that came as a shock?"

I feel her finger push against my nipple ring and I remind myself why I need to calm my dick and be the sensitive boyfriend who listens instead of just fucks his woman every time she breathes near him.

Easier said than done.

When she gives it another tweak, I almost forget all my good intentions.

"I'm honestly not shocked. I've always wondered why she stayed with him, but she didn't have the best life growing up and I think she stuck around out of fear of being alone."

"I could kick his ass for her."

Her laughter tickles my skin, and I have to clench my jaw not to shiver like a little girl.

"That's sweet, honey, but I think her honor is safe and all that."

"Is she going to be okay?"

Ember lifts off my chest and shifts so that her lips press against mine.

"She'll be fine. She's a strong one. Just needed to get it out. Don't be surprised if she never brings it up again and just moves on like she hadn't just been betrayed by a man she had spent the last few years loving."

"That's not healthy, baby."

"I know it's not. She works on things her own way and I just make sure I'm there if she needs me."

"And what do you need?"

Her smile is instant. "Just you."

"Always."

She curls back against my body, her hand going still a few minutes later as her exhaustion wins. It's been a crazy night, but hopefully, it helped distract the nerves that she's been fighting as her show gets closer.

It's been on the tip of my tongue the last few nights, especially after the fire, to tell her how I feel, but because of the bullshit I had done in the past to hurt her, I know that she needs to be shown. I fucked up and because of that, my biggest fear is that my words won't be enough. Actually, that's a lie. The thought that I might feel what she did all those years ago when she bared her soul and I let the pain come to it is a very real insecurity for me. I know deep down that won't happen, but until I can make her say it again and prove to her that I won't take that gift for granted, I'm going to keep proving my feelings for her.

Hell, any fool can say those three little words but not all can show it. It took me a while to figure out what I needed to do was demonstrate that having all of her is something I not only want but also crave. Turning her down will always be one of my biggest regrets—even if it was the best thing for her at the time—because now that I have her, I know the only way I would have ever felt true happiness is in her arms.

Everything I have ever wanted is coming true. I have Dirty, and already, I know with no doubts that place will continue to thrive. My family is healthy. I have my own home, a badass truck, and friends with a bond that most people would kill to have. Everything that money could buy, I have. But getting the gift of Ember's love will without a doubt solidify that I've made it.

Nothing in the world is worth having if it isn't with her.

I know that now, and it's my job to make sure that any lingering doubts she might have are erased.

With a smile on my face and a plan forming in my mind, I pull her a little closer and drift off to sleep.

Tomorrow is going to be fun.

Chapter 29
Ember

"Would you sit still!" my sister yells, throwing another Q-tip down on the kitchen table. "I swear to God, Ember, you act like you've never put eyeliner on before."

Blinking back some of the tears in my eyes, I look up at her and smile, or try to, but my nerves are going nuts in my gut and I'm too focused on trying not to puke.

"You're lucky I love you," she fumes.

Nate wisely left when the girls showed up earlier. I think he would have stuck around, but when his sister started talking about her night with Cohen, he gagged and left with the promise to be back in time to escort me to the gallery.

"When is Stella getting here?" Dani asks, twirling another lock of my hair around her flat iron. I've always wondered how she got those amazing curls to stay so long but never thought it would be a flat iron doing the trick.

"Dunno," Maddi hums, her breath hitting my face as she attempts to put my liner on—again—and I fight the urge to blink when she starts to come at me with the pointy end again.

"She had better hurry; she's got my dress," I mumble. When I realized that the fire had destroyed the one I had picked out, I knew Stella, or her father rather, was my only hope.

"What happened to the one you bought?"

I look over at Dani with a sad smile. "It was hanging on the molding in the doorway to my kitchen. I accidentally brought it in there with the groceries and just decided to leave it there." Even though I've come to terms with what I lost in the fire, it still hurts. My studio being the biggest of heartaches. But everything besides that room that had meant something to me was salvageable, so I need to focus on that and not on what I lost.

"Damn, sorry, Em," Dani mumbles.

"It's okay. Things are coming along with the construction, according to my dad. I've slowly started to rebuild my supplies, so I'll be fine."

"And luckily she kept a lot of her overflow in the guest room, so not all was lost, right Em?"

I smile at my sister and nod my head.

"That's good. You should take over a place here," Dani contemplates out loud.

It isn't something I haven't thought about, but I don't want to take over Nate's space with my stuff. He has a bonus room upstairs that has so much natural lighting and a huge picture window overlooking his backyard. When I first walked into the room, something that he had been using for a man cave type game room, I couldn't help but think of what a perfect space it would be to set up my easel and get lost.

His property is set away from the road, gated and secluded. When you stand in that room and look out the window, all you can see is the beautiful woods, the small creek, and the birds flying around. The trees aren't heavy back there, not like they are around the sides and front of his property, so the sun just gives a shadowed grayness to the land.

I've already decided that I would be painting it soon. My phone was quickly filling up with various angles and images from his woods and property in general.

"I'm here!"

All three of us turn when Stella comes bursting into the kitchen, where we have currently set up command central to get me ready for the show tonight. She rushes into the room and I notice that she's empty-handed, making what nerves I had been able to settle pick back up.

"Uh," I start.

"It's coming. I had a tagalong that I just couldn't shake when it was discovered where I was headed."

That's when I notice the heavy clicks of heels against the floor. There is only one person I know who takes that heavy of a step when in heels.

Sway.

Or Dilbert 'Sway' Harrison III.

He's not only one-half of Stella's fathers, as in plural, but he also owns the very popular salon, Sway's, that my sister, Dani, and Stella work at. He's gotten a lot of hype after the reality show aired a few years ago, *Sway All the Way*, and things just keep getting bigger and bigger for him and the girls at the salon.

But more importantly, he knows what he's talking about when it comes to fashion. I've known him my whole life and never thought anything but the best of the man who rocked designer fashions better than anyone else did. I've seen pictures of him from before all of our parents had kids, and this has always been him. Back then, he was always rocking a long blond wig, but these days, he has it shaped into a shoulder-length stylized mess of wavy curls.

Just because he's a gay man who prefers the tight clothing from the women's section doesn't mean he can't pull off jeans and a tee shirt from his husband's closet too. He just has it all.

"Looking good, Sway," Dani calls over my shoulder, and she isn't wrong.

He has on some tight flare-legged black pants with a white button-down shirt tucked into his trim waist. He used to be a little overweight, but nowadays, he's trimmed up and put on some muscle. Instead of his normal blond locks, though, he has his natural shaved black hair on display, something I know that even though he usually has covered up, he takes great pains to make sure his grays don't ever show.

"Of course, Sway does, darlin'. Would you expect any less?"

"I suppose not." She giggles.

"What are you wearing?" He gasps and continues to look at Dani.

"Uh … clothes?"

"Those," he puffs, "are not clothes and should be thrown out immediately. What have I told you about hiding that luscious body?"

"I know, I know, but give it a rest today. I was in a rush, and Owen spilled his breakfast on me, so I just threw something on. I'm going home to change when I finish her hair."

"You had better be," he fusses.

"And you," he says to me with a smile. "I have the best dress ever for you. Tight and black, but covers everything from shoulders to knees. I even have a gold shawl if you decide that bare arms aren't what you want. Finish that up with some gold heels that are just marvelous. I knew you wouldn't want something too flashy, even if flashy is my middle name, even though you should show off that body too. I'll let it pass tonight because you should flatter your art and not overshadow it with your beauty. So hurry up so Sway can get you all beautified for tonight."

I don't get a chance to talk because his face lights up and he starts bouncing in his spot.

"Oh! And now, tell me all about the hunky prince who owns this house. I always knew with parents as striking as Axel and Izzy that boy would be a jaw dropper. Even as a baby he was just the most handsome thing in the world, I tell you. Just the sweetest face, like his mama. But it was his daddy and those brawny, mouthwatering muscles that I knew would win out with his only son. That jaw, my lord. And his hair. I've been itching to get my hands on him for way too long, oh yes, I have. Tell Sway everything, if you know what I mean." He finishes with a dreamy sigh and drops into the seat in front of me, pushing Maddi out of the way. "I bet he is a dream in bed!"

"Oh my God, Sway! I'm going to puke!" Dani whines, making a gagging noise.

"Something is wrong with you," Maddi snaps and nudges him out of the way with her hip.

Sway continues to wag his brows at me, and I have to fight to keep my giggles in. I just give him a wink and hope that's enough to keep him quiet while Dani and Maddi finish my hair and makeup.

Chapter 30
Ember

After being fussed over, buffed, and stuffed, the girls—and Sway—deemed me 'perfect' and left shortly after to get ready themselves. I still have another three hours before the gallery doors open, but I hope Nate gets back soon so I can get over there. The anxious anticipation for tonight hit a fever pitch when I took my first look in the mirror after getting dressed.

Sway wasn't wrong about the dress. It's perfect, understated, and classy.

It's also skintight, and because of that, I had to forgo any undergarments. Every step I take on the tall heels has me fighting the urge to look and see if my big boobs are swaying around. Sway assured me that it was designed to 'hug the girls tightly,' and even if I decided to jump up and down, they would stay put. Now, I just need to make sure Nate doesn't make my nipples hard, and I should be good to go.

The black fabric has a high neck, covering me as promised from my collarbone to the end of the pencil skirt at my knees. My arms are bare, which is perfect to keep me cool if I start to get the nervous sweats. My hips are outlined in a way that I look like the perfect model for an hourglass figure. That is until I turn to the side and you can't help but notice my butt. I've always thought it was one of my worst features, having more than a handful, but seeing how it's accented, I know it's probably one of my best. Lord knows, Nate can't keep his hands off it. Not quite a Kardashian butt, but close.

Dani took all my hair, curled loosely, and after twisting a few pieces at my temple, pinned one side back so all it hangs over my right shoulder.

My makeup is light, except for the light smoky effect that Maddi had created around my eyes. The normally dull brown color looks more like melted chocolate with the outline of black.

I look good. No, I look damn good. Just standing in front of the mirror in Nate's room has helped to ease a little of my tension about tonight because of the confidence my appearance brings forth.

"Fuck me," a deep voice moans, breaking through my thoughts.

I turn, my red lips smiling as Nate stands in the doorway breathing heavily.

"Well, hello to you too," I joke.

"How long is the show again?"

"A few hours. Why?"

"I just need to know how long I'm going to have to wait before I can peel that skirt over your ass and bend you over. Fuck, Ember. I'm going to be tenting my pants all night."

I laugh, walking over to him, and his eyes zero in on my heels.

"Those will stay on. All night. I have plans for those." He adjusts his crotch, moving the very noticeable erection around with a groan before holding his hand up to stop my movements. "Don't get near me. If you do, we'll never get out of here. Be a good girl and go wait for me downstairs while I get dressed."

He shifts, jumping away from the doorway when I take another step, making me throw back my head with a laugh as I walk out of the bedroom and down to let Bam outside to take care of his business before we leave for the night.

Thirty minutes later, he comes downstairs and gives me a narrowed eye look full of accusations.

"What?" I ask, tossing the magazine I had been thumbing through down on the couch next to me.

"What, she says," he grumbles. "Acting like you didn't plan this with your tempting body on display for me." He points at his crotch, and I can just see the outline of his hard cock still tenting the fabric.

My giggles bubble out and he puts his hands on his hips, the fabric of his black dress shirt pulling tight on the muscles in his arm.

I lick my lips as my eyes travel back to the black slacks hiding—or rather, not hiding—his erection.

"Not helping, Ember," he says through clenched teeth.

I hold up my hands and have to stifle the bubble of laughter that is threatening to burst out. "I didn't plan anything. Promise. This is all thanks to Sway." I point at my dress.

"Sway did this?"

I nod.

"Hmm. Remind me to send him a thank-you note then," he mutters under his breath.

"Just a second ago, you were ready to spank me for having the nerve to wear this dress! Now, you're talking about sending thank-you notes?"

"Oh, I'm still spanking your ass, but I'm going to make sure and thank him for giving me a whole new list of fantasies when it comes to how I want to fuck you."

My jaw drops. "I think that's an inappropriate thank-you note, Nate."

"You're right. I should send him an edible arrangement and mention how he should enjoy eating something delicious as fuck for giving me my own mouthwatering treat."

"You're incorrigible."

"I'm horny! You have no idea what that dress is doing to me. In fact, after I fuck you in it tonight, I might have the damn thing bronzed."

Speechless, I just shake my head and turn to gather my clutch and phone, smiling to myself when he makes a noise low in his throat.

Maybe I'll send Sway a thank-you note of my own.

"I'm so proud of you, sweetheart," my mom praises and gives me a big hug.

I look over her shoulder and let her admiration sink in. The nerves I had been fighting leading up to this moment had left the second Annabelle's gallery filled to the point of bursting earlier, and I haven't been able to stop smiling since.

When I got here, she had everything already set up, and with nothing to do but wait, I spent the quiet time I had walking the room with Nate, showing him all of my work.

The catering company Annabelle had hired had been working the room, passing out champagne flutes and light canapés. I've been enjoying a glorious buzz thanks to that. The low hum of classical music that was playing through the speakers earlier can't even be heard over the light babble of this many people filling the room.

She had sent out something like two hundred invitations, not counting the huge crowd that came from my personal guest list, and it looked as if almost every single person had shown up.

The only thing I was still anxious about was hearing what ended up selling at the end of the night. Optimistically, I was hoping for at least half of my collection to sell, but I really would be happy with anything. Just being here and seeing my work on display as everyone visibly appreciates my pieces is the most wonderful gift to my soul.

"Thank you, Mom. It's a little overwhelming but so exciting to see everyone loving my work."

"What's not to love?" my dad says from behind me, and I turn to smile up at him. "Except that woman wouldn't let me buy one."

My brow furrows. "Annabelle?"

"Snotty blond woman who looks like a stick is permanently wedged up her-"

My mom slaps her hand over his mouth, not letting him continue to complain, and gives me an apologetic look.

"That's Annabelle. Did she give you a reason?" My mind races with reasons why she would deny a sale, to my own father of all people.

"Sure as hell did," he answers against my mom's hand, his lips turning up as he smiles brightly at me.

When my mom feels his smile, she drops her hand immediately and looks up at him with one of her own. It's rare that he gives us this look, especially in public, so to see his stoic mask slip I know she is soaking it in too.

"Okay?"

"Sold out, my sweet girl. Every single fucking piece is sold." His smile gets even larger as his chest puffs with pride.

"What?" I gasp.

"Oh my God, Emberlyn!" my mom exclaims, pulling me back into her arms with a bruising hug.

My dad wraps his arms around us both and hoarsely gives me the words that make my eyes prick with emotion. "Proud of you, honey. So damn proud."

I've never doubted his pride, but I know he's always worried about me since my career started out so quick. I had so much success with my work before I even left my teenage years behind, and when I left art school after two years to pursue my dreams, his worrying didn't ease up. But this, tonight, goes a long way to extinguishing those thoughts in his mind.

"I need to go tell Nate," I tell them, pulling out of her embrace.

My dad, shockingly, gives a nod of agreement. "You did good," he states low and slowly follows with a smile that almost looks sad.

"Thank you?" I respond a little confused. He just said he was proud of me, so I'm not sure why he now looks sad about it.

"Talking about the man, not your night."

"Oh."

"Like I said, you did good. He did better, but you still did good. And if he makes you cry again, I'll kill him."

My nose tingles, and I look up at my big, strong father as I fight not to start crying. Maddi would kill me if I messed up my makeup, but I know my father would be upset if he was the reason I shed a tear … even if they were happy ones.

"I did do better, didn't I?" I give a wobbly laugh when he winks, taking my mom's hand and pulling her into the crowd over to where the Reids are—well, one-half of them since I don't see Nate's dad, Axel. The Becketts, Coopers, and Cages are laughing and smiling in the back corner.

Their children scattered around the room, as well, but I only have eyes for the long-haired man in black standing in front of *A Beautiful War* with his father at his side.

I'm stopped a few times on the way to him. A few critics from the local paper and the *Atlanta Journal-Constitution* stop me for a few quick questions, making my high for the night climb even higher. The *AJC*? Holy crap. That's huge for them to feature an Atlanta artist! By the time I'm stepping up behind the Reid men, I might as well be walking on clouds I'm so happy.

"You going to tell her tonight?" I hear Axel ask his son.

"Yeah. I can't wait any longer. It's killing me to keep it from her."

My heart seizes in my chest, and I drop the hand that had been reaching for Nate's shoulder as I wait to hear what else they have to say. If they wanted privacy, well, then they should have had this conversation somewhere else.

"Good you don't wait any longer. Women don't appreciate that shit."

Nate nods, still looking at the canvas in front of him.

"Didn't want it to come to this, but I can't keep it in anymore."

This time Axel bobs his head, taking a swallow of the champagne in his hand. After a few seconds—minutes maybe—Axel gives him a slap on his shoulder and turns. He stumbles a little in his step when he sees me behind them but just bends to kiss my temple, covering his misstep.

"Congratulations, Ember," he acknowledges softly.

Nate's shoulders tense, but he doesn't turn. After his father walks away, I wait for it, but he still doesn't give me his eyes. Their words run through my mind and instead of feeling the overwhelming desolation I would have expected to feel, I have too much faith in him to just walk away without demanding an explanation.

I haven't come this far to just give up. If he's going to end it, he's going to tell me right now to my face.

Squaring my shoulders and taking a deep breath, I step around him, standing between him and the wall holding *A Beautiful War*. A fitting place, if there ever was one. Even if the crowd is milling about just a few feet away.

"Nate?" His eyes roam over the piece behind me for a second before looking at me, giving me his attention, and the fierceness in his gaze almost makes my knees buckle. "What is it?"

He studies my face before looking back over my shoulder. "That's us."

Not a question.

"That *was* us," I correct.

"And what changed?" he continues as his attention stays focused on the painting.

"Everything," I breathe.

With a deep inhale, I finally get his stunning green eyes. "Give me more than that, Emberlyn. What changed to end our *beautiful war*?"

Time to go for broke. We've been leading up to this for weeks now, and after everything that we've been through to get to this point, I just need to take a leap and pray this time things will end differently than it did the last time I told him how I felt.

"My head collided with my heart."

His pupils dilate, his eyes getting stormy as his nostrils flare. "Give me more," he demands, taking a step toward me until just the smallest of space separates us from touching.

"Love won."

His chest heaves, jolting at my words, and he dips until we're nose to nose. "*More*."

"I love you." I softly comply with his demand, my voice steady, strong, and true. "I love you. And even though that has never changed through the years, regardless of my fears and hurt, what made everything change was when I realized you not only wanted my heart, but you would also protect it when I took the last step toward you and asked for yours in return again."

"I have all of you?"

"I think you always have."

His hand snakes out, going around my middle to pull me to him as he straightens to stand, my feet lifting to dangle above the ground. I reach up, curling my fingers over his shoulders as our breath mingles between us.

"Tell me again." The hunger in his eyes betrays the calmness in his voice.

"I love you."

His eyes close, and he presses his forehead against mine.

"Nate?" I whisper when he doesn't move.

"I had it all planned." His words just barely a whisper. "Everything I wanted to say to you, show you, and give you … all planned. It was getting so hard to keep it from you, though. I took one look at this painting, and I knew I couldn't wait any longer. It was killing me to keep those plans from you, but I just had to be patient."

I think back to the conversation I had overheard between him and his father when he finishes talking, and my body jolts when I realize what had really been going on.

"I knew that tonight I had to tell you, regardless if I had proven myself worthy of getting it in return, and I had to take a chance that you were ready to give that back to me. Then I see this and I knew that even if you weren't ready, I was more than prepared to give you enough to last for the both of us until you were."

Finally opening his eyes, I gasp when I see the blazing brightness illuminated by the slight dampness in them.

"My God," I wheeze when his arms tighten around me, wishing we were alone so that I could wrap my legs around him and never let go.

"I love you, Emberlyn Locke. I can't change that we lost us for a while, but I can promise you with everything that I am that you will never, not for one second for the rest of our lives, know another day without that love."

"Oh, Nate."

His mouth presses against mine. Not in a deep kiss, but the soft touch of his lips against mine is all I need to feel like we're the only ones in a crowded room. Taking my hands from his shoulders, I wrap them around his neck and take a deep pull of air through my nose, my eyes watering as every single crack I had ever had in my heart repairs itself with the power of us winning our beautiful war.

In his arms, I know that no matter what, as long as I'm with him, we can win any fight that is in our path.

Chapter 31
Ember

"I don't understand."

Annabelle gives me a sly smile before looking over my shoulder. I turn and follow the path to see Nate standing with our group, and Dani and Cohen laughing at something he's said. Maddi is standing with Cohen's sisters as they talk to Liam and Megan. The rest of our group—Stella, Zac, and Jax, as well as Cohen's brothers—left when the doors locked.

Turning back to Annabelle, I try to make sense of her last words.

"It is quite unorthodox but not unheard of."

"You're telling me, and not joking, that every single one of my paintings was sold before anyone arrived?"

There's no way. I mean sure we had sent out a little teaser to the guests before the show, but there is no way that someone would have even had time to see the whole collection, let alone enough people to buy the whole damn thing.

"I didn't say no one had arrived, just that every piece was paid for before the show started."

"Can you please stop talking in riddles and just let me see the purchase orders."

Her smile grows, and I look behind me when I feel Nate press against my back.

"What's going on?"

I turn slightly to look up at him while I sink into his hold, loving the way his hard muscles feel against my body.

"I'm trying to get Annabelle to tell me why, when my dad tried to buy a painting earlier, he was denied. She said that was because everything was sold, but Nate"—I take a deep breath after rushing that out quickly—"he tried to make a purchase less than thirty minutes after people started arriving."

"I see," he responds, his eyes alive with mirth. "Well, Annabelle?"

Pulling my attention back to her, I watch in confusion as she throws her head back and laughs.

"You," she says and points at him. "Are trouble."

"You might as well just show her the purchase order, so I can get my girl home to celebrate."

"Trouble," she huffs under her breath, shifting some things around on her desk before handing me the purchase orders.

Expecting to see a spreadsheet of orders or, at the very least, more than one single sheet of paper, my brain freezes.

"Oh my God," I stutter, seeing the words but not really understanding them.

"I told you I wanted every piece of you, and I'll be damned if I share this part of your stunning mind with anyone else."

"What have you done?" Still mumbling, my eyes rake over every word. It really isn't a question since not only can I see it with my own eyes, but also the only thing I'm capable of getting past the huge lump of emotion burning my throat.

"I have all of you now, Ember."

"Oh, my God."

Tears burn my eyes and I look up to an elated Annabelle. I'm sure she's thrilled that she sold every piece. After all, her commission alone is worth being excited about, but she looks like my reaction alone is worth more to her than any money she made tonight.

His deep chuckles at my shock vibrate against my back, and with a hitch in my breath, I turn with a leap and bury my head in the crook of his neck and cry the happiest tears I've ever shed.

"You're crazy," I tell him.

"Crazy for you."

"That … God, Nate. Do you have any idea how much money you just spent?"

He shrugs.

"Where are you even planning to put all of these?" My question is a hushed whisper against his smiling lips.

"I guess we can give one to your dad," he answers in complete seriousness. "But *our* war is going home with us. That's mine."

"There are still over thirty paintings that you now own, Nate."

His lips part, his teeth showing as he smiles big. "Looks like we're about to have some full walls then."

"I love you, you crazy man."

"I know."

I raise a brow, his laughter booming around us. "I love you, too."

"Nate!" I scream when his hand smacks against my exposed ass. "Please," I beg.

"If I would have known you were walking around bare under this dress." His words come out so deep and full of lust that he sounds animalistic.

My fingers flex against the wall in front of me, wishing he had, at least, pushed me against the couch instead so I would have something to grip. We didn't even make it a step inside the door before he was pushing me against the wall and making true to his promise earlier when he pulled my dress's tight skirt over my hips.

Then he discovered just what I had on underneath. Or, rather, what I didn't.

And that is where we are now. He's standing behind me panting while one palm between my shoulders pins me against the wall as his other continues to spank each of my naked cheeks.

He takes a handful of my flesh and gives me a painful squeeze, the feeling shooting something so heavenly between my legs. He lets go, brings his hand down again over the heated skin, and shifts so I can feel his pants-covered erection between my cheeks.

"You look so fucking hot wearing my marks," he utters against my shoulder before his teeth take a hard nip.

"Oh, God." I gasp.

He continues to play with me, nipping and licking at my shoulder and neck while rocking against me.

"Please. I need you, Nate," I whine, pushing against him.

"My mouth or my cock?"

My mouth moves, and between pants and incoherent mumbling, I try to answer. My legs are shaking so violently; the release I so desperately need is just within reach, rendering me incapable of conscious thought, let alone speech.

"You're soaking my pants, Ember. You need me, baby?"

I give him a nod, my forehead hitting the wall softly. With no strength left, I leave it there and sigh.

Nate continues his tantalizing movements with hips rocking against my backside. The burn of his pants against my heated flesh only spikes my growing need for him with each rub. His hands come up to roughly grab my breasts through the dress, pinching my nipples harshly. I whine and he answers with a coarse laugh.

With quick movements, he has me turned. My back hits the wall as my legs come up to hook behind his back. The second his hips connect with my core, I notice that at some point he had shed his pants, the hard heat of his bare erection hitting the spot that needs him the most, and I whimper shamelessly.

With our faces level, noses touching with each deep inhale, it's as if we both feel the need to be as close as possible and our hands move. Mine slowly travel up his chest until the tips of my fingers are in his silky hair and my thumbs are at his cheekbones. He moves slower, stabilizing our weight with his body before framing my face, his thumbs sweeping over my cheek slowly.

His luminous eyes burn their gaze into mine as he stares at me with raw hunger. Our mingled breaths rush between parted lips, just inches from touching, as we continue to gaze at each other. What had started as a desperate desire to feel each other changes in that instant; it's no longer about the hunger to find our releases, but to share something more intense than we ever had before.

I gasp when he lifts his body from mine; taking his cock from the hug my lips had been giving it, I mourn the loss. With our faces so close, I see his hooded eyes darken to a mossy green that burns brightly, reminding me of a rain-soaked field after a hard downpour.

Hypnotizing.

Alluring.

All-consuming.

The second he enters my body, we both call out. His fingers flex on my neck and pull my forehead to his without breaking eye contact.

He moves slowly, each inch entering my body with unhurried measured thrusts that have a new burn crawling up my skin, leaving goose bumps in its wake. I tighten my thighs, trying to bring him closer, or speed him up, but he ignores me. Even as my whimpers turn to an aroused whine, he doesn't take me harder than the slow glide he had created. The sounds of our breaths echoing around us mingle with the wet sounds of him entering and exiting my body.

"More," I say breathily.

His forehead rocks against mine as that mossy green brightness takes on a blaze from within. His nostrils flaring and his breathing labored.

"More," I beg.

His movements still with his cock buried deep. I whimper, the fullness stretching me. He twitches but still doesn't move. Just bores into me with an expression that causes my heart to gallop at dangerous speeds.

"I love you." His voice is guttural, hoarse from the intense moment we're sharing.

"I love you, too. So much."

Not breaking eye contact and his cock still deep inside me, he closes the small distance to my lips. Only when our tongues make contact does he start to move again. The same slow—painfully slow—infiltration of mind, body, heart, and soul.

I pull my mouth from his when the intimacy becomes too much. My hands fall from his face to his neck, and I feel my eyes wet when I realize that, at this moment, we're as close as anyone could ever get to experience paradise.

Not even completely nude and with me against the wall, Nate

makes love to my body. And if there was any doubt about him owning all of me before now, it was obliterated the second I clamped down on him with a scream as his own grunt of completion rumbled from deep in his chest.

Chapter 32

Nate

It's been two weeks since Ember's art show.

Two weeks since I earned the right to have her heart back and gave her mine in return. Sometimes, I feel like the biggest pussy-whipped bastard around because all it takes is one sly smile from her and I'm ready to drop to my knees and promise her the fucking world.

And I love every single second of it.

She's still at my house, and honestly, I wasn't kidding when I had told her that it was where I wanted her. Fuck rushed. I don't see the point in changing the way things are now just because society has some misconception on how fast two people in love should move. Ember and me, we aren't conventional. Our past proves that, and just because we haven't been together that long—almost two months—we've known each other our whole lives. We're closer than most couples who have been married for years.

So if I want my girl with me, I'm going to make sure I do whatever it takes to convince her to stay.

However, judging by how quick her dad is moving the construction on her house along, I have a feeling that *he* isn't too happy with his daughter 'living in sin.'

I make a mental note to have a conversation with him tonight at our first family dinner together as a couple. I would be a fool if I weren't a little worried that he might kick my ass just for suggesting it.

But it's a chance I'm willing to take.

Even though everyone had come out to her show, our parents knew that we were together now, but they haven't actually come face-to-face with just how together we really are. There hasn't been time before tonight. She's been busy working in my guest room on some more pieces Annabelle had commissioned out, and I've been busy with Dirty.

Thankfully, Dirty is running so smoothly with Shane and Dent managing the club that I've been able to really take a step back. I still go in every day, but I trust my team, and I've been able to be home early more often than not. My girl got the dates she deserved, and it's rare that I miss one of her home-cooked meals. Sometimes, she comes with me when I go over at night, and sometimes, she doesn't. All that matters is that we found our stride and it's fucking perfect.

"Hey, handsome," I hear and look up from the socks I had been pulling on to see Ember standing in the bedroom doorway, Bam panting at her side.

Pulling my jeans legs down, I grab my shoes and slip them on before standing to get my hands on her. She laughs when I bend and grab her ass to pull her up so that I can take her mouth. The sound muffles against my lips, and I smile, breaking the kiss to look at her.

"Hey baby, you ready?" Her face heats and she pulls one plump lip between her teeth. Well, shit. I thought she had gotten over her nerves about tonight, but apparently not. "What is it?"

"Nothing really. I just stupidly let some nerves take root."

"I told you, Ember, you have nothing to feel uneasy about."

She gives me an adorable pout, and I have to remind myself that we really don't have time for me to fuck her. Even if we did, I'm pretty sure her father *would* kill me if we show up smelling like sex, regardless of me having his blessing to be with his little girl.

"I know, logically. I just can't help it."

"What are you really worried about?"

She sighs. "I don't know. Maybe that they won't agree with our relationship. Or that it will be awkward."

"And would it be a problem if someone did have an issue with us being together?" I ask. To me, fuck no, but Ember has always been treated a little differently as the baby of the group. The overprotective father acting like a giant guard more often than not, and I understand where she is coming from because of that. After all, I did use that as a reason for us not to be together in the past.

"Not even a little, to me, but like I said … it would be awkward."

"Good thing for you, awkward is my middle name."

She laughs, the mood lifting, and I give her another brief kiss before placing her on her feet.

"I love you, Ember, but so does every single other person who will be there tonight. They won't even think twice because they can see with their own eyes that not only do you have my love, but I have yours. Give them the benefit of the doubt until they prove otherwise, and if they do, then we will deal. Together."

"Together," she echoes.

"You're stuck with me, baby. If they give you any lip, then just light the fuse on that little firecracker temper of yours and put them in their place."

She barks out a laugh, the heaviness of her mood dissipating instantly.

"I'll go take Bam out. Come get me when you're ready to leave."

"Okay, Nate."

The second her body passes by mine when she walks into the room, I let my hand fall back and give her ass a loud smack. She jumps and turns quickly. I wag my finger at her.

"Not fair, Nate!" she whines, the sound falling on my back as I walk out of the room.

"Foreplay is a good thing," I call back, laughing to myself as I walk through the house and start tossing Bam his ball in the backyard.

"Everyone is already here," she softly observes, looking through the windshield of my truck at the vehicles that line my parents' driveway.

"Well, that's what happens when your beast of a dog decides that he would rather hunt his own dinner than have that bag shit."

She laughs nervously.

"Calm down. It's going to be fine."

Her head moves, but her eyes stay focused on the driveway.

"How many times do I have to remind you that this isn't the first time they've seen us together?"

"My show doesn't count. I hardly had time away from Annabelle parading me around to even be at your side."

I hum, not responding. She has to work this out on her own, and nothing I say will ease her mind.

"Plus, this is so much different. This is our *family,* Nate. Someone is bound to say something. I just don't want to cause any issues."

Again, I just nod and make a noise in my throat.

"Then again, our parents are the only ones who it could cause issues with and they know about us, so it will probably be fine. I mean we've had the group over to the house and they've seen us together, so it's not as if this is going to be shocking. But all of our parents, I mean … yeah, they haven't really seen us together. But you know what, you're right. We love each other and that's all that matters. If someone has a problem with it, then screw them."

Her head finally turns as she slides her hand into mine.

"Firecracker."

She smiles brightly, happiness clear on her face, and I know she's ready.

We walk up the driveway, having parked all the way at the end, hand in hand. I give her one more look before pushing the door open and stepping into my parents' house. She follows behind; I'm not sure if she's using me to hide behind or if I'm just too pumped to be here *with* her that I'm rushing, but when I stop walking a few feet in to shut the door behind us, she crashes into my back with an oomph.

I turn and look down at her. She looks up with a glare.

"Would you rather I just jump on your back so that you don't have to drag me around?" she says sarcastically.

I drop her hand and bend to hold her face between my palms. "The only time I want you jumping on me is when you're taking my cock in your tight cunt." My voice is low, for her ears only. When her cheeks pink and eyes darken, I drop my mouth to hers for a deep, wet kiss. Her hands grab onto my tee shirt and I feel her try to pull me closer, completely forgetting where we are.

That is until a tiny little angelic voice screams out.

"OH! Mommy! Nate has his tongue in Ember's mouth! That's *bad*. Mommy *and* Daddy said so. You have to keep your tongue in your mouth and only when you are married can you do *that*! Oh, boy. You're in trouble! Mommy!"

I regrettably break away from Ember and give her shocked eyes a wink before looking down at Molly. I've loved this kid since the day I met her, but right now, I'm having a hard time remembering why. I give her a smile before bending down. Not willing to give Ember a chance to freak out again, I grab her hand and pull her to my side. She almost stumbles but keeps her hand in mine while standing next to my crouched form. Molly's eyes move from my face to our joined hands. Her mischievous expression gets a little wonky before she replaces it with a sickeningly sweet smile. Her little angelic act isn't fooling me, though; I know she's up to something.

"You have spit germs in your mouth now," she scolds. "You could be sick."

"I'm used to spit germs in my mouth."

"You had your hand on her booty. That's a no-touch place. Daddy said so."

"I can touch her booty."

"You might put a baby in her belly if you keep putting your tongue in her mouth, and Mommy said you have to be married to tongue touch spit germs and put babies in bellies. That's how I got my baby Jack. Daddy told me so."

"I think we're going to be okay, Molly-Wolly."

She tilts her head and studies my face. "I don't like that lipstick on you."

I look up at Ember at that, confused, and see her giggling. She points to her own dark pink lips before I realize what Molly means.

"My apologies, your highness. I vow to never wear another woman's lipstick other than the one you deem worthy of my complexion."

Molly giggles.

"Molly? Why don't you let Nate and Ember come in now?"

I look up and see Molly's mom, Megan, a few feet away. Behind her, I see my sister, Cohen, and Molly's dad, Lee, losing the fight to keep their laughter in.

Assholes.

"It's not that funny," I tell them after Megan had taken Molly away from the group.

"It's freaking hilarious," Dani wheezes through her laughter. "Oh, Nate, I sure hope you didn't tongue a baby into Ember." She doubles over, and I narrow my eyes at her.

"Danielle Cage."

She still doesn't stop.

"I mean maybe you could keep wearing that pretty lipstick and your 'tongue spit germ baby' can call you mommy too."

My jaw ticks.

"Mommy Nate," she snorts.

Cohen backs up with one look at me, knowing that if he sticks behind his wife, he's going to take a foot to the balls when I pick her bratty ass up. Ember lets my hand go, and I make a mental note to spank her ass later for laughing along with Dani. The second my shoulder goes into her stomach, she lets out one ungodly loud scream, but I just stomp through the entryway and into the kitchen before turning and depositing her on her feet right inside the living room. Her shoulders are turned first, and then I push her nose against the wall.

"Five minutes. Time-out, brat."

Turning from my sister, I see Ember standing behind me with her chest still moving in silent laughter.

"Keep laughing. You've earned my palm later, Emberlyn."

Her jaw drops at my growled words, and I take way too much satisfaction in seeing the blush that crawls up her chest. The minimal coverage of her sundress is not hiding how much she loves my words.

"Hey, you guys," Maddi calls, walking from the back porch into the kitchen. "Why is Dani in the corner?"

"Because she doesn't know how to keep her damn mouth shut," I respond, still looking at Ember as she licks her lips. I have to bite my tongue to keep my cock in line.

"Righttttt." Maddi laughs. "Well, I was sent to drag you outside before Molly had a chance to tell anyone other than Lyn and Lila that you two were in here making spit germ babies."

"Oh my God," Ember gasps in embarrassment. I, with no other option, throw my head back and laugh.

"Let's go," I tell her, taking her hand in mine and walking out the door.

We stand on the deck, overlooking the backyard, and I give her a reassuring squeeze. Her smile comes instantly, even if she still looks slightly self-conscious from her sister's comment.

"I love you," I express, offering her that reassurance of *us* if she needs it.

With a deep breath, her plump lips spread and she gives me one hell of a blinding smile. "I love you, too."

"Yeah, yeah … everyone loves each other. Jerk." Dani brushes past me with a shoulder bump meant to knock me off balance, but she stumbles against my unmoving body.

We walk down the steps, together, hand in hand.

Chelcie and Asher give us both a wave when we walk past them. Their boys, Zac and Jax, stop tossing the football around to call out a greeting before returning to their game.

Dani, now standing next to her husband and in-laws, is still glaring at me. I ignore her and give Cohen a lift of my chin.

"Hey, Melissa." I address his mom, bending down to kiss her cheek.

"Hey, honey." She grins at me before looking at Ember, her happiness spreading to her eyes, which squint slightly. She steps away from her husband and I'm forced to let Ember's hand go when Melissa wraps her in a hug.

Looking over at her husband, I give Greg the same lift of my chin that his son got.

"Give me a damn hug, boy."

I shake my head but give him the hug he demanded with a slap of my hand against his back.

"I'm sure her father already told you, but you make her cry and I'll kill you," he says before pulling away, giving me a stern smile to cover up the fact he just threatened my life. "Good to see you, Nate."

"Yeah, likewise, Greg." My chest moves with my silent laughter.

Ember pulls from Melissa, and I see a slight wobble to her chin. Melissa cups her cheek. "You wear love beautifully, honey." Her words are low, and I know she didn't mean for anyone to overhear them, so I just wait for Ember to step away before taking her hand back in mine.

When we turn, Beck and his wife, Dee, are right behind us. They give their hellos much like Greg and Melissa did. By the time we step away from them and walk to where Liam is standing, I've already had two men threaten to kill me if I hurt Ember. I wouldn't have it any other way. If I somehow hurt her, I would welcome their anger.

Lyn, Lila, Stella, and Maddi are laughing with Megan and Molly. By the glances they keep sending my way, I'm sure there is still talk about spit babies by that girl.

"You sure do know how to make an entrance." Lee laughs. "Hey, Em." He gives her a hug.

"Yeah, seems so."

I look around and see Cohen's brothers have now joined the Cooper boys with the football; they're too wrapped up in their game, so I skirt my eyes around them to see my and Ember's parents standing by the grill looking at us. Both our moms have big smiles on their faces, and if I'm not mistaken, tears in their eyes.

"Well, aren't you looking handsome today?"

I look away from our parents and laugh at Sway.

"I always look handsome."

"Just as cocky as your father. Come wrap those big strong arms of yours around Sway and give me a proper hello."

I bend, giving him the hug he wants. "Hey, Davey," I tell his husband over his shoulder and wait for him to finally let go.

Finally, he does, but not before I get a kiss on my cheek. Ember is at my side laughing at his antics, and I would gladly let that man kiss me again if it means she's no longer feeling unsure about how we will be received today.

"I think we should probably go finish the rounds," I whisper in her ear after stepping away from Sway.

She looks up before following my eyes to our parents and gives me a nod. This time, she takes my hand before leading the way. You couldn't have stopped the grin that came over me at her claim of ownership. My mom passes my nephew, Owen, to my father before walking from their foursome and meeting us halfway. Instead of giving her baby boy a hug, though, she approaches Ember.

She places her hands on Ember's biceps and says, "Hey, sweetheart. You look beautiful." I clear my throat and raise my brow when she looks up at me. "What? Do you want me to tell you that you look beautiful too, son?"

"That would be lovely. Yes, you can tell me how beautiful I am."

She shakes her head and looks back at my girl. "I'm so happy for you two."

I don't need to look at Ember to know that her happiness does, in fact, make her look beautiful.

"Thanks, Izzy," she says softly. "You have no idea how much it means to hear you say that."

I give a mock gasp. "You mean you doubted my own mother thought her baby boy was beautiful?"

Ember pulls her hand from mine to give me a playful smack against my chest at the same time my mother does, and we all three laugh.

"Go on," she tells us before turning and calling Owen's name. He jumps from my dad's arms and starts rushing to his grandma. "Don't let those big men intimidate you," she warns before walking away.

"Let's go, baby."

We move until we're standing in front of them. My dad reaches out and hooks my shoulder before pulling me to his body. With just a few inches separating our height, his mouth turns to my ear. "Don't make me hurt my own boy by doing something stupid as fuck to his woman. Got it?"

"Yes, sir," I lament, shoving off him playfully and turning to Ember's dad.

He has his arms crossed over his chest and his face gives nothing away as to what he is thinking. It doesn't matter that he knows about us. It doesn't even matter that I have his blessing to be with his daughter. Right now, he's playing the part of a father that is, in a sense, letting go of the daughter he has loved and raised for twenty-one years and giving her to the man who will spend the rest of her life being the one to make sure no harm comes to her heart.

"Maddox." I nod.

"Nate." He doesn't move.

"Mind if I have a word?"

His nostrils flare; the only tell he gives me before nodding. I step back and watch him wrap his arms around Ember before giving both her and Emmy a kiss on their foreheads. Ember looks up at me, worried, but I just smile. Then enjoy the fuck out of the growl that I hear from her dad when I pull her into my arms and give her a deep kiss.

"Be right back, baby."

Chapter 33

Nate

We walk to the side of my parents' house, out of view and earshot, and I turn to stand tall in front of her frowning father.

"I love her," I blurt without any lead-up.

I wait for him to speak, but he doesn't.

"You gave me your blessing once, but I need you to understand just what you were giving me when you did. I love your daughter with every fiber in my body. Her happiness is the only thing that matters to me. Her smile will never die again if I have anything to do with it. I promised myself that I would prove to her that I was worthy of her love, and even though her opinion is really the only one that matters, I'm asking you again to respect the love we share and let me have her."

"What exactly are you trying to say, Nate?"

I take a deep breath. "I don't want to spend another day without her by my side. The same goes for her. I will be her supporter in every aspect of her life personally and professionally. No cheerleader in her corner will yell louder. I will make sure she never doubts the love we share and her choice to give me a chance. I would give my life for her, Maddox. One day soon, I pray to God that I'm lucky enough to have you walking her down the aisle. But most importantly, I want all of that to happen with you not only giving me your blessing to make sure it does but with you being happy that you did."

"If I told you I would cut your arm from your body if you caused her a second of pain, what would you say?"

I stand a little straighter and keep my face as impassive as his. "I would hand you the knife."

"If I told you that you didn't deserve her?"

"I would agree. She deserves the world, but she's just getting me, and with me, she's going to get a man who works his ass off to hand the world to her."

He continues his stare down when I finish speaking, and then he gives me something that not once in my damn life have I been on the receiving end of.

His smile.

"I always knew this day would come. Out of my two girls, Ember was the one I always knew would use her head and find a good man. Still, I thought I would hate the bastard. You're a good kid, Nate. You always have been. I can't say I'm happy that you're asking to take my girl from me, but I am happy that she's found a man who will always make sure she comes first daily and goes to sleep knowing that she's got a blessed life. The only thing I've ever wanted for her."

My shoulders drop some when I let out the breath I had been holding.

"I'm going to marry her," I declare and raise my hand to stop him when he opens his mouth, smile gone. "Don't tell me I couldn't possibly know that after only having her love for just under two months. I just want you to know that this is where it's heading, and it's heading there real fast."

"I wasn't going to say that." I raise a brow and he gruffs out a chuckle. "Time is a fickle motherfucker, Nate. I had my own experience with it before I made Emmy mine, so if anyone gets you, it's me. I realized not too long ago that this—you and Ember—has been a long time coming. You had your reasons for pushing her away the first time, and I can respect the hell out of them, but now, you know what you've spent years missing out and you would be an idiot to waste a second more now. That being said, if you think I'm happy about my girl being under your roof without you taking the steps to make her yours completely, you might actually be a dumb shit."

I shake my head. "No, sir. She's an independent woman, but I hope that I can rectify this situation by the time her house is done. If I have it my way, her storage unit full of belongings will just be making one stop, and that's to my house."

"I've enjoyed watching you turn into the man standing in front of me, Nate. You have a good head on your shoulders and your heart's in the right place. You want my blessing, all the cards now on the table, well … you've got it."

Hearing those words from him and knowing that he means it fills my chest with happiness. "So do we hug now?"

"Jesus Christ," he grumbles. "Seems like her sass is wearing the fuck off." He uncrosses his arms and tags the back of my neck, and shockingly, Maddox Locke gives me a hug. "Welcome to the family," he rumbles and lets go.

"Thank you," I tell him after pulling back. "Thank you for letting her go and trusting that I'm going to make sure you never regret that."

His throat moves, but he doesn't speak. With a look demanding I follow and a small smile on his face, he starts walking.

When we walk around the side of the house, I see Ember standing with our mothers and wringing her hands in front of her. The second she sees the looks on our faces, though, she drops her hands to her side and starts running. Maddox stops and I move to the side so she can go to him.

But to my utter shock, and everyone else watching, she passes him with a huge smile and leaps into my arms. I curl my arms around her back as her legs wrap tight around me and contentment like I've never known settles over me.

"I love you," she repeats over and over, not giving me a chance to say a word.

I look at her dad, expecting to see his fury, but instead, I once again find myself on the receiving end of his smile.

Chapter 34
Ember

"I'm so excited to go to Dirty with you!" I exclaim, pulling one of my black heels on and jumping off the bench in front of Nate's bed.

He takes a long sweep of my body, spending a little time on my dress, before looking back up at me, the hunger in his eyes shining brightly.

"You can't wear that."

I look down and try to see what about my simple black lace dress is so offensive, but I come up blank, so I look back up at him.

"You really can't wear that."

"Why?"

"Because if you wear that, the only thing that is going to get done tonight will be you, and as much as it pains me to say this, I really have to get some work done."

I toss my head back and laugh loudly. When I look back at him, he's licking his lips and staring at my legs. "You're crazy."

"Baby," he groans, adjusting himself. "You can wear that any other night, but please not tonight. If I can get all my shit done, that means I don't work all weekend and I have plans to lock you in this room and not leave for forty-eight long, sweaty hours."

"Oh."

"Yeah," he gulps. "Please change?"

"All right, honey." I walk over and stand on my toes to give him a kiss before walking to the closet and looking through what clothes I have here. I settle on a pair of leather leggings and a black halter-style top. Surely, he can't complain about every inch of skin except for the top of my back being covered.

Hobbling on one foot, I pull on the other black heel I had discarded to change and step back into the bedroom. He groans again, and I snap my head up to see what his problem is now.

"Now you look like a sexy dominatrix."

"You going to let me tie you up later?" I joke.

"Not a fucking chance, but if you want some rope play, I'll make sure you get it. Come on, we need to leave."

"Take Bam out, please!" I call after him. "I just need to finish my hair."

He calls out to Bam, and I walk into the bathroom, pulling my hair into a high ponytail as I go. I add a little dark shadow to my eyes to give them more of a smoky look to what had been subtle before when I was wearing the dress. These leather pants have always made me feel like a different person. One who wears her self-assurance. Before now, I had worn that confidence and faked the hell out of it, but now, I don't need to fake a thing. And I have Nate to thank for that. The way he looks at me added with the way he worships my body—all of that has turned me into a whole new person.

I love it.

He is unsure, on a good day, if he's going to let me leave the house because of it. Something about not sharing what's his.

Again, I love it.

Ever since what our families refer to as our 'coming out dinner' a month ago, we've grown even closer. We've even had both of our families over for dinner a few times. Once again, I was nervous about that, but each time, we all ended the evening with loud laughter filling the house.

The only thing that we've disagreed on lately is if I'll be returning to my house in two weeks when it's done. Nate seems to think my moving in permanently is a done deal, but I'm not so sure. I figure we would address it when it became a reality; until then, there was no sense in fighting about it.

That being said, a big part of me doesn't want to leave, and I have a feeling when it comes down to it, I won't be able to. Not when I've come to think of his house as *our* home.

"Ember!"

Rolling my eyes, I give my red lips a pucker and smile at my reflection.

The crowd is thick and the music is loud.

Like every other time I've been to Dirty, things are` a flurry of activity. Each of the dance floors is crammed with bodies, no room between them, as they move with the music. With the view I have from Nate's office, I'm able to see just how crazy everyone gets each time there is a bar dance from the bartenders. It's like watching ants move, but the second one of the guys jumps on the glossy wood, they all move as one to try and get a front-row spot.

Dirty Dog is a beast.

"Things are crazy, honey," I call over my shoulder to Nate.

We got here a few hours ago, and he's been at his desk pretty much the whole time. I've been content watching the madness below because I know he's not only catching up on some paperwork but making sure all the orders and inventory is squared away for the next week to ensure we have more time together at home.

"Hmm?"

Turning, I look over at him as his brow pulls in. He looks at some of the papers beside his computer before punching a few more keys. He looks so hot right now. The glasses that he put on before starting to look over the paperwork have had me hot for him since he started.

I'm tired of waiting.

He doesn't notice as I kick off my shoes and kneel. His desk, a sleek black design with no back, puts his legs in view when I drop to my hands and crawl under. His scent is strong down here, and it just bumps my desire for him higher.

I crouch, keeping my back bent so I don't bump my head, and reach out to place both hands on the inside of his thighs.

He jolts. "What the hell?"

"Sit back and let me give you something to help you relax."

"Fuck me."

He shifts, coming down a little more, but just enough for me to be able to undo his belt and pants. I take his velvety smooth cock in my hands, licking my lips when the tip juts out toward my mouth.

I take him deep in my mouth and smile around his flesh when I hear something slam on the desk above me. Because of my position, I can't do more than fist the base of his cock and swallow a few inches of him, but I work him with my hand and mouth until he's cursing and tensing.

"Come up here and let me fuck your pussy."

I ignore the command, hitting my head on the top of his desk when I pick up my speed. My saliva runs down his shaft until my fist is slick. When I graze him softly with my teeth, he lets out a groan as his legs straighten and I feel him clench his ass.

If I were in a better position, I would push my hand down my pants, but I know he would be pissed if I took my 'sweetness' from him. Instead, I just shift a little and enjoy the way my pants rub against my swollen clit.

Humming my pleasure, I speed up and grip him tighter.

He starts making rough sounds above the desk, and I know he's close. Pulling back, I kiss the tip and blow against the skin. He hisses loudly, causing me to smile.

"Suck my cock, Ember."

Not one to disobey—much—I do as I'm told and take him back in my mouth.

It doesn't take long before my jaw relaxes as I sense him close to the edge before I take him as deep as I can and use my throat muscles to constrict against his cock.

He shouts out my name and then bathes the back of my throat with his come. I pull back slightly when he keeps coming so I don't choke. I continue to slowly move my mouth up and down his shaft, waiting for the last twitch before licking the tip once more and pulling him from my mouth.

He doesn't move when I back up and crawl out from under his

desk. When I stand, I look down at him and feel a rush of power from what I've done. He's slouched in his chair, his head resting against the back and his eyes closed.

I turn and walk to the bathroom in the corner to wash my hands and fix my hair and makeup before returning to his office, finding him standing and tucking his semi-hard cock back into his pants.

"Not that I'm complaining, but what was that for?" he questions, color still high on his cheeks.

"No reason. You looked tense, and I couldn't have that."

He laughs, the sound like a low rumble of thunder, and walks toward me. "Next time you're in deep concentration on one of your paintings, I'm going to have a lot of fucking fun returning the favor, baby."

I sway in his arms and lick my lips, his eyes following the movement of my tongue.

"I just have to get payroll submitted and then we're out of here. I'm going to fuck you hard all night."

"Promises, promises."

He kisses my forehead, and after another moment of searching my eyes, he walks back to the desk.

"Do you mind if I head down to get a drink at the bar?"

He pauses, half down in his seat before nodding. "Let me text Shane and have him send someone up to escort you. I don't want you fighting through that crowd on your own."

I nod. "Thanks, love."

He presses a few buttons on his phone, and I wait for someone, who is security I'm assuming, to come up. It takes almost ten minutes, but finally a mountain of a man enters the office after a brief knock. His black shirt says SECURITY in bold white letters.

"Sir?"

Nate looks up and frowns slightly. "Are you new?"

"Yes, sir," he replies, his tone dark.

"Joe, right?"

The huge man gives a grunt in response.

"Right, well, Joe, this is my girl, and she wants to head down for a drink. Make sure she gets to the bar without any trouble. Shane knows you're coming and is waiting for her at the main bar."

Another noise from Joe.

"Love you, honey," I call to Nate and walk over to the scary-as-hell Joe.

"Love you too, Ember."

Joe doesn't speak. He gives me about two seconds of attention, his ice-blue eyes sweeping my whole body in about a second, before turning to open the door. I step out with one last wave to Nate and wait for Joe to close the door and lead the way. If I know Nate, he's now standing behind that wall of black windows, watching our every move.

The crowd might have looked crazy from his office, but being down here and trying to move around takes it to a whole new level. I keep my eyes trained on Joe as he seems to part the sea of people with no effort at all. It's as if they sense the danger coming toward them and want to get as far away as possible.

We make it to the bar with no issue, and after a nod to Shane, Joe walks away and over to the entrance to the holding room. His back goes to the wall as his massive arms cross over his chest. Whoever hired him did one hell of a job on making sure they had not only the muscle but the fear factor as well.

"Hey, Ember," Shane yells over the music.

"Hey!"

"What can I make you?"

With a smile, hoping Nate is still watching, I point up to the sign where *my* drink is still written above the bar. Shane laughs, shakes his head, and turns to get everything he needs.

Once the flames stop, I take the drink down quickly, and this time, ask Shane to just make me something fruity. He gets busy and I turn around to survey the crowd. I smile when I take in everything around me. I still think it's a beast, but this beast is just proof of how successful my man is and I couldn't be more proud of him.

The music changes and my eyes widen when the dance floor I just walked around seems to come alive and not in a good way. Bodies start colliding, and it isn't long before I hear someone scream something about a fight. I look around, seeing Joe start stalking into the fury, but I lose him the second he enters the tangling bodies.

I was just about to turn around and ask Shane to get me back up to Nate when I feel someone bump my side. I jump when something pokes me in the ribs and turn to look up at the man next to me.

What I see has my heart seizing in raw fear.

He bends, making it look like he's about to call over a bartender. The shift digs whatever is at my side deeper until I cry out slightly. Then he turns his head and looks at me sinisterly.

"Get up and walk to that back hallway. Don't even think of doing shit to make anyone get curious."

My blood runs cold, and I risk a glance toward Nate's black wall of windows, hoping that he still has his eyes on me, but I feel a palm shove between my bare shoulders and the movement pulls my eyes away when I almost fall to the ground.

With each step I take toward the hallway, my panic starts to take over until I feel like I'm going to pass out from the fear alone. I know nothing good can come of this, but when one bruising hard hand wraps around my bicep, I fear there is nothing I can do but follow.

I stumble down the hallway as he drags me with him. He moves me around like a ragdoll, my arm aching from his hold, until he slams open the back door and the cool night air hits my tear-streaked face.

Then with a rough shove, he pushes me until I tumble to my knees with a cry of pain.

"Levi, you don't want to do this," I weep, my words hitching as my sobs grow. I fall on my ass when he takes a step toward me and I start to crab crawl backward.

"Wrong move, bitch."

He reaches down and pulls me off the pavement with a rough hold of his hand at my throat. I claw at his arm when the air to my lungs cuts off instantly, but I'm no match for him. Before I know what's happening, he's holding me up off the ground with just his hand squeezing tightly around my throat. Tears fall and I kick my legs frantically as I fight to take a breath.

He grunts when my legs connect with his body and throws me back with all his strength. My back scrapes roughly against the pavement and my head hits the unforgiving surface with teeth-rattling force. My vision goes black for a second, but I struggle until I can see him again, fighting against the dizziness.

"All you had to do was listen, Emberlyn. I gave you plenty of chances to come running back. You just kept ignoring them. Cleaning up my *presents* instead of being scared and calling *me* for help! You called him, though. Spread your whore legs for him without a second glance at ME!"

Oh, my God. All those things that I thought were just weird accidents. It had been Levi the whole time.

"I should have killed that fucking mutt of yours the night you used a headache as an excuse to go home. I still have his teeth marks on my ass from when I brought you back. I couldn't even fuck you because he took that away from me."

"Levi," I moan in pain when I try to move from the pavement. Not wanting to have him this close now that I see he's holding a knife in his hand. "You don't want to do this. Let's talk?"

"You're fucking wrong. I'm going to fuck you right here under his nose, and by the time he finds you, he's not going to want you. You're going to be used up, and if you're lucky, you might be alive."

"Please," I beg, holding my hands up when he stands above me and bends over my body. I keep fighting with the blurred darkness that is trying to suck me under, blinking rapidly as my head swims.

"You were supposed to run into my arms after I made sure your old ass house had some wires cross. That was my chance to come to save you!" His spit hits my face and mixes with the tears running down my cheeks. "I had just enough time to start that fucking shit and rush over to the station so I could be in the right place at the right fucking time, but you still didn't listen, and I'm done waiting. If I can't have you, bitch, no one can!"

His hand comes up, the one with the knife, and I sob louder knowing that this is how it's all going to end. I bring my hands and arms up to shield my face from the knife that is shining in the moonlight, and I pray.

"You mother*fucker*!" I hear roared. It takes me a second to realize that the blow I had been waiting for didn't come, and I try to blink back some of the darkness that had been edging in my vision.

But once I hear Nate, it's as if that was all my mind needed to give up, and with a rushed exhale of relief, I pass out.

Chapter 35

Nate

I stand in the dark hospital room and keep my eyes on Ember. I haven't looked away since the doctor assured me that she was going to be okay. Other than the handprint to her throat and the few scrapes and redness on her back, she has no outward signs of what happened earlier.

But the blow to her head left her with one hell of a concussion.

She's been sleeping peacefully under my watchful eyes for the last three hours, and all I've been able to do is pass the time by planning.

When I saw him leading her away from the bar, I rushed after her. The fight had kept me from getting through the club floor quickly, and all I could do was pray as the dread consumed me and I worried I wouldn't make it in time.

I can still feel the jolts shooting up my legs as I ran as fast as I fucking could through the crowd and then down the hallway. When I finally got to her, seeing that motherfucker she used to date standing over her with a knife, I saw red. I was ready to kill him with my bare hands.

But when he took off running, I had to pick between him and my sweet girl and *that* had been an easy pick.

And now, I'm left with the need for vengeance that rivals the hunger of a starved man. Now that I know she's going to be okay, all I've been able to do is plan for that vengeance and thank God she wasn't taken from me.

"Son? Why don't you go get something to eat?"

I don't look at my mom.

"Nate, we won't leave her side."

I blink at my father's tone but keep my eyes on Ember's face.

"Leave him be."

That voice gets my attention, and I look up to see Ember's father standing on the other side of her bed. Emmy's in Maddox's arms as she cries silently, but what I see in his eyes lets me breathe for the first time since I picked her up and rushed her to the hospital. Some of the fear made tension easing off my chest when I realize he isn't trying to get me to leave or to calm down. He's accepting my need for blood, and if anything, giving me his silent support. I give him a nod but look back at Ember.

Our sisters are sitting behind me on the bench by the window, but they've been silent since they arrived.

Meanwhile, I wait.

It isn't for another hour that I know it's time. My parents had stepped out to get me some food since I refused to leave, and Dani had left to call her husband and check on her kids.

I waited for the nurse to check her and give us a small nod. I heard her tell me that she still had stable vitals and was just sleeping. I stayed put with my eyes on her until the doctor came in to say that as long as everything was clear on her scans later, she would be released in the morning.

Then I made my move.

I stood, silently, and bent to kiss her slack lips. Without a word or a glance to the people around me, I started to stalk down the hallway. I had one thing on my mind, and I wasn't going to rest until I had retribution for every scrape and bump on her body.

I knew from the background check I had run on him after the fire that the sorry fuck only spent time in three places—the station, the gym, or his house—and seeing that it was three in the goddamn morning, I was going with the last option.

Lucky for me, his house butted up to a road so I parked my truck on the shoulder and moved through the woods separating me from my prey. I tagged his SUV in the driveway first. Walking around the side, I felt nothing but hatred as I moved to the back of his house. His back door was older, and with a solid kick at the knob, it gave and crashed open.

I hunted inside. My eyes searched through the darkness as I moved. When I rounded the corner, entering what looked like his living room, I found him jacking off. The porn was turned up so loud that it's no wonder the motherfucker didn't hear me enter.

"Get up!" I thunder and watch him jump.

The lube he had been about to squirt on his small ass dick came out with a rush when his startled movements made his fist tighten.

He moves to stand, getting hung up on the pants around his ankles, and I wait for him to stand completely, pulling his pants up roughly as he goes.

"I'm going to kill you," I fume through clenched teeth. When he doesn't move, I feel my rage spike even higher. "Can't hold your own against a man?"

"What the fuck are you doing in my house?" he screams, but I see the fear in his eyes, and I let it fuel me.

"I'm here to show you what it feels like when you mess with the wrong man's woman. I'm here to make sure that you feel the pain she did, but the difference is, I'm going to fucking kill you."

I stomp toward him, and he finally gets with the program and tries to rush me. But I have the power of a man set to avenge his love right now because as I crack my fist against his nose, he tries to fight back, but I keep pounding into him with an inhuman speed. Each blow to his body makes him stumble until I have him flat against the wall, holding him up for me as I use him as a punching bag for every second of panic, fear, and pain that Ember felt.

"Stop."

At the voice behind me, I halt and let this sorry fuck slide to the ground.

"Why are you here?" I ask, my chest heaving with exertion.

He ignores me. "You do my daughter no good if you end up in prison for murder. Get the fuck out of here, clean yourself up, and get back to her."

When I hesitate, he moves forward, and with a meaty hand to my neck, he shoves me toward the back of the house.

"You got what you needed; now, get the fuck back to your girl before she wakes up needing the one person not there!"

With one last look at the passed out man on the floor, I give Maddox a nod and walk out of the house.

My first stop is my house. I let Bam out quickly before I rush to wipe the sweat and fear from my skin with a damp washcloth. I run to my closet and move some shit around before I grab what I need. I change my clothes quickly before rushing to the laundry room and throwing the ones I had on in the washer. After making sure Bam is back inside with a full bowl of water, I'm on my way out of the house with a squeal of my tires as I head back to the hospital.

No one says a word when I walk back into Ember's hospital room two hours after I had left. Not one mention of my new clothes or the fact that two knuckles are now split with dry blood. And not one damn word is said when I stop on the opposite side of the bed from my chair to take her hand in mine, slipping the diamond ring on her finger before placing a kiss on her hand and laying it gently back down.

Not one word.

I sit back in the chair I had left earlier, and with my eyes back on her sleeping face, I take my first deep breath of the night.

Nothing will ever take her from me.

Not one damn thing.

Chapter 36
Ember

"I'm okay," I tell my fussing mother as she pulls the covers up to my chin.

"Yes. You're okay, sweetheart." Her voice wobbles, and I just sigh, letting her fret if that's what she needs to assure herself that I'm okay.

"Emmy, leave her alone." I look over her bent head and smile at my dad.

"I'm not going to leave her alone. She's been through something traumatic and then had to sit there while the police questioned her as if she had done something wrong. She is not *okay*!"

I whine when her voice gets louder; the slight headache that I've felt since I woke up this morning had followed me all the way to where I am now in Nate's bed.

Dad walks over to the side of the bed, and I follow his movements. I lose his eyes when he bends to place a soft kiss on the top of my head.

"It's time to go, Emmy. Let Nate take over. He's what she needs now."

My heart flips at his words and the bigger meaning behind them, and I feel my chin quiver with emotion.

He's letting me go. Completely letting me go to give me to another man.

And … he's happy about it.

I watch in awe as he pulls my mom away and walks to where Nate is leaning against the doorframe with his arms over his chest. He pulls him in for a quick hug before letting go and looking into his eyes. The flipping in my heart starts to turn into summersaults as I watch something heavy move between them.

They leave with one last look over their shoulder, and I watch as Nate moves over to sit at my side.

"Are you going to cry?"

I blink a few times but don't answer. I'm sure, without a doubt, that if I were to open my mouth to speak, I *would* cry.

"Are you really okay?"

I clear my throat. "I am now. Thanks to you."

He looks down, holding my hand in his. "I've never felt the kind of fear that I did when I thought I was too late, Ember. Just the thought of spending one second without you is more pain than I care to ever feel."

"Nate, baby, I'm here. I'm *okay*."

"I can't, Ember. Not one second or any day. I can't be without you."

I can't see his face with his hair hanging like a curtain shielding him from me, but I don't miss the tear that falls down from his eyes to his lap.

"Get up, Nate."

I shift to the side and wait for him to stand. He doesn't argue with me; instead, he climbs to his feet and looks down at me. My heart clenches when I see the expression on his face. Eyes wet with unshed tears and full of fear as they look down at me. His strong chest is moving with the force of his harsh breathing. I see his hands shake before he clenches them into a tight, white-knuckled fist.

"Come."

I make sure my tone is hard and unbending, giving him no doubts that I mean what I'm telling him.

His fists release, and with shaky movements, he pulls his pants off and his shirt over his head. With just his black boxers on, he lifts the corner of the sheet and folds his tall body down next to me. I move to my side, facing him, and with the hand that is against the bed, I slide it up until I'm holding one of his. My other hand moves up his arm until I can curl it around his neck and focus on his face.

I stare into his eyes. "I'm not going anywhere."

His breath hitches.

"You saved me, Nate. You saved me long before last night when you showed me just how much your love completed me. I won't lie to you and brush last night under the rug. I was scared out of my mind, but I'm going to look at it as the last battle in our beautiful war. It's fought, now over, and we won. It's up to us how we move on and turn that beautiful war won into a beautiful love."

"God, Ember. I mean it, baby. Not one more day can I spend without you."

I smile, feeling the ring on my left finger move when my hand shifts against the mattress, and I know in an instant what it will take to get him to realize that no matter how horrible last night was, I'm still here and never leaving.

"So here's what we do. I apparently gained a fiancé last night, so he's going to sit with me as I plan a wedding. I'll have my dad put my house on the market and you make sure all my stuff stuck in storage is filling this house. I'm going to take over your man cave and you're going to turn Dirty into the biggest club the South has ever seen. Then, the way I see it, we spend the next ten years making babies or practicing to make babies. I'll let you know when I decide how we're going to spend the next fifty plus years after that. Is *that* enough to convince you that you won't have to spend another day without me?"

His eyes change and he looks at me with wonderment instead of sad trepidation.

"Is that all?" His voice is thick with emotion.

I shrug. "All for now."

"I think that's a great start, baby."

He pulls me into his arms, and with a deep breath from us both, we fall asleep knowing that as long as we're together, in each other's arms, we will feel the beauty of our beautiful war won.

I woke up the next morning feeling a lot better than I had the day before. My headache was gone and my back no longer hurt. The scrapes I had were small and the slight redness was the only thing left. My neck looked bad, the bruising something that I would have to face for days before it faded away, but at least I could move without pain.

True to my word, when we woke up this morning, I had my dad contact a realtor. He didn't question my decision, and I had a feeling that he was proud of the choice I had made.

I look down at the huge diamond on my hand and smile. Leave it to Nate to not even ask, but to slide the ring on and not mention it. He's crazy, but I love him for it.

"Hey, Nate," I call over to him. He turns, looking at me from the kitchen as I stay sitting on the couch, curled in the softest blanket I've ever felt. "Just in case our kids ask one day, I said yes."

He tips his head to the side and looks at me as if I'm the crazy one. I hold my hand up and enjoy the hell out of seeing his face get soft when he looks at the engagement ring on my hand.

"But just out of curiosity, were you even going to ask me?"

He pauses in his dinner preparations and leans both hands down on the island. "There was no doubt in my mind, Ember, so I figured asking was just a formality. I'm sure I could have thought of something romantic, spent an hour after trying to dry your tears when you were overcome with happiness, and then taken you home and fucked you until you passed out with nothing but bliss in your eyes. But I didn't want to see you cry any kind of tears, so I went with my gut and just took what's mine."

I laugh, the sound making him smile. "I love you, you crazy man."

"I know; I'm easy to love."

"I wouldn't have cried for an hour," I add a few minutes later.

He looks up from his chopping with a face that tells me he knows I'm lying through my teeth, his eyes sparkling with mirth. "You're right, baby. It would have probably been more like two."

I open my mouth to respond but stop when the doorbell sounds, waving him off and standing from the couch.

My parents come in and greet me with a hug, followed by Nate's.

"How are you, honey?" Izzy asks after we move to sit around the kitchen table.

"I really am okay. It happened and it sucked, but I have to move on."

Nate gives me a hard look

"Have the police found that man yet?" I look over at my mom and shrug.

"They won't be bringing him in."

Everyone looks over at Axel after his comment, and I feel a little spark of worry.

"And why the hell not?" His wife gasps.

I look over at Nate, terrified for what this might mean, and wait for him to take the lead, but he isn't looking at me.

"He died last night. Lost control of his car and hit a tree head-on," Axel answers.

"Good riddance," my mom mumbles.

"I hope he suffered," Izzy adds, nodding at her.

"Oh, I'm sure he did since his engine caught fire. From what the ME says, he didn't die until after that." Axel finishes talking, and I can see from his face that he's happy that Levi didn't die instantly.

I move my attention to Nate. He's stopped his hands completely, hovering over the cutting board. I would have missed it had I not been looking at him, but he struggles slightly to keep his face blank before lifting one brow slowly. I follow his eyes and see my father looking at him with the same intensity. And then, to my utter confusion, he winks, causing Nate to let out a rushed breath. I snap my eyes back and see him nod with a small grin on his lips.

"Accidents happen," my dad grumbles under his breath, still looking at Nate. He turns his head and looks over at me. "He can rot six feet under now instead of in prison. Ember's safe from him, and that's all that matters."

What the hell was that? I look back at Nate, but he's not looking up. He's also not moving, just focusing on the vegetables he had been chopping with his chest moving with harsh deep breaths.

"Ember?"

Nate looks up when my mom calls my name, carefully masking his expression before giving me a look of pure adoration. Whatever just passed between him and my father is gone, and all I see now is that love he has for me shining brightly.

I shake off whatever I just witnessed. If he wants me to know, he'll tell me, but all I care about in this instant is that we really can move on from this moment and put it behind us. Move on and spend the rest of our lives with this being a tiny little black dot in our past.

"You know what? I'm starved." I stand from the table and walk over to him. He lifts one arm and I curl into his side. "What can I do to help, Nate?"

"I've got it," he answers in a deep rumble, looking down at me with a smile.

"I love you."

He swallows thickly. "Right back at you, baby."

Chapter 37
Ember

"Did my dad say anything to you about my call this morning?" I ask, thinking about the fleeting comment my dad made about needing to get my stuff moved over from storage since I had finally decided where I wanted to be. A weird comment from him, but one Nate took with a huge smile.

He pauses, his fingers stopping the soothing brushing of them through my hair. "Not exactly."

I turn my head in his lap, looking away from the episode of *Chopped* we had been watching, and smirk at him. "Oh, really? What does that mean?"

His eyes dance. "He just pointed out a few things."

He grunts when I shift and my head brushes against the bulge in his sweats, and he moves his arm away when I lift my body off the couch. I have to pause to pull the shirt I had changed into after our parents left down as it starts to ride up. His eyes follow my hands, and I just roll mine when he lets out a sound of complaint when my panties are covered up.

When I turn and climb into his lap, this time with my legs straddling his thick thighs, his muffled complaint turns into a noise of pleasure the second my lap settles against his.

"Let's try that again," I start, placing my hands on his shoulders as his hooded eyes darken. "What did my dad say to you about my call to him this morning?"

He shifts, his erection rubbing against me, and I have to fight back a moan.

"Nate?" I question when his attention strays to my now exposed again lace panties.

"Uh." He clears his throat. "He might have said something about a ring not making an honest woman out of you."

My jaw drops. "Focus, honey."

He snaps his eyes up and his full lips tip up slightly. "I might have said something about not giving a shit because you were where you belonged, honest woman or not, and that I would make sure to rectify that before I put babies in you."

"You didn't!" I tease.

"Like I said, that *might* have happened."

"You are a crazy man," I joke.

"Not a surprise, Ember." His lighthearted expression is full of unmasked happiness.

"I *am* surprised, however, that you didn't get your ass kicked for talking about *putting babies in me*."

He shrugs. "In all seriousness, he knows you're happy and that I will do everything in my power to make sure you stay that way. He's a smart man, baby, and he knows where you belong."

"I guess I expected more of a show from him. He didn't even blink an eye when I called to tell him to get my house on the market because I was officially moving in."

Nate's shoulders shake. "Oh, trust me, the show happened. It just happened long before I put my ring on your finger."

"Want to explain *that*?"

"Not really. We had a few man-to-man chats. He's known where this was headed for a while now. Hell, I'm pretty sure he knew well before we did."

I study his face and think about his words. My dad has always been ten feet ahead of everything, so that's not far off the mark.

"Ember," Nate says, breaking through my thoughts, and I concentrate back on him. "He really is okay with it. All joking aside, he understands that it's time to let you go. You've been on your own since you graduated and have accomplished more success at your age than some people ever will. He knows that you have one hell of a good head on your shoulders and nothing you do will ever be without the knowledge that it's the right move for you."

"Don't make me cry," I warn, sniffing a few times.

"It's true. I've given him everything he needs to witness with his own eyes and hear with his own ears. He *knows* that we're ready to start living our lives together."

I drop my head, our foreheads touching, and breathe deeply through my nose.

"I'm still not going to waste any time making an honest woman out of you. Even with his acceptance of us—blessing given or not—I'm not going to risk him cutting off my dick for dragging my feet a second longer. We lost years, Ember, a fact I don't have to remind you of, and now, *this* is our time."

"If we have a shotgun wedding, people will think you knocked me up."

His eyes flare and I suck in a breath. "I do not really see how that would be a problem."

"Nate," I breathe. "It's way too soon for that kind of talk."

When our eyes connect, I almost gasp when I see the seriousness in his. "Ember, I'm almost thirty years old. I want a house full of kids with you, and I really don't want to have to wait to make that happen."

"We just got engaged, Nate. Besides that, we've been together for only a few months."

"If you need my last name before you let me put babies in here"—his big hands move from my hips to press lightly on my belly—"then that's going to happen sooner than later."

"You're stuck on this?"

He nods.

"Let's revisit this conversation in six months, okay?" I can tell that isn't what he wants to hear, so I rush to finish. "Give me six months, Nate. We have time to get settled in *our* home and with each other. I want to have that time to show you how much I love you this time."

His eyes flare. "Six months and not a day longer. You have that long to make my house our home and then I'm going to start doing my best to put babies in you."

"We'll see," I hum, kissing his lips softly before bending to rest my head on his shoulder.

His arms curl around me, the strength of him soaking into my skin. We stay like that for a while, him just holding me tightly.

When he pulls one arm up and his hand gently grips the back of my head, I feel him take a deep breath. "How are you with what we found out before dinner?"

I think about what he's asking and answer him honestly. "I'm okay, I think. A man lost his life, and as much as I hate to think it, let alone say it, he deserved the karma that he got. Would I have wished death on him for what he did? Probably not, but it happened and we both know he made his own path of destruction."

"Hmm." He doesn't say more, and I lift up to look at him, his hand falling from my head to rest back at my hips.

"You heard what I told the police at the hospital. The things he had done even before setting the fire proved he wasn't right in the head, but even if you and I hadn't gotten together, I would never have gone back to Levi." His expression turns hard when I bring up his name. "I know he knew that too. We weren't together long, but I feel like, had he not died, he wouldn't have given up, and I realize now that nothing I could have done differently would have changed things in his head."

"I'm not sorry that he died. I just wish I would have been the one to end his life."

I smile sadly. "Yeah, then he would have taken you away from me anyway."

"Never," he says heatedly.

"It could have been worse, Nate. I don't want to downplay it, but I also don't want to give what he did any more power by continuing to let it affect me—us. His death means we get instant closure, and as we start this new chapter in our lives, we do it without anyone being able to taint it."

"God, you're one strong woman."

"Nate." I smile with a sigh. "Don't you see? When I'm with you, there isn't anything I can't overcome."

His eyes close at my words. When he opens them again, I feel a lump of emotion form in my throat. There is so much love hitting me from just that look alone.

"Promise me, Ember, that if you start to feel the darkness of what happened ever touch you, you'll tell me. I don't care how big or small those shadows might be; I want you to know that I'm here to shield you and protect you from anything."

He brushes a tear from my cheek and I nod. "I promise, honey."

When he pulls me forward, I brace myself with my palms to his chest and open my mouth to deepen our kiss the second our lips touch. He doesn't make any move to take things further than the intimacy of our kiss, but the second his tongue slides against mine, I know I need to feel all of him.

Breaking away from him with a small shove, both of our chests rising rapidly, I quickly pull the shirt up and over my head. The desperation I feel to be filled by him hits a fever pitch, and I shift my hips until I can place my feet on the ground to stand before him. I rip my panties down my legs at the same time he lifts off the back of the couch and silently pulls his shirt off. I rock on my feet while he pulls at the waistband of his sweatpants. The second his erection springs out, I pounce, not even giving him a chance to get his sweats past mid-thigh.

When I get back in his lap, his shaft hits my folds, and I moan deep in my chest. I thread my fingers into his hair and pull him to me as I restart our kiss. There is no slow speed for us right now. No need for a gentle buildup of seduction with our hands. We both need this, his hunger just as fierce as mine is.

I push off the couch with my knees, and he helps me with one hand at his cock. When I sink down on his length, we both cry out. My body welcomes his thickness with a tight hug as our lips feast on each other.

No words are needed. His normal control-fueled demands are silent. He lets my body set the pace only tightening his hold on my hips when my pleasure becomes too much to handle and I lose the ability to make love to him. He bottoms out with each thrust of his hips off the couch, hitting something so deep inside me that I swear I could pass out from the intensity of that alone.

This is so much more than just making love to each other. I've never imagined that our already powerful bond could grow, but as my body clamps around him with a hoarse cry from my lips, he thunders out his release as his heat fills me.

I know at that moment what we just shared was our souls colliding with the power of our love, solidifying our unbreakable and unshakable bond. A bond that guarantees we will only feel the beauty of it as long as we're together.

"I love you with everything I am, Ember."

"As do I, Nate. As do I."

Six months and sixteen days later

I can't have an erection at the altar.

I can't have an erection at the altar.

I can't have an erection at the altar.

"I can't have an erection at the altar."

"Uh, I'm thinking you probably shouldn't think about having one at the altar, either."

I turn my head from where Ember will be walking at any second and give Cohen a confused look. Shane, my other groomsman, is having a hard time holding in his laughter. Cohen, the bastard, laughs softly as he looks around the church, and shifts a little closer to me.

"You have been mumbling about not getting hard for the last five minutes. I figured you might want to shut up with all that before your bride-to-be makes her walk down the aisle or you'll be saying 'I'm hard' instead of 'I do.'"

"Fuck," I hiss.

"Yeah, probably shouldn't say that either."

Before I can think of a comeback, the soft music, which had been playing since I stepped out from some secret room on the side of the altar, changes.

"Get ready," Cohen whispers, straightening himself up.

I don't turn to look at him. Instead, I watch as Molly and Owen start walking down the aisle. Owen, giving no fucks whatsoever, starts some weird run waddle thing. Hell, I don't blame him. I don't even want to be wearing this damn monkey suit, so I can't imagine the little dude does either.

My mom, laughing softly, stands from her front-row seat and kneels at the end of the aisle. Owen runs right to her while laughing his ass off.

I look back at where Molly is still standing in the doorway to the sanctuary. Only this time, she looks annoyed that Owen doesn't know how to do his 'job.' Finally realizing that the attention is back on her, she wipes the snotty look off her face and her beautiful smile takes over. Never one to miss a moment to shine, she starts tossing the flower petals from her basket all fancy-like, almost falling on her ass because she's twirling with each toss. Hell, I'm shocked she didn't demand to wear the tiara she's been sporting since Ember showed her what her flower girl dress looked like.

She looks like a mini-bride. The white dress is puffed out around her with some shiny beads or something all over the top, straps, and skirt. But that smile alone is worth the ridiculous price Ember paid for that thing.

Molly's had a hard time adjusting to my and Ember's relationship. She's always loved Ember, but when she realized what Ember was to *me,* there was some weird jealousy for a while. Ember took it in stride, but I hated it. Molly might not be my blood niece, but I love her like she was. Luckily, she realized real quick that just because she isn't number one in my heart, she still has a big place.

It didn't hurt that I spent four hours letting her paint my face and nails with all that girly shit. And took her to the movies dressed like a goddamn princess.

"Nate! I look like a princess," she whisper-yells before standing next to Maddi and Dani on the other side of the little stage we're all on.

I give her a wink but look away the second I hear the music change again and the pastor asking everyone to stand.

I can't have an erection at the altar.

I can't have an erection at the altar.

I can't have an erection at the altar.

Then I see her.

The woman that, for almost a year, has shown me a love that almost brings me to my knees daily.

All previous thoughts disappear from my mind when I get my first good look at her. The skintight white dress fits her mouthwatering curves like a glove. The tiny straps at her shoulders look like they would snap with one tug by me.

Maybe with my teeth. I'll have to try that later.

The small flare that starts at her knees comes up slightly at the bottom when she takes her first step, and I can just see the tip of a sparkly shoe.

My eyes roam back up the white fabric, following the intricate lace design until I'm looking at her chest. She takes another step, and they bounce. I have to look away before I embarrass myself.

When I see her face, though, that's when I feel like my heart might stop. She's crying, and even though I know it's because she's over the moon happy right now, I hate seeing her tears. But it's the look of pure fucking love, for me, that has my heart restarting and thumping wildly in my chest. Each step she takes makes the rhythm crank up until I feel like I can't breathe.

I swat at my cheeks when I feel my own emotion trickling from my eyes. I have no shame in my tears, not one fucking ounce. I want the world to see what this woman does to me.

When she takes her next step, bringing her to my side, I have to swallow the huge lump in my throat. The pastor says something, I couldn't tell you what, and she continues to smile through her tears at me.

"Her mother and I do," I hear.

I lose her beautiful face when she turns, and for the first time since she walked through that doorway, I see her father. He kisses her temple and pulls her into a hug while looking over her shoulder at me. I'm not sure what I expected from him right now, but seeing his own eyes wet wasn't even in the realm of possibilities. Hell, I was still anticipating him coming down the aisle guns blazing and refusing to give her away.

Ember steps back and he straightens. Instead of turning to go sit next to his wife, he reaches his hand out. I close mine around his and almost fall on my face when he pulls me forward. His hand tightens as he pulls his other around me with a strong smack against my back.

Then his head turns slightly. "I couldn't be more proud that my girl found a man worthy of her. You're a great man, Nate. Enjoy this blessed life."

He steps away, and I watch his back until he sits next to Emmy. She hands him a tissue and he wipes at his eyes, eyes that I notice are now letting those tears fall freely.

I give him a nod and then … then I turn.

"Hey," she whispers.

My mouth twitches, and I whisper back, "You look hot."

Her eyes widen, and I notice my mistake instantly when I hear the pastor clear his throat into the mic. I just shrug, not ashamed at all because she does look hot.

With her hand in mine, not even hearing a damn thing that is said, I follow the cues and speak when I'm told. The whole time my heart grows a little bigger, filling my chest until I'm convinced it will burst.

"And I now pronounce you man and wife. Nate, you may kiss your bride."

She's in my arms before he finishes. I get an ear full of flowers when she wraps her arms around my neck, and I tighten my hold around her waist to bring her up off her feet.

And I kiss my wife deeply and thoroughly.

I would have kept kissing her, had I not gotten a nudge on my back. I make a mental note to kill Cohen later, then place her gently back down on the ground. Her lipstick is slightly smudged, and when her free hand comes up to wipe at my lips, I'm sure I'm wearing some now too.

Her eyes dance, and she smiles up at me before crooking a finger at me.

She turns obviously wiser than I am when it comes to the damn mic and I feel her breath against my ear. "You said not a day over six months and I should have believed you … Daddy."

I can't move.

I'm not even sure I'm breathing.

Nope, I'm lightheaded, definitely not breathing.

"It's my pleasure to now introduce to you, Mr. and Mrs. Nathaniel Gregory Reid."

I hear the pastor talk, but fuck if I'm not dumbstruck.

Her giggles bring me back to my senses, and I have to choke back a sob as I stand to my full height to look down at her. She's smiling through her tears as she wipes my own away with her finger.

"Come on, husband."

"I didn't think I could ever love you more, but you proved me wrong, wife."

I turn, the tears still falling, and after her arm loops through the crook of my waiting elbow, we walk down the aisle. This isn't the first time I've felt the intoxicating power that loving her brings me, and it damn well won't be the last.

Eight Months and Seven Days Later

"I'm never letting you *put a baby in me* again!"

I bite my tongue when her hand clamps down on mine with the strength of ten men. Fucking hell, I think she might actually break my hand before she gives birth.

"Okay, firecracker. No more babies."

Hell, I would agree with her if she told me the sky was purple and the grass was black at this point. Anything to get her to stop looking at me like the devil has possessed her body.

Her eyes tear, and her face changes. Instead of anger, she looks like I just told her that all the puppies in the world are dead. "You don't want more babies with me?"

I look over at the doctor between her legs when he snickers, and I try to figure out how to answer that without pissing her off more. Her hand tightens as another contraction hits, and the doctor tells her to push. I welcome the pain of my crushing bones since they just saved me from potentially saying something to make her head start spinning.

"That's great, Ember. One more just like that."

"Good job, baby," I soothingly say. "Just a few more."

I hope.

Almost thirty minutes later, Ember is worn out and still pushing like a champ. I know everyone warned us that this takes time, but seeing her in so much pain is killing me.

"One more, Ember. One more strong push."

I tighten the hold I have on one of her legs. She takes a deep breath and lifts her back off the hospital bed, curling into her round stomach. Her face reddens and she clamps her eyes tight as she pushes with every ounce of strength she has left. I count like I was told to and push her sweat-dampened hair out of her face with my free hand.

She falls back the second a loud cry starts to fill the room. She looks up, a tired smile on her face, and I bend to kiss her lips.

"It's a girl!" the doctor announces and then places our baby on Ember's chest.

I blink a few times to clear the emotion out of my eyes and give her another kiss before looking down at our child.

For the second time in my life, I gave my heart away. When I looked down at the cone-headed, blood-and-white-goo-covered, scrunched-in-anger face … I fell head over heels in love with our daughter.

I'm not sure who was crying more by the time the nurses took her off Ember's chest to clean her up—Ember, me, or the baby. When I looked down, torn with staying at her side or going with the baby, Ember just reached out and gave me a shove.

One more kiss to my wife's lips, and I stumbled like I was drunk over to where the nurses were working on my still very angry daughter. I stood by, my heart in my chest, and watched them. I feel powerless as she continues to cry, getting more pissed as they wipe her skin, and I have to clench my fists so I don't knock them all to the ground and steal my child back.

Then, finally, I hear the words I've been waiting to hear since Ember told me she was pregnant.

"Would you like to hold your daughter?"

I nod, I think, and hold my arms up as she places her into the safety of her daddy's arms. Her cries stop almost instantly as I make my way over to Ember. I got one glance at the doctor still working between her legs, and I quickly covered my shock at what I saw coming out of my wife before Ember noticed.

"Hey, Mommy," I say softly to Ember, bending down to place the baby in her arms.

"Oh, Nate," she coos. "She's so beautiful."

I run my fingertip over her satiny-smooth cheek. "Yeah," I weakly respond.

"So tiny," she muses.

I pull my eyes from our daughter and look at Ember. She's smiling down at her with pure wonderment. Once again, my chest swells with love as I see my woman holding our girl. The two most important ladies in my world are right in front of me.

"Thank you, Emberlyn." My voice wavers and she stops kissing our baby to look up at me. "You've once again made me the happiest man in the world. Thank you for providing me this kind of love and for giving us the most beautiful little girl."

"Oh, honey."

I bend over the bedrail and give her a deep kiss. When I pull away, I bend to bring my lips to our daughter's forehead.

"Quinnly Grace," I softly mummer. "We're going to love you so much, baby. Mommy and Daddy are so happy you're here."

Six months and two weeks later

"Why are you looking at me like that?" I drop my brush and turn to look where Nate is standing in the doorway of our bathroom.

"What way?"

I roll my eyes. "Like you're starving."

He pushes off the door jam and starts to stalk toward where I'm standing in front of the vanity. "Quinnie is sleeping," he rasps. "I miss your belly round with my baby, Em. My little queen is growing too fast and she told me she wants a sister." The gravelly tone to his voice is working its magic on my body even though I'm determined not to give in.

I hold the brush between us like a weapon. "Oh, she did, huh?"

He nods.

"Our daughter, the one who can only babble and drool, told you she wants a sister?"

He nods, his smile turning wicked.

"She's just now crawling, Nate. We agreed, two years between children."

He takes another step, frowning now.

"I'm going to give her what she wants."

"You mean what *you* want." I laugh, dropping the brush when he pulls me into his arms.

“I don’t see a difference here.”

His mouth drops to mine in one hell of a toe-curling kiss. I find my protests falling on deaf ears when he pulls my sundress over my head and cups my naked breasts; the feel of his hands on me never fails to render me incapable of speech.

“Are you going to give us what we want?” he whispers against my neck, trailing his tongue down to my shoulder to give me a light nip of his teeth.

“Usually, it’s the woman with the ticking biological clock, you know?”

His soft chuckles tickle my skin. “You knew I wanted a house full of babies, Em. The way you look when you’re pregnant, I can’t even put it into words. Just knowing that you’re growing our love in there unmans me. Straight to my knees, baby.”

“Quinnly is so little, Nate,” I weakly add, and judging by the ear-splitting grin on his face, he knows I’m going to give him what he wants.

“Just think about how close she will be to her sister.”

I laugh. “You can’t guarantee her a sister, you know?”

His handsome face brightens instantly. He looks down at my naked chest and bites his lip, the bright teeth peeking out for a brief second before he releases it. When he looks back up at me, the look of rapture in his eyes makes me gasp softly.

“Watch me,” he rumbles against my mouth before literally sweeping me off my feet when they give out in a rush of desire.

When he pulls me from the bathroom and pushes me down on the mattress, I look up at him and lick my lips as he pulls his sweats down and yanks his shirt off, blindly tossing them in the corner.

Ever since Quinnly was born, we’ve been using condoms. I didn’t want to go back on the pill while breastfeeding, regardless of how safe it was. Call me weird, but I wasn’t willing to take a chance that she got traces of that when I nursed. I had started to wean her two weeks ago when she started to prefer the formula that we had to supplement when I got the flu. I was heartbroken, but I knew it was time.

Nate’s been dropping hints ever since about starting to try for another child. Hints that I've been ignoring, but judging by the hungry look on his face as he looks down at me, he's going to do his best to make sure I'm pregnant by the end of tonight.

He leans down, placing his hands on my knees before slowly dragging them up. The slow seduction of his touch makes me squirm, eager to feel him against me. He rubs his nose against my lace covered pussy, and I almost die of need when I hear him moan as if the smell of me alone is the best thing he's ever smelled.

"Nate," I whine.

"Hush," he scolds, looking up with a smirk. "I'm enjoying my wife."

He spends the next painfully long five minutes doing just that. I know because I whine every time the clock turns over a new number, my oversensitive skin burning with every touch of his fingers, mouth, and tongue. Each nip of his teeth causes me to cry out against the palm he placed over my mouth when it became obvious I wasn't going to be able to quiet my screams of pleasure.

And we learned the hard way over the last six months, babies seem to sense when the worst possible time to wake up will be. Which is usually the second he pushes his thick erection inside me.

"Please," I beg, muffled against his hand.

He looks up from the nipple he had been teasing, and he must sense how high my need is for him because the next second, he's holding my legs up by the back of my knees and pushing into my body with one powerful thrust.

I whimper, rolling my lips together and biting down on the flesh to keep from screaming as he pounds into me with deep, rough, measured drives. Of course, when he pulls out, grabs my hips, and flips me over, I let out a loud yelp. That yelp turns into a scream of ecstasy when he slaps my ass while pushing back into me, even deeper than before.

His balls slap against my aching clit as he continues to push into me; swiveling his hips each time, he bottoms out and only lets go of my hips to smack my ass.

The painful smart of his palm mixing and mingling with the frenzied rush of pleasure he's creating every time he hits that spot deep inside my body becomes overwhelming in its power. My fingers hurt from the grip I have on our sheets, and I start rocking back to slam into his hips, welcoming each thrust he makes. We both let out grunts and cries as we climb the peak, ready to tumble over the edge of what promises to be one hell of a powerful climax.

"Fuck, your pussy is so tight, baby. I can feel you hugging and pulling me deeper. You want me to fuck you harder?"

I make, what I hope, is a sound of agreement. I know words aren't going to cut it, not when I feel like I'm about to burst into a million tiny pieces.

"Hold on," he rumbles, tightening his hold on my hips with his fingers digging into the soft skin as he starts to piston into my body rapidly.

"Yes! Oh God, yes!"

He grows impossibly hard inside me, and the second his hand lifts off my hips to give me another one of those smacks that I love, I detonate. When he feels my walls start to flutter, he pushes in deep and even through the haze of my orgasm, I feel the delicious hot rush of him emptying inside me.

Hours later, after a quick late-night bottle to Quinnly and one delicious coupling, I rest my head on his sweaty chest and sigh contently.

"You know, I think I'm going to enjoy this whole practicing for another baby thing."

He huffs. "No practicing, baby. My baby is already in there."

I roll my eyes and curl into him more. "Whatever."

His chest moves and the arm around me tightens. "Go to sleep, mama."

He doesn't have to tell me twice.

Epilogue Four

Ember

Four years, seven months, and two days later

"Quinnie, baby, where is Mommy's makeup bag?"

She turns and looks at me over her shoulder with a face that is so much like her father's, it's almost like looking in the mirror, and shrugs. Her chestnut ringlets dance around her face with the motion.

"Right dare," Brooklynn, our four-year-old, says and points at her sister. Her sweet little lips turn into a sassy grin before she sticks her tongue out at her big sister.

"Brookie!" Quinnly shouts and finally turns so I can see what she was trying her hardest to hide.

My mouth falls open as I look at the mess she's created.

"I made a princess."

Kaylee, our two-year-old, gives a little clap and looks back and forth between her two sisters and me with the happiest of expressions on her face.

I have no idea how Quinnly managed to cover so much of her baby sister, but I'm fairly confident some splattering of various colors covers every bit of her. My makeup bag is wide open in front of her with just about every item that was inside of it spread in Kaylee's lap.

"I see, Quinnie."

She beams, looking quite proud of herself.

"Kaykay," I coo, bending to pick up my messy daughter. "Want to take a bubble bath before Daddy gets home? He's going to want his *princess* all clean so he can give you tons of kisses."

She lets out a loud squeal of joy at the mention of her father. The blond curls bounce around her. We still don't know how she ended up with those beautiful locks, but they make her already angelic face look like she has a halo on when the sun hits her head. Of course, that wouldn't be the case right now since different shades of red and pink currently streak through it.

"Quinnie, honey?"

She smiles up at me.

"Did you put lipstick in your sister's hair?"

She nods and that smile grows huge and wonky. One little dimple coming out in her left cheek.

"And why did you think you should put it there?" I laugh because really, what else can I do?

"Because Uncle Sway taught me how to do highs lights."

Ah. And that will teach me to let my sister bring her niece to work with her. I thought it would be fun since Quinnly loves to play in my makeup, something that started during one of the many tea parties her daddy and little Molly Beckett had with her.

"Okay, sweet girl. You did a wonderful job, but let's get this all cleaned up before Daddy gets home from work, okay?"

She nods, her smile still huge, and with the help of Brooklynn, they start cleaning up my makeup.

It takes me almost thirty minutes to get everything off Kaylee, and she loved every second of it. Her laughter never stopping. By the time I finish with her bath, I'm just as wet as she is.

Just when I'm pulling a new shirt over her head, I hear Nate arrive home. His thunder of a greeting to the girls is something that never fails to bring a smile to my face.

"Where is your mom and sister, my beautiful, enchanted fair maidens?"

"Right here, honey."

"Goldilocks!" he booms and holds his hands out to Kaylee, who of course gives a loud scream before diving from my arms to his when he steps in front of us. She curls into his chest and sticks her thumb in her mouth, looking up at him as if he hung the moon.

I understand how she feels. There is no greater feeling than being in his arms. Which is probably how I ended up with three children in five years. I wouldn't change a thing, even though I give him a hard time about it.

He pulls me into his side and places a kiss on my head. "I missed you."

I snort, looking up. "You've only been gone a few hours."

"Yeah, but the last thing I want to do on a Saturday is spend a few hours doing payroll at Dirty when all my girls are at home having fun without me."

"Yeah, you could have been here almost an hour ago to see your daughter turn this one into a makeup experiment."

He looks down at Kaylee and gives her a wet kiss on her cheek, making her little Tinker Bell giggles erupt. "I bet she looked beautiful."

"She looked something, that's for sure." I yawn, and he brings his attention back to me.

"You look tired." I narrow my eyes, and he holds up his hands. "I just meant; shit, never mind."

"I *am* tired, but only because I had the paintings Annabelle commissioned two months ago to finish. I'm lucky she's so understanding. I just hope she continues to be that way."

He frowns in confusion. "I thought you didn't have anything else due after you finished this last painting? We have the Disney trip coming up this summer."

I turn when Brooklynn screams at her sister, telling them to stop running around the living room. Chuck, our one-year-old Lab, is chasing them and making just as much noise. It's at times like this that I find myself missing Bam more and more. His age caught up with him just after Brooklynn was born, and after watching him struggle for months, we made the painful decision to put him to sleep.

Chuck was Nate's idea, and even though I love having his crazy butt around, I still miss my beautiful beast.

"Ember?"

I look back up at Nate, forgetting what we had been talking about, and give him a raised brow and secretive smirk.

"Why don't you let Kaylee play with her sisters without my make-up," I add in Quinnie's direction. "I need to show you something."

He still looks beyond confused, but with one more kiss, he places her on her feet where she joins her sisters and Chuck as they dance around the living room. I grab Nate's hand and pull him into the kitchen, giving us a moment of quiet so I can talk to him.

I walk around the island, using it as a shield between us and slide the little rectangular card toward him. He looks down, and I see it the second he registers what's written on the card.

"Oh, hell no!" He looks up, and I can see that he is about as far from happy as one could get. Not that I blame him.

"Now, listen to me, honey." He opens his mouth to complain, but I give him the same look that I give the girls when they're out of line. "We agreed you would take care of this. Our family is complete. It's time, big boy."

He places both his hands on the island and gives me a hard glare. "It is most certainly *not*! I'm not letting some jackass cut into my cock when I still have work to do with it."

I roll my eyes. "You're being unreasonable."

"Uh, no. I told you last week when you brought it up that I wasn't getting fixed. No fucking way. Not until I have my boy in your belly. You need to call and cancel this appointment." He picks up the card, and like the very presence of it offends him, he walks to the sink and shoves it down the disposal before turning the water on and flipping the switch. The whole time it's making its shredding noise, he looks at me as if he's won.

Oh, how wrong he is.

"Nate," I warn when he shuts everything off and stomps over to me. "Don't you dare."

He, of course, doesn't listen, and before I can get another word in edgewise, he has me over his shoulder—gently—as he walks into the madness where our girls are still laughing and playing. They stop instantly when we walk in, and I'm sure if I could see them, they would be standing there just waiting to see what crazy thing their daddy is doing now.

He places me on my feet, and I open my mouth to give him some attitude, but it comes out as a squeak when he spins me and I'm looking at the gray wall.

"Five minutes, Ember. Time-out for trying to keep my boy from me."

"Oh, Mommy is in trouble!" Quinnie laughs.

I hear Brooklynn snicker, but I just start to count as a huge, happy-as-hell smile pulls at my lips. I start counting out the minutes in my head, playing into Nate's craziness as I enjoy his grumbling behind me.

Over the years, with each birth of our children, achievement with the club, or with my artwork, our love has just continued to grow. We rarely fight, and when we do, it is usually always about when we will stop having children. I think, if Nate had his way, he would continue having them until I physically couldn't, but I knew it was time.

Especially now.

And since I love seeing him get all riled up, I figured this would be the funniest way to bring it up. And if everything goes as planned, I'm going to enjoy the benefits of provoking him later.

I hit the three-minute mark and turn my head to the side. I see the painting of *A Beautiful War* that Nate had bought all those years ago and my eyes mist. He made sure that was the focal point in our family room. Luckily, we have the space with our vaulted ceilings because it takes up the whole top half of that wall. I let my mind wander to the large photo canvas that is over our bed, my heart filling with love.

Nate surprised me a few weeks after our wedding with a canvas portrait I didn't even know was taken. It eerily looks just like the painting in our living room; only it's a picture of us on our wedding day.

The center being our hands, clasped together at our hips as we both look to the side and into each other's eyes. You can't see anything else but half our bodies as we hold hands and look at each other with so much love.

"Honey?" I call from my spot in the corner, having had enough, and I'm ready to knock my handsome husband down a few pegs.

"What?" he snaps.

I turn and look over at where he is petting Chuck with Kaylee hanging on his back.

"I don't need to cancel that appointment."

He stands and puts his hands on his hips. Kaylee giggles and I have to fight with my desire to look at the way his muscles always bulge when he does that.

"I don't need to cancel because I never made one. I picked up an appointment card when I was leaving my gynecologist last week. She shares an office with the urologist."

"I'm not following." He looks so damn hot that I struggle not to rush into his arms and kiss him hungrily.

"The way I see it," I continue as if he hadn't spoken. "If you get your boy this time, we can make the appointment then. If not, we'll talk about you giving up on that boy and enjoying a house full of women."

His eyes widen, and he woodenly starts to walk over to me. Kaylee still laughing and squealing on his back as she continues to act like she's a monkey. When he's standing in front of me, he reaches out and I feel his knuckles brush against my belly before reaching up to take my face between his hands.

"My boy is in there?"

"Or girl, but yes." I smile through my tears. Even though this will be my fourth pregnancy, I'm still overcome with emotion when I think about how far we've come together as the proof of our love grows in my belly.

"God, I love you, woman."

I don't get a chance to tell him that I love him too because his mouth is instantly on mine. Our girls all start yelling and laughing at their parents as we kiss deeply, my tears mingling with his.

I sink into him and, not for the first time, I realize just how lucky I am to have the love of a man like Nate Reid. True to his word, he's never stopped making sure that he gave me the world. He thinks I give that to him, but standing there with his mouth on mine while our girls dance around happily, I know that will never be the case.

Eight months later, our world grew with even more love when our son, Elijah, was born and Nate got his boy.

The End

Leaving Your Mark

Ember

"Ember!"

I roll my eyes at Nate's bellow and continue into the house, dropping my purse and keys on the kitchen table before walking through the living room.

"Where are you?" I call out.

"Upstairs."

I puff out a breath in annoyance at his lacking response.

I roll my eyes at his response.

Things have been crazy in the last couple of months since I moved in. The success of my art has grown leaps and bounds in such a short time, and I already have another show scheduled with Annabelle. It's been a stressor for me lately, something that Nate hasn't missed. Not that I don't love living here, but I miss my old studio. I don't miss my old house as much as I thought I would, not with Nate by my side, but that studio was my dream room. It's been hard to find my mojo since it burned down.

Of course, planning our wedding on top of the stress I have over painting—or painters block, I should say—is probably another reason that I've been going insane lately. Nate's even cut back his hours at Dirty to be an active supporter and help during the planning process, something I love him even more for. Hell, I would be happy at this point to just go to the courthouse and call it a day.

"Are you coming or not, woman?"

"I wish I was coming," I mumble to myself.

"Heard that! Get your sweet ass up here, and I'll help you out, firecracker."

"Smartass."

"Heard that, too!"

"I wasn't trying to hide it from you! Where are you, anyway?" I call back, looking up the stairs just in time to see him slide into view with a wag of his brows.

"Right here," he says with a smartass grin on his face.

I shake my head but laugh at him. As always, my man looks hot as hell. He's wearing a pair of old, worn jeans. You know the kind. The jeans that mold and hug every single delicious bit of a man's body, highlighting all those bits in the most mouthwatering way. Yeah, those. His shirt is off, and I can tell he's been doing something physical because his muscular chest has just the slightest bit of sweat dampening his skin.

I lick my lips.

"As much as I love it when you eat me with those eyes of yours, I'm more than just a piece of man meat, baby."

"Right now, you're the juiciest steak I've ever seen, and I've been starving for months."

His mouth opens and then closes, clearly shocked by my words. He's usually the dirty talker, but I can't help it. We've been so busy I feel like it's been weeks since he took me. In reality, it's only been a few days, but when you have a man like Nate Reid, a few days without making love to him feels like decades.

"Well, the feast has to wait," he says, his voice just a tad deeper than normal, and my smile deepens, knowing that I've got him right where I want him.

"Why?"

"Because I have a surprise for you, and no matter how much I want that sweetness, you have to wait."

"You suck." I continue up the stairs with a huff.

"Not yet, but I will, firecracker."

"Tease," I snap when I take the last step and wrap my arms around his neck.

"Nah, Em, that was a promise."

He bends his head and gives me a light kiss before pulling my arms from his neck and turning me. His hands remain at my hips while we walk together down the hallway toward his man cave.

"Open it," he tells me when we reach the closed door.

I look over my shoulder at him in confusion before reaching out and turning the knob. What I see when the door opens has me thankful that Nate is still holding my hips because, otherwise, I would have melted into a puddle at his feet.

Complete awe.

That's what I feel when I see what he's clearly been working hard to create. Something I had no idea he was even doing.

"How? What? God," I breathe, unable to even form a complete thought.

"It wasn't that hard to hide from you, baby. You never came into my man cave, and I worked on it when you were out. It took us a few days, but I think it turned out perfect."

"You … you made me a studio?" My tears fall down my cheek unchecked. I can't be bothered to dry my eyes when I'm too busy looking at the heaven Nate's created for me.

"I would give you the world," Nate mumbles, bringing his lips to my neck and peppering kisses down to my shoulder. "Do you like it?"

"It's perfect," I gasp, turning in his arms to look up at him.

His handsome face studies mine before giving me another brief kiss. "Let me show you where everything is," he whispers, pulling me into the room.

He spends the next fifteen minutes giving me a tour. He kept the white theme that I had at my old place. A large and ridiculously cozy looking chair sits in the corner, and an easel is propped on the opposite side of the room—sandwiched between the two large windows. The biggest upgrade from my old studio is the huge wall of organized supplies and canvases.

"Did you make that?" I ask, pointing at the shelving unit. There is no way this is store bought. Three large doors cover the whole bottom half. When I pull on them, they drop to reveal deep pockets full of various sized canvases. On top of that are three shelves, each full of paints, brushes, and palettes.

"Yeah. Took me forever to figure out how to get your canvases in here with everything else, but I figured these little hidden drawers would be perfect. Anything you want to be changed or added, we can figure out."

"God, I love you."

"I love you, too, but you aren't finished."

He spins me around, and when I see what he has me facing, my tears pick up again. On the same wall as the door, I see the same chest that my father made me; the same chest that I thought was gone forever when the fire hit my old house.

"It doesn't serve the same purpose as the last one, but when I told your dad what I wanted, he didn't waste a second making sure it was in this room—where it belongs. I figure you'll figure out a use for it. I know how much your old chest meant to you, so I wanted a piece of that here, in our house."

"Nate," I start but have to stop when my voice cracks. How do you say thank you for something like this?

"I know, baby," he says, reading my mind. "How about you show me how much you like it and get to painting?" he suggests.

I turn to look at him. He's standing in the middle of the room; the only color in the solid white room is his tan skin, black hair, and jeans. An idea pops into my head, and I give him a wicked smile. He doesn't move, but I know he sees something in my eyes because he stands a little taller before bringing his hand to his crotch and adjusting his cock.

"Don't move," I tell him, walking from my chest to the wall of paints and brushes. I feel his eyes on me the whole time, but I don't look away from my task. I pick up a palette and fill it with a rainbow of color before grabbing a brush and walking over to Nate.

He hasn't moved, but his breathing has picked up.

Looking into his eyes, I blindly drag the brush against the palette, not even caring that I'm most likely mixing the colors, before reaching up and swiping the brush down his chest and over his abs before it hits his jeans.

His nostrils flare.

I repeat the process until his whole chest, back, and arms are a kaleidoscope of color. I can see how hard he has to hold himself back. His fists have been clenched since the third stroke of my brush. His breathing went wild around stroke fifteen. When I trailed my brush across his collarbone, I watched in fascination as his veins seemed to throb.

Dropping to my knees, I place the palette on the ground and put the brush between my teeth before looking up and meeting his eyes. The stormy depths darkened with desire spark when I begin to unbutton his pants.

He rips the brush from my mouth the second I push his jeans down his legs, stepping out briefly to kick them to the side, while his cock bounces from its jutted position right in front of my face. I hear the brush crash to the floor at the same second that my lips wrap around his thick length and I pull him deep into my mouth. I work him with my hands and mouth until he's groaning deep in his throat then I let go with a loud pop and lean down to coat my hands in paint. I run them up his legs, covering each in blue and purple paint before reaching behind him and grabbing his ass to pull him forward. His cock goes back into my mouth, and with my paint-covered hands, I hold him where I want him.

We continue like that, me stopping only to get more paint until I hear him panting. His hand comes out and grabs my head by my ponytail to rip me off his cock. "I'm not coming in your fucking mouth," he commands before his hands are under my armpits and pulling me to my feet. He doesn't waste a second, and in the next breath, I'm naked and yanked against his paint-covered body. I feel the sticky wetness coating my skin, and I moan, rubbing against him.

He steps back and gives me a wicked smile before rubbing his hands from his chest down to his hips, covering his hands in paint before he cups my breasts. I look down to see his rainbow of color against my skin. Not happy with the amount of paint he's able to transfer, he bends and scoops globs of his own paint. Starting at my ankles, he pulls the color up both legs. It isn't long before I'm just as covered as he is, and when his paint-covered hands grab my ass, I leap, taking him off guard and to the ground. He lands on his back and looks up at me in shock. I reach out to grab my shirt and use that to guide his cock to my entrance.

He looks at me weird, and I just shrug. "Don't want your cock covered in paint when it's about to be inside my body."

His response is lost on a groan, though, because I drop my body and impale myself on his cock, screaming out his name when I feel him deep. His hands grab my hips to help me move when my paint-covered knees keep sliding against the white wooden floor. My own hands reach out and use his chest to balance myself before I ride him, hard.

It doesn't take long before we're both calling out our releases and I collapse onto his chest, sweat and paint making me slide against his skin.

"So … can I make a request that all thank-yous are given like that?" he pants against my temple.

I laugh, feeling our combined releases start to fall from my body. "Come on, handsome, come let me show you some more thank-yous in the shower while we clean up. Our parents are coming over for dinner tonight."

Later that night, long after we said thank you, twice, in the shower, our parents arrive. We spent the night in the kitchen and living room, talking after our dinner before I remembered I wanted to show off the new studio. Of course, had I not had a few glasses of wine with dinner, I might have remembered the mess that we left behind earlier. But I didn't, so when we opened the door, the first thing that our parents saw was the large imprint of Nate's body—including his very clear ass print—in various paint colors dead center on the floor. To make it worse, it didn't take any imagination to figure out how that print got there—not since you could see the clear prints of my legs on either side of his body and my handprints scattered around the top of his body's shadow.

I was too embarrassed to look, but when Nate bellows out a laugh, I can't help but smile. I hear our mothers giggling before movement of all of them leaving filter around us.

Nate, still laughing, bends down. "I'm going to be sealing that floor so it never fades, firecracker."

I close my eyes, but even my embarrassment couldn't touch the love I feel for this man at my side—or under me, as it was.

Thank Yous

To my family: Thank you for every ounce of support. I love you guys and your love for me keeps me going. You guys might be the only people that love me more than Felicia does. ☺

Felicia Lynn: HA, you thought there would be something here, didn't you? I dedicated the book to you – so you get nothing more! :P

To my amazing readers: I would be nothing without you all. Your support keeps me going every single step of the way.

To my amazing publicist, Danielle Sanchez: I'm so beyond lucky to have you in my life. Thank you for ALL that you have done and continue to do for me.

To the women behind making my books shine: Lauren Perry, Sommer Stein, Jenny Sims, Ellie McLove, and Stacey Blake – I would be lost without each and every one of you!

A special thanks to my beta reader and friend, Lara Feldstein. You've been with me through so many books and I can honestly say I value your opinion to the moon. You're incredible.

A special thank you to JM Walker. I love you, Jo-Anna. Thank you so much for all those 'pretties' and for loving my crew! You're the best.

To Contact Harper:

Email: Authorharpersloan@gmail.com
Website: www.authorharpersloan.com
Facebook: www.facebook.com/harpersloanbooks

Other Books by Harper Sloan:

Corps Security Series:
Axel
Cage
Beck
Uncaged
Cooper
Locke

Hope Town Series:
Unexpected Fate
Bleeding Love
When I'm With You

Standalones:
Perfectly Imperfect

Keep reading for a preview of *Jaded Hearts*, book 1 in the Loaded Replay series.

Prologue

Signing with the record company of our dreams should have been the best thing that ever happened to us. And it was . . . for a short while. While the glitz and glamour of the fame's promise was shining as bright as our stage lights we could forget where we came from and live in the glory. The money bought us every happiness we ever craved. Those false securities that you think will make your life better. The instant friends, lovers—you name it-would do whatever we asked just to spend a second in our presence.

We had it all.

The only problem was when we had those quiet moments in between the insanity. When we were slapped in the face with the reality that all we really had—all we could count on—was each other.

My brother, Weston, is the only constant I've ever had in my life. He's the person that I know will never let me down and will always be my biggest support. We grew up with parents that hated us. Really . . . it sounds ridiculous, the notion that parents could hate their children, but ours do. They made no secret of it when we were younger. And continue to attempt to pick at our very souls like the vultures that they are.

My earliest memory of them is somewhere around third or fourth grade when they would scream at us about how we ruined it all for them. How *they* were on the edge of fame and then we came along and it all went down hill. We were essentially their bad luck.

When we hit middle school it got worse, but only because they knew that they could leave us for long periods and we wouldn't die.

Our parents, like us, were born to be stars . . . or at least they assumed they were and they had no qualms about reminding us that fact daily. Unfortunately for them, they lacked the drive and ambition to never back down until they had everything they ever wanted. The first challenge that was thrown in their path they decided to take the low road full of scavengers and sinners.

Like I said, vultures through and through.

Our dad knocked up mom in the early eighties, when big hair rock bands were all the rage and theirs was seconds away from signing the record deal that would make their careers.

Then they found out about us.

The twins that ruined it all.

And all those long nights performing in whatever local hole they could find, bouncing from town to town just waiting for their big break was washed away.

Mom was no longer the singer that men would lust over. Not when we ruined her body. And our dad was so deep in the bottle I'm not sure he realized he was swimming in it.

And when the band fell apart, they decided hating us was almost easier than hating each other. They had a common goal in their blame and right or wrong, to them we would never be anything other than a reminder of why they aren't living their dream.

Their band mates obviously didn't share the same bond that Weston and I have with Jamison and Luke. God forbid I ever found myself in a position like that they would band together and the show would go on. Because for us, this is it. This is our future's promise of a better life and even if for me it's starting to look like more of a curse than a promise, it's something that we would die before we gave up.

Unfortunately for me, I'm pretty sure that there are a few people that would love to make that happen.

Who am I?

I'm Wrenlee Davenport, lead singer of Loaded Replay, and I've learned the hard way that there is plenty of people in the world that would love to have a piece of me, but they don't give one shit about the person behind the voice.

They see the persona. The *fake* me that the record label loves to market as the sexy singer with the voice of a saint, but for me—I'm probably always going to be that stupid little girl that believes that my prince charming will come riding in on his black horse—because really, black horses are so much more badass than white ones—and prove to me that every little jaded piece of my heart is worth loving.

And *he* will love me for me. For *Wren*. And not the *Wrenlee* that has more times than I care to admit has to drink herself stupid just to face this fucking life I'm living.

Yeah . . . fame and fortune is far from everything I ever dreamed it was.

It's my own personal hell and I pray that there's something or someone out there that can prove to me that the world isn't screwed because the majority of humanity is too busy licking the windows on the outside to see the beauty behind it. All they care about is what's at face value when what matters is skin deep.

I should feel bad for prince charming. My knight in tarnished armor. Because he'll have one giant battle on his hands to make me believe that there might be someone left out there that doesn't just want a piece of me.

Release date for *Jaded Hearts* is tentatively set for December 2016.

CPSIA information can be obtained
at www.ICGtesting.com
Printed in the USA
BVHW041213050721
611158BV00025B/1340

9 781539 660088